COMBO EDITIONS

Great way to get the books you want for a lower overall price! Excellent reading.

JACK LONDON COMBO #3

THE IRON HEEL
MARTIN EDEN
BURNING DAYLIGHT

JACK LONDON

2013

Jack London Combo #3

The Iron Heel (1907)
Martin Eden (1909)
Burning Daylight (1910)

This edition prepared in 2013

ISBN-13: 978-1492816713
ISBN-10: 149281671X

THE IRON HEEL

"At first, this Earth, a stage so gloomed with woe
You almost sicken at the shifting of the scenes.
And yet be patient. Our Playwright may show
In some fifth act what this Wild Drama means."

FOREWORD

It cannot be said that the Everhard Manuscript is an important historical document. To the historian it bristles with errors—not errors of fact, but errors of interpretation. Looking back across the seven centuries that have lapsed since Avis Everhard completed her manuscript, events, and the bearings of events, that were confused and veiled to her, are clear to us. She lacked perspective. She was too close to the events she writes about. Nay, she was merged in the events she has described.

Nevertheless, as a personal document, the Everhard Manuscript is of inestimable value. But here again enter error of perspective, and vitiation due to the bias of love. Yet we smile, indeed, and forgive Avis Everhard for the heroic lines upon which she modelled her husband. We know to-day that he was not so colossal, and that he loomed among the events of his times less largely than the Manuscript would lead us to believe.

We know that Ernest Everhard was an exceptionally strong man, but not so exceptional as his wife thought him to be. He was, after all, but one of a large number of heroes who, throughout the world, devoted their lives to the Revolution; though it must be conceded that he did unusual work, especially in his elaboration and interpretation of working-class philosophy. "Proletarian science" and "proletarian philosophy" were his phrases for it, and therein he shows the provincialism of his mind—a defect, however, that was due to the times and that none in that day could escape.

But to return to the Manuscript. Especially valuable is it in communicating to us the FEEL of those terrible times. Nowhere do we find more vividly portrayed the psychology of the persons that lived in that turbulent period embraced between the years 1912 and 1932—their mistakes and ignorance, their doubts and fears and misapprehensions, their ethical delusions, their violent passions, their inconceivable sordidness and selfishness. These are the things that are so hard for us of this enlightened age to understand. History tells us that these things were, and biology and psychology tell us why they were; but history and biology and psychology do not make these things alive. We accept them as facts, but we are left without sympathetic comprehension of them.

This sympathy comes to us, however, as we peruse the Everhard Manuscript. We enter into the minds of the actors in that long-ago world-drama, and for the time being their mental processes are our mental processes. Not alone do we understand Avis Everhard's love for her hero-husband, but we feel, as he felt, in those first days, the vague and terrible loom of the Oligarchy. The Iron Heel (well named) we feel descending upon and crushing mankind.

And in passing we note that that historic phrase, the Iron Heel, originated in Ernest Everhard's mind. This, we may say, is the one moot question that this new-found document clears up. Previous to this, the earliest-known use of the phrase occurred in the pamphlet, "Ye Slaves," written by George Milford and published in December, 1912. This George Milford was an obscure agitator about whom nothing is known, save the one additional bit of information gained from the Manuscript, which mentions that he was shot in the Chicago Commune. Evidently he had heard Ernest Everhard make use of the phrase in some public speech, most probably when he was running for Congress in the fall of 1912. From the Manuscript we learn that Everhard used the phrase at a private dinner in the spring of 1912. This is, without discussion, the earliest-known occasion on which the Oligarchy was so designated.

The rise of the Oligarchy will always remain a cause of secret wonder to the historian and the philosopher. Other great historical events have their place in social evolution. They were inevitable. Their coming could have been predicted with the same certitude that astronomers to-day predict the outcome of the movements of stars. Without these other great historical events, social evolution could not have proceeded. Primitive communism, chattel slavery, serf slavery, and wage slavery were necessary stepping-stones in the evolution of society. But it were ridiculous to assert that the Iron Heel was a necessary stepping-stone. Rather, to-day, is it adjudged a step aside, or a step backward, to the social tyrannies that made the early world a hell, but that were as necessary as the Iron Heel was unnecessary.

Black as Feudalism was, yet the coming of it was inevitable. What else than Feudalism could have followed upon the breakdown of that great centralized governmental machine known as the Roman Empire? Not so, however, with the Iron Heel. In the orderly procedure of social evolution there was no place for it. It was not necessary, and it was not inevitable. It must always remain the great curiosity of history—a whim, a fantasy, an apparition, a thing unexpected and undreamed; and it should serve as a warning to those rash political theorists of to-day who speak with certitude of social processes.

Capitalism was adjudged by the sociologists of the time to be the culmination of bourgeois rule, the ripened fruit of the bourgeois revolution. And we of to-day can but applaud that judgment. Following upon Capitalism, it was held, even by such intellectual and antagonistic giants as Herbert Spencer, that Socialism would come. Out of the decay of self-seeking capitalism, it was held, would arise that flower of the ages, the Brotherhood of Man. Instead of which, appalling alike to us who look back and to those that lived at the time, capitalism, rotten-ripe, sent forth that monstrous offshoot, the Oligarchy.

Too late did the socialist movement of the early twentieth century divine the coming of the Oligarchy. Even as it was divined, the Oligarchy was there—a fact established in blood, a stupendous and awful reality. Nor even then, as the Everhard Manuscript well shows, was any permanence attributed to the Iron Heel. Its overthrow was a matter of a few short years, was the judgment of the revolutionists. It is true, they realized that the Peasant Revolt was unplanned, and that the First Revolt was premature; but they little realized that the Second Revolt, planned and mature, was doomed to equal futility and more terrible punishment.

It is apparent that Avis Everhard completed the Manuscript during the last days of preparation for the Second Revolt; hence the fact that there is no mention of the disastrous outcome of the Second Revolt. It is quite clear that she intended the Manuscript for immediate publication, as soon as the Iron Heel was overthrown, so that her husband, so recently dead, should receive full credit for all that he had ventured and accomplished. Then came the frightful crushing of the Second Revolt, and it is probable that in the moment of danger, ere she fled or was captured by the Mercenaries, she hid the Manuscript in the hollow oak at Wake Robin Lodge.

Of Avis Everhard there is no further record. Undoubtedly she was executed by the Mercenaries; and, as is well known, no record of such executions was kept by the Iron Heel. But little did she realize, even then, as she hid the Manuscript and prepared to flee, how terrible had been the breakdown of the Second Revolt. Little did she realize that the tortuous and distorted evolution of the next three centuries would compel a Third Revolt and a Fourth Revolt, and many Revolts, all drowned in seas of blood, ere the world-movement of labor should come into its own. And little did she dream that for seven long centuries the tribute of her love to Ernest Everhard would repose undisturbed in the heart of the ancient oak of Wake Robin Lodge.

ANTHONY MEREDITH
Ardis,
November 27, 419 B.O.M.

CHAPTER I

MY EAGLE

The soft summer wind stirs the redwoods, and Wild-Water ripples sweet cadences over its mossy stones. There are butterflies in the sunshine, and from everywhere arises the drowsy hum of bees. It is so quiet and peaceful, and I sit here, and ponder, and am restless. It is the quiet that makes me restless. It seems unreal. All the world is quiet, but it is the quiet before the storm. I strain my ears, and all my senses, for some betrayal of that impending storm. Oh, that it may not be premature! That it may not be premature!*

> * The Second Revolt was largely the work of Ernest Everhard, though he cooperated, of course, with the European leaders. The capture and secret execution of Everhard was the great event of the spring of 1932 A.D. Yet so thoroughly had he prepared for the revolt, that his fellow-conspirators were able, with little confusion or delay, to carry out his plans. It was after Everhard's execution that his wife went to Wake Robin Lodge, a small bungalow in the Sonoma Hills of California.

Small wonder that I am restless. I think, and think, and I cannot cease from thinking. I have been in the thick of life so long that I am oppressed by the peace and quiet, and I cannot forbear from dwelling upon that mad maelstrom of death and destruction so soon to burst forth. In my ears are the cries of the stricken; and I can see, as I have seen in the past,* all the marring and mangling of the sweet, beautiful flesh, and the souls torn with violence from proud bodies and hurled to God. Thus do we poor humans attain our ends, striving through carnage and destruction to bring lasting peace and happiness upon the earth.

> * Without doubt she here refers to the Chicago Commune.

And then I am lonely. When I do not think of what is to come, I think of what has been and is no more—my Eagle, beating with tireless wings the void, soaring toward what was ever his sun, the flaming ideal of human freedom. I cannot sit idly by and wait the great event that is his making, though he is not here to see. He devoted all the years of his manhood to it, and for it he gave his life. It is his handiwork. He made it.*

> * With all respect to Avis Everhard, it must be pointed out that Everhard was but one of many able leaders who planned the Second Revolt. And we to-day, looking back across the centuries, can safely say that even had he lived, the Second

> Revolt would not have been less calamitous in its outcome than it was.

And so it is, in this anxious time of waiting, that I shall write of my husband. There is much light that I alone of all persons living can throw upon his character, and so noble a character cannot be blazoned forth too brightly. His was a great soul, and, when my love grows unselfish, my chiefest regret is that he is not here to witness tomorrow's dawn. We cannot fail. He has built too stoutly and too surely for that. Woe to the Iron Heel! Soon shall it be thrust back from off prostrate humanity. When the word goes forth, the labor hosts of all the world shall rise. There has been nothing like it in the history of the world. The solidarity of labor is assured, and for the first time will there be an international revolution wide as the world is wide.*

> * The Second Revolt was truly international. It was a colossal plan—too colossal to be wrought by the genius of one man alone. Labor, in all the oligarchies of the world, was prepared to rise at the signal. Germany, Italy, France, and all Australasia were labor countries—socialist states. They were ready to lend aid to the revolution. Gallantly they did; and it was for this reason, when the Second Revolt was crushed, that they, too, were crushed by the united oligarchies of the world, their socialist governments being replaced by oligarchical governments.

You see, I am full of what is impending. I have lived it day and night utterly and for so long that it is ever present in my mind. For that matter, I cannot think of my husband without thinking of it. He was the soul of it, and how can I possibly separate the two in thought?

As I have said, there is much light that I alone can throw upon his character. It is well known that he toiled hard for liberty and suffered sore. How hard he toiled and how greatly he suffered, I well know; for I have been with him during these twenty anxious years and I know his patience, his untiring effort, his infinite devotion to the Cause for which, only two months gone, he laid down his life.

I shall try to write simply and to tell here how Ernest Everhard entered my life—how I first met him, how he grew until I became a part of him, and the tremendous changes he wrought in my life. In this way may you look at him through my eyes and learn him as I learned him—in all save the things too secret and sweet for me to tell.

It was in February, 1912, that I first met him, when, as a guest of my father's* at dinner, he came to our house in Berkeley. I cannot say that my very first impression of him was favorable. He was one of many at dinner, and in the drawing-room where we gathered and waited for all to arrive, he made a rather incongruous appearance. It was "preacher's night," as my father privately called it, and Ernest was certainly out of place in the midst of the churchmen.

> * John Cunningham, Avis Everhard's father, was a professor at the State University at Berkeley, California. His chosen

field was physics, and in addition he did much original
research and was greatly distinguished as a scientist. His
chief contribution to science was his studies of the
electron and his monumental work on the "Identification of
Matter and Energy," wherein he established, beyond cavil and
for all time, that the ultimate unit of matter and the
ultimate unit of force were identical. This idea had been
earlier advanced, but not demonstrated, by Sir Oliver Lodge
and other students in the new field of radio-activity.

In the first place, his clothes did not fit him. He wore a ready-made suit of dark cloth that was ill adjusted to his body. In fact, no ready-made suit of clothes ever could fit his body. And on this night, as always, the cloth bulged with his muscles, while the coat between the shoulders, what of the heavy shoulder-development, was a maze of wrinkles. His neck was the neck of a prize-fighter,* thick and strong. So this was the social philosopher and ex-horseshoer my father had discovered, was my thought. And he certainly looked it with those bulging muscles and that bull-throat. Immediately I classified him—a sort of prodigy, I thought, a Blind Tom** of the working class.

* In that day it was the custom of men to compete for purses
of money. They fought with their hands. When one was
beaten into insensibility or killed, the survivor took the
money.

** This obscure reference applies to a blind negro musician
who took the world by storm in the latter half of the
nineteenth century of the Christian Era.

And then, when he shook hands with me! His handshake was firm and strong, but he looked at me boldly with his black eyes—too boldly, I thought. You see, I was a creature of environment, and at that time had strong class instincts. Such boldness on the part of a man of my own class would have been almost unforgivable. I know that I could not avoid dropping my eyes, and I was quite relieved when I passed him on and turned to greet Bishop Morehouse—a favorite of mine, a sweet and serious man of middle age, Christ-like in appearance and goodness, and a scholar as well.

But this boldness that I took to be presumption was a vital clew to the nature of Ernest Everhard. He was simple, direct, afraid of nothing, and he refused to waste time on conventional mannerisms. "You pleased me," he explained long afterward; "and why should I not fill my eyes with that which pleases me?" I have said that he was afraid of nothing. He was a natural aristocrat—and this in spite of the fact that he was in the camp of the non-aristocrats. He was a superman, a blond beast such as Nietzsche* has described, and in addition he was aflame with democracy.

* Friederich Nietzsche, the mad philosopher of the
nineteenth century of the Christian Era, who caught wild
glimpses of truth, but who, before he was done, reasoned
himself around the great circle of human thought and off
into madness.

In the interest of meeting the other guests, and what of my unfavorable impression, I forgot all about the working-class philosopher, though once or twice at table I noticed him—especially the twinkle in his eye as he listened to the talk first of one minister and then of another. He has humor, I thought, and I almost forgave him his clothes. But the time went by, and the dinner went by, and he never opened his mouth to speak, while the ministers talked interminably about the working class and its relation to the church, and what the church had done and was doing for it. I noticed that my father was annoyed because Ernest did not talk. Once father took advantage of a lull and asked him to say something; but Ernest shrugged his shoulders and with an "I have nothing to say" went on eating salted almonds.

But father was not to be denied. After a while he said:

"We have with us a member of the working class. I am sure that he can present things from a new point of view that will be interesting and refreshing. I refer to Mr. Everhard."

The others betrayed a well-mannered interest, and urged Ernest for a statement of his views. Their attitude toward him was so broadly tolerant and kindly that it was really patronizing. And I saw that Ernest noted it and was amused. He looked slowly about him, and I saw the glint of laughter in his eyes.

"I am not versed in the courtesies of ecclesiastical controversy," he began, and then hesitated with modesty and indecision.

"Go on," they urged, and Dr. Hammerfield said: "We do not mind the truth that is in any man. If it is sincere," he amended.

"Then you separate sincerity from truth?" Ernest laughed quickly.

Dr. Hammerfield gasped, and managed to answer, "The best of us may be mistaken, young man, the best of us."

Ernest's manner changed on the instant. He became another man.

"All right, then," he answered; "and let me begin by saying that you are all mistaken. You know nothing, and worse than nothing, about the working class. Your sociology is as vicious and worthless as is your method of thinking."

It was not so much what he said as how he said it. I roused at the first sound of his voice. It was as bold as his eyes. It was a clarion-call that thrilled me. And the whole table was aroused, shaken alive from monotony and drowsiness.

"What is so dreadfully vicious and worthless in our method of thinking, young man?" Dr. Hammerfield demanded, and already there was something unpleasant in his voice and manner of utterance.

"You are metaphysicians. You can prove anything by metaphysics; and having done so, every metaphysician can prove every other metaphysician wrong—to his own satisfaction. You are anarchists in the realm of thought. And you are mad cosmos-makers. Each of you dwells in a cosmos of his own making, created out of his own fancies and desires. You do not know the real world in which you live, and your thinking has no place in the real world except in so far as it is phenomena of mental aberration.

"Do you know what I was reminded of as I sat at table and listened to you talk and talk? You reminded me for all the world of the scholastics of the Middle Ages who gravely and learnedly debated the absorbing question of how many angels could dance on the point of a needle. Why, my dear sirs, you are as remote from the intellectual life of the twentieth century as an Indian medicine-man making incantation in the primeval forest ten thousand years ago."

As Ernest talked he seemed in a fine passion; his face glowed, his eyes snapped and flashed, and his chin and jaw were eloquent with aggressiveness. But it was only a way he had. It always aroused people. His smashing, sledge-hammer manner of attack invariably made them forget themselves. And they were forgetting themselves now. Bishop Morehouse was leaning forward and listening intently. Exasperation and anger were flushing the face of Dr. Hammerfield. And others were exasperated, too, and some were smiling in an amused and superior way. As for myself, I found it most enjoyable. I glanced at father, and I was afraid he was going to giggle at the effect of this human bombshell he had been guilty of launching amongst us.

"Your terms are rather vague," Dr. Hammerfield interrupted. "Just precisely what do you mean when you call us metaphysicians?"

"I call you metaphysicians because you reason metaphysically," Ernest went on. "Your method of reasoning is the opposite to that of science. There is no validity to your conclusions. You can prove everything and nothing, and no two of you can agree upon anything. Each of you goes into his own consciousness to explain himself and the universe. As well may you lift yourselves by your own bootstraps as to explain consciousness by consciousness."

"I do not understand," Bishop Morehouse said. "It seems to me that all things of the mind are metaphysical. That most exact and convincing of all sciences, mathematics, is sheerly metaphysical. Each and every thought-process of the scientific reasoner is metaphysical. Surely you will agree with me?"

"As you say, you do not understand," Ernest replied. "The metaphysician reasons deductively out of his own subjectivity. The scientist reasons inductively from the facts of experience. The metaphysician reasons from theory to facts, the scientist reasons from facts to theory. The metaphysician explains the universe by himself, the scientist explains himself by the universe."

"Thank God we are not scientists," Dr. Hammerfield murmured complacently.

"What are you then?" Ernest demanded.

"Philosophers."

"There you go," Ernest laughed. "You have left the real and solid earth and are up in the air with a word for a flying machine. Pray come down to earth and tell me precisely what you do mean by philosophy."

"Philosophy is—" (Dr. Hammerfield paused and cleared his throat)—"something that cannot be defined comprehensively except to such minds and temperaments as are philosophical. The narrow scientist with his nose in a test-tube cannot understand philosophy."

Ernest ignored the thrust. It was always his way to turn the point back upon an opponent, and he did it now, with a beaming brotherliness of face and utterance.

"Then you will undoubtedly understand the definition I shall now make of philosophy. But before I make it, I shall challenge you to point out error in it or to remain a silent metaphysician. Philosophy is merely the widest science of all. Its reasoning method is the same as that of any particular science and of all particular sciences. And by that same method of reasoning, the inductive method, philosophy fuses all particular sciences into one great science. As Spencer says, the data of any particular science are partially unified knowledge. Philosophy unifies the knowledge that is contributed by all the sciences. Philosophy is the science of science, the master science, if you please. How do you like my definition?"

"Very creditable, very creditable," Dr. Hammerfield muttered lamely.

But Ernest was merciless.

"Remember," he warned, "my definition is fatal to metaphysics. If you do not now point out a flaw in my definition, you are disqualified later on from advancing metaphysical arguments. You must go through life seeking that flaw and remaining metaphysically silent until you have found it."

Ernest waited. The silence was painful. Dr. Hammerfield was pained. He was also puzzled. Ernest's sledge-hammer attack disconcerted him. He was not used to the simple and direct method of controversy. He looked appealingly around the table, but no one answered for him. I caught father grinning into his napkin.

"There is another way of disqualifying the metaphysicians," Ernest said, when he had rendered Dr. Hammerfield's discomfiture complete. "Judge them by their works. What have they done for mankind beyond the spinning of airy fancies and the mistaking of their own shadows for gods? They have added to the gayety of mankind, I grant; but what tangible good have they wrought for mankind? They philosophized, if you will pardon my misuse of the word, about the heart as the seat of the emotions, while the scientists were formulating the circulation of the blood. They declaimed about famine and pestilence as being scourges of God, while the scientists were building granaries and draining cities. They built gods in their own shapes and out of their own desires, while the scientists were building roads and bridges. They were describing the earth as the centre of the universe, while the scientists were discovering America and probing space for the stars and the laws of the stars. In short, the metaphysicians have done nothing, absolutely nothing, for mankind. Step by step, before the advance of science, they have been driven back. As fast as the ascertained facts of science have overthrown their subjective explanations of things, they have made new subjective explanations of things, including explanations of the latest ascertained facts. And this, I doubt not, they will go on doing to the end of time. Gentlemen, a metaphysician is a medicine man. The difference between you and the Eskimo who makes a fur-clad blubber-eating god is merely a difference of several thousand years of ascertained facts. That is all."

"Yet the thought of Aristotle ruled Europe for twelve centuries," Dr. Ballingford announced pompously. "And Aristotle was a metaphysician."

Dr. Ballingford glanced around the table and was rewarded by nods and smiles of approval.

"Your illustration is most unfortunate," Ernest replied. "You refer to a very dark period in human history. In fact, we call that period the Dark Ages. A period wherein science was raped by the metaphysicians, wherein physics became a search for the Philosopher's Stone, wherein chemistry became alchemy, and astronomy became astrology. Sorry the domination of Aristotle's thought!"

Dr. Ballingford looked pained, then he brightened up and said:

"Granted this horrible picture you have drawn, yet you must confess that metaphysics was inherently potent in so far as it drew humanity out of this dark period and on into the illumination of the succeeding centuries."

"Metaphysics had nothing to do with it," Ernest retorted.

"What?" Dr. Hammerfield cried. "It was not the thinking and the speculation that led to the voyages of discovery?"

"Ah, my dear sir," Ernest smiled, "I thought you were disqualified. You have not yet picked out the flaw in my definition of philosophy. You are now on an unsubstantial basis. But it is the way of the metaphysicians, and I forgive you. No, I repeat, metaphysics had nothing to do with it. Bread and butter, silks and jewels, dollars and cents, and, incidentally, the closing up of the overland trade-routes to India, were the things that caused the voyages of discovery. With the fall of Constantinople, in 1453, the Turks blocked the way of the caravans to India. The traders of Europe had to find another route. Here was the original cause for the voyages of discovery. Columbus sailed to find a new route to the Indies. It is so stated in all the history books. Incidentally, new facts were learned about the nature, size, and form of the earth, and the Ptolemaic system went glimmering."

Dr. Hammerfield snorted.

"You do not agree with me?" Ernest queried. "Then wherein am I wrong?"

"I can only reaffirm my position," Dr. Hammerfield retorted tartly. "It is too long a story to enter into now."

"No story is too long for the scientist," Ernest said sweetly. "That is why the scientist gets to places. That is why he got to America."

I shall not describe the whole evening, though it is a joy to me to recall every moment, every detail, of those first hours of my coming to know Ernest Everhard.

Battle royal raged, and the ministers grew red-faced and excited, especially at the moments when Ernest called them romantic philosophers, shadow-projectors, and similar things. And always he checked them back to facts. "The fact, man, the irrefragable fact!" he would proclaim triumphantly, when he had brought one of them a cropper. He bristled with facts. He tripped them up with facts, ambuscaded them with facts, bombarded them with broadsides of facts.

"You seem to worship at the shrine of fact," Dr. Hammerfield taunted him.

"There is no God but Fact, and Mr. Everhard is its prophet," Dr. Ballingford paraphrased.

Ernest smilingly acquiesced.

"I'm like the man from Texas," he said. And, on being solicited, he explained. "You see, the man from Missouri always says, 'You've got to show me.' But the man from Texas says, 'You've got to put it in my hand.' From which it is apparent that he is no metaphysician."

Another time, when Ernest had just said that the metaphysical philosophers could never stand the test of truth, Dr. Hammerfield suddenly demanded:

"What is the test of truth, young man? Will you kindly explain what has so long puzzled wiser heads than yours?"

"Certainly," Ernest answered. His cocksureness irritated them. "The wise heads have puzzled so sorely over truth because they went up into the air after it. Had they remained on the solid earth, they would have found it easily enough—ay, they would have found that they themselves were precisely testing truth with every practical act and thought of their lives."

"The test, the test," Dr. Hammerfield repeated impatiently. "Never mind the preamble. Give us that which we have sought so long—the test of truth. Give it us, and we will be as gods."

There was an impolite and sneering scepticism in his words and manner that secretly pleased most of them at the table, though it seemed to bother Bishop Morehouse.

"Dr. Jordan* has stated it very clearly," Ernest said. "His test of truth is: 'Will it work? Will you trust your life to it?'"

> * A noted educator of the late nineteenth and early
> twentieth centuries of the Christian Era. He was president
> of the Stanford University, a private benefaction of the
> times.

"Pish!" Dr. Hammerfield sneered. "You have not taken Bishop Berkeley* into account. He has never been answered."

> * An idealistic monist who long puzzled the philosophers of
> that time with his denial of the existence of matter, but
> whose clever argument was finally demolished when the new
> empiric facts of science were philosophically generalized.

"The noblest metaphysician of them all," Ernest laughed. "But your example is unfortunate. As Berkeley himself attested, his metaphysics didn't work."

Dr. Hammerfield was angry, righteously angry. It was as though he had caught Ernest in a theft or a lie.

"Young man," he trumpeted, "that statement is on a par with all you have uttered tonight. It is a base and unwarranted assumption."

"I am quite crushed," Ernest murmured meekly. "Only I don't know what hit me. You'll have to put it in my hand, Doctor."

"I will, I will," Dr. Hammerfield spluttered. "How do you know? You do not know that Bishop Berkeley attested that his metaphysics did not work. You have no proof. Young man, they have always worked."

"I take it as proof that Berkeley's metaphysics did not work, because—" Ernest paused calmly for a moment. "Because Berkeley made an invariable practice of going through doors instead of walls. Because he trusted his life to solid bread and butter and roast beef. Because he shaved himself with a razor that worked when it removed the hair from his face."

"But those are actual things!" Dr. Hammerfield cried. "Metaphysics is of the mind."

"And they work—in the mind?" Ernest queried softly.

The other nodded.

"And even a multitude of angels can dance on the point of a needle—in the mind," Ernest went on reflectively. "And a blubber-eating, fur-clad god can exist and work—in the mind; and there are no proofs to the contrary—in the mind. I suppose, Doctor, you live in the mind?"

"My mind to me a kingdom is," was the answer.

"That's another way of saying that you live up in the air. But you come back to earth at meal-time, I am sure, or when an earthquake happens along. Or, tell me, Doctor, do you have no apprehension in an earthquake that that incorporeal body of yours will be hit by an immaterial brick?"

Instantly, and quite unconsciously, Dr. Hammerfield's hand shot up to his head, where a scar disappeared under the hair. It happened that Ernest had blundered on an apposite illustration. Dr. Hammerfield had been nearly killed in the Great Earthquake* by a falling chimney. Everybody broke out into roars of laughter.

   * The Great Earthquake of 1906 A.D. that destroyed San
     Francisco.

"Well?" Ernest asked, when the merriment had subsided. "Proofs to the contrary?"

And in the silence he asked again, "Well?" Then he added, "Still well, but not so well, that argument of yours."

But Dr. Hammerfield was temporarily crushed, and the battle raged on in new directions. On point after point, Ernest challenged the ministers. When they affirmed that they knew the working class, he told them fundamental truths about the working class that they did not know, and challenged them for disproofs. He gave them facts, always facts, checked their excursions into the air, and brought them back to the solid earth and its facts.

How the scene comes back to me! I can hear him now, with that war-note in his voice, flaying them with his facts, each fact a lash that stung and stung again. And he was merciless. He took no quarter,* and gave none. I can never forget the flaying he gave them at the end:

> * This figure arises from the customs of the times. When, among men fighting to the death in their wild-animal way, a beaten man threw down his weapons, it was at the option of the victor to slay him or spare him.

"You have repeatedly confessed to-night, by direct avowal or ignorant statement, that you do not know the working class. But you are not to be blamed for this. How can you know anything about the working class? You do not live in the same locality with the working class. You herd with the capitalist class in another locality. And why not? It is the capitalist class that pays you, that feeds you, that puts the very clothes on your backs that you are wearing to-night. And in return you preach to your employers the brands of metaphysics that are especially acceptable to them; and the especially acceptable brands are acceptable because they do not menace the established order of society."

Here there was a stir of dissent around the table.

"Oh, I am not challenging your sincerity," Ernest continued. "You are sincere. You preach what you believe. There lies your strength and your value—to the capitalist class. But should you change your belief to something that menaces the established order, your preaching would be unacceptable to your employers, and you would be discharged. Every little while some one or another of you is so discharged.* Am I not right?"

> * During this period there were many ministers cast out of the church for preaching unacceptable doctrine. Especially were they cast out when their preaching became tainted with socialism.

This time there was no dissent. They sat dumbly acquiescent, with the exception of Dr. Hammerfield, who said:

"It is when their thinking is wrong that they are asked to resign."

"Which is another way of saying when their thinking is unacceptable," Ernest answered, and then went on. "So I say to you, go ahead and preach and earn your pay, but for goodness' sake leave the working class alone. You belong in the enemy's camp. You have nothing in common with the working class. Your hands are soft with the work others have performed for you. Your stomachs are round with the plenitude of eating." (Here Dr. Ballingford winced, and every eye glanced at his prodigious girth. It was said he had not seen his own feet in years.) "And your minds are filled with doctrines that are buttresses of the established order. You are as much mercenaries (sincere mercenaries, I grant) as were the men of the Swiss Guard.* Be true to your salt and your hire; guard, with your preaching, the interests of your employers; but do not come down to the working class and serve as false leaders. You cannot honestly be in the two camps at once. The working class has done without you. Believe me, the working class will continue to do without you. And, furthermore, the working class can do better without you than with you."

    * The hired foreign palace guards of Louis XVI, a king of
    France that was beheaded by his people.

CHAPTER II

CHALLENGES.

After the guests had gone, father threw himself into a chair and gave vent to roars of Gargantuan laughter. Not since the death of my mother had I known him to laugh so heartily.

"I'll wager Dr. Hammerfield was never up against anything like it in his life," he laughed. "'The courtesies of ecclesiastical controversy!' Did you notice how he began like a lamb—Everhard, I mean, and how quickly he became a roaring lion? He has a splendidly disciplined mind. He would have made a good scientist if his energies had been directed that way."

I need scarcely say that I was deeply interested in Ernest Everhard. It was not alone what he had said and how he had said it, but it was the man himself. I had never met a man like him. I suppose that was why, in spite of my twenty-four years, I had not married. I liked him; I had to confess it to myself. And my like for him was founded on things beyond intellect and argument. Regardless of his bulging muscles and prize-fighter's throat, he impressed me as an ingenuous boy. I felt that under the guise of an intellectual swashbuckler was a delicate and sensitive spirit. I sensed this, in ways I knew not, save that they were my woman's intuitions.

There was something in that clarion-call of his that went to my heart. It still rang in my ears, and I felt that I should like to hear it again—and to see again that glint of laughter in his eyes that belied the impassioned seriousness of his face. And there were further reaches of vague and indeterminate feelings that stirred in me. I almost loved him then, though I am confident, had I never seen him again, that the vague feelings would have passed away and that I should easily have forgotten him.

But I was not destined never to see him again. My father's new-born interest in sociology and the dinner parties he gave would not permit. Father was not a sociologist. His marriage with my mother had been very happy, and in the researches of his own science, physics, he had been very happy. But when mother died, his own work could not fill the emptiness. At first, in a mild way, he had dabbled in philosophy; then, becoming interested, he had drifted on into economics and sociology. He had a strong sense of justice, and he soon became fired with a passion to redress wrong. It was with gratitude that I hailed these signs of a new interest in life, though I little dreamed what the outcome would be. With the enthusiasm of a boy he plunged excitedly into these new pursuits, regardless of whither they led him.

He had been used always to the laboratory, and so it was that he turned the dining room into a sociological laboratory. Here came to dinner all sorts and conditions of men,—scientists, politicians, bankers, merchants, professors, labor leaders, socialists, and anarchists. He stirred them to discussion, and analyzed their thoughts of life and society.

He had met Ernest shortly prior to the "preacher's night." And after the guests were gone, I learned how he had met him, passing down a street at night and stopping to listen to a man on a soap-box who was addressing a crowd of workingmen. The man on the box was Ernest. Not that he was a mere soap-box orator. He stood high in the councils of the socialist party, was one of the leaders, and was the acknowledged leader in the philosophy of socialism. But he had a certain clear way of stating the abstruse in simple language, was a born expositor and teacher, and was not above the soap-box as a means of interpreting economics to the workingmen.

My father stopped to listen, became interested, effected a meeting, and, after quite an acquaintance, invited him to the ministers' dinner. It was after the dinner that father told me what little he knew about him. He had been born in the working class, though he was a descendant of the old line of Everhards that for over two hundred years had lived in America.* At ten years of age he had gone to work in the mills, and later he served his apprenticeship and became a horseshoer. He was self-educated, had taught himself German and French, and at that time was earning a meagre living by translating scientific and philosophical works for a struggling socialist publishing house in Chicago. Also, his earnings were added to by the royalties from the small sales of his own economic and philosophic works.

> * The distinction between being native born and foreign born was sharp and invidious in those days.

This much I learned of him before I went to bed, and I lay long awake, listening in memory to the sound of his voice. I grew frightened at my thoughts. He was so unlike the men of my own class, so alien and so strong. His masterfulness delighted me and terrified me, for my fancies wantonly roved until I found myself considering him as a lover, as a husband. I had always heard that the strength of men was an irresistible attraction to women; but he was too strong. "No! no!" I cried out. "It is impossible, absurd!" And on the morrow I awoke to find in myself a longing to see him again. I wanted to see him mastering men in discussion, the war-note in his voice; to see him, in all his certitude and strength, shattering their complacency, shaking them out of their ruts of thinking. What if he did swashbuckle? To use his own phrase, "it worked," it produced effects. And, besides, his swashbuckling was a fine thing to see. It stirred one like the onset of battle.

Several days passed during which I read Ernest's books, borrowed from my father. His written word was as his spoken word, clear and convincing. It was its absolute simplicity that convinced even while one continued to doubt. He had the gift of lucidity. He was the perfect expositor. Yet, in spite of his style, there was much that I did not like. He laid too great stress on what he called the class struggle, the antagonism between labor and capital, the conflict of interest.

Father reported with glee Dr. Hammerfield's judgment of Ernest, which was to the effect that he was "an insolent young puppy, made bumptious by a little and very inadequate learning." Also, Dr. Hammerfield declined to meet Ernest again.

But Bishop Morehouse turned out to have become interested in Ernest, and was anxious for another meeting. "A strong young man," he said; "and very much alive, very much alive. But he is too sure, too sure."

Ernest came one afternoon with father. The Bishop had already arrived, and we were having tea on the veranda. Ernest's continued presence in Berkeley, by the way, was accounted for by the fact that he was taking special courses in biology at the university, and also that he was hard at work on a new book entitled "Philosophy and Revolution."*

> * This book continued to be secretly printed throughout the
> three centuries of the Iron Heel. There are several copies
> of various editions in the National Library of Ardis.

The veranda seemed suddenly to have become small when Ernest arrived. Not that he was so very large—he stood only five feet nine inches; but that he seemed to radiate an atmosphere of largeness. As he stopped to meet me, he betrayed a certain slight awkwardness that was strangely at variance with his bold-looking eyes and his firm, sure hand that clasped for a moment in greeting. And in that moment his eyes were just as steady and sure. There seemed a question in them this time, and as before he looked at me over long.

"I have been reading your 'Working-class Philosophy,'" I said, and his eyes lighted in a pleased way.

"Of course," he answered, "you took into consideration the audience to which it was addressed."

"I did, and it is because I did that I have a quarrel with you," I challenged.

"I, too, have a quarrel with you, Mr. Everhard," Bishop Morehouse said.

Ernest shrugged his shoulders whimsically and accepted a cup of tea.

The Bishop bowed and gave me precedence.

"You foment class hatred," I said. "I consider it wrong and criminal to appeal to all that is narrow and brutal in the working class. Class hatred is anti-social, and, it seems to me, anti-socialistic."

"Not guilty," he answered. "Class hatred is neither in the text nor in the spirit of anything I have every written."

"Oh!" I cried reproachfully, and reached for his book and opened it.

He sipped his tea and smiled at me while I ran over the pages.

"Page one hundred and thirty-two," I read aloud: "'The class struggle, therefore, presents itself in the present stage of social development between the wage-paying and the wage-paid classes.'"

I looked at him triumphantly.

"No mention there of class hatred," he smiled back.

"But," I answered, "you say 'class struggle.'"

"A different thing from class hatred," he replied. "And, believe me, we foment no hatred. We say that the class struggle is a law of social development. We are not responsible for it. We do not make the class struggle. We merely explain it, as Newton explained gravitation. We explain the nature of the conflict of interest that produces the class struggle."

"But there should be no conflict of interest!" I cried.

"I agree with you heartily," he answered. "That is what we socialists are trying to bring about,—the abolition of the conflict of interest. Pardon me. Let me read an extract." He took his book and turned back several pages. "Page one hundred and twenty-six: 'The cycle of class struggles which began with the dissolution of rude, tribal communism and the rise of private property will end with the passing of private property in the means of social existence.'"

"But I disagree with you," the Bishop interposed, his pale, ascetic face betraying by a faint glow the intensity of his feelings. "Your premise is wrong. There is no such thing as a conflict of interest between labor and capital—or, rather, there ought not to be."

"Thank you," Ernest said gravely. "By that last statement you have given me back my premise."

"But why should there be a conflict?" the Bishop demanded warmly.

Ernest shrugged his shoulders. "Because we are so made, I guess."

"But we are not so made!" cried the other.

"Are you discussing the ideal man?" Ernest asked, "—unselfish and godlike, and so few in numbers as to be practically non-existent, or are you discussing the common and ordinary average man?"

"The common and ordinary man," was the answer.

"Who is weak and fallible, prone to error?"

Bishop Morehouse nodded.

"And petty and selfish?"

Again he nodded.

"Watch out!" Ernest warned. "I said 'selfish.'"

"The average man IS selfish," the Bishop affirmed valiantly.

"Wants all he can get?"

"Wants all he can get—true but deplorable."

"Then I've got you." Ernest's jaw snapped like a trap. "Let me show you. Here is a man who works on the street railways."

"He couldn't work if it weren't for capital," the Bishop interrupted.

"True, and you will grant that capital would perish if there were no labor to earn the dividends."

The Bishop was silent.

"Won't you?" Ernest insisted.

The Bishop nodded.

"Then our statements cancel each other," Ernest said in a matter-of-fact tone, "and we are where we were. Now to begin again. The workingmen on the street railway furnish the labor. The stockholders furnish the capital. By the joint effort of the workingmen and the capital, money is earned.* They divide between them this money that is earned. Capital's share is called 'dividends.' Labor's share is called 'wages.'"

> * In those days, groups of predatory individuals controlled all the means of transportation, and for the use of same levied toll upon the public.

"Very good," the Bishop interposed. "And there is no reason that the division should not be amicable."

"You have already forgotten what we had agreed upon," Ernest replied. "We agreed that the average man is selfish. He is the man that is. You have gone up in the air and are arranging a division between the kind of men that ought to be but are not. But to return to the earth, the workingman, being selfish, wants all he can get in the division. The capitalist, being selfish, wants all he can get in the division. When there is only so much of the same thing, and when two men want all they can get of the same thing, there is a conflict of interest between labor and capital. And it is an irreconcilable conflict. As long as workingmen and capitalists exist, they will continue to quarrel over the division. If you were in San Francisco this afternoon, you'd have to walk. There isn't a street car running."

"Another strike?"* the Bishop queried with alarm.

> * These quarrels were very common in those irrational and anarchic times. Sometimes the laborers refused to work. Sometimes the capitalists refused to let the laborers work. In the violence and turbulence of such disagreements much property was destroyed and many lives lost. All this is inconceivable to us—as inconceivable as another custom of that time, namely, the habit the men of the lower classes had of breaking the furniture when they quarrelled with their wives.

"Yes, they're quarrelling over the division of the earnings of the street railways."

Bishop Morehouse became excited.

"It is wrong!" he cried. "It is so short-sighted on the part of the workingmen. How can they hope to keep our sympathy—"

"When we are compelled to walk," Ernest said slyly.

But Bishop Morehouse ignored him and went on:

"Their outlook is too narrow. Men should be men, not brutes. There will be violence and murder now, and sorrowing widows and orphans. Capital and labor should be friends. They should work hand in hand and to their mutual benefit."

"Ah, now you are up in the air again," Ernest remarked dryly. "Come back to earth. Remember, we agreed that the average man is selfish."

"But he ought not to be!" the Bishop cried.

"And there I agree with you," was Ernest's rejoinder. "He ought not to be selfish, but he will continue to be selfish as long as he lives in a social system that is based on pig-ethics."

The Bishop was aghast, and my father chuckled.

"Yes, pig-ethics," Ernest went on remorselessly. "That is the meaning of the capitalist system. And that is what your church is standing for, what you are preaching for every time you get up in the pulpit. Pig-ethics! There is no other name for it."

Bishop Morehouse turned appealingly to my father, but he laughed and nodded his head.

"I'm afraid Mr. Everhard is right," he said. "LAISSEZ-FAIRE, the let-alone policy of each for himself and devil take the hindmost. As Mr. Everhard said the other night, the function you churchmen perform is to maintain the established order of society, and society is established on that foundation."

"But that is not the teaching of Christ!" cried the Bishop.

"The Church is not teaching Christ these days," Ernest put in quickly. "That is why the workingmen will have nothing to do with the Church. The Church condones the frightful brutality and savagery with which the capitalist class treats the working class."

"The Church does not condone it," the Bishop objected.

"The Church does not protest against it," Ernest replied. "And in so far as the Church does not protest, it condones, for remember the Church is supported by the capitalist class."

"I had not looked at it in that light," the Bishop said naively. "You must be wrong. I know that there is much that is sad and wicked in this world. I know that the Church has lost the—what you call the proletariat."*

> * Proletariat: Derived originally from the Latin PROLETARII,
> the name given in the census of Servius Tullius to those who
> were of value to the state only as the rearers of offspring
> (PROLES); in other words, they were of no importance either
> for wealth, or position, or exceptional ability.

"You never had the proletariat," Ernest cried. "The proletariat has grown up outside the Church and without the Church."

"I do not follow you," the Bishop said faintly.

"Then let me explain. With the introduction of machinery and the factory system in the latter part of the eighteenth century, the great mass of the working people was separated from the land. The old system of labor was broken down. The working people were driven from their villages and herded in factory towns. The mothers and children were put to work at the new machines. Family life ceased. The conditions were frightful. It is a tale of blood."

"I know, I know," Bishop Morehouse interrupted with an agonized expression on his face. "It was terrible. But it occurred a century and a half ago."

"And there, a century and a half ago, originated the modern proletariat," Ernest continued. "And the Church ignored it. While a slaughter-house was made of the nation by the capitalist, the Church was dumb. It did not protest, as to-day it does not protest. As Austin Lewis* says, speaking of that time, those to whom the command 'Feed my lambs' had been given, saw those lambs sold into slavery and worked to death without a protest.** The Church was dumb, then, and before I go on I want you either flatly to agree with me or flatly to disagree with me. Was the Church dumb then?"

* Candidate for Governor of California on the Socialist
ticket in the fall election of 1906 Christian Era. An
Englishman by birth, a writer of many books on political
economy and philosophy, and one of the Socialist leaders of
the times.

** There is no more horrible page in history than the
treatment of the child and women slaves in the English
factories in the latter half of the eighteenth century of
the Christian Era. In such industrial hells arose some of
the proudest fortunes of that day.

Bishop Morehouse hesitated. Like Dr. Hammerfield, he was unused to this fierce "infighting," as Ernest called it.

"The history of the eighteenth century is written," Ernest prompted. "If the Church was not dumb, it will be found not dumb in the books."

"I am afraid the Church was dumb," the Bishop confessed.

"And the Church is dumb to-day."

"There I disagree," said the Bishop.

Ernest paused, looked at him searchingly, and accepted the challenge.

"All right," he said. "Let us see. In Chicago there are women who toil all the week for ninety cents. Has the Church protested?"

"This is news to me," was the answer. "Ninety cents per week! It is horrible!"

"Has the Church protested?" Ernest insisted.

"The Church does not know." The Bishop was struggling hard.

"Yet the command to the Church was, 'Feed my lambs,'" Ernest sneered. And then, the next moment, "Pardon my sneer, Bishop. But can you wonder that we lose patience with you? When have you protested to your capitalistic congregations at the working of children in the Southern cotton mills?* Children, six and seven years of age, working every night at twelve-hour shifts? They never see the blessed sunshine. They die like flies. The dividends are paid out of their blood. And out of the dividends magnificent churches are built in New England, wherein your kind preaches pleasant platitudes to the sleek, full-bellied recipients of those dividends."

* Everhard might have drawn a better illustration from the Southern Church's outspoken defence of chattel slavery prior to what is known as the "War of the Rebellion." Several such illustrations, culled from the documents of the times, are here appended. In 1835 A.D., the General Assembly of the Presbyterian Church resolved that: "slavery is recognized in both the Old and the New Testaments, and is not condemned by the authority of God." The Charleston Baptist Association issued the following, in an address, in 1835 A.D.: "The right of masters to dispose of the time of their slaves has been distinctly recognized by the Creator of all things, who is surely at liberty to vest the right of property over any object whomsoever He pleases." The Rev. E. D. Simon, Doctor of Divinity and professor in the Randolph-Macon Methodist College of Virginia, wrote: "Extracts from Holy Writ unequivocally assert the right of property in slaves, together with the usual incidents to that right. The right to buy and sell is clearly stated. Upon the whole, then, whether we consult the Jewish policy instituted by God himself, or the uniform opinion and practice of mankind in all ages, or the injunctions of the New Testament and the moral law, we are brought to the conclusion that slavery is not immoral. Having established the point that the first African slaves were legally brought into bondage, the right to detain their children in bondage follows as an indispensable consequence. Thus we see that the slavery that exists in America was founded in right."

It is not at all remarkable that this same note should have been struck by the Church a generation or so later in relation to the defence of capitalistic property. In the great museum at Asgard there is a book entitled "Essays in Application," written by Henry van Dyke. The book was published in 1905 of the Christian Era. From what we can make out, Van Dyke must have been a churchman. The book is a good example of what Everhard would have called bourgeois thinking. Note the similarity between the utterance of the Charleston Baptist Association quoted above, and the following utterance of Van Dyke seventy years later: "The Bible teaches that God owns the world. He distributes to every man according to His own good pleasure, conformably to general laws."

"I did not know," the Bishop murmured faintly. His face was pale, and he seemed suffering from nausea.

"Then you have not protested?"

The Bishop shook his head.

"Then the Church is dumb to-day, as it was in the eighteenth century?"

The Bishop was silent, and for once Ernest forbore to press the point.

"And do not forget, whenever a churchman does protest, that he is discharged."

"I hardly think that is fair," was the objection.

"Will you protest?" Ernest demanded.

"Show me evils, such as you mention, in our own community, and I will protest."

"I'll show you," Ernest said quietly. "I am at your disposal. I will take you on a journey through hell."

"And I shall protest." The Bishop straightened himself in his chair, and over his gentle face spread the harshness of the warrior. "The Church shall not be dumb!"

"You will be discharged," was the warning.

"I shall prove the contrary," was the retort. "I shall prove, if what you say is so, that the Church has erred through ignorance. And, furthermore, I hold that whatever is horrible in industrial society is due to the ignorance of the capitalist class. It will mend all that is wrong as soon as it receives the message. And this message it shall be the duty of the Church to deliver."

Ernest laughed. He laughed brutally, and I was driven to the Bishop's defence.

"Remember," I said, "you see but one side of the shield. There is much good in us, though you give us credit for no good at all. Bishop Morehouse is right. The industrial wrong, terrible as you say it is, is due to ignorance. The divisions of society have become too widely separated."

"The wild Indian is not so brutal and savage as the capitalist class," he answered; and in that moment I hated him.

"You do not know us," I answered. "We are not brutal and savage."

"Prove it," he challenged.

"How can I prove it . . . to you?" I was growing angry.

He shook his head. "I do not ask you to prove it to me. I ask you to prove it to yourself."

"I know," I said.

"You know nothing," was his rude reply.

"There, there, children," father said soothingly.

"I don't care—" I began indignantly, but Ernest interrupted.

"I understand you have money, or your father has, which is the same thing—money invested in the Sierra Mills."

"What has that to do with it?" I cried.

"Nothing much," he began slowly, "except that the gown you wear is stained with blood. The food you eat is a bloody stew. The blood of little children and of strong men is dripping from your very roof-beams. I can close my eyes, now, and hear it drip, drop, drip, drop, all about me."

And suiting the action to the words, he closed his eyes and leaned back in his chair. I burst into tears of mortification and hurt vanity. I had never been so brutally treated in my life. Both the Bishop and my father were embarrassed and perturbed. They tried to lead the conversation away into easier channels; but Ernest opened his eyes, looked at me, and waved them aside. His mouth was stern, and his eyes too; and in the latter there was no glint of laughter. What he was about to say, what terrible castigation he was going to give me, I never knew; for at that moment a man, passing along the sidewalk, stopped and glanced in at us. He was a large man, poorly dressed, and on his back was a great load of rattan and bamboo stands, chairs, and screens. He looked at the house as if debating whether or not he should come in and try to sell some of his wares.

"That man's name is Jackson," Ernest said.

"With that strong body of his he should be at work, and not peddling,"* I answered curtly.

> * In that day there were many thousands of these poor merchants called PEDLERS. They carried their whole stock in trade from door to door. It was a most wasteful expenditure of energy. Distribution was as confused and irrational as the whole general system of society.

"Notice the sleeve of his left arm," Ernest said gently.

I looked, and saw that the sleeve was empty.

"It was some of the blood from that arm that I heard dripping from your roof-beams," Ernest said with continued gentleness. "He lost his arm in the Sierra Mills, and like a broken-down horse you turned him out on the highway to die. When I say 'you,' I mean the superintendent and the officials that you and the other stockholders pay to manage the mills for you. It was an accident. It was caused by his trying to save the company a few dollars. The toothed drum of the picker caught his arm. He might have let the small flint that he saw in the teeth go through. It would have smashed out a double row of spikes. But he reached for the flint, and his arm was picked and clawed to shreds from the finger tips to the shoulder. It was at night. The mills were working overtime. They paid a fat dividend that quarter. Jackson had been working many hours, and his muscles had lost their resiliency and snap. They made his movements a bit slow. That was why the machine caught him. He had a wife and three children."

"And what did the company do for him?" I asked.

"Nothing. Oh, yes, they did do something. They successfully fought the damage suit he brought when he came out of hospital. The company employs very efficient lawyers, you know."

"You have not told the whole story," I said with conviction. "Or else you do not know the whole story. Maybe the man was insolent."

"Insolent! Ha! ha!" His laughter was Mephistophelian. "Great God! Insolent! And with his arm chewed off! Nevertheless he was a meek and lowly servant, and there is no record of his having been insolent."

"But the courts," I urged. "The case would not have been decided against him had there been no more to the affair than you have mentioned."

"Colonel Ingram is leading counsel for the company. He is a shrewd lawyer." Ernest looked at me intently for a moment, then went on. "I'll tell you what you do, Miss Cunningham. You investigate Jackson's case."

"I had already determined to," I said coldly.

"All right," he beamed good-naturedly, "and I'll tell you where to find him. But I tremble for you when I think of all you are to prove by Jackson's arm."

And so it came about that both the Bishop and I accepted Ernest's challenges. They went away together, leaving me smarting with a sense of injustice that had been done me and my class. The man was a beast. I hated him, then, and consoled myself with the thought that his behavior was what was to be expected from a man of the working class.

CHAPTER III

JACKSON'S ARM.

Little did I dream the fateful part Jackson's arm was to play in my life. Jackson himself did not impress me when I hunted him out. I found him in a crazy, ramshackle* house down near the bay on the edge of the marsh. Pools of stagnant water stood around the house, their surfaces covered with a green and putrid-looking scum, while the stench that arose from them was intolerable.

   * An adjective descriptive of ruined and dilapidated houses
in which great numbers of the working people found shelter
in those days. They invariably paid rent, and, considering
the value of such houses, enormous rent, to the landlords.

I found Jackson the meek and lowly man he had been described. He was making some sort of rattan-work, and he toiled on stolidly while I talked with him. But in spite of his meekness and lowliness, I fancied I caught the first note of a nascent bitterness in him when he said:

"They might a-given me a job as watchman,* anyway."

   * In those days thievery was incredibly prevalent.
Everybody stole property from everybody else. The lords of
society stole legally or else legalized their stealing,
while the poorer classes stole illegally. Nothing was safe
unless guarded. Enormous numbers of men were employed as
watchmen to protect property. The houses of the well-to-do
were a combination of safe deposit vault and fortress. The
appropriation of the personal belongings of others by our
own children of to-day is looked upon as a rudimentary
survival of the theft-characteristic that in those early
times was universal.

I got little out of him. He struck me as stupid, and yet the deftness with which he worked with his one hand seemed to belie his stupidity. This suggested an idea to me.

"How did you happen to get your arm caught in the machine?" I asked.

He looked at me in a slow and pondering way, and shook his head. "I don't know. It just happened."

"Carelessness?" I prompted.

"No," he answered, "I ain't for callin' it that. I was workin' overtime, an' I guess I was tired out some. I worked seventeen years in them mills, an' I've took notice that most of the accidents happens just before whistle-blow.* I'm willin' to bet that more accidents happens in the hour before whistle-blow than in all the rest of the day. A man ain't so quick after workin' steady for hours. I've seen too many of 'em cut up an' gouged an' chawed not to know."

> * The laborers were called to work and dismissed by savage, screaming, nerve-racking steam-whistles.

"Many of them?" I queried.

"Hundreds an' hundreds, an' children, too."

With the exception of the terrible details, Jackson's story of his accident was the same as that I had already heard. When I asked him if he had broken some rule of working the machinery, he shook his head.

"I chucked off the belt with my right hand," he said, "an' made a reach for the flint with my left. I didn't stop to see if the belt was off. I thought my right hand had done it—only it didn't. I reached quick, and the belt wasn't all the way off. And then my arm was chewed off."

"It must have been painful," I said sympathetically.

"The crunchin' of the bones wasn't nice," was his answer.

His mind was rather hazy concerning the damage suit. Only one thing was clear to him, and that was that he had not got any damages. He had a feeling that the testimony of the foremen and the superintendent had brought about the adverse decision of the court. Their testimony, as he put it, "wasn't what it ought to have ben." And to them I resolved to go.

One thing was plain, Jackson's situation was wretched. His wife was in ill health, and he was unable to earn, by his rattan-work and peddling, sufficient food for the family. He was back in his rent, and the oldest boy, a lad of eleven, had started to work in the mills.

"They might a-given me that watchman's job," were his last words as I went away.

By the time I had seen the lawyer who had handled Jackson's case, and the two foremen and the superintendent at the mills who had testified, I began to feel that there was something after all in Ernest's contention.

He was a weak and inefficient-looking man, the lawyer, and at sight of him I did not wonder that Jackson's case had been lost. My first thought was that it had served Jackson right for getting such a lawyer. But the next moment two of Ernest's statements came flashing into my consciousness: "The company employs very efficient lawyers" and "Colonel Ingram is a shrewd lawyer." I did some rapid thinking. It dawned upon me that of course the company could afford finer legal talent than could a workingman like Jackson. But this was merely a minor detail. There was some very good reason, I was sure, why Jackson's case had gone against him.

"Why did you lose the case?" I asked.

The lawyer was perplexed and worried for a moment, and I found it in my heart to pity the wretched little creature. Then he began to whine. I do believe his whine was congenital. He was a man beaten at birth. He whined about the testimony. The witnesses had given only the evidence that helped the other side. Not one word could he get out of them that would have helped Jackson. They knew which side their bread was buttered on. Jackson was a fool. He had been brow-beaten and confused by Colonel Ingram. Colonel Ingram was brilliant at cross-examination. He had made Jackson answer damaging questions.

"How could his answers be damaging if he had the right on his side?" I demanded.

"What's right got to do with it?" he demanded back. "You see all those books." He moved his hand over the array of volumes on the walls of his tiny office. "All my reading and studying of them has taught me that law is one thing and right is another thing. Ask any lawyer. You go to Sunday-school to learn what is right. But you go to those books to learn . . . law."

"Do you mean to tell me that Jackson had the right on his side and yet was beaten?" I queried tentatively. "Do you mean to tell me that there is no justice in Judge Caldwell's court?"

The little lawyer glared at me a moment, and then the belligerence faded out of his face.

"I hadn't a fair chance," he began whining again. "They made a fool out of Jackson and out of me, too. What chance had I? Colonel Ingram is a great lawyer. If he wasn't great, would he have charge of the law business of the Sierra Mills, of the Erston Land Syndicate, of the Berkeley Consolidated, of the Oakland, San Leandro, and Pleasanton Electric? He's a corporation lawyer, and corporation lawyers are not paid for being fools.* What do you think the Sierra Mills alone give him twenty thousand dollars a year for? Because he's worth twenty thousand dollars a year to them, that's what for. I'm not worth that much. If I was, I wouldn't be on the outside, starving and taking cases like Jackson's. What do you think I'd have got if I'd won Jackson's case?"

> * The function of the corporation lawyer was to serve, by corrupt methods, the money-grabbing propensities of the corporations. It is on record that Theodore Roosevelt, at that time President of the United States, said in 1905 A.D., in his address at Harvard Commencement: "We all know that, as things actually are, many of the most influential and most highly remunerated members of the Bar in every centre of wealth, make it their special task to work out bold and ingenious schemes by which their wealthy clients, individual or corporate, can evade the laws which were made to regulate, in the interests of the public, the uses of great wealth."

"You'd have robbed him, most probably," I answered.

"Of course I would," he cried angrily. "I've got to live, haven't I?"*

> * A typical illustration of the internecine strife that permeated all society. Men preyed upon one another like ravening wolves. The big wolves ate the little wolves, and in the social pack Jackson was one of the least of the

little wolves.

"He has a wife and children," I chided.

"So have I a wife and children," he retorted. "And there's not a soul in this world except myself that cares whether they starve or not."

His face suddenly softened, and he opened his watch and showed me a small photograph of a woman and two little girls pasted inside the case.

"There they are. Look at them. We've had a hard time, a hard time. I had hoped to send them away to the country if I'd won Jackson's case. They're not healthy here, but I can't afford to send them away."

When I started to leave, he dropped back into his whine.

"I hadn't the ghost of a chance. Colonel Ingram and Judge Caldwell are pretty friendly. I'm not saying that if I'd got the right kind of testimony out of their witnesses on cross-examination, that friendship would have decided the case. And yet I must say that Judge Caldwell did a whole lot to prevent my getting that very testimony. Why, Judge Caldwell and Colonel Ingram belong to the same lodge and the same club. They live in the same neighborhood—one I can't afford. And their wives are always in and out of each other's houses. They're always having whist parties and such things back and forth."

"And yet you think Jackson had the right of it?" I asked, pausing for the moment on the threshold.

"I don't think; I know it," was his answer. "And at first I thought he had some show, too. But I didn't tell my wife. I didn't want to disappoint her. She had her heart set on a trip to the country hard enough as it was."

"Why did you not call attention to the fact that Jackson was trying to save the machinery from being injured?" I asked Peter Donnelly, one of the foremen who had testified at the trial.

He pondered a long time before replying. Then he cast an anxious look about him and said:

"Because I've a good wife an' three of the sweetest children ye ever laid eyes on, that's why."

"I do not understand," I said.

"In other words, because it wouldn't a-ben healthy," he answered.

"You mean—" I began.

But he interrupted passionately.

"I mean what I said. It's long years I've worked in the mills. I began as a little lad on the spindles. I worked up ever since. It's by hard work I got to my present exalted position. I'm a foreman, if you please. An' I doubt me if there's a man in the mills that'd put out a hand to drag me from drownin'. I used to belong to the union. But I've stayed by the company through two strikes. They called me 'scab.' There's not a man among 'em to-day to take a drink with me if I asked him. D'ye see the scars on me head where

I was struck with flying bricks? There ain't a child at the spindles but what would curse me name. Me only friend is the company. It's not me duty, but me bread an' butter an' the life of me children to stand by the mills. That's why."

"Was Jackson to blame?" I asked.

"He should a-got the damages. He was a good worker an' never made trouble."

"Then you were not at liberty to tell the whole truth, as you had sworn to do?"

He shook his head.

"The truth, the whole truth, and nothing but the truth?" I said solemnly.

Again his face became impassioned, and he lifted it, not to me, but to heaven.

"I'd let me soul an' body burn in everlastin' hell for them children of mine," was his answer.

Henry Dallas, the superintendent, was a vulpine-faced creature who regarded me insolently and refused to talk. Not a word could I get from him concerning the trial and his testimony. But with the other foreman I had better luck. James Smith was a hard-faced man, and my heart sank as I encountered him. He, too, gave me the impression that he was not a free agent, as we talked I began to see that he was mentally superior to the average of his kind. He agreed with Peter Donnelly that Jackson should have got damages, and he went farther and called the action heartless and cold-blooded that had turned the worker adrift after he had been made helpless by the accident. Also, he explained that there were many accidents in the mills, and that the company's policy was to fight to the bitter end all consequent damage suits.

"It means hundreds of thousands a year to the stockholders," he said; and as he spoke I remembered the last dividend that had been paid my father, and the pretty gown for me and the books for him that had been bought out of that dividend. I remembered Ernest's charge that my gown was stained with blood, and my flesh began to crawl underneath my garments.

"When you testified at the trial, you didn't point out that Jackson received his accident through trying to save the machinery from damage?" I said.

"No, I did not," was the answer, and his mouth set bitterly. "I testified to the effect that Jackson injured himself by neglect and carelessness, and that the company was not in any way to blame or liable."

"Was it carelessness?" I asked.

"Call it that, or anything you want to call it. The fact is, a man gets tired after he's been working for hours."

I was becoming interested in the man. He certainly was of a superior kind.

"You are better educated than most workingmen," I said.

"I went through high school," he replied. "I worked my way through doing janitor-work. I wanted to go through the university. But my father died, and I came to work in the mills.

"I wanted to become a naturalist," he explained shyly, as though confessing a weakness. "I love animals. But I came to work in the mills. When I was promoted to foreman I got married, then the family came, and . . . well, I wasn't my own boss any more."

"What do you mean by that?" I asked.

"I was explaining why I testified at the trial the way I did—why I followed instructions."

"Whose instructions?"

"Colonel Ingram. He outlined the evidence I was to give."

"And it lost Jackson's case for him."

He nodded, and the blood began to rise darkly in his face.

"And Jackson had a wife and two children dependent on him."

"I know," he said quietly, though his face was growing darker.

"Tell me," I went on, "was it easy to make yourself over from what you were, say in high school, to the man you must have become to do such a thing at the trial?"

The suddenness of his outburst startled and frightened me. He ripped* out a savage oath, and clenched his fist as though about to strike me.

> * It is interesting to note the virilities of language that
> were common speech in that day, as indicative of the life,
> 'red of claw and fang,' that was then lived. Reference is
> here made, of course, not to the oath of Smith, but to the
> verb ripped used by Avis Everhard.

"I beg your pardon," he said the next moment. "No, it was not easy. And now I guess you can go away. You've got all you wanted out of me. But let me tell you this before you go. It won't do you any good to repeat anything I've said. I'll deny it, and there are no witnesses. I'll deny every word of it; and if I have to, I'll do it under oath on the witness stand."

After my interview with Smith I went to my father's office in the Chemistry Building and there encountered Ernest. It was quite unexpected, but he met me with his bold eyes and firm hand-clasp, and with that curious blend of his awkwardness and ease. It was as though our last stormy meeting was forgotten; but I was not in the mood to have it forgotten.

"I have been looking up Jackson's case," I said abruptly.

He was all interested attention, and waited for me to go on, though I could see in his eyes the certitude that my convictions had been shaken.

"He seems to have been badly treated," I confessed. "I—I—think some of his blood is dripping from our roof-beams."

"Of course," he answered. "If Jackson and all his fellows were treated mercifully, the dividends would not be so large."

"I shall never be able to take pleasure in pretty gowns again," I added.

I felt humble and contrite, and was aware of a sweet feeling that Ernest was a sort of father confessor. Then, as ever after, his strength appealed to me. It seemed to radiate a promise of peace and protection.

"Nor will you be able to take pleasure in sackcloth," he said gravely. "There are the jute mills, you know, and the same thing goes on there. It goes on everywhere. Our boasted civilization is based upon blood, soaked in blood, and neither you nor I nor any of us can escape the scarlet stain. The men you talked with—who were they?"

I told him all that had taken place.

"And not one of them was a free agent," he said. "They were all tied to the merciless industrial machine. And the pathos of it and the tragedy is that they are tied by their heartstrings. Their children—always the young life that it is their instinct to protect. This instinct is stronger than any ethic they possess. My father! He lied, he stole, he did all sorts of dishonorable things to put bread into my mouth and into the mouths of my brothers and sisters. He was a slave to the industrial machine, and it stamped his life out, worked him to death."

"But you," I interjected. "You are surely a free agent."

"Not wholly," he replied. "I am not tied by my heartstrings. I am often thankful that I have no children, and I dearly love children. Yet if I married I should not dare to have any."

"That surely is bad doctrine," I cried.

"I know it is," he said sadly. "But it is expedient doctrine. I am a revolutionist, and it is a perilous vocation."

I laughed incredulously.

"If I tried to enter your father's house at night to steal his dividends from the Sierra Mills, what would he do?"

"He sleeps with a revolver on the stand by the bed," I answered. "He would most probably shoot you."

"And if I and a few others should lead a million and a half of men* into the houses of all the well-to-do, there would be a great deal of shooting, wouldn't there?"

> * This reference is to the socialist vote cast in the United
> States in 1910. The rise of this vote clearly indicates the
> swift growth of the party of revolution. Its voting
> strength in the United States in 1888 was 2068; in 1902,
> 127,713; in 1904, 435,040; in 1908, 1,108,427; and in 1910,
> 1,688,211.

"Yes, but you are not doing that," I objected.

"It is precisely what I am doing. And we intend to take, not the mere wealth in the houses, but all the sources of that wealth, all the mines, and railroads, and factories, and banks, and stores. That is the revolution. It is truly perilous. There will be more shooting, I am afraid, than even I dream of. But as I was saying, no one to-day is a free agent. We are all caught up in the wheels and cogs of the industrial machine. You found that you were, and that the men you talked with were. Talk with more of them. Go and see Colonel Ingram. Look up the reporters that kept Jackson's case out of the papers, and the editors that run the papers. You will find them all slaves of the machine."

A little later in our conversation I asked him a simple little question about the liability of workingmen to accidents, and received a statistical lecture in return.

"It is all in the books," he said. "The figures have been gathered, and it has been proved conclusively that accidents rarely occur in the first hours of the morning work, but that they increase rapidly in the succeeding hours as the workers grow tired and slower in both their muscular and mental processes.

"Why, do you know that your father has three times as many chances for safety of life and limb than has a working-man? He has. The insurance* companies know. They will charge him four dollars and twenty cents a year on a thousand-dollar accident policy, and for the same policy they will charge a laborer fifteen dollars."

> * In the terrible wolf-struggle of those centuries, no man
> was permanently safe, no matter how much wealth he amassed.
> Out of fear for the welfare of their families, men devised
> the scheme of insurance. To us, in this intelligent age,
> such a device is laughably absurd and primitive. But in
> that age insurance was a very serious matter. The amusing
> part of it is that the funds of the insurance companies were
> frequently plundered and wasted by the very officials who
> were intrusted with the management of them.

"And you?" I asked; and in the moment of asking I was aware of a solicitude that was something more than slight.

"Oh, as a revolutionist, I have about eight chances to the workingman's one of being injured or killed," he answered carelessly. "The insurance companies charge the highly trained chemists that handle explosives eight times what they charge the workingmen. I don't think they'd insure me at all. Why did you ask?"

My eyes fluttered, and I could feel the blood warm in my face. It was not that he had caught me in my solicitude, but that I had caught myself, and in his presence.

Just then my father came in and began making preparations to depart with me. Ernest returned some books he had borrowed, and went away first. But just as he was going, he turned and said:

"Oh, by the way, while you are ruining your own peace of mind and I am ruining the Bishop's, you'd better look up Mrs. Wickson and Mrs. Pertonwaithe. Their husbands, you know, are the two principal stockholders in the Mills. Like all the rest of humanity, those two women are tied to the machine, but they are so tied that they sit on top of it."

CHAPTER IV

SLAVES OF THE MACHINE

The more I thought of Jackson's arm, the more shaken I was. I was confronted by the concrete. For the first time I was seeing life. My university life, and study and culture, had not been real. I had learned nothing but theories of life and society that looked all very well on the printed page, but now I had seen life itself. Jackson's arm was a fact of life. "The fact, man, the irrefragable fact!" of Ernest's was ringing in my consciousness.

It seemed monstrous, impossible, that our whole society was based upon blood. And yet there was Jackson. I could not get away from him. Constantly my thought swung back to him as the compass to the Pole. He had been monstrously treated. His blood had not been paid for in order that a larger dividend might be paid. And I knew a score of happy complacent families that had received those dividends and by that much had profited by Jackson's blood. If one man could be so monstrously treated and society move on its way unheeding, might not many men be so monstrously treated? I remembered Ernest's women of Chicago who toiled for ninety cents a week, and the child slaves of the Southern cotton mills he had described. And I could see their wan white hands, from which the blood had been pressed, at work upon the cloth out of which had been made my gown. And then I thought of the Sierra Mills and the dividends that had been paid, and I saw the blood of Jackson upon my gown as well. Jackson I could not escape. Always my meditations led me back to him.

Down in the depths of me I had a feeling that I stood on the edge of a precipice. It was as though I were about to see a new and awful revelation of life. And not I alone. My whole world was turning over. There was my father. I could see the effect Ernest was beginning to have on him. And then there was the Bishop. When I had last seen him he had looked a sick man. He was at high nervous tension, and in his eyes there was unspeakable horror. From the little I learned I knew that Ernest had been keeping his promise of taking him through hell. But what scenes of hell the Bishop's eyes had seen, I knew not, for he seemed too stunned to speak about them.

Once, the feeling strong upon me that my little world and all the world was turning over, I thought of Ernest as the cause of it; and also I thought, "We were so happy and peaceful before he came!" And the next moment I was aware that the thought was a treason against truth, and Ernest rose before me transfigured, the apostle of truth, with shining brows and the fearlessness of one of Gods own angels, battling for the truth and the right, and battling for the succor of the poor and lonely and oppressed. And then there arose before me another figure, the Christ! He, too, had taken the part of the lowly and oppressed, and against all the established power of priest and pharisee. And I remembered his end upon the cross, and my heart contracted with a pang as I thought of Ernest. Was he, too, destined for a cross?—he, with his clarion call and war-noted voice, and all the fine man's vigor of him!

And in that moment I knew that I loved him, and that I was melting with desire to comfort him. I thought of his life. A sordid, harsh, and meagre life it must have been. And I thought of his father, who had lied and stolen for him and been worked to death. And he himself had gone into the mills when he was ten! All my heart seemed bursting with desire to fold my arms around him, and to rest his head on my breast—his head that must be weary with so many thoughts; and to give him rest—just rest—and easement and forgetfulness for a tender space.

I met Colonel Ingram at a church reception. Him I knew well and had known well for many years. I trapped him behind large palms and rubber plants, though he did not know he was trapped. He met me with the conventional gayety and gallantry. He was ever a graceful man, diplomatic, tactful, and considerate. And as for appearance, he was the most distinguished-looking man in our society. Beside him even the venerable head of the university looked tawdry and small.

And yet I found Colonel Ingram situated the same as the unlettered mechanics. He was not a free agent. He, too, was bound upon the wheel. I shall never forget the change in him when I mentioned Jackson's case. His smiling good nature vanished like a ghost. A sudden, frightful expression distorted his well-bred face. I felt the same alarm that I had felt when James Smith broke out. But Colonel Ingram did not curse. That was the slight difference that was left between the workingman and him. He was famed as a wit, but he had no wit now. And, unconsciously, this way and that he glanced for avenues of escape. But he was trapped amid the palms and rubber trees.

Oh, he was sick of the sound of Jackson's name. Why had I brought the matter up? He did not relish my joke. It was poor taste on my part, and very inconsiderate. Did I not know that in his profession personal feelings did not count? He left his personal feelings at home when he went down to the office. At the office he had only professional feelings.

"Should Jackson have received damages?" I asked.

"Certainly," he answered. "That is, personally, I have a feeling that he should. But that has nothing to do with the legal aspects of the case."

He was getting his scattered wits slightly in hand.

"Tell me, has right anything to do with the law?" I asked.

"You have used the wrong initial consonant," he smiled in answer.

"Might?" I queried; and he nodded his head. "And yet we are supposed to get justice by means of the law?"

"That is the paradox of it," he countered. "We do get justice."

"You are speaking professionally now, are you not?" I asked.

Colonel Ingram blushed, actually blushed, and again he looked anxiously about him for a way of escape. But I blocked his path and did not offer to move.

"Tell me," I said, "when one surrenders his personal feelings to his professional feelings, may not the action be defined as a sort of spiritual mayhem?"

I did not get an answer. Colonel Ingram had ingloriously bolted, overturning a palm in his flight.

Next I tried the newspapers. I wrote a quiet, restrained, dispassionate account of Jackson's case. I made no charges against the men with whom I had talked, nor, for that matter, did I even mention them. I gave the actual facts of the case, the long years Jackson had worked in the mills, his effort to save the machinery from damage and the consequent accident, and his own present wretched and starving condition. The three local newspapers rejected my communication, likewise did the two weeklies.

I got hold of Percy Layton. He was a graduate of the university, had gone in for journalism, and was then serving his apprenticeship as reporter on the most influential of the three newspapers. He smiled when I asked him the reason the newspapers suppressed all mention of Jackson or his case.

"Editorial policy," he said. "We have nothing to do with that. It's up to the editors."

"But why is it policy?" I asked.

"We're all solid with the corporations," he answered. "If you paid advertising rates, you couldn't get any such matter into the papers. A man who tried to smuggle it in would lose his job. You couldn't get it in if you paid ten times the regular advertising rates."

"How about your own policy?" I questioned. "It would seem your function is to twist truth at the command of your employers, who, in turn, obey the behests of the corporations."

"I haven't anything to do with that." He looked uncomfortable for the moment, then brightened as he saw his way out. "I, myself, do not write untruthful things. I keep square all right with my own conscience. Of course, there's lots that's repugnant in the course of the day's work. But then, you see, that's all part of the day's work," he wound up boyishly.

"Yet you expect to sit at an editor's desk some day and conduct a policy."

"I'll be case-hardened by that time," was his reply.

"Since you are not yet case-hardened, tell me what you think right now about the general editorial policy."

"I don't think," he answered quickly. "One can't kick over the ropes if he's going to succeed in journalism. I've learned that much, at any rate."

And he nodded his young head sagely.

"But the right?" I persisted.

"You don't understand the game. Of course it's all right, because it comes out all right, don't you see?"

"Delightfully vague," I murmured; but my heart was aching for the youth of him, and I felt that I must either scream or burst into tears.

I was beginning to see through the appearances of the society in which I had always lived, and to find the frightful realities that were beneath. There seemed a tacit conspiracy against Jackson, and I was aware of a thrill of sympathy for the whining lawyer who had ingloriously fought his case. But this tacit conspiracy grew large. Not alone was it aimed against Jackson. It was aimed against every workingman who was maimed in the mills. And if against every man in the mills, why not against every man in all the other mills and factories? In fact, was it not true of all the industries?

And if this was so, then society was a lie. I shrank back from my own conclusions. It was too terrible and awful to be true. But there was Jackson, and Jackson's arm, and the blood that stained my gown and dripped from my own roof-beams. And there were many Jacksons—hundreds of them in the mills alone, as Jackson himself had said. Jackson I could not escape.

I saw Mr. Wickson and Mr. Pertonwaithe, the two men who held most of the stock in the Sierra Mills. But I could not shake them as I had shaken the mechanics in their employ. I discovered that they had an ethic superior to that of the rest of society. It was what I may call the aristocratic ethic or the master ethic.* They talked in large ways of policy, and they identified policy and right. And to me they talked in fatherly ways, patronizing my youth and inexperience. They were the most hopeless of all I had encountered in my quest. They believed absolutely that their conduct was right. There was no question about it, no discussion. They were convinced that they were the saviours of society, and that it was they who made happiness for the many. And they drew pathetic pictures of what would be the sufferings of the working class were it not for the employment that they, and they alone, by their wisdom, provided for it.

 * Before Avis Everhard was born, John Stuart Mill, in his
 essay, ON LIBERTY, wrote: "Wherever there is an ascendant
 class, a large portion of the morality emanates from its
 class interests and its class feelings of superiority."

Fresh from these two masters, I met Ernest and related my experience. He looked at me with a pleased expression, and said:

"Really, this is fine. You are beginning to dig truth for yourself. It is your own empirical generalization, and it is correct. No man in the industrial machine is a free-will agent, except the large capitalist, and he isn't, if you'll pardon the Irishism.* You see, the masters are quite sure that they are right in what they are doing. That is the crowning absurdity of the whole situation. They are so tied by their human nature that they can't do a thing unless they think it is right. They must have a sanction for their acts.

 * Verbal contradictions, called BULLS, were long an amiable

weakness of the ancient Irish.

"When they want to do a thing, in business of course, they must wait till there arises in their brains, somehow, a religious, or ethical, or scientific, or philosophic, concept that the thing is right. And then they go ahead and do it, unwitting that one of the weaknesses of the human mind is that the wish is parent to the thought. No matter what they want to do, the sanction always comes. They are superficial casuists. They are Jesuitical. They even see their way to doing wrong that right may come of it. One of the pleasant and axiomatic fictions they have created is that they are superior to the rest of mankind in wisdom and efficiency. Therefrom comes their sanction to manage the bread and butter of the rest of mankind. They have even resurrected the theory of the divine right of kings—commercial kings in their case.*

> * The newspapers, in 1902 of that era, credited the president of the Anthracite Coal Trust, George F. Baer, with the enunciation of the following principle: "The rights and interests of the laboring man will be protected by the Christian men to whom God in His infinite wisdom has given the property interests of the country."

"The weakness in their position lies in that they are merely business men. They are not philosophers. They are not biologists nor sociologists. If they were, of course all would be well. A business man who was also a biologist and a sociologist would know, approximately, the right thing to do for humanity. But, outside the realm of business, these men are stupid. They know only business. They do not know mankind nor society, and yet they set themselves up as arbiters of the fates of the hungry millions and all the other millions thrown in. History, some day, will have an excruciating laugh at their expense."

I was not surprised when I had my talk out with Mrs. Wickson and Mrs. Pertonwaithe. They were society women.* Their homes were palaces. They had many homes scattered over the country, in the mountains, on lakes, and by the sea. They were tended by armies of servants, and their social activities were bewildering. They patronized the university and the churches, and the pastors especially bowed at their knees in meek subservience.** They were powers, these two women, what of the money that was theirs. The power of subsidization of thought was theirs to a remarkable degree, as I was soon to learn under Ernest's tuition.

> * SOCIETY is here used in a restricted sense, a common usage of the times to denote the gilded drones that did no labor, but only glutted themselves at the honey-vats of the workers. Neither the business men nor the laborers had time or opportunity for SOCIETY. SOCIETY was the creation of the idle rich who toiled not and who in this way played.

> ** "Bring on your tainted money," was the expressed sentiment of the Church during this period.

They aped their husbands, and talked in the same large ways about policy, and the duties and responsibilities of the rich. They were swayed by the same ethic that dominated their husbands—the ethic of their class; and they uttered glib phrases that their own ears did not understand.

Also, they grew irritated when I told them of the deplorable condition of Jackson's family, and when I wondered that they had made no voluntary provision for the man. I was told that they thanked no one for instructing them in their social duties. When I asked them flatly to assist Jackson, they as flatly refused. The astounding thing about it was that they refused in almost identically the same language, and this in face of the fact that I interviewed them separately and that one did not know that I had seen or was going to see the other. Their common reply was that they were glad of the opportunity to make it perfectly plain that no premium would ever be put on carelessness by them; nor would they, by paying for accident, tempt the poor to hurt themselves in the machinery.*

> * In the files of the OUTLOOK, a critical weekly of the period, in the number dated August 18, 1906, is related the circumstance of a workingman losing his arm, the details of which are quite similar to those of Jackson's case as related by Avis Everhard.

And they were sincere, these two women. They were drunk with conviction of the superiority of their class and of themselves. They had a sanction, in their own class-ethic, for every act they performed. As I drove away from Mrs. Pertonwaithe's great house, I looked back at it, and I remembered Ernest's expression that they were bound to the machine, but that they were so bound that they sat on top of it.

CHAPTER V

THE PHILOMATHS

Ernest was often at the house. Nor was it my father, merely, nor the controversial dinners, that drew him there. Even at that time I flattered myself that I played some part in causing his visits, and it was not long before I learned the correctness of my surmise. For never was there such a lover as Ernest Everhard. His gaze and his hand-clasp grew firmer and steadier, if that were possible; and the question that had grown from the first in his eyes, grew only the more imperative.

My impression of him, the first time I saw him, had been unfavorable. Then I had found myself attracted toward him. Next came my repulsion, when he so savagely attacked my class and me. After that, as I saw that he had not maligned my class, and that the harsh and bitter things he said about it were justified, I had drawn closer to him again. He became my oracle. For me he tore the sham from the face of society and gave me glimpses of reality that were as unpleasant as they were undeniably true.

As I have said, there was never such a lover as he. No girl could live in a university town till she was twenty-four and not have love experiences. I had been made love to by beardless sophomores and gray professors, and by the athletes and the football giants. But not one of them made love to me as Ernest did. His arms were around me before I knew. His lips were on mine before I could protest or resist. Before his earnestness conventional maiden dignity was ridiculous. He swept me off my feet by the splendid invincible rush of him. He did not propose. He put his arms around me and kissed me and took it for granted that we should be married. There was no discussion about it. The only discussion—and that arose afterward—was when we should be married.

It was unprecedented. It was unreal. Yet, in accordance with Ernest's test of truth, it worked. I trusted my life to it. And fortunate was the trust. Yet during those first days of our love, fear of the future came often to me when I thought of the violence and impetuosity of his love-making. Yet such fears were groundless. No woman was ever blessed with a gentler, tenderer husband. This gentleness and violence on his part was a curious blend similar to the one in his carriage of awkwardness and ease. That slight awkwardness! He never got over it, and it was delicious. His behavior in our drawing-room reminded me of a careful bull in a china shop.*

> * In those days it was still the custom to fill the living
> rooms with bric-a-brac. They had not discovered simplicity
> of living. Such rooms were museums, entailing endless labor
> to keep clean. The dust-demon was the lord of the household.

> There were a myriad devices for catching dust, and only a few devices for getting rid of it.

It was at this time that vanished my last doubt of the completeness of my love for him (a subconscious doubt, at most). It was at the Philomath Club—a wonderful night of battle, wherein Ernest bearded the masters in their lair. Now the Philomath Club was the most select on the Pacific Coast. It was the creation of Miss Brentwood, an enormously wealthy old maid; and it was her husband, and family, and toy. Its members were the wealthiest in the community, and the strongest-minded of the wealthy, with, of course, a sprinkling of scholars to give it intellectual tone.

The Philomath had no club house. It was not that kind of a club. Once a month its members gathered at some one of their private houses to listen to a lecture. The lecturers were usually, though not always, hired. If a chemist in New York made a new discovery in say radium, all his expenses across the continent were paid, and as well he received a princely fee for his time. The same with a returning explorer from the polar regions, or the latest literary or artistic success. No visitors were allowed, while it was the Philomath's policy to permit none of its discussions to get into the papers. Thus great statesmen—and there had been such occasions—were able fully to speak their minds.

I spread before me a wrinkled letter, written to me by Ernest twenty years ago, and from it I copy the following:

"Your father is a member of the Philomath, so you are able to come. Therefore come next Tuesday night. I promise you that you will have the time of your life. In your recent encounters, you failed to shake the masters. If you come, I'll shake them for you. I'll make them snarl like wolves. You merely questioned their morality. When their morality is questioned, they grow only the more complacent and superior. But I shall menace their money-bags. That will shake them to the roots of their primitive natures. If you can come, you will see the cave-man, in evening dress, snarling and snapping over a bone. I promise you a great caterwauling and an illuminating insight into the nature of the beast.

"They've invited me in order to tear me to pieces. This is the idea of Miss Brentwood. She clumsily hinted as much when she invited me. She's given them that kind of fun before. They delight in getting trustful-souled gentle reformers before them. Miss Brentwood thinks I am as mild as a kitten and as good-natured and stolid as the family cow. I'll not deny that I helped to give her that impression. She was very tentative at first, until she divined my harmlessness. I am to receive a handsome fee—two hundred and fifty dollars—as befits the man who, though a radical, once ran for governor. Also, I am to wear evening dress. This is compulsory. I never was so apparelled in my life. I suppose I'll have to hire one somewhere. But I'd do more than that to get a chance at the Philomaths."

Of all places, the Club gathered that night at the Pertonwaithe house. Extra chairs had been brought into the great drawing-room, and in all there must have been two hundred Philomaths that sat down to hear Ernest. They were truly lords of society. I amused myself with running over in my mind the sum of the fortunes represented, and it ran well into the hundreds of millions. And the possessors were not of the idle rich. They were men of affairs who took most active parts in industrial and political life.

We were all seated when Miss Brentwood brought Ernest in. They moved at once to the head of the room, from where he was to speak. He was in evening dress, and, what of his broad shoulders and kingly head, he looked magnificent. And then there was that faint and unmistakable touch of awkwardness in his movements. I almost think I could have loved him for that alone. And as I looked at him I was aware of a great joy. I felt again the pulse of his palm on mine, the touch of his lips; and such pride was mine that I felt I must rise up and cry out to the assembled company: "He is mine! He has held me in his arms, and I, mere I, have filled that mind of his to the exclusion of all his multitudinous and kingly thoughts!"

At the head of the room, Miss Brentwood introduced him to Colonel Van Gilbert, and I knew that the latter was to preside. Colonel Van Gilbert was a great corporation lawyer. In addition, he was immensely wealthy. The smallest fee he would deign to notice was a hundred thousand dollars. He was a master of law. The law was a puppet with which he played. He moulded it like clay, twisted and distorted it like a Chinese puzzle into any design he chose. In appearance and rhetoric he was old-fashioned, but in imagination and knowledge and resource he was as young as the latest statute. His first prominence had come when he broke the Shardwell will.* His fee for this one act was five hundred thousand dollars. From then on he had risen like a rocket. He was often called the greatest lawyer in the country—corporation lawyer, of course; and no classification of the three greatest lawyers in the United States could have excluded him.

> * This breaking of wills was a peculiar feature of the period. With the accumulation of vast fortunes, the problem of disposing of these fortunes after death was a vexing one to the accumulators. Will-making and will-breaking became complementary trades, like armor-making and gun-making. The shrewdest will-making lawyers were called in to make wills that could not be broken. But these wills were always broken, and very often by the very lawyers that had drawn them up. Nevertheless the delusion persisted in the wealthy class that an absolutely unbreakable will could be cast; and so, through the generations, clients and lawyers pursued the illusion. It was a pursuit like unto that of the Universal Solvent of the mediaeval alchemists.

He arose and began, in a few well-chosen phrases that carried an undertone of faint irony, to introduce Ernest. Colonel Van Gilbert was subtly facetious in his introduction of the social reformer and member of the working class, and the audience smiled. It made me angry, and I glanced at Ernest. The sight of him made me doubly angry. He did not seem to resent the delicate slurs. Worse than that, he did not seem to be aware of them. There he sat, gentle, and stolid, and somnolent. He really looked stupid. And for a moment the thought rose in my mind, What if he were overawed by this imposing array of power and brains? Then I smiled. He couldn't fool me. But he fooled the others, just as he had fooled Miss Brentwood. She occupied a chair right up to the front, and several times she turned her head toward one or another of her CONFRERES and smiled her appreciation of the remarks.

Colonel Van Gilbert done, Ernest arose and began to speak. He began in a low voice, haltingly and modestly, and with an air of evident embarrassment. He spoke of his birth in the working class, and of the sordidness and wretchedness of his environment, where flesh and spirit were alike starved and tormented. He described his ambitions and ideals, and his conception of the paradise wherein lived the people of the upper classes. As he said:

"Up above me, I knew, were unselfishnesses of the spirit, clean and noble thinking, keen intellectual living. I knew all this because I read 'Seaside Library'* novels, in which, with the exception of the villains and adventuresses, all men and women thought beautiful thoughts, spoke a beautiful tongue, and performed glorious deeds. In short, as I accepted the rising of the sun, I accepted that up above me was all that was fine and noble and gracious, all that gave decency and dignity to life, all that made life worth living and that remunerated one for his travail and misery."

> * A curious and amazing literature that served to make the working class utterly misapprehend the nature of the leisure class.

He went on and traced his life in the mills, the learning of the horseshoeing trade, and his meeting with the socialists. Among them, he said, he had found keen intellects and brilliant wits, ministers of the Gospel who had been broken because their Christianity was too wide for any congregation of mammon-worshippers, and professors who had been broken on the wheel of university subservience to the ruling class. The socialists were revolutionists, he said, struggling to overthrow the irrational society of the present and out of the material to build the rational society of the future. Much more he said that would take too long to write, but I shall never forget how he described the life among the revolutionists. All halting utterance vanished. His voice grew strong and confident, and it glowed as he glowed, and as the thoughts glowed that poured out from him. He said:

"Amongst the revolutionists I found, also, warm faith in the human, ardent idealism, sweetnesses of unselfishness, renunciation, and martyrdom—all the splendid, stinging things of the spirit. Here life was clean, noble, and alive. I was in touch with great souls who exalted flesh and spirit over dollars and cents, and to whom the thin wail of the starved slum child meant more than all the pomp and circumstance of commercial expansion and world empire. All about me were nobleness of purpose and heroism of effort, and my days and nights were sunshine and starshine, all fire and dew, with before my eyes, ever burning and blazing, the Holy Grail, Christ's own Grail, the warm human, long-suffering and maltreated but to be rescued and saved at the last."

As before I had seen him transfigured, so now he stood transfigured before me. His brows were bright with the divine that was in him, and brighter yet shone his eyes from the midst of the radiance that seemed to envelop him as a mantle. But the others did not see this radiance, and I assumed that it was due to the tears of joy and love that dimmed my vision. At any rate, Mr. Wickson, who sat behind me, was unaffected, for I heard him sneer aloud, "Utopian."*

> * The people of that age were phrase slaves. The abjectness
> of their servitude is incomprehensible to us. There was a
> magic in words greater than the conjurer's art. So
> befuddled and chaotic were their minds that the utterance of
> a single word could negative the generalizations of a
> lifetime of serious research and thought. Such a word was
> the adjective UTOPIAN. The mere utterance of it could damn
> any scheme, no matter how sanely conceived, of economic
> amelioration or regeneration. Vast populations grew
> frenzied over such phrases as "an honest dollar" and "a full
> dinner pail." The coinage of such phrases was considered
> strokes of genius.

Ernest went on to his rise in society, till at last he came in touch with members of the upper classes, and rubbed shoulders with the men who sat in the high places. Then came his disillusionment, and this disillusionment he described in terms that did not flatter his audience. He was surprised at the commonness of the clay. Life proved not to be fine and gracious. He was appalled by the selfishness he encountered, and what had surprised him even more than that was the absence of intellectual life. Fresh from his revolutionists, he was shocked by the intellectual stupidity of the master class. And then, in spite of their magnificent churches and well-paid preachers, he had found the masters, men and women, grossly material. It was true that they prattled sweet little ideals and dear little moralities, but in spite of their prattle the dominant key of the life they lived was materialistic. And they were without real morality—for instance, that which Christ had preached but which was no longer preached.

"I met men," he said, "who invoked the name of the Prince of Peace in their diatribes against war, and who put rifles in the hands of Pinkertons* with which to shoot down strikers in their own factories. I met men incoherent with indignation at the brutality of prize-fighting, and who, at the same time, were parties to the adulteration of food that killed each year more babes than even red-handed Herod had killed.

> * Originally, they were private detectives; but they quickly
> became hired fighting men of the capitalists, and ultimately

developed into the Mercenaries of the Oligarchy.

"This delicate, aristocratic-featured gentleman was a dummy director and a tool of corporations that secretly robbed widows and orphans. This gentleman, who collected fine editions and was a patron of literature, paid blackmail to a heavy-jowled, black-browed boss of a municipal machine. This editor, who published patent medicine advertisements, called me a scoundrelly demagogue because I dared him to print in his paper the truth about patent medicines.* This man, talking soberly and earnestly about the beauties of idealism and the goodness of God, had just betrayed his comrades in a business deal. This man, a pillar of the church and heavy contributor to foreign missions, worked his shop girls ten hours a day on a starvation wage and thereby directly encouraged prostitution. This man, who endowed chairs in universities and erected magnificent chapels, perjured himself in courts of law over dollars and cents. This railroad magnate broke his word as a citizen, as a gentleman, and as a Christian, when he granted a secret rebate, and he granted many secret rebates. This senator was the tool and the slave, the little puppet, of a brutal uneducated machine boss;** so was this governor and this supreme court judge; and all three rode on railroad passes; and, also, this sleek capitalist owned the machine, the machine boss, and the railroads that issued the passes.

> * PATENT MEDICINES were patent lies, but, like the charms
> and indulgences of the Middle Ages, they deceived the
> people. The only difference lay in that the patent
> medicines were more harmful and more costly.
>
> ** Even as late as 1912, A.D., the great mass of the people
> still persisted in the belief that they ruled the country by
> virtue of their ballots. In reality, the country was ruled
> by what were called POLITICAL MACHINES. At first the
> machine bosses charged the master capitalists extortionate
> tolls for legislation; but in a short time the master
> capitalists found it cheaper to own the political machines
> themselves and to hire the machine bosses.

"And so it was, instead of in paradise, that I found myself in the arid desert of commercialism. I found nothing but stupidity, except for business. I found none clean, noble, and alive, though I found many who were alive—with rottenness. What I did find was monstrous selfishness and heartlessness, and a gross, gluttonous, practised, and practical materialism."

Much more Ernest told them of themselves and of his disillusionment. Intellectually they had bored him; morally and spiritually they had sickened him; so that he was glad to go back to his revolutionists, who were clean, noble, and alive, and all that the capitalists were not.

"And now," he said, "let me tell you about that revolution."

But first I must say that his terrible diatribe had not touched them. I looked about me at their faces and saw that they remained complacently superior to what he had charged. And I remembered what he had told me: that no indictment of their morality could shake them. However, I could see that the boldness of his language had affected Miss Brentwood. She was looking worried and apprehensive.

Ernest began by describing the army of revolution, and as he gave the figures of its strength (the votes cast in the various countries), the assemblage began to grow restless. Concern showed in their faces, and I noticed a tightening of lips. At last the gage of battle had been thrown down. He described the international organization of the socialists that united the million and a half in the United States with the twenty-three millions and a half in the rest of the world.

"Such an army of revolution," he said, "twenty-five millions strong, is a thing to make rulers and ruling classes pause and consider. The cry of this army is: 'No quarter! We want all that you possess. We will be content with nothing less than all that you possess. We want in our hands the reins of power and the destiny of mankind. Here are our hands. They are strong hands. We are going to take your governments, your palaces, and all your purpled ease away from you, and in that day you shall work for your bread even as the peasant in the field or the starved and runty clerk in your metropolises. Here are our hands. They are strong hands!'"

And as he spoke he extended from his splendid shoulders his two great arms, and the horseshoer's hands were clutching the air like eagle's talons. He was the spirit of regnant labor as he stood there, his hands outreaching to rend and crush his audience. I was aware of a faintly perceptible shrinking on the part of the listeners before this figure of revolution, concrete, potential, and menacing. That is, the women shrank, and fear was in their faces. Not so with the men. They were of the active rich, and not the idle, and they were fighters. A low, throaty rumble arose, lingered on the air a moment, and ceased. It was the forerunner of the snarl, and I was to hear it many times that night—the token of the brute in man, the earnest of his primitive passions. And they were unconscious that they had made this sound. It was the growl of the pack, mouthed by the pack, and mouthed in all unconsciousness. And in that moment, as I saw the harshness form in their faces and saw the fight-light flashing in their eyes, I realized that not easily would they let their lordship of the world be wrested from them.

Ernest proceeded with his attack. He accounted for the existence of the million and a half of revolutionists in the United States by charging the capitalist class with having mismanaged society. He sketched the economic condition of the cave-man and of the savage peoples of to-day, pointing out that they possessed neither tools nor machines, and possessed only a natural efficiency of one in producing power. Then he traced the development of machinery and social organization so that to-day the producing power of civilized man was a thousand times greater than that of the savage.

"Five men," he said, "can produce bread for a thousand. One man can produce cotton cloth for two hundred and fifty people, woollens for three hundred, and boots and shoes for a thousand. One would conclude from this that under a capable management of society modern civilized man would be a great deal better off than the cave-man. But is he? Let us see. In the United States to-day there are fifteen million* people living in poverty; and by poverty is meant that condition in life in which, through lack of food and adequate shelter, the mere standard of working efficiency cannot be maintained. In the United States to-day, in spite of all your so-called labor legislation, there are three millions of child laborers.** In twelve years their numbers have been doubled. And in passing I will ask you managers of society why you did not make public the census figures of 1910? And I will answer for you, that you were afraid. The figures of misery would have precipitated the revolution that even now is gathering.

    * Robert Hunter, in 1906, in a book entitled "Poverty,"
pointed out that at that time there were ten millions in the
United States living in poverty.

    ** In the United States Census of 1900 (the last census the
figures of which were made public), the number of child
laborers was placed at 1,752,187.

"But to return to my indictment. If modern man's producing power is a thousand times greater than that of the cave-man, why then, in the United States to-day, are there fifteen million people who are not properly sheltered and properly fed? Why then, in the United States to-day, are there three million child laborers? It is a true indictment. The capitalist class has mismanaged. In face of the facts that modern man lives more wretchedly than the cave-man, and that his producing power is a thousand times greater than that of the cave-man, no other conclusion is possible than that the capitalist class has mismanaged, that you have mismanaged, my masters, that you have criminally and selfishly mismanaged. And on this count you cannot answer me here to-night, face to face, any more than can your whole class answer the million and a half of revolutionists in the United States. You cannot answer. I challenge you to answer. And furthermore, I dare to say to you now that when I have finished you will not answer. On that point you will be tongue-tied, though you will talk wordily enough about other things.

"You have failed in your management. You have made a shambles of civilization. You have been blind and greedy. You have risen up (as you to-day rise up), shamelessly, in our legislative halls, and declared that profits were impossible without the toil of children and babes. Don't take my word for it. It is all in the records against you. You have lulled your conscience to sleep with prattle of sweet ideals and dear moralities. You are fat with power and possession, drunken with success; and you have no more hope against us than have the drones, clustered about the honey-vats, when the worker-bees spring upon them to end their rotund existence. You have failed in your management of society, and your management is to be taken away from you. A million and a half of the men of the working class say that they are going to get the rest of the working class to join with them and take the management away from you. This is the revolution, my masters. Stop it if you can."

For an appreciable lapse of time Ernest's voice continued to ring through the great room. Then arose the throaty rumble I had heard before, and a dozen men were on their feet clamoring for recognition from Colonel Van Gilbert. I noticed Miss Brentwood's shoulders moving convulsively, and for the moment I was angry, for I thought that she was laughing at Ernest. And then I discovered that it was not laughter, but hysteria. She was appalled by what she had done in bringing this firebrand before her blessed Philomath Club.

Colonel Van Gilbert did not notice the dozen men, with passion-wrought faces, who strove to get permission from him to speak. His own face was passion-wrought. He sprang to his feet, waving his arms, and for a moment could utter only incoherent sounds. Then speech poured from him. But it was not the speech of a one-hundred-thousand-dollar lawyer, nor was the rhetoric old-fashioned.

"Fallacy upon fallacy!" he cried. "Never in all my life have I heard so many fallacies uttered in one short hour. And besides, young man, I must tell you that you have said nothing new. I learned all that at college before you were born. Jean Jacques Rousseau enunciated your socialistic theory nearly two centuries ago. A return to the soil, forsooth! Reversion! Our biology teaches the absurdity of it. It has been truly said that a little learning is a dangerous thing, and you have exemplified it to-night with your madcap theories. Fallacy upon fallacy! I was never so nauseated in my life with overplus of fallacy. That for your immature generalizations and childish reasonings!"

He snapped his fingers contemptuously and proceeded to sit down. There were lip-exclamations of approval on the part of the women, and hoarser notes of confirmation came from the men. As for the dozen men who were clamoring for the floor, half of them began speaking at once. The confusion and babel was indescribable. Never had Mrs. Pertonwaithe's spacious walls beheld such a spectacle. These, then, were the cool captains of industry and lords of society, these snarling, growling savages in evening clothes. Truly Ernest had shaken them when he stretched out his hands for their moneybags, his hands that had appeared in their eyes as the hands of the fifteen hundred thousand revolutionists.

But Ernest never lost his head in a situation. Before Colonel Van Gilbert had succeeded in sitting down, Ernest was on his feet and had sprung forward.

"One at a time!" he roared at them.

The sound arose from his great lungs and dominated the human tempest. By sheer compulsion of personality he commanded silence.

"One at a time," he repeated softly. "Let me answer Colonel Van Gilbert. After that the rest of you can come at me—but one at a time, remember. No mass-plays here. This is not a football field.

"As for you," he went on, turning toward Colonel Van Gilbert, "you have replied to nothing I have said. You have merely made a few excited and dogmatic assertions about my mental caliber. That may serve you in your business, but you can't talk to me like that. I am not a workingman, cap in hand, asking you to increase my wages or to protect me from the machine at which I work. You cannot be dogmatic with truth when you deal with me. Save that for dealing with your wage-slaves. They will not dare reply to you because you hold their bread and butter, their lives, in your hands.

"As for this return to nature that you say you learned at college before I was born, permit me to point out that on the face of it you cannot have learned anything since. Socialism has no more to do with the state of nature than has differential calculus with a Bible class. I have called your class stupid when outside the realm of business. You, sir, have brilliantly exemplified my statement."

This terrible castigation of her hundred-thousand-dollar lawyer was too much for Miss Brentwood's nerves. Her hysteria became violent, and she was helped, weeping and laughing, out of the room. It was just as well, for there was worse to follow.

"Don't take my word for it," Ernest continued, when the interruption had been led away. "Your own authorities with one unanimous voice will prove you stupid. Your own hired purveyors of knowledge will tell you that you are wrong. Go to your meekest little assistant instructor of sociology and ask him what is the difference between Rousseau's theory of the return to nature and the theory of socialism; ask your greatest orthodox bourgeois political economists and sociologists; question through the pages of every text-book written on the subject and stored on the shelves of your subsidized libraries; and from one and all the answer will be that there is nothing congruous between the return to nature and socialism. On the other hand, the unanimous affirmative answer will be that the return to nature and socialism are diametrically opposed to each other. As I say, don't take my word for it. The record of your stupidity is there in the books, your own books that you never read. And so far as your stupidity is concerned, you are but the exemplar of your class.

"You know law and business, Colonel Van Gilbert. You know how to serve corporations and increase dividends by twisting the law. Very good. Stick to it. You are quite a figure. You are a very good lawyer, but you are a poor historian, you know nothing of sociology, and your biology is contemporaneous with Pliny."

Here Colonel Van Gilbert writhed in his chair. There was perfect quiet in the room. Everybody sat fascinated—paralyzed, I may say. Such fearful treatment of the great Colonel Van Gilbert was unheard of, undreamed of, impossible to believe—the great Colonel Van Gilbert before whom judges trembled when he arose in court. But Ernest never gave quarter to an enemy.

"This is, of course, no reflection on you," Ernest said. "Every man to his trade. Only you stick to your trade, and I'll stick to mine. You have specialized. When it comes to a knowledge of the law, of how best to evade the law or make new law for the benefit of thieving corporations, I am down in the dirt at your feet. But when it comes to sociology—my trade—you are down in the dirt at my feet. Remember that. Remember, also, that your law is the stuff of a day, and that you are not versatile in the stuff of more than a day. Therefore your dogmatic assertions and rash generalizations on things historical and sociological are not worth the breath you waste on them."

Ernest paused for a moment and regarded him thoughtfully, noting his face dark and twisted with anger, his panting chest, his writhing body, and his slim white hands nervously clenching and unclenching.

"But it seems you have breath to use, and I'll give you a chance to use it. I indicted your class. Show me that my indictment is wrong. I pointed out to you the wretchedness of modern man—three million child slaves in the United States, without whose labor profits would not be possible, and fifteen million under-fed, ill-clothed, and worse-housed people. I pointed out that modern man's producing power through social organization and the use of machinery was a thousand times greater than that of the cave-man. And I stated that from these two facts no other conclusion was possible than that the capitalist class had mismanaged. This was my indictment, and I specifically and at length challenged you to answer it. Nay, I did more. I prophesied that you would not answer. It remains for your breath to smash my prophecy. You called my speech fallacy. Show the fallacy, Colonel Van Gilbert. Answer the indictment that I and my fifteen hundred thousand comrades have brought against your class and you."

Colonel Van Gilbert quite forgot that he was presiding, and that in courtesy he should permit the other clamorers to speak. He was on his feet, flinging his arms, his rhetoric, and his control to the winds, alternately abusing Ernest for his youth and demagoguery, and savagely attacking the working class, elaborating its inefficiency and worthlessness.

"For a lawyer, you are the hardest man to keep to a point I ever saw," Ernest began his answer to the tirade. "My youth has nothing to do with what I have enunciated. Nor has the worthlessness of the working class. I charged the capitalist class with having mismanaged society. You have not answered. You have made no attempt to answer. Why? Is it because you have no answer? You are the champion of this whole audience. Every one here, except me, is hanging on your lips for that answer. They are hanging on your lips for that answer because they have no answer themselves. As for me, as I said before, I know that you not only cannot answer, but that you will not attempt an answer."

"This is intolerable!" Colonel Van Gilbert cried out. "This is insult!"

"That you should not answer is intolerable," Ernest replied gravely. "No man can be intellectually insulted. Insult, in its very nature, is emotional. Recover yourself. Give me an intellectual answer to my intellectual charge that the capitalist class has mismanaged society."

Colonel Van Gilbert remained silent, a sullen, superior expression on his face, such as will appear on the face of a man who will not bandy words with a ruffian.

"Do not be downcast," Ernest said. "Take consolation in the fact that no member of your class has ever yet answered that charge." He turned to the other men who were anxious to speak. "And now it's your chance. Fire away, and do not forget that I here challenge you to give the answer that Colonel Van Gilbert has failed to give."

It would be impossible for me to write all that was said in the discussion. I never realized before how many words could be spoken in three short hours. At any rate, it was glorious. The more his opponents grew excited, the more Ernest deliberately excited them. He had an encyclopaedic command of the field of knowledge, and by a word or a phrase, by delicate rapier thrusts, he punctured them. He named the points of their illogic. This was a false syllogism, that conclusion had no connection with the premise, while that next premise was an impostor because it had cunningly hidden in it the conclusion that was being attempted to be proved. This was an error, that was an assumption, and the next was an assertion contrary to ascertained truth as printed in all the text-books.

And so it went. Sometimes he exchanged the rapier for the club and went smashing amongst their thoughts right and left. And always he demanded facts and refused to discuss theories. And his facts made for them a Waterloo. When they attacked the working class, he always retorted, "The pot calling the kettle black; that is no answer to the charge that your own face is dirty." And to one and all he said: "Why have you not answered the charge that your class has mismanaged? You have talked about other things and things concerning other things, but you have not answered. Is it because you have no answer?"

It was at the end of the discussion that Mr. Wickson spoke. He was the only one that was cool, and Ernest treated him with a respect he had not accorded the others.

"No answer is necessary," Mr. Wickson said with slow deliberation. "I have followed the whole discussion with amazement and disgust. I am disgusted with you gentlemen, members of my class. You have behaved like foolish little schoolboys, what with intruding ethics and the thunder of the common politician into such a discussion. You have been outgeneralled and outclassed. You have been very wordy, and all you have done is buzz. You have buzzed like gnats about a bear. Gentlemen, there stands the bear" (he pointed at Ernest), "and your buzzing has only tickled his ears.

"Believe me, the situation is serious. That bear reached out his paws tonight to crush us. He has said there are a million and a half of revolutionists in the United States. That is a fact. He has said that it is their intention to take away from us our governments, our palaces, and all our purpled ease. That, also, is a fact. A change, a great change, is coming in society; but, haply, it may not be the change the bear anticipates. The bear has said that he will crush us. What if we crush the bear?"

The throat-rumble arose in the great room, and man nodded to man with indorsement and certitude. Their faces were set hard. They were fighters, that was certain.

"But not by buzzing will we crush the bear," Mr. Wickson went on coldly and dispassionately. "We will hunt the bear. We will not reply to the bear in words. Our reply shall be couched in terms of lead. We are in power. Nobody will deny it. By virtue of that power we shall remain in power."

He turned suddenly upon Ernest. The moment was dramatic.

"This, then, is our answer. We have no words to waste on you. When you reach out your vaunted strong hands for our palaces and purpled ease, we will show you what strength is. In roar of shell and shrapnel and in whine of machine-guns will our answer be couched.* We will grind you revolutionists down under our heel, and we shall walk upon your faces. The world is ours, we are its lords, and ours it shall remain. As for the host of labor, it has been in the dirt since history began, and I read history aright. And in the dirt it shall remain so long as I and mine and those that come after us have the power. There is the word. It is the king of words—Power. Not God, not Mammon, but Power. Pour it over your tongue till it tingles with it. Power."

* To show the tenor of thought, the following definition is
quoted from "The Cynic's Word Book" (1906 A.D.), written by
one Ambrose Bierce, an avowed and confirmed misanthrope of
the period: "Grapeshot, n. An argument which the future is
preparing in answer to the demands of American Socialism."

"I am answered," Ernest said quietly. "It is the only answer that could be given. Power. It is what we of the working class preach. We know, and well we know by bitter experience, that no appeal for the right, for justice, for humanity, can ever touch you. Your hearts are hard as your heels with which you tread upon the faces of the poor. So we have preached power. By the power of our ballots on election day will we take your government away from you—"

"What if you do get a majority, a sweeping majority, on election day?" Mr. Wickson broke in to demand. "Suppose we refuse to turn the government over to you after you have captured it at the ballot-box?"

"That, also, have we considered," Ernest replied. "And we shall give you an answer in terms of lead. Power you have proclaimed the king of words. Very good. Power it shall be. And in the day that we sweep to victory at the ballot-box, and you refuse to turn over to us the government we have constitutionally and peacefully captured, and you demand what we are going to do about it—in that day, I say, we shall answer you;

and in roar of shell and shrapnel and in whine of machine-guns shall our answer be couched.

"You cannot escape us. It is true that you have read history aright. It is true that labor has from the beginning of history been in the dirt. And it is equally true that so long as you and yours and those that come after you have power, that labor shall remain in the dirt. I agree with you. I agree with all that you have said. Power will be the arbiter, as it always has been the arbiter. It is a struggle of classes. Just as your class dragged down the old feudal nobility, so shall it be dragged down by my class, the working class. If you will read your biology and your sociology as clearly as you do your history, you will see that this end I have described is inevitable. It does not matter whether it is in one year, ten, or a thousand—your class shall be dragged down. And it shall be done by power. We of the labor hosts have conned that word over till our minds are all a-tingle with it. Power. It is a kingly word."

And so ended the night with the Philomaths.

CHAPTER VI

ADUMBRATIONS

It was about this time that the warnings of coming events began to fall about us thick and fast. Ernest had already questioned father's policy of having socialists and labor leaders at his house, and of openly attending socialist meetings; and father had only laughed at him for his pains. As for myself, I was learning much from this contact with the working-class leaders and thinkers. I was seeing the other side of the shield. I was delighted with the unselfishness and high idealism I encountered, though I was appalled by the vast philosophic and scientific literature of socialism that was opened up to me. I was learning fast, but I learned not fast enough to realize then the peril of our position.

There were warnings, but I did not heed them. For instance, Mrs. Pertonwaithe and Mrs. Wickson exercised tremendous social power in the university town, and from them emanated the sentiment that I was a too-forward and self-assertive young woman with a mischievous penchant for officiousness and interference in other persons' affairs. This I thought no more than natural, considering the part I had played in investigating the case of Jackson's arm. But the effect of such a sentiment, enunciated by two such powerful social arbiters, I underestimated.

True, I noticed a certain aloofness on the part of my general friends, but this I ascribed to the disapproval that was prevalent in my circles of my intended marriage with Ernest. It was not till some time afterward that Ernest pointed out to me clearly that this general attitude of my class was something more than spontaneous, that behind it were the hidden springs of an organized conduct. "You have given shelter to an enemy of your class," he said. "And not alone shelter, for you have given your love, yourself. This is treason to your class. Think not that you will escape being penalized."

But it was before this that father returned one afternoon. Ernest was with me, and we could see that father was angry—philosophically angry. He was rarely really angry; but a certain measure of controlled anger he allowed himself. He called it a tonic. And we could see that he was tonic-angry when he entered the room.

"What do you think?" he demanded. "I had luncheon with Wilcox."

Wilcox was the superannuated president of the university, whose withered mind was stored with generalizations that were young in 1870, and which he had since failed to revise.

"I was invited," father announced. "I was sent for."

He paused, and we waited.

"Oh, it was done very nicely, I'll allow; but I was reprimanded. I! And by that old fossil!"

"I'll wager I know what you were reprimanded for," Ernest said.

"Not in three guesses," father laughed.

"One guess will do," Ernest retorted. "And it won't be a guess. It will be a deduction. You were reprimanded for your private life."

"The very thing!" father cried. "How did you guess?"

"I knew it was coming. I warned you before about it."

"Yes, you did," father meditated. "But I couldn't believe it. At any rate, it is only so much more clinching evidence for my book."

"It is nothing to what will come," Ernest went on, "if you persist in your policy of having these socialists and radicals of all sorts at your house, myself included."

"Just what old Wilcox said. And of all unwarranted things! He said it was in poor taste, utterly profitless, anyway, and not in harmony with university traditions and policy. He said much more of the same vague sort, and I couldn't pin him down to anything specific. I made it pretty awkward for him, and he could only go on repeating himself and telling me how much he honored me, and all the world honored me, as a scientist. It wasn't an agreeable task for him. I could see he didn't like it."

"He was not a free agent," Ernest said. "The leg-bar* is not always worn graciously."

> * LEG-BAR—the African slaves were so manacled; also criminals. It was not until the coming of the Brotherhood of Man that the leg-bar passed out of use.

"Yes. I got that much out of him. He said the university needed ever so much more money this year than the state was willing to furnish; and that it must come from wealthy personages who could not but be offended by the swerving of the university from its high ideal of the passionless pursuit of passionless intelligence. When I tried to pin him down to what my home life had to do with swerving the university from its high ideal, he offered me a two years' vacation, on full pay, in Europe, for recreation and research. Of course I couldn't accept it under the circumstances."

"It would have been far better if you had," Ernest said gravely.

"It was a bribe," father protested; and Ernest nodded.

"Also, the beggar said that there was talk, tea-table gossip and so forth, about my daughter being seen in public with so notorious a character as you, and that it was not in keeping with university tone and dignity. Not that he personally objected—oh, no; but that there was talk and that I would understand."

Ernest considered this announcement for a moment, and then said, and his face was very grave, withal there was a sombre wrath in it:

"There is more behind this than a mere university ideal. Somebody has put pressure on President Wilcox."

"Do you think so?" father asked, and his face showed that he was interested rather than frightened.

"I wish I could convey to you the conception that is dimly forming in my own mind," Ernest said. "Never in the history of the world was society in so terrific flux as it is right now. The swift changes in our industrial system are causing equally swift changes in our religious, political, and social structures. An unseen and fearful revolution is taking place in the fibre and structure of society. One can only dimly feel these things. But they are in the air, now, to-day. One can feel the loom of them—things vast, vague, and terrible. My mind recoils from contemplation of what they may crystallize into. You heard Wickson talk the other night. Behind what he said were the same nameless, formless things that I feel. He spoke out of a superconscious apprehension of them."

"You mean . . . ?" father began, then paused.

"I mean that there is a shadow of something colossal and menacing that even now is beginning to fall across the land. Call it the shadow of an oligarchy, if you will; it is the nearest I dare approximate it. What its nature may be I refuse to imagine.* But what I wanted to say was this: You are in a perilous position—a peril that my own fear enhances because I am not able even to measure it. Take my advice and accept the vacation."

> * Though, like Everhard, they did not dream of the nature of it, there were men, even before his time, who caught glimpses of the shadow. John C. Calhoun said: "A power has risen up in the government greater than the people themselves, consisting of many and various and powerful interests, combined into one mass, and held together by the cohesive power of the vast surplus in the banks." And that great humanist, Abraham Lincoln, said, just before his assassination: "I see in the near future a crisis approaching that unnerves me and causes me to tremble for the safety of my country. . . . Corporations have been enthroned, an era of corruption in high places will follow, and the money-power of the country will endeavor to prolong its reign by working upon the prejudices of the people until the wealth is aggregated in a few hands and the Republic is destroyed."

"But it would be cowardly," was the protest.

"Not at all. You are an old man. You have done your work in the world, and a great work. Leave the present battle to youth and strength. We young fellows have our work yet to do. Avis will stand by my side in what is to come. She will be your representative in the battle-front."

"But they can't hurt me," father objected. "Thank God I am independent. Oh, I assure you, I know the frightful persecution they can wage on a professor who is economically dependent on his university. But I am independent. I have not been a professor for the sake of my salary. I can get along very comfortably on my own income, and the salary is all they can take away from me."

"But you do not realize," Ernest answered. "If all that I fear be so, your private income, your principal itself, can be taken from you just as easily as your salary."

Father was silent for a few minutes. He was thinking deeply, and I could see the lines of decision forming in his face. At last he spoke.

"I shall not take the vacation." He paused again. "I shall go on with my book.* You may be wrong, but whether you are wrong or right, I shall stand by my guns."

> * This book, "Economics and Education," was published in
> that year. Three copies of it are extant; two at Ardis, and
> one at Asgard. It dealt, in elaborate detail, with one
> factor in the persistence of the established, namely, the
> capitalistic bias of the universities and common schools.
> It was a logical and crushing indictment of the whole system
> of education that developed in the minds of the students
> only such ideas as were favorable to the capitalistic
> regime, to the exclusion of all ideas that were inimical and
> subversive. The book created a furor, and was promptly
> suppressed by the Oligarchy.

"All right," Ernest said. "You are travelling the same path that Bishop Morehouse is, and toward a similar smash-up. You'll both be proletarians before you're done with it."

The conversation turned upon the Bishop, and we got Ernest to explain what he had been doing with him.

"He is soul-sick from the journey through hell I have given him. I took him through the homes of a few of our factory workers. I showed him the human wrecks cast aside by the industrial machine, and he listened to their life stories. I took him through the slums of San Francisco, and in drunkenness, prostitution, and criminality he learned a deeper cause than innate depravity. He is very sick, and, worse than that, he has got out of hand. He is too ethical. He has been too severely touched. And, as usual, he is unpractical. He is up in the air with all kinds of ethical delusions and plans for mission work among the cultured. He feels it is his bounden duty to resurrect the ancient spirit of the Church and to deliver its message to the masters. He is overwrought. Sooner or later he is going to break out, and then there's going to be a smash-up. What form it will take I can't even guess. He is a pure, exalted soul, but he is so unpractical. He's beyond me. I can't keep his feet on the earth. And through the air he is rushing on to his Gethsemane. And after this his crucifixion. Such high souls are made for crucifixion."

"And you?" I asked; and beneath my smile was the seriousness of the anxiety of love.

"Not I," he laughed back. "I may be executed, or assassinated, but I shall never be crucified. I am planted too solidly and stolidly upon the earth."

"But why should you bring about the crucifixion of the Bishop?" I asked. "You will not deny that you are the cause of it."

"Why should I leave one comfortable soul in comfort when there are millions in travail and misery?" he demanded back.

"Then why did you advise father to accept the vacation?"

"Because I am not a pure, exalted soul," was the answer. "Because I am solid and stolid and selfish. Because I love you and, like Ruth of old, thy people are my people. As for the Bishop, he has no daughter. Besides, no matter how small the good, nevertheless his little inadequate wail will be productive of some good in the revolution, and every little bit counts."

I could not agree with Ernest. I knew well the noble nature of Bishop Morehouse, and I could not conceive that his voice raised for righteousness would be no more than a little inadequate wail. But I did not yet have the harsh facts of life at my fingers' ends as Ernest had. He saw clearly the futility of the Bishop's great soul, as coming events were soon to show as clearly to me.

It was shortly after this day that Ernest told me, as a good story, the offer he had received from the government, namely, an appointment as United States Commissioner of Labor. I was overjoyed. The salary was comparatively large, and would make safe our marriage. And then it surely was congenial work for Ernest, and, furthermore, my jealous pride in him made me hail the proffered appointment as a recognition of his abilities.

Then I noticed the twinkle in his eyes. He was laughing at me.

"You are not going to . . . to decline?" I quavered.

"It is a bribe," he said. "Behind it is the fine hand of Wickson, and behind him the hands of greater men than he. It is an old trick, old as the class struggle is old—stealing the captains from the army of labor. Poor betrayed labor! If you but knew how many of its leaders have been bought out in similar ways in the past. It is cheaper, so much cheaper, to buy a general than to fight him and his whole army. There was—but I'll not call any names. I'm bitter enough over it as it is. Dear heart, I am a captain of labor. I could not sell out. If for no other reason, the memory of my poor old father and the way he was worked to death would prevent."

The tears were in his eyes, this great, strong hero of mine. He never could forgive the way his father had been malformed—the sordid lies and the petty thefts he had been compelled to, in order to put food in his children's mouths.

"My father was a good man," Ernest once said to me. "The soul of him was good, and yet it was twisted, and maimed, and blunted by the savagery of his life. He was made into a broken-down beast by his masters, the arch-beasts. He should be alive to-day, like your father. He had a strong constitution. But he was caught in the machine and worked to death—for profit. Think of it. For profit—his life blood transmuted into a wine-supper, or a jewelled gewgaw, or some similar sense-orgy of the parasitic and idle rich, his masters, the arch-beasts."

CHAPTER VII

THE BISHOP'S VISION

"The Bishop is out of hand," Ernest wrote me. "He is clear up in the air. Tonight he is going to begin putting to rights this very miserable world of ours. He is going to deliver his message. He has told me so, and I cannot dissuade him. To-night he is chairman of the I.P.H.,* and he will embody his message in his introductory remarks.

>   * There is no clew to the name of the organization for which
>   these initials stand.

"May I bring you to hear him? Of course, he is foredoomed to futility. It will break your heart—it will break his; but for you it will be an excellent object lesson. You know, dear heart, how proud I am because you love me. And because of that I want you to know my fullest value, I want to redeem, in your eyes, some small measure of my unworthiness. And so it is that my pride desires that you shall know my thinking is correct and right. My views are harsh; the futility of so noble a soul as the Bishop will show you the compulsion for such harshness. So come to-night. Sad though this night's happening will be, I feel that it will but draw you more closely to me."

The I.P.H. held its convention that night in San Francisco.* This convention had been called to consider public immorality and the remedy for it. Bishop Morehouse presided. He was very nervous as he sat on the platform, and I could see the high tension he was under. By his side were Bishop Dickinson; H. H. Jones, the head of the ethical department in the University of California; Mrs. W. W. Hurd, the great charity organizer; Philip Ward, the equally great philanthropist; and several lesser luminaries in the field of morality and charity. Bishop Morehouse arose and abruptly began:

>   * It took but a few minutes to cross by ferry from Berkeley
>   to San Francisco. These, and the other bay cities,
>   practically composed one community.

"I was in my brougham, driving through the streets. It was night-time. Now and then I looked through the carriage windows, and suddenly my eyes seemed to be opened, and I saw things as they really are. At first I covered my eyes with my hands to shut out the awful sight, and then, in the darkness, the question came to me: What is to be done? What is to be done? A little later the question came to me in another way: What would the Master do? And with the question a great light seemed to fill the place, and I saw my duty sun-clear, as Saul saw his on the way to Damascus.

"I stopped the carriage, got out, and, after a few minutes' conversation, persuaded two of the public women to get into the brougham with me. If Jesus was right, then these two unfortunates were my sisters, and the only hope of their purification was in my affection and tenderness.

"I live in one of the loveliest localities of San Francisco. The house in which I live cost a hundred thousand dollars, and its furnishings, books, and works of art cost as much more. The house is a mansion. No, it is a palace, wherein there are many servants. I never knew what palaces were good for. I had thought they were to live in. But now I know. I took the two women of the street to my palace, and they are going to stay with me. I hope to fill every room in my palace with such sisters as they."

The audience had been growing more and more restless and unsettled, and the faces of those that sat on the platform had been betraying greater and greater dismay and consternation. And at this point Bishop Dickinson arose, and with an expression of disgust on his face, fled from the platform and the hall. But Bishop Morehouse, oblivious to all, his eyes filled with his vision, continued:

"Oh, sisters and brothers, in this act of mine I find the solution of all my difficulties. I didn't know what broughams were made for, but now I know. They are made to carry the weak, the sick, and the aged; they are made to show honor to those who have lost the sense even of shame.

"I did not know what palaces were made for, but now I have found a use for them. The palaces of the Church should be hospitals and nurseries for those who have fallen by the wayside and are perishing."

He made a long pause, plainly overcome by the thought that was in him, and nervous how best to express it.

"I am not fit, dear brethren, to tell you anything about morality. I have lived in shame and hypocrisies too long to be able to help others; but my action with those women, sisters of mine, shows me that the better way is easy to find. To those who believe in Jesus and his gospel there can be no other relation between man and man than the relation of affection. Love alone is stronger than sin—stronger than death. I therefore say to the rich among you that it is their duty to do what I have done and am doing. Let each one of you who is prosperous take into his house some thief and treat him as his brother, some unfortunate and treat her as his sister, and San Francisco will need no police force and no magistrates; the prisons will be turned into hospitals, and the criminal will disappear with his crime.

"We must give ourselves and not our money alone. We must do as Christ did; that is the message of the Church today. We have wandered far from the Master's teaching. We are consumed in our own flesh-pots. We have put mammon in the place of Christ. I have here a poem that tells the whole story. I should like to read it to you. It was written by an erring soul who yet saw clearly.* It must not be mistaken for an attack upon the Catholic Church. It is an attack upon all churches, upon the pomp and splendor of all churches that have wandered from the Master's path and hedged themselves in from his lambs. Here it is:

"The silver trumpets rang across the Dome;
    The people knelt upon the ground with awe;
    And borne upon the necks of men I saw,
Like some great God, the Holy Lord of Rome.

"Priest-like, he wore a robe more white than foam,
    And, king-like, swathed himself in royal red,
    Three crowns of gold rose high upon his head;
In splendor and in light the Pope passed home.

"My heart stole back across wide wastes of years
    To One who wandered by a lonely sea;
And sought in vain for any place of rest:
'Foxes have holes, and every bird its nest,
    I, only I, must wander wearily,
And bruise my feet, and drink wine salt with tears.'"

* Oscar Wilde, one of the lords of language of the nineteenth century of the Christian Era.

The audience was agitated, but unresponsive. Yet Bishop Morehouse was not aware of it. He held steadily on his way.

"And so I say to the rich among you, and to all the rich, that bitterly you oppress the Master's lambs. You have hardened your hearts. You have closed your ears to the voices that are crying in the land—the voices of pain and sorrow that you will not hear but that some day will be heard. And so I say—"

But at this point H. H. Jones and Philip Ward, who had already risen from their chairs, led the Bishop off the platform, while the audience sat breathless and shocked.

Ernest laughed harshly and savagely when he had gained the street. His laughter jarred upon me. My heart seemed ready to burst with suppressed tears.

"He has delivered his message," Ernest cried. "The manhood and the deep-hidden, tender nature of their Bishop burst out, and his Christian audience, that loved him, concluded that he was crazy! Did you see them leading him so solicitously from the platform? There must have been laughter in hell at the spectacle."

"Nevertheless, it will make a great impression, what the Bishop did and said to-night," I said.

"Think so?" Ernest queried mockingly.

"It will make a sensation," I asserted. "Didn't you see the reporters scribbling like mad while he was speaking?"

"Not a line of which will appear in to-morrow's papers."

"I can't believe it," I cried.

"Just wait and see," was the answer. "Not a line, not a thought that he uttered. The daily press? The daily suppressage!"

"But the reporters," I objected. "I saw them."

"Not a word that he uttered will see print. You have forgotten the editors. They draw their salaries for the policy they maintain. Their policy is to print nothing that is a vital menace to the established. The Bishop's utterance was a violent assault upon the established morality. It was heresy. They led him from the platform to prevent him from uttering more heresy. The newspapers will purge his heresy in the oblivion of silence. The press of the United States? It is a parasitic growth that battens on the capitalist class. Its function is to serve the established by moulding public opinion, and right well it serves it.

"Let me prophesy. To-morrow's papers will merely mention that the Bishop is in poor health, that he has been working too hard, and that he broke down last night. The next mention, some days hence, will be to the effect that he is suffering from nervous prostration and has been given a vacation by his grateful flock. After that, one of two things will happen: either the Bishop will see the error of his way and return from his vacation a well man in whose eyes there are no more visions, or else he will persist in his madness, and then you may expect to see in the papers, couched pathetically and tenderly, the announcement of his insanity. After that he will be left to gibber his visions to padded walls."

"Now there you go too far!" I cried out.

"In the eyes of society it will truly be insanity," he replied. "What honest man, who is not insane, would take lost women and thieves into his house to dwell with him sisterly and brotherly? True, Christ died between two thieves, but that is another story. Insanity? The mental processes of the man with whom one disagrees, are always wrong. Therefore the mind of the man is wrong. Where is the line between wrong mind and insane mind? It is inconceivable that any sane man can radically disagree with one's most sane conclusions.

"There is a good example of it in this evening's paper. Mary McKenna lives south of Market Street. She is a poor but honest woman. She is also patriotic. But she has erroneous ideas concerning the American flag and the protection it is supposed to symbolize. And here's what happened to her. Her husband had an accident and was laid up in hospital three months. In spite of taking in washing, she got behind in her rent. Yesterday they evicted her. But first, she hoisted an American flag, and from under its folds she announced that by virtue of its protection they could not turn her out on to the cold street. What was done? She was arrested and arraigned for insanity. To-day she was examined by the regular insanity experts. She was found insane. She was consigned to the Napa Asylum."

"But that is far-fetched," I objected. "Suppose I should disagree with everybody about the literary style of a book. They wouldn't send me to an asylum for that."

"Very true," he replied. "But such divergence of opinion would constitute no menace to society. Therein lies the difference. The divergence of opinion on the parts of Mary McKenna and the Bishop do menace society. What if all the poor people should refuse to pay rent and shelter themselves under the American flag? Landlordism would go crumbling. The Bishop's views are just as perilous to society. Ergo, to the asylum with him."

But still I refused to believe.

"Wait and see," Ernest said, and I waited.

Next morning I sent out for all the papers. So far Ernest was right. Not a word that Bishop Morehouse had uttered was in print. Mention was made in one or two of the papers that he had been overcome by his feelings. Yet the platitudes of the speakers that followed him were reported at length.

Several days later the brief announcement was made that he had gone away on a vacation to recover from the effects of overwork. So far so good, but there had been no hint of insanity, nor even of nervous collapse. Little did I dream the terrible road the Bishop was destined to travel—the Gethsemane and crucifixion that Ernest had pondered about.

CHAPTER VIII

THE MACHINE BREAKERS

It was just before Ernest ran for Congress, on the socialist ticket, that father gave what he privately called his "Profit and Loss" dinner. Ernest called it the dinner of the Machine Breakers. In point of fact, it was merely a dinner for business men—small business men, of course. I doubt if one of them was interested in any business the total capitalization of which exceeded a couple of hundred thousand dollars. They were truly representative middle-class business men.

There was Owen, of Silverberg, Owen & Company—a large grocery firm with several branch stores. We bought our groceries from them. There were both partners of the big drug firm of Kowalt & Washburn, and Mr. Asmunsen, the owner of a large granite quarry in Contra Costa County. And there were many similar men, owners or part-owners in small factories, small businesses and small industries—small capitalists, in short.

They were shrewd-faced, interesting men, and they talked with simplicity and clearness. Their unanimous complaint was against the corporations and trusts. Their creed was, "Bust the Trusts." All oppression originated in the trusts, and one and all told the same tale of woe. They advocated government ownership of such trusts as the railroads and telegraphs, and excessive income taxes, graduated with ferocity, to destroy large accumulations. Likewise they advocated, as a cure for local ills, municipal ownership of such public utilities as water, gas, telephones, and street railways.

Especially interesting was Mr. Asmunsen's narrative of his tribulations as a quarry owner. He confessed that he never made any profits out of his quarry, and this, in spite of the enormous volume of business that had been caused by the destruction of San Francisco by the big earthquake. For six years the rebuilding of San Francisco had been going on, and his business had quadrupled and octupled, and yet he was no better off.

"The railroad knows my business just a little bit better than I do," he said. "It knows my operating expenses to a cent, and it knows the terms of my contracts. How it knows these things I can only guess. It must have spies in my employ, and it must have access to the parties to all my contracts. For look you, when I place a big contract, the terms of which favor me a goodly profit, the freight rate from my quarry to market is promptly raised. No explanation is made. The railroad gets my profit. Under such circumstances I have never succeeded in getting the railroad to reconsider its raise. On the other hand, when there have been accidents, increased expenses of operating, or contracts with less profitable terms, I have always succeeded in getting the railroad to lower its rate. What is the result? Large or small, the railroad always gets my profits."

"What remains to you over and above," Ernest interrupted to ask, "would roughly be the equivalent of your salary as a manager did the railroad own the quarry."

"The very thing," Mr. Asmunsen replied. "Only a short time ago I had my books gone through for the past ten years. I discovered that for those ten years my gain was just equivalent to a manager's salary. The railroad might just as well have owned my quarry and hired me to run it."

"But with this difference," Ernest laughed; "the railroad would have had to assume all the risk which you so obligingly assumed for it."

"Very true," Mr. Asmunsen answered sadly.

Having let them have they say, Ernest began asking questions right and left. He began with Mr. Owen.

"You started a branch store here in Berkeley about six months ago?"

"Yes," Mr. Owen answered.

"And since then I've noticed that three little corner groceries have gone out of business. Was your branch store the cause of it?"

Mr. Owen affirmed with a complacent smile. "They had no chance against us."

"Why not?"

"We had greater capital. With a large business there is always less waste and greater efficiency."

"And your branch store absorbed the profits of the three small ones. I see. But tell me, what became of the owners of the three stores?"

"One is driving a delivery wagon for us. I don't know what happened to the other two."

Ernest turned abruptly on Mr. Kowalt.

"You sell a great deal at cut-rates.* What have become of the owners of the small drug stores that you forced to the wall?"

> * A lowering of selling price to cost, and even to less than
> cost. Thus, a large company could sell at a loss for a
> longer period than a small company, and so drive the small
> company out of business. A common device of competition.

"One of them, Mr. Haasfurther, has charge now of our prescription department," was the answer.

"And you absorbed the profits they had been making?"

"Surely. That is what we are in business for."

"And you?" Ernest said suddenly to Mr. Asmunsen. "You are disgusted because the railroad has absorbed your profits?"

Mr. Asmunsen nodded.

"What you want is to make profits yourself?"

Again Mr. Asmunsen nodded.

"Out of others?"

There was no answer.

"Out of others?" Ernest insisted.

"That is the way profits are made," Mr. Asmunsen replied curtly.

"Then the business game is to make profits out of others, and to prevent others from making profits out of you. That's it, isn't it?"

Ernest had to repeat his question before Mr. Asmunsen gave an answer, and then he said:

"Yes, that's it, except that we do not object to the others making profits so long as they are not extortionate."

"By extortionate you mean large; yet you do not object to making large profits yourself? . . . Surely not?"

And Mr. Asmunsen amiably confessed to the weakness. There was one other man who was quizzed by Ernest at this juncture, a Mr. Calvin, who had once been a great dairy-owner.

"Some time ago you were fighting the Milk Trust," Ernest said to him; "and now you are in Grange politics.* How did it happen?"

> * Many efforts were made during this period to organize the
> perishing farmer class into a political party, the aim of
> which was destroy the trusts and corporations by drastic
> legislation. All such attempts ended in failure.

"Oh, I haven't quit the fight," Mr. Calvin answered, and he looked belligerent enough. "I'm fighting the Trust on the only field where it is possible to fight—the political field. Let me show you. A few years ago we dairymen had everything our own way."

"But you competed among yourselves?" Ernest interrupted.

"Yes, that was what kept the profits down. We did try to organize, but independent dairymen always broke through us. Then came the Milk Trust."

"Financed by surplus capital from Standard Oil,"* Ernest said.

> * The first successful great trust—almost a generation in
> advance of the rest.

"Yes," Mr. Calvin acknowledged. "But we did not know it at the time. Its agents approached us with a club. "Come in and be fat," was their proposition, "or stay out and starve." Most of us came in. Those that didn't, starved. Oh, it paid us . . . at first. Milk was raised a cent a quart. One-quarter of this cent came to us. Three-quarters of it went to the Trust. Then milk was raised another cent, only we didn't get any of that cent. Our complaints were useless. The Trust was in control. We discovered that we were pawns. Finally, the additional quarter of a cent was denied us. Then the Trust began to squeeze us out. What could we do? We were squeezed out. There were no dairymen, only a Milk Trust."

"But with milk two cents higher, I should think you could have competed," Ernest suggested slyly.

"So we thought. We tried it." Mr. Calvin paused a moment. "It broke us. The Trust could put milk upon the market more cheaply than we. It could sell still at a slight profit when we were selling at actual loss. I dropped fifty thousand dollars in that venture. Most of us went bankrupt.* The dairymen were wiped out of existence."

> * Bankruptcy—a peculiar institution that enabled an individual, who had failed in competitive industry, to forego paying his debts. The effect was to ameliorate the too savage conditions of the fang-and-claw social struggle.

"So the Trust took your profits away from you," Ernest said, "and you've gone into politics in order to legislate the Trust out of existence and get the profits back?"

Mr. Calvin's face lighted up. "That is precisely what I say in my speeches to the farmers. That's our whole idea in a nutshell."

"And yet the Trust produces milk more cheaply than could the independent dairymen?" Ernest queried.

"Why shouldn't it, with the splendid organization and new machinery its large capital makes possible?"

"There is no discussion," Ernest answered. "It certainly should, and, furthermore, it does."

Mr. Calvin here launched out into a political speech in exposition of his views. He was warmly followed by a number of the others, and the cry of all was to destroy the trusts.

"Poor simple folk," Ernest said to me in an undertone. "They see clearly as far as they see, but they see only to the ends of their noses."

A little later he got the floor again, and in his characteristic way controlled it for the rest of the evening.

"I have listened carefully to all of you," he began, "and I see plainly that you play the business game in the orthodox fashion. Life sums itself up to you in profits. You have a firm and abiding belief that you were created for the sole purpose of making profits. Only there is a hitch. In the midst of your own profit-making along comes the trust and takes your profits away from you. This is a dilemma that interferes somehow with the aim of creation, and the only way out, as it seems to you, is to destroy that which takes from you your profits.

"I have listened carefully, and there is only one name that will epitomize you. I shall call you that name. You are machine-breakers. Do you know what a machine-breaker is? Let me tell you. In the eighteenth century, in England, men and women wove cloth on hand-looms in their own cottages. It was a slow, clumsy, and costly way of weaving cloth, this cottage system of manufacture. Along came the steam-engine and labor-saving machinery. A thousand looms assembled in a large factory, and driven by a central engine wove cloth vastly more cheaply than could the cottage weavers on their hand-looms. Here in the factory was combination, and before it competition faded away. The men and women who had worked the hand-looms for themselves now went into the factories and worked the machine-looms, not for themselves, but for the capitalist owners. Furthermore, little children went to work on the machine-looms, at lower wages, and displaced the men. This made hard times for the men. Their standard of living fell. They starved. And they said it was all the fault of the machines. Therefore, they proceeded to break the machines. They did not succeed, and they were very stupid.

"Yet you have not learned their lesson. Here are you, a century and a half later, trying to break machines. By your own confession the trust machines do the work more efficiently and more cheaply than you can. That is why you cannot compete with them. And yet you would break those machines. You are even more stupid than the stupid workmen of England. And while you maunder about restoring competition, the trusts go on destroying you.

"One and all you tell the same story,—the passing away of competition and the coming on of combination. You, Mr. Owen, destroyed competition here in Berkeley when your branch store drove the three small groceries out of business. Your combination was more effective. Yet you feel the pressure of other combinations on you, the trust combinations, and you cry out. It is because you are not a trust. If you were a grocery trust for the whole United States, you would be singing another song. And the song would be, 'Blessed are the trusts.' And yet again, not only is your small combination not a trust, but you are aware yourself of its lack of strength. You are beginning to divine your own end. You feel yourself and your branch stores a pawn in the game. You see the powerful interests rising and growing more powerful day by day; you feel their mailed hands descending upon your profits and taking a pinch here and a pinch there—the railroad trust, the oil trust, the steel trust, the coal trust; and you know that in the end they will destroy you, take away from you the last per cent of your little profits.

"You, sir, are a poor gamester. When you squeezed out the three small groceries here in Berkeley by virtue of your superior combination, you swelled out your chest, talked about efficiency and enterprise, and sent your wife to Europe on the profits you had gained by eating up the three small groceries. It is dog eat dog, and you ate them up. But, on the other hand, you are being eaten up in turn by the bigger dogs, wherefore you squeal. And what I say to you is true of all of you at this table. You are all squealing. You are all playing the losing game, and you are all squealing about it.

"But when you squeal you don't state the situation flatly, as I have stated it. You don't say that you like to squeeze profits out of others, and that you are making all the row because others are squeezing your profits out of you. No, you are too cunning for that. You say something else. You make small-capitalist political speeches such as Mr. Calvin made. What did he say? Here are a few of his phrases I caught: 'Our original principles are all right,' 'What this country requires is a return to fundamental American methods—free opportunity for all,' 'The spirit of liberty in which this nation was born,' 'Let us return to the principles of our forefathers.'

"When he says 'free opportunity for all,' he means free opportunity to squeeze profits, which freedom of opportunity is now denied him by the great trusts. And the absurd thing about it is that you have repeated these phrases so often that you believe them. You want opportunity to plunder your fellow-men in your own small way, but you hypnotize yourselves into thinking you want freedom. You are piggish and acquisitive, but the magic of your phrases leads you to believe that you are patriotic. Your desire for profits, which is sheer selfishness, you metamorphose into altruistic solicitude for suffering humanity. Come on now, right here amongst ourselves, and be honest for once. Look the matter in the face and state it in direct terms."

There were flushed and angry faces at the table, and withal a measure of awe. They were a little frightened at this smooth-faced young fellow, and the swing and smash of his words, and his dreadful trait of calling a spade a spade. Mr. Calvin promptly replied.

"And why not?" he demanded. "Why can we not return to ways of our fathers when this republic was founded? You have spoken much truth, Mr. Everhard, unpalatable though it has been. But here amongst ourselves let us speak out. Let us throw off all disguise and accept the truth as Mr. Everhard has flatly stated it. It is true that we smaller capitalists are after profits, and that the trusts are taking our profits away from us. It is true that we want to destroy the trusts in order that our profits may remain to us. And why can we not do it? Why not? I say, why not?"

"Ah, now we come to the gist of the matter," Ernest said with a pleased expression. "I'll try to tell you why not, though the telling will be rather hard. You see, you fellows have studied business, in a small way, but you have not studied social evolution at all. You are in the midst of a transition stage now in economic evolution, but you do not understand it, and that's what causes all the confusion. Why cannot you return? Because you can't. You can no more make water run up hill than can you cause the tide of economic evolution to flow back in its channel along the way it came. Joshua made the sun stand still upon Gibeon, but you would outdo Joshua. You would make the sun go backward in the sky. You would have time retrace its steps from noon to morning.

"In the face of labor-saving machinery, of organized production, of the increased efficiency of combination, you would set the economic sun back a whole generation or so to the time when there were no great capitalists, no great machinery, no railroads—a time when a host of little capitalists warred with each other in economic anarchy, and when production was primitive, wasteful, unorganized, and costly. Believe me, Joshua's task was easier, and he had Jehovah to help him. But God has forsaken you small capitalists. The sun of the small capitalists is setting. It will never rise again. Nor is it in your power even to make it stand still. You are perishing, and you are doomed to perish utterly from the face of society.

"This is the fiat of evolution. It is the word of God. Combination is stronger than competition. Primitive man was a puny creature hiding in the crevices of the rocks. He combined and made war upon his carnivorous enemies. They were competitive beasts. Primitive man was a combinative beast, and because of it he rose to primacy over all the animals. And man has been achieving greater and greater combinations ever since. It is combination versus competition, a thousand centuries long struggle, in which competition has always been worsted. Whoso enlists on the side of competition perishes."

"But the trusts themselves arose out of competition," Mr. Calvin interrupted.

"Very true," Ernest answered. "And the trusts themselves destroyed competition. That, by your own word, is why you are no longer in the dairy business."

The first laughter of the evening went around the table, and even Mr. Calvin joined in the laugh against himself.

"And now, while we are on the trusts," Ernest went on, "let us settle a few things. I shall make certain statements, and if you disagree with them, speak up. Silence will mean agreement. Is it not true that a machine-loom will weave more cloth and weave more cheaply than a hand-loom?" He paused, but nobody spoke up. "Is it not then highly irrational to break the machine-loom and go back to the clumsy and more costly hand-loom method of weaving?" Heads nodded in acquiescence. "Is it not true that that known as a trust produces more efficiently and cheaply than can a thousand competing small concerns?" Still no one objected. "Then is it not irrational to destroy that cheap and efficient combination?"

No one answered for a long time. Then Mr. Kowalt spoke.

"What are we to do, then?" he demanded. "To destroy the trusts is the only way we can see to escape their domination."

Ernest was all fire and aliveness on the instant.

"I'll show you another way!" he cried. "Let us not destroy those wonderful machines that produce efficiently and cheaply. Let us control them. Let us profit by their efficiency and cheapness. Let us run them for ourselves. Let us oust the present owners of the wonderful machines, and let us own the wonderful machines ourselves. That, gentlemen, is socialism, a greater combination than the trusts, a greater economic and social combination than any that has as yet appeared on the planet. It is in line with evolution. We meet combination with greater combination. It is the winning side. Come on over with us socialists and play on the winning side."

Here arose dissent. There was a shaking of heads, and mutterings arose.

"All right, then, you prefer to be anachronisms," Ernest laughed. "You prefer to play atavistic roles. You are doomed to perish as all atavisms perish. Have you ever asked what will happen to you when greater combinations than even the present trusts arise?

Have you ever considered where you will stand when the great trusts themselves combine into the combination of combinations—into the social, economic, and political trust?"

He turned abruptly and irrelevantly upon Mr. Calvin.

"Tell me," Ernest said, "if this is not true. You are compelled to form a new political party because the old parties are in the hands of the trusts. The chief obstacle to your Grange propaganda is the trusts. Behind every obstacle you encounter, every blow that smites you, every defeat that you receive, is the hand of the trusts. Is this not so? Tell me."

Mr. Calvin sat in uncomfortable silence.

"Go ahead," Ernest encouraged.

"It is true," Mr. Calvin confessed. "We captured the state legislature of Oregon and put through splendid protective legislation, and it was vetoed by the governor, who was a creature of the trusts. We elected a governor of Colorado, and the legislature refused to permit him to take office. Twice we have passed a national income tax, and each time the supreme court smashed it as unconstitutional. The courts are in the hands of the trusts. We, the people, do not pay our judges sufficiently. But there will come a time—"

"When the combination of the trusts will control all legislation, when the combination of the trusts will itself be the government," Ernest interrupted.

"Never! never!" were the cries that arose. Everybody was excited and belligerent.

"Tell me," Ernest demanded, "what will you do when such a time comes?"

"We will rise in our strength!" Mr. Asmunsen cried, and many voices backed his decision.

"That will be civil war," Ernest warned them.

"So be it, civil war," was Mr. Asmunsen's answer, with the cries of all the men at the table behind him. "We have not forgotten the deeds of our forefathers. For our liberties we are ready to fight and die."

Ernest smiled.

"Do not forget," he said, "that we had tacitly agreed that liberty in your case, gentlemen, means liberty to squeeze profits out of others."

The table was angry, now, fighting angry; but Ernest controlled the tumult and made himself heard.

"One more question. When you rise in your strength, remember, the reason for your rising will be that the government is in the hands of the trusts. Therefore, against your strength the government will turn the regular army, the navy, the militia, the police—in short, the whole organized war machinery of the United States. Where will your strength be then?"

Dismay sat on their faces, and before they could recover, Ernest struck again.

"Do you remember, not so long ago, when our regular army was only fifty thousand? Year by year it has been increased until to-day it is three hundred thousand."

Again he struck.

"Nor is that all. While you diligently pursued that favorite phantom of yours, called profits, and moralized about that favorite fetich of yours, called competition, even greater and more direful things have been accomplished by combination. There is the militia."

"It is our strength!" cried Mr. Kowalt. "With it we would repel the invasion of the regular army."

"You would go into the militia yourself," was Ernest's retort, "and be sent to Maine, or Florida, or the Philippines, or anywhere else, to drown in blood your own comrades civil-warring for their liberties. While from Kansas, or Wisconsin, or any other state, your own comrades would go into the militia and come here to California to drown in blood your own civil-warring."

Now they were really shocked, and they sat wordless, until Mr. Owen murmured:

"We would not go into the militia. That would settle it. We would not be so foolish."

Ernest laughed outright.

"You do not understand the combination that has been effected. You could not help yourself. You would be drafted into the militia."

"There is such a thing as civil law," Mr. Owen insisted.

"Not when the government suspends civil law. In that day when you speak of rising in your strength, your strength would be turned against yourself. Into the militia you would go, willy-nilly. Habeas corpus, I heard some one mutter just now. Instead of habeas corpus you would get post mortems. If you refused to go into the militia, or to obey after you were in, you would be tried by drumhead court martial and shot down like dogs. It is the law."

"It is not the law!" Mr. Calvin asserted positively. "There is no such law. Young man, you have dreamed all this. Why, you spoke of sending the militia to the Philippines. That is unconstitutional. The Constitution especially states that the militia cannot be sent out of the country."

"What's the Constitution got to do with it?" Ernest demanded. "The courts interpret the Constitution, and the courts, as Mr. Asmunsen agreed, are the creatures of the trusts. Besides, it is as I have said, the law. It has been the law for years, for nine years, gentlemen."

"That we can be drafted into the militia?" Mr. Calvin asked incredulously. "That they can shoot us by drumhead court martial if we refuse?"

"Yes," Ernest answered, "precisely that."

"How is it that we have never heard of this law?" my father asked, and I could see that it was likewise new to him.

"For two reasons," Ernest said. "First, there has been no need to enforce it. If there had, you'd have heard of it soon enough. And secondly, the law was rushed through Congress and the Senate secretly, with practically no discussion. Of course, the newspapers made no mention of it. But we socialists knew about it. We published it in our papers. But you never read our papers."

"I still insist you are dreaming," Mr. Calvin said stubbornly. "The country would never have permitted it."

"But the country did permit it," Ernest replied. "And as for my dreaming—" he put his hand in his pocket and drew out a small pamphlet—"tell me if this looks like dream-stuff."

He opened it and began to read:

"'Section One, be it enacted, and so forth and so forth, that the militia shall consist of every able-bodied male citizen of the respective states, territories, and District of Columbia, who is more than eighteen and less than forty-five years of age.'

"'Section Seven, that any officer or enlisted man'—remember Section One, gentlemen, you are all enlisted men—'that any enlisted man of the militia who shall refuse or neglect to present himself to such mustering officer upon being called forth as herein prescribed, shall be subject to trial by court martial, and shall be punished as such court martial shall direct.'

"'Section Eight, that courts martial, for the trial of officers or men of the militia, shall be composed of militia officers only.'

"'Section Nine, that the militia, when called into the actual service of the United States, shall be subject to the same rules and articles of war as the regular troops of the United States.'

"There you are gentlemen, American citizens, and fellow-militiamen. Nine years ago we socialists thought that law was aimed against labor. But it would seem that it was aimed against you, too. Congressman Wiley, in the brief discussion that was permitted, said that the bill 'provided for a reserve force to take the mob by the throat'—you're the mob, gentlemen—'and protect at all hazards life, liberty, and property.' And in the time to come, when you rise in your strength, remember that you will be rising against the property of the trusts, and the liberty of the trusts, according to the law, to squeeze you. Your teeth are pulled, gentlemen. Your claws are trimmed. In the day you rise in your strength, toothless and clawless, you will be as harmless as any army of clams."

"I don't believe it!" Kowalt cried. "There is no such law. It is a canard got up by you socialists."

"This bill was introduced in the House of Representatives on July 30, 1902," was the reply. "It was introduced by Representative Dick of Ohio. It was rushed through. It was passed unanimously by the Senate on January 14, 1903. And just seven days afterward was approved by the President of the United States."*

* Everhard was right in the essential particulars, though his date of the introduction of the bill is in error. The bill was introduced on June 30, and not on July 30. The Congressional Record is here in Ardis, and a reference to it shows mention of the bill on the following dates: June 30, December 9, 15, 16, and 17, 1902, and January 7 and 14, 1903. The ignorance evidenced by the business men at the dinner was nothing unusual. Very few people knew of the existence of this law. E. Untermann, a revolutionist, in July, 1903, published a pamphlet at Girard, Kansas, on the "Militia Bill." This pamphlet had a small circulation among workingmen; but already had the segregation of classes proceeded so far, that the members of the middle class never heard of the pamphlet at all, and so remained in ignorance of the law.

CHAPTER IX

THE MATHEMATICS OF A DREAM

In the midst of the consternation his revelation had produced, Ernest began again to speak.

"You have said, a dozen of you to-night, that socialism is impossible. You have asserted the impossible, now let me demonstrate the inevitable. Not only is it inevitable that you small capitalists shall pass away, but it is inevitable that the large capitalists, and the trusts also, shall pass away. Remember, the tide of evolution never flows backward. It flows on and on, and it flows from competition to combination, and from little combination to large combination, and from large combination to colossal combination, and it flows on to socialism, which is the most colossal combination of all.

"You tell me that I dream. Very good. I'll give you the mathematics of my dream; and here, in advance, I challenge you to show that my mathematics are wrong. I shall develop the inevitability of the breakdown of the capitalist system, and I shall demonstrate mathematically why it must break down. Here goes, and bear with me if at first I seem irrelevant.

"Let us, first of all, investigate a particular industrial process, and whenever I state something with which you disagree, please interrupt me. Here is a shoe factory. This factory takes leather and makes it into shoes. Here is one hundred dollars' worth of leather. It goes through the factory and comes out in the form of shoes, worth, let us say, two hundred dollars. What has happened? One hundred dollars has been added to the value of the leather. How was it added? Let us see.

"Capital and labor added this value of one hundred dollars. Capital furnished the factory, the machines, and paid all the expenses. Labor furnished labor. By the joint effort of capital and labor one hundred dollars of value was added. Are you all agreed so far?"

Heads nodded around the table in affirmation.

"Labor and capital having produced this one hundred dollars, now proceed to divide it. The statistics of this division are fractional; so let us, for the sake of convenience, make them roughly approximate. Capital takes fifty dollars as its share, and labor gets in wages fifty dollars as its share. We will not enter into the squabbling over the division.* No matter how much squabbling takes place, in one percentage or another the division is arranged. And take notice here, that what is true of this particular industrial process is true of all industrial processes. Am I right?"

* Everhard here clearly develops the cause of all the labor

troubles of that time. In the division of the joint-product, capital wanted all it could get, and labor wanted all it could get. This quarrel over the division was irreconcilable. So long as the system of capitalistic production existed, labor and capital continued to quarrel over the division of the joint-product. It is a ludicrous spectacle to us, but we must not forget that we have seven centuries' advantage over those that lived in that time.

Again the whole table agreed with Ernest.

"Now, suppose labor, having received its fifty dollars, wanted to buy back shoes. It could only buy back fifty dollars' worth. That's clear, isn't it?

"And now we shift from this particular process to the sum total of all industrial processes in the United States, which includes the leather itself, raw material, transportation, selling, everything. We will say, for the sake of round figures, that the total production of wealth in the United States is one year is four billion dollars. Then labor has received in wages, during the same period, two billion dollars. Four billion dollars has been produced. How much of this can labor buy back? Two billions. There is no discussion of this, I am sure. For that matter, my percentages are mild. Because of a thousand capitalistic devices, labor cannot buy back even half of the total product.

"But to return. We will say labor buys back two billions. Then it stands to reason that labor can consume only two billions. There are still two billions to be accounted for, which labor cannot buy back and consume."

"Labor does not consume its two billions, even," Mr. Kowalt spoke up. "If it did, it would not have any deposits in the savings banks."

"Labor's deposits in the savings banks are only a sort of reserve fund that is consumed as fast as it accumulates. These deposits are saved for old age, for sickness and accident, and for funeral expenses. The savings bank deposit is simply a piece of the loaf put back on the shelf to be eaten next day. No, labor consumes all of the total product that its wages will buy back.

"Two billions are left to capital. After it has paid its expenses, does it consume the remainder? Does capital consume all of its two billions?"

Ernest stopped and put the question point blank to a number of the men. They shook their heads.

"I don't know," one of them frankly said.

"Of course you do," Ernest went on. "Stop and think a moment. If capital consumed its share, the sum total of capital could not increase. It would remain constant. If you will look at the economic history of the United States, you will see that the sum total of capital has continually increased. Therefore capital does not consume its share. Do you remember when England owned so much of our railroad bonds? As the years went by, we bought back those bonds. What does that mean? That part of capital's unconsumed share bought back the bonds. What is the meaning of the fact that to-day the capitalists of the United States own hundreds and hundreds of millions of dollars of Mexican bonds, Russian bonds, Italian bonds, Grecian bonds? The meaning is that those hundreds and hundreds of millions were part of capital's share which capital did not consume. Furthermore, from the very beginning of the capitalist system, capital has never consumed all of its share.

"And now we come to the point. Four billion dollars of wealth is produced in one year in the United States. Labor buys back and consumes two billions. Capital does not consume the remaining two billions. There is a large balance left over unconsumed. What is done with this balance? What can be done with it? Labor cannot consume any of it, for labor has already spent all its wages. Capital will not consume this balance, because, already, according to its nature, it has consumed all it can. And still remains the balance. What can be done with it? What is done with it?"

"It is sold abroad," Mr. Kowalt volunteered.

"The very thing," Ernest agreed. "Because of this balance arises our need for a foreign market. This is sold abroad. It has to be sold abroad. There is no other way of getting rid of it. And that unconsumed surplus, sold abroad, becomes what we call our favorable balance of trade. Are we all agreed so far?"

"Surely it is a waste of time to elaborate these A B C's of commerce," Mr. Calvin said tartly. "We all understand them."

"And it is by these A B C's I have so carefully elaborated that I shall confound you," Ernest retorted. "There's the beauty of it. And I'm going to confound you with them right now. Here goes.

"The United States is a capitalist country that has developed its resources. According to its capitalist system of industry, it has an unconsumed surplus that must be got rid of, and that must be got rid of abroad.* What is true of the United States is true of every other capitalist country with developed resources. Every one of such countries has an unconsumed surplus. Don't forget that they have already traded with one another, and that these surpluses yet remain. Labor in all these countries has spent it wages, and cannot buy any of the surpluses. Capital in all these countries has already consumed all it is able according to its nature. And still remain the surpluses. They cannot dispose of these surpluses to one another. How are they going to get rid of them?"

* Theodore Roosevelt, President of the United States a few years prior to this time, made the following public declaration: "A more liberal and extensive reciprocity in the purchase and sale of commodities is necessary, so that the overproduction of the United States can be satisfactorily disposed of to foreign countries." Of course, this overproduction he mentions was the profits of the capitalist system over and beyond the consuming power of the capitalists. It was at this time that Senator Mark Hanna said: "The production of wealth in the United States

is one-third larger annually than its consumption." Also a fellow-Senator, Chauncey Depew, said: "The American people produce annually two billions more wealth than they consume."

"Sell them to countries with undeveloped resources," Mr. Kowalt suggested.

"The very thing. You see, my argument is so clear and simple that in your own minds you carry it on for me. And now for the next step. Suppose the United States disposes of its surplus to a country with undeveloped resources like, say, Brazil. Remember this surplus is over and above trade, which articles of trade have been consumed. What, then, does the United States get in return from Brazil?"

"Gold," said Mr. Kowalt.

"But there is only so much gold, and not much of it, in the world," Ernest objected.

"Gold in the form of securities and bonds and so forth," Mr. Kowalt amended.

"Now you've struck it," Ernest said. "From Brazil the United States, in return for her surplus, gets bonds and securities. And what does that mean? It means that the United States is coming to own railroads in Brazil, factories, mines, and lands in Brazil. And what is the meaning of that in turn?"

Mr. Kowalt pondered and shook his head.

"I'll tell you," Ernest continued. "It means that the resources of Brazil are being developed. And now, the next point. When Brazil, under the capitalist system, has developed her resources, she will herself have an unconsumed surplus. Can she get rid of this surplus to the United States? No, because the United States has herself a surplus. Can the United States do what she previously did—get rid of her surplus to Brazil? No, for Brazil now has a surplus, too.

"What happens? The United States and Brazil must both seek out other countries with undeveloped resources, in order to unload the surpluses on them. But by the very process of unloading the surpluses, the resources of those countries are in turn developed. Soon they have surpluses, and are seeking other countries on which to unload. Now, gentlemen, follow me. The planet is only so large. There are only so many countries in the world. What will happen when every country in the world, down to the smallest and last, with a surplus in its hands, stands confronting every other country with surpluses in their hands?"

He paused and regarded his listeners. The bepuzzlement in their faces was delicious. Also, there was awe in their faces. Out of abstractions Ernest had conjured a vision and made them see it. They were seeing it then, as they sat there, and they were frightened by it.

"We started with A B C, Mr. Calvin," Ernest said slyly. "I have now given you the rest of the alphabet. It is very simple. That is the beauty of it. You surely have the answer forthcoming. What, then, when every country in the world has an unconsumed surplus? Where will your capitalist system be then?"

But Mr. Calvin shook a troubled head. He was obviously questing back through Ernest's reasoning in search of an error.

"Let me briefly go over the ground with you again," Ernest said. "We began with a particular industrial process, the shoe factory. We found that the division of the joint product that took place there was similar to the division that took place in the sum total of all industrial processes. We found that labor could buy back with its wages only so much of the product, and that capital did not consume all of the remainder of the product. We found that when labor had consumed to the full extent of its wages, and when capital had consumed all it wanted, there was still left an unconsumed surplus. We agreed that this surplus could only be disposed of abroad. We agreed, also, that the effect of unloading this surplus on another country would be to develop the resources of that country, and that in a short time that country would have an unconsumed surplus. We extended this process to all the countries on the planet, till every country was producing every year, and every day, an unconsumed surplus, which it could dispose of to no other country. And now I ask you again, what are we going to do with those surpluses?"

Still no one answered.

"Mr. Calvin?" Ernest queried.

"It beats me," Mr. Calvin confessed.

"I never dreamed of such a thing," Mr. Asmunsen said. "And yet it does seem clear as print."

It was the first time I had ever heard Karl Marx's* doctrine of surplus value elaborated, and Ernest had done it so simply that I, too, sat puzzled and dumbfounded.

> * Karl Marx—the great intellectual hero of Socialism. A
> German Jew of the nineteenth century. A contemporary of
> John Stuart Mill. It seems incredible to us that whole
> generations should have elapsed after the enunciation of
> Marx's economic discoveries, in which time he was sneered at
> by the world's accepted thinkers and scholars. Because of
> his discoveries he was banished from his native country, and
> he died an exile in England.

"I'll tell you a way to get rid of the surplus," Ernest said. "Throw it into the sea. Throw every year hundreds of millions of dollars' worth of shoes and wheat and clothing and all the commodities of commerce into the sea. Won't that fix it?"

"It will certainly fix it," Mr. Calvin answered. "But it is absurd for you to talk that way."

Ernest was upon him like a flash.

"Is it a bit more absurd than what you advocate, you machine-breaker, returning to the antediluvian ways of your forefathers? What do you propose in order to get rid of the surplus? You would escape the problem of the surplus by not producing any surplus. And how do you propose to avoid producing a surplus? By returning to a primitive method of production, so confused and disorderly and irrational, so wasteful and costly, that it will be impossible to produce a surplus."

Mr. Calvin swallowed. The point had been driven home. He swallowed again and cleared his throat.

"You are right," he said. "I stand convicted. It is absurd. But we've got to do something. It is a case of life and death for us of the middle class. We refuse to perish. We elect to be absurd and to return to the truly crude and wasteful methods of our forefathers. We will put back industry to its pre-trust stage. We will break the machines. And what are you going to do about it?"

"But you can't break the machines," Ernest replied. "You cannot make the tide of evolution flow backward. Opposed to you are two great forces, each of which is more powerful than you of the middle class. The large capitalists, the trusts, in short, will not let you turn back. They don't want the machines destroyed. And greater than the trusts, and more powerful, is labor. It will not let you destroy the machines. The ownership of the world, along with the machines, lies between the trusts and labor. That is the battle alignment. Neither side wants the destruction of the machines. But each side wants to possess the machines. In this battle the middle class has no place. The middle class is a pygmy between two giants. Don't you see, you poor perishing middle class, you are caught between the upper and nether millstones, and even now has the grinding begun.

"I have demonstrated to you mathematically the inevitable breakdown of the capitalist system. When every country stands with an unconsumed and unsalable surplus on its hands, the capitalist system will break down under the terrific structure of profits that it itself has reared. And in that day there won't be any destruction of the machines. The struggle then will be for the ownership of the machines. If labor wins, your way will be easy. The United States, and the whole world for that matter, will enter upon a new and tremendous era. Instead of being crushed by the machines, life will be made fairer, and happier, and nobler by them. You of the destroyed middle class, along with labor—there will be nothing but labor then; so you, and all the rest of labor, will participate in the equitable distribution of the products of the wonderful machines. And we, all of us, will make new and more wonderful machines. And there won't be any unconsumed surplus, because there won't be any profits."

"But suppose the trusts win in this battle over the ownership of the machines and the world?" Mr. Kowalt asked.

"Then," Ernest answered, "you, and labor, and all of us, will be crushed under the iron heel of a despotism as relentless and terrible as any despotism that has blackened the pages of the history of man. That will be a good name for that despotism, the Iron Heel."*

> * The earliest known use of that name to designate the
> Oligarchy.

There was a long pause, and every man at the table meditated in ways unwonted and profound.

"But this socialism of yours is a dream," Mr. Calvin said; and repeated, "a dream."

"I'll show you something that isn't a dream, then," Ernest answered. "And that something I shall call the Oligarchy. You call it the Plutocracy. We both mean the same thing, the large capitalists or the trusts. Let us see where the power lies today. And in order to do so, let us apportion society into its class divisions.

"There are three big classes in society. First comes the Plutocracy, which is composed of wealthy bankers, railway magnates, corporation directors, and trust magnates. Second, is the middle class, your class, gentlemen, which is composed of farmers, merchants, small manufacturers, and professional men. And third and last comes my class, the proletariat, which is composed of the wage-workers.*

> * This division of society made by Everhard is in accordance
> with that made by Lucien Sanial, one of the statistical
> authorities of that time. His calculation of the membership
> of these divisions by occupation, from the United States
> Census of 1900, is as follows: Plutocratic class, 250,251;
> Middle class, 8,429,845; and Proletariat class, 20,393,137.

"You cannot but grant that the ownership of wealth constitutes essential power in the United States to-day. How is this wealth owned by these three classes? Here are the figures. The Plutocracy owns sixty-seven billions of wealth. Of the total number of persons engaged in occupations in the United States, only nine-tenths of one per cent are from the Plutocracy, yet the Plutocracy owns seventy per cent of the total wealth. The middle class owns twenty-four billions. Twenty-nine per cent of those in occupations are from the middle class, and they own twenty-five per cent of the total wealth. Remains the proletariat. It owns four billions. Of all persons in occupations, seventy per cent come from the proletariat; and the proletariat owns four per cent of the total wealth. Where does the power lie, gentlemen?"

"From your own figures, we of the middle class are more powerful than labor," Mr. Asmunsen remarked.

"Calling us weak does not make you stronger in the face of the strength of the Plutocracy," Ernest retorted. "And furthermore, I'm not done with you. There is a greater strength than wealth, and it is greater because it cannot be taken away. Our strength, the strength of the proletariat, is in our muscles, in our hands to cast ballots, in our fingers to pull triggers. This strength we cannot be stripped of. It is the primitive strength, it is the strength that is to life germane, it is the strength that is stronger than wealth, and that wealth cannot take away.

"But your strength is detachable. It can be taken away from you. Even now the Plutocracy is taking it away from you. In the end it will take it all away from you. And then you will cease to be the middle class. You will descend to us. You will become proletarians. And the beauty of it is that you will then add to our strength. We will hail you brothers, and we will fight shoulder to shoulder in the cause of humanity.

"You see, labor has nothing concrete of which to be despoiled. Its share of the wealth of the country consists of clothes and household furniture, with here and there, in very rare cases, an unencumbered home. But you have the concrete wealth, twenty-four billions of it, and the Plutocracy will take it away from you. Of course, there is the large likelihood that the proletariat will take it away first. Don't you see your position, gentlemen? The middle class is a wobbly little lamb between a lion and a tiger. If one doesn't get you, the other will. And if the Plutocracy gets you first, why it's only a matter of time when the Proletariat gets the Plutocracy.

"Even your present wealth is not a true measure of your power. The strength of your wealth at this moment is only an empty shell. That is why you are crying out your feeble little battle-cry, 'Return to the ways of our fathers.' You are aware of your impotency. You know that your strength is an empty shell. And I'll show you the emptiness of it.

"What power have the farmers? Over fifty per cent are thralls by virtue of the fact that they are merely tenants or are mortgaged. And all of them are thralls by virtue of the fact that the trusts already own or control (which is the same thing only better)—own and control all the means of marketing the crops, such as cold storage, railroads, elevators, and steamship lines. And, furthermore, the trusts control the markets. In all this the farmers are without power. As regards their political and governmental power, I'll take that up later, along with the political and governmental power of the whole middle class.

"Day by day the trusts squeeze out the farmers as they squeezed out Mr. Calvin and the rest of the dairymen. And day by day are the merchants squeezed out in the same way. Do you remember how, in six months, the Tobacco Trust squeezed out over four hundred cigar stores in New York City alone? Where are the old-time owners of the coal fields? You know today, without my telling you, that the Railroad Trust owns or controls the entire anthracite and bituminous coal fields. Doesn't the Standard Oil Trust* own a score of the ocean lines? And does it not also control copper, to say nothing of running a smelter trust as a little side enterprise? There are ten thousand cities in the United States to-night lighted by the companies owned or controlled by Standard Oil, and in as many cities all the electric transportation,—urban, suburban, and interurban,—is in the hands of Standard Oil. The small capitalists who were in these thousands of enterprises are gone. You know that. It's the same way that you are going.

  * Standard Oil and Rockefeller—see upcoming footnote:
  "Rockefeller began as a member . . ."

"The small manufacturer is like the farmer; and small manufacturers and farmers to-day are reduced, to all intents and purposes, to feudal tenure. For that matter, the professional men and the artists are at this present moment villeins in everything but name, while the politicians are henchmen. Why do you, Mr. Calvin, work all your nights and days to organize the farmers, along with the rest of the middle class, into a new political party? Because the politicians of the old parties will have nothing to do with your atavistic ideas; and with your atavistic ideas, they will have nothing to do because they are what I said they are, henchmen, retainers of the Plutocracy.

"I spoke of the professional men and the artists as villeins. What else are they? One and all, the professors, the preachers, and the editors, hold their jobs by serving the Plutocracy, and their service consists of propagating only such ideas as are either harmless to or commendatory of the Plutocracy. Whenever they propagate ideas that menace the Plutocracy, they lose their jobs, in which case, if they have not provided for the rainy day, they descend into the proletariat and either perish or become working-class agitators. And don't forget that it is the press, the pulpit, and the university that mould public opinion, set the thought-pace of the nation. As for the artists, they merely pander to the little less than ignoble tastes of the Plutocracy.

"But after all, wealth in itself is not the real power; it is the means to power, and power is governmental. Who controls the government to-day? The proletariat with its twenty millions engaged in occupations? Even you laugh at the idea. Does the middle class, with its eight million occupied members? No more than the proletariat. Who, then, controls the government? The Plutocracy, with its paltry quarter of a million of occupied members. But this quarter of a million does not control the government, though it renders yeoman service. It is the brain of the Plutocracy that controls the government, and this brain consists of seven* small and powerful groups of men. And do not forget that these groups are working to-day practically in unison.

> * Even as late as 1907, it was considered that eleven groups dominated the country, but this number was reduced by the amalgamation of the five railroad groups into a supreme combination of all the railroads. These five groups so amalgamated, along with their financial and political allies, were (1) James J. Hill with his control of the Northwest; (2) the Pennsylvania railway group, Schiff financial manager, with big banking firms of Philadelphia and New York; (3) Harriman, with Frick for counsel and Odell as political lieutenant, controlling the central continental, Southwestern and Southern Pacific Coast lines of transportation; (4) the Gould family railway interests; and (5) Moore, Reid, and Leeds, known as the "Rock Island crowd." These strong oligarchs arose out of the conflict of competition and travelled the inevitable road toward combination.

"Let me point out the power of but one of them, the railroad group. It employs forty thousand lawyers to defeat the people in the courts. It issues countless thousands of free passes to judges, bankers, editors, ministers, university men, members of state legislatures, and of Congress. It maintains luxurious lobbies* at every state capital, and at the national capital; and in all the cities and towns of the land it employs an immense army of pettifoggers and small politicians whose business is to attend primaries, pack conventions, get on juries, bribe judges, and in every way to work for its interests.**

> * Lobby—a peculiar institution for bribing, bulldozing, and corrupting the legislators who were supposed to represent the people's interests.
>
> ** A decade before this speech of Everhard's, the New York Board of Trade issued a report from which the following is quoted: "The railroads control absolutely the legislatures of a majority of the states of the Union; they make and unmake United States Senators, congressmen, and governors, and are practically dictators of the governmental policy of the United States."

"Gentlemen, I have merely sketched the power of one of the seven groups that constitute the brain of the Plutocracy.* Your twenty-four billions of wealth does not give you twenty-five cents' worth of governmental power. It is an empty shell, and soon even the empty shell will be taken away from you. The Plutocracy has all power in its hands to-day. It to-day makes the laws, for it owns the Senate, Congress, the courts, and the state legislatures. And not only that. Behind law must be force to execute the law. To-day the Plutocracy makes the law, and to enforce the law it has at its beck and call the, police, the army, the navy, and, lastly, the militia, which is you, and me, and all of us."

> * Rockefeller began as a member of the proletariat, and through thrift and cunning succeeded in developing the first perfect trust, namely that known as Standard Oil. We cannot forbear giving the following remarkable page from the history of the times, to show how the need for reinvestment of the Standard Oil surplus crushed out small capitalists and hastened the breakdown of the capitalist system. David Graham Phillips was a radical writer of the period, and the quotation, by him, is taken from a copy of the Saturday Evening Post, dated October 4, 1902 A.D. This is the only copy of this publication that has come down to us, and yet, from its appearance and content, we cannot but conclude that it was one of the popular periodicals with a large circulation. The quotation here follows:
>
> "About ten years ago Rockefeller's income was given as thirty millions by an excellent authority. He had reached the limit of profitable investment of profits in the oil industry. Here, then, were these enormous sums in cash pouring in—more than $2,000,000 a month for John Davison Rockefeller alone. The problem of reinvestment became more

serious. It became a nightmare. The oil income was swelling, swelling, and the number of sound investments limited, even more limited than it is now. It was through no special eagerness for more gains that the Rockefellers began to branch out from oil into other things. They were forced, swept on by this inrolling tide of wealth which their monopoly magnet irresistibly attracted. They developed a staff of investment seekers and investigators. It is said that the chief of this staff has a salary of $125,000 a year.

"The first conspicuous excursion and incursion of the Rockefellers was into the railway field. By 1895 they controlled one-fifth of the railway mileage of the country. What do they own or, through dominant ownership, control to-day? They are powerful in all the great railways of New York, north, east, and west, except one, where their share is only a few millions. They are in most of the great railways radiating from Chicago. They dominate in several of the systems that extend to the Pacific. It is their votes that make Mr. Morgan so potent, though, it may be added, they need his brains more than he needs their votes—at present, and the combination of the two constitutes in large measure the 'community of interest.'

"But railways could not alone absorb rapidly enough those mighty floods of gold. Presently John D. Rockefeller's $2,500,000 a month had increased to four, to five, to six millions a month, to $75,000,000 a year. Illuminating oil was becoming all profit. The reinvestments of income were adding their mite of many annual millions.

"The Rockefellers went into gas and electricity when those industries had developed to the safe investment stage. And now a large part of the American people must begin to enrich the Rockefellers as soon as the sun goes down, no matter what form of illuminant they use. They went into farm mortgages. It is said that when prosperity a few years ago enabled the farmers to rid themselves of their mortgages, John D. Rockefeller was moved almost to tears; eight millions which he had thought taken care of for years to come at a good interest were suddenly dumped upon his doorstep and there set up a-squawking for a new home. This unexpected addition to his worriments in finding places for the progeny of his petroleum and their progeny and their progeny's progeny was too much for the equanimity of a man without a digestion. . . .

"The Rockefellers went into mines—iron and coal and copper and lead; into other industrial companies; into street railways, into national, state, and municipal bonds; into steamships and steamboats and telegraphy; into real estate, into skyscrapers and residences and hotels and business blocks; into life insurance, into banking. There was soon literally no field of industry where their millions were not at work. . . .

"The Rockefeller bank—the National City Bank—is by itself far and away the biggest bank in the United States. It is exceeded in the world only by the Bank of England and the Bank of France. The deposits average more than one hundred millions a day; and it dominates the call loan market on Wall Street and the stock market. But it is not alone; it is the head of the Rockefeller chain of banks, which includes fourteen banks and trust companies in New York City, and banks of great strength and influence in every large money center in the country.

"John D. Rockefeller owns Standard Oil stock worth between four and five hundred millions at the market quotations. He has a hundred millions in the steel trust, almost as much in a single western railway system, half as much in a second, and so on and on and on until the mind wearies of the cataloguing. His income last year was about $100,000,000— it is doubtful if the incomes of all the Rothschilds together make a greater sum. And it is going up by leaps and bounds."

Little discussion took place after this, and the dinner soon broke up. All were quiet and subdued, and leave-taking was done with low voices. It seemed almost that they were scared by the vision of the times they had seen.

"The situation is, indeed, serious," Mr. Calvin said to Ernest. "I have little quarrel with the way you have depicted it. Only I disagree with you about the doom of the middle class. We shall survive, and we shall overthrow the trusts."

"And return to the ways of your fathers," Ernest finished for him.

"Even so," Mr. Calvin answered gravely. "I know it's a sort of machine-breaking, and that it is absurd. But then life seems absurd to-day, what of the machinations of the Plutocracy. And at any rate, our sort of machine-breaking is at least practical and possible, which your dream is not. Your socialistic dream is . . . well, a dream. We cannot follow you."

"I only wish you fellows knew a little something about evolution and sociology," Ernest said wistfully, as they shook hands. "We would be saved so much trouble if you did."

CHAPTER X

THE VORTEX

Following like thunder claps upon the Business Men's dinner, occurred event after event of terrifying moment; and I, little I, who had lived so placidly all my days in the quiet university town, found myself and my personal affairs drawn into the vortex of the great world-affairs. Whether it was my love for Ernest, or the clear sight he had given me of the society in which I lived, that made me a revolutionist, I know not; but a revolutionist I became, and I was plunged into a whirl of happenings that would have been inconceivable three short months before.

The crisis in my own fortunes came simultaneously with great crises in society. First of all, father was discharged from the university. Oh, he was not technically discharged. His resignation was demanded, that was all. This, in itself, did not amount to much. Father, in fact, was delighted. He was especially delighted because his discharge had been precipitated by the publication of his book, "Economics and Education." It clinched his argument, he contended. What better evidence could be advanced to prove that education was dominated by the capitalist class?

But this proof never got anywhere. Nobody knew he had been forced to resign from the university. He was so eminent a scientist that such an announcement, coupled with the reason for his enforced resignation, would have created somewhat of a furor all over the world. The newspapers showered him with praise and honor, and commended him for having given up the drudgery of the lecture room in order to devote his whole time to scientific research.

At first father laughed. Then he became angry—tonic angry. Then came the suppression of his book. This suppression was performed secretly, so secretly that at first we could not comprehend. The publication of the book had immediately caused a bit of excitement in the country. Father had been politely abused in the capitalist press, the tone of the abuse being to the effect that it was a pity so great a scientist should leave his field and invade the realm of sociology, about which he knew nothing and wherein he had promptly become lost. This lasted for a week, while father chuckled and said the book had touched a sore spot on capitalism. And then, abruptly, the newspapers and the critical magazines ceased saying anything about the book at all. Also, and with equal suddenness, the book disappeared from the market. Not a copy was obtainable from any bookseller. Father wrote to the publishers and was informed that the plates had been accidentally injured. An unsatisfactory correspondence followed. Driven finally to an unequivocal stand, the publishers stated that they could not see their way to putting the book into type again, but that they were willing to relinquish their rights in it.

"And you won't find another publishing house in the country to touch it," Ernest said. "And if I were you, I'd hunt cover right now. You've merely got a foretaste of the Iron Heel."

But father was nothing if not a scientist. He never believed in jumping to conclusions. A laboratory experiment was no experiment if it were not carried through in all its details. So he patiently went the round of the publishing houses. They gave a multitude of excuses, but not one house would consider the book.

When father became convinced that the book had actually been suppressed, he tried to get the fact into the newspapers; but his communications were ignored. At a political meeting of the socialists, where many reporters were present, father saw his chance. He arose and related the history of the suppression of the book. He laughed next day when he read the newspapers, and then he grew angry to a degree that eliminated all tonic qualities. The papers made no mention of the book, but they misreported him beautifully. They twisted his words and phrases away from the context, and turned his subdued and controlled remarks into a howling anarchistic speech. It was done artfully. One instance, in particular, I remember. He had used the phrase "social revolution." The reporter merely dropped out "social." This was sent out all over the country in an Associated Press despatch, and from all over the country arose a cry of alarm. Father was branded as a nihilist and an anarchist, and in one cartoon that was copied widely he was portrayed waving a red flag at the head of a mob of long-haired, wild-eyed men who bore in their hands torches, knives, and dynamite bombs.

He was assailed terribly in the press, in long and abusive editorials, for his anarchy, and hints were made of mental breakdown on his part. This behavior, on the part of the capitalist press, was nothing new, Ernest told us. It was the custom, he said, to send reporters to all the socialist meetings for the express purpose of misreporting and distorting what was said, in order to frighten the middle class away from any possible affiliation with the proletariat. And repeatedly Ernest warned father to cease fighting and to take to cover.

The socialist press of the country took up the fight, however, and throughout the reading portion of the working class it was known that the book had been suppressed. But this knowledge stopped with the working class. Next, the "Appeal to Reason," a big socialist publishing house, arranged with father to bring out the book. Father was jubilant, but Ernest was alarmed.

"I tell you we are on the verge of the unknown," he insisted. "Big things are happening secretly all around us. We can feel them. We do not know what they are, but they are there. The whole fabric of society is a-tremble with them. Don't ask me. I don't know myself. But out of this flux of society something is about to crystallize. It is crystallizing now. The suppression of the book is a precipitation. How many books have been suppressed? We haven't the least idea. We are in the dark. We have no way of learning. Watch out next for the suppression of the socialist press and socialist publishing houses. I'm afraid it's coming. We are going to be throttled."

Ernest had his hand on the pulse of events even more closely than the rest of the socialists, and within two days the first blow was struck. The Appeal to Reason was a weekly, and its regular circulation amongst the proletariat was seven hundred and fifty thousand. Also, it very frequently got out special editions of from two to five millions. These great editions were paid for and distributed by the small army of voluntary workers who had marshalled around the Appeal. The first blow was aimed at these special editions, and it was a crushing one. By an arbitrary ruling of the Post Office, these editions were decided to be not the regular circulation of the paper, and for that reason were denied admission to the mails.

A week later the Post Office Department ruled that the paper was seditious, and barred it entirely from the mails. This was a fearful blow to the socialist propaganda. The Appeal was desperate. It devised a plan of reaching its subscribers through the express companies, but they declined to handle it. This was the end of the Appeal. But not quite. It prepared to go on with its book publishing. Twenty thousand copies of father's book were in the bindery, and the presses were turning off more. And then, without warning, a mob arose one night, and, under a waving American flag, singing patriotic songs, set fire to the great plant of the Appeal and totally destroyed it.

Now Girard, Kansas, was a quiet, peaceable town. There had never been any labor troubles there. The Appeal paid union wages; and, in fact, was the backbone of the town, giving employment to hundreds of men and women. It was not the citizens of Girard that composed the mob. This mob had risen up out of the earth apparently, and to all intents and purposes, its work done, it had gone back into the earth. Ernest saw in the affair the most sinister import.

"The Black Hundreds* are being organized in the United States," he said. "This is the beginning. There will be more of it. The Iron Heel is getting bold."

> * The Black Hundreds were reactionary mobs organized by the perishing Autocracy in the Russian Revolution. These reactionary groups attacked the revolutionary groups, and also, at needed moments, rioted and destroyed property so as to afford the Autocracy the pretext of calling out the Cossacks.

And so perished father's book. We were to see much of the Black Hundreds as the days went by. Week by week more of the socialist papers were barred from the mails, and in a number of instances the Black Hundreds destroyed the socialist presses. Of course, the newspapers of the land lived up to the reactionary policy of the ruling class, and the destroyed socialist press was misrepresented and vilified, while the Black Hundreds were represented as true patriots and saviours of society. So convincing was all this misrepresentation that even sincere ministers in the pulpit praised the Black Hundreds while regretting the necessity of violence.

History was making fast. The fall elections were soon to occur, and Ernest was nominated by the socialist party to run for Congress. His chance for election was most favorable. The street-car strike in San Francisco had been broken. And following upon it the teamsters' strike had been broken. These two defeats had been very disastrous to organized labor. The whole Water Front Federation, along with its allies in the structural trades, had backed up the teamsters, and all had smashed down ingloriously. It had been a bloody strike. The police had broken countless heads with their riot clubs; and the death list had been augmented by the turning loose of a machine-gun on the strikers from the barns of the Marsden Special Delivery Company.

In consequence, the men were sullen and vindictive. They wanted blood, and revenge. Beaten on their chosen field, they were ripe to seek revenge by means of political action. They still maintained their labor organization, and this gave them strength in the political struggle that was on. Ernest's chance for election grew stronger and stronger. Day by day unions and more unions voted their support to the socialists, until even Ernest laughed when the Undertakers' Assistants and the Chicken Pickers fell into line. Labor became mulish. While it packed the socialist meetings with mad enthusiasm, it was impervious to the wiles of the old-party politicians. The old-party orators were usually greeted with empty halls, though occasionally they encountered full halls where they were so roughly handled that more than once it was necessary to call out the police reserves.

History was making fast. The air was vibrant with things happening and impending. The country was on the verge of hard times,* caused by a series of prosperous years wherein the difficulty of disposing abroad of the unconsumed surplus had become increasingly difficult. Industries were working short time; many great factories were standing idle against the time when the surplus should be gone; and wages were being cut right and left.

> * Under the capitalist regime these periods of hard times were as inevitable as they were absurd. Prosperity always brought calamity. This, of course, was due to the excess of unconsumed profits that was piled up.

Also, the great machinist strike had been broken. Two hundred thousand machinists, along with their five hundred thousand allies in the metalworking trades, had been defeated in as bloody a strike as had ever marred the United States. Pitched battles had been fought with the small armies of armed strike-breakers* put in the field by the employers' associations; the Black Hundreds, appearing in scores of wide-scattered places, had destroyed property; and, in consequence, a hundred thousand regular soldiers of the United States has been called out to put a frightful end to the whole affair. A number of the labor leaders had been executed; many others had been sentenced to prison, while thousands of the rank and file of the strikers had been herded into bull-pens** and abominably treated by the soldiers.

* Strike-breakers—these were, in purpose and practice and everything except name, the private soldiers of the capitalists. They were thoroughly organized and well armed, and they were held in readiness to be hurled in special trains to any part of the country where labor went on strike or was locked out by the employers. Only those curious times could have given rise to the amazing spectacle of one, Farley, a notorious commander of strike-breakers, who, in 1906, swept across the United States in special trains from New York to San Francisco with an army of twenty-five hundred men, fully armed and equipped, to break a strike of the San Francisco street-car men. Such an act was in direct violation of the laws of the land. The fact that this act, and thousands of similar acts, went unpunished, goes to show how completely the judiciary was the creature of the Plutocracy.

** Bull-pen—in a miners' strike in Idaho, in the latter part of the nineteenth century, it happened that many of the strikers were confined in a bull-pen by the troops. The practice and the name continued in the twentieth century.

The years of prosperity were now to be paid for. All markets were glutted; all markets were falling; and amidst the general crumble of prices the price of labor crumbled fastest of all. The land was convulsed with industrial dissensions. Labor was striking here, there, and everywhere; and where it was not striking, it was being turned out by the capitalists. The papers were filled with tales of violence and blood. And through it all the Black Hundreds played their part. Riot, arson, and wanton destruction of property was their function, and well they performed it. The whole regular army was in the field, called there by the actions of the Black Hundreds.* All cities and towns were like armed camps, and laborers were shot down like dogs. Out of the vast army of the unemployed the strike-breakers were recruited; and when the strike-breakers were worsted by the labor unions, the troops always appeared and crushed the unions. Then there was the militia. As yet, it was not necessary to have recourse to the secret militia law. Only the regularly organized militia was out, and it was out everywhere. And in this time of terror, the regular army was increased an additional hundred thousand by the government.

* The name only, and not the idea, was imported from Russia. The Black Hundreds were a development out of the secret agents of the capitalists, and their use arose in the labor struggles of the nineteenth century. There is no discussion of this. No less an authority of the times than Carroll D. Wright, United States Commissioner of Labor, is responsible for the statement. From his book, entitled "The Battles of

Labor," is quoted the declaration that "in some of the great historic strikes the employers themselves have instigated acts of violence;" that manufacturers have deliberately provoked strikes in order to get rid of surplus stock; and that freight cars have been burned by employers' agents during railroad strikes in order to increase disorder. It was out of these secret agents of the employers that the Black Hundreds arose; and it was they, in turn, that later became that terrible weapon of the Oligarchy, the agents-provocateurs.

Never had labor received such an all-around beating. The great captains of industry, the oligarchs, had for the first time thrown their full weight into the breach the struggling employers' associations had made. These associations were practically middle-class affairs, and now, compelled by hard times and crashing markets, and aided by the great captains of industry, they gave organized labor an awful and decisive defeat. It was an all-powerful alliance, but it was an alliance of the lion and the lamb, as the middle class was soon to learn.

Labor was bloody and sullen, but crushed. Yet its defeat did not put an end to the hard times. The banks, themselves constituting one of the most important forces of the Oligarchy, continued to call in credits. The Wall Street* group turned the stock market into a maelstrom where the values of all the land crumbled away almost to nothingness. And out of all the rack and ruin rose the form of the nascent Oligarchy, imperturbable, indifferent, and sure. Its serenity and certitude was terrifying. Not only did it use its own vast power, but it used all the power of the United States Treasury to carry out its plans.

* Wall Street—so named from a street in ancient New York, where was situated the stock exchange, and where the irrational organization of society permitted underhanded manipulation of all the industries of the country.

The captains of industry had turned upon the middle class. The employers' associations, that had helped the captains of industry to tear and rend labor, were now torn and rent by their quondam allies. Amidst the crashing of the middle men, the small business men and manufacturers, the trusts stood firm. Nay, the trusts did more than stand firm. They were active. They sowed wind, and wind, and ever more wind; for they alone knew how to reap the whirlwind and make a profit out of it. And such profits! Colossal profits! Strong enough themselves to weather the storm that was largely their own brewing, they turned loose and plundered the wrecks that floated about them. Values were pitifully and inconceivably shrunken, and the trusts added hugely to their holdings, even extending their enterprises into many new fields—and always at the expense of the middle class.

Thus the summer of 1912 witnessed the virtual death-thrust to the middle class. Even Ernest was astounded at the quickness with which it had been done. He shook his head ominously and looked forward without hope to the fall elections.

"It's no use," he said. "We are beaten. The Iron Heel is here. I had hoped for a peaceable victory at the ballot-box. I was wrong. Wickson was right. We shall be robbed of our few remaining liberties; the Iron Heel will walk upon our faces; nothing remains but a bloody revolution of the working class. Of course we will win, but I shudder to think of it."

And from then on Ernest pinned his faith in revolution. In this he was in advance of his party. His fellow-socialists could not agree with him. They still insisted that victory could be gained through the elections. It was not that they were stunned. They were too cool-headed and courageous for that. They were merely incredulous, that was all. Ernest could not get them seriously to fear the coming of the Oligarchy. They were stirred by him, but they were too sure of their own strength. There was no room in their theoretical social evolution for an oligarchy, therefore the Oligarchy could not be.

"We'll send you to Congress and it will be all right," they told him at one of our secret meetings.

"And when they take me out of Congress," Ernest replied coldly, "and put me against a wall, and blow my brains out—what then?"

"Then we'll rise in our might," a dozen voices answered at once.

"Then you'll welter in your gore," was his retort. "I've heard that song sung by the middle class, and where is it now in its might?"

CHAPTER XI

THE GREAT ADVENTURE

Mr. Wickson did not send for father. They met by chance on the ferry-boat to San Francisco, so that the warning he gave father was not premeditated. Had they not met accidentally, there would not have been any warning. Not that the outcome would have been different, however. Father came of stout old Mayflower* stock, and the blood was imperative in him.

> * One of the first ships that carried colonies to America, after the discovery of the New World. Descendants of these original colonists were for a while inordinately proud of their genealogy; but in time the blood became so widely diffused that it ran in the veins practically of all Americans.

"Ernest was right," he told me, as soon as he had returned home. "Ernest is a very remarkable young man, and I'd rather see you his wife than the wife of Rockefeller himself or the King of England."

"What's the matter?" I asked in alarm.

"The Oligarchy is about to tread upon our faces—yours and mine. Wickson as much as told me so. He was very kind—for an oligarch. He offered to reinstate me in the university. What do you think of that? He, Wickson, a sordid money-grabber, has the power to determine whether I shall or shall not teach in the university of the state. But he offered me even better than that—offered to make me president of some great college of physical sciences that is being planned—the Oligarchy must get rid of its surplus somehow, you see.

"'Do you remember what I told that socialist lover of your daughter's?' he said. 'I told him that we would walk upon the faces of the working class. And so we shall. As for you, I have for you a deep respect as a scientist; but if you throw your fortunes in with the working class—well, watch out for your face, that is all.' And then he turned and left me."

"It means we'll have to marry earlier than you planned," was Ernest's comment when we told him.

I could not follow his reasoning, but I was soon to learn it. It was at this time that the quarterly dividend of the Sierra Mills was paid—or, rather, should have been paid, for father did not receive his. After waiting several days, father wrote to the secretary. Promptly came the reply that there was no record on the books of father's owning any stock, and a polite request for more explicit information.

"I'll make it explicit enough, confound him," father declared, and departed for the bank to get the stock in question from his safe-deposit box.

"Ernest is a very remarkable man," he said when he got back and while I was helping him off with his overcoat. "I repeat, my daughter, that young man of yours is a very remarkable young man."

I had learned, whenever he praised Ernest in such fashion, to expect disaster.

"They have already walked upon my face," father explained. "There was no stock. The box was empty. You and Ernest will have to get married pretty quickly."

Father insisted on laboratory methods. He brought the Sierra Mills into court, but he could not bring the books of the Sierra Mills into court. He did not control the courts, and the Sierra Mills did. That explained it all. He was thoroughly beaten by the law, and the bare-faced robbery held good.

It is almost laughable now, when I look back on it, the way father was beaten. He met Wickson accidentally on the street in San Francisco, and he told Wickson that he was a damned scoundrel. And then father was arrested for attempted assault, fined in the police court, and bound over to keep the peace. It was all so ridiculous that when he got home he had to laugh himself. But what a furor was raised in the local papers! There was grave talk about the bacillus of violence that infected all men who embraced socialism; and father, with his long and peaceful life, was instanced as a shining example of how the bacillus of violence worked. Also, it was asserted by more than one paper that father's mind had weakened under the strain of scientific study, and confinement in a state asylum for the insane was suggested. Nor was this merely talk. It was an imminent peril. But father was wise enough to see it. He had the Bishop's experience to lesson from, and he lessoned well. He kept quiet no matter what injustice was perpetrated on him, and really, I think, surprised his enemies.

There was the matter of the house—our home. A mortgage was foreclosed on it, and we had to give up possession. Of course there wasn't any mortgage, and never had been any mortgage. The ground had been bought outright, and the house had been paid for when it was built. And house and lot had always been free and unencumbered. Nevertheless there was the mortgage, properly and legally drawn up and signed, with a record of the payments of interest through a number of years. Father made no outcry. As he had been robbed of his money, so was he now robbed of his home. And he had no recourse. The machinery of society was in the hands of those who were bent on breaking him. He was a philosopher at heart, and he was no longer even angry.

"I am doomed to be broken," he said to me; "but that is no reason that I should not try to be shattered as little as possible. These old bones of mine are fragile, and I've learned my lesson. God knows I don't want to spend my last days in an insane asylum."

Which reminds me of Bishop Morehouse, whom I have neglected for many pages. But first let me tell of my marriage. In the play of events, my marriage sinks into insignificance, I know, so I shall barely mention it.

"Now we shall become real proletarians," father said, when we were driven from our home. "I have often envied that young man of yours for his actual knowledge of the proletariat. Now I shall see and learn for myself."

Father must have had strong in him the blood of adventure. He looked upon our catastrophe in the light of an adventure. No anger nor bitterness possessed him. He was too philosophic and simple to be vindictive, and he lived too much in the world of mind to miss the creature comforts we were giving up. So it was, when we moved to San Francisco into four wretched rooms in the slum south of Market Street, that he embarked upon the adventure with the joy and enthusiasm of a child—combined with the clear sight and mental grasp of an extraordinary intellect. He really never crystallized mentally. He had no false sense of values. Conventional or habitual values meant nothing to him. The only values he recognized were mathematical and scientific facts. My father was a great man. He had the mind and the soul that only great men have. In ways he was even greater than Ernest, than whom I have known none greater.

Even I found some relief in our change of living. If nothing else, I was escaping from the organized ostracism that had been our increasing portion in the university town ever since the enmity of the nascent Oligarchy had been incurred. And the change was to me likewise adventure, and the greatest of all, for it was love-adventure. The change in our fortunes had hastened my marriage, and it was as a wife that I came to live in the four rooms on Pell Street, in the San Francisco slum.

And this out of all remains: I made Ernest happy. I came into his stormy life, not as a new perturbing force, but as one that made toward peace and repose. I gave him rest. It was the guerdon of my love for him. It was the one infallible token that I had not failed. To bring forgetfulness, or the light of gladness, into those poor tired eyes of his—what greater joy could have blessed me than that?

Those dear tired eyes. He toiled as few men ever toiled, and all his lifetime he toiled for others. That was the measure of his manhood. He was a humanist and a lover. And he, with his incarnate spirit of battle, his gladiator body and his eagle spirit—he was as gentle and tender to me as a poet. He was a poet. A singer in deeds. And all his life he sang the song of man. And he did it out of sheer love of man, and for man he gave his life and was crucified.

And all this he did with no hope of future reward. In his conception of things there was no future life. He, who fairly burnt with immortality, denied himself immortality—such was the paradox of him. He, so warm in spirit, was dominated by that cold and forbidding philosophy, materialistic monism. I used to refute him by telling him that I measured his immortality by the wings of his soul, and that I should have to live endless aeons in order to achieve the full measurement. Whereat he would laugh, and his arms would leap out to me, and he would call me his sweet metaphysician; and the tiredness would pass out of his eyes, and into them would flood the happy love-light that was in itself a new and sufficient advertisement of his immortality.

Also, he used to call me his dualist, and he would explain how Kant, by means of pure reason, had abolished reason, in order to worship God. And he drew the parallel and included me guilty of a similar act. And when I pleaded guilty, but defended the act as highly rational, he but pressed me closer and laughed as only one of God's own lovers could laugh. I was wont to deny that heredity and environment could explain his own originality and genius, any more than could the cold groping finger of science catch and analyze and classify that elusive essence that lurked in the constitution of life itself.

I held that space was an apparition of God, and that soul was a projection of the character of God; and when he called me his sweet metaphysician, I called him my immortal materialist. And so we loved and were happy; and I forgave him his materialism because of his tremendous work in the world, performed without thought of soul-gain thereby, and because of his so exceeding modesty of spirit that prevented him from having pride and regal consciousness of himself and his soul.

But he had pride. How could he have been an eagle and not have pride? His contention was that it was finer for a finite mortal speck of life to feel Godlike, than for a god to feel godlike; and so it was that he exalted what he deemed his mortality. He was fond of quoting a fragment from a certain poem. He had never seen the whole poem, and he had tried vainly to learn its authorship. I here give the fragment, not alone because he loved it, but because it epitomized the paradox that he was in the spirit of him, and his conception of his spirit. For how can a man, with thrilling, and burning, and exaltation, recite the following and still be mere mortal earth, a bit of fugitive force, an evanescent form? Here it is:

"Joy upon joy and gain upon gain
Are the destined rights of my birth,
And I shout the praise of my endless days
To the echoing edge of the earth.
Though I suffer all deaths that a man can die
To the uttermost end of time,
I have deep-drained this, my cup of bliss,
In every age and clime—

"The froth of Pride, the tang of Power,
The sweet of Womanhood!
I drain the lees upon my knees,
For oh, the draught is good;
I drink to Life, I drink to Death,
And smack my lips with song,
For when I die, another 'I' shall pass the cup along.

"The man you drove from Eden's grove
   Was I, my Lord, was I,
And I shall be there when the earth and the air

    Are rent from sea to sky;
For it is my world, my gorgeous world,
    The world of my dearest woes,
From the first faint cry of the newborn
    To the rack of the woman's throes.

"Packed with the pulse of an unborn race,
Torn with a world's desire,
The surging flood of my wild young blood
Would quench the judgment fire.
I am Man, Man, Man, from the tingling flesh
To the dust of my earthly goal,
From the nestling gloom of the pregnant womb
To the sheen of my naked soul.
Bone of my bone and flesh of my flesh
The whole world leaps to my will,
And the unslaked thirst of an Eden cursed
Shall harrow the earth for its fill.
Almighty God, when I drain life's glass
Of all its rainbow gleams,
The hapless plight of eternal night
Shall be none too long for my dreams.

"The man you drove from Eden's grove
    Was I, my Lord, was I,
And I shall be there when the earth and the air
    Are rent from sea to sky;
For it is my world, my gorgeous world,
    The world of my dear delight,
From the brightest gleam of the Arctic stream
    To the dusk of my own love-night."

Ernest always overworked. His wonderful constitution kept him up; but even that constitution could not keep the tired look out of his eyes. His dear, tired eyes! He never slept more than four and one-half hours a night; yet he never found time to do all the work he wanted to do. He never ceased from his activities as a propagandist, and was always scheduled long in advance for lectures to workingmen's organizations. Then there was the campaign. He did a man's full work in that alone. With the suppression of the socialist publishing houses, his meagre royalties ceased, and he was hard-put to make a living; for he had to make a living in addition to all his other labor. He did a great deal of translating for the magazines on scientific and philosophic subjects; and, coming home late at night, worn out from the strain of the campaign, he would plunge into his translating and toil on well into the morning hours. And in addition to everything, there was his studying. To the day of his death he kept up his studies, and he studied prodigiously.

And yet he found time in which to love me and make me happy. But this was accomplished only through my merging my life completely into his. I learned shorthand and typewriting, and became his secretary. He insisted that I succeeded in cutting his work in half; and so it was that I schooled myself to understand his work. Our interests became mutual, and we worked together and played together.

And then there were our sweet stolen moments in the midst of our work—just a word, or caress, or flash of love-light; and our moments were sweeter for being stolen. For we lived on the heights, where the air was keen and sparkling, where the toil was for humanity, and where sordidness and selfishness never entered. We loved love, and our love was never smirched by anything less than the best. And this out of all remains: I did not fail. I gave him rest—he who worked so hard for others, my dear, tired-eyed mortalist.

CHAPTER XII

THE BISHOP

It was after my marriage that I chanced upon Bishop Morehouse. But I must give the events in their proper sequence. After his outbreak at the I. P. H. Convention, the Bishop, being a gentle soul, had yielded to the friendly pressure brought to bear upon him, and had gone away on a vacation. But he returned more fixed than ever in his determination to preach the message of the Church. To the consternation of his congregation, his first sermon was quite similar to the address he had given before the Convention. Again he said, and at length and with distressing detail, that the Church had wandered away from the Master's teaching, and that Mammon had been instated in the place of Christ.

And the result was, willy-nilly, that he was led away to a private sanitarium for mental disease, while in the newspapers appeared pathetic accounts of his mental breakdown and of the saintliness of his character. He was held a prisoner in the sanitarium. I called repeatedly, but was denied access to him; and I was terribly impressed by the tragedy of a sane, normal, saintly man being crushed by the brutal will of society. For the Bishop was sane, and pure, and noble. As Ernest said, all that was the matter with him was that he had incorrect notions of biology and sociology, and because of his incorrect notions he had not gone about it in the right way to rectify matters.

What terrified me was the Bishop's helplessness. If he persisted in the truth as he saw it, he was doomed to an insane ward. And he could do nothing. His money, his position, his culture, could not save him. His views were perilous to society, and society could not conceive that such perilous views could be the product of a sane mind. Or, at least, it seems to me that such was society's attitude.

But the Bishop, in spite of the gentleness and purity of his spirit, was possessed of guile. He apprehended clearly his danger. He saw himself caught in the web, and he tried to escape from it. Denied help from his friends, such as father and Ernest and I could have given, he was left to battle for himself alone. And in the enforced solitude of the sanitarium he recovered. He became again sane. His eyes ceased to see visions; his brain was purged of the fancy that it was the duty of society to feed the Master's lambs.

As I say, he became well, quite well, and the newspapers and the church people hailed his return with joy. I went once to his church. The sermon was of the same order as the ones he had preached long before his eyes had seen visions. I was disappointed, shocked. Had society then beaten him into submission? Was he a coward? Had he been bulldozed into recanting? Or had the strain been too great for him, and had he meekly surrendered to the juggernaut of the established?

I called upon him in his beautiful home. He was woefully changed. He was thinner, and there were lines on his face which I had never seen before. He was manifestly distressed by my coming. He plucked nervously at his sleeve as we talked; and his eyes were restless, fluttering here, there, and everywhere, and refusing to meet mine. His mind seemed preoccupied, and there were strange pauses in his conversation, abrupt changes of topic, and an inconsecutiveness that was bewildering. Could this, then, be the firm-poised, Christ-like man I had known, with pure, limpid eyes and a gaze steady and unfaltering as his soul? He had been man-handled; he had been cowed into subjection. His spirit was too gentle. It had not been mighty enough to face the organized wolf-pack of society.

I felt sad, unutterably sad. He talked ambiguously, and was so apprehensive of what I might say that I had not the heart to catechise him. He spoke in a far-away manner of his illness, and we talked disjointedly about the church, the alterations in the organ, and about petty charities; and he saw me depart with such evident relief that I should have laughed had not my heart been so full of tears.

The poor little hero! If I had only known! He was battling like a giant, and I did not guess it. Alone, all alone, in the midst of millions of his fellow-men, he was fighting his fight. Torn by his horror of the asylum and his fidelity to truth and the right, he clung steadfastly to truth and the right; but so alone was he that he did not dare to trust even me. He had learned his lesson well—too well.

But I was soon to know. One day the Bishop disappeared. He had told nobody that he was going away; and as the days went by and he did not reappear, there was much gossip to the effect that he had committed suicide while temporarily deranged. But this idea was dispelled when it was learned that he had sold all his possessions,—his city mansion, his country house at Menlo Park, his paintings, and collections, and even his cherished library. It was patent that he had made a clean and secret sweep of everything before he disappeared.

This happened during the time when calamity had overtaken us in our own affairs; and it was not till we were well settled in our new home that we had opportunity really to wonder and speculate about the Bishop's doings. And then, everything was suddenly made clear. Early one evening, while it was yet twilight, I had run across the street and into the butcher-shop to get some chops for Ernest's supper. We called the last meal of the day "supper" in our new environment.

Just at the moment I came out of the butcher-shop, a man emerged from the corner grocery that stood alongside. A queer sense familiarity made me look again. But the man had turned and was walking rapidly away. There was something about the slope of the shoulders and the fringe of silver hair between coat collar and slouch hat that aroused vague memories. Instead of crossing the street, I hurried after the man. I quickened my pace, trying not to think the thoughts that formed unbidden in my brain. No, it was impossible. It could not be—not in those faded overalls, too long in the legs and frayed at the bottoms.

I paused, laughed at myself, and almost abandoned the chase. But the haunting familiarity of those shoulders and that silver hair! Again I hurried on. As I passed him, I shot a keen look at his face; then I whirled around abruptly and confronted—the Bishop.

He halted with equal abruptness, and gasped. A large paper bag in his right hand fell to the sidewalk. It burst, and about his feet and mine bounced and rolled a flood of potatoes. He looked at me with surprise and alarm, then he seemed to wilt away; the shoulders drooped with dejection, and he uttered a deep sigh.

I held out my hand. He shook it, but his hand felt clammy. He cleared his throat in embarrassment, and I could see the sweat starting out on his forehead. It was evident that he was badly frightened.

"The potatoes," he murmured faintly. "They are precious."

Between us we picked them up and replaced them in the broken bag, which he now held carefully in the hollow of his arm. I tried to tell him my gladness at meeting him and that he must come right home with me.

"Father will be rejoiced to see you," I said. "We live only a stone's throw away."

"I can't," he said, "I must be going. Good-by."

He looked apprehensively about him, as though dreading discovery, and made an attempt to walk on.

"Tell me where you live, and I shall call later," he said, when he saw that I walked beside him and that it was my intention to stick to him now that he was found.

"No," I answered firmly. "You must come now."

He looked at the potatoes spilling on his arm, and at the small parcels on his other arm.

"Really, it is impossible," he said. "Forgive me for my rudeness. If you only knew."

He looked as if he were going to break down, but the next moment he had himself in control.

"Besides, this food," he went on. "It is a sad case. It is terrible. She is an old woman. I must take it to her at once. She is suffering from want of it. I must go at once. You understand. Then I will return. I promise you."

"Let me go with you," I volunteered. "Is it far?"

He sighed again, and surrendered.

"Only two blocks," he said. "Let us hasten."

Under the Bishop's guidance I learned something of my own neighborhood. I had not dreamed such wretchedness and misery existed in it. Of course, this was because I did not concern myself with charity. I had become convinced that Ernest was right when he sneered at charity as a poulticing of an ulcer. Remove the ulcer, was his remedy; give to the worker his product; pension as soldiers those who grow honorably old in their toil, and there will be no need for charity. Convinced of this, I toiled with him at the revolution, and did not exhaust my energy in alleviating the social ills that continuously arose from the injustice of the system.

I followed the Bishop into a small room, ten by twelve, in a rear tenement. And there we found a little old German woman—sixty-four years old, the Bishop said. She was surprised at seeing me, but she nodded a pleasant greeting and went on sewing on the pair of men's trousers in her lap. Beside her, on the floor, was a pile of trousers. The Bishop discovered there was neither coal nor kindling, and went out to buy some.

I took up a pair of trousers and examined her work.

"Six cents, lady," she said, nodding her head gently while she went on stitching. She stitched slowly, but never did she cease from stitching. She seemed mastered by the verb "to stitch."

"For all that work?" I asked. "Is that what they pay? How long does it take you?"

"Yes," she answered, "that is what they pay. Six cents for finishing. Two hours' sewing on each pair."

"But the boss doesn't know that," she added quickly, betraying a fear of getting him into trouble. "I'm slow. I've got the rheumatism in my hands. Girls work much faster. They finish in half that time. The boss is kind. He lets me take the work home, now that I am old and the noise of the machine bothers my head. If it wasn't for his kindness, I'd starve.

"Yes, those who work in the shop get eight cents. But what can you do? There is not enough work for the young. The old have no chance. Often one pair is all I can get. Sometimes, like to-day, I am given eight pair to finish before night."

I asked her the hours she worked, and she said it depended on the season.

"In the summer, when there is a rush order, I work from five in the morning to nine at night. But in the winter it is too cold. The hands do not early get over the stiffness. Then you must work later—till after midnight sometimes.

"Yes, it has been a bad summer. The hard times. God must be angry. This is the first work the boss has given me in a week. It is true, one cannot eat much when there is no work. I am used to it. I have sewed all my life, in the old country and here in San Francisco—thirty-three years.

"If you are sure of the rent, it is all right. The houseman is very kind, but he must have his rent. It is fair. He only charges three dollars for this room. That is cheap. But it is not easy for you to find all of three dollars every month."

She ceased talking, and, nodding her head, went on stitching.

"You have to be very careful as to how you spend your earnings," I suggested.

She nodded emphatically.

"After the rent it's not so bad. Of course you can't buy meat. And there is no milk for the coffee. But always there is one meal a day, and often two."

She said this last proudly. There was a smack of success in her words. But as she stitched on in silence, I noticed the sadness in her pleasant eyes and the droop of her mouth. The look in her eyes became far away. She rubbed the dimness hastily out of them; it interfered with her stitching.

"No, it is not the hunger that makes the heart ache," she explained. "You get used to being hungry. It is for my child that I cry. It was the machine that killed her. It is true she worked hard, but I cannot understand. She was strong. And she was young—only forty; and she worked only thirty years. She began young, it is true; but my man died. The boiler exploded down at the works. And what were we to do? She was ten, but she was very strong. But the machine killed her. Yes, it did. It killed her, and she was the fastest worker in the shop. I have thought about it often, and I know. That is why I cannot work in the shop. The machine bothers my head. Always I hear it saying, 'I did it, I did it.' And it says that all day long. And then I think of my daughter, and I cannot work."

The moistness was in her old eyes again, and she had to wipe it away before she could go on stitching.

I heard the Bishop stumbling up the stairs, and I opened the door. What a spectacle he was. On his back he carried half a sack of coal, with kindling on top. Some of the coal dust had coated his face, and the sweat from his exertions was running in streaks. He dropped his burden in the corner by the stove and wiped his face on a coarse bandana handkerchief. I could scarcely accept the verdict of my senses. The Bishop, black as a coal-heaver, in a workingman's cheap cotton shirt (one button was missing from the throat), and in overalls! That was the most incongruous of all—the overalls, frayed at the bottoms, dragged down at the heels, and held up by a narrow leather belt around the hips such as laborers wear.

Though the Bishop was warm, the poor swollen hands of the old woman were already cramping with the cold; and before we left her, the Bishop had built the fire, while I had peeled the potatoes and put them on to boil. I was to learn, as time went by, that there were many cases similar to hers, and many worse, hidden away in the monstrous depths of the tenements in my neighborhood.

We got back to find Ernest alarmed by my absence. After the first surprise of greeting was over, the Bishop leaned back in his chair, stretched out his overall-covered legs, and actually sighed a comfortable sigh. We were the first of his old friends he had met since his disappearance, he told us; and during the intervening weeks he must have suffered greatly from loneliness. He told us much, though he told us more of the joy he had experienced in doing the Master's bidding.

"For truly now," he said, "I am feeding his lambs. And I have learned a great lesson. The soul cannot be ministered to till the stomach is appeased. His lambs must be fed bread and butter and potatoes and meat; after that, and only after that, are their spirits ready for more refined nourishment."

He ate heartily of the supper I cooked. Never had he had such an appetite at our table in the old days. We spoke of it, and he said that he had never been so healthy in his life.

"I walk always now," he said, and a blush was on his cheek at the thought of the time when he rode in his carriage, as though it were a sin not lightly to be laid.

"My health is better for it," he added hastily. "And I am very happy—indeed, most happy. At last I am a consecrated spirit."

And yet there was in his face a permanent pain, the pain of the world that he was now taking to himself. He was seeing life in the raw, and it was a different life from what he had known within the printed books of his library.

"And you are responsible for all this, young man," he said directly to Ernest.

Ernest was embarrassed and awkward.

"I—I warned you," he faltered.

"No, you misunderstand," the Bishop answered. "I speak not in reproach, but in gratitude. I have you to thank for showing me my path. You led me from theories about life to life itself. You pulled aside the veils from the social shams. You were light in my darkness, but now I, too, see the light. And I am very happy, only . . ." he hesitated painfully, and in his eyes fear leaped large. "Only the persecution. I harm no one. Why will they not let me alone? But it is not that. It is the nature of the persecution. I shouldn't mind if they cut my flesh with stripes, or burned me at the stake, or crucified me head—downward. But it is the asylum that frightens me. Think of it! Of me—in an asylum for the insane! It is revolting. I saw some of the cases at the sanitarium. They were violent. My blood chills when I think of it. And to be imprisoned for the rest of my life amid scenes of screaming madness! No! no! Not that! Not that!"

It was pitiful. His hands shook, his whole body quivered and shrank away from the picture he had conjured. But the next moment he was calm.

"Forgive me," he said simply. "It is my wretched nerves. And if the Master's work leads there, so be it. Who am I to complain?"

I felt like crying aloud as I looked at him: "Great Bishop! O hero! God's hero!"

As the evening wore on we learned more of his doings.

"I sold my house—my houses, rather," he said, "all my other possessions. I knew I must do it secretly, else they would have taken everything away from me. That would have been terrible. I often marvel these days at the immense quantity of potatoes two or three hundred thousand dollars will buy, or bread, or meat, or coal and kindling." He turned to Ernest. "You are right, young man. Labor is dreadfully underpaid. I never did a bit of work in my life, except to appeal aesthetically to Pharisees—I thought I was preaching the message—and yet I was worth half a million dollars. I never knew what half a million dollars meant until I realized how much potatoes and bread and butter and meat it could buy. And then I realized something more. I realized that all those potatoes and that bread and butter and meat were mine, and that I had not worked to make them. Then it was clear to me, some one else had worked and made them and been robbed of them. And when I came down amongst the poor I found those who had been robbed and who were hungry and wretched because they had been robbed."

We drew him back to his narrative.

"The money? I have it deposited in many different banks under different names. It can never be taken away from me, because it can never be found. And it is so good, that money. It buys so much food. I never knew before what money was good for."

"I wish we could get some of it for the propaganda," Ernest said wistfully. "It would do immense good."

"Do you think so?" the Bishop said. "I do not have much faith in politics. In fact, I am afraid I do not understand politics."

Ernest was delicate in such matters. He did not repeat his suggestion, though he knew only too well the sore straits the Socialist Party was in through lack of money.

"I sleep in cheap lodging houses," the Bishop went on. "But I am afraid, and never stay long in one place. Also, I rent two rooms in workingmen's houses in different quarters of the city. It is a great extravagance, I know, but it is necessary. I make up for it in part by doing my own cooking, though sometimes I get something to eat in cheap coffee-houses. And I have made a discovery. Tamales* are very good when the air grows chilly late at night. Only they are so expensive. But I have discovered a place where I can get three for ten cents. They are not so good as the others, but they are very warming.

> * A Mexican dish, referred to occasionally in the literature
> of the times. It is supposed that it was warmly seasoned.
> No recipe of it has come down to us.

"And so I have at last found my work in the world, thanks to you, young man. It is the Master's work." He looked at me, and his eyes twinkled. "You caught me feeding his lambs, you know. And of course you will all keep my secret."

He spoke carelessly enough, but there was real fear behind the speech. He promised to call upon us again. But a week later we read in the newspaper of the sad case of Bishop Morehouse, who had been committed to the Napa Asylum and for whom there were still hopes held out. In vain we tried to see him, to have his case reconsidered or investigated. Nor could we learn anything about him except the reiterated statements that slight hopes were still held for his recovery.

"Christ told the rich young man to sell all he had," Ernest said bitterly. "The Bishop obeyed Christ's injunction and got locked up in a madhouse. Times have changed since Christ's day. A rich man to-day who gives all he has to the poor is crazy. There is no discussion. Society has spoken."

CHAPTER XIII

THE GENERAL STRIKE

Of course Ernest was elected to Congress in the great socialist landslide that took place in the fall of 1912. One great factor that helped to swell the socialist vote was the destruction of Hearst.* This the Plutocracy found an easy task. It cost Hearst eighteen million dollars a year to run his various papers, and this sum, and more, he got back from the middle class in payment for advertising. The source of his financial strength lay wholly in the middle class. The trusts did not advertise.** To destroy Hearst, all that was necessary was to take away from him his advertising.

* William Randolph Hearst—a young California millionaire who became the most powerful newspaper owner in the country. His newspapers were published in all the large cities, and they appealed to the perishing middle class and to the proletariat. So large was his following that he managed to take possession of the empty shell of the old Democratic Party. He occupied an anomalous position, preaching an emasculated socialism combined with a nondescript sort of petty bourgeois capitalism. It was oil and water, and there was no hope for him, though for a short period he was a source of serious apprehension to the Plutocrats.

** The cost of advertising was amazing in those helter-skelter times. Only the small capitalists competed, and therefore they did the advertising. There being no competition where there was a trust, there was no need for the trusts to advertise.

The whole middle class had not yet been exterminated. The sturdy skeleton of it remained; but it was without power. The small manufacturers and small business men who still survived were at the complete mercy of the Plutocracy. They had no economic nor political souls of their own. When the fiat of the Plutocracy went forth, they withdrew their advertisements from the Hearst papers.

Hearst made a gallant fight. He brought his papers out at a loss of a million and a half each month. He continued to publish the advertisements for which he no longer received pay. Again the fiat of the Plutocracy went forth, and the small business men and manufacturers swamped him with a flood of notices that he must discontinue running their old advertisements. Hearst persisted. Injunctions were served on him. Still he persisted. He received six months' imprisonment for contempt of court in disobeying the injunctions, while he was bankrupted by countless damage suits. He had no chance. The Plutocracy had passed sentence on him. The courts were in the hands of the Plutocracy to carry the sentence out. And with Hearst crashed also to destruction the Democratic Party that he had so recently captured.

With the destruction of Hearst and the Democratic Party, there were only two paths for his following to take. One was into the Socialist Party; the other was into the Republican Party. Then it was that we socialists reaped the fruit of Hearst's pseudo-socialistic preaching; for the great Majority of his followers came over to us.

The expropriation of the farmers that took place at this time would also have swelled our vote had it not been for the brief and futile rise of the Grange Party. Ernest and the socialist leaders fought fiercely to capture the farmers; but the destruction of the socialist press and publishing houses constituted too great a handicap, while the mouth-to-mouth propaganda had not yet been perfected. So it was that politicians like Mr. Calvin, who were themselves farmers long since expropriated, captured the farmers and threw their political strength away in a vain campaign.

"The poor farmers," Ernest once laughed savagely; "the trusts have them both coming and going."

And that was really the situation. The seven great trusts, working together, had pooled their enormous surpluses and made a farm trust. The railroads, controlling rates, and the bankers and stock exchange gamesters, controlling prices, had long since bled the farmers into indebtedness. The bankers, and all the trusts for that matter, had likewise long since loaned colossal amounts of money to the farmers. The farmers were in the net. All that remained to be done was the drawing in of the net. This the farm trust proceeded to do.

The hard times of 1912 had already caused a frightful slump in the farm markets. Prices were now deliberately pressed down to bankruptcy, while the railroads, with extortionate rates, broke the back of the farmer-camel. Thus the farmers were compelled to borrow more and more, while they were prevented from paying back old loans. Then ensued the great foreclosing of mortgages and enforced collection of notes. The farmers simply surrendered the land to the farm trust. There was nothing else for them to do. And having surrendered the land, the farmers next went to work for the farm trust, becoming managers, superintendents, foremen, and common laborers. They worked for wages. They became villeins, in short—serfs bound to the soil by a living wage. They could not leave their masters, for their masters composed the Plutocracy. They could not go to the cities, for there, also, the Plutocracy was in control. They had but one alternative,—to leave the soil and become vagrants, in brief, to starve. And even there they were frustrated, for stringent vagrancy laws were passed and rigidly enforced.

Of course, here and there, farmers, and even whole communities of farmers, escaped expropriation by virtue of exceptional conditions. But they were merely strays and did not count, and they were gathered in anyway during the following year.*

* The destruction of the Roman yeomanry proceeded far less rapidly than the destruction of the American farmers and small capitalists. There was momentum in the twentieth century, while there was practically none in ancient Rome.

Numbers of the farmers, impelled by an insane lust for the soil, and willing to show what beasts they could become, tried to escape expropriation by withdrawing from any and all market-dealing. They sold nothing. They bought nothing. Among themselves a primitive barter began to spring up. Their privation and hardships were terrible, but they persisted. It became quite a movement, in fact. The manner in which they were beaten was unique and logical and simple. The Plutocracy, by virtue of its possession of the government, raised their taxes. It was the weak joint in their armor. Neither buying nor selling, they had no money, and in the end their land was sold to pay the taxes.

Thus it was that in the fall of 1912 the socialist leaders, with the exception of Ernest, decided that the end of capitalism had come. What of the hard times and the consequent vast army of the unemployed; what of the destruction of the farmers and the middle class; and what of the decisive defeat administered all along the line to the labor unions; the socialists were really justified in believing that the end of capitalism had come and in themselves throwing down the gauntlet to the Plutocracy.

Alas, how we underestimated the strength of the enemy! Everywhere the socialists proclaimed their coming victory at the ballot-box, while, in unmistakable terms, they stated the situation. The Plutocracy accepted the challenge. It was the Plutocracy, weighing and balancing, that defeated us by dividing our strength. It was the Plutocracy, through its secret agents, that raised the cry that socialism was sacrilegious and atheistic; it was the Plutocracy that whipped the churches, and especially the Catholic Church, into line, and robbed us of a portion of the labor vote. And it was the Plutocracy, through its secret agents of course, that encouraged the Grange Party and even spread it to the cities into the ranks of the dying middle class.

Nevertheless the socialist landslide occurred. But, instead of a sweeping victory with chief executive officers and majorities in all legislative bodies, we found ourselves in the minority. It is true, we elected fifty Congressmen; but when they took their seats in the spring of 1913, they found themselves without power of any sort. Yet they were more fortunate than the Grangers, who captured a dozen state governments, and who, in the spring, were not permitted to take possession of the captured offices. The incumbents refused to retire, and the courts were in the hands of the Oligarchy. But this is too far in advance of events. I have yet to tell of the stirring times of the winter of 1912.

The hard times at home had caused an immense decrease in consumption. Labor, out of work, had no wages with which to buy. The result was that the Plutocracy found a greater surplus than ever on its hands. This surplus it was compelled to dispose of abroad, and, what of its colossal plans, it needed money. Because of its strenuous efforts to dispose of the surplus in the world market, the Plutocracy clashed with Germany. Economic clashes were usually succeeded by wars, and this particular clash was no exception. The great German war-lord prepared, and so did the United States prepare.

The war-cloud hovered dark and ominous. The stage was set for a world-catastrophe, for in all the world were hard times, labor troubles, perishing middle classes, armies of unemployed, clashes of economic interests in the world-market, and mutterings and rumblings of the socialist revolution.*

> * For a long time these mutterings and rumblings had been heard. As far back as 1906 A.D., Lord Avebury, an Englishman, uttered the following in the House of Lords: "The unrest in Europe, the spread of socialism, and the ominous rise of Anarchism, are warnings to the governments and the ruling classes that the condition of the working classes in Europe is becoming intolerable, and that if a revolution is to be avoided some steps must be taken to increase wages, reduce the hours of labor, and lower the prices of the necessaries of life." The Wall Street Journal, a stock gamesters' publication, in commenting upon Lord Avebury's speech, said: "These words were spoken by an aristocrat and a member of the most conservative body in all Europe. That gives them all the more significance. They contain more valuable political economy than is to be found in most of the books. They sound a note of warning. Take heed, gentlemen of the war and navy departments!"
>
> At the same time, Sydney Brooks, writing in America, in Harper's Weekly, said: "You will not hear the socialists mentioned in Washington. Why should you? The politicians are always the last people in this country to see what is going on under their noses. They will jeer at me when I prophesy, and prophesy with the utmost confidence, that at the next presidential election the socialists will poll over a million votes."

The Oligarchy wanted the war with Germany. And it wanted the war for a dozen reasons. In the juggling of events such a war would cause, in the reshuffling of the international cards and the making of new treaties and alliances, the Oligarchy had much to gain. And, furthermore, the war would consume many national surpluses, reduce the armies of unemployed that menaced all countries, and give the Oligarchy a breathing space in which to perfect its plans and carry them out. Such a war would virtually put the Oligarchy in possession of the world-market. Also, such a war would create a large standing army that need never be disbanded, while in the minds of the people would be substituted the issue, "America versus Germany," in place of "Socialism versus Oligarchy."

And truly the war would have done all these things had it not been for the socialists. A secret meeting of the Western leaders was held in our four tiny rooms in Pell Street. Here was first considered the stand the socialists were to take. It was not the first time we had put our foot down upon war,* but it was the first time we had done so in the United States. After our secret meeting we got in touch with the national organization, and soon our code cables were passing back and forth across the Atlantic between us and the International Bureau.

* It was at the very beginning of the twentieth century A.D., that the international organization of the socialists finally formulated their long-maturing policy on war. Epitomized their doctrine was: "Why should the workingmen of one country fight with the workingmen of another country for the benefit of their capitalist masters?"

On May 21, 1905 A.D., when war threatened between Austria and Italy, the socialists of Italy, Austria, and Hungary held a conference at Trieste, and threatened a general strike of the workingmen of both countries in case war was declared. This was repeated the following year, when the "Morocco Affair" threatened to involve France, Germany, and England.

The German socialists were ready to act with us. There were over five million of them, many of them in the standing army, and, in addition, they were on friendly terms with the labor unions. In both countries the socialists came out in bold declaration against the war and threatened the general strike. And in the meantime they made preparation for the general strike. Furthermore, the revolutionary parties in all countries gave public utterance to the socialist principle of international peace that must be preserved at all hazards, even to the extent of revolt and revolution at home.

The general strike was the one great victory we American socialists won. On the 4th of December the American minister was withdrawn from the German capital. That night a German fleet made a dash on Honolulu, sinking three American cruisers and a revenue cutter, and bombarding the city. Next day both Germany and the United States declared war, and within an hour the socialists called the general strike in both countries.

For the first time the German war-lord faced the men of his empire who made his empire go. Without them he could not run his empire. The novelty of the situation lay in that their revolt was passive. They did not fight. They did nothing. And by doing nothing they tied their war-lord's hands. He would have asked for nothing better than an opportunity to loose his war-dogs on his rebellious proletariat. But this was denied him. He could not loose his war-dogs. Neither could he mobilize his army to go forth to war, nor could he punish his recalcitrant subjects. Not a wheel moved in his empire. Not a train ran, not a telegraphic message went over the wires, for the telegraphers and railroad men had ceased work along with the rest of the population.

And as it was in Germany, so it was in the United States. At last organized labor had learned its lesson. Beaten decisively on its own chosen field, it had abandoned that field and come over to the political field of the socialists; for the general strike was a political strike. Besides, organized labor had been so badly beaten that it did not care. It joined in the general strike out of sheer desperation. The workers threw down their tools and left their tasks by the millions. Especially notable were the machinists. Their heads were bloody, their organization had apparently been destroyed, yet out they came, along with their allies in the metal-working trades.

Even the common laborers and all unorganized labor ceased work. The strike had tied everything up so that nobody could work. Besides, the women proved to be the strongest promoters of the strike. They set their faces against the war. They did not want their men to go forth to die. Then, also, the idea of the general strike caught the mood of the people. It struck their sense of humor. The idea was infectious. The children struck in all the schools, and such teachers as came, went home again from deserted class rooms. The general strike took the form of a great national picnic. And the idea of the solidarity of labor, so evidenced, appealed to the imagination of all. And, finally, there was no danger to be incurred by the colossal frolic. When everybody was guilty, how was anybody to be punished?

The United States was paralyzed. No one knew what was happening. There were no newspapers, no letters, no despatches. Every community was as completely isolated as though ten thousand miles of primeval wilderness stretched between it and the rest of the world. For that matter, the world had ceased to exist. And for a week this state of affairs was maintained.

In San Francisco we did not know what was happening even across the bay in Oakland or Berkeley. The effect on one's sensibilities was weird, depressing. It seemed as though some great cosmic thing lay dead. The pulse of the land had ceased to beat. Of a truth the nation had died. There were no wagons rumbling on the streets, no factory whistles, no hum of electricity in the air, no passing of street cars, no cries of news-boys—nothing but persons who at rare intervals went by like furtive ghosts, themselves oppressed and made unreal by the silence.

And during that week of silence the Oligarchy was taught its lesson. And well it learned the lesson. The general strike was a warning. It should never occur again. The Oligarchy would see to that.

At the end of the week, as had been prearranged, the telegraphers of Germany and the United States returned to their posts. Through them the socialist leaders of both countries presented their ultimatum to the rulers. The war should be called off, or the general strike would continue. It did not take long to come to an understanding. The war was declared off, and the populations of both countries returned to their tasks.

It was this renewal of peace that brought about the alliance between Germany and the United States. In reality, this was an alliance between the Emperor and the Oligarchy, for the purpose of meeting their common foe, the revolutionary proletariat of both countries. And it was this alliance that the Oligarchy afterward so treacherously broke when the German socialists rose and drove the war-lord from his throne. It was the very thing the Oligarchy had played for—the destruction of its great rival in the world-market. With the German Emperor out of the way, Germany would have no surplus to sell abroad. By the very nature of the socialist state, the German population would consume all that it produced. Of course, it would trade abroad certain things it produced for things it did not produce; but this would be quite different from an unconsumable surplus.

"I'll wager the Oligarchy finds justification," Ernest said, when its treachery to the German Emperor became known. "As usual, the Oligarchy will believe it has done right."

And sure enough. The Oligarchy's public defence for the act was that it had done it for the sake of the American people whose interests it was looking out for. It had flung its hated rival out of the world-market and enabled us to dispose of our surplus in that market.

"And the howling folly of it is that we are so helpless that such idiots really are managing our interests," was Ernest's comment. "They have enabled us to sell more abroad, which means that we'll be compelled to consume less at home."

CHAPTER XIV

THE BEGINNING OF THE END

As early as January, 1913, Ernest saw the true trend of affairs, but he could not get his brother leaders to see the vision of the Iron Heel that had arisen in his brain. They were too confident. Events were rushing too rapidly to culmination. A crisis had come in world affairs. The American Oligarchy was practically in possession of the world-market, and scores of countries were flung out of that market with unconsumable and unsalable surpluses on their hands. For such countries nothing remained but reorganization. They could not continue their method of producing surpluses. The capitalistic system, so far as they were concerned, had hopelessly broken down.

The reorganization of these countries took the form of revolution. It was a time of confusion and violence. Everywhere institutions and governments were crashing. Everywhere, with the exception of two or three countries, the erstwhile capitalist masters fought bitterly for their possessions. But the governments were taken away from them by the militant proletariat. At last was being realized Karl Marx's classic: "The knell of private capitalist property sounds. The expropriators are expropriated." And as fast as capitalistic governments crashed, cooperative commonwealths arose in their place.

"Why does the United States lag behind?"; "Get busy, you American revolutionists!"; "What's the matter with America?"—were the messages sent to us by our successful comrades in other lands. But we could not keep up. The Oligarchy stood in the way. Its bulk, like that of some huge monster, blocked our path.

"Wait till we take office in the spring," we answered. "Then you'll see."

Behind this lay our secret. We had won over the Grangers, and in the spring a dozen states would pass into their hands by virtue of the elections of the preceding fall. At once would be instituted a dozen cooperative commonwealth states. After that, the rest would be easy.

"But what if the Grangers fail to get possession?" Ernest demanded. And his comrades called him a calamity howler.

But this failure to get possession was not the chief danger that Ernest had in mind. What he foresaw was the defection of the great labor unions and the rise of the castes.

"Ghent has taught the oligarchs how to do it," Ernest said. "I'll wager they've made a text-book out of his 'Benevolent Feudalism.'"*

* "Our Benevolent Feudalism," a book published in 1902 A.D.,
by W. J. Ghent. It has always been insisted that Ghent put
the idea of the Oligarchy into the minds of the great

capitalists. This belief persists throughout the literature
of the three centuries of the Iron Heel, and even in the
literature of the first century of the Brotherhood of Man.
To-day we know better, but our knowledge does not overcome
the fact that Ghent remains the most abused innocent man in
all history.

Never shall I forget the night when, after a hot discussion with half a dozen labor leaders, Ernest turned to me and said quietly: "That settles it. The Iron Heel has won. The end is in sight."

This little conference in our home was unofficial; but Ernest, like the rest of his comrades, was working for assurances from the labor leaders that they would call out their men in the next general strike. O'Connor, the president of the Association of Machinists, had been foremost of the six leaders present in refusing to give such assurance.

"You have seen that you were beaten soundly at your old tactics of strike and boycott," Ernest urged.

O'Connor and the others nodded their heads.

"And you saw what a general strike would do," Ernest went on. "We stopped the war with Germany. Never was there so fine a display of the solidarity and the power of labor. Labor can and will rule the world. If you continue to stand with us, we'll put an end to the reign of capitalism. It is your only hope. And what is more, you know it. There is no other way out. No matter what you do under your old tactics, you are doomed to defeat, if for no other reason because the masters control the courts."*

* As a sample of the decisions of the courts adverse to
labor, the following instances are given. In the coal-
mining regions the employment of children was notorious. In
1905 A.D., labor succeeded in getting a law passed in
Pennsylvania providing that proof of the age of the child
and of certain educational qualifications must accompany the
oath of the parent. This was promptly declared
unconstitutional by the Luzerne County Court, on the ground
that it violated the Fourteenth Amendment in that it
discriminated between individuals of the same class—namely,
children above fourteen years of age and children below.
The state court sustained the decision. The New York Court
of Special Sessions, in 1905 A.D., declared unconstitutional
the law prohibiting minors and women from working in
factories after nine o'clock at night, the ground taken
being that such a law was "class legislation." Again, the
bakers of that time were terribly overworked. The New York
Legislature passed a law restricting work in bakeries to ten
hours a day. In 1906 A.D., the Supreme Court of the United
States declared this law to be unconstitutional. In part
the decision read: "There is no reasonable ground for
interfering with the liberty of persons or the right of free

contract by determining the hours of labor in the occupation of a baker."

"You run ahead too fast," O'Connor answered. "You don't know all the ways out. There is another way out. We know what we're about. We're sick of strikes. They've got us beaten that way to a frazzle. But I don't think we'll ever need to call our men out again."

"What is your way out?" Ernest demanded bluntly.

O'Connor laughed and shook his head. "I can tell you this much: We've not been asleep. And we're not dreaming now."

"There's nothing to be afraid of, or ashamed of, I hope," Ernest challenged.

"I guess we know our business best," was the retort.

"It's a dark business, from the way you hide it," Ernest said with growing anger.

"We've paid for our experience in sweat and blood, and we've earned all that's coming to us," was the reply. "Charity begins at home."

"If you're afraid to tell me your way out, I'll tell it to you." Ernest's blood was up. "You're going in for grab-sharing. You've made terms with the enemy, that's what you've done. You've sold out the cause of labor, of all labor. You are leaving the battle-field like cowards."

"I'm not saying anything," O'Connor answered sullenly. "Only I guess we know what's best for us a little bit better than you do."

"And you don't care a cent for what is best for the rest of labor. You kick it into the ditch."

"I'm not saying anything," O'Connor replied, "except that I'm president of the Machinists' Association, and it's my business to consider the interests of the men I represent, that's all."

And then, when the labor leaders had left, Ernest, with the calmness of defeat, outlined to me the course of events to come.

"The socialists used to foretell with joy," he said, "the coming of the day when organized labor, defeated on the industrial field, would come over on to the political field. Well, the Iron Heel has defeated the labor unions on the industrial field and driven them over to the political field; and instead of this being joyful for us, it will be a source of grief. The Iron Heel learned its lesson. We showed it our power in the general strike. It has taken steps to prevent another general strike."

"But how?" I asked.

"Simply by subsidizing the great unions. They won't join in the next general strike. Therefore it won't be a general strike."

"But the Iron Heel can't maintain so costly a programme forever," I objected.

"Oh, it hasn't subsidized all of the unions. That's not necessary. Here is what is going to happen. Wages are going to be advanced and hours shortened in the railroad unions, the iron and steel workers unions, and the engineer and machinist unions. In these unions more favorable conditions will continue to prevail. Membership in these unions will become like seats in Paradise."

"Still I don't see," I objected. "What is to become of the other unions? There are far more unions outside of this combination than in it."

"The other unions will be ground out of existence—all of them. For, don't you see, the railway men, machinists and engineers, iron and steel workers, do all of the vitally essential work in our machine civilization. Assured of their faithfulness, the Iron Heel can snap its fingers at all the rest of labor. Iron, steel, coal, machinery, and transportation constitute the backbone of the whole industrial fabric."

"But coal?" I queried. "There are nearly a million coal miners."

They are practically unskilled labor. They will not count. Their wages will go down and their hours will increase. They will be slaves like all the rest of us, and they will become about the most bestial of all of us. They will be compelled to work, just as the farmers are compelled to work now for the masters who robbed them of their land. And the same with all the other unions outside the combination. Watch them wobble and go to pieces, and their members become slaves driven to toil by empty stomachs and the law of the land.

"Do you know what will happen to Farley* and his strike-breakers? I'll tell you. Strike-breaking as an occupation will cease. There won't be any more strikes. In place of strikes will be slave revolts. Farley and his gang will be promoted to slave-driving. Oh, it won't be called that; it will be called enforcing the law of the land that compels the laborers to work. It simply prolongs the fight, this treachery of the big unions. Heaven only knows now where and when the Revolution will triumph."

> * James Farley—a notorious strike-breaker of the period. A man more courageous than ethical, and of undeniable ability. He rose high under the rule of the Iron Heel and finally was translated into the oligarch class. He was assassinated in 1932 by Sarah Jenkins, whose husband, thirty years before, had been killed by Farley's strike-breakers.

"But with such a powerful combination as the Oligarchy and the big unions, is there any reason to believe that the Revolution will ever triumph?" I queried. "May not the combination endure forever?"

He shook his head. "One of our generalizations is that every system founded upon class and caste contains within itself the germs of its own decay. When a system is founded upon class, how can caste be prevented? The Iron Heel will not be able to prevent it, and in the end caste will destroy the Iron Heel. The oligarchs have already developed caste among themselves; but wait until the favored unions develop caste. The Iron Heel will use all its power to prevent it, but it will fail.

"In the favored unions are the flower of the American workingmen. They are strong, efficient men. They have become members of those unions through competition for place. Every fit workman in the United States will be possessed by the ambition to become a member of the favored unions. The Oligarchy will encourage such ambition and the consequent competition. Thus will the strong men, who might else be revolutionists, be won away and their strength used to bolster the Oligarchy.

"On the other hand, the labor castes, the members of the favored unions, will strive to make their organizations into close corporations. And they will succeed. Membership in the labor castes will become hereditary. Sons will succeed fathers, and there will be no inflow of new strength from that eternal reservoir of strength, the common people. This will mean deterioration of the labor castes, and in the end they will become weaker and weaker. At the same time, as an institution, they will become temporarily all-powerful. They will be like the guards of the palace in old Rome, and there will be palace revolutions whereby the labor castes will seize the reins of power. And there will be counter-palace revolutions of the oligarchs, and sometimes the one, and sometimes the other, will be in power. And through it all the inevitable caste-weakening will go on, so that in the end the common people will come into their own."

This foreshadowing of a slow social evolution was made when Ernest was first depressed by the defection of the great unions. I never agreed with him in it, and I disagree now, as I write these lines, more heartily than ever; for even now, though Ernest is gone, we are on the verge of the revolt that will sweep all oligarchies away. Yet I have here given Ernest's prophecy because it was his prophecy. In spite of his belief in it, he worked like a giant against it, and he, more than any man, has made possible the revolt that even now waits the signal to burst forth.*

> * Everhard's social foresight was remarkable. As clearly as
> in the light of past events, he saw the defection of the
> favored unions, the rise and the slow decay of the labor
> castes, and the struggle between the decaying oligarchs and
> labor castes for control of the great governmental machine.

"But if the Oligarchy persists," I asked him that evening, "what will become of the great surpluses that will fall to its share every year?"

"The surpluses will have to be expended somehow," he answered; "and trust the oligarchs to find a way. Magnificent roads will be built. There will be great achievements in science, and especially in art. When the oligarchs have completely mastered the people, they will have time to spare for other things. They will become worshippers of beauty. They will become art-lovers. And under their direction and generously rewarded, will toil the artists. The result will be great art; for no longer, as up to yesterday, will the artists pander to the bourgeois taste of the middle class. It will be great art, I tell you, and wonder cities will arise that will make tawdry and cheap the cities of old time. And in these cities will the oligarchs dwell and worship beauty.*

> * We cannot but marvel at Everhard's foresight. Before ever
> the thought of wonder cities like Ardis and Asgard entered
> the minds of the oligarchs, Everhard saw those cities and
> the inevitable necessity for their creation.

"Thus will the surplus be constantly expended while labor does the work. The building of these great works and cities will give a starvation ration to millions of common laborers, for the enormous bulk of the surplus will compel an equally enormous expenditure, and the oligarchs will build for a thousand years—ay, for ten thousand years. They will build as the Egyptians and the Babylonians never dreamed of building; and when the oligarchs have passed away, their great roads and their wonder cities will remain for the brotherhood of labor to tread upon and dwell within.*

> * And since that day of prophecy, have passed away the three centuries of the Iron Heel and the four centuries of the Brotherhood of Man, and to-day we tread the roads and dwell in the cities that the oligarchs built. It is true, we are even now building still more wonderful wonder cities, but the wonder cities of the oligarchs endure, and I write these lines in Ardis, one of the most wonderful of them all.

"These things the oligarchs will do because they cannot help doing them. These great works will be the form their expenditure of the surplus will take, and in the same way that the ruling classes of Egypt of long ago expended the surplus they robbed from the people by the building of temples and pyramids. Under the oligarchs will flourish, not a priest class, but an artist class. And in place of the merchant class of bourgeoisie will be the labor castes. And beneath will be the abyss, wherein will fester and starve and rot, and ever renew itself, the common people, the great bulk of the population. And in the end, who knows in what day, the common people will rise up out of the abyss; the labor castes and the Oligarchy will crumble away; and then, at last, after the travail of the centuries, will it be the day of the common man. I had thought to see that day; but now I know that I shall never see it."

He paused and looked at me, and added:

"Social evolution is exasperatingly slow, isn't it, sweetheart?"

My arms were about him, and his head was on my breast.

"Sing me to sleep," he murmured whimsically. "I have had a visioning, and I wish to forget."

CHAPTER XV

LAST DAYS

It was near the end of January, 1913, that the changed attitude of the Oligarchy toward the favored unions was made public. The newspapers published information of an unprecedented rise in wages and shortening of hours for the railroad employees, the iron and steel workers, and the engineers and machinists. But the whole truth was not told. The oligarchs did not dare permit the telling of the whole truth. In reality, the wages had been raised much higher, and the privileges were correspondingly greater. All this was secret, but secrets will out. Members of the favored unions told their wives, and the wives gossiped, and soon all the labor world knew what had happened.

It was merely the logical development of what in the nineteenth century had been known as grab-sharing. In the industrial warfare of that time, profit-sharing had been tried. That is, the capitalists had striven to placate the workers by interesting them financially in their work. But profit-sharing, as a system, was ridiculous and impossible. Profit-sharing could be successful only in isolated cases in the midst of a system of industrial strife; for if all labor and all capital shared profits, the same conditions would obtain as did obtain when there was no profit-sharing.

So, out of the unpractical idea of profit-sharing, arose the practical idea of grab-sharing. "Give us more pay and charge it to the public," was the slogan of the strong unions.* And here and there this selfish policy worked successfully. In charging it to the public, it was charged to the great mass of unorganized labor and of weakly organized labor. These workers actually paid the increased wages of their stronger brothers who were members of unions that were labor monopolies. This idea, as I say, was merely carried to its logical conclusion, on a large scale, by the combination of the oligarchs and the favored unions.

> * All the railroad unions entered into this combination with the oligarchs, and it is of interest to note that the first definite application of the policy of profit-grabbing was made by a railroad union in the nineteenth century A.D., namely, the Brotherhood of Locomotive Engineers. P. M. Arthur was for twenty years Grand Chief of the Brotherhood. After the strike on the Pennsylvania Railroad in 1877, he broached a scheme to have the Locomotive Engineers make terms with the railroads and to "go it alone" so far as the rest of the labor unions were concerned. This scheme was eminently successful. It was as successful as it was selfish, and out of it was coined the word "arthurization," to denote grab-sharing on the part of labor unions. This

word "arthurization" has long puzzled the etymologists, but
its derivation, I hope, is now made clear.

As soon as the secret of the defection of the favored unions leaked out, there were rumblings and mutterings in the labor world. Next, the favored unions withdrew from the international organizations and broke off all affiliations. Then came trouble and violence. The members of the favored unions were branded as traitors, and in saloons and brothels, on the streets and at work, and, in fact, everywhere, they were assaulted by the comrades they had so treacherously deserted.

Countless heads were broken, and there were many killed. No member of the favored unions was safe. They gathered together in bands in order to go to work or to return from work. They walked always in the middle of the street. On the sidewalk they were liable to have their skulls crushed by bricks and cobblestones thrown from windows and house-tops. They were permitted to carry weapons, and the authorities aided them in every way. Their persecutors were sentenced to long terms in prison, where they were harshly treated; while no man, not a member of the favored unions, was permitted to carry weapons. Violation of this law was made a high misdemeanor and punished accordingly.

Outraged labor continued to wreak vengeance on the traitors. Caste lines formed automatically. The children of the traitors were persecuted by the children of the workers who had been betrayed, until it was impossible for the former to play on the streets or to attend the public schools. Also, the wives and families of the traitors were ostracized, while the corner groceryman who sold provisions to them was boycotted.

As a result, driven back upon themselves from every side, the traitors and their families became clannish. Finding it impossible to dwell in safety in the midst of the betrayed proletariat, they moved into new localities inhabited by themselves alone. In this they were favored by the oligarchs. Good dwellings, modern and sanitary, were built for them, surrounded by spacious yards, and separated here and there by parks and playgrounds. Their children attended schools especially built for them, and in these schools manual training and applied science were specialized upon. Thus, and unavoidably, at the very beginning, out of this segregation arose caste. The members of the favored unions became the aristocracy of labor. They were set apart from the rest of labor. They were better housed, better clothed, better fed, better treated. They were grab-sharing with a vengeance.

In the meantime, the rest of the working class was more harshly treated. Many little privileges were taken away from it, while its wages and its standard of living steadily sank down. Incidentally, its public schools deteriorated, and education slowly ceased to be compulsory. The increase in the younger generation of children who could not read nor write was perilous.

The capture of the world-market by the United States had disrupted the rest of the world. Institutions and governments were everywhere crashing or transforming.

Germany, Italy, France, Australia, and New Zealand were busy forming cooperative commonwealths. The British Empire was falling apart. England's hands were full. In India revolt was in full swing. The cry in all Asia was, "Asia for the Asiatics!" And behind this cry was Japan, ever urging and aiding the yellow and brown races against the white. And while Japan dreamed of continental empire and strove to realize the dream, she suppressed her own proletarian revolution. It was a simple war of the castes, Coolie versus Samurai, and the coolie socialists were executed by tens of thousands. Forty thousand were killed in the street-fighting of Tokio and in the futile assault on the Mikado's palace. Kobe was a shambles; the slaughter of the cotton operatives by machine-guns became classic as the most terrific execution ever achieved by modern war machines. Most savage of all was the Japanese Oligarchy that arose. Japan dominated the East, and took to herself the whole Asiatic portion of the world-market, with the exception of India.

England managed to crush her own proletarian revolution and to hold on to India, though she was brought to the verge of exhaustion. Also, she was compelled to let her great colonies slip away from her. So it was that the socialists succeeded in making Australia and New Zealand into cooperative commonwealths. And it was for the same reason that Canada was lost to the mother country. But Canada crushed her own socialist revolution, being aided in this by the Iron Heel. At the same time, the Iron Heel helped Mexico and Cuba to put down revolt. The result was that the Iron Heel was firmly established in the New World. It had welded into one compact political mass the whole of North America from the Panama Canal to the Arctic Ocean.

And England, at the sacrifice of her great colonies, had succeeded only in retaining India. But this was no more than temporary. The struggle with Japan and the rest of Asia for India was merely delayed. England was destined shortly to lose India, while behind that event loomed the struggle between a united Asia and the world.

And while all the world was torn with conflict, we of the United States were not placid and peaceful. The defection of the great unions had prevented our proletarian revolt, but violence was everywhere. In addition to the labor troubles, and the discontent of the farmers and of the remnant of the middle class, a religious revival had blazed up. An offshoot of the Seventh Day Adventists sprang into sudden prominence, proclaiming the end of the world.

"Confusion thrice confounded!" Ernest cried. "How can we hope for solidarity with all these cross purposes and conflicts?"

And truly the religious revival assumed formidable proportions. The people, what of their wretchedness, and of their disappointment in all things earthly, were ripe and eager for a heaven where industrial tyrants entered no more than camels passed through needle-eyes. Wild-eyed itinerant preachers swarmed over the land; and despite the prohibition of the civil authorities, and the persecution for disobedience, the flames of religious frenzy were fanned by countless camp-meetings.

It was the last days, they claimed, the beginning of the end of the world. The four winds had been loosed. God had stirred the nations to strife. It was a time of visions and miracles, while seers and prophetesses were legion. The people ceased work by hundreds of thousands and fled to the mountains, there to await the imminent coming of God and the rising of the hundred and forty and four thousand to heaven. But in the meantime God did not come, and they starved to death in great numbers. In their desperation they ravaged the farms for food, and the consequent tumult and anarchy in the country districts but increased the woes of the poor expropriated farmers.

Also, the farms and warehouses were the property of the Iron Heel. Armies of troops were put into the field, and the fanatics were herded back at the bayonet point to their tasks in the cities. There they broke out in ever recurring mobs and riots. Their leaders were executed for sedition or confined in madhouses. Those who were executed went to their deaths with all the gladness of martyrs. It was a time of madness. The unrest spread. In the swamps and deserts and waste places, from Florida to Alaska, the small groups of Indians that survived were dancing ghost dances and waiting the coming of a Messiah of their own.

And through it all, with a serenity and certitude that was terrifying, continued to rise the form of that monster of the ages, the Oligarchy. With iron hand and iron heel it mastered the surging millions, out of confusion brought order, out of the very chaos wrought its own foundation and structure.

"Just wait till we get in," the Grangers said—Calvin said it to us in our Pell Street quarters. "Look at the states we've captured. With you socialists to back us, we'll make them sing another song when we take office."

"The millions of the discontented and the impoverished are ours," the socialists said. "The Grangers have come over to us, the farmers, the middle class, and the laborers. The capitalist system will fall to pieces. In another month we send fifty men to Congress. Two years hence every office will be ours, from the President down to the local dog-catcher."

To all of which Ernest would shake his head and say:

"How many rifles have you got? Do you know where you can get plenty of lead? When it comes to powder, chemical mixtures are better than mechanical mixtures, you take my word."

CHAPTER XVI

THE END

When it came time for Ernest and me to go to Washington, father did not accompany us. He had become enamoured of proletarian life. He looked upon our slum neighborhood as a great sociological laboratory, and he had embarked upon an apparently endless orgy of investigation. He chummed with the laborers, and was an intimate in scores of homes. Also, he worked at odd jobs, and the work was play as well as learned investigation, for he delighted in it and was always returning home with copious notes and bubbling over with new adventures. He was the perfect scientist.

There was no need for his working at all, because Ernest managed to earn enough from his translating to take care of the three of us. But father insisted on pursuing his favorite phantom, and a protean phantom it was, judging from the jobs he worked at. I shall never forget the evening he brought home his street pedler's outfit of shoe-laces and suspenders, nor the time I went into the little corner grocery to make some purchase and had him wait on me. After that I was not surprised when he tended bar for a week in the saloon across the street. He worked as a night watchman, hawked potatoes on the street, pasted labels in a cannery warehouse, was utility man in a paper-box factory, and water-carrier for a street railway construction gang, and even joined the Dishwashers' Union just before it fell to pieces.

I think the Bishop's example, so far as wearing apparel was concerned, must have fascinated father, for he wore the cheap cotton shirt of the laborer and the overalls with the narrow strap about the hips. Yet one habit remained to him from the old life; he always dressed for dinner, or supper, rather.

I could be happy anywhere with Ernest; and father's happiness in our changed circumstances rounded out my own happiness.

"When I was a boy," father said, "I was very curious. I wanted to know why things were and how they came to pass. That was why I became a physicist. The life in me to-day is just as curious as it was in my boyhood, and it's the being curious that makes life worth living."

Sometimes he ventured north of Market Street into the shopping and theatre district, where he sold papers, ran errands, and opened cabs. There, one day, closing a cab, he encountered Mr. Wickson. In high glee father described the incident to us that evening.

"Wickson looked at me sharply when I closed the door on him, and muttered, 'Well, I'll be damned.' Just like that he said it, 'Well, I'll be damned.' His face turned red and he was so confused that he forgot to tip me. But he must have recovered himself quickly, for the cab hadn't gone fifty feet before it turned around and came back. He leaned out of the door.

"'Look here, Professor,' he said, 'this is too much. What can I do for you?'

"'I closed the cab door for you,' I answered. 'According to common custom you might give me a dime.'

"'Bother that!' he snorted. 'I mean something substantial.'

"He was certainly serious—a twinge of ossified conscience or something; and so I considered with grave deliberation for a moment.

"His face was quite expectant when I began my answer, but you should have seen it when I finished.

"'You might give me back my home,' I said, 'and my stock in the Sierra Mills.'"

Father paused.

"What did he say?" I questioned eagerly.

"What could he say? He said nothing. But I said. 'I hope you are happy.' He looked at me curiously. 'Tell me, are you happy?'" I asked.

"He ordered the cabman to drive on, and went away swearing horribly. And he didn't give me the dime, much less the home and stock; so you see, my dear, your father's street-arab career is beset with disappointments."

And so it was that father kept on at our Pell Street quarters, while Ernest and I went to Washington. Except for the final consummation, the old order had passed away, and the final consummation was nearer than I dreamed. Contrary to our expectation, no obstacles were raised to prevent the socialist Congressmen from taking their seats. Everything went smoothly, and I laughed at Ernest when he looked upon the very smoothness as something ominous.

We found our socialist comrades confident, optimistic of their strength and of the things they would accomplish. A few Grangers who had been elected to Congress increased our strength, and an elaborate programme of what was to be done was prepared by the united forces. In all of which Ernest joined loyally and energetically, though he could not forbear, now and again, from saying, apropos of nothing in particular, "When it comes to powder, chemical mixtures are better than mechanical mixtures, you take my word."

The trouble arose first with the Grangers in the various states they had captured at the last election. There were a dozen of these states, but the Grangers who had been elected were not permitted to take office. The incumbents refused to get out. It was very simple. They merely charged illegality in the elections and wrapped up the whole situation in the interminable red tape of the law. The Grangers were powerless. The courts were in the hands of their enemies.

This was the moment of danger. If the cheated Grangers became violent, all was lost. How we socialists worked to hold them back! There were days and nights when Ernest never closed his eyes in sleep. The big leaders of the Grangers saw the peril and were with us to a man. But it was all of no avail. The Oligarchy wanted violence, and it set its agents-provocateurs to work. Without discussion, it was the agents-provocateurs who caused the Peasant Revolt.

In a dozen states the revolt flared up. The expropriated farmers took forcible possession of the state governments. Of course this was unconstitutional, and of course the United States put its soldiers into the field. Everywhere the agents-provocateurs urged the people on. These emissaries of the Iron Heel disguised themselves as artisans, farmers, and farm laborers. In Sacramento, the capital of California, the Grangers had succeeded in maintaining order. Thousands of secret agents were rushed to the devoted city. In mobs composed wholly of themselves, they fired and looted buildings and factories. They worked the people up until they joined them in the pillage. Liquor in large quantities was distributed among the slum classes further to inflame their minds. And then, when all was ready, appeared upon the scene the soldiers of the United States, who were, in reality, the soldiers of the Iron Heel. Eleven thousand men, women, and children were shot down on the streets of Sacramento or murdered in their houses. The national government took possession of the state government, and all was over for California.

And as with California, so elsewhere. Every Granger state was ravaged with violence and washed in blood. First, disorder was precipitated by the secret agents and the Black Hundreds, then the troops were called out. Rioting and mob-rule reigned throughout the rural districts. Day and night the smoke of burning farms, warehouses, villages, and cities filled the sky. Dynamite appeared. Railroad bridges and tunnels were blown up and trains were wrecked. The poor farmers were shot and hanged in great numbers. Reprisals were bitter, and many plutocrats and army officers were murdered. Blood and vengeance were in men's hearts. The regular troops fought the farmers as savagely as had they been Indians. And the regular troops had cause. Twenty-eight hundred of them had been annihilated in a tremendous series of dynamite explosions in Oregon, and in a similar manner, a number of train loads, at different times and places, had been destroyed. So it was that the regular troops fought for their lives as well as did the farmers.

As for the militia, the militia law of 1903 was put into effect, and the workers of one state were compelled, under pain of death, to shoot down their comrade-workers in other states. Of course, the militia law did not work smoothly at first. Many militia officers were murdered, and many militiamen were executed by drumhead court martial. Ernest's prophecy was strikingly fulfilled in the cases of Mr. Kowalt and Mr. Asmunsen. Both were eligible for the militia, and both were drafted to serve in the punitive expedition that was despatched from California against the farmers of Missouri. Mr. Kowalt and Mr. Asmunsen refused to serve. They were given short shrift. Drumhead court martial was their portion, and military execution their end. They were shot with their backs to the firing squad.

Many young men fled into the mountains to escape serving in the militia. There they became outlaws, and it was not until more peaceful times that they received their punishment. It was drastic. The government issued a proclamation for all law-abiding citizens to come in from the mountains for a period of three months. When the proclaimed date arrived, half a million soldiers were sent into the mountainous districts everywhere. There was no investigation, no trial. Wherever a man was encountered, he was shot down on the spot. The troops operated on the basis that no man not an outlaw remained in the mountains. Some bands, in strong positions, fought gallantly, but in the end every deserter from the militia met death.

A more immediate lesson, however, was impressed on the minds of the people by the punishment meted out to the Kansas militia. The great Kansas Mutiny occurred at the very beginning of military operations against the Grangers. Six thousand of the militia mutinied. They had been for several weeks very turbulent and sullen, and for that reason had been kept in camp. Their open mutiny, however, was without doubt precipitated by the agents-provocateurs.

On the night of the 22d of April they arose and murdered their officers, only a small remnant of the latter escaping. This was beyond the scheme of the Iron Heel, for the agents-provocateurs had done their work too well. But everything was grist to the Iron Heel. It had prepared for the outbreak, and the killing of so many officers gave it justification for what followed. As by magic, forty thousand soldiers of the regular army surrounded the malcontents. It was a trap. The wretched militiamen found that their machine-guns had been tampered with, and that the cartridges from the captured magazines did not fit their rifles. They hoisted the white flag of surrender, but it was ignored. There were no survivors. The entire six thousand were annihilated. Common shell and shrapnel were thrown in upon them from a distance, and, when, in their desperation, they charged the encircling lines, they were mowed down by the machine-guns. I talked with an eye-witness, and he said that the nearest any militiaman approached the machine-guns was a hundred and fifty yards. The earth was carpeted with the slain, and a final charge of cavalry, with trampling of horses' hoofs, revolvers, and sabres, crushed the wounded into the ground.

Simultaneously with the destruction of the Grangers came the revolt of the coal miners. It was the expiring effort of organized labor. Three-quarters of a million of miners went out on strike. But they were too widely scattered over the country to advantage from their own strength. They were segregated in their own districts and beaten into submission. This was the first great slave-drive. Pocock* won his spurs as a slave-driver and earned the undying hatred of the proletariat. Countless attempts were made upon his life, but he seemed to bear a charmed existence. It was he who was responsible for the introduction of the Russian passport system among the miners, and the denial of their right of removal from one part of the country to another.

* Albert Pocock, another of the notorious strike-breakers of

earlier years, who, to the day of his death, successfully held all the coal-miners of the country to their task. He was succeeded by his son, Lewis Pocock, and for five generations this remarkable line of slave-drivers handled the coal mines. The elder Pocock, known as Pocock I., has been described as follows: "A long, lean head, semicircled by a fringe of brown and gray hair, with big cheek-bones and a heavy chin, . . . a pale face, lustreless gray eyes, a metallic voice, and a languid manner." He was born of humble parents, and began his career as a bartender. He next became a private detective for a street railway corporation, and by successive steps developed into a professional strikebreaker. Pocock V., the last of the line, was blown up in a pump-house by a bomb during a petty revolt of the miners in the Indian Territory. This occurred in 2073 A.D.

In the meantime, the socialists held firm. While the Grangers expired in flame and blood, and organized labor was disrupted, the socialists held their peace and perfected their secret organization. In vain the Grangers pleaded with us. We rightly contended that any revolt on our part was virtually suicide for the whole Revolution. The Iron Heel, at first dubious about dealing with the entire proletariat at one time, had found the work easier than it had expected, and would have asked nothing better than an uprising on our part. But we avoided the issue, in spite of the fact that agents-provocateurs swarmed in our midst. In those early days, the agents of the Iron Heel were clumsy in their methods. They had much to learn and in the meantime our Fighting Groups weeded them out. It was bitter, bloody work, but we were fighting for life and for the Revolution, and we had to fight the enemy with its own weapons. Yet we were fair. No agent of the Iron Heel was executed without a trial. We may have made mistakes, but if so, very rarely. The bravest, and the most combative and self-sacrificing of our comrades went into the Fighting Groups. Once, after ten years had passed, Ernest made a calculation from figures furnished by the chiefs of the Fighting Groups, and his conclusion was that the average life of a man or woman after becoming a member was five years. The comrades of the Fighting Groups were heroes all, and the peculiar thing about it was that they were opposed to the taking of life. They violated their own natures, yet they loved liberty and knew of no sacrifice too great to make for the Cause.*

* These Fighting groups were modelled somewhat after the Fighting Organization of the Russian Revolution, and, despite the unceasing efforts of the Iron Heel, these groups persisted throughout the three centuries of its existence. Composed of men and women actuated by lofty purpose and unafraid to die, the Fighting Groups exercised tremendous influence and tempered the savage brutality of the rulers. Not alone was their work confined to unseen warfare with the

secret agents of the Oligarchy. The oligarchs themselves were compelled to listen to the decrees of the Groups, and often, when they disobeyed, were punished by death—and likewise with the subordinates of the oligarchs, with the officers of the army and the leaders of the labor castes.

Stern justice was meted out by these organized avengers, but most remarkable was their passionless and judicial procedure. There were no snap judgments. When a man was captured he was given fair trial and opportunity for defence. Of necessity, many men were tried and condemned by proxy, as in the case of General Lampton. This occurred in 2138 A.D. Possibly the most bloodthirsty and malignant of all the mercenaries that ever served the Iron Heel, he was informed by the Fighting Groups that they had tried him, found him guilty, and condemned him to death—and this, after three warnings for him to cease from his ferocious treatment of the proletariat. After his condemnation he surrounded himself with a myriad protective devices. Years passed, and in vain the Fighting Groups strove to execute their decree. Comrade after comrade, men and women, failed in their attempts, and were cruelly executed by the Oligarchy. It was the case of General Lampton that revived crucifixion as a legal method of execution. But in the end the condemned man found his executioner in the form of a slender girl of seventeen, Madeline Provence, who, to accomplish her purpose, served two years in his palace as a seamstress to the household. She died in solitary confinement after horrible and prolonged torture; but to-day she stands in imperishable bronze in the Pantheon of Brotherhood in the wonder city of Serles.

We, who by personal experience know nothing of bloodshed, must not judge harshly the heroes of the Fighting Groups. They gave up their lives for humanity, no sacrifice was too great for them to accomplish, while inexorable necessity compelled them to bloody expression in an age of blood. The Fighting Groups constituted the one thorn in the side of the Iron Heel that the Iron Heel could never remove. Everhard was the father of this curious army, and its accomplishments and successful persistence for three hundred years bear witness to the wisdom with which he organized and the solid foundation he laid for the succeeding generations to build upon. In some respects, despite his great economic and sociological contributions, and his work as a general leader in the Revolution, his organization of the Fighting Groups must be regarded as his greatest achievement.

The task we set ourselves was threefold. First, the weeding out from our circles of the secret agents of the Oligarchy. Second, the organizing of the Fighting Groups, and outside of them, of the general secret organization of the Revolution. And third, the introduction of our own secret agents into every branch of the Oligarchy—into the labor castes and especially among the telegraphers and secretaries and clerks, into the army, the agents-provocateurs, and the slave-drivers. It was slow work, and perilous, and often were our efforts rewarded with costly failures.

The Iron Heel had triumphed in open warfare, but we held our own in the new warfare, strange and awful and subterranean, that we instituted. All was unseen, much was unguessed; the blind fought the blind; and yet through it all was order, purpose, control. We permeated the entire organization of the Iron Heel with our agents, while our own organization was permeated with the agents of the Iron Heel. It was warfare dark and devious, replete with intrigue and conspiracy, plot and counterplot. And behind all, ever menacing, was death, violent and terrible. Men and women disappeared, our nearest and dearest comrades. We saw them to-day. To-morrow they were gone; we never saw them again, and we knew that they had died.

There was no trust, no confidence anywhere. The man who plotted beside us, for all we knew, might be an agent of the Iron Heel. We mined the organization of the Iron Heel with our secret agents, and the Iron Heel countermined with its secret agents inside its own organization. And it was the same with our organization. And despite the absence of confidence and trust we were compelled to base our every effort on confidence and trust. Often were we betrayed. Men were weak. The Iron Heel could offer money, leisure, the joys and pleasures that waited in the repose of the wonder cities. We could offer nothing but the satisfaction of being faithful to a noble ideal. As for the rest, the wages of those who were loyal were unceasing peril, torture, and death.

Men were weak, I say, and because of their weakness we were compelled to make the only other reward that was within our power. It was the reward of death. Out of necessity we had to punish our traitors. For every man who betrayed us, from one to a dozen faithful avengers were loosed upon his heels. We might fail to carry out our decrees against our enemies, such as the Pococks, for instance; but the one thing we could not afford to fail in was the punishment of our own traitors. Comrades turned traitor by permission, in order to win to the wonder cities and there execute our sentences on the real traitors. In fact, so terrible did we make ourselves, that it became a greater peril to betray us than to remain loyal to us.

The Revolution took on largely the character of religion. We worshipped at the shrine of the Revolution, which was the shrine of liberty. It was the divine flashing through us. Men and women devoted their lives to the Cause, and new-born babes were sealed to it as of old they had been sealed to the service of God. We were lovers of Humanity.

CHAPTER XVII

THE SCARLET LIVERY

With the destruction of the Granger states, the Grangers in Congress disappeared. They were being tried for high treason, and their places were taken by the creatures of the Iron Heel. The socialists were in a pitiful minority, and they knew that their end was near. Congress and the Senate were empty pretences, farces. Public questions were gravely debated and passed upon according to the old forms, while in reality all that was done was to give the stamp of constitutional procedure to the mandates of the Oligarchy.

Ernest was in the thick of the fight when the end came. It was in the debate on the bill to assist the unemployed. The hard times of the preceding year had thrust great masses of the proletariat beneath the starvation line, and the continued and wide-reaching disorder had but sunk them deeper. Millions of people were starving, while the oligarchs and their supporters were surfeiting on the surplus.* We called these wretched people the people of the abyss,** and it was to alleviate their awful suffering that the socialists had introduced the unemployed bill. But this was not to the fancy of the Iron Heel. In its own way it was preparing to set these millions to work, but the way was not our way, wherefore it had issued its orders that our bill should be voted down. Ernest and his fellows knew that their effort was futile, but they were tired of the suspense. They wanted something to happen. They were accomplishing nothing, and the best they hoped for was the putting of an end to the legislative farce in which they were unwilling players. They knew not what end would come, but they never anticipated a more disastrous end than the one that did come.

* The same conditions obtained in the nineteenth century A.D. under British rule in India. The natives died of starvation by the million, while their rulers robbed them of the fruits of their toil and expended it on magnificent pageants and mumbo-jumbo fooleries. Perforce, in this enlightened age, we have much to blush for in the acts of our ancestors. Our only consolation is philosophic. We must accept the capitalistic stage in social evolution as about on a par with the earlier monkey stage. The human had to pass through those stages in its rise from the mire and slime of low organic life. It was inevitable that much of the mire and slime should cling and be not easily shaken off.

** The people of the abyss—this phrase was struck out by

the genius of H. G. Wells in the late nineteenth century
A.D. Wells was a sociological seer, sane and normal as well
as warm human. Many fragments of his work have come down to us, while two of his greatest achievements, "Anticipations"
and "Mankind in the Making," have come down intact. Before
the oligarchs, and before Everhard, Wells speculated upon
the building of the wonder cities, though in his writings
they are referred to as "pleasure cities."

I sat in the gallery that day. We all knew that something terrible was imminent. It was in the air, and its presence was made visible by the armed soldiers drawn up in lines in the corridors, and by the officers grouped in the entrances to the House itself. The Oligarchy was about to strike. Ernest was speaking. He was describing the sufferings of the unemployed, as if with the wild idea of in some way touching their hearts and consciences; but the Republican and Democratic members sneered and jeered at him, and there was uproar and confusion. Ernest abruptly changed front.

"I know nothing that I may say can influence you," he said. "You have no souls to be influenced. You are spineless, flaccid things. You pompously call yourselves Republicans and Democrats. There is no Republican Party. There is no Democratic Party. There are no Republicans nor Democrats in this House. You are lick-spittlers and panderers, the creatures of the Plutocracy. You talk verbosely in antiquated terminology of your love of liberty, and all the while you wear the scarlet livery of the Iron Heel."

Here the shouting and the cries of "Order! order!" drowned his voice, and he stood disdainfully till the din had somewhat subsided. He waved his hand to include all of them, turned to his own comrades, and said:

"Listen to the bellowing of the well-fed beasts."

Pandemonium broke out again. The Speaker rapped for order and glanced expectantly at the officers in the doorways. There were cries of "Sedition!" and a great, rotund New York member began shouting "Anarchist!" at Ernest. And Ernest was not pleasant to look at. Every fighting fibre of him was quivering, and his face was the face of a fighting animal, withal he was cool and collected.

"Remember," he said, in a voice that made itself heard above the din, "that as you show mercy now to the proletariat, some day will that same proletariat show mercy to you."

The cries of "Sedition!" and "Anarchist!" redoubled.

"I know that you will not vote for this bill," Ernest went on. "You have received the command from your masters to vote against it. And yet you call me anarchist. You, who have destroyed the government of the people, and who shamelessly flaunt your scarlet shame in public places, call me anarchist. I do not believe in hell-fire and brimstone; but in moments like this I regret my unbelief. Nay, in moments like this I almost do believe. Surely there must be a hell, for in no less place could it be possible for you to receive punishment adequate to your crimes. So long as you exist, there is a vital need for hell-fire in the Cosmos."

There was movement in the doorways. Ernest, the Speaker, all the members turned to see.

"Why do you not call your soldiers in, Mr. Speaker, and bid them do their work?" Ernest demanded. "They should carry out your plan with expedition."

"There are other plans afoot," was the retort. "That is why the soldiers are present."

"Our plans, I suppose," Ernest sneered. "Assassination or something kindred."

But at the word "assassination" the uproar broke out again. Ernest could not make himself heard, but he remained on his feet waiting for a lull. And then it happened. From my place in the gallery I saw nothing except the flash of the explosion. The roar of it filled my ears and I saw Ernest reeling and falling in a swirl of smoke, and the soldiers rushing up all the aisles. His comrades were on their feet, wild with anger, capable of any violence. But Ernest steadied himself for a moment, and waved his arms for silence.

"It is a plot!" his voice rang out in warning to his comrades. "Do nothing, or you will be destroyed."

Then he slowly sank down, and the soldiers reached him. The next moment soldiers were clearing the galleries and I saw no more.

Though he was my husband, I was not permitted to get to him. When I announced who I was, I was promptly placed under arrest. And at the same time were arrested all socialist Congressmen in Washington, including the unfortunate Simpson, who lay ill with typhoid fever in his hotel.

The trial was prompt and brief. The men were foredoomed. The wonder was that Ernest was not executed. This was a blunder on the part of the Oligarchy, and a costly one. But the Oligarchy was too confident in those days. It was drunk with success, and little did it dream that that small handful of heroes had within them the power to rock it to its foundations. To-morrow, when the Great Revolt breaks out and all the world resounds with the tramp, tramp of the millions, the Oligarchy, will realize, and too late, how mightily that band of heroes has grown.*

> * Avis Everhard took for granted that her narrative would be read in her own day, and so omits to mention the outcome of the trial for high treason. Many other similar disconcerting omissions will be noticed in the Manuscript. Fifty-two socialist Congressmen were tried, and all were found guilty. Strange to relate, not one received the death sentence. Everhard and eleven others, among whom were Theodore Donnelson and Matthew Kent, received life imprisonment. The remaining forty received sentences varying from thirty to forty-five years; while Arthur Simpson, referred to in the Manuscript as being ill of typhoid fever at the time of the explosion, received only

> fifteen years. It is the tradition that he died of starvation in solitary confinement, and this harsh treatment is explained as having been caused by his uncompromising stubbornness and his fiery and tactless hatred for all men that served the despotism. He died in Cabanas in Cuba, where three of his comrades were also confined. The fifty-two socialist Congressmen were confined in military fortresses scattered all over the United States. Thus, Du Bois and Woods were held in Porto Rico, while Everhard and Merryweather were placed in Alcatraz, an island in San Francisco Bay that had already seen long service as a military prison.

As a revolutionist myself, as one on the inside who knew the hopes and fears and secret plans of the revolutionists, I am fitted to answer, as very few are, the charge that they were guilty of exploding the bomb in Congress. And I can say flatly, without qualification or doubt of any sort, that the socialists, in Congress and out, had no hand in the affair. Who threw the bomb we do not know, but the one thing we are absolutely sure of is that we did not throw it.

On the other hand, there is evidence to show that the Iron Heel was responsible for the act. Of course, we cannot prove this. Our conclusion is merely presumptive. But here are such facts as we do know. It had been reported to the Speaker of the House, by secret-service agents of the government, that the Socialist Congressmen were about to resort to terroristic tactics, and that they had decided upon the day when their tactics would go into effect. This day was the very day of the explosion. Wherefore the Capitol had been packed with troops in anticipation. Since we knew nothing about the bomb, and since a bomb actually was exploded, and since the authorities had prepared in advance for the explosion, it is only fair to conclude that the Iron Heel did know. Furthermore, we charge that the Iron Heel was guilty of the outrage, and that the Iron Heel planned and perpetrated the outrage for the purpose of foisting the guilt on our shoulders and so bringing about our destruction.

From the Speaker the warning leaked out to all the creatures in the House that wore the scarlet livery. They knew, while Ernest was speaking, that some violent act was to be committed. And to do them justice, they honestly believed that the act was to be committed by the socialists. At the trial, and still with honest belief, several testified to having seen Ernest prepare to throw the bomb, and that it exploded prematurely. Of course they saw nothing of the sort. In the fevered imagination of fear they thought they saw, that was all.

As Ernest said at the trial: "Does it stand to reason, if I were going to throw a bomb, that I should elect to throw a feeble little squib like the one that was thrown? There wasn't enough powder in it. It made a lot of smoke, but hurt no one except me. It exploded right at my feet, and yet it did not kill me. Believe me, when I get to throwing bombs, I'll do damage. There'll be more than smoke in my petards."

In return it was argued by the prosecution that the weakness of the bomb was a blunder on the part of the socialists, just as its premature explosion, caused by Ernest's losing his nerve and dropping it, was a blunder. And to clinch the argument, there were the several Congressmen who testified to having seen Ernest fumble and drop the bomb.

As for ourselves, not one of us knew how the bomb was thrown. Ernest told me that the fraction of an instant before it exploded he both heard and saw it strike at his feet. He testified to this at the trial, but no one believed him. Besides, the whole thing, in popular slang, was "cooked up." The Iron Heel had made up its mind to destroy us, and there was no withstanding it.

There is a saying that truth will out. I have come to doubt that saying. Nineteen years have elapsed, and despite our untiring efforts, we have failed to find the man who really did throw the bomb. Undoubtedly he was some emissary of the Iron Heel, but he has escaped detection. We have never got the slightest clew to his identity. And now, at this late date, nothing remains but for the affair to take its place among the mysteries of history.*

> * Avis Everhard would have had to live for many generations
> ere she could have seen the clearing up of this particular
> mystery. A little less than a hundred years ago, and a
> little more than six hundred years after the death, the
> confession of Pervaise was discovered in the secret archives
> of the Vatican. It is perhaps well to tell a little
> something about this obscure document, which, in the main,
> is of interest to the historian only.
>
> Pervaise was an American, of French descent, who in 1913
> A.D., was lying in the Tombs Prison, New York City, awaiting
> trial for murder. From his confession we learn that he was
> not a criminal. He was warm-blooded, passionate, emotional.
> In an insane fit of jealousy he killed his wife—a very
> common act in those times. Pervaise was mastered by the fear
> of death, all of which is recounted at length in his
> confession. To escape death he would have done anything,
> and the police agents prepared him by assuring him that he
> could not possibly escape conviction of murder in the first
> degree when his trial came off. In those days, murder in
> the first degree was a capital offense. The guilty man or
> woman was placed in a specially constructed death-chair,
> and, under the supervision of competent physicians, was
> destroyed by a current of electricity. This was called
> electrocution, and it was very popular during that period.
> Anaesthesia, as a mode of compulsory death, was not
> introduced until later.
>
> This man, good at heart but with a ferocious animalism close

at the surface of his being, lying in jail and expectant of nothing less than death, was prevailed upon by the agents of the Iron Heel to throw the bomb in the House of Representatives. In his confession he states explicitly that he was informed that the bomb was to be a feeble thing and that no lives would be lost. This is directly in line with the fact that the bomb was lightly charged, and that its explosion at Everhard's feet was not deadly.

Pervaise was smuggled into one of the galleries ostensibly closed for repairs. He was to select the moment for the throwing of the bomb, and he naively confesses that in his interest in Everhard's tirade and the general commotion raised thereby, he nearly forgot his mission.

Not only was he released from prison in reward for his deed, but he was granted an income for life. This he did not long enjoy. In 1914 A.D., in September, he was stricken with rheumatism of the heart and lived for three days. It was then that he sent for the Catholic priest, Father Peter Durban, and to him made confession. So important did it seem to the priest, that he had the confession taken down in writing and sworn to. What happened after this we can only surmise. The document was certainly important enough to find its way to Rome. Powerful influences must have been brought to bear, hence its suppression. For centuries no hint of its existence reached the world. It was not until in the last century that Lorbia, the brilliant Italian scholar, stumbled upon it quite by chance during his researches in the Vatican.

There is to-day no doubt whatever that the Iron Heel was responsible for the bomb that exploded in the House of Representatives in 1913 A.D. Even though the Pervaise confession had never come to light, no reasonable doubt could obtain; for the act in question, that sent fifty-two Congressmen to prison, was on a par with countless other acts committed by the oligarchs, and, before them, by the capitalists.

There is the classic instance of the ferocious and wanton judicial murder of the innocent and so-called Haymarket Anarchists in Chicago in the penultimate decade of the nineteenth century A.D. In a category by itself is the deliberate burning and destruction of capitalist property by the capitalists themselves. For such destruction of property innocent men were frequently punished—"railroaded" in the parlance of the times.

In the labor troubles of the first decade of the twentieth century A.D., between the capitalists and the Western Federation of Miners, similar but more bloody tactics were employed. The railroad station at Independence was blown up by the agents of the capitalists. Thirteen men were killed, and many more were wounded. And then the capitalists, controlling the legislative and judicial machinery of the state of Colorado, charged the miners with the crime and came very near to convicting them. Romaines, one of the tools in this affair, like Pervaise, was lying in jail in another state, Kansas, awaiting trial, when he was approached by the agents of the capitalists. But, unlike Pervaise the confession of Romaines was made public in his own time.

Then, during this same period, there was the case of Moyer and Haywood, two strong, fearless leaders of labor. One was president and the other was secretary of the Western Federation of Miners. The ex-governor of Idaho had been mysteriously murdered. The crime, at the time, was openly charged to the mine owners by the socialists and miners. Nevertheless, in violation of the national and state constitutions, and by means of conspiracy on the parts of the governors of Idaho and Colorado, Moyer and Haywood were kidnapped, thrown into jail, and charged with the murder. It was this instance that provoked from Eugene V. Debs, national leader of the American socialists at the time, the following words: "The labor leaders that cannot be bribed nor bullied, must be ambushed and murdered. The only crime of Moyer and Haywood is that they have been unswervingly true to the working class. The capitalists have stolen our country, debauched our politics, defiled our judiciary, and ridden over us rough-shod, and now they propose to murder those who will not abjectly surrender to their brutal dominion. The governors of Colorado and Idaho are but
> executing the mandates of their masters, the Plutocracy. The issue is the Workers versus the Plutocracy. If they strike the first violent blow, we will strike the last."

CHAPTER XVIII

IN THE SHADOW OF SONOMA

Of myself, during this period, there is not much to say. For six months I was kept in prison, though charged with no crime. I was a suspect—a word of fear that all revolutionists were soon to come to know. But our own nascent secret service was beginning to work. By the end of my second month in prison, one of the jailers made himself known as a revolutionist in touch with the organization. Several weeks later, Joseph Parkhurst, the prison doctor who had just been appointed, proved himself to be a member of one of the Fighting Groups.

Thus, throughout the organization of the Oligarchy, our own organization, weblike and spidery, was insinuating itself. And so I was kept in touch with all that was happening in the world without. And furthermore, every one of our imprisoned leaders was in contact with brave comrades who masqueraded in the livery of the Iron Heel. Though Ernest lay in prison three thousand miles away, on the Pacific Coast, I was in unbroken communication with him, and our letters passed regularly back and forth.

The leaders, in prison and out, were able to discuss and direct the campaign. It would have been possible, within a few months, to have effected the escape of some of them; but since imprisonment proved no bar to our activities, it was decided to avoid anything premature. Fifty-two Congressmen were in prison, and fully three hundred more of our leaders. It was planned that they should be delivered simultaneously. If part of them escaped, the vigilance of the oligarchs might be aroused so as to prevent the escape of the remainder. On the other hand, it was held that a simultaneous jail-delivery all over the land would have immense psychological influence on the proletariat. It would show our strength and give confidence.

So it was arranged, when I was released at the end of six months, that I was to disappear and prepare a secure hiding-place for Ernest. To disappear was in itself no easy thing. No sooner did I get my freedom than my footsteps began to be dogged by the spies of the Iron Heel. It was necessary that they should be thrown off the track, and that I should win to California. It is laughable, the way this was accomplished.

Already the passport system, modelled on the Russian, was developing. I dared not cross the continent in my own character. It was necessary that I should be completely lost if ever I was to see Ernest again, for by trailing me after he escaped, he would be caught once more. Again, I could not disguise myself as a proletarian and travel. There remained the disguise of a member of the Oligarchy. While the arch-oligarchs were no more than a handful, there were myriads of lesser ones of the type, say, of Mr.

Wickson—men, worth a few millions, who were adherents of the arch-oligarchs. The wives and daughters of these lesser oligarchs were legion, and it was decided that I should assume the disguise of such a one. A few years later this would have been impossible, because the passport system was to become so perfect that no man, woman, nor child in all the land was unregistered and unaccounted for in his or her movements.

When the time was ripe, the spies were thrown off my track. An hour later Avis Everhard was no more. At that time one Felice Van Verdighan, accompanied by two maids and a lap-dog, with another maid for the lap-dog,* entered a drawing-room on a Pullman,** and a few minutes later was speeding west.

> * This ridiculous picture well illustrates the heartless conduct of the masters. While people starved, lap-dogs were waited upon by maids. This was a serious masquerade on the part of Avis Everhard. Life and death and the Cause were in the issue; therefore the picture must be accepted as a true picture. It affords a striking commentary of the times.

> ** Pullman—the designation of the more luxurious railway cars of the period and so named from the inventor.

The three maids who accompanied me were revolutionists. Two were members of the Fighting Groups, and the third, Grace Holbrook, entered a group the following year, and six months later was executed by the Iron Heel. She it was who waited upon the dog. Of the other two, Bertha Stole disappeared twelve years later, while Anna Roylston still lives and plays an increasingly important part in the Revolution.*

> * Despite continual and almost inconceivable hazards, Anna Roylston lived to the royal age of ninety-one. As the Pococks defied the executioners of the Fighting Groups, so she defied the executioners of the Iron Heel. She bore a charmed life and prospered amid dangers and alarms. She herself was an executioner for the Fighting Groups, and, known as the Red Virgin, she became one of the inspired figures of the Revolution. When she was an old woman of sixty-nine she shot "Bloody" Halcliffe down in the midst of his armed escort and got away unscathed. In the end she died peaceably of old age in a secret refuge of the revolutionists in the Ozark mountains.

Without adventure we crossed the United States to California. When the train stopped at Sixteenth Street Station, in Oakland, we alighted, and there Felice Van Verdighan, with her two maids, her lap-dog, and her lap-dog's maid, disappeared forever. The maids, guided by trusty comrades, were led away. Other comrades took charge of me. Within half an hour after leaving the train I was on board a small fishing boat and out on the waters of San Francisco Bay. The winds baffled, and we drifted aimlessly the greater part of the night. But I saw the lights of Alcatraz where Ernest lay, and found comfort in the thought of nearness to him. By dawn, what with the rowing of the fishermen, we made the Marin Islands. Here we lay in hiding all day, and on the following night, swept on by a flood tide and a fresh wind, we crossed San Pablo Bay in two hours and ran up Petaluma Creek.

Here horses were ready and another comrade, and without delay we were away through the starlight. To the north I could see the loom of Sonoma Mountain, toward which we rode. We left the old town of Sonoma to the right and rode up a canyon that lay between outlying buttresses of the mountain. The wagon-road became a wood-road, the wood-road became a cow-path, and the cow-path dwindled away and ceased among the upland pastures. Straight over Sonoma Mountain we rode. It was the safest route. There was no one to mark our passing.

Dawn caught us on the northern brow, and in the gray light we dropped down through chaparral into redwood canyons deep and warm with the breath of passing summer. It was old country to me that I knew and loved, and soon I became the guide. The hiding-place was mine. I had selected it. We let down the bars and crossed an upland meadow. Next, we went over a low, oak-covered ridge and descended into a smaller meadow. Again we climbed a ridge, this time riding under red-limbed madronos and manzanitas of deeper red. The first rays of the sun streamed upon our backs as we climbed. A flight of quail thrummed off through the thickets. A big jackrabbit crossed our path, leaping swiftly and silently like a deer. And then a deer, a many-pronged buck, the sun flashing red-gold from neck and shoulders, cleared the crest of the ridge before us and was gone.

We followed in his wake a space, then dropped down a zigzag trail that he disdained into a group of noble redwoods that stood about a pool of water murky with minerals from the mountain side. I knew every inch of the way. Once a writer friend of mine had owned the ranch; but he, too, had become a revolutionist, though more disastrously than I, for he was already dead and gone, and none knew where nor how. He alone, in the days he had lived, knew the secret of the hiding-place for which I was bound. He had bought the ranch for beauty, and paid a round price for it, much to the disgust of the local farmers. He used to tell with great glee how they were wont to shake their heads mournfully at the price, to accomplish ponderously a bit of mental arithmetic, and then to say, "But you can't make six per cent on it."

But he was dead now, nor did the ranch descend to his children. Of all men, it was now the property of Mr. Wickson, who owned the whole eastern and northern slopes of Sonoma Mountain, running from the Spreckels estate to the divide of Bennett Valley. Out of it he had made a magnificent deer-park, where, over thousands of acres of sweet slopes and glades and canyons, the deer ran almost in primitive wildness. The people who had owned the soil had been driven away. A state home for the feeble-minded had also been demolished to make room for the deer.

To cap it all, Wickson's hunting lodge was a quarter of a mile from my hiding-place. This, instead of being a danger, was an added security. We were sheltered under the very aegis of one of the minor oligarchs. Suspicion, by the nature of the situation, was turned aside. The last place in the world the spies of the Iron Heel would dream of looking for me, and for Ernest when he joined me, was Wickson's deer-park.

We tied our horses among the redwoods at the pool. From a cache behind a hollow rotting log my companion brought out a variety of things,—a fifty-pound sack of flour, tinned foods of all sorts, cooking utensils, blankets, a canvas tarpaulin, books and writing material, a great bundle of letters, a five-gallon can of kerosene, an oil stove, and, last and most important, a large coil of stout rope. So large was the supply of things that a number of trips would be necessary to carry them to the refuge.

But the refuge was very near. Taking the rope and leading the way, I passed through a glade of tangled vines and bushes that ran between two wooded knolls. The glade ended abruptly at the steep bank of a stream. It was a little stream, rising from springs, and the hottest summer never dried it up. On every hand were tall wooded knolls, a group of them, with all the seeming of having been flung there from some careless Titan's hand. There was no bed-rock in them. They rose from their bases hundreds of feet, and they were composed of red volcanic earth, the famous wine-soil of Sonoma. Through these the tiny stream had cut its deep and precipitous channel.

It was quite a scramble down to the stream bed, and, once on the bed, we went down stream perhaps for a hundred feet. And then we came to the great hole. There was no warning of the existence of the hole, nor was it a hole in the common sense of the word. One crawled through tight-locked briers and branches, and found oneself on the very edge, peering out and down through a green screen. A couple of hundred feet in length and width, it was half of that in depth. Possibly because of some fault that had occurred when the knolls were flung together, and certainly helped by freakish erosion, the hole had been scooped out in the course of centuries by the wash of water. Nowhere did the raw earth appear. All was garmented by vegetation, from tiny maidenhair and gold-back ferns to mighty redwood and Douglas spruces. These great trees even sprang out from the walls of the hole. Some leaned over at angles as great as forty-five degrees, though the majority towered straight up from the soft and almost perpendicular earth walls.

It was a perfect hiding-place. No one ever came there, not even the village boys of Glen Ellen. Had this hole existed in the bed of a canyon a mile long, or several miles long, it would have been well known. But this was no canyon. From beginning to end the length of the stream was no more than five hundred yards. Three hundred yards above the hole the stream took its rise in a spring at the foot of a flat meadow. A hundred yards below the hole the stream ran out into open country, joining the main stream and flowing across rolling and grass-covered land.

My companion took a turn of the rope around a tree, and with me fast on the other end lowered away. In no time I was on the bottom. And in but a short while he had carried all the articles from the cache and lowered them down to me. He hauled the rope up and hid it, and before he went away called down to me a cheerful parting.

Before I go on I want to say a word for this comrade, John Carlson, a humble figure of the Revolution, one of the countless faithful ones in the ranks. He worked for Wickson, in the stables near the hunting lodge. In fact, it was on Wickson's horses that we had ridden over Sonoma Mountain. For nearly twenty years now John Carlson has been custodian of the refuge. No thought of disloyalty, I am sure, has ever entered his mind during all that time. To betray his trust would have been in his mind a thing undreamed. He was phlegmatic, stolid to such a degree that one could not but wonder how the Revolution had any meaning to him at all. And yet love of freedom glowed sombrely and steadily in his dim soul. In ways it was indeed good that he was not flighty and imaginative. He never lost his head. He could obey orders, and he was neither curious nor garrulous. Once I asked how it was that he was a revolutionist.

"When I was a young man I was a soldier," was his answer. "It was in Germany. There all young men must be in the army. So I was in the army. There was another soldier there, a young man, too. His father was what you call an agitator, and his father was in jail for lese majesty—what you call speaking the truth about the Emperor. And the young man, the son, talked with me much about people, and work, and the robbery of the people by the capitalists. He made me see things in new ways, and I became a socialist. His talk was very true and good, and I have never forgotten. When I came to the United States I hunted up the socialists. I became a member of a section—that was in the day of the S. L. P. Then later, when the split came, I joined the local of the S. P. I was working in a livery stable in San Francisco then. That was before the Earthquake. I have paid my dues for twenty-two years. I am yet a member, and I yet pay my dues, though it is very secret now. I will always pay my dues, and when the cooperative commonwealth comes, I will be glad."

Left to myself, I proceeded to cook breakfast on the oil stove and to prepare my home. Often, in the early morning, or in the evening after dark, Carlson would steal down to the refuge and work for a couple of hours. At first my home was the tarpaulin. Later, a small tent was put up. And still later, when we became assured of the perfect security of the place, a small house was erected. This house was completely hidden from any chance eye that might peer down from the edge of the hole. The lush vegetation of that sheltered spot make a natural shield. Also, the house was built against the perpendicular wall; and in the wall itself, shored by strong timbers, well drained and ventilated, we excavated two small rooms. Oh, believe me, we had many comforts. When Biedenbach, the German terrorist, hid with us some time later, he installed a smoke-consuming device that enabled us to sit by crackling wood fires on winter nights.

And here I must say a word for that gentle-souled terrorist, than whom there is no comrade in the Revolution more fearfully misunderstood. Comrade Biedenbach did not betray the Cause. Nor was he executed by the comrades as is commonly supposed. This canard was circulated by the creatures of the Oligarchy. Comrade Biedenbach was absent-minded, forgetful. He was shot by one of our lookouts at the cave-refuge at Carmel, through failure on his part to remember the secret signals. It was all a sad mistake. And that he betrayed his Fighting Group is an absolute lie. No truer, more loyal man ever labored for the Cause.*

* Search as we may through all the material of those times that has come down to us, we can find no clew to the Biedenbach here referred to. No mention is made of him anywhere save in the Everhard Manuscript.
*

For nineteen years now the refuge that I selected had been almost continuously occupied, and in all that time, with one exception, it has never been discovered by an outsider. And yet it was only a quarter of a mile from Wickson's hunting-lodge, and a short mile from the village of Glen Ellen. I was able, always, to hear the morning and evening trains arrive and depart, and I used to set my watch by the whistle at the brickyards.*

* If the curious traveller will turn south from Glen Ellen, he will find himself on a boulevard that is identical with the old country road seven centuries ago. A quarter of a mile from Glen Ellen, after the second bridge is passed, to the right will be noticed a barranca that runs like a scar across the rolling land toward a group of wooded knolls. The barranca is the site of the ancient right of way that in the time of private property in land ran across the holding of one Chauvet, a French pioneer of California who came from his native country in the fabled days of gold. The wooded knolls are the same knolls referred to by Avis Everhard.

The Great Earthquake of 2368 A.D. broke off the side of one of these knolls and toppled it into the hole where the Everhards made their refuge. Since the finding of the Manuscript excavations have been made, and the house, the two cave rooms, and all the accumulated rubbish of long occupancy have been brought to light. Many valuable relics have been found, among which, curious to relate, is the smoke-consuming device of Biedenbach's mentioned in the narrative. Students interested in such matters should read the brochure of Arnold Bentham soon to be published.

A mile northwest from the wooded knolls brings one to the site of Wake Robin Lodge at the junction of Wild-Water and Sonoma Creeks. It may be noticed, in passing, that Wild-

Water was originally called Graham Creek and was so named on the early local maps. But the later name sticks. It was at Wake Robin Lodge that Avis Everhard later lived for short periods, when, disguised as an agent-provocateur of the Iron Heel, she was enabled to play with impunity her part among men and events. The official permission to occupy Wake Robin Lodge is still on the records, signed by no less a man than Wickson, the minor oligarch of the Manuscript.

CHAPTER XIX

TRANSFORMATION

"You must make yourself over again," Ernest wrote to me. "You must cease to be. You must become another woman—and not merely in the clothes you wear, but inside your skin under the clothes. You must make yourself over again so that even I would not know you—your voice, your gestures, your mannerisms, your carriage, your walk, everything."

This command I obeyed. Every day I practised for hours in burying forever the old Avis Everhard beneath the skin of another woman whom I may call my other self. It was only by long practice that such results could be obtained. In the mere detail of voice intonation I practised almost perpetually till the voice of my new self became fixed, automatic. It was this automatic assumption of a role that was considered imperative. One must become so adept as to deceive oneself. It was like learning a new language, say the French. At first speech in French is self-conscious, a matter of the will. The student thinks in English and then transmutes into French, or reads in French but transmutes into English before he can understand. Then later, becoming firmly grounded, automatic, the student reads, writes, and THINKS in French, without any recourse to English at all.

And so with our disguises. It was necessary for us to practise until our assumed roles became real; until to be our original selves would require a watchful and strong exercise of will. Of course, at first, much was mere blundering experiment. We were creating a new art, and we had much to discover. But the work was going on everywhere; masters in the art were developing, and a fund of tricks and expedients was being accumulated. This fund became a sort of text-book that was passed on, a part of the curriculum, as it were, of the school of Revolution.*

> * Disguise did become a veritable art during that period. The revolutionists maintained schools of acting in all their refuges. They scorned accessories, such as wigs and beards, false eyebrows, and such aids of the theatrical actors. The game of revolution was a game of life and death, and mere accessories were traps. Disguise had to be fundamental, intrinsic, part and parcel of one's being, second nature. The Red Virgin is reported to have been one of the most adept in the art, to which must be ascribed her long and successful career.

It was at this time that my father disappeared. His letters, which had come to me regularly, ceased. He no longer appeared at our Pell Street quarters. Our comrades sought him everywhere. Through our secret service we ransacked every prison in the land. But he was lost as completely as if the earth had swallowed him up, and to this day no clew to his end has been discovered.*

> * Disappearance was one of the horrors of the time. As a
> motif, in song and story, it constantly crops up. It was an
> inevitable concomitant of the subterranean warfare that
> raged through those three centuries. This phenomenon was
> almost as common in the oligarch class and the labor castes,
> as it was in the ranks of the revolutionists. Without
> warning, without trace, men and women, and even children,
> disappeared and were seen no more, their end shrouded in
> mystery.

Six lonely months I spent in the refuge, but they were not idle months. Our organization went on apace, and there were mountains of work always waiting to be done. Ernest and his fellow-leaders, from their prisons, decided what should be done; and it remained for us on the outside to do it. There was the organization of the mouth-to-mouth propaganda; the organization, with all its ramifications, of our spy system; the establishment of our secret printing-presses; and the establishment of our underground railways, which meant the knitting together of all our myriads of places of refuge, and the formation of new refuges where links were missing in the chains we ran over all the land.

So I say, the work was never done. At the end of six months my loneliness was broken by the arrival of two comrades. They were young girls, brave souls and passionate lovers of liberty: Lora Peterson, who disappeared in 1922, and Kate Bierce, who later married Du Bois,* and who is still with us with eyes lifted to to-morrow's sun, that heralds in the new age.

> * Du Bois, the present librarian of Ardis, is a lineal
> descendant of this revolutionary pair.

The two girls arrived in a flurry of excitement, danger, and sudden death. In the crew of the fishing boat that conveyed them across San Pablo Bay was a spy. A creature of the Iron Heel, he had successfully masqueraded as a revolutionist and penetrated deep into the secrets of our organization. Without doubt he was on my trail, for we had long since learned that my disappearance had been cause of deep concern to the secret service of the Oligarchy. Luckily, as the outcome proved, he had not divulged his discoveries to any one. He had evidently delayed reporting, preferring to wait until he had brought things to a successful conclusion by discovering my hiding-place and capturing me. His information died with him. Under some pretext, after the girls had landed at Petaluma Creek and taken to the horses, he managed to get away from the boat.

Part way up Sonoma Mountain, John Carlson let the girls go on, leading his horse, while he went back on foot. His suspicions had been aroused. He captured the spy, and as to what then happened, Carlson gave us a fair idea.

"I fixed him," was Carlson's unimaginative way of describing the affair. "I fixed him," he repeated, while a sombre light burnt in his eyes, and his huge, toil-distorted hands opened and closed eloquently. "He made no noise. I hid him, and tonight I will go back and bury him deep."

During that period I used to marvel at my own metamorphosis. At times it seemed impossible, either that I had ever lived a placid, peaceful life in a college town, or else that I had become a revolutionist inured to scenes of violence and death. One or the other could not be. One was real, the other was a dream, but which was which? Was this present life of a revolutionist, hiding in a hole, a nightmare? or was I a revolutionist who had somewhere, somehow, dreamed that in some former existence I have lived in Berkeley and never known of life more violent than teas and dances, debating societies, and lectures rooms? But then I suppose this was a common experience of all of us who had rallied under the red banner of the brotherhood of man.

I often remembered figures from that other life, and, curiously enough, they appeared and disappeared, now and again, in my new life. There was Bishop Morehouse. In vain we searched for him after our organization had developed. He had been transferred from asylum to asylum. We traced him from the state hospital for the insane at Napa to the one in Stockton, and from there to the one in the Santa Clara Valley called Agnews, and there the trail ceased. There was no record of his death. In some way he must have escaped. Little did I dream of the awful manner in which I was to see him once again—the fleeting glimpse of him in the whirlwind carnage of the Chicago Commune.

Jackson, who had lost his arm in the Sierra Mills and who had been the cause of my own conversion into a revolutionist, I never saw again; but we all knew what he did before he died. He never joined the revolutionists. Embittered by his fate, brooding over his wrongs, he became an anarchist—not a philosophic anarchist, but a mere animal, mad with hate and lust for revenge. And well he revenged himself. Evading the guards, in the nighttime while all were asleep, he blew the Pertonwaithe palace into atoms. Not a soul escaped, not even the guards. And in prison, while awaiting trial, he suffocated himself under his blankets.

Dr. Hammerfield and Dr. Ballingford achieved quite different fates from that of Jackson. They have been faithful to their salt, and they have been correspondingly rewarded with ecclesiastical palaces wherein they dwell at peace with the world. Both are apologists for the Oligarchy. Both have grown very fat. "Dr. Hammerfield," as Ernest once said, "has succeeded in modifying his metaphysics so as to give God's sanction to the Iron Heel, and also to include much worship of beauty and to reduce to an invisible wraith the gaseous vertebrate described by Haeckel—the difference between Dr. Hammerfield and Dr. Ballingford being that the latter has made the God of the oligarchs a little more gaseous and a little less vertebrate."

Peter Donnelly, the scab foreman at the Sierra Mills whom I encountered while investigating the case of Jackson, was a surprise to all of us. In 1918 I was present at a meeting of the 'Frisco Reds. Of all our Fighting Groups this one was the most formidable, ferocious, and merciless. It was really not a part of our organization. Its members were fanatics, madmen. We dared not encourage such a spirit. On the other hand, though they did not belong to us, we remained on friendly terms with them. It was a matter of vital importance that brought me there that night. I, alone in the midst of a score of men, was the only person unmasked. After the business that brought me there was transacted, I was led away by one of them. In a dark passage this guide struck a match, and, holding it close to his face, slipped back his mask. For a moment I gazed upon the passion-wrought features of Peter Donnelly. Then the match went out.

"I just wanted you to know it was me," he said in the darkness. "D'you remember Dallas, the superintendent?"

I nodded at recollection of the vulpine-face superintendent of the Sierra Mills.

"Well, I got him first," Donnelly said with pride. "'Twas after that I joined the Reds."

"But how comes it that you are here?" I queried. "Your wife and children?"

"Dead," he answered. "That's why. No," he went on hastily, "'tis not revenge for them. They died easily in their beds—sickness, you see, one time and another. They tied my arms while they lived. And now that they're gone, 'tis revenge for my blasted manhood I'm after. I was once Peter Donnelly, the scab foreman. But to-night I'm Number 27 of the 'Frisco Reds. Come on now, and I'll get you out of this."

More I heard of him afterward. In his own way he had told the truth when he said all were dead. But one lived, Timothy, and him his father considered dead because he had taken service with the Iron Heel in the Mercenaries.* A member of the 'Frisco Reds pledged himself to twelve annual executions. The penalty for failure was death. A member who failed to complete his number committed suicide. These executions were not haphazard. This group of madmen met frequently and passed wholesale judgments upon offending members and servitors of the Oligarchy. The executions were afterward apportioned by lot.

> * In addition to the labor castes, there arose another caste, the military. A standing army of professional soldiers was created, officered by members of the Oligarchy and known as the Mercenaries. This institution took the place of the militia, which had proved impracticable under the new regime. Outside the regular secret service of the Iron Heel, there was further established a secret service of the Mercenaries, this latter forming a connecting link between the police and the military.

In fact, the business that brought me there the night of my visit was such a trial. One of our own comrades, who for years had successfully maintained himself in a clerical position in the local bureau of the secret service of the Iron Heel, had fallen under the ban of the 'Frisco Reds and was being tried. Of course he was not present, and of course his judges did not know that he was one of our men. My mission had been to testify to his identity and loyalty. It may be wondered how we came to know of the affair at all. The explanation is simple. One of our secret agents was a member of the 'Frisco Reds. It was necessary for us to keep an eye on friend as well as foe, and this group of madmen was not too unimportant to escape our surveillance.

But to return to Peter Donnelly and his son. All went well with Donnelly until, in the following year, he found among the sheaf of executions that fell to him the name of Timothy Donnelly. Then it was that that clannishness, which was his to so extraordinary a degree, asserted itself. To save his son, he betrayed his comrades. In this he was partially blocked, but a dozen of the 'Frisco Reds were executed, and the group was well-nigh destroyed. In retaliation, the survivors meted out to Donnelly the death he had earned by his treason.

Nor did Timothy Donnelly long survive. The 'Frisco Reds pledged themselves to his execution. Every effort was made by the Oligarchy to save him. He was transferred from one part of the country to another. Three of the Reds lost their lives in vain efforts to get him. The Group was composed only of men. In the end they fell back on a woman, one of our comrades, and none other than Anna Roylston. Our Inner Circle forbade her, but she had ever a will of her own and disdained discipline. Furthermore, she was a genius and lovable, and we could never discipline her anyway. She is in a class by herself and not amenable to the ordinary standards of the revolutionists.

Despite our refusal to grant permission to do the deed, she went on with it. Now Anna Roylston was a fascinating woman. All she had to do was to beckon a man to her. She broke the hearts of scores of our young comrades, and scores of others she captured, and by their heart-strings led into our organization. Yet she steadfastly refused to marry. She dearly loved children, but she held that a child of her own would claim her from the Cause, and that it was the Cause to which her life was devoted.

It was an easy task for Anna Roylston to win Timothy Donnelly. Her conscience did not trouble her, for at that very time occurred the Nashville Massacre, when the Mercenaries, Donnelly in command, literally murdered eight hundred weavers of that city. But she did not kill Donnelly. She turned him over, a prisoner, to the 'Frisco Reds. This happened only last year, and now she had been renamed. The revolutionists everywhere are calling her the "Red Virgin."*

> * It was not until the Second Revolt was crushed, that the 'Frisco Reds flourished again. And for two generations the Group flourished. Then an agent of the Iron Heel managed to become a member, penetrated all its secrets, and brought about its total annihilation. This occurred in 2002 A.D. The members were executed one at a time, at intervals of three weeks, and their bodies exposed in the labor-ghetto of

San Francisco.

Colonel Ingram and Colonel Van Gilbert are two more familiar figures that I was later to encounter. Colonel Ingram rose high in the Oligarchy and became Minister to Germany. He was cordially detested by the proletariat of both countries. It was in Berlin that I met him, where, as an accredited international spy of the Iron Heel, I was received by him and afforded much assistance. Incidentally, I may state that in my dual role I managed a few important things for the Revolution.

Colonel Van Gilbert became known as "Snarling" Van Gilbert. His important part was played in drafting the new code after the Chicago Commune. But before that, as trial judge, he had earned sentence of death by his fiendish malignancy. I was one of those that tried him and passed sentence upon him. Anna Roylston carried out the execution.

Still another figure arises out of the old life—Jackson's lawyer. Least of all would I have expected again to meet this man, Joseph Hurd. It was a strange meeting. Late at night, two years after the Chicago Commune, Ernest and I arrived together at the Benton Harbor refuge. This was in Michigan, across the lake from Chicago. We arrived just at the conclusion of the trial of a spy. Sentence of death had been passed, and he was being led away. Such was the scene as we came upon it. The next moment the wretched man had wrenched free from his captors and flung himself at my feet, his arms clutching me about the knees in a vicelike grip as he prayed in a frenzy for mercy. As he turned his agonized face up to me, I recognized him as Joseph Hurd. Of all the terrible things I have witnessed, never have I been so unnerved as by this frantic creature's pleading for life. He was mad for life. It was pitiable. He refused to let go of me, despite the hands of a dozen comrades. And when at last he was dragged shrieking away, I sank down fainting upon the floor. It is far easier to see brave men die than to hear a coward beg for life.*

> * The Benton Harbor refuge was a catacomb, the entrance of which was cunningly contrived by way of a well. It has been maintained in a fair state of preservation, and the curious visitor may to-day tread its labyrinths to the assembly hall, where, without doubt, occurred the scene described by Avis Everhard. Farther on are the cells where the prisoners were confined, and the death chamber where the executions took place. Beyond is the cemetery—long, winding galleries hewn out of the solid rock, with recesses on either hand, wherein, tier above tier, lie the revolutionists just as they were laid away by their comrades long years agone.

CHAPTER XX

A LOST OLIGARCH

But in remembering the old life I have run ahead of my story into the new life. The wholesale jail delivery did not occur until well along into 1915. Complicated as it was, it was carried through without a hitch, and as a very creditable achievement it cheered us on in our work. From Cuba to California, out of scores of jails, military prisons, and fortresses, in a single night, we delivered fifty-one of our fifty-two Congressmen, and in addition over three hundred other leaders. There was not a single instance of miscarriage. Not only did they escape, but every one of them won to the refuges as planned. The one comrade Congressman we did not get was Arthur Simpson, and he had already died in Cabanas after cruel tortures.

The eighteen months that followed was perhaps the happiest of my life with Ernest. During that time we were never apart. Later, when we went back into the world, we were separated much. Not more impatiently do I await the flame of to-morrow's revolt than did I that night await the coming of Ernest. I had not seen him for so long, and the thought of a possible hitch or error in our plans that would keep him still in his island prison almost drove me mad. The hours passed like ages. I was all alone. Biedenbach, and three young men who had been living in the refuge, were out and over the mountain, heavily armed and prepared for anything. The refuges all over the land were quite empty, I imagine, of comrades that night.

Just as the sky paled with the first warning of dawn, I heard the signal from above and gave the answer. In the darkness I almost embraced Biedenbach, who came down first; but the next moment I was in Ernest's arms. And in that moment, so complete had been my transformation, I discovered it was only by an effort of will that I could be the old Avis Everhard, with the old mannerisms and smiles, phrases and intonations of voice. It was by strong effort only that I was able to maintain my old identity; I could not allow myself to forget for an instant, so automatically imperative had become the new personality I had created.

Once inside the little cabin, I saw Ernest's face in the light. With the exception of the prison pallor, there was no change in him—at least, not much. He was my same lover-husband and hero. And yet there was a certain ascetic lengthening of the lines of his face. But he could well stand it, for it seemed to add a certain nobility of refinement to the riotous excess of life that had always marked his features. He might have been a trifle graver than of yore, but the glint of laughter still was in his eyes. He was twenty pounds lighter, but in splendid physical condition. He had kept up exercise during the whole period of confinement, and his muscles were like iron. In truth, he was in better condition than when he had entered prison. Hours passed before his head touched pillow and I had soothed him off to sleep. But there was no sleep for me. I was too happy, and the fatigue of jail-breaking and riding horseback had not been mine.

While Ernest slept, I changed my dress, arranged my hair differently, and came back to my new automatic self. Then, when Biedenbach and the other comrades awoke, with their aid I concocted a little conspiracy. All was ready, and we were in the cave-room that served for kitchen and dining room when Ernest opened the door and entered. At that moment Biedenbach addressed me as Mary, and I turned and answered him. Then I glanced at Ernest with curious interest, such as any young comrade might betray on seeing for the first time so noted a hero of the Revolution. But Ernest's glance took me in and questioned impatiently past and around the room. The next moment I was being introduced to him as Mary Holmes.

To complete the deception, an extra plate was laid, and when we sat down to table one chair was not occupied. I could have cried with joy as I noted Ernest's increasing uneasiness and impatience. Finally he could stand it no longer.

"Where's my wife?" he demanded bluntly.

"She is still asleep," I answered.

It was the crucial moment. But my voice was a strange voice, and in it he recognized nothing familiar. The meal went on. I talked a great deal, and enthusiastically, as a hero-worshipper might talk, and it was obvious that he was my hero. I rose to a climax of enthusiasm and worship, and, before he could guess my intention, threw my arms around his neck and kissed him on the lips. He held me from him at arm's length and stared about in annoyance and perplexity. The four men greeted him with roars of laughter, and explanations were made. At first he was sceptical. He scrutinized me keenly and was half convinced, then shook his head and would not believe. It was not until I became the old Avis Everhard and whispered secrets in his ear that none knew but he and Avis Everhard, that he accepted me as his really, truly wife.

It was later in the day that he took me in his arms, manifesting great embarrassment and claiming polygamous emotions.

"You are my Avis," he said, "and you are also some one else. You are two women, and therefore you are my harem. At any rate, we are safe now. If the United States becomes too hot for us, why I have qualified for citizenship in Turkey."*

 * At that time polygamy was still practised in Turkey.

Life became for me very happy in the refuge. It is true, we worked hard and for long hours; but we worked together. We had each other for eighteen precious months, and we were not lonely, for there was always a coming and going of leaders and comrades—strange voices from the under-world of intrigue and revolution, bringing stranger tales of strife and war from all our battle-line. And there was much fun and delight. We were not mere gloomy conspirators. We toiled hard and suffered greatly, filled the gaps in our ranks and went on, and through all the labour and the play and interplay of life and death we found time to laugh and love. There were artists, scientists, scholars, musicians, and poets among us; and in that hole in the ground culture was higher and finer than in the palaces of wonder-cities of the oligarchs. In truth, many of our comrades toiled at making beautiful those same palaces and wonder-cities.*

> * This is not braggadocio on the part of Avis Everhard. The flower of the artistic and intellectual world were revolutionists. With the exception of a few of the musicians and singers, and of a few of the oligarchs, all the great creators of the period whose names have come down to us, were revolutionists.

Nor were we confined to the refuge itself. Often at night we rode over the mountains for exercise, and we rode on Wickson's horses. If only he knew how many revolutionists his horses have carried! We even went on picnics to isolated spots we knew, where we remained all day, going before daylight and returning after dark. Also, we used Wickson's cream and butter,* and Ernest was not above shooting Wickson's quail and rabbits, and, on occasion, his young bucks.

> * Even as late as that period, cream and butter were still crudely extracted from cow's milk. The laboratory preparation of foods had not yet begun.

Indeed, it was a safe refuge. I have said that it was discovered only once, and this brings me to the clearing up of the mystery of the disappearance of young Wickson. Now that he is dead, I am free to speak. There was a nook on the bottom of the great hole where the sun shone for several hours and which was hidden from above. Here we had carried many loads of gravel from the creek-bed, so that it was dry and warm, a pleasant basking place; and here, one afternoon, I was drowsing, half asleep, over a volume of Mendenhall.* I was so comfortable and secure that even his flaming lyrics failed to stir me.

> * In all the extant literature and documents of that period, continual reference is made to the poems of Rudolph Mendenhall. By his comrades he was called "The Flame." He was undoubtedly a great genius; yet, beyond weird and haunting fragments of his verse, quoted in the writings of others, nothing of his has come down to us. He was executed by the Iron Heel in 1928 A.D.

I was aroused by a clod of earth striking at my feet. Then from above, I heard a sound of scrambling. The next moment a young man, with a final slide down the crumbling wall, alighted at my feet. It was Philip Wickson, though I did not know him at the time. He looked at me coolly and uttered a low whistle of surprise.

"Well," he said; and the next moment, cap in hand, he was saying, "I beg your pardon. I did not expect to find any one here."

I was not so cool. I was still a tyro so far as concerned knowing how to behave in desperate circumstances. Later on, when I was an international spy, I should have been less clumsy, I am sure. As it was, I scrambled to my feet and cried out the danger call.

"Why did you do that?" he asked, looking at me searchingly.

It was evident that he had no suspicion of our presence when making the descent. I recognized this with relief.

"For what purpose do you think I did it?" I countered. I was indeed clumsy in those days.

"I don't know," he answered, shaking his head. "Unless you've got friends about. Anyway, you've got some explanations to make. I don't like the look of it. You are trespassing. This is my father's land, and—"

But at that moment, Biedenbach, every polite and gentle, said from behind him in a low voice, "Hands up, my young sir."

Young Wickson put his hands up first, then turned to confront Biedenbach, who held a thirty-thirty automatic rifle on him. Wickson was imperturbable.

"Oh, ho," he said, "a nest of revolutionists—and quite a hornet's nest it would seem. Well, you won't abide here long, I can tell you."

"Maybe you'll abide here long enough to reconsider that statement," Biedenbach said quietly. "And in the meanwhile I must ask you to come inside with me."

"Inside?" The young man was genuinely astonished. "Have you a catacomb here? I have heard of such things."

"Come and see," Biedenbach answered with his adorable accent.

"But it is unlawful," was the protest.

"Yes, by your law," the terrorist replied significantly. "But by our law, believe me, it is quite lawful. You must accustom yourself to the fact that you are in another world than the one of oppression and brutality in which you have lived."

"There is room for argument there," Wickson muttered.

"Then stay with us and discuss it."

The young fellow laughed and followed his captor into the house. He was led into the inner cave-room, and one of the young comrades left to guard him, while we discussed the situation in the kitchen.

Biedenbach, with tears in his eyes, held that Wickson must die, and was quite relieved when we outvoted him and his horrible proposition. On the other hand, we could not dream of allowing the young oligarch to depart.

"I'll tell you what to do," Ernest said. "We'll keep him and give him an education."

"I bespeak the privilege, then, of enlightening him in jurisprudence," Biedenbach cried.

And so a decision was laughingly reached. We would keep Philip Wickson a prisoner and educate him in our ethics and sociology. But in the meantime there was work to be done. All trace of the young oligarch must be obliterated. There were the marks he had left when descending the crumbling wall of the hole. This task fell to Biedenbach, and, slung on a rope from above, he toiled cunningly for the rest of the day till no sign remained. Back up the canyon from the lip of the hole all marks were likewise removed. Then, at twilight, came John Carlson, who demanded Wickson's shoes.

The young man did not want to give up his shoes, and even offered to fight for them, till he felt the horseshoer's strength in Ernest's hands. Carlson afterward reported several blisters and much grievous loss of skin due to the smallness of the shoes, but he succeeded in doing gallant work with them. Back from the lip of the hole, where ended the young man's obliterated trial, Carlson put on the shoes and walked away to the left. He walked for miles, around knolls, over ridges and through canyons, and finally covered the trail in the running water of a creek-bed. Here he removed the shoes, and, still hiding trail for a distance, at last put on his own shoes. A week later Wickson got back his shoes.

That night the hounds were out, and there was little sleep in the refuge. Next day, time and again, the baying hounds came down the canyon, plunged off to the left on the trail Carlson had made for them, and were lost to ear in the farther canyons high up the mountain. And all the time our men waited in the refuge, weapons in hand—automatic revolvers and rifles, to say nothing of half a dozen infernal machines of Biedenbach's manufacture. A more surprised party of rescuers could not be imagined, had they ventured down into our hiding-place.

I have now given the true disappearance of Philip Wickson, one-time oligarch, and, later, comrade in the Revolution. For we converted him in the end. His mind was fresh and plastic, and by nature he was very ethical. Several months later we rode him, on one of his father's horses, over Sonoma Mountains to Petaluma Creek and embarked him in a small fishing-launch. By easy stages we smuggled him along our underground railway to the Carmel refuge.

There he remained eight months, at the end of which time, for two reasons, he was loath to leave us. One reason was that he had fallen in love with Anna Roylston, and the other was that he had become one of us. It was not until he became convinced of the hopelessness of his love affair that he acceded to our wishes and went back to his father. Ostensibly an oligarch until his death, he was in reality one of the most valuable of our agents. Often and often has the Iron Heel been dumbfounded by the miscarriage of its plans and operations against us. If it but knew the number of its own members who are our agents, it would understand. Young Wickson never wavered in his loyalty to the Cause. In truth, his very death was incurred by his devotion to duty. In the great storm of 1927, while attending a meeting of our leaders, he contracted the pneumonia of which he died.*

> * The case of this young man was not unusual. Many young men of the Oligarchy, impelled by sense of right conduct, or

their imaginations captured by the glory of the Revolution, ethically or romantically devoted their lives to it. In similar way, many sons of the Russian nobility played their parts in the earlier and protracted revolution in that country.

CHAPTER XXI

THE ROARING ABYSMAL BEAST

During the long period of our stay in the refuge, we were kept closely in touch with what was happening in the world without, and we were learning thoroughly the strength of the Oligarchy with which we were at war. Out of the flux of transition the new institutions were forming more definitely and taking on the appearance and attributes of permanence. The oligarchs had succeeded in devising a governmental machine, as intricate as it was vast, that worked—and this despite all our efforts to clog and hamper.

This was a surprise to many of the revolutionists. They had not conceived it possible. Nevertheless the work of the country went on. The men toiled in the mines and fields—perforce they were no more than slaves. As for the vital industries, everything prospered. The members of the great labor castes were contented and worked on merrily. For the first time in their lives they knew industrial peace. No more were they worried by slack times, strike and lockout, and the union label. They lived in more comfortable homes and in delightful cities of their own—delightful compared with the slums and ghettos in which they had formerly dwelt. They had better food to eat, less hours of labor, more holidays, and a greater amount and variety of interests and pleasures. And for their less fortunate brothers and sisters, the unfavored laborers, the driven people of the abyss, they cared nothing. An age of selfishness was dawning upon mankind. And yet this is not altogether true. The labor castes were honeycombed by our agents—men whose eyes saw, beyond the belly-need, the radiant figure of liberty and brotherhood.

Another great institution that had taken form and was working smoothly was the Mercenaries. This body of soldiers had been evolved out of the old regular army and was now a million strong, to say nothing of the colonial forces. The Mercenaries constituted a race apart. They dwelt in cities of their own which were practically self-governed, and they were granted many privileges. By them a large portion of the perplexing surplus was consumed. They were losing all touch and sympathy with the rest of the people, and, in fact, were developing their own class morality and consciousness. And yet we had thousands of our agents among them.*

* The Mercenaries, in the last days of the Iron Heel, played
an important role. They constituted the balance of power in
the struggles between the labor castes and the oligarchs,
and now to one side and now to the other, threw their
strength according to the play of intrigue and conspiracy.

The oligarchs themselves were going through a remarkable and, it must be confessed, unexpected development. As a class, they disciplined themselves. Every member had his work to do in the world, and this work he was compelled to do. There were no more idle-rich young men. Their strength was used to give united strength to the Oligarchy. They served as leaders of troops and as lieutenants and captains of industry. They found careers in applied science, and many of them became great engineers. They went into the multitudinous divisions of the government, took service in the colonial possessions, and by tens of thousands went into the various secret services. They were, I may say, apprenticed to education, to art, to the church, to science, to literature; and in those fields they served the important function of moulding the thought-processes of the nation in the direction of the perpetuity of the Oligarchy.

They were taught, and later they in turn taught, that what they were doing was right. They assimilated the aristocratic idea from the moment they began, as children, to receive impressions of the world. The aristocratic idea was woven into the making of them until it became bone of them and flesh of them. They looked upon themselves as wild-animal trainers, rulers of beasts. From beneath their feet rose always the subterranean rumbles of revolt. Violent death ever stalked in their midst; bomb and knife and bullet were looked upon as so many fangs of the roaring abysmal beast they must dominate if humanity were to persist. They were the saviours of humanity, and they regarded themselves as heroic and sacrificing laborers for the highest good.

They, as a class, believed that they alone maintained civilization. It was their belief that if ever they weakened, the great beast would ingulf them and everything of beauty and wonder and joy and good in its cavernous and slime-dripping maw. Without them, anarchy would reign and humanity would drop backward into the primitive night out of which it had so painfully emerged. The horrid picture of anarchy was held always before their child's eyes until they, in turn, obsessed by this cultivated fear, held the picture of anarchy before the eyes of the children that followed them. This was the beast to be stamped upon, and the highest duty of the aristocrat was to stamp upon it. In short, they alone, by their unremitting toil and sacrifice, stood between weak humanity and the all-devouring beast; and they believed it, firmly believed it.

I cannot lay too great stress upon this high ethical righteousness of the whole oligarch class. This has been the strength of the Iron Heel, and too many of the comrades have been slow or loath to realize it. Many of them have ascribed the strength of the Iron Heel to its system of reward and punishment. This is a mistake. Heaven and hell may be the prime factors of zeal in the religion of a fanatic; but for the great majority of the religious, heaven and hell are incidental to right and wrong. Love of the right, desire for the right, unhappiness with anything less than the right—in short, right conduct, is the prime factor of religion. And so with the Oligarchy. Prisons, banishment and degradation, honors and palaces and wonder-cities, are all incidental.

The great driving force of the oligarchs is the belief that they are doing right. Never mind the exceptions, and never mind the oppression and injustice in which the Iron Heel was conceived. All is granted. The point is that the strength of the Oligarchy today lies in its satisfied conception of its own righteousness.*

* Out of the ethical incoherency and inconsistency of capitalism, the oligarchs emerged with a new ethics, coherent and definite, sharp and severe as steel, the most absurd and unscientific and at the same time the most potent ever possessed by any tyrant class. The oligarchs believed their ethics, in spite of the fact that biology and evolution gave them the lie; and, because of their faith, for three centuries they were able to hold back the mighty tide of human progress—a spectacle, profound, tremendous, puzzling to the metaphysical moralist, and one that to the materialist is the cause of many doubts and reconsiderations.

For that matter, the strength of the Revolution, during these frightful twenty years, has resided in nothing else than the sense of righteousness. In no other way can be explained our sacrifices and martyrdoms. For no other reason did Rudolph Mendenhall flame out his soul for the Cause and sing his wild swan-song that last night of life. For no other reason did Hurlbert die under torture, refusing to the last to betray his comrades. For no other reason has Anna Roylston refused blessed motherhood. For no other reason has John Carlson been the faithful and unrewarded custodian of the Glen Ellen Refuge. It does not matter, young or old, man or woman, high or low, genius or clod, go where one will among the comrades of the Revolution, the motor-force will be found to be a great and abiding desire for the right.

But I have run away from my narrative. Ernest and I well understood, before we left the refuge, how the strength of the Iron Heel was developing. The labor castes, the Mercenaries, and the great hordes of secret agents and police of various sorts were all pledged to the Oligarchy. In the main, and ignoring the loss of liberty, they were better off than they had been. On the other hand, the great helpless mass of the population, the people of the abyss, was sinking into a brutish apathy of content with misery. Whenever strong proletarians asserted their strength in the midst of the mass, they were drawn away from the mass by the oligarchs and given better conditions by being made members of the labor castes or of the Mercenaries. Thus discontent was lulled and the proletariat robbed of its natural leaders.

The condition of the people of the abyss was pitiable. Common school education, so far as they were concerned, had ceased. They lived like beasts in great squalid labor-ghettos, festering in misery and degradation. All their old liberties were gone. They were labor-slaves. Choice of work was denied them. Likewise was denied them the right to move from place to place, or the right to bear or possess arms. They were not land serfs like the farmers. They were machine-serfs and labor-serfs. When unusual needs arose for them, such as the building of the great highways and air-lines, of canals, tunnels, subways, and fortifications, levies were made on the labor-ghettos, and tens of thousands of serfs, willy-nilly, were transported to the scene of operations. Great armies of them are toiling now at the building of Ardis, housed in wretched barracks where family life cannot exist, and where decency is displaced by dull bestiality. In all truth, there in the labor-ghettos is the roaring abysmal beast the oligarchs fear so dreadfully—but it is the beast of their own making. In it they will not let the ape and tiger die.

And just now the word has gone forth that new levies are being imposed for the building of Asgard, the projected wonder-city that will far exceed Ardis when the latter is completed.* We of the Revolution will go on with that great work, but it will not be done by the miserable serfs. The walls and towers and shafts of that fair city will arise to the sound of singing, and into its beauty and wonder will be woven, not sighs and groans, but music and laughter.

> * Ardis was completed in 1942 A.D., Asgard was not completed until 1984 A.D. It was fifty-two years in the building, during which time a permanent army of half a million serfs was employed. At times these numbers swelled to over a million—without any account being taken of the hundreds of thousands of the labor castes and the artists.

Ernest was madly impatient to be out in the world and doing, for our ill-fated First Revolt, that had miscarried in the Chicago Commune, was ripening fast. Yet he possessed his soul with patience, and during this time of his torment, when Hadly, who had been brought for the purpose from Illinois, made him over into another man* he revolved great plans in his head for the organization of the learned proletariat, and for the maintenance of at least the rudiments of education amongst the people of the abyss—all this of course in the event of the First Revolt being a failure.

> * Among the Revolutionists were many surgeons, and in vivisection they attained marvellous proficiency. In Avis Everhard's words, they could literally make a man over. To them the elimination of scars and disfigurements was a trivial detail. They changed the features with such microscopic care that no traces were left of their handiwork. The nose was a favorite organ to work upon. Skin-grafting and hair-transplanting were among their commonest devices. The changes in expression they accomplished were wizard-like. Eyes and eyebrows, lips, mouths, and ears, were radically altered. By cunning operations on tongue, throat, larynx, and nasal cavities a man's whole enunciation and manner of speech could be changed. Desperate times give need for desperate remedies, and the surgeons of the Revolution rose to the need. Among other things, they could increase an adult's stature by as much as four or five inches and decrease it by one or two

> inches. What they did is to-day a lost art. We have no need for it.

It was not until January, 1917, that we left the refuge. All had been arranged. We took our place at once as agents-provocateurs in the scheme of the Iron Heel. I was supposed to be Ernest's sister. By oligarchs and comrades on the inside who were high in authority, place had been made for us, we were in possession of all necessary documents, and our pasts were accounted for. With help on the inside, this was not difficult, for in that shadow-world of secret service identity was nebulous. Like ghosts the agents came and went, obeying commands, fulfilling duties, following clews, making their reports often to officers they never saw or cooperating with other agents they had never seen before and would never see again.

CHAPTER XXII

THE CHICAGO COMMUNE

As agents-provocateurs, not alone were we able to travel a great deal, but our very work threw us in contact with the proletariat and with our comrades, the revolutionists. Thus we were in both camps at the same time, ostensibly serving the Iron Heel and secretly working with all our might for the Cause. There were many of us in the various secret services of the Oligarchy, and despite the shakings-up and reorganizations the secret services have undergone, they have never been able to weed all of us out.

Ernest had largely planned the First Revolt, and the date set had been somewhere early in the spring of 1918. In the fall of 1917 we were not ready; much remained to be done, and when the Revolt was precipitated, of course it was doomed to failure. The plot of necessity was frightfully intricate, and anything premature was sure to destroy it. This the Iron Heel foresaw and laid its schemes accordingly.

We had planned to strike our first blow at the nervous system of the Oligarchy. The latter had remembered the general strike, and had guarded against the defection of the telegraphers by installing wireless stations, in the control of the Mercenaries. We, in turn, had countered this move. When the signal was given, from every refuge, all over the land, and from the cities, and towns, and barracks, devoted comrades were to go forth and blow up the wireless stations. Thus at the first shock would the Iron Heel be brought to earth and lie practically dismembered.

At the same moment, other comrades were to blow up the bridges and tunnels and disrupt the whole network of railroads. Still further, other groups of comrades, at the signal, were to seize the officers of the Mercenaries and the police, as well as all Oligarchs of unusual ability or who held executive positions. Thus would the leaders of the enemy be removed from the field of the local battles that would inevitably be fought all over the land.

Many things were to occur simultaneously when the signal went forth. The Canadian and Mexican patriots, who were far stronger than the Iron Heel dreamed, were to duplicate our tactics. Then there were comrades (these were the women, for the men would be busy elsewhere) who were to post the proclamations from our secret presses. Those of us in the higher employ of the Iron Heel were to proceed immediately to make confusion and anarchy in all our departments. Inside the Mercenaries were thousands of our comrades. Their work was to blow up the magazines and to destroy the delicate mechanism of all the war machinery. In the cities of the Mercenaries and of the labor castes similar programmes of disruption were to be carried out.

In short, a sudden, colossal, stunning blow was to be struck. Before the paralyzed Oligarchy could recover itself, its end would have come. It would have meant terrible times and great loss of life, but no revolutionist hesitates at such things. Why, we even depended much, in our plan, on the unorganized people of the abyss. They were to be loosed on the palaces and cities of the masters. Never mind the destruction of life and property. Let the abysmal brute roar and the police and Mercenaries slay. The abysmal brute would roar anyway, and the police and Mercenaries would slay anyway. It would merely mean that various dangers to us were harmlessly destroying one another. In the meantime we would be doing our own work, largely unhampered, and gaining control of all the machinery of society.

Such was our plan, every detail of which had to be worked out in secret, and, as the day drew near, communicated to more and more comrades. This was the danger point, the stretching of the conspiracy. But that danger-point was never reached. Through its spy-system the Iron Heel got wind of the Revolt and prepared to teach us another of its bloody lessons. Chicago was the devoted city selected for the instruction, and well were we instructed.

Chicago* was the ripest of all—Chicago which of old time was the city of blood and which was to earn anew its name. There the revolutionary spirit was strong. Too many bitter strikes had been curbed there in the days of capitalism for the workers to forget and forgive. Even the labor castes of the city were alive with revolt. Too many heads had been broken in the early strikes. Despite their changed and favorable conditions, their hatred for the master class had not died. This spirit had infected the Mercenaries, of which three regiments in particular were ready to come over to us en masse.

> * Chicago was the industrial inferno of the nineteenth century A.D. A curious anecdote has come down to us of John Burns, a great English labor leader and one time member of the British Cabinet. In Chicago, while on a visit to the United States, he was asked by a newspaper reporter for his opinion of that city. "Chicago," he answered, "is a pocket edition of hell." Some time later, as he was going aboard his steamer to sail to England, he was approached by another reporter, who wanted to know if he had changed his opinion of Chicago. "Yes, I have," was his reply. "My present opinion is that hell is a pocket edition of Chicago."

Chicago had always been the storm-centre of the conflict between labor and capital, a city of street-battles and violent death, with a class-conscious capitalist organization and a class-conscious workman organization, where, in the old days, the very school-teachers were formed into labor unions and affiliated with the hod-carriers and bricklayers in the American Federation of Labor. And Chicago became the storm-centre of the premature First Revolt.

The trouble was precipitated by the Iron Heel. It was cleverly done. The whole population, including the favored labor castes, was given a course of outrageous treatment. Promises and agreements were broken, and most drastic punishments visited upon even petty offenders. The people of the abyss were tormented out of their apathy. In fact, the Iron Heel was preparing to make the abysmal beast roar. And hand in hand with this, in all precautionary measures in Chicago, the Iron Heel was inconceivably careless. Discipline was relaxed among the Mercenaries that remained, while many regiments had been withdrawn and sent to various parts of the country.

It did not take long to carry out this programme—only several weeks. We of the Revolution caught vague rumors of the state of affairs, but had nothing definite enough for an understanding. In fact, we thought it was a spontaneous spirit of revolt that would require careful curbing on our part, and never dreamed that it was deliberately manufactured—and it had been manufactured so secretly, from the very innermost circle of the Iron Heel, that we had got no inkling. The counter-plot was an able achievement, and ably carried out.

I was in New York when I received the order to proceed immediately to Chicago. The man who gave me the order was one of the oligarchs, I could tell that by his speech, though I did not know his name nor see his face. His instructions were too clear for me to make a mistake. Plainly I read between the lines that our plot had been discovered, that we had been countermined. The explosion was ready for the flash of powder, and countless agents of the Iron Heel, including me, either on the ground or being sent there, were to supply that flash. I flatter myself that I maintained my composure under the keen eye of the oligarch, but my heart was beating madly. I could almost have shrieked and flown at his throat with my naked hands before his final, cold-blooded instructions were given.

Once out of his presence, I calculated the time. I had just the moments to spare, if I were lucky, to get in touch with some local leader before catching my train. Guarding against being trailed, I made a rush of it for the Emergency Hospital. Luck was with me, and I gained access at once to comrade Galvin, the surgeon-in-chief. I started to gasp out my information, but he stopped me.

"I already know," he said quietly, though his Irish eyes were flashing. "I knew what you had come for. I got the word fifteen minutes ago, and I have already passed it along. Everything shall be done here to keep the comrades quiet. Chicago is to be sacrificed, but it shall be Chicago alone."

"Have you tried to get word to Chicago?" I asked.

He shook his head. "No telegraphic communication. Chicago is shut off. It's going to be hell there."

He paused a moment, and I saw his white hands clinch. Then he burst out:

"By God! I wish I were going to be there!"

"There is yet a chance to stop it," I said, "if nothing happens to the train and I can get there in time. Or if some of the other secret-service comrades who have learned the truth can get there in time."

"You on the inside were caught napping this time," he said.

I nodded my head humbly.

"It was very secret," I answered. "Only the inner chiefs could have known up to to-day. We haven't yet penetrated that far, so we couldn't escape being kept in the dark. If only Ernest were here. Maybe he is in Chicago now, and all is well."

Dr. Galvin shook his head. "The last news I heard of him was that he had been sent to Boston or New Haven. This secret service for the enemy must hamper him a lot, but it's better than lying in a refuge."

I started to go, and Galvin wrung my hand.

"Keep a stout heart," were his parting words. "What if the First Revolt is lost? There will be a second, and we will be wiser then. Good-by and good luck. I don't know whether I'll ever see you again. It's going to be hell there, but I'd give ten years of my life for your chance to be in it."

The Twentieth Century* left New York at six in the evening, and was supposed to arrive at Chicago at seven next morning. But it lost time that night. We were running behind another train. Among the travellers in my Pullman was comrade Hartman, like myself in the secret service of the Iron Heel. He it was who told me of the train that immediately preceded us. It was an exact duplicate of our train, though it contained no passengers. The idea was that the empty train should receive the disaster were an attempt made to blow up the Twentieth Century. For that matter there were very few people on the train—only a baker's dozen in our car.

* This was reputed to be the fastest train in the world then. It was quite a famous train.

"There must be some big men on board," Hartman concluded. "I noticed a private car on the rear."

Night had fallen when we made our first change of engine, and I walked down the platform for a breath of fresh air and to see what I could see. Through the windows of the private car I caught a glimpse of three men whom I recognized. Hartman was right. One of the men was General Altendorff; and the other two were Mason and Vanderbold, the brains of the inner circle of the Oligarchy's secret service.

It was a quiet moonlight night, but I tossed restlessly and could not sleep. At five in the morning I dressed and abandoned my bed.

I asked the maid in the dressing-room how late the train was, and she told me two hours. She was a mulatto woman, and I noticed that her face was haggard, with great circles under the eyes, while the eyes themselves were wide with some haunting fear.

"What is the matter?" I asked.

"Nothing, miss; I didn't sleep well, I guess," was her reply.

I looked at her closely, and tried her with one of our signals. She responded, and I made sure of her.

"Something terrible is going to happen in Chicago," she said. "There's that fake* train in front of us. That and the troop-trains have made us late."

    * False.

"Troop-trains?" I queried.

She nodded her head. "The line is thick with them. We've been passing them all night. And they're all heading for Chicago. And bringing them over the air-line—that means business.

"I've a lover in Chicago," she added apologetically. "He's one of us, and he's in the Mercenaries, and I'm afraid for him."

Poor girl. Her lover was in one of the three disloyal regiments.

Hartman and I had breakfast together in the dining car, and I forced myself to eat. The sky had clouded, and the train rushed on like a sullen thunderbolt through the gray pall of advancing day. The very negroes that waited on us knew that something terrible was impending. Oppression sat heavily upon them; the lightness of their natures had ebbed out of them; they were slack and absent-minded in their service, and they whispered gloomily to one another in the far end of the car next to the kitchen. Hartman was hopeless over the situation.

"What can we do?" he demanded for the twentieth time, with a helpless shrug of the shoulders.

He pointed out of the window. "See, all is ready. You can depend upon it that they're holding them like this, thirty or forty miles outside the city, on every road."

He had reference to troop-trains on the side-track. The soldiers were cooking their breakfasts over fires built on the ground beside the track, and they looked up curiously at us as we thundered past without slackening our terrific speed.

All was quiet as we entered Chicago. It was evident nothing had happened yet. In the suburbs the morning papers came on board the train. There was nothing in them, and yet there was much in them for those skilled in reading between the lines that it was intended the ordinary reader should read into the text. The fine hand of the Iron Heel was apparent in every column. Glimmerings of weakness in the armor of the Oligarchy were given. Of course, there was nothing definite. It was intended that the reader should feel his way to these glimmerings. It was cleverly done. As fiction, those morning papers of October 27th were masterpieces.

The local news was missing. This in itself was a masterstroke. It shrouded Chicago in mystery, and it suggested to the average Chicago reader that the Oligarchy did not dare give the local news. Hints that were untrue, of course, were given of insubordination all over the land, crudely disguised with complacent references to punitive measures to be taken. There were reports of numerous wireless stations that had been blown up, with heavy rewards offered for the detection of the perpetrators. Of course no wireless stations had been blown up. Many similar outrages, that dovetailed with the plot of the revolutionists, were given. The impression to be made on the minds of the Chicago comrades was that the general Revolt was beginning, albeit with a confusing miscarriage in many details. It was impossible for one uninformed to escape the vague yet certain feeling that all the land was ripe for the revolt that had already begun to break out.

It was reported that the defection of the Mercenaries in California had become so serious that half a dozen regiments had been disbanded and broken, and that their members with their families had been driven from their own city and on into the labor-ghettos. And the California Mercenaries were in reality the most faithful of all to their salt! But how was Chicago, shut off from the rest of the world, to know? Then there was a ragged telegram describing an outbreak of the populace in New York City, in which the labor castes were joining, concluding with the statement (intended to be accepted as a bluff*) that the troops had the situation in hand.

* A lie.

And as the oligarchs had done with the morning papers, so had they done in a thousand other ways. These we learned afterward, as, for example, the secret messages of the oligarchs, sent with the express purpose of leaking to the ears of the revolutionists, that had come over the wires, now and again, during the first part of the night.

"I guess the Iron Heel won't need our services," Hartman remarked, putting down the paper he had been reading, when the train pulled into the central depot. "They wasted their time sending us here. Their plans have evidently prospered better than they expected. Hell will break loose any second now."

He turned and looked down the train as we alighted.

"I thought so," he muttered. "They dropped that private car when the papers came aboard."

Hartman was hopelessly depressed. I tried to cheer him up, but he ignored my effort and suddenly began talking very hurriedly, in a low voice, as we passed through the station. At first I could not understand.

"I have not been sure," he was saying, "and I have told no one. I have been working on it for weeks, and I cannot make sure. Watch out for Knowlton. I suspect him. He knows the secrets of a score of our refuges. He carries the lives of hundreds of us in his hands, and I think he is a traitor. It's more a feeling on my part than anything else. But I thought I marked a change in him a short while back. There is the danger that he has sold us out, or is going to sell us out. I am almost sure of it. I wouldn't whisper my suspicions to a soul, but, somehow, I don't think I'll leave Chicago alive. Keep your eye on Knowlton. Trap him. Find out. I don't know anything more. It is only an intuition, and so far I have failed to find the slightest clew." We were just stepping out upon the sidewalk. "Remember," Hartman concluded earnestly. "Keep your eyes upon Knowlton."

And Hartman was right. Before a month went by Knowlton paid for his treason with his life. He was formally executed by the comrades in Milwaukee.

All was quiet on the streets—too quiet. Chicago lay dead. There was no roar and rumble of traffic. There were not even cabs on the streets. The surface cars and the elevated were not running. Only occasionally, on the sidewalks, were there stray pedestrians, and these pedestrians did not loiter. They went their ways with great haste and definiteness, withal there was a curious indecision in their movements, as though they expected the buildings to topple over on them or the sidewalks to sink under their feet or fly up in the air. A few gamins, however, were around, in their eyes a suppressed eagerness in anticipation of wonderful and exciting things to happen.

From somewhere, far to the south, the dull sound of an explosion came to our ears. That was all. Then quiet again, though the gamins had startled and listened, like young deer, at the sound. The doorways to all the buildings were closed; the shutters to the shops were up. But there were many police and watchmen in evidence, and now and again automobile patrols of the Mercenaries slipped swiftly past.

Hartman and I agreed that it was useless to report ourselves to the local chiefs of the secret service. Our failure so to report would be excused, we knew, in the light of subsequent events. So we headed for the great labor-ghetto on the South Side in the hope of getting in contact with some of the comrades. Too late! We knew it. But we could not stand still and do nothing in those ghastly, silent streets. Where was Ernest? I was wondering. What was happening in the cities of the labor castes and Mercenaries? In the fortresses?

As if in answer, a great screaming roar went up, dim with distance, punctuated with detonation after detonation.

"It's the fortresses," Hartman said. "God pity those three regiments!"

At a crossing we noticed, in the direction of the stockyards, a gigantic pillar of smoke. At the next crossing several similar smoke pillars were rising skyward in the direction of the West Side. Over the city of the Mercenaries we saw a great captive war-balloon that burst even as we looked at it, and fell in flaming wreckage toward the earth. There was no clew to that tragedy of the air. We could not determine whether the balloon had been manned by comrades or enemies. A vague sound came to our ears, like the bubbling of a gigantic caldron a long way off, and Hartman said it was machine-guns and automatic rifles.

And still we walked in immediate quietude. Nothing was happening where we were. The police and the automobile patrols went by, and once half a dozen fire-engines, returning evidently from some conflagration. A question was called to the fireman by an officer in an automobile, and we heard one shout in reply: "No water! They've blown up the mains!"

"We've smashed the water supply," Hartman cried excitedly to me. "If we can do all this in a premature, isolated, abortive attempt, what can't we do in a concerted, ripened effort all over the land?"

The automobile containing the officer who had asked the question darted on. Suddenly there was a deafening roar. The machine, with its human freight, lifted in an upburst of smoke, and sank down a mass of wreckage and death.

Hartman was jubilant. "Well done! well done!" he was repeating, over and over, in a whisper. "The proletariat gets its lesson to-day, but it gives one, too."

Police were running for the spot. Also, another patrol machine had halted. As for myself, I was in a daze. The suddenness of it was stunning. How had it happened? I knew not how, and yet I had been looking directly at it. So dazed was I for the moment that I was scarcely aware of the fact that we were being held up by the police. I abruptly saw that a policeman was in the act of shooting Hartman. But Hartman was cool and was giving the proper passwords. I saw the levelled revolver hesitate, then sink down, and heard the disgusted grunt of the policeman. He was very angry, and was cursing the whole secret service. It was always in the way, he was averring, while Hartman was talking back to him and with fitting secret-service pride explaining to him the clumsiness of the police.

The next moment I knew how it had happened. There was quite a group about the wreck, and two men were just lifting up the wounded officer to carry him to the other machine. A panic seized all of them, and they scattered in every direction, running in blind terror, the wounded officer, roughly dropped, being left behind. The cursing policeman alongside of me also ran, and Hartman and I ran, too, we knew not why, obsessed with the same blind terror to get away from that particular spot.

Nothing really happened then, but everything was explained. The flying men were sheepishly coming back, but all the while their eyes were raised apprehensively to the many-windowed, lofty buildings that towered like the sheer walls of a canyon on each side of the street. From one of those countless windows the bomb had been thrown, but which window? There had been no second bomb, only a fear of one.

Thereafter we looked with speculative comprehension at the windows. Any of them contained possible death. Each building was a possible ambuscade. This was warfare in that modern jungle, a great city. Every street was a canyon, every building a mountain. We had not changed much from primitive man, despite the war automobiles that were sliding by.

Turning a corner, we came upon a woman. She was lying on the pavement, in a pool of blood. Hartman bent over and examined her. As for myself, I turned deathly sick. I was to see many dead that day, but the total carnage was not to affect me as did this first forlorn body lying there at my feet abandoned on the pavement. "Shot in the breast," was Hartman's report. Clasped in the hollow of her arm, as a child might be clasped, was a bundle of printed matter. Even in death she seemed loath to part with that which had caused her death; for when Hartman had succeeded in withdrawing the bundle, we found that it consisted of large printed sheets, the proclamations of the revolutionists.

"A comrade," I said.

But Hartman only cursed the Iron Heel, and we passed on. Often we were halted by the police and patrols, but our passwords enabled us to proceed. No more bombs fell from the windows, the last pedestrians seemed to have vanished from the streets, and our immediate quietude grew more profound; though the gigantic caldron continued to bubble in the distance, dull roars of explosions came to us from all directions, and the smoke-pillars were towering more ominously in the heavens.

CHAPTER XXIII

THE PEOPLE OF THE ABYSS

Suddenly a change came over the face of things. A tingle of excitement ran along the air. Automobiles fled past, two, three, a dozen, and from them warnings were shouted to us. One of the machines swerved wildly at high speed half a block down, and the next moment, already left well behind it, the pavement was torn into a great hole by a bursting bomb. We saw the police disappearing down the cross-streets on the run, and knew that something terrible was coming. We could hear the rising roar of it.

"Our brave comrades are coming," Hartman said.

We could see the front of their column filling the street from gutter to gutter, as the last war-automobile fled past. The machine stopped for a moment just abreast of us. A soldier leaped from it, carrying something carefully in his hands. This, with the same care, he deposited in the gutter. Then he leaped back to his seat and the machine dashed on, took the turn at the corner, and was gone from sight. Hartman ran to the gutter and stooped over the object.

"Keep back," he warned me.

I could see he was working rapidly with his hands. When he returned to me the sweat was heavy on his forehead.

"I disconnected it," he said, "and just in the nick of time. The soldier was clumsy. He intended it for our comrades, but he didn't give it enough time. It would have exploded prematurely. Now it won't explode at all."

Everything was happening rapidly now. Across the street and half a block down, high up in a building, I could see heads peering out. I had just pointed them out to Hartman, when a sheet of flame and smoke ran along that portion of the face of the building where the heads had appeared, and the air was shaken by the explosion. In places the stone facing of the building was torn away, exposing the iron construction beneath. The next moment similar sheets of flame and smoke smote the front of the building across the street opposite it. Between the explosions we could hear the rattle of the automatic pistols and rifles. For several minutes this mid-air battle continued, then died out. It was patent that our comrades were in one building, that Mercenaries were in the other, and that they were fighting across the street. But we could not tell which was which—which building contained our comrades and which the Mercenaries.

By this time the column on the street was almost on us. As the front of it passed under the warring buildings, both went into action again—one building dropping bombs into the street, being attacked from across the street, and in return replying to that attack. Thus we learned which building was held by our comrades, and they did good work, saving those in the street from the bombs of the enemy.

Hartman gripped my arm and dragged me into a wide entrance.

"They're not our comrades," he shouted in my ear.

The inner doors to the entrance were locked and bolted. We could not escape. The next moment the front of the column went by. It was not a column, but a mob, an awful river that filled the street, the people of the abyss, mad with drink and wrong, up at last and roaring for the blood of their masters. I had seen the people of the abyss before, gone through its ghettos, and thought I knew it; but I found that I was now looking on it for the first time. Dumb apathy had vanished. It was now dynamic—a fascinating spectacle of dread. It surged past my vision in concrete waves of wrath, snarling and growling, carnivorous, drunk with whiskey from pillaged warehouses, drunk with hatred, drunk with lust for blood—men, women, and children, in rags and tatters, dim ferocious intelligences with all the godlike blotted from their features and all the fiendlike stamped in, apes and tigers, anaemic consumptives and great hairy beasts of burden, wan faces from which vampire society had sucked the juice of life, bloated forms swollen with physical grossness and corruption, withered hags and death's-heads bearded like patriarchs, festering youth and festering age, faces of fiends, crooked, twisted, misshapen monsters blasted with the ravages of disease and all the horrors of chronic innutrition—the refuse and the scum of life, a raging, screaming, screeching, demoniacal horde.

And why not? The people of the abyss had nothing to lose but the misery and pain of living. And to gain?—nothing, save one final, awful glut of vengeance. And as I looked the thought came to me that in that rushing stream of human lava were men, comrades and heroes, whose mission had been to rouse the abysmal beast and to keep the enemy occupied in coping with it.

And now a strange thing happened to me. A transformation came over me. The fear of death, for myself and for others, left me. I was strangely exalted, another being in another life. Nothing mattered. The Cause for this one time was lost, but the Cause would be here to-morrow, the same Cause, ever fresh and ever burning. And thereafter, in the orgy of horror that raged through the succeeding hours, I was able to take a calm interest. Death meant nothing, life meant nothing. I was an interested spectator of events, and, sometimes swept on by the rush, was myself a curious participant. For my mind had leaped to a star-cool altitude and grasped a passionless transvaluation of values. Had it not done this, I know that I should have died.

Half a mile of the mob had swept by when we were discovered. A woman in fantastic rags, with cheeks cavernously hollow and with narrow black eyes like burning gimlets, caught a glimpse of Hartman and me. She let out a shrill shriek and bore in upon us. A section of the mob tore itself loose and surged in after her. I can see her now, as I write these lines, a leap in advance, her gray hair flying in thin tangled strings, the blood dripping down her forehead from some wound in the scalp, in her right hand a hatchet, her left hand, lean and wrinkled, a yellow talon, gripping the air convulsively. Hartman sprang in front of me. This was no time for explanations. We were well dressed, and that was enough. His fist shot out, striking the woman between her burning eyes. The impact of the blow drove her backward, but she struck the wall of her on-coming fellows and bounced forward again, dazed and helpless, the brandished hatchet falling feebly on Hartman's shoulder.

The next moment I knew not what was happening. I was overborne by the crowd. The confined space was filled with shrieks and yells and curses. Blows were falling on me. Hands were ripping and tearing at my flesh and garments. I felt that I was being torn to pieces. I was being borne down, suffocated. Some strong hand gripped my shoulder in the thick of the press and was dragging fiercely at me. Between pain and pressure I fainted. Hartman never came out of that entrance. He had shielded me and received the first brunt of the attack. This had saved me, for the jam had quickly become too dense for anything more than the mad gripping and tearing of hands.

I came to in the midst of wild movement. All about me was the same movement. I had been caught up in a monstrous flood that was sweeping me I knew not whither. Fresh air was on my cheek and biting sweetly in my lungs. Faint and dizzy, I was vaguely aware of a strong arm around my body under the arms, and half-lifting me and dragging me along. Feebly my own limbs were helping me. In front of me I could see the moving back of a man's coat. It had been slit from top to bottom along the centre seam, and it pulsed rhythmically, the slit opening and closing regularly with every leap of the wearer. This phenomenon fascinated me for a time, while my senses were coming back to me. Next I became aware of stinging cheeks and nose, and could feel blood dripping on my face. My hat was gone. My hair was down and flying, and from the stinging of the scalp I managed to recollect a hand in the press of the entrance that had torn at my hair. My chest and arms were bruised and aching in a score of places.

My brain grew clearer, and I turned as I ran and looked at the man who was holding me up. He it was who had dragged me out and saved me. He noticed my movement.

"It's all right!" he shouted hoarsely. "I knew you on the instant."

I failed to recognize him, but before I could speak I trod upon something that was alive and that squirmed under my foot. I was swept on by those behind and could not look down and see, and yet I knew that it was a woman who had fallen and who was being trampled into the pavement by thousands of successive feet.

"It's all right," he repeated. "I'm Garthwaite."

He was bearded and gaunt and dirty, but I succeeded in remembering him as the stalwart youth that had spent several months in our Glen Ellen refuge three years before. He passed me the signals of the Iron Heel's secret service, in token that he, too, was in its employ.

"I'll get you out of this as soon as I can get a chance," he assured me. "But watch your footing. On your life don't stumble and go down."

All things happened abruptly on that day, and with an abruptness that was sickening the mob checked itself. I came in violent collision with a large woman in front of me (the man with the split coat had vanished), while those behind collided against me. A devilish pandemonium reigned,—shrieks, curses, and cries of death, while above all rose the churning rattle of machine-guns and the put-a-put, put-a-put of rifles. At first I could make out nothing. People were falling about me right and left. The woman in front doubled up and went down, her hands on her abdomen in a frenzied clutch. A man was quivering against my legs in a death-struggle.

It came to me that we were at the head of the column. Half a mile of it had disappeared—where or how I never learned. To this day I do not know what became of that half-mile of humanity—whether it was blotted out by some frightful bolt of war, whether it was scattered and destroyed piecemeal, or whether it escaped. But there we were, at the head of the column instead of in its middle, and we were being swept out of life by a torrent of shrieking lead.

As soon as death had thinned the jam, Garthwaite, still grasping my arm, led a rush of survivors into the wide entrance of an office building. Here, at the rear, against the doors, we were pressed by a panting, gasping mass of creatures. For some time we remained in this position without a change in the situation.

"I did it beautifully," Garthwaite was lamenting to me. "Ran you right into a trap. We had a gambler's chance in the street, but in here there is no chance at all. It's all over but the shouting. Vive la Revolution!"

Then, what he expected, began. The Mercenaries were killing without quarter. At first, the surge back upon us was crushing, but as the killing continued the pressure was eased. The dead and dying went down and made room. Garthwaite put his mouth to my ear and shouted, but in the frightful din I could not catch what he said. He did not wait. He seized me and threw me down. Next he dragged a dying woman over on top of me, and, with much squeezing and shoving, crawled in beside me and partly over me. A mound of dead and dying began to pile up over us, and over this mound, pawing and moaning, crept those that still survived. But these, too, soon ceased, and a semi-silence settled down, broken by groans and sobs and sounds of strangulation.

I should have been crushed had it not been for Garthwaite. As it was, it seemed inconceivable that I could bear the weight I did and live. And yet, outside of pain, the only feeling I possessed was one of curiosity. How was it going to end? What would death be like? Thus did I receive my red baptism in that Chicago shambles. Prior to that, death to me had been a theory; but ever afterward death has been a simple fact that does not matter, it is so easy.

But the Mercenaries were not content with what they had done. They invaded the entrance, killing the wounded and searching out the unhurt that, like ourselves, were playing dead. I remember one man they dragged out of a heap, who pleaded abjectly until a revolver shot cut him short. Then there was a woman who charged from a heap, snarling and shooting. She fired six shots before they got her, though what damage she did we could not know. We could follow these tragedies only by the sound. Every little while flurries like this occurred, each flurry culminating in the revolver shot that put an end to it. In the intervals we could hear the soldiers talking and swearing as they rummaged among the carcasses, urged on by their officers to hurry up.

At last they went to work on our heap, and we could feel the pressure diminish as they dragged away the dead and wounded. Garthwaite began uttering aloud the signals. At first he was not heard. Then he raised his voice.

"Listen to that," we heard a soldier say. And next the sharp voice of an officer. "Hold on there! Careful as you go!"

Oh, that first breath of air as we were dragged out! Garthwaite did the talking at first, but I was compelled to undergo a brief examination to prove service with the Iron Heel.

"Agents-provocateurs all right," was the officer's conclusion. He was a beardless young fellow, a cadet, evidently, of some great oligarch family.

"It's a hell of a job," Garthwaite grumbled. "I'm going to try and resign and get into the army. You fellows have a snap."

"You've earned it," was the young officer's answer. "I've got some pull, and I'll see if it can be managed. I can tell them how I found you."

He took Garthwaite's name and number, then turned to me.

"And you?"

"Oh, I'm going to be married," I answered lightly, "and then I'll be out of it all."

And so we talked, while the killing of the wounded went on. It is all a dream, now, as I look back on it; but at the time it was the most natural thing in the world. Garthwaite and the young officer fell into an animated conversation over the difference between so-called modern warfare and the present street-fighting and sky-scraper fighting that was taking place all over the city. I followed them intently, fixing up my hair at the same time and pinning together my torn skirts. And all the time the killing of the wounded went on. Sometimes the revolver shots drowned the voices of Garthwaite and the officer, and they were compelled to repeat what they had been saying.

I lived through three days of the Chicago Commune, and the vastness of it and of the slaughter may be imagined when I say that in all that time I saw practically nothing outside the killing of the people of the abyss and the mid-air fighting between sky-scrapers. I really saw nothing of the heroic work done by the comrades. I could hear the explosions of their mines and bombs, and see the smoke of their conflagrations, and that was all. The mid-air part of one great deed I saw, however, and that was the balloon attacks made by our comrades on the fortresses. That was on the second day. The three disloyal regiments had been destroyed in the fortresses to the last man. The fortresses were crowded with Mercenaries, the wind blew in the right direction, and up went our balloons from one of the office buildings in the city.

Now Biedenbach, after he left Glen Ellen, had invented a most powerful explosive—"expedite" he called it. This was the weapon the balloons used. They were only hot-air balloons, clumsily and hastily made, but they did the work. I saw it all from the top of an office building. The first balloon missed the fortresses completely and disappeared into the country; but we learned about it afterward. Burton and O'Sullivan were in it. As they were descending they swept across a railroad directly over a troop-train that was heading at full speed for Chicago. They dropped their whole supply of expedite upon the locomotive. The resulting wreck tied the line up for days. And the best of it was that, released from the weight of expedite, the balloon shot up into the air and did not come down for half a dozen miles, both heroes escaping unharmed.

The second balloon was a failure. Its flight was lame. It floated too low and was shot full of holes before it could reach the fortresses. Herford and Guinness were in it, and they were blown to pieces along with the field into which they fell. Biedenbach was in despair—we heard all about it afterward—and he went up alone in the third balloon. He, too, made a low flight, but he was in luck, for they failed seriously to puncture his balloon. I can see it now as I did then, from the lofty top of the building—that inflated bag drifting along the air, and that tiny speck of a man clinging on beneath. I could not see the fortress, but those on the roof with me said he was directly over it. I did not see the expedite fall when he cut it loose. But I did see the balloon suddenly leap up into the sky. An appreciable time after that the great column of the explosion towered in the air, and after that, in turn, I heard the roar of it. Biedenbach the gentle had destroyed a fortress. Two other balloons followed at the same time. One was blown to pieces in the air, the expedite exploding, and the shock of it disrupted the second balloon, which fell prettily into the remaining fortress. It couldn't have been better planned, though the two comrades in it sacrificed their lives.

But to return to the people of the abyss. My experiences were confined to them. They raged and slaughtered and destroyed all over the city proper, and were in turn destroyed; but never once did they succeed in reaching the city of the oligarchs over on the west side. The oligarchs had protected themselves well. No matter what destruction was wreaked in the heart of the city, they, and their womenkind and children, were to escape hurt. I am told that their children played in the parks during those terrible days and that their favorite game was an imitation of their elders stamping upon the proletariat.

But the Mercenaries found it no easy task to cope with the people of the abyss and at the same time fight with the comrades. Chicago was true to her traditions, and though a generation of revolutionists was wiped out, it took along with it pretty close to a generation of its enemies. Of course, the Iron Heel kept the figures secret, but, at a very conservative estimate, at least one hundred and thirty thousand Mercenaries were slain. But the comrades had no chance. Instead of the whole country being hand in hand in revolt, they were all alone, and the total strength of the Oligarchy could have been directed against them if necessary. As it was, hour after hour, day after day, in endless train-loads, by hundreds of thousands, the Mercenaries were hurled into Chicago.

And there were so many of the people of the abyss! Tiring of the slaughter, a great herding movement was begun by the soldiers, the intent of which was to drive the street mobs, like cattle, into Lake Michigan. It was at the beginning of this movement that Garthwaite and I had encountered the young officer. This herding movement was practically a failure, thanks to the splendid work of the comrades. Instead of the great host the Mercenaries had hoped to gather together, they succeeded in driving no more than forty thousand of the wretches into the lake. Time and again, when a mob of them was well in hand and being driven along the streets to the water, the comrades would create a diversion, and the mob would escape through the consequent hole torn in the encircling net.

Garthwaite and I saw an example of this shortly after meeting with the young officer. The mob of which we had been a part, and which had been put in retreat, was prevented from escaping to the south and east by strong bodies of troops. The troops we had fallen in with had held it back on the west. The only outlet was north, and north it went toward the lake, driven on from east and west and south by machine-gun fire and automatics. Whether it divined that it was being driven toward the lake, or whether it was merely a blind squirm of the monster, I do not know; but at any rate the mob took a cross street to the west, turned down the next street, and came back upon its track, heading south toward the great ghetto.

Garthwaite and I at that time were trying to make our way westward to get out of the territory of street-fighting, and we were caught right in the thick of it again. As we came to the corner we saw the howling mob bearing down upon us. Garthwaite seized my arm and we were just starting to run, when he dragged me back from in front of the wheels of half a dozen war automobiles, equipped with machine-guns, that were rushing for the spot. Behind them came the soldiers with their automatic rifles. By the time they took position, the mob was upon them, and it looked as though they would be overwhelmed before they could get into action.

Here and there a soldier was discharging his rifle, but this scattered fire had no effect in checking the mob. On it came, bellowing with brute rage. It seemed the machine-guns could not get started. The automobiles on which they were mounted blocked the street, compelling the soldiers to find positions in, between, and on the sidewalks. More and more soldiers were arriving, and in the jam we were unable to get away. Garthwaite held me by the arm, and we pressed close against the front of a building.

The mob was no more than twenty-five feet away when the machine-guns opened up; but before that flaming sheet of death nothing could live. The mob came on, but it could not advance. It piled up in a heap, a mound, a huge and growing wave of dead and dying. Those behind urged on, and the column, from gutter to gutter, telescoped upon itself. Wounded creatures, men and women, were vomited over the top of that awful wave and fell squirming down the face of it till they threshed about under the automobiles and against the legs of the soldiers. The latter bayoneted the struggling wretches, though one I saw who gained his feet and flew at a soldier's throat with his teeth. Together they went down, soldier and slave, into the welter.

The firing ceased. The work was done. The mob had been stopped in its wild attempt to break through. Orders were being given to clear the wheels of the war-machines. They could not advance over that wave of dead, and the idea was to run them down the cross street. The soldiers were dragging the bodies away from the wheels when it happened. We learned afterward how it happened. A block distant a hundred of our comrades had been holding a building. Across roofs and through buildings they made their way, till they found themselves looking down upon the close-packed soldiers. Then it was counter-massacre.

Without warning, a shower of bombs fell from the top of the building. The automobiles were blown to fragments, along with many soldiers. We, with the survivors, swept back in mad retreat. Half a block down another building opened fire on us. As the soldiers had carpeted the street with dead slaves, so, in turn, did they themselves become carpet. Garthwaite and I bore charmed lives. As we had done before, so again we sought shelter in an entrance. But he was not to be caught napping this time. As the roar of the bombs died away, he began peering out.

"The mob's coming back!" he called to me. "We've got to get out of this!"

We fled, hand in hand, down the bloody pavement, slipping and sliding, and making for the corner. Down the cross street we could see a few soldiers still running. Nothing was happening to them. The way was clear. So we paused a moment and looked back. The mob came on slowly. It was busy arming itself with the rifles of the slain and killing the wounded. We saw the end of the young officer who had rescued us. He painfully lifted himself on his elbow and turned loose with his automatic pistol.

"There goes my chance of promotion," Garthwaite laughed, as a woman bore down on the wounded man, brandishing a butcher's cleaver. "Come on. It's the wrong direction, but we'll get out somehow."

And we fled eastward through the quiet streets, prepared at every cross street for anything to happen. To the south a monster conflagration was filling the sky, and we knew that the great ghetto was burning. At last I sank down on the sidewalk. I was exhausted and could go no farther. I was bruised and sore and aching in every limb; yet I could not escape smiling at Garthwaite, who was rolling a cigarette and saying:

"I know I'm making a mess of rescuing you, but I can't get head nor tail of the situation. It's all a mess. Every time we try to break out, something happens and we're turned back. We're only a couple of blocks now from where I got you out of that entrance. Friend and foe are all mixed up. It's chaos. You can't tell who is in those darned buildings. Try to find out, and you get a bomb on your head. Try to go peaceably on your way, and you run into a mob and are killed by machine-guns, or you run into the Mercenaries and are killed by your own comrades from a roof. And on the top of it all the mob comes along and kills you, too."

He shook his head dolefully, lighted his cigarette, and sat down beside me.

"And I'm that hungry," he added, "I could eat cobblestones."

The next moment he was on his feet again and out in the street prying up a cobblestone. He came back with it and assaulted the window of a store behind us.

"It's ground floor and no good," he explained as he helped me through the hole he had made; "but it's the best we can do. You get a nap and I'll reconnoitre. I'll finish this rescue all right, but I want time, time, lots of it—and something to eat."

It was a harness store we found ourselves in, and he fixed me up a couch of horse blankets in the private office well to the rear. To add to my wretchedness a splitting headache was coming on, and I was only too glad to close my eyes and try to sleep.

"I'll be back," were his parting words. "I don't hope to get an auto, but I'll surely bring some grub,* anyway."

    * Food.

And that was the last I saw of Garthwaite for three years. Instead of coming back, he was carried away to a hospital with a bullet through his lungs and another through the fleshy part of his neck.

CHAPTER XXIV

NIGHTMARE

I had not closed my eyes the night before on the Twentieth Century, and what of that and of my exhaustion I slept soundly. When I first awoke, it was night. Garthwaite had not returned. I had lost my watch and had no idea of the time. As I lay with my eyes closed, I heard the same dull sound of distant explosions. The inferno was still raging. I crept through the store to the front. The reflection from the sky of vast conflagrations made the street almost as light as day. One could have read the finest print with ease. From several blocks away came the crackle of small hand-bombs and the churning of machine-guns, and from a long way off came a long series of heavy explosions. I crept back to my horse blankets and slept again.

When next I awoke, a sickly yellow light was filtering in on me. It was dawn of the second day. I crept to the front of the store. A smoke pall, shot through with lurid gleams, filled the sky. Down the opposite side of the street tottered a wretched slave. One hand he held tightly against his side, and behind him he left a bloody trail. His eyes roved everywhere, and they were filled with apprehension and dread. Once he looked straight across at me, and in his face was all the dumb pathos of the wounded and hunted animal. He saw me, but there was no kinship between us, and with him, at least, no sympathy of understanding; for he cowered perceptibly and dragged himself on. He could expect no aid in all God's world. He was a helot in the great hunt of helots that the masters were making. All he could hope for, all he sought, was some hole to crawl away in and hide like any animal. The sharp clang of a passing ambulance at the corner gave him a start. Ambulances were not for such as he. With a groan of pain he threw himself into a doorway. A minute later he was out again and desperately hobbling on.

I went back to my horse blankets and waited an hour for Garthwaite. My headache had not gone away. On the contrary, it was increasing. It was by an effort of will only that I was able to open my eyes and look at objects. And with the opening of my eyes and the looking came intolerable torment. Also, a great pulse was beating in my brain. Weak and reeling, I went out through the broken window and down the street, seeking to escape, instinctively and gropingly, from the awful shambles. And thereafter I lived nightmare. My memory of what happened in the succeeding hours is the memory one would have of nightmare. Many events are focussed sharply on my brain, but between these indelible pictures I retain are intervals of unconsciousness. What occurred in those intervals I know not, and never shall know.

I remember stumbling at the corner over the legs of a man. It was the poor hunted wretch that had dragged himself past my hiding-place. How distinctly do I remember his poor, pitiful, gnarled hands as he lay there on the pavement—hands that were more hoof and claw than hands, all twisted and distorted by the toil of all his days, with on the palms a horny growth of callous a half inch thick. And as I picked myself up and started on, I looked into the face of the thing and saw that it still lived; for the eyes, dimly intelligent, were looking at me and seeing me.

After that came a kindly blank. I knew nothing, saw nothing, merely tottered on in my quest for safety. My next nightmare vision was a quiet street of the dead. I came upon it abruptly, as a wanderer in the country would come upon a flowing stream. Only this stream I gazed upon did not flow. It was congealed in death. From pavement to pavement, and covering the sidewalks, it lay there, spread out quite evenly, with only here and there a lump or mound of bodies to break the surface. Poor driven people of the abyss, hunted helots—they lay there as the rabbits in California after a drive.* Up the street and down I looked. There was no movement, no sound. The quiet buildings looked down upon the scene from their many windows. And once, and once only, I saw an arm that moved in that dead stream. I swear I saw it move, with a strange writhing gesture of agony, and with it lifted a head, gory with nameless horror, that gibbered at me and then lay down again and moved no more.

* In those days, so sparsely populated was the land that
wild animals often became pests. In California the custom
of rabbit-driving obtained. On a given day all the farmers
in a locality would assemble and sweep across the country in
converging lines, driving the rabbits by scores of thousands
into a prepared enclosure, where they were clubbed to death
by men and boys.

I remember another street, with quiet buildings on either side, and the panic that smote me into consciousness as again I saw the people of the abyss, but this time in a stream that flowed and came on. And then I saw there was nothing to fear. The stream moved slowly, while from it arose groans and lamentations, cursings, babblings of senility, hysteria, and insanity; for these were the very young and the very old, the feeble and the sick, the helpless and the hopeless, all the wreckage of the ghetto. The burning of the great ghetto on the South Side had driven them forth into the inferno of the street-fighting, and whither they wended and whatever became of them I did not know and never learned.*

* It was long a question of debate, whether the burning of
the South Side ghetto was accidental, or whether it was done
by the Mercenaries; but it is definitely settled now that
the ghetto was fired by the Mercenaries under orders from
their chiefs.

I have faint memories of breaking a window and hiding in some shop to escape a street mob that was pursued by soldiers. Also, a bomb burst near me, once, in some still street, where, look as I would, up and down, I could see no human being. But my next sharp recollection begins with the crack of a rifle and an abrupt becoming aware that I am being fired at by a soldier in an automobile. The shot missed, and the next moment I was screaming and motioning the signals. My memory of riding in the automobile is very hazy, though this ride, in turn, is broken by one vivid picture. The crack of the rifle of the soldier sitting beside me made me open my eyes, and I saw George Milford, whom I had known in the Pell Street days, sinking slowly down to the sidewalk. Even as he sank the soldier fired again, and Milford doubled in, then flung his body out, and fell sprawling. The soldier chuckled, and the automobile sped on.

The next I knew after that I was awakened out of a sound sleep by a man who walked up and down close beside me. His face was drawn and strained, and the sweat rolled down his nose from his forehead. One hand was clutched tightly against his chest by the other hand, and blood dripped down upon the floor as he walked. He wore the uniform of the Mercenaries. From without, as through thick walls, came the muffled roar of bursting bombs. I was in some building that was locked in combat with some other building.

A surgeon came in to dress the wounded soldier, and I learned that it was two in the afternoon. My headache was no better, and the surgeon paused from his work long enough to give me a powerful drug that would depress the heart and bring relief. I slept again, and the next I knew I was on top of the building. The immediate fighting had ceased, and I was watching the balloon attack on the fortresses. Some one had an arm around me and I was leaning close against him. It came to me quite as a matter of course that this was Ernest, and I found myself wondering how he had got his hair and eyebrows so badly singed.

It was by the merest chance that we had found each other in that terrible city. He had had no idea that I had left New York, and, coming through the room where I lay asleep, could not at first believe that it was I. Little more I saw of the Chicago Commune. After watching the balloon attack, Ernest took me down into the heart of the building, where I slept the afternoon out and the night. The third day we spent in the building, and on the fourth, Ernest having got permission and an automobile from the authorities, we left Chicago.

My headache was gone, but, body and soul, I was very tired. I lay back against Ernest in the automobile, and with apathetic eyes watched the soldiers trying to get the machine out of the city. Fighting was still going on, but only in isolated localities. Here and there whole districts were still in possession of the comrades, but such districts were surrounded and guarded by heavy bodies of troops. In a hundred segregated traps were the comrades thus held while the work of subjugating them went on. Subjugation meant death, for no quarter was given, and they fought heroically to the last man.*

* Numbers of the buildings held out over a week, while one
 held out eleven days. Each building had to be stormed like

> a fort, and the Mercenaries fought their way upward floor by floor. It was deadly fighting. Quarter was neither given nor taken, and in the fighting the revolutionists had the advantage of being above. While the revolutionists were wiped out, the loss was not one-sided. The proud Chicago proletariat lived up to its ancient boast. For as many of itself as were killed, it killed that many of the enemy.

Whenever we approached such localities, the guards turned us back and sent us around. Once, the only way past two strong positions of the comrades was through a burnt section that lay between. From either side we could hear the rattle and roar of war, while the automobile picked its way through smoking ruins and tottering walls. Often the streets were blocked by mountains of debris that compelled us to go around. We were in a labyrinth of ruin, and our progress was slow.

The stockyards (ghetto, plant, and everything) were smouldering ruins. Far off to the right a wide smoke haze dimmed the sky,—the town of Pullman, the soldier chauffeur told us, or what had been the town of Pullman, for it was utterly destroyed. He had driven the machine out there, with despatches, on the afternoon of the third day. Some of the heaviest fighting had occurred there, he said, many of the streets being rendered impassable by the heaps of the dead.

Swinging around the shattered walls of a building, in the stockyards district, the automobile was stopped by a wave of dead. It was for all the world like a wave tossed up by the sea. It was patent to us what had happened. As the mob charged past the corner, it had been swept, at right angles and point-blank range, by the machine-guns drawn up on the cross street. But disaster had come to the soldiers. A chance bomb must have exploded among them, for the mob, checked until its dead and dying formed the wave, had white-capped and flung forward its foam of living, fighting slaves. Soldiers and slaves lay together, torn and mangled, around and over the wreckage of the automobiles and guns.

Ernest sprang out. A familiar pair of shoulders in a cotton shirt and a familiar fringe of white hair had caught his eye. I did not watch him, and it was not until he was back beside me and we were speeding on that he said:

"It was Bishop Morehouse."

Soon we were in the green country, and I took one last glance back at the smoke-filled sky. Faint and far came the low thud of an explosion. Then I turned my face against Ernest's breast and wept softly for the Cause that was lost. Ernest's arm about me was eloquent with love.

"For this time lost, dear heart," he said, "but not forever. We have learned. To-morrow the Cause will rise again, strong with wisdom and discipline."

The automobile drew up at a railroad station. Here we would catch a train to New York. As we waited on the platform, three trains thundered past, bound west to Chicago. They were crowded with ragged, unskilled laborers, people of the abyss.

"Slave-levies for the rebuilding of Chicago," Ernest said. "You see, the Chicago slaves are all killed."

CHAPTER XXV

THE TERRORISTS

It was not until Ernest and I were back in New York, and after weeks had elapsed, that we were able to comprehend thoroughly the full sweep of the disaster that had befallen the Cause. The situation was bitter and bloody. In many places, scattered over the country, slave revolts and massacres had occurred. The roll of the martyrs increased mightily. Countless executions took place everywhere. The mountains and waste regions were filled with outlaws and refugees who were being hunted down mercilessly. Our own refuges were packed with comrades who had prices on their heads. Through information furnished by its spies, scores of our refuges were raided by the soldiers of the Iron Heel.

Many of the comrades were disheartened, and they retaliated with terroristic tactics. The set-back to their hopes made them despairing and desperate. Many terrorist organizations unaffiliated with us sprang into existence and caused us much trouble.* These misguided people sacrificed their own lives wantonly, very often made our own plans go astray, and retarded our organization.

* The annals of this short-lived era of despair make bloody reading. Revenge was the ruling motive, and the members of the terroristic organizations were careless of their own lives and hopeless about the future. The Danites, taking their name from the avenging angels of the Mormon mythology, sprang up in the mountains of the Great West and spread over the Pacific Coast from Panama to Alaska. The Valkyries were women. They were the most terrible of all. No woman was eligible for membership who had not lost near relatives at the hands of the Oligarchy. They were guilty of torturing their prisoners to death. Another famous organization of women was The Widows of War. A companion organization to the Valkyries was the Berserkers. These men placed no value whatever upon their own lives, and it was they who totally destroyed the great Mercenary city of Bellona along with its population of over a hundred thousand souls. The Bedlamites and the Helldamites were twin slave organizations, while a new religious sect that did not flourish long was called The Wrath of God. Among others, to show the whimsicality of their deadly seriousness, may be mentioned the following: The Bleeding Hearts, Sons of the Morning, the Morning Stars, The Flamingoes, The Triple Triangles, The Three Bars, The Rubonics, The Vindicators, The Comanches, and the

Erebusites.

And through it all moved the Iron Heel, impassive and deliberate, shaking up the whole fabric of the social structure in its search for the comrades, combing out the Mercenaries, the labor castes, and all its secret services, punishing without mercy and without malice, suffering in silence all retaliations that were made upon it, and filling the gaps in its fighting line as fast as they appeared. And hand in hand with this, Ernest and the other leaders were hard at work reorganizing the forces of the Revolution. The magnitude of the task may be understood when it is taken into.*

* This is the end of the Everhard Manuscript. It breaks off abruptly in the middle of a sentence. She must have received warning of the coming of the Mercenaries, for she had time safely to hide the Manuscript before she fled or was captured. It is to be regretted that she did not live to complete her narrative, for then, undoubtedly, would have been cleared away the mystery that has shrouded for seven centuries the execution of Ernest Everhard.

MARTIN EDEN

CHAPTER I

The one opened the door with a latch-key and went in, followed by a young fellow who awkwardly removed his cap. He wore rough clothes that smacked of the sea, and he was manifestly out of place in the spacious hall in which he found himself. He did not know what to do with his cap, and was stuffing it into his coat pocket when the other took it from him. The act was done quietly and naturally, and the awkward young fellow appreciated it. "He understands," was his thought. "He'll see me through all right."

He walked at the other's heels with a swing to his shoulders, and his legs spread unwittingly, as if the level floors were tilting up and sinking down to the heave and lunge of the sea. The wide rooms seemed too narrow for his rolling gait, and to himself he was in terror lest his broad shoulders should collide with the doorways or sweep the bric-a-brac from the low mantel. He recoiled from side to side between the various objects and multiplied the hazards that in reality lodged only in his mind. Between a grand piano and a centre-table piled high with books was space for a half a dozen to walk abreast, yet he essayed it with trepidation. His heavy arms hung loosely at his sides. He did not know what to do with those arms and hands, and when, to his excited vision, one arm seemed liable to brush against the books on the table, he lurched away like a frightened horse, barely missing the piano stool. He watched the easy walk of the other in front of him, and for the first time realized that his walk was different from that of other men. He experienced a momentary pang of shame that he should walk so uncouthly. The sweat burst through the skin of his forehead in tiny beads, and he paused and mopped his bronzed face with his handkerchief.

"Hold on, Arthur, my boy," he said, attempting to mask his anxiety with facetious utterance. "This is too much all at once for yours truly. Give me a chance to get my nerve. You know I didn't want to come, an' I guess your fam'ly ain't hankerin' to see me neither."

"That's all right," was the reassuring answer. "You mustn't be frightened at us. We're just homely people—Hello, there's a letter for me."

He stepped back to the table, tore open the envelope, and began to read, giving the stranger an opportunity to recover himself. And the stranger understood and appreciated. His was the gift of sympathy, understanding; and beneath his alarmed exterior that sympathetic process went on. He mopped his forehead dry and glanced about him with a controlled face, though in the eyes there was an expression such as wild animals betray when they fear the trap. He was surrounded by the unknown, apprehensive of what might happen, ignorant of what he should do, aware that he walked and bore himself awkwardly, fearful that every attribute and power of him was similarly afflicted. He was keenly sensitive, hopelessly self-conscious, and the amused glance that the other stole privily at him over the top of the letter burned into him like a dagger-thrust. He saw the glance, but he gave no sign, for among the things he had learned was discipline. Also, that dagger-thrust went to his pride. He cursed himself for having come, and at the same time resolved that, happen what would, having come, he would carry it through. The lines of his face hardened, and into his eyes came a fighting light. He looked about more unconcernedly, sharply observant, every detail of the pretty interior registering itself on his brain. His eyes were wide apart; nothing in their field of vision escaped; and as they drank in the beauty before them the fighting light died out and a warm glow took its place. He was responsive to beauty, and here was cause to respond.

An oil painting caught and held him. A heavy surf thundered and burst over an outjutting rock; lowering storm-clouds covered the sky; and, outside the line of surf, a pilot-schooner, close-hauled, heeled over till every detail of her deck was visible, was surging along against a stormy sunset sky. There was beauty, and it drew him irresistibly. He forgot his awkward walk and came closer to the painting, very close. The beauty faded out of the canvas. His face expressed his bepuzzlement. He stared at what seemed a careless daub of paint, then stepped away. Immediately all the beauty flashed back into the canvas. "A trick picture," was his thought, as he dismissed it, though in the midst of the multitudinous impressions he was receiving he found time to feel a prod of indignation that so much beauty should be sacrificed to make a trick. He did not know painting. He had been brought up on chromos and lithographs that were always definite and sharp, near or far. He had seen oil paintings, it was true, in the show windows of shops, but the glass of the windows had prevented his eager eyes from approaching too near.

He glanced around at his friend reading the letter and saw the books on the table. Into his eyes leaped a wistfulness and a yearning as promptly as the yearning leaps into the eyes of a starving man at sight of food. An impulsive stride, with one lurch to right and left of the shoulders, brought him to the table, where he began affectionately handling the books. He glanced at the titles and the authors' names, read fragments of text, caressing the volumes with his eyes and hands, and, once, recognized a book he had read. For the rest, they were strange books and strange authors. He chanced upon a volume of Swinburne and began reading steadily, forgetful of where he was, his face glowing. Twice he closed the book on his forefinger to look at the name of the author. Swinburne! he would remember that name. That fellow had eyes, and he had certainly seen color and flashing light. But who was Swinburne? Was he dead a hundred years or so, like most of the poets? Or was he alive still, and writing? He turned to the title-page . . . yes, he had written other books; well, he would go to the free library the first thing in the morning and try to get hold of some of Swinburne's stuff. He went back to the text and lost himself. He did not notice that a young woman had entered the room. The first he knew was when he heard Arthur's voice saying:-

"Ruth, this is Mr. Eden."

The book was closed on his forefinger, and before he turned he was thrilling to the first new impression, which was not of the girl, but of her brother's words. Under that muscled body of his he was a mass of quivering sensibilities. At the slightest impact of the outside world upon his consciousness, his thoughts, sympathies, and emotions leapt and played like lambent flame. He was extraordinarily receptive and responsive, while his imagination, pitched high, was ever at work establishing relations of likeness and difference. "Mr. Eden," was what he had thrilled to—he who had been called "Eden," or "Martin Eden," or just "Martin," all his life. And "*Mister*!" It was certainly going some, was his internal comment. His mind seemed to turn, on the instant, into a vast camera obscura, and he saw arrayed around his consciousness endless pictures from his life, of stoke-holes and forecastles, camps and beaches, jails and boozing-kens, fever-hospitals and slum streets, wherein the thread of association was the fashion in which he had been addressed in those various situations.

And then he turned and saw the girl. The phantasmagoria of his brain vanished at sight of her. She was a pale, ethereal creature, with wide, spiritual blue eyes and a wealth of golden hair. He did not know how she was dressed, except that the dress was as wonderful as she. He likened her to a pale gold flower upon a slender stem. No, she was a spirit, a divinity, a goddess; such sublimated beauty was not of the earth. Or perhaps the books were right, and there were many such as she in the upper walks of life. She might well be sung by that chap, Swinburne. Perhaps he had had somebody like her in mind when he painted that girl, Iseult, in the book there on the table. All this plethora of sight, and feeling, and thought occurred on the instant. There was no pause of the realities wherein he moved. He saw her hand coming out to his, and she looked him straight in the eyes as she shook hands, frankly, like a man. The women he had known did not shake hands that way. For that matter, most of them did not shake hands at all. A flood of associations, visions of various ways he had made the acquaintance of women, rushed into his mind and threatened to swamp it. But he shook them aside and looked at her. Never had he seen such a woman. The women he had known! Immediately, beside her, on either hand, ranged the women he had known. For an eternal second he stood in the midst of a portrait gallery, wherein she occupied the central place, while about her were limned many women, all to be weighed and measured by a fleeting glance, herself the unit of weight and measure. He saw the weak and sickly faces of the girls of the factories, and the simpering, boisterous girls from the south of Market. There were women of the cattle camps, and swarthy cigarette-smoking women of Old Mexico. These, in turn, were crowded out by Japanese women, doll-like, stepping mincingly on wooden clogs; by Eurasians, delicate featured, stamped with degeneracy; by full-bodied South-Sea-Island women, flower-crowned and brown-skinned. All these were blotted out by a grotesque and terrible nightmare brood—frowsy, shuffling creatures from the pavements of Whitechapel, gin-bloated hags of the stews, and all the vast hell's following of harpies, vile-mouthed and filthy, that under the guise of monstrous female form prey upon sailors, the scrapings of the ports, the scum and slime of the human pit.

"Won't you sit down, Mr. Eden?" the girl was saying. "I have been looking forward to meeting you ever since Arthur told us. It was brave of you—"

He waved his hand deprecatingly and muttered that it was nothing at all, what he had done, and that any fellow would have done it. She noticed that the hand he waved was covered with fresh abrasions, in the process of healing, and a glance at the other loose-hanging hand showed it to be in the same condition. Also, with quick, critical eye, she noted a scar on his cheek, another that peeped out from under the hair of the forehead, and a third that ran down and disappeared under the starched collar. She repressed a smile at sight of the red line that marked the chafe of the collar against the bronzed neck. He was evidently unused to stiff collars. Likewise her feminine eye took in the clothes he wore, the cheap and unaesthetic cut, the wrinkling of the coat across the shoulders, and the series of wrinkles in the sleeves that advertised bulging biceps muscles.

While he waved his hand and muttered that he had done nothing at all, he was obeying her behest by trying to get into a chair. He found time to admire the ease with which she sat down, then lurched toward a chair facing her, overwhelmed with consciousness of the awkward figure he was cutting. This was a new experience for him. All his life, up to then, he had been unaware of being either graceful or awkward. Such thoughts of self had never entered his mind. He sat down gingerly on the edge of the chair, greatly worried by his hands. They were in the way wherever he put them. Arthur was leaving the room, and Martin Eden followed his exit with longing eyes. He felt lost, alone there in the room with that pale spirit of a woman.

There was no bar-keeper upon whom to call for drinks, no small boy to send around the corner for a can of beer and by means of that social fluid start the amenities of friendship flowing.

"You have such a scar on your neck, Mr. Eden," the girl was saying. "How did it happen? I am sure it must have been some adventure."

"A Mexican with a knife, miss," he answered, moistening his parched lips and clearing hip throat. "It was just a fight. After I got the knife away, he tried to bite off my nose."

Baldly as he had stated it, in his eyes was a rich vision of that hot, starry night at Salina Cruz, the white strip of beach, the lights of the sugar steamers in the harbor, the voices of the drunken sailors in the distance, the jostling stevedores, the flaming passion in the Mexican's face, the glint of the beast-eyes in the starlight, the sting of the steel in his neck, and the rush of blood, the crowd and the cries, the two bodies, his and the Mexican's, locked together, rolling over and over and tearing up the sand, and from away off somewhere the mellow tinkling of a guitar. Such was the picture, and he thrilled to the memory of it, wondering if the man could paint it who had painted the pilot-schooner on the wall. The white beach, the stars, and the lights of the sugar steamers would look great, he thought, and midway on the sand the dark group of figures that surrounded the fighters. The knife occupied a place in the picture, he decided, and would show well, with a sort of gleam, in the light of the stars. But of all this no hint had crept into his speech. "He tried to bite off my nose," he concluded.

"Oh," the girl said, in a faint, far voice, and he noticed the shock in her sensitive face.

He felt a shock himself, and a blush of embarrassment shone faintly on his sunburned cheeks, though to him it burned as hotly as when his cheeks had been exposed to the open furnace-door in the fire-room. Such sordid things as stabbing affrays were evidently not fit subjects for conversation with a lady. People in the books, in her walk of life, did not talk about such things—perhaps they did not know about them, either.

There was a brief pause in the conversation they were trying to get started. Then she asked tentatively about the scar on his cheek. Even as she asked, he realized that she was making an effort to talk his talk, and he resolved to get away from it and talk hers.

"It was just an accident," he said, putting his hand to his cheek. "One night, in a calm, with a heavy sea running, the main-boom-lift carried away, an' next the tackle. The lift was wire, an' it was threshin' around like a snake. The whole watch was tryin' to grab it, an' I rushed in an' got swatted."

"Oh," she said, this time with an accent of comprehension, though secretly his speech had been so much Greek to her and she was wondering what a *lift* was and what *swatted* meant.

"This man Swineburne," he began, attempting to put his plan into execution and pronouncing the *i* long.

"Who?"

"Swineburne," he repeated, with the same mispronunciation. "The poet."

"Swinburne," she corrected.

"Yes, that's the chap," he stammered, his cheeks hot again. "How long since he died?"

"Why, I haven't heard that he was dead." She looked at him curiously. "Where did you make his acquaintance?"

"I never clapped eyes on him," was the reply. "But I read some of his poetry out of that book there on the table just before you come in. How do you like his poetry?"

And thereat she began to talk quickly and easily upon the subject he had suggested. He felt better, and settled back slightly from the edge of the chair, holding tightly to its arms with his hands, as if it might get away from him and buck him to the floor. He had succeeded in making her talk her talk, and while she rattled on, he strove to follow her, marvelling at all the knowledge that was stowed away in that pretty head of hers, and drinking in the pale beauty of her face. Follow her he did, though bothered by unfamiliar words that fell glibly from her lips and by critical phrases and thought-processes that were foreign to his mind, but that nevertheless stimulated his mind and set it tingling. Here was intellectual life, he thought, and here was beauty, warm and wonderful as he had never dreamed it could be. He forgot himself and stared at her with hungry eyes. Here was something to live for, to win to, to fight for—ay, and die for. The books were true. There were such women in the world. She was one of them. She lent wings to his imagination, and great, luminous canvases spread themselves before him whereon loomed vague, gigantic figures of love and romance, and of heroic deeds for woman's sake—for a pale woman, a flower of gold. And through the swaying, palpitant vision, as through a fairy mirage, he stared at the real woman, sitting there and talking of literature and art. He listened as well, but he stared, unconscious of the fixity of his gaze or of the fact that all that was essentially masculine in his nature was shining in his eyes. But she, who knew little of the world of men, being a woman, was keenly aware of his burning eyes. She had never had men look at her in such fashion, and it embarrassed her. She stumbled and halted in her utterance. The thread of argument slipped from her. He frightened her, and at the same time it was strangely pleasant to be so looked upon. Her training warned her of peril and of wrong, subtle, mysterious, luring; while her instincts rang clarion-voiced through her being, impelling her to hurdle caste and place and gain to this traveller from another world, to this uncouth young fellow with lacerated hands and a line of raw red caused by the unaccustomed linen at his throat, who, all too evidently, was soiled and tainted by ungracious existence. She was clean, and her cleanness revolted; but she was woman, and she was just beginning to learn the paradox of woman.

"As I was saying—what was I saying?" She broke off abruptly and laughed merrily at her predicament.

"You was saying that this man Swinburne failed bein' a great poet because—an' that was as far as you got, miss," he prompted, while to himself he seemed suddenly hungry, and delicious little thrills crawled up and down his spine at the sound of her laughter. Like silver, he thought to himself, like tinkling silver bells; and on the instant, and for an instant, he was transported to a far land, where under pink cherry blossoms, he smoked a cigarette and listened to the bells of the peaked pagoda calling straw-sandalled devotees to worship.

"Yes, thank you," she said. "Swinburne fails, when all is said, because he is, well, indelicate. There are many of his poems that should never be read. Every line of the really great poets is filled with beautiful truth, and calls to all that is high and noble in the human. Not a line of the great poets can be spared without impoverishing the world by that much."

"I thought it was great," he said hesitatingly, "the little I read. I had no idea he was such a—a scoundrel. I guess that crops out in his other books."

"There are many lines that could be spared from the book you were reading," she said, her voice primly firm and dogmatic.

"I must 'a' missed 'em," he announced. "What I read was the real goods. It was all lighted up an' shining, an' it shun right into me an' lighted me up inside, like the sun or a searchlight. That's the way it landed on me, but I guess I ain't up much on poetry, miss."

He broke off lamely. He was confused, painfully conscious of his inarticulateness. He had felt the bigness and glow of life in what he had read, but his speech was inadequate. He could not express what he felt, and to himself he likened himself to a sailor, in a strange ship, on a dark night, groping about in the unfamiliar running rigging. Well, he decided, it was up to him to get acquainted in this new world. He had never seen anything that he couldn't get the hang of when he wanted to and it was about time for him to want to learn to talk the things that were inside of him so that she could understand. *She* was bulking large on his horizon.

"Now Longfellow—" she was saying.

"Yes, I've read 'm," he broke in impulsively, spurred on to exhibit and make the most of his little store of book knowledge, desirous of showing her that he was not wholly a stupid clod. "'The Psalm of Life,' 'Excelsior,' an' . . . I guess that's all."

She nodded her head and smiled, and he felt, somehow, that her smile was tolerant, pitifully tolerant. He was a fool to attempt to make a pretence that way. That Longfellow chap most likely had written countless books of poetry.

"Excuse me, miss, for buttin' in that way. I guess the real facts is that I don't know nothin' much about such things. It ain't in my class. But I'm goin' to make it in my class."

It sounded like a threat. His voice was determined, his eyes were flashing, the lines of his face had grown harsh. And to her it seemed that the angle of his jaw had changed; its pitch had become unpleasantly aggressive. At the same time a wave of intense virility seemed to surge out from him and impinge upon her.

"I think you could make it in—in your class," she finished with a laugh. "You are very strong."

Her gaze rested for a moment on the muscular neck, heavy corded, almost bull-like, bronzed by the sun, spilling over with rugged health and strength. And though he sat there, blushing and humble, again she felt drawn to him. She was surprised by a wanton thought that rushed into her mind. It seemed to her that if she could lay her two hands upon that neck that all its strength and vigor would flow out to her. She was shocked by this thought. It seemed to reveal to her an undreamed depravity in her nature. Besides, strength to her was a gross and brutish thing. Her ideal of masculine beauty had always been slender gracefulness. Yet the thought still persisted. It bewildered her that she should desire to place her hands on that sunburned neck. In truth, she was far from robust, and the need of her body and mind was for strength. But she did not know it. She knew only that no man had ever affected her before as this one had, who shocked her from moment to moment with his awful grammar.

"Yes, I ain't no invalid," he said. "When it comes down to hard-pan, I can digest scrap-iron. But just now I've got dyspepsia. Most of what you was sayin' I can't digest. Never trained that way, you see. I like books and poetry, and what time I've had I've read 'em, but I've never thought about 'em the way you have. That's why I can't talk about 'em. I'm like a navigator adrift on a strange sea without chart or compass. Now I want to get my bearin's. Mebbe you can put me right. How did you learn all this you've ben talkin'?"

"By going to school, I fancy, and by studying," she answered.

"I went to school when I was a kid," he began to object.

"Yes; but I mean high school, and lectures, and the university."

"You've gone to the university?" he demanded in frank amazement. He felt that she had become remoter from him by at least a million miles.

"I'm going there now. I'm taking special courses in English."

He did not know what "English" meant, but he made a mental note of that item of ignorance and passed on.

"How long would I have to study before I could go to the university?" he asked.

She beamed encouragement upon his desire for knowledge, and said: "That depends upon how much studying you have already done. You have never attended high school? Of course not. But did you finish grammar school?"

"I had two years to run, when I left," he answered. "But I was always honorably promoted at school."

The next moment, angry with himself for the boast, he had gripped the arms of the chair so savagely that every finger-end was stinging. At the same moment he became aware that a woman was entering the room. He saw the girl leave her chair and trip swiftly across the floor to the newcomer. They kissed each other, and, with arms around each other's waists, they advanced toward him. That must be her mother, he thought. She was a tall, blond woman, slender, and stately, and beautiful. Her gown was what he might expect in such a house. His eyes delighted in the graceful lines of it. She and her dress together reminded him of women on the stage. Then he remembered seeing similar grand ladies and gowns entering the London theatres while he stood and watched and the policemen shoved him back into the drizzle beyond the awning. Next his mind leaped to the Grand Hotel at Yokohama, where, too, from the sidewalk, he had seen grand ladies. Then the city and the harbor of Yokohama, in a thousand pictures, began flashing before his eyes. But he swiftly dismissed the kaleidoscope of memory, oppressed by the urgent need of the present. He knew that he must stand up to be introduced, and he struggled painfully to his feet, where he stood with trousers bagging at the knees, his arms loose-hanging and ludicrous, his face set hard for the impending ordeal.

CHAPTER II

The process of getting into the dining room was a nightmare to him. Between halts and stumbles, jerks and lurches, locomotion had at times seemed impossible. But at last he had made it, and was seated alongside of Her. The array of knives and forks frightened him. They bristled with unknown perils, and he gazed at them, fascinated, till their dazzle became a background across which moved a succession of forecastle pictures, wherein he and his mates sat eating salt beef with sheath-knives and fingers, or scooping thick pea-soup out of pannikins by means of battered iron spoons. The stench of bad beef was in his nostrils, while in his ears, to the accompaniment of creaking timbers and groaning bulkheads, echoed the loud mouth-noises of the eaters. He watched them eating, and decided that they ate like pigs. Well, he would be careful here. He would make no noise. He would keep his mind upon it all the time.

He glanced around the table. Opposite him was Arthur, and Arthur's brother, Norman. They were her brothers, he reminded himself, and his heart warmed toward them. How they loved each other, the members of this family! There flashed into his mind the picture of her mother, of the kiss of greeting, and of the pair of them walking toward him with arms entwined. Not in his world were such displays of affection between parents and children made. It was a revelation of the heights of existence that were attained in the world above. It was the finest thing yet that he had seen in this small glimpse of that world. He was moved deeply by appreciation of it, and his heart was melting with sympathetic tenderness. He had starved for love all his life. His nature craved love. It was an organic demand of his being. Yet he had gone without, and hardened himself in the process. He had not known that he needed love. Nor did he know it now. He merely saw it in operation, and thrilled to it, and thought it fine, and high, and splendid.

He was glad that Mr. Morse was not there. It was difficult enough getting acquainted with her, and her mother, and her brother, Norman. Arthur he already knew somewhat. The father would have been too much for him, he felt sure. It seemed to him that he had never worked so hard in his life. The severest toil was child's play compared with this. Tiny nodules of moisture stood out on his forehead, and his shirt was wet with sweat from the exertion of doing so many unaccustomed things at once. He had to eat as he had never eaten before, to handle strange tools, to glance surreptitiously about and learn how to accomplish each new thing, to receive the flood of impressions that was pouring in upon him and being mentally annotated and classified; to be conscious of a yearning for her that perturbed him in the form of a dull, aching restlessness; to feel the prod of desire to win to the walk in life whereon she trod, and to have his mind ever and again straying off in speculation and vague plans of how to reach to her. Also, when his secret glance went across to Norman opposite him, or to any one else, to ascertain just what knife or fork was to be used in any particular occasion, that person's features were seized upon by his mind, which automatically strove to appraise them and to divine what they were—all in relation to her. Then he had to talk, to hear what was said to him and what was said back and forth, and to answer, when it was necessary, with a tongue prone to looseness of speech that required a constant curb. And to add confusion to confusion, there was the servant, an unceasing menace, that appeared noiselessly at his shoulder, a dire Sphinx that propounded puzzles and conundrums demanding instantaneous solution. He was oppressed throughout the meal by the thought of finger-bowls. Irrelevantly, insistently, scores of times, he wondered when they would come on and what they looked like. He had heard of such things, and now, sooner or later, somewhere in the next few minutes, he would see them, sit at table with exalted beings who used them—ay, and he would use them himself. And most important of all, far down and yet always at the surface of his thought, was the problem of how he should comport himself toward these persons. What should his attitude be? He wrestled continually and anxiously with the problem. There were cowardly suggestions that he should make believe, assume a part; and there were still more cowardly suggestions that warned him he would fail in such course, that his nature was not fitted to live up to it, and that he would make a fool of himself.

It was during the first part of the dinner, struggling to decide upon his attitude, that he was very quiet. He did not know that his quietness was giving the lie to Arthur's words of the day before, when that brother of hers had announced that he was going to bring a wild man home to dinner and for them not to be alarmed, because they would find him an interesting wild man. Martin Eden could not have found it in him, just then, to believe that her brother could be guilty of such treachery—especially when he had been the means of getting this particular brother out of an unpleasant row. So he sat at table, perturbed by his own unfitness and at the same time charmed by all that went on about him. For the first time he realized that eating was something more than a utilitarian function. He was unaware of what he ate. It was merely food. He was feasting his love of beauty at this table where eating was an aesthetic function. It was an intellectual function, too. His mind was stirred. He heard words spoken that were meaningless to him, and other words that he had seen only in books and that no man or woman he had known was of large enough mental caliber to pronounce. When he heard such words dropping carelessly from the lips of the members of this marvellous family, her family, he thrilled with delight. The romance, and beauty, and high vigor of the books were coming true. He was in that rare and blissful state wherein a man sees his dreams stalk out from the crannies of fantasy and become fact.

Never had he been at such an altitude of living, and he kept himself in the background, listening, observing, and pleasuring, replying in reticent monosyllables, saying, "Yes, miss," and "No, miss," to her, and "Yes, ma'am," and "No, ma'am," to her mother. He curbed the impulse, arising out of his sea-training, to say "Yes, sir," and "No, sir," to her brothers. He felt that it would be inappropriate and a confession of inferiority on his part—which would never do if he was to win to her. Also, it was a dictate of his pride. "By God!" he cried to himself, once; "I'm just as good as them, and if they do know lots that I don't, I could learn 'm a few myself, all the same!" And the next moment, when she or her mother addressed him as "Mr. Eden," his aggressive pride was forgotten, and he was glowing and warm with delight. He was a civilized man, that was what he was, shoulder to shoulder, at dinner, with people he had read about in books. He was in the books himself, adventuring through the printed pages of bound volumes.

But while he belied Arthur's description, and appeared a gentle lamb rather than a wild man, he was racking his brains for a course of action. He was no gentle lamb, and the part of second fiddle would never do for the high-pitched dominance of his nature. He talked only when he had to, and then his speech was like his walk to the table, filled with jerks and halts as he groped in his polyglot vocabulary for words, debating over words he knew were fit but which he feared he could not pronounce, rejecting other words he knew would not be understood or would be raw and harsh. But all the time he was oppressed by the consciousness that this carefulness of diction was making a booby of him, preventing him from expressing what he had in him. Also, his love of freedom chafed against the restriction in much the same way his neck chafed against the starched fetter of a collar. Besides, he was confident that he could not keep it up. He was by nature powerful of thought and sensibility, and the creative spirit was restive and urgent. He was swiftly mastered by the concept or sensation in him that struggled in birth-throes to receive expression and form, and then he forgot himself and where he was, and the old words—the tools of speech he knew—slipped out.

Once, he declined something from the servant who interrupted and pestered at his shoulder, and he said, shortly and emphatically, "Pew!"

On the instant those at the table were keyed up and expectant, the servant was smugly pleased, and he was wallowing in mortification. But he recovered himself quickly.

"It's the Kanaka for 'finish,'" he explained, "and it just come out naturally. It's spelt p-a-u."

He caught her curious and speculative eyes fixed on his hands, and, being in explanatory mood, he said:-

"I just come down the Coast on one of the Pacific mail steamers. She was behind time, an' around the Puget Sound ports we worked like niggers, storing cargo-mixed freight, if you know what that means. That's how the skin got knocked off."

"Oh, it wasn't that," she hastened to explain, in turn. "Your hands seemed too small for your body."

His cheeks were hot. He took it as an exposure of another of his deficiencies.

"Yes," he said depreciatingly. "They ain't big enough to stand the strain. I can hit like a mule with my arms and shoulders. They are too strong, an' when I smash a man on the jaw the hands get smashed, too."

He was not happy at what he had said. He was filled with disgust at himself. He had loosed the guard upon his tongue and talked about things that were not nice.

"It was brave of you to help Arthur the way you did—and you a stranger," she said tactfully, aware of his discomfiture though not of the reason for it.

He, in turn, realized what she had done, and in the consequent warm surge of gratefulness that overwhelmed him forgot his loose-worded tongue.

"It wasn't nothin' at all," he said. "Any guy 'ud do it for another. That bunch of hoodlums was lookin' for trouble, an' Arthur wasn't botherin' 'em none. They butted in on 'm, an' then I butted in on them an' poked a few. That's where some of the skin off my hands went, along with some of the teeth of the gang. I wouldn't 'a' missed it for anything. When I seen—"

He paused, open-mouthed, on the verge of the pit of his own depravity and utter worthlessness to breathe the same air she did. And while Arthur took up the tale, for the twentieth time, of his adventure with the drunken hoodlums on the ferry-boat and of how Martin Eden had rushed in and rescued him, that individual, with frowning brows, meditated upon the fool he had made of himself, and wrestled more determinedly with the problem of how he should conduct himself toward these people. He certainly had not succeeded so far. He wasn't of their tribe, and he couldn't talk their lingo, was the way he put it to himself. He couldn't fake being their kind. The masquerade would fail, and besides, masquerade was foreign to his nature. There was no room in him for sham or artifice. Whatever happened, he must be real. He couldn't talk their talk just yet, though in time he would. Upon that he was resolved. But in the meantime, talk he must, and it must be his own talk, toned down, of course, so as to be comprehensible to them and so as not to shook them too much. And furthermore, he wouldn't claim, not even by tacit acceptance, to be familiar with anything that was unfamiliar. In pursuance of this decision, when the two brothers, talking university shop, had used "trig" several times, Martin Eden demanded:-

"What is *trig*?"

"Trignometry," Norman said; "a higher form of math."

"And what is math?" was the next question, which, somehow, brought the laugh on Norman.

"Mathematics, arithmetic," was the answer.

Martin Eden nodded. He had caught a glimpse of the apparently illimitable vistas of knowledge. What he saw took on tangibility. His abnormal power of vision made abstractions take on concrete form. In the alchemy of his brain, trigonometry and mathematics and the whole field of knowledge which they betokened were transmuted into so much landscape. The vistas he saw were vistas of green foliage and forest glades, all softly luminous or shot through with flashing lights. In the distance, detail was veiled and blurred by a purple haze, but behind this purple haze, he knew, was the glamour of the unknown, the lure of romance. It was like wine to him. Here was adventure, something to do with head and hand, a world to conquer—and straightway from the back of his consciousness rushed the thought, *conquering, to win to her, that lily-pale spirit sitting beside him.*

The glimmering vision was rent asunder and dissipated by Arthur, who, all evening, had been trying to draw his wild man out. Martin Eden remembered his decision. For the first time he became himself, consciously and deliberately at first, but soon lost in the joy of creating in making life as he knew it appear before his listeners' eyes. He had been a member of the crew of the smuggling schooner *Halcyon* when she was captured by a revenue cutter. He saw with wide eyes, and he could tell what he saw. He brought the pulsing sea before them, and the men and the ships upon the sea. He communicated his power of vision, till they saw with his eyes what he had seen. He selected from the vast mass of detail with an artist's touch, drawing pictures of life that glowed and burned with light and color, injecting movement so that his listeners surged along with him on the flood of rough eloquence, enthusiasm, and power. At times he shocked them with the vividness of the narrative and his terms of speech, but beauty always followed fast upon the heels of violence, and tragedy was relieved by humor, by interpretations of the strange twists and quirks of sailors' minds.

And while he talked, the girl looked at him with startled eyes. His fire warmed her. She wondered if she had been cold all her days. She wanted to lean toward this burning, blazing man that was like a volcano spouting forth strength, robustness, and health. She felt that she must lean toward him, and resisted by an effort. Then, too, there was the counter impulse to shrink away from him. She was repelled by those lacerated hands, grimed by toil so that the very dirt of life was ingrained in the flesh itself, by that red chafe of the collar and those bulging muscles. His roughness frightened her; each roughness of speech was an insult to her ear, each rough phase of his life an insult to her soul. And ever and again would come the draw of him, till she thought he must be evil to have such power over her. All that was most firmly established in her mind was rocking. His romance and adventure were battering at the conventions. Before his facile perils and ready laugh, life was no longer an affair of serious effort and restraint, but a toy, to be played with and turned topsy-turvy, carelessly to be lived and pleasured in, and carelessly to be flung aside. "Therefore, play!" was the cry that rang through her. "Lean toward him, if so you will, and place your two hands upon his neck!" She wanted to cry out at the recklessness of the thought, and in vain she appraised her own cleanness and culture and balanced all that she was against what he was not. She glanced about her and saw the others gazing at him with rapt attention; and she would have despaired had not she seen horror in her mother's eyes—fascinated horror, it was true, but none the less horror. This man from outer darkness was evil. Her mother saw it, and her mother was right. She would trust her mother's judgment in this as she had always trusted it in all things. The fire of him was no longer warm, and the fear of him was no longer poignant.

Later, at the piano, she played for him, and at him, aggressively, with the vague intent of emphasizing the impassableness of the gulf that separated them. Her music was a club that she swung brutally upon his head; and though it stunned him and crushed him down, it incited him. He gazed upon her in awe. In his mind, as in her own, the gulf widened; but faster than it widened, towered his ambition to win across it. But he was too complicated a plexus of sensibilities to sit staring at a gulf a whole evening, especially when there was music. He was remarkably susceptible to music. It was like strong drink, firing him to audacities of feeling,— a drug that laid hold of his imagination and went cloud-soaring through the sky. It banished sordid fact, flooded his mind with beauty, loosed romance and to its heels added wings. He did not understand the music she played. It was different from the dance-hall piano-banging and blatant brass bands he had heard. But he had caught hints of such music from the books, and he accepted her playing largely on faith, patiently waiting, at first, for the lifting measures of pronounced and simple rhythm, puzzled because those measures were not long continued. Just as he caught the swing of them and started, his imagination attuned in flight, always they vanished away in a chaotic scramble of sounds that was meaningless to him, and that dropped his imagination, an inert weight, back to earth.

Once, it entered his mind that there was a deliberate rebuff in all this. He caught her spirit of antagonism and strove to divine the message that her hands pronounced upon the keys. Then he dismissed the thought as unworthy and impossible, and yielded himself more freely to the music. The old delightful condition began to be induced. His feet were no longer clay, and his flesh became spirit; before his eyes and behind his eyes shone a great glory; and then the scene before him vanished and he was away, rocking over the world that was to him a very dear world. The known and the unknown were commingled in the dream-pageant that thronged his vision. He entered strange ports of sun-washed lands, and trod market-places among barbaric peoples that no man had ever seen. The scent of the spice islands was in his nostrils as he had known it on warm, breathless nights at sea, or he beat up against the southeast trades through long tropic days, sinking palm-tufted coral islets in the turquoise sea behind and lifting palm-tufted coral islets in the turquoise sea ahead. Swift as thought the pictures came and went. One instant he was astride a broncho and flying through the fairy-colored Painted Desert country; the next instant he was gazing down through shimmering heat into the whited sepulchre of Death Valley, or pulling an oar on a freezing ocean where great ice islands towered and glistened in the sun. He lay on a coral beach where the cocoanuts grew down to the mellow-sounding surf. The hulk of an ancient wreck burned with blue fires, in the light of which danced the *hula* dancers to the barbaric love-calls of the singers, who chanted to tinkling *ukuleles* and rumbling tom-toms. It was a sensuous, tropic night. In the background a volcano crater was silhouetted against the stars. Overhead drifted a pale crescent moon, and the Southern Cross burned low in the sky.

He was a harp; all life that he had known and that was his consciousness was the strings; and the flood of music was a wind that poured against those strings and set them vibrating with memories and dreams. He did not merely feel. Sensation invested itself in form and color and radiance, and what his imagination dared, it objectified in some sublimated and magic way. Past, present, and future mingled; and he went on oscillating across the broad, warm world, through high adventure and noble deeds to Her—ay, and with her, winning her, his arm about her, and carrying her on in flight through the empery of his mind.

And she, glancing at him across her shoulder, saw something of all this in his face. It was a transfigured face, with great shining eyes that gazed beyond the veil of sound and saw behind it the leap and pulse of life and the gigantic phantoms of the spirit. She was startled. The raw, stumbling lout was gone. The ill-fitting clothes, battered hands, and sunburned face remained; but these seemed the prison-bars through which she saw a great soul looking forth, inarticulate and dumb because of those feeble lips that would not give it speech. Only for a flashing moment did she see this, then she saw the lout returned, and she laughed at the whim of her fancy. But the impression of that fleeting glimpse lingered, and when the time came for him to beat a stumbling retreat and go, she lent him the volume of Swinburne, and another of Browning—she was studying Browning in one of her English courses. He seemed such a boy, as he stood blushing and stammering his thanks, that a wave of pity, maternal in its prompting, welled up in her. She did not remember the lout, nor the imprisoned soul, nor the man who had stared at her in all masculineness and delighted and frightened her. She saw before her only a boy, who was shaking her hand with a hand so calloused that it felt like a nutmeg-grater and rasped her skin, and who was saying jerkily:-

"The greatest time of my life. You see, I ain't used to things. . . " He looked about him helplessly. "To people and houses like this. It's all new to me, and I like it."

"I hope you'll call again," she said, as he was saying good night to her brothers.

He pulled on his cap, lurched desperately through the doorway, and was gone.

"Well, what do you think of him?" Arthur demanded.

"He is most interesting, a whiff of ozone," she answered. "How old is he?"

"Twenty—almost twenty-one. I asked him this afternoon. I didn't think he was that young."

And I am three years older, was the thought in her mind as she kissed her brothers goodnight.

CHAPTER III

As Martin Eden went down the steps, his hand dropped into his coat pocket. It came out with a brown rice paper and a pinch of Mexican tobacco, which were deftly rolled together into a cigarette. He drew the first whiff of smoke deep into his lungs and expelled it in a long and lingering exhalation. "By God!" he said aloud, in a voice of awe and wonder. "By God!" he repeated. And yet again he murmured, "By God!" Then his hand went to his collar, which he ripped out of the shirt and stuffed into his pocket. A cold drizzle was falling, but he bared his head to it and unbuttoned his vest, swinging along in splendid unconcern. He was only dimly aware that it was raining. He was in an ecstasy, dreaming dreams and reconstructing the scenes just past.

He had met the woman at last—the woman that he had thought little about, not being given to thinking about women, but whom he had expected, in a remote way, he would sometime meet. He had sat next to her at table. He had felt her hand in his, he had looked into her eyes and caught a vision of a beautiful spirit;—but no more beautiful than the eyes through which it shone, nor than the flesh that gave it expression and form. He did not think of her flesh as flesh,—which was new to him; for of the women he had known that was the only way he thought. Her flesh was somehow different. He did not conceive of her body as a body, subject to the ills and frailties of bodies. Her body was more than the garb of her spirit. It was an emanation of her spirit, a pure and gracious crystallization of her divine essence. This feeling of the divine startled him. It shocked him from his dreams to sober thought. No word, no clew, no hint, of the divine had ever reached him before. He had never believed in the divine. He had always been irreligious, scoffing good-naturedly at the sky-pilots and their immortality of the soul. There was no life beyond, he had contended; it was here and now, then darkness everlasting. But what he had seen in her eyes was soul—immortal soul that could never die. No man he had known, nor any woman, had given him the message of immortality. But she had. She had whispered it to him the first moment she looked at him. Her face shimmered before his eyes as he walked along,—pale and serious, sweet and sensitive, smiling with pity and tenderness as only a spirit could smile, and pure as he had never dreamed purity could be. Her purity smote him like a blow. It startled him. He had known good and bad; but purity, as an attribute of existence, had never entered his mind. And now, in her, he conceived purity to be the superlative of goodness and of cleanness, the sum of which constituted eternal life.

And promptly urged his ambition to grasp at eternal life. He was not fit to carry water for her—he knew that; it was a miracle of luck and a fantastic stroke that had enabled him to see her and be with her and talk with her that night. It was accidental. There was no merit in it. He did not deserve such fortune. His mood was essentially religious. He was humble and meek, filled with self-disparagement and abasement. In such frame of mind sinners come to the penitent form. He was convicted of sin. But as the meek and lowly at the penitent form catch splendid glimpses of their future lordly existence, so did he catch similar glimpses of the state he would gain to by possessing her. But this possession of her was dim and nebulous and totally different from possession as he had known it. Ambition soared on mad wings, and he saw himself climbing the heights with her, sharing thoughts with her, pleasuring in beautiful and noble things with her. It was a soul-possession he dreamed, refined beyond any grossness, a free comradeship of spirit that he could not put into definite thought. He did not think it. For that matter, he did not think at all. Sensation usurped reason, and he was quivering and palpitant with emotions he had never known, drifting deliciously on a sea of sensibility where feeling itself was exalted and spiritualized and carried beyond the summits of life.

He staggered along like a drunken man, murmuring fervently aloud: "By God! By God!"

A policeman on a street corner eyed him suspiciously, then noted his sailor roll.

"Where did you get it?" the policeman demanded.

Martin Eden came back to earth. His was a fluid organism, swiftly adjustable, capable of flowing into and filling all sorts of nooks and crannies. With the policeman's hail he was immediately his ordinary self, grasping the situation clearly.

"It's a beaut, ain't it?" he laughed back. "I didn't know I was talkin' out loud."

"You'll be singing next," was the policeman's diagnosis.

"No, I won't. Gimme a match an' I'll catch the next car home."

He lighted his cigarette, said good night, and went on. "Now wouldn't that rattle you?" he ejaculated under his breath. "That copper thought I was drunk." He smiled to himself and meditated. "I guess I was," he added; "but I didn't think a woman's face'd do it."

He caught a Telegraph Avenue car that was going to Berkeley. It was crowded with youths and young men who were singing songs and ever and again barking out college yells. He studied them curiously. They were university boys. They went to the same university that she did, were in her class socially, could know her, could see her every day if they wanted to. He wondered that they did not want to, that they had been out having a good time instead of being with her that evening, talking with her, sitting around her in a worshipful and adoring circle. His thoughts wandered on. He noticed one with narrow-slitted eyes and a loose-lipped mouth. That fellow was vicious, he decided. On shipboard he would be a sneak, a whiner, a tattler. He, Martin Eden, was a better man than that fellow. The thought cheered him. It seemed to draw him nearer to Her. He began comparing himself with the students. He grew conscious of the muscled mechanism of his body and felt confident that he was physically their master. But their heads were filled with knowledge that enabled them to talk her talk,—the thought depressed him. But what was a brain for? he demanded passionately. What they had done, he could do. They had been studying about life from the books while he had been busy living life. His brain was just as full of knowledge as theirs, though it was a different kind of knowledge. How many of them could tie a lanyard knot, or take a wheel or a lookout? His life spread out before him in a series of pictures of danger and daring, hardship and toil. He remembered his failures and scrapes in the process of learning. He was that much to the good, anyway. Later on they would have to begin living life and going through the mill as he had gone. Very well. While they were busy with that, he could be learning the other side of life from the books.

As the car crossed the zone of scattered dwellings that separated Oakland from Berkeley, he kept a lookout for a familiar, two-story building along the front of which ran the proud sign, HIGGINBOTHAM'S CASH STORE. Martin Eden got off at this corner. He stared up for a moment at the sign. It carried a message to him beyond its mere wording. A personality of smallness and egotism and petty underhandedness seemed to emanate from the letters themselves. Bernard Higginbotham had married his sister, and he knew him well. He let himself in with a latch-key and climbed the stairs to the second floor. Here lived his brother-in-law. The grocery was below. There was a smell of stale vegetables in the air. As he groped his way across the hall he stumbled over a toy-cart, left there by one of his numerous nephews and nieces, and brought up against a door with a resounding bang. "The pincher," was his thought; "too miserly to burn two cents' worth of gas and save his boarders' necks."

He fumbled for the knob and entered a lighted room, where sat his sister and Bernard Higginbotham. She was patching a pair of his trousers, while his lean body was distributed over two chairs, his feet dangling in dilapidated carpet-slippers over the edge of the second chair. He glanced across the top of the paper he was reading, showing a pair of dark, insincere, sharp-staring eyes. Martin Eden never looked at him without experiencing a sense of repulsion. What his sister had seen in the man was beyond him. The other affected him as so much vermin, and always aroused in him an impulse to crush him under his foot. "Some day I'll beat the face off of him," was the way he often consoled himself for enduring the man's existence. The eyes, weasel-like and cruel, were looking at him complainingly.

"Well," Martin demanded. "Out with it."

"I had that door painted only last week," Mr. Higginbotham half whined, half bullied; "and you know what union wages are. You should be more careful."

Martin had intended to reply, but he was struck by the hopelessness of it. He gazed across the monstrous sordidness of soul to a chromo on the wall. It surprised him. He had always liked it, but it seemed that now he was seeing it for the first time. It was cheap, that was what it was, like everything else in this house. His mind went back to the house he had just left, and he saw, first, the paintings, and next, Her, looking at him with melting sweetness as she shook his hand at leaving. He forgot where he was and Bernard Higginbotham's existence, till that gentleman demanded:-

"Seen a ghost?"

Martin came back and looked at the beady eyes, sneering, truculent, cowardly, and there leaped into his vision, as on a screen, the same eyes when their owner was making a sale in the store below—subservient eyes, smug, and oily, and flattering.

"Yes," Martin answered. "I seen a ghost. Good night. Good night, Gertrude."

He started to leave the room, tripping over a loose seam in the slatternly carpet.

"Don't bang the door," Mr. Higginbotham cautioned him.

He felt the blood crawl in his veins, but controlled himself and closed the door softly behind him.

Mr. Higginbotham looked at his wife exultantly.

"He's ben drinkin'," he proclaimed in a hoarse whisper. "I told you he would."

She nodded her head resignedly.

"His eyes was pretty shiny," she confessed; "and he didn't have no collar, though he went away with one. But mebbe he didn't have more'n a couple of glasses."

"He couldn't stand up straight," asserted her husband. "I watched him. He couldn't walk across the floor without stumblin'. You heard 'm yourself almost fall down in the hall."

"I think it was over Alice's cart," she said. "He couldn't see it in the dark."

Mr. Higginbotham's voice and wrath began to rise. All day he effaced himself in the store, reserving for the evening, with his family, the privilege of being himself.

"I tell you that precious brother of yours was drunk."

His voice was cold, sharp, and final, his lips stamping the enunciation of each word like the die of a machine. His wife sighed and remained silent. She was a large, stout woman, always dressed slatternly and always tired from the burdens of her flesh, her work, and her husband.

"He's got it in him, I tell you, from his father," Mr. Higginbotham went on accusingly. "An' he'll croak in the gutter the same way. You know that."

She nodded, sighed, and went on stitching. They were agreed that Martin had come home drunk. They did not have it in their souls to know beauty, or they would have known that those shining eyes and that glowing face betokened youth's first vision of love.

"Settin' a fine example to the children," Mr. Higginbotham snorted, suddenly, in the silence for which his wife was responsible and which he resented. Sometimes he almost wished she would oppose him more. "If he does it again, he's got to get out. Understand! I won't put up with his shinanigan—debotchin' innocent children with his boozing." Mr. Higginbotham liked the word, which was a new one in his vocabulary, recently gleaned from a newspaper column. "That's what it is, debotchin'—there ain't no other name for it."

Still his wife sighed, shook her head sorrowfully, and stitched on. Mr. Higginbotham resumed the newspaper.

"Has he paid last week's board?" he shot across the top of the newspaper.

She nodded, then added, "He still has some money."

"When is he goin' to sea again?"

"When his pay-day's spent, I guess," she answered. "He was over to San Francisco yesterday looking for a ship. But he's got money, yet, an' he's particular about the kind of ship he signs for."

"It's not for a deck-swab like him to put on airs," Mr. Higginbotham snorted. "Particular! Him!"

"He said something about a schooner that's gettin' ready to go off to some outlandish place to look for buried treasure, that he'd sail on her if his money held out."

"If he only wanted to steady down, I'd give him a job drivin' the wagon," her husband said, but with no trace of benevolence in his voice. "Tom's quit."

His wife looked alarm and interrogation.

"Quit to-night. Is goin' to work for Carruthers. They paid 'm more'n I could afford."

"I told you you'd lose 'm," she cried out. "He was worth more'n you was giving him."

"Now look here, old woman," Higginbotham bullied, "for the thousandth time I've told you to keep your nose out of the business. I won't tell you again."

"I don't care," she sniffled. "Tom was a good boy." Her husband glared at her. This was unqualified defiance.

"If that brother of yours was worth his salt, he could take the wagon," he snorted.

"He pays his board, just the same," was the retort. "An' he's my brother, an' so long as he don't owe you money you've got no right to be jumping on him all the time. I've got some feelings, if I have been married to you for seven years."

"Did you tell 'm you'd charge him for gas if he goes on readin' in bed?" he demanded.

Mrs. Higginbotham made no reply. Her revolt faded away, her spirit wilting down into her tired flesh. Her husband was triumphant. He had her. His eyes snapped vindictively, while his ears joyed in the sniffles she emitted. He extracted great happiness from squelching her, and she squelched easily these days, though it had been different in the first years of their married life, before the brood of children and his incessant nagging had sapped her energy.

"Well, you tell 'm to-morrow, that's all," he said. "An' I just want to tell you, before I forget it, that you'd better send for Marian to-morrow to take care of the children. With Tom quit, I'll have to be out on the wagon, an' you can make up your mind to it to be down below waitin' on the counter."

"But to-morrow's wash day," she objected weakly.

"Get up early, then, an' do it first. I won't start out till ten o'clock."

He crinkled the paper viciously and resumed his reading.

CHAPTER IV

Martin Eden, with blood still crawling from contact with his brother-in-law, felt his way along the unlighted back hall and entered his room, a tiny cubbyhole with space for a bed, a wash-stand, and one chair. Mr. Higginbotham was too thrifty to keep a servant when his wife could do the work. Besides, the servant's room enabled them to take in two boarders instead of one. Martin placed the Swinburne and Browning on the chair, took off his coat, and sat down on the bed. A screeching of asthmatic springs greeted the weight of his body, but he did not notice them. He started to take off his shoes, but fell to staring at the white plaster wall opposite him, broken by long streaks of dirty brown where rain had leaked through the roof. On this befouled background visions began to flow and burn. He forgot his shoes and stared long, till his lips began to move and he murmured, "Ruth."

"Ruth." He had not thought a simple sound could be so beautiful. It delighted his ear, and he grew intoxicated with the repetition of it. "Ruth." It was a talisman, a magic word to conjure with. Each time he murmured it, her face shimmered before him, suffusing the foul wall with a golden radiance. This radiance did not stop at the wall. It extended on into infinity, and through its golden depths his soul went questing after hers. The best that was in him was out in splendid flood. The very thought of her ennobled and purified him, made him better, and made him want to be better. This was new to him. He had never known women who had made him better. They had always had the counter effect of making him beastly. He did not know that many of them had done their best, bad as it was. Never having been conscious of himself, he did not know that he had that in his being that drew love from women and which had been the cause of their reaching out for his youth. Though they had often bothered him, he had never bothered about them; and he would never have dreamed that there were women who had been better because of him. Always in sublime carelessness had he lived, till now, and now it seemed to him that they had always reached out and dragged at him with vile hands. This was not just to them, nor to himself. But he, who for the first time was becoming conscious of himself, was in no condition to judge, and he burned with shame as he stared at the vision of his infamy.

He got up abruptly and tried to see himself in the dirty looking-glass over the wash-stand. He passed a towel over it and looked again, long and carefully. It was the first time he had ever really seen himself. His eyes were made for seeing, but up to that moment they had been filled with the ever changing panorama of the world, at which he had been too busy gazing, ever to gaze at himself. He saw the head and face of a young fellow of twenty, but, being unused to such appraisement, he did not know how to value it. Above a square-domed forehead he saw a mop of brown hair, nut-brown, with a wave to it and hints of curls that were a delight to any woman, making hands tingle to stroke it and fingers tingle to pass caresses through it. But he passed it by as without merit, in Her eyes, and dwelt long and thoughtfully on the high, square forehead,—striving to penetrate it and learn the quality of its content. What kind of a brain lay behind there? was his insistent interrogation. What was it capable of? How far would it take him? Would it take him to her?

He wondered if there was soul in those steel-gray eyes that were often quite blue of color and that were strong with the briny airs of the sun-washed deep. He wondered, also, how his eyes looked to her. He tried to imagine himself she, gazing into those eyes of his, but failed in the jugglery. He could successfully put himself inside other men's minds, but they had to be men whose ways of life he knew. He did not know her way of life. She was wonder and mystery, and how could he guess one thought of hers? Well, they were honest eyes, he concluded, and in them was neither smallness nor meanness. The brown sunburn of his face surprised him. He had not dreamed he was so black. He rolled up his shirt-sleeve and compared the white underside if the arm with his face. Yes, he was a white man, after all. But the arms were sunburned, too. He twisted his arm, rolled the biceps over with his other hand, and gazed underneath where he was least touched by the sun. It was very white. He laughed at his bronzed face in the glass at the thought that it was once as white as the underside of his arm; nor did he dream that in the world there were few pale spirits of women who could boast fairer or smoother skins than he—fairer than where he had escaped the ravages of the sun.

His might have been a cherub's mouth, had not the full, sensuous lips a trick, under stress, of drawing firmly across the teeth. At times, so tightly did they draw, the mouth became stern and harsh, even ascetic. They were the lips of a fighter and of a lover. They could taste the sweetness of life with relish, and they could put the sweetness aside and command life. The chin and jaw, strong and just hinting of square aggressiveness, helped the lips to command life. Strength balanced sensuousness and had upon it a tonic effect, compelling him to love beauty that was healthy and making him vibrate to sensations that were wholesome. And between the lips were teeth that had never known nor needed the dentist's care. They were white and strong and regular, he decided, as he looked at them. But as he looked, he began to be troubled. Somewhere, stored away in the recesses of his mind and vaguely remembered, was the impression that there were people who washed their teeth every day. They were the people from up above—people in her class. She must wash her teeth every day, too. What would she think if she learned that he had never washed his teeth in all the days of his life? He resolved to get a tooth-brush and form the habit. He would begin at once, to-morrow. It was not by mere achievement that he could hope to win to her. He must make a personal reform in all things, even to tooth-washing and neck-gear, though a starched collar affected him as a renunciation of freedom.

He held up his hand, rubbing the ball of the thumb over the calloused palm and gazing at the dirt that was ingrained in the flesh itself and which no brush could scrub away. How different was her palm! He thrilled deliciously at the remembrance. Like a rose-petal, he thought; cool and soft as a snowflake. He had never thought that a mere woman's hand could be so sweetly soft. He caught himself imagining the wonder of a caress from such a hand, and flushed guiltily. It was too gross a thought for her. In ways it seemed to impugn her high spirituality. She was a pale, slender spirit, exalted far beyond the flesh; but nevertheless the softness of her palm persisted in his thoughts. He was used to the harsh callousness of factory girls and working women. Well he knew why their hands were rough; but this hand of hers . . . It was soft because she had never used it to work with. The gulf yawned between her and him at the awesome thought of a person who did not have to work for a living. He suddenly saw the aristocracy of the people who did not labor. It towered before him on the wall, a figure in brass, arrogant and powerful. He had worked himself; his first memories seemed connected with work, and all his family had worked. There was Gertrude. When her hands were not hard from the endless housework, they were swollen and red like boiled beef, what of the washing.

And there was his sister Marian. She had worked in the cannery the preceding summer, and her slim, pretty hands were all scarred with the tomato-knives. Besides, the tips of two of her fingers had been left in the cutting machine at the paper-box factory the preceding winter. He remembered the hard palms of his mother as she lay in her coffin. And his father had worked to the last fading gasp; the horned growth on his hands must have been half an inch thick when he died. But Her hands were soft, and her mother's hands, and her brothers'. This last came to him as a surprise; it was tremendously indicative of the highness of their caste, of the enormous distance that stretched between her and him.

He sat back on the bed with a bitter laugh, and finished taking off his shoes. He was a fool; he had been made drunken by a woman's face and by a woman's soft, white hands. And then, suddenly, before his eyes, on the foul plaster-wall appeared a vision. He stood in front of a gloomy tenement house. It was night-time, in the East End of London, and before him stood Margey, a little factory girl of fifteen. He had seen her home after the bean-feast. She lived in that gloomy tenement, a place not fit for swine. His hand was going out to hers as he said good night. She had put her lips up to be kissed, but he wasn't going to kiss her. Somehow he was afraid of her. And then her hand closed on his and pressed feverishly. He felt her callouses grind and grate on his, and a great wave of pity welled over him. He saw her yearning, hungry eyes, and her ill-fed female form which had been rushed from childhood into a frightened and ferocious maturity; then he put his arms about her in large tolerance and stooped and kissed her on the lips. Her glad little cry rang in his ears, and he felt her clinging to him like a cat. Poor little starveling! He continued to stare at the vision of what had happened in the long ago. His flesh was crawling as it had crawled that night when she clung to him, and his heart was warm with pity. It was a gray scene, greasy gray, and the rain drizzled greasily on the pavement stones. And then a radiant glory shone on the wall, and up through the other vision, displacing it, glimmered Her pale face under its crown of golden hair, remote and inaccessible as a star.

He took the Browning and the Swinburne from the chair and kissed them. Just the same, she told me to call again, he thought. He took another look at himself in the glass, and said aloud, with great solemnity:-

"Martin Eden, the first thing to-morrow you go to the free library an' read up on etiquette. Understand!"

He turned off the gas, and the springs shrieked under his body.

"But you've got to quit cussin', Martin, old boy; you've got to quit cussin'," he said aloud.

Then he dozed off to sleep and to dream dreams that for madness and audacity rivalled those of poppy-eaters.

CHAPTER V

He awoke next morning from rosy scenes of dream to a steamy atmosphere that smelled of soapsuds and dirty clothes, and that was vibrant with the jar and jangle of tormented life. As he came out of his room he heard the slosh of water, a sharp exclamation, and a resounding smack as his sister visited her irritation upon one of her numerous progeny. The squall of the child went through him like a knife. He was aware that the whole thing, the very air he breathed, was repulsive and mean. How different, he thought, from the atmosphere of beauty and repose of the house wherein Ruth dwelt. There it was all spiritual. Here it was all material, and meanly material.

"Come here, Alfred," he called to the crying child, at the same time thrusting his hand into his trousers pocket, where he carried his money loose in the same large way that he lived life in general. He put a quarter in the youngster's hand and held him in his arms a moment, soothing his sobs. "Now run along and get some candy, and don't forget to give some to your brothers and sisters. Be sure and get the kind that lasts longest."

His sister lifted a flushed face from the wash-tub and looked at him.

"A nickel'd ha' ben enough," she said. "It's just like you, no idea of the value of money. The child'll eat himself sick."

"That's all right, sis," he answered jovially. "My money'll take care of itself. If you weren't so busy, I'd kiss you good morning."

He wanted to be affectionate to this sister, who was good, and who, in her way, he knew, loved him. But, somehow, she grew less herself as the years went by, and more and more baffling. It was the hard work, the many children, and the nagging of her husband, he decided, that had changed her. It came to him, in a flash of fancy, that her nature seemed taking on the attributes of stale vegetables, smelly soapsuds, and of the greasy dimes, nickels, and quarters she took in over the counter of the store.

"Go along an' get your breakfast," she said roughly, though secretly pleased. Of all her wandering brood of brothers he had always been her favorite. "I declare I *will* kiss you," she said, with a sudden stir at her heart.

With thumb and forefinger she swept the dripping suds first from one arm and then from the other. He put his arms round her massive waist and kissed her wet steamy lips. The tears welled into her eyes—not so much from strength of feeling as from the weakness of chronic overwork. She shoved him away from her, but not before he caught a glimpse of her moist eyes.

"You'll find breakfast in the oven," she said hurriedly. "Jim ought to be up now. I had to get up early for the washing. Now get along with you and get out of the house early. It won't be nice to-day, what of Tom quittin' an' nobody but Bernard to drive the wagon."

Martin went into the kitchen with a sinking heart, the image of her red face and slatternly form eating its way like acid into his brain. She might love him if she only had some time, he concluded. But she was worked to death. Bernard Higginbotham was a brute to work her so hard. But he could not help but feel, on the other hand, that there had not been anything beautiful in that kiss. It was true, it was an unusual kiss. For years she had kissed him only when he returned from voyages or departed on voyages. But this kiss had tasted soapsuds, and the lips, he had noticed, were flabby. There had been no quick, vigorous lip-pressure such as should accompany any kiss. Hers was the kiss of a tired woman who had been tired so long that she had forgotten how to kiss. He remembered her as a girl, before her marriage, when she would dance with the best, all night, after a hard day's work at the laundry, and think nothing of leaving the dance to go to another day's hard work. And then he thought of Ruth and the cool sweetness that must reside in her lips as it resided in all about her. Her kiss would be like her hand-shake or the way she looked at one, firm and frank. In imagination he dared to think of her lips on his, and so vividly did he imagine that he went dizzy at the thought and seemed to rift through clouds of rose-petals, filling his brain with their perfume.

In the kitchen he found Jim, the other boarder, eating mush very languidly, with a sick, far-away look in his eyes. Jim was a plumber's apprentice whose weak chin and hedonistic temperament, coupled with a certain nervous stupidity, promised to take him nowhere in the race for bread and butter.

"Why don't you eat?" he demanded, as Martin dipped dolefully into the cold, half-cooked oatmeal mush. "Was you drunk again last night?"

Martin shook his head. He was oppressed by the utter squalidness of it all. Ruth Morse seemed farther removed than ever.

"I was," Jim went on with a boastful, nervous giggle. "I was loaded right to the neck. Oh, she was a daisy. Billy brought me home."

Martin nodded that he heard,—it was a habit of nature with him to pay heed to whoever talked to him,—and poured a cup of lukewarm coffee.

"Goin' to the Lotus Club dance to-night?" Jim demanded. "They're goin' to have beer, an' if that Temescal bunch comes, there'll be a rough-house. I don't care, though. I'm takin' my lady friend just the same. Cripes, but I've got a taste in my mouth!"

He made a wry face and attempted to wash the taste away with coffee.

"D'ye know Julia?"

Martin shook his head.

"She's my lady friend," Jim explained, "and she's a peach. I'd introduce you to her, only you'd win her. I don't see what the girls see in you, honest I don't; but the way you win them away from the fellers is sickenin'."

"I never got any away from you," Martin answered uninterestedly. The breakfast had to be got through somehow.

"Yes, you did, too," the other asserted warmly. "There was Maggie."

"Never had anything to do with her. Never danced with her except that one night."

"Yes, an' that's just what did it," Jim cried out. "You just danced with her an' looked at her, an' it was all off. Of course you didn't mean nothin' by it, but it settled me for keeps. Wouldn't look at me again. Always askin' about you. She'd have made fast dates enough with you if you'd wanted to."

"But I didn't want to."

"Wasn't necessary. I was left at the pole." Jim looked at him admiringly. "How d'ye do it, anyway, Mart?"

"By not carin' about 'em," was the answer.

"You mean makin' b'lieve you don't care about them?" Jim queried eagerly.

Martin considered for a moment, then answered, "Perhaps that will do, but with me I guess it's different. I never have cared—much. If you can put it on, it's all right, most likely."

"You should 'a' ben up at Riley's barn last night," Jim announced inconsequently. "A lot of the fellers put on the gloves. There was a peach from West Oakland. They called 'm 'The Rat.' Slick as silk. No one could touch 'm. We was all wishin' you was there. Where was you anyway?"

"Down in Oakland," Martin replied.

"To the show?"

Martin shoved his plate away and got up.

"Comin' to the dance to-night?" the other called after him.

"No, I think not," he answered.

He went downstairs and out into the street, breathing great breaths of air. He had been suffocating in that atmosphere, while the apprentice's chatter had driven him frantic. There had been times when it was all he could do to refrain from reaching over and mopping Jim's face in the mush-plate. The more he had chattered, the more remote had Ruth seemed to him. How could he, herding with such cattle, ever become worthy of her? He was appalled at the problem confronting him, weighted down by the incubus of his working-class station. Everything reached out to hold him down—his sister, his sister's house and family, Jim the apprentice, everybody he knew, every tie of life. Existence did not taste good in his mouth. Up to then he had accepted existence, as he had lived it with all about him, as a good thing. He had never questioned it, except when he read books; but then, they were only books, fairy stories of a fairer and impossible world. But now he had seen that world, possible and real, with a flower of a woman called Ruth in the midmost centre of it; and thenceforth he must know bitter tastes, and longings sharp as pain, and hopelessness that tantalized because it fed on hope.

He had debated between the Berkeley Free Library and the Oakland Free Library, and decided upon the latter because Ruth lived in Oakland. Who could tell?—a library was a most likely place for her, and he might see her there. He did not know the way of libraries, and he wandered through endless rows of fiction, till the delicate-featured French-looking girl who seemed in charge, told him that the reference department was upstairs. He did not know enough to ask the man at the desk, and began his adventures in the philosophy alcove. He had heard of book philosophy, but had not imagined there had been so much written about it. The high, bulging shelves of heavy tomes humbled him and at the same time stimulated him. Here was work for the vigor of his brain. He found books on trigonometry in the mathematics section, and ran the pages, and stared at the meaningless formulas and figures. He could read English, but he saw there an alien speech. Norman and Arthur knew that speech. He had heard them talking it. And they were her brothers. He left the alcove in despair. From every side the books seemed to press upon him and crush him.

He had never dreamed that the fund of human knowledge bulked so big. He was frightened. How could his brain ever master it all? Later, he remembered that there were other men, many men, who had mastered it; and he breathed a great oath, passionately, under his breath, swearing that his brain could do what theirs had done.

And so he wandered on, alternating between depression and elation as he stared at the shelves packed with wisdom. In one miscellaneous section he came upon a "Norrie's

Epitome." He turned the pages reverently. In a way, it spoke a kindred speech. Both he and it were of the sea. Then he found a "Bowditch" and books by Lecky and Marshall. There it was; he would teach himself navigation. He would quit drinking, work up, and become a captain. Ruth seemed very near to him in that moment. As a captain, he could marry her (if she would have him). And if she wouldn't, well—he would live a good life among men, because of Her, and he would quit drinking anyway. Then he remembered the underwriters and the owners, the two masters a captain must serve, either of which could and would break him and whose interests were diametrically opposed. He cast his eyes about the room and closed the lids down on a vision of ten thousand books. No; no more of the sea for him. There was power in all that wealth of books, and if he would do great things, he must do them on the land. Besides, captains were not allowed to take their wives to sea with them.

Noon came, and afternoon. He forgot to eat, and sought on for the books on etiquette; for, in addition to career, his mind was vexed by a simple and very concrete problem: *When you meet a young lady and she asks you to call, how soon can you call*? was the way he worded it to himself. But when he found the right shelf, he sought vainly for the answer. He was appalled at the vast edifice of etiquette, and lost himself in the mazes of visiting-card conduct between persons in polite society. He abandoned his search. He had not found what he wanted, though he had found that it would take all of a man's time to be polite, and that he would have to live a preliminary life in which to learn how to be polite.

"Did you find what you wanted?" the man at the desk asked him as he was leaving.

"Yes, sir," he answered. "You have a fine library here."

The man nodded. "We should be glad to see you here often. Are you a sailor?"

"Yes, sir," he answered. "And I'll come again."

Now, how did he know that? he asked himself as he went down the stairs.

And for the first block along the street he walked very stiff and straight and awkwardly, until he forgot himself in his thoughts, whereupon his rolling gait gracefully returned to him.

CHAPTER VI

A terrible restlessness that was akin to hunger afflicted Martin Eden. He was famished for a sight of the girl whose slender hands had gripped his life with a giant's grasp. He could not steel himself to call upon her. He was afraid that he might call too soon, and so be guilty of an awful breach of that awful thing called etiquette. He spent long hours in the Oakland and Berkeley libraries, and made out application blanks for membership for himself, his sisters Gertrude and Marian, and Jim, the latter's consent being obtained at the expense of several glasses of beer. With four cards permitting him to draw books, he burned the gas late in the servant's room, and was charged fifty cents a week for it by Mr. Higginbotham.

The many books he read but served to whet his unrest. Every page of every book was a peep-hole into the realm of knowledge. His hunger fed upon what he read, and increased. Also, he did not know where to begin, and continually suffered from lack of preparation. The commonest references, that he could see plainly every reader was expected to know, he did not know. And the same was true of the poetry he read which maddened him with delight. He read more of Swinburne than was contained in the volume Ruth had lent him; and "Dolores" he understood thoroughly. But surely Ruth did not understand it, he concluded. How could she, living the refined life she did? Then he chanced upon Kipling's poems, and was swept away by the lilt and swing and glamour with which familiar things had been invested. He was amazed at the man's sympathy with life and at his incisive psychology. *Psychology* was a new word in Martin's vocabulary. He had bought a dictionary, which deed had decreased his supply of money and brought nearer the day on which he must sail in search of more. Also, it incensed Mr. Higginbotham, who would have preferred the money taking the form of board.

He dared not go near Ruth's neighborhood in the daytime, but night found him lurking like a thief around the Morse home, stealing glimpses at the windows and loving the very walls that sheltered her. Several times he barely escaped being caught by her brothers, and once he trailed Mr. Morse down town and studied his face in the lighted streets, longing all the while for some quick danger of death to threaten so that he might spring in and save her father. On another night, his vigil was rewarded by a glimpse of Ruth through a second-story window. He saw only her head and shoulders, and her arms raised as she fixed her hair before a mirror. It was only for a moment, but it was a long moment to him, during which his blood turned to wine and sang through his veins. Then she pulled down the shade. But it was her room—he had learned that; and thereafter he strayed there often, hiding under a dark tree on the opposite side of the street and smoking countless cigarettes. One afternoon he saw her mother coming out of a bank, and received another proof of the enormous distance that separated Ruth from him. She was of the class that dealt with banks. He had never been inside a bank in his life, and he had an idea that such institutions were frequented only by the very rich and the very powerful.

In one way, he had undergone a moral revolution. Her cleanness and purity had reacted upon him, and he felt in his being a crying need to be clean. He must be that if he were ever to be worthy of breathing the same air with her. He washed his teeth, and scrubbed his hands with a kitchen scrub-brush till he saw a nail-brush in a drug-store window and divined its use. While purchasing it, the clerk glanced at his nails, suggested a nail-file, and so he became possessed of an additional toilet-tool. He ran across a book in the library on the care of the body, and promptly developed a penchant for a cold-water bath every morning, much to the amazement of Jim, and to the bewilderment of Mr. Higginbotham, who was not in sympathy with such high-fangled notions and who seriously debated whether or not he should charge Martin extra for the water. Another stride was in the direction of creased trousers. Now that Martin was aroused in such matters, he swiftly noted the difference between the baggy knees of the trousers worn by the working class and the straight line from knee to foot of those worn by the men above the working class. Also, he learned the reason why, and invaded his sister's kitchen in search of irons and ironing-board. He had misadventures at first, hopelessly burning one pair and buying another, which expenditure again brought nearer the day on which he must put to sea.

But the reform went deeper than mere outward appearance. He still smoked, but he drank no more. Up to that time, drinking had seemed to him the proper thing for men to do, and he had prided himself on his strong head which enabled him to drink most men under the table. Whenever he encountered a chance shipmate, and there were many in San Francisco, he treated them and was treated in turn, as of old, but he ordered for himself root beer or ginger ale and good-naturedly endured their chaffing. And as they waxed maudlin he studied them, watching the beast rise and master them and thanking God that he was no longer as they. They had their limitations to forget, and when they were drunk, their dim, stupid spirits were even as gods, and each ruled in his heaven of intoxicated desire. With Martin the need for strong drink had vanished. He was drunken in new and more profound ways—with Ruth, who had fired him with love and with a glimpse of higher and eternal life; with books, that had set a myriad maggots of desire gnawing in his brain; and with the sense of personal cleanliness he was achieving, that gave him even more superb health than what he had enjoyed and that made his whole body sing with physical well-being.

One night he went to the theatre, on the blind chance that he might see her there, and from the second balcony he did see her. He saw her come down the aisle, with Arthur and a strange young man with a football mop of hair and eyeglasses, the sight of whom spurred him to instant apprehension and jealousy. He saw her take her seat in the orchestra circle, and little else than her did he see that night—a pair of slender white shoulders and a mass of pale gold hair, dim with distance. But there were others who saw, and now and again, glancing at those about him, he noted two young girls who looked back from the row in front, a dozen seats along, and who smiled at him with bold eyes. He had always been easy-going. It was not in his nature to give rebuff. In the old days he would have smiled back, and gone further and encouraged smiling. But now it was different. He did smile back, then looked away, and looked no more deliberately. But several times, forgetting the existence of the two girls, his eyes caught their smiles. He could not re-thumb himself in a day, nor could he violate the intrinsic kindliness of his nature; so, at such moments, he smiled at the girls in warm human friendliness. It was nothing new to him. He knew they were reaching out their woman's hands to him. But it was different now. Far down there in the orchestra circle was the one woman in all the world, so different, so terrifically different, from these two girls of his class, that he could feel for them only pity and sorrow. He had it in his heart to wish that they could possess, in some small measure, her goodness and glory. And not for the world could he hurt them because of their outreaching. He was not flattered by it; he even felt a slight shame at his lowliness that permitted it. He knew, did he belong in Ruth's class, that there would be no overtures from these girls; and with each glance of theirs he felt the fingers of his own class clutching at him to hold him down.

He left his seat before the curtain went down on the last act, intent on seeing Her as she passed out. There were always numbers of men who stood on the sidewalk outside, and he could pull his cap down over his eyes and screen himself behind some one's shoulder so that she should not see him. He emerged from the theatre with the first of the crowd; but scarcely had he taken his position on the edge of the sidewalk when the two girls appeared. They were looking for him, he knew; and for the moment he could have cursed that in him which drew women. Their casual edging across the sidewalk to the curb, as they drew near, apprised him of discovery. They slowed down, and were in the thick of the crown as they came up with him. One of them brushed against him and apparently for the first time noticed him. She was a slender, dark girl, with black, defiant eyes. But they smiled at him, and he smiled back.

"Hello," he said.

It was automatic; he had said it so often before under similar circumstances of first meetings. Besides, he could do no less. There was that large tolerance and sympathy in his nature that would permit him to do no less. The black-eyed girl smiled gratification and greeting, and showed signs of stopping, while her companion, arm linked in arm, giggled and likewise showed signs of halting. He thought quickly. It would never do for Her to come out and see him talking there with them. Quite naturally, as a matter of course, he swung in alongside the dark-eyed one and walked with her. There was no awkwardness on his part, no numb tongue. He was at home here, and he held his own royally in the badinage, bristling with slang and sharpness, that was always the preliminary to getting acquainted in these swift-moving affairs. At the corner where the main stream of people flowed onward, he started to edge out into the cross street. But the girl with the black eyes caught his arm, following him and dragging her companion after her, as she cried:

"Hold on, Bill! What's yer rush? You're not goin' to shake us so sudden as all that?"

He halted with a laugh, and turned, facing them. Across their shoulders he could see the moving throng passing under the street lamps. Where he stood it was not so light, and, unseen, he would be able to see Her as she passed by. She would certainly pass by, for that way led home.

"What's her name?" he asked of the giggling girl, nodding at the dark-eyed one.

"You ask her," was the convulsed response.

"Well, what is it?" he demanded, turning squarely on the girl in question.

"You ain't told me yours, yet," she retorted.

"You never asked it," he smiled. "Besides, you guessed the first rattle. It's Bill, all right, all right."

"Aw, go 'long with you." She looked him in the eyes, her own sharply passionate and inviting. "What is it, honest?"

Again she looked. All the centuries of woman since sex began were eloquent in her eyes. And he measured her in a careless way, and knew, bold now, that she would begin to retreat, coyly and delicately, as he pursued, ever ready to reverse the game should he turn fainthearted. And, too, he was human, and could feel the draw of her, while his ego could not but appreciate the flattery of her kindness. Oh, he knew it all, and knew them well, from A to Z. Good, as goodness might be measured in their particular class, hard-working for meagre wages and scorning the sale of self for easier ways, nervously desirous for some small pinch of happiness in the desert of existence, and facing a future that was a gamble between the ugliness of unending toil and the black pit of more terrible wretchedness, the way whereto being briefer though better paid.

"Bill," he answered, nodding his head. "Sure, Pete, Bill an' no other."

"No joshin'?" she queried.

"It ain't Bill at all," the other broke in.

"How do you know?" he demanded. "You never laid eyes on me before."

"No need to, to know you're lyin'," was the retort.

"Straight, Bill, what is it?" the first girl asked.

"Bill'll do," he confessed.

She reached out to his arm and shook him playfully. "I knew you was lyin', but you look good to me just the same."

He captured the hand that invited, and felt on the palm familiar markings and distortions.

"When'd you chuck the cannery?" he asked.

"How'd yeh know?" and, "My, ain't cheh a mind-reader!" the girls chorussed.

And while he exchanged the stupidities of stupid minds with them, before his inner sight towered the book-shelves of the library, filled with the wisdom of the ages. He smiled bitterly at the incongruity of it, and was assailed by doubts. But between inner vision and outward pleasantry he found time to watch the theatre crowd streaming by. And then he saw Her, under the lights, between her brother and the strange young man with glasses, and his heart seemed to stand still. He had waited long for this moment. He had time to note the light, fluffy something that hid her queenly head, the tasteful lines of her wrapped figure, the gracefulness of her carriage and of the hand that caught up her skirts; and then she was gone and he was left staring at the two girls of the cannery, at their tawdry attempts at prettiness of dress, their tragic efforts to be clean and trim, the cheap cloth, the cheap ribbons, and the cheap rings on the fingers. He felt a tug at his arm, and heard a voice saying:-

"Wake up, Bill! What's the matter with you?"

"What was you sayin'?" he asked.

"Oh, nothin'," the dark girl answered, with a toss of her head. "I was only remarkin'—"

"What?"

"Well, I was whisperin' it'd be a good idea if you could dig up a gentleman friend—for her" (indicating her companion), "and then, we could go off an' have ice-cream soda somewhere, or coffee, or anything."

He was afflicted by a sudden spiritual nausea. The transition from Ruth to this had been too abrupt. Ranged side by side with the bold, defiant eyes of the girl before him, he saw Ruth's clear, luminous eyes, like a saint's, gazing at him out of unplumbed depths of purity. And, somehow, he felt within him a stir of power. He was better than this. Life meant more to him than it meant to these two girls whose thoughts did not go beyond ice-cream and a gentleman friend. He remembered that he had led always a secret life in his thoughts. These thoughts he had tried to share, but never had he found a woman capable of understanding—nor a man. He had tried, at times, but had only puzzled his listeners. And as his thoughts had been beyond them, so, he argued now, he must be beyond them. He felt power move in him, and clenched his fists. If life meant more to him, then it was for him to demand more from life, but he could not demand it from such companionship as this. Those bold black eyes had nothing to offer. He knew the thoughts behind them—of ice-cream and of something else. But those saint's eyes alongside—they offered all he knew and more than he could guess. They offered books and painting, beauty and repose, and all the fine elegance of higher existence. Behind those black eyes he knew every thought process. It was like clockwork. He could watch every wheel go around. Their bid was low pleasure, narrow as the grave, that palled, and the grave was at the end of it. But the bid of the saint's eyes was mystery, and wonder unthinkable, and eternal life. He had caught glimpses of the soul in them, and glimpses of his own soul, too.

"There's only one thing wrong with the programme," he said aloud. "I've got a date already."

The girl's eyes blazed her disappointment.

"To sit up with a sick friend, I suppose?" she sneered.

"No, a real, honest date with—" he faltered, "with a girl."

"You're not stringin' me?" she asked earnestly.

He looked her in the eyes and answered: "It's straight, all right. But why can't we meet some other time? You ain't told me your name yet. An' where d'ye live?"

"Lizzie," she replied, softening toward him, her hand pressing his arm, while her body leaned against his. "Lizzie Connolly. And I live at Fifth an' Market."

He talked on a few minutes before saying good night. He did not go home immediately; and under the tree where he kept his vigils he looked up at a window and murmured: "That date was with you, Ruth. I kept it for you."

CHAPTER VII

A week of heavy reading had passed since the evening he first met Ruth Morse, and still he dared not call. Time and again he nerved himself up to call, but under the doubts that assailed him his determination died away. He did not know the proper time to call, nor was there any one to tell him, and he was afraid of committing himself to an irretrievable blunder. Having shaken himself free from his old companions and old ways of life, and having no new companions, nothing remained for him but to read, and the long hours he devoted to it would have ruined a dozen pairs of ordinary eyes. But his eyes were strong, and they were backed by a body superbly strong. Furthermore, his mind was fallow. It had lain fallow all his life so far as the abstract thought of the books was concerned, and it was ripe for the sowing. It had never been jaded by study, and it bit hold of the knowledge in the books with sharp teeth that would not let go.

It seemed to him, by the end of the week, that he had lived centuries, so far behind were the old life and outlook. But he was baffled by lack of preparation. He attempted to read books that required years of preliminary specialization. One day he would read a book of antiquated philosophy, and the next day one that was ultra-modern, so that his head would be whirling with the conflict and contradiction of ideas. It was the same with the economists. On the one shelf at the library he found Karl Marx, Ricardo, Adam Smith, and Mill, and the abstruse formulas of the one gave no clew that the ideas of another were obsolete. He was bewildered, and yet he wanted to know. He had become interested, in a day, in economics, industry, and politics. Passing through the City Hall Park, he had noticed a group of men, in the centre of which were half a dozen, with flushed faces and raised voices, earnestly carrying on a discussion. He joined the listeners, and heard a new, alien tongue in the mouths of the philosophers of the people. One was a tramp, another was a labor agitator, a third was a law-school student, and the remainder was composed of wordy workingmen. For the first time he heard of socialism, anarchism, and single tax, and learned that there were warring social philosophies. He heard hundreds of technical words that were new to him, belonging to fields of thought that his meagre reading had never touched upon. Because of this he could not follow the arguments closely, and he could only guess at and surmise the ideas wrapped up in such strange expressions. Then there was a black-eyed restaurant waiter who was a theosophist, a union baker who was an agnostic, an old man who baffled all of them with the strange philosophy that *what is is right*, and another old man who discoursed interminably about the cosmos and the father-atom and the mother-atom.

Martin Eden's head was in a state of addlement when he went away after several hours, and he hurried to the library to look up the definitions of a dozen unusual words. And when he left the library, he carried under his arm four volumes: Madam Blavatsky's "Secret Doctrine," "Progress and Poverty," "The Quintessence of Socialism," and, "Warfare of Religion and Science." Unfortunately, he began on the "Secret Doctrine." Every line bristled with many-syllabled words he did not understand. He sat up in bed, and the dictionary was in front of him more often than the book. He looked up so many new words that when they recurred, he had forgotten their meaning and had to look them up again. He devised the plan of writing the definitions in a note-book, and filled page after page with them. And still he could not understand. He read until three in the morning, and his brain was in a turmoil, but not one essential thought in the text had he grasped. He looked up, and it seemed that the room was lifting, heeling, and plunging like a ship upon the sea. Then he hurled the "Secret Doctrine" and many curses across the room, turned off the gas, and composed himself to sleep. Nor did he have much better luck with the other three books. It was not that his brain was weak or incapable; it could think these thoughts were it not for lack of training in thinking and lack of the thought-tools with which to think. He guessed this, and for a while entertained the idea of reading nothing but the dictionary until he had mastered every word in it.

Poetry, however, was his solace, and he read much of it, finding his greatest joy in the simpler poets, who were more understandable. He loved beauty, and there he found beauty. Poetry, like music, stirred him profoundly, and, though he did not know it, he was preparing his mind for the heavier work that was to come. The pages of his mind were blank, and, without effort, much he read and liked, stanza by stanza, was impressed upon those pages, so that he was soon able to extract great joy from chanting aloud or under his breath the music and the beauty of the printed words he had read. Then he stumbled upon Gayley's "Classic Myths" and Bulfinch's "Age of Fable," side by side on a library shelf. It was illumination, a great light in the darkness of his ignorance, and he read poetry more avidly than ever.

The man at the desk in the library had seen Martin there so often that he had become quite cordial, always greeting him with a smile and a nod when he entered. It was because of this that Martin did a daring thing. Drawing out some books at the desk, and while the man was stamping the cards, Martin blurted out:-

"Say, there's something I'd like to ask you."

The man smiled and paid attention.

"When you meet a young lady an' she asks you to call, how soon can you call?"

Martin felt his shirt press and cling to his shoulders, what of the sweat of the effort.

"Why I'd say any time," the man answered.

"Yes, but this is different," Martin objected. "She—I—well, you see, it's this way: maybe she won't be there. She goes to the university."

"Then call again."

"What I said ain't what I meant," Martin confessed falteringly, while he made up his mind to throw himself wholly upon the other's mercy. "I'm just a rough sort of a fellow, an' I ain't never seen anything of society. This girl is all that I ain't, an' I ain't anything that she is. You don't think I'm playin' the fool, do you?" he demanded abruptly.

"No, no; not at all, I assure you," the other protested. "Your request is not exactly in the scope of the reference department, but I shall be only too pleased to assist you."

Martin looked at him admiringly.

"If I could tear it off that way, I'd be all right," he said.

"I beg pardon?"

"I mean if I could talk easy that way, an' polite, an' all the rest."

"Oh," said the other, with comprehension.

"What is the best time to call? The afternoon?—not too close to meal-time? Or the evening? Or Sunday?"

"I'll tell you," the librarian said with a brightening face. "You call her up on the telephone and find out."

"I'll do it," he said, picking up his books and starting away.

He turned back and asked:-

"When you're speakin' to a young lady—say, for instance, Miss Lizzie Smith—do you say 'Miss Lizzie'? or 'Miss Smith'?"

"Say 'Miss Smith,'" the librarian stated authoritatively. "Say 'Miss Smith' always—until you come to know her better."

So it was that Martin Eden solved the problem.

"Come down any time; I'll be at home all afternoon," was Ruth's reply over the telephone to his stammered request as to when he could return the borrowed books.

She met him at the door herself, and her woman's eyes took in immediately the creased trousers and the certain slight but indefinable change in him for the better. Also, she was struck by his face. It was almost violent, this health of his, and it seemed to rush out of him and at her in waves of force. She felt the urge again of the desire to lean toward him for warmth, and marvelled again at the effect his presence produced upon her. And he, in turn, knew again the swimming sensation of bliss when he felt the contact of her hand in greeting. The difference between them lay in that she was cool and self-possessed while his face flushed to the roots of the hair. He stumbled with his old awkwardness after her, and his shoulders swung and lurched perilously.

Once they were seated in the living-room, he began to get on easily—more easily by far than he had expected. She made it easy for him; and the gracious spirit with which she did it made him love her more madly than ever. They talked first of the borrowed books, of the Swinburne he was devoted to, and of the Browning he did not understand; and she led the conversation on from subject to subject, while she pondered the problem of how she could be of help to him. She had thought of this often since their first meeting. She wanted to help him. He made a call upon her pity and tenderness that no one had ever made before, and the pity was not so much derogatory of him as maternal in her. Her pity could not be of the common sort, when the man who drew it was so much man as to shock her with maidenly fears and set her mind and pulse thrilling with strange thoughts and feelings. The old fascination of his neck was there, and there was sweetness in the thought of laying her hands upon it. It seemed still a wanton impulse, but she had grown more used to it. She did not dream that in such guise new-born love would epitomize itself. Nor did she dream that the feeling he excited in her was love. She thought she was merely interested in him as an unusual type possessing various potential excellencies, and she even felt philanthropic about it.

She did not know she desired him; but with him it was different. He knew that he loved her, and he desired her as he had never before desired anything in his life. He had loved poetry for beauty's sake; but since he met her the gates to the vast field of love-poetry had been opened wide. She had given him understanding even more than Bulfinch and Gayley. There was a line that a week before he would not have favored with a second thought—"God's own mad lover dying on a kiss"; but now it was ever insistent in his mind. He marvelled at the wonder of it and the truth; and as he gazed upon her he knew that he could die gladly upon a kiss. He felt himself God's own mad lover, and no accolade of knighthood could have given him greater pride. And at last he knew the meaning of life and why he had been born.

As he gazed at her and listened, his thoughts grew daring. He reviewed all the wild delight of the pressure of her hand in his at the door, and longed for it again. His gaze wandered often toward her lips, and he yearned for them hungrily. But there was nothing gross or earthly about this yearning. It gave him exquisite delight to watch every movement and play of those lips as they enunciated the words she spoke; yet they were not ordinary lips such as all men and women had. Their substance was not mere human clay. They were lips of pure spirit, and his desire for them seemed absolutely different from the desire that had led him to other women's lips. He could kiss her lips, rest his own physical lips upon them, but it would be with the lofty and awful fervor with which one would kiss the robe of God. He was not conscious of this transvaluation of values that had taken place in him, and was unaware that the light that shone in his eyes when he looked at her was quite the same light that shines in all men's eyes when the desire of love is upon them. He did not dream how ardent and masculine his gaze was, nor that the warm flame of it was affecting the alchemy of her spirit. Her penetrative virginity exalted and disguised his own emotions, elevating his thoughts to a star-cool chastity, and he would have been startled to learn that there was that shining out of his eyes, like warm waves, that flowed through her and kindled a kindred warmth. She was subtly perturbed by it, and more than once, though she knew not why, it disrupted her train of thought with its delicious intrusion and compelled her to grope for the remainder of ideas partly uttered. Speech was always easy with her, and these interruptions would have puzzled her had she not decided that it was because he was a remarkable type. She was very sensitive to impressions, and it was not strange, after all, that this aura of a traveller from another world should so affect her.

The problem in the background of her consciousness was how to help him, and she turned the conversation in that direction; but it was Martin who came to the point first.

"I wonder if I can get some advice from you," he began, and received an acquiescence of willingness that made his heart bound. "You remember the other time I was here I said I couldn't talk about books an' things because I didn't know how? Well, I've ben doin' a lot of thinkin' ever since. I've ben to the library a whole lot, but most of the books I've tackled have ben over my head. Mebbe I'd better begin at the beginnin'. I ain't never had no advantages. I've worked pretty hard ever since I was a kid, an' since I've ben to the library, lookin' with new eyes at books—an' lookin' at new books, too—I've just about concluded that I ain't ben reading the right kind. You know the books you find in cattle-camps an' fo'c's'ls ain't the same you've got in this house, for instance. Well, that's the sort of readin' matter I've ben accustomed to. And yet—an' I ain't just makin' a brag of it—I've ben different from the people I've herded with. Not that I'm any better than the sailors an' cow-punchers I travelled with,—I was cow-punchin' for a short time, you know,—but I always liked books, read everything I could lay hands on, an'—well, I guess I think differently from most of 'em.

"Now, to come to what I'm drivin' at. I was never inside a house like this. When I come a week ago, an' saw all this, an' you, an' your mother, an' brothers, an' everything—well, I liked it. I'd heard about such things an' read about such things in some of the books, an' when I looked around at your house, why, the books come true. But the thing I'm after is I liked it. I wanted it. I want it now. I want to breathe air like you get in this house—air that is filled with books, and pictures, and beautiful things, where people talk in low voices an' are clean, an' their thoughts are clean. The air I always breathed was mixed up with grub an' house-rent an' scrappin' an booze an' that's all they talked about, too. Why, when you was crossin' the room to kiss your mother, I thought it was the most beautiful thing I ever seen. I've seen a whole lot of life, an' somehow I've seen a whole lot more of it than most of them that was with me. I like to see, an' I want to see more, an' I want to see it different.

"But I ain't got to the point yet. Here it is. I want to make my way to the kind of life you have in this house. There's more in life than booze, an' hard work, an' knockin' about. Now, how am I goin' to get it? Where do I take hold an' begin? I'm willin' to work my passage, you know, an' I can make most men sick when it comes to hard work. Once I get started, I'll work night an' day. Mebbe you think it's funny, me askin' you about all this. I know you're the last person in the world I ought to ask, but I don't know anybody else I could ask—unless it's Arthur. Mebbe I ought to ask him. If I was—"

His voice died away. His firmly planned intention had come to a halt on the verge of the horrible probability that he should have asked Arthur and that he had made a fool of himself. Ruth did not speak immediately. She was too absorbed in striving to reconcile the stumbling, uncouth speech and its simplicity of thought with what she saw in his face. She had never looked in eyes that expressed greater power. Here was a man who could do anything, was the message she read there, and it accorded ill with the weakness of his spoken thought. And for that matter so complex and quick was her own mind that she did not have a just appreciation of simplicity. And yet she had caught an impression of power in the very groping of this mind. It had seemed to her like a giant writhing and straining at the bonds that held him down. Her face was all sympathy when she did speak.

"What you need, you realize yourself, and it is education. You should go back and finish grammar school, and then go through to high school and university."

"But that takes money," he interrupted.

"Oh!" she cried. "I had not thought of that. But then you have relatives, somebody who could assist you?"

He shook his head.

"My father and mother are dead. I've two sisters, one married, an' the other'll get married soon, I suppose. Then I've a string of brothers,—I'm the youngest,—but they never helped nobody. They've just knocked around over the world, lookin' out for number one. The oldest died in India. Two are in South Africa now, an' another's on a whaling voyage, an' one's travellin' with a circus—he does trapeze work. An' I guess I'm just like them. I've taken care of myself since I was eleven—that's when my mother died. I've got to study by myself, I guess, an' what I want to know is where to begin."

"I should say the first thing of all would be to get a grammar. Your grammar is—" She had intended saying "awful," but she amended it to "is not particularly good."

He flushed and sweated.

"I know I must talk a lot of slang an' words you don't understand. But then they're the only words I know—how to speak. I've got other words in my mind, picked 'em up from books, but I can't pronounce 'em, so I don't use 'em."

"It isn't what you say, so much as how you say it. You don't mind my being frank, do you? I don't want to hurt you."

"No, no," he cried, while he secretly blessed her for her kindness. "Fire away. I've got to know, an' I'd sooner know from you than anybody else."

"Well, then, you say, 'You was'; it should be, 'You were.' You say 'I seen' for 'I saw.' You use the double negative—"

"What's the double negative?" he demanded; then added humbly, "You see, I don't even understand your explanations."

"I'm afraid I didn't explain that," she smiled. "A double negative is—let me see—well, you say, 'never helped nobody.' 'Never' is a negative. 'Nobody' is another negative. It is a rule that two negatives make a positive. 'Never helped nobody' means that, not helping nobody, they must have helped somebody."

"That's pretty clear," he said. "I never thought of it before. But it don't mean they *must* have helped somebody, does it? Seems to me that 'never helped nobody' just naturally fails to say whether or not they helped somebody. I never thought of it before, and I'll never say it again."

She was pleased and surprised with the quickness and surety of his mind. As soon as he had got the clew he not only understood but corrected her error.

"You'll find it all in the grammar," she went on. "There's something else I noticed in your speech. You say 'don't' when you shouldn't. 'Don't' is a contraction and stands for two words. Do you know them?"

He thought a moment, then answered, "'Do not.'"

She nodded her head, and said, "And you use 'don't' when you mean 'does not.'"

He was puzzled over this, and did not get it so quickly.

"Give me an illustration," he asked.

"Well—" She puckered her brows and pursed up her mouth as she thought, while he looked on and decided that her expression was most adorable. "'It don't do to be hasty.' Change 'don't' to 'do not,' and it reads, 'It do not do to be hasty,' which is perfectly absurd."

He turned it over in his mind and considered.

"Doesn't it jar on your ear?" she suggested.

"Can't say that it does," he replied judicially.

"Why didn't you say, 'Can't say that it do'?" she queried.

"That sounds wrong," he said slowly. "As for the other I can't make up my mind. I guess my ear ain't had the trainin' yours has."

"There is no such word as 'ain't,'" she said, prettily emphatic.

Martin flushed again.

"And you say 'ben' for 'been,'" she continued; "'come' for 'came'; and the way you chop your endings is something dreadful."

"How do you mean?" He leaned forward, feeling that he ought to get down on his knees before so marvellous a mind. "How do I chop?"

"You don't complete the endings. 'A-n-d' spells 'and.' You pronounce it 'an'.' 'I-n-g' spells 'ing.' Sometimes you pronounce it 'ing' and sometimes you leave off the 'g.' And then you slur by dropping initial letters and diphthongs. 'T-h-e-m' spells 'them.' You pronounce it—oh, well, it is not necessary to go over all of them. What you need is the grammar. I'll get one and show you how to begin."

As she arose, there shot through his mind something that he had read in the etiquette books, and he stood up awkwardly, worrying as to whether he was doing the right thing, and fearing that she might take it as a sign that he was about to go.

"By the way, Mr. Eden," she called back, as she was leaving the room. "What is *booze*? You used it several times, you know."

"Oh, booze," he laughed. "It's slang. It means whiskey an' beer—anything that will make you drunk."

"And another thing," she laughed back. "Don't use 'you' when you are impersonal. 'You' is very personal, and your use of it just now was not precisely what you meant."

"I don't just see that."

"Why, you said just now, to me, 'whiskey and beer—anything that will make you drunk'—make me drunk, don't you see?"

"Well, it would, wouldn't it?"

"Yes, of course," she smiled. "But it would be nicer not to bring me into it. Substitute 'one' for 'you' and see how much better it sounds."

When she returned with the grammar, she drew a chair near his—he wondered if he should have helped her with the chair—and sat down beside him. She turned the pages of the grammar, and their heads were inclined toward each other. He could hardly follow her outlining of the work he must do, so amazed was he by her delightful propinquity. But when she began to lay down the importance of conjugation, he forgot all about her. He had never heard of conjugation, and was fascinated by the glimpse he was catching into the tie-ribs of language. He leaned closer to the page, and her hair touched his cheek. He had fainted but once in his life, and he thought he was going to faint again. He could scarcely breathe, and his heart was pounding the blood up into his throat and suffocating him. Never had she seemed so accessible as now. For the moment the great gulf that separated them was bridged. But there was no diminution in the loftiness of his feeling for her. She had not descended to him. It was he who had been caught up into the clouds and carried to her. His reverence for her, in that moment, was of the same order as religious awe and fervor. It seemed to him that he had intruded upon the holy of holies, and slowly and carefully he moved his head aside from the contact which thrilled him like an electric shock and of which she had not been aware.

CHAPTER VIII

Several weeks went by, during which Martin Eden studied his grammar, reviewed the books on etiquette, and read voraciously the books that caught his fancy. Of his own class he saw nothing. The girls of the Lotus Club wondered what had become of him and worried Jim with questions, and some of the fellows who put on the glove at Riley's were glad that Martin came no more. He made another discovery of treasure-trove in the library. As the grammar had shown him the tie-ribs of language, so that book showed him the tie-ribs of poetry, and he began to learn metre and construction and form, beneath the beauty he loved finding the why and wherefore of that beauty. Another modern book he found treated poetry as a representative art, treated it exhaustively, with copious illustrations from the best in literature. Never had he read fiction with so keen zest as he studied these books. And his fresh mind, untaxed for twenty years and impelled by maturity of desire, gripped hold of what he read with a virility unusual to the student mind.

When he looked back now from his vantage-ground, the old world he had known, the world of land and sea and ships, of sailor-men and harpy-women, seemed a very small world; and yet it blended in with this new world and expanded. His mind made for unity, and he was surprised when at first he began to see points of contact between the two worlds. And he was ennobled, as well, by the loftiness of thought and beauty he found in the books. This led him to believe more firmly than ever that up above him, in society like Ruth and her family, all men and women thought these thoughts and lived them. Down below where he lived was the ignoble, and he wanted to purge himself of the ignoble that had soiled all his days, and to rise to that sublimated realm where dwelt the upper classes. All his childhood and youth had been troubled by a vague unrest; he had never known what he wanted, but he had wanted something that he had hunted vainly for until he met Ruth. And now his unrest had become sharp and painful, and he knew at last, clearly and definitely, that it was beauty, and intellect, and love that he must have.

During those several weeks he saw Ruth half a dozen times, and each time was an added inspiration. She helped him with his English, corrected his pronunciation, and started him on arithmetic. But their intercourse was not all devoted to elementary study. He had seen too much of life, and his mind was too matured, to be wholly content with fractions, cube root, parsing, and analysis; and there were times when their conversation turned on other themes—the last poetry he had read, the latest poet she had studied. And when she read aloud to him her favorite passages, he ascended to the topmost heaven of delight. Never, in all the women he had heard speak, had he heard a voice like hers. The least sound of it was a stimulus to his love, and he thrilled and throbbed with every word she uttered. It was the quality of it, the repose, and the musical modulation—the soft, rich, indefinable product of culture and a gentle soul. As he listened to her, there rang in the ears of his memory the harsh cries of barbarian women and of hags, and, in lesser degrees of harshness, the strident voices of working women and of the girls of his own class. Then the chemistry of vision would begin to work, and they would troop in review across his mind, each, by contrast, multiplying Ruth's glories. Then, too, his bliss was heightened by the knowledge that her mind was comprehending what she read and was quivering with appreciation of the beauty of the written thought. She read to him much from "The Princess," and often he saw her eyes swimming with tears, so finely was her aesthetic nature strung. At such moments her own emotions elevated him till he was as a god, and, as he gazed at her and listened, he seemed gazing on the face of life and reading its deepest secrets. And then, becoming aware of the heights of exquisite sensibility he attained, he decided that this was love and that love was the greatest thing in the world. And in review would pass along the corridors of memory all previous thrills and burnings he had known,—the drunkenness of wine, the caresses of women, the rough play and give and take of physical contests,—and they seemed trivial and mean compared with this sublime ardor he now enjoyed.

The situation was obscured to Ruth. She had never had any experiences of the heart. Her only experiences in such matters were of the books, where the facts of ordinary day were translated by fancy into a fairy realm of unreality; and she little knew that this rough sailor was creeping into her heart and storing there pent forces that would some day burst forth and surge through her in waves of fire. She did not know the actual fire of love. Her knowledge of love was purely theoretical, and she conceived of it as lambent flame, gentle as the fall of dew or the ripple of quiet water, and cool as the velvet-dark of summer nights. Her idea of love was more that of placid affection, serving the loved one softly in an atmosphere, flower-scented and dim-lighted, of ethereal calm. She did not dream of the volcanic convulsions of love, its scorching heat and sterile wastes of parched ashes. She knew neither her own potencies, nor the potencies of the world; and the deeps of life were to her seas of illusion. The conjugal affection of her father and mother constituted her ideal of love-affinity, and she looked forward some day to emerging, without shock or friction, into that same quiet sweetness of existence with a loved one.

So it was that she looked upon Martin Eden as a novelty, a strange individual, and she identified with novelty and strangeness the effects he produced upon her. It was only natural. In similar ways she had experienced unusual feelings when she looked at wild animals in the menagerie, or when she witnessed a storm of wind, or shuddered at the bright-ribbed lightning. There was something cosmic in such things, and there was something cosmic in him. He came to her breathing of large airs and great spaces. The blaze of tropic suns was in his face, and in his swelling, resilient muscles was the primordial vigor of life. He was marred and scarred by that mysterious world of rough men and rougher deeds, the outposts of which began beyond her horizon. He was untamed, wild, and in secret ways her vanity was touched by the fact that he came so mildly to her hand. Likewise she was stirred by the common impulse to tame the wild thing. It was an unconscious impulse, and farthest from her thoughts that her desire was to re-thumb the clay of him into a likeness of her father's image, which image she believed to be the finest in the world. Nor was there any way, out of her inexperience, for her to know that the cosmic feel she caught of him was that most cosmic of things, love, which with equal power drew men and women together across the world, compelled stags to kill each other in the rutting season, and drove even the elements irresistibly to unite.

His swift development was a source of surprise and interest. She detected unguessed finenesses in him that seemed to bud, day by day, like flowers in congenial soil. She read Browning aloud to him, and was often puzzled by the strange interpretations he gave to mooted passages. It was beyond her to realize that, out of his experience of men and women and life, his interpretations were far more frequently correct than hers. His conceptions seemed naive to her, though she was often fired by his daring flights of comprehension, whose orbit-path was so wide among the stars that she could not follow and could only sit and thrill to the impact of unguessed power. Then she played to him—no longer at him—and probed him with music that sank to depths beyond her plumb-line. His nature opened to music as a flower to the sun, and the transition was quick from his working-class rag-time and jingles to her classical display pieces that she knew nearly by heart. Yet he betrayed a democratic fondness for Wagner, and the "Tannhäuser" overture, when she had given him the clew to it, claimed him as nothing else she played. In an immediate way it personified his life. All his past was the *Venusburg* motif, while her he identified somehow with the *Pilgrim's Chorus* motif; and from the exalted state this elevated him to, he swept onward and upward into that vast shadow-realm of spirit-groping, where good and evil war eternally.

Sometimes he questioned, and induced in her mind temporary doubts as to the correctness of her own definitions and conceptions of music. But her singing he did not question. It was too wholly her, and he sat always amazed at the divine melody of her pure soprano voice. And he could not help but contrast it with the weak pipings and shrill quaverings of factory girls, ill-nourished and untrained, and with the raucous shriekings from gin-cracked throats of the women of the seaport towns. She enjoyed singing and playing to him. In truth, it was the first time she had ever had a human soul to play with, and the plastic clay of him was a delight to mould; for she thought she was moulding it, and her intentions were good. Besides, it was pleasant to be with him. He did not repel her. That first repulsion had been really a fear of her undiscovered self, and the fear had gone to sleep. Though she did not know it, she had a feeling in him of proprietary right. Also, he had a tonic effect upon her. She was studying hard at the university, and it seemed to strengthen her to emerge from the dusty books and have the fresh sea-breeze of his personality blow upon her. Strength! Strength was what she needed, and he gave it to her in generous measure. To come into the same room with him, or to meet him at the door, was to take heart of life. And when he had gone, she would return to her books with a keener zest and fresh store of energy.

She knew her Browning, but it had never sunk into her that it was an awkward thing to play with souls. As her interest in Martin increased, the remodelling of his life became a passion with her.

"There is Mr. Butler," she said one afternoon, when grammar and arithmetic and poetry had been put aside.

"He had comparatively no advantages at first. His father had been a bank cashier, but he lingered for years, dying of consumption in Arizona, so that when he was dead, Mr. Butler, Charles Butler he was called, found himself alone in the world. His father had come from Australia, you know, and so he had no relatives in California. He went to work in a printing-office,—I have heard him tell of it many times,—and he got three dollars a week, at first. His income to-day is at least thirty thousand a year. How did he do it? He was honest, and faithful, and industrious, and economical. He denied himself the enjoyments that most boys indulge in. He made it a point to save so much every week, no matter what he had to do without in order to save it. Of course, he was soon earning more than three dollars a week, and as his wages increased he saved more and more.

"He worked in the daytime, and at night he went to night school. He had his eyes fixed always on the future. Later on he went to night high school. When he was only seventeen, he was earning excellent wages at setting type, but he was ambitious. He wanted a career, not a livelihood, and he was content to make immediate sacrifices for his ultimate again. He decided upon the law, and he entered father's office as an office boy—think of that!—and got only four dollars a week. But he had learned how to be economical, and out of that four dollars he went on saving money."

She paused for breath, and to note how Martin was receiving it. His face was lighted up with interest in the youthful struggles of Mr. Butler; but there was a frown upon his face as well.

"I'd say they was pretty hard lines for a young fellow," he remarked. "Four dollars a week! How could he live on it? You can bet he didn't have any frills. Why, I pay five dollars a week for board now, an' there's nothin' excitin' about it, you can lay to that. He must have lived like a dog. The food he ate—"

"He cooked for himself," she interrupted, "on a little kerosene stove."

"The food he ate must have been worse than what a sailor gets on the worst-feedin' deep-water ships, than which there ain't much that can be possibly worse."

"But think of him now!" she cried enthusiastically. "Think of what his income affords him. His early denials are paid for a thousand-fold."

Martin looked at her sharply.

"There's one thing I'll bet you," he said, "and it is that Mr. Butler is nothin' gay-hearted now in his fat days. He fed himself like that for years an' years, on a boy's stomach, an' I bet his stomach's none too good now for it."

Her eyes dropped before his searching gaze.

"I'll bet he's got dyspepsia right now!" Martin challenged.

"Yes, he has," she confessed; "but—"

"An' I bet," Martin dashed on, "that he's solemn an' serious as an old owl, an' doesn't care a rap for a good time, for all his thirty thousand a year. An' I'll bet he's not particularly joyful at seein' others have a good time. Ain't I right?"

She nodded her head in agreement, and hastened to explain:-

"But he is not that type of man. By nature he is sober and serious. He always was that."

"You can bet he was," Martin proclaimed. "Three dollars a week, an' four dollars a week, an' a young boy cookin' for himself on an oil-burner an' layin' up money, workin' all day an' studyin' all night, just workin' an' never playin', never havin' a good time, an' never learnin' how to have a good time—of course his thirty thousand came along too late."

His sympathetic imagination was flashing upon his inner sight all the thousands of details of the boy's existence and of his narrow spiritual development into a thirty-thousand-dollar-a-year man. With the swiftness and wide-reaching of multitudinous thought Charles Butler's whole life was telescoped upon his vision.

"Do you know," he added, "I feel sorry for Mr. Butler. He was too young to know better, but he robbed himself of life for the sake of thirty thousand a year that's clean wasted upon him. Why, thirty thousand, lump sum, wouldn't buy for him right now what ten cents he was layin' up would have bought him, when he was a kid, in the way of candy an' peanuts or a seat in nigger heaven."

It was just such uniqueness of points of view that startled Ruth. Not only were they new to her, and contrary to her own beliefs, but she always felt in them germs of truth that threatened to unseat or modify her own convictions. Had she been fourteen instead of twenty-four, she might have been changed by them; but she was twenty-four, conservative by nature and upbringing, and already crystallized into the cranny of life where she had been born and formed. It was true, his bizarre judgments troubled her in the moments they were uttered, but she ascribed them to his novelty of type and strangeness of living, and they were soon forgotten. Nevertheless, while she disapproved of them, the strength of their utterance, and the flashing of eyes and earnestness of face that accompanied them, always thrilled her and drew her toward him. She would never have guessed that this man who had come from beyond her horizon, was, in such moments, flashing on beyond her horizon with wider and deeper concepts. Her own limits were the limits of her horizon; but limited minds can recognize limitations only in others. And so she felt that her outlook was very wide indeed, and that where his conflicted with hers marked his limitations; and she dreamed of helping him to see as she saw, of widening his horizon until it was identified with hers.

"But I have not finished my story," she said. "He worked, so father says, as no other office boy he ever had. Mr. Butler was always eager to work. He never was late, and he was usually at the office a few minutes before his regular time. And yet he saved his time. Every spare moment was devoted to study. He studied book-keeping and type-writing, and he paid for lessons in shorthand by dictating at night to a court reporter who needed practice. He quickly became a clerk, and he made himself invaluable. Father appreciated him and saw that he was bound to rise. It was on father's suggestion that he went to law college. He became a lawyer, and hardly was he back in the office when father took him in as junior partner. He is a great man. He refused the United States Senate several times, and father says he could become a justice of the Supreme Court any time a vacancy occurs, if he wants to. Such a life is an inspiration to all of us. It shows us that a man with will may rise superior to his environment."

"He is a great man," Martin said sincerely.

But it seemed to him there was something in the recital that jarred upon his sense of beauty and life. He could not find an adequate motive in Mr. Butler's life of pinching and privation. Had he done it for love of a woman, or for attainment of beauty, Martin would have understood. God's own mad lover should do anything for the kiss, but not for thirty thousand dollars a year. He was dissatisfied with Mr. Butler's career. There was something paltry about it, after all. Thirty thousand a year was all right, but dyspepsia and inability to be humanly happy robbed such princely income of all its value.

Much of this he strove to express to Ruth, and shocked her and made it clear that more remodelling was necessary. Hers was that common insularity of mind that makes human creatures believe that their color, creed, and politics are best and right and that other human creatures scattered over the world are less fortunately placed than they. It was the same insularity of mind that made the ancient Jew thank God he was not born a woman, and sent the modern missionary god-substituting to the ends of the earth; and it made Ruth desire to shape this man from other crannies of life into the likeness of the men who lived in her particular cranny of life.

CHAPTER IX

Back from sea Martin Eden came, homing for California with a lover's desire. His store of money exhausted, he had shipped before the mast on the treasure-hunting schooner; and the Solomon Islands, after eight months of failure to find treasure, had witnessed the breaking up of the expedition. The men had been paid off in Australia, and Martin had immediately shipped on a deep-water vessel for San Francisco. Not alone had those eight months earned him enough money to stay on land for many weeks, but they had enabled him to do a great deal of studying and reading.

His was the student's mind, and behind his ability to learn was the indomitability of his nature and his love for Ruth. The grammar he had taken along he went through again and again until his unjaded brain had mastered it. He noticed the bad grammar used by his shipmates, and made a point of mentally correcting and reconstructing their crudities of speech. To his great joy he discovered that his ear was becoming sensitive and that he was developing grammatical nerves. A double negative jarred him like a discord, and often, from lack of practice, it was from his own lips that the jar came. His tongue refused to learn new tricks in a day.

After he had been through the grammar repeatedly, he took up the dictionary and added twenty words a day to his vocabulary. He found that this was no light task, and at wheel or lookout he steadily went over and over his lengthening list of pronunciations and definitions, while he invariably memorized himself to sleep. "Never did anything," "if I were," and "those things," were phrases, with many variations, that he repeated under his breath in order to accustom his tongue to the language spoken by Ruth. "And" and "ing," with the "d" and "g" pronounced emphatically, he went over thousands of times; and to his surprise he noticed that he was beginning to speak cleaner and more correct English than the officers themselves and the gentleman-adventurers in the cabin who had financed the expedition.

The captain was a fishy-eyed Norwegian who somehow had fallen into possession of a complete Shakespeare, which he never read, and Martin had washed his clothes for him and in return been permitted access to the precious volumes. For a time, so steeped was he in the plays and in the many favorite passages that impressed themselves almost without effort on his brain, that all the world seemed to shape itself into forms of Elizabethan tragedy or comedy and his very thoughts were in blank verse. It trained his ear and gave him a fine appreciation for noble English; withal it introduced into his mind much that was archaic and obsolete.

The eight months had been well spent, and, in addition to what he had learned of right speaking and high thinking, he had learned much of himself. Along with his humbleness because he knew so little, there arose a conviction of power. He felt a sharp gradation between himself and his shipmates, and was wise enough to realize that the difference lay in potentiality rather than achievement. What he could do,—they could do; but within him he felt a confused ferment working that told him there was more in him than he had done. He was tortured by the exquisite beauty of the world, and wished that Ruth were there to share it with him. He decided that he would describe to her many of the bits of South Sea beauty. The creative spirit in him flamed up at the thought and urged that he recreate this beauty for a wider audience than Ruth. And then, in splendor and glory, came the great idea. He would write. He would be one of the eyes through which the world saw, one of the ears through which it heard, one of the hearts through which it felt. He would write—everything—poetry and prose, fiction and description, and plays like Shakespeare. There was career and the way to win to Ruth. The men of literature were the world's giants, and he conceived them to be far finer than the Mr. Butlers who earned thirty thousand a year and could be Supreme Court justices if they wanted to.

Once the idea had germinated, it mastered him, and the return voyage to San Francisco was like a dream. He was drunken with unguessed power and felt that he could do anything. In the midst of the great and lonely sea he gained perspective. Clearly, and for the first lime, he saw Ruth and her world. It was all visualized in his mind as a concrete thing which he could take up in his two hands and turn around and about and examine. There was much that was dim and nebulous in that world, but he saw it as a whole and not in detail, and he saw, also, the way to master it. To write! The thought was fire in him. He would begin as soon as he got back. The first thing he would do would be to describe the voyage of the treasure-hunters. He would sell it to some San Francisco newspaper. He would not tell Ruth anything about it, and she would be surprised and pleased when she saw his name in print. While he wrote, he could go on studying. There were twenty-four hours in each day. He was invincible. He knew how to work, and the citadels would go down before him. He would not have to go to sea again—as a sailor; and for the instant he caught a vision of a steam yacht. There were other writers who possessed steam yachts. Of course, he cautioned himself, it would be slow succeeding at first, and for a time he would be content to earn enough money by his writing to enable him to go on studying. And then, after some time,—a very indeterminate time,—when he had learned and prepared himself, he would write the great things and his name would be on all men's lips. But greater than that, infinitely greater and greatest of all, he would have proved himself worthy of Ruth. Fame was all very well, but it was for Ruth that his splendid dream arose. He was not a fame-monger, but merely one of God's mad lovers.

Arrived in Oakland, with his snug pay-day in his pocket, he took up his old room at Bernard Higginbotham's and set to work. He did not even let Ruth know he was back. He would go and see her when he finished the article on the treasure-hunters. It was not so difficult to abstain from seeing her, because of the violent heat of creative fever that burned in him. Besides, the very article he was writing would bring her nearer to him. He did not know how long an article he should write, but he counted the words in a double-page article in the Sunday supplement of the *San Francisco Examiner*, and guided himself by that. Three days, at white heat, completed his narrative; but when he had copied it carefully, in a large scrawl that was easy to read, he learned from a rhetoric he picked up in the library that there were such things as paragraphs and quotation marks. He had never thought of such things before; and he promptly set to work writing the article over, referring continually to the pages of the rhetoric and learning more in a day about composition than the average schoolboy in a year. When he had copied the article a second time and rolled it up carefully, he read in a newspaper an item on hints to beginners, and discovered the iron law that manuscripts should never be rolled and that they should be written on one side of the paper. He had violated the law on both counts. Also, he learned from the item that first-class papers paid a minimum of ten dollars a column. So, while he copied the manuscript a third time, he consoled himself by multiplying ten columns by ten dollars. The product was always the same, one hundred dollars, and he decided that that was better than seafaring. If it hadn't been for his blunders, he would have finished the article in three days. One hundred dollars in three days! It would have taken him three months and longer on the sea to earn a similar amount. A man was a fool to go to sea when he could write, he concluded, though the money in itself meant nothing to him. Its value was in the liberty it would get him, the presentable garments it would buy him, all of which would bring him nearer, swiftly nearer, to the slender, pale girl who had turned his life back upon itself and given him inspiration.

He mailed the manuscript in a flat envelope, and addressed it to the editor of the *San Francisco Examiner*. He had an idea that anything accepted by a paper was published immediately, and as he had sent the manuscript in on Friday he expected it to come out on the following Sunday. He conceived that it would be fine to let that event apprise Ruth of his return. Then, Sunday afternoon, he would call and see her. In the meantime he was occupied by another idea, which he prided himself upon as being a particularly sane, careful, and modest idea. He would write an adventure story for boys and sell it to *The Youth's Companion*. He went to the free reading-room and looked through the files of *The Youth's Companion*. Serial stories, he found, were usually published in that weekly in five instalments of about three thousand words each. He discovered several serials that ran to seven instalments, and decided to write one of that length.

He had been on a whaling voyage in the Arctic, once—a voyage that was to have been for three years and which had terminated in shipwreck at the end of six months. While his imagination was fanciful, even fantastic at times, he had a basic love of reality that compelled him to write about the things he knew. He knew whaling, and out of the real materials of his knowledge he proceeded to manufacture the fictitious adventures of the two boys he intended to use as joint heroes. It was easy work, he decided on Saturday evening. He had completed on that day the first instalment of three thousand words—much to the amusement of Jim, and to the open derision of Mr. Higginbotham, who sneered throughout meal-time at the "litery" person they had discovered in the family.

Martin contented himself by picturing his brother-in-law's surprise on Sunday morning when he opened his *Examiner* and saw the article on the treasure-hunters. Early that morning he was out himself to the front door, nervously racing through the many-sheeted newspaper. He went through it a second time, very carefully, then folded it up and left it where he had found it. He was glad he had not told any one about his article. On second thought he concluded that he had been wrong about the speed with which things found their way into newspaper columns. Besides, there had not been any news value in his article, and most likely the editor would write to him about it first.

After breakfast he went on with his serial. The words flowed from his pen, though he broke off from the writing frequently to look up definitions in the dictionary or to refer to the rhetoric. He often read or re-read a chapter at a time, during such pauses; and he consoled himself that while he was not writing the great things he felt to be in him, he was learning composition, at any rate, and training himself to shape up and express his thoughts. He toiled on till dark, when he went out to the reading-room and explored magazines and weeklies until the place closed at ten o'clock. This was his programme for a week. Each day he did three thousand words, and each evening he puzzled his way through the magazines, taking note of the stories, articles, and poems that editors saw fit to publish. One thing was certain: What these multitudinous writers did he could do, and only give him time and he would do what they could not do. He was cheered to read in *Book News*, in a paragraph on the payment of magazine writers, not that Rudyard Kipling received a dollar per word, but that the minimum rate paid by first-class magazines was two cents a word. *The Youth's Companion* was certainly first class, and at that rate the three thousand words he had written that day would bring him sixty dollars—two months' wages on the sea!

On Friday night he finished the serial, twenty-one thousand words long. At two cents a word, he calculated, that would bring him four hundred and twenty dollars. Not a bad week's work. It was more money than he had ever possessed at one time. He did not know how he could spend it all. He had tapped a gold mine. Where this came from he could always get more. He planned to buy some more clothes, to subscribe to many magazines, and to buy dozens of reference books that at present he was compelled to go to the library to consult. And still there was a large portion of the four hundred and twenty dollars unspent. This worried him until the thought came to him of hiring a servant for Gertrude and of buying a bicycle for Marion.

He mailed the bulky manuscript to *The Youth's Companion*, and on Saturday afternoon, after having planned an article on pearl-diving, he went to see Ruth. He had telephoned, and she went herself to greet him at the door. The old familiar blaze of health rushed out from him and struck her like a blow. It seemed to enter into her body and course through her veins in a liquid glow, and to set her quivering with its imparted strength. He flushed warmly as he took her hand and looked into her blue eyes, but the fresh bronze of eight months of sun hid the flush, though it did not protect the neck from the gnawing chafe of the stiff collar. She noted the red line of it with amusement which quickly vanished as she glanced at his clothes. They really fitted him,—it was his first made-to-order suit,—and he seemed slimmer and better modelled. In addition, his cloth cap had been replaced by a soft hat, which she commanded him to put on and then complimented him on his appearance. She did not remember when she had felt so happy. This change in him was her handiwork, and she was proud of it and fired with ambition further to help him.

But the most radical change of all, and the one that pleased her most, was the change in his speech. Not only did he speak more correctly, but he spoke more easily, and there were many new words in his vocabulary. When he grew excited or enthusiastic, however, he dropped back into the old slurring and the dropping of final consonants. Also, there was an awkward hesitancy, at times, as he essayed the new words he had learned. On the other hand, along with his ease of expression, he displayed a lightness and facetiousness of thought that delighted her. It was his old spirit of humor and badinage that had made him a favorite in his own class, but which he had hitherto been unable to use in her presence through lack of words and training. He was just beginning to orientate himself and to feel that he was not wholly an intruder. But he was very tentative, fastidiously so, letting Ruth set the pace of sprightliness and fancy, keeping up with her but never daring to go beyond her.

He told her of what he had been doing, and of his plan to write for a livelihood and of going on with his studies. But he was disappointed at her lack of approval. She did not think much of his plan.

"You see," she said frankly, "writing must be a trade, like anything else. Not that I know anything about it, of course. I only bring common judgment to bear. You couldn't hope to be a blacksmith without spending three years at learning the trade—or is it five years! Now writers are so much better paid than blacksmiths that there must be ever so many more men who would like to write, who—try to write."

"But then, may not I be peculiarly constituted to write?" he queried, secretly exulting at the language he had used, his swift imagination throwing the whole scene and atmosphere upon a vast screen along with a thousand other scenes from his life—scenes that were rough and raw, gross and bestial.

The whole composite vision was achieved with the speed of light, producing no pause in the conversation, nor interrupting his calm train of thought. On the screen of his imagination he saw himself and this sweet and beautiful girl, facing each other and conversing in good English, in a room of books and paintings and tone and culture, and all illuminated by a bright light of steadfast brilliance; while ranged about and fading away to the remote edges of the screen were antithetical scenes, each scene a picture, and he the onlooker, free to look at will upon what he wished. He saw these other scenes through drifting vapors and swirls of sullen fog dissolving before shafts of red and garish light. He saw cowboys at the bar, drinking fierce whiskey, the air filled with obscenity and ribald language, and he saw himself with them drinking and cursing with the wildest, or sitting at table with them, under smoking kerosene lamps, while the chips clicked and clattered and the cards were dealt around. He saw himself, stripped to the waist, with naked fists, fighting his great fight with Liverpool Red in the forecastle of the *Susquehanna*; and he saw the bloody deck of the *John Rogers*, that gray morning of attempted mutiny, the mate kicking in death-throes on the main-hatch, the revolver in the old man's hand spitting fire and smoke, the men with passion-wrenched faces, of brutes screaming vile blasphemies and falling about him—and then he returned to the central scene, calm and clean in the steadfast light, where Ruth sat and talked with him amid books and paintings; and he saw the grand piano upon which she would later play to him; and he heard the echoes of his own selected and correct words, "But then, may I not be peculiarly constituted to write?"

"But no matter how peculiarly constituted a man may be for blacksmithing," she was laughing, "I never heard of one becoming a blacksmith without first serving his apprenticeship."

"What would you advise?" he asked. "And don't forget that I feel in me this capacity to write—I can't explain it; I just know that it is in me."

"You must get a thorough education," was the answer, "whether or not you ultimately become a writer. This education is indispensable for whatever career you select, and it must not be slipshod or sketchy. You should go to high school."

"Yes—" he began; but she interrupted with an afterthought:-

"Of course, you could go on with your writing, too."

"I would have to," he said grimly.

"Why?" She looked at him, prettily puzzled, for she did not quite like the persistence with which he clung to his notion.

"Because, without writing there wouldn't be any high school. I must live and buy books and clothes, you know."

"I'd forgotten that," she laughed. "Why weren't you born with an income?"

"I'd rather have good health and imagination," he answered. "I can make good on the income, but the other things have to be made good for—" He almost said "you," then amended his sentence to, "have to be made good for one."

"Don't say 'make good,'" she cried, sweetly petulant. "It's slang, and it's horrid."

He flushed, and stammered, "That's right, and I only wish you'd correct me every time."

"I—I'd like to," she said haltingly. "You have so much in you that is good that I want to see you perfect."

He was clay in her hands immediately, as passionately desirous of being moulded by her as she was desirous of shaping him into the image of her ideal of man. And when she pointed out the opportuneness of the time, that the entrance examinations to high school began on the following Monday, he promptly volunteered that he would take them.

Then she played and sang to him, while he gazed with hungry yearning at her, drinking in her loveliness and marvelling that there should not be a hundred suitors listening there and longing for her as he listened and longed.

CHAPTER X

He stopped to dinner that evening, and, much to Ruth's satisfaction, made a favorable impression on her father. They talked about the sea as a career, a subject which Martin had at his finger-ends, and Mr. Morse remarked afterward that he seemed a very clear-headed young man. In his avoidance of slang and his search after right words, Martin was compelled to talk slowly, which enabled him to find the best thoughts that were in him. He was more at ease than that first night at dinner, nearly a year before, and his shyness and modesty even commended him to Mrs. Morse, who was pleased at his manifest improvement.

"He is the first man that ever drew passing notice from Ruth," she told her husband. "She has been so singularly backward where men are concerned that I have been worried greatly."

Mr. Morse looked at his wife curiously.

"You mean to use this young sailor to wake her up?" he questioned.

"I mean that she is not to die an old maid if I can help it," was the answer. "If this young Eden can arouse her interest in mankind in general, it will be a good thing."

"A very good thing," he commented. "But suppose,—and we must suppose, sometimes, my dear,—suppose he arouses her interest too particularly in him?"

"Impossible," Mrs. Morse laughed. "She is three years older than he, and, besides, it is impossible. Nothing will ever come of it. Trust that to me."

And so Martin's rôle was arranged for him, while he, led on by Arthur and Norman, was meditating an extravagance. They were going out for a ride into the hills Sunday morning on their wheels, which did not interest Martin until he learned that Ruth, too, rode a wheel and was going along. He did not ride, nor own a wheel, but if Ruth rode, it was up to him to begin, was his decision; and when he said good night, he stopped in at a cyclery on his way home and spent forty dollars for a wheel. It was more than a month's hard-earned wages, and it reduced his stock of money amazingly; but when he added the hundred dollars he was to receive from the *Examiner* to the four hundred and twenty dollars that was the least *The Youth's Companion* could pay him, he felt that he had reduced the perplexity the unwonted amount of money had caused him. Nor did he mind, in the course of learning to ride the wheel home, the fact that he ruined his suit of clothes. He caught the tailor by telephone that night from Mr. Higginbotham's store and ordered another suit. Then he carried the wheel up the narrow stairway that clung like a fire-escape to the rear wall of the building, and when he had moved his bed out from the wall, found there was just space enough in the small room for himself and the wheel.

Sunday he had intended to devote to studying for the high school examination, but the pearl-diving article lured him away, and he spent the day in the white-hot fever of re-creating the beauty and romance that burned in him. The fact that the *Examiner* of that morning had failed to publish his treasure-hunting article did not dash his spirits. He was at too great a height for that, and having been deaf to a twice-repeated summons, he went without the heavy Sunday dinner with which Mr. Higginbotham invariably graced his table. To Mr. Higginbotham such a dinner was advertisement of his worldly achievement and prosperity, and he honored it by delivering platitudinous sermonettes upon American institutions and the opportunity said institutions gave to any hard-working man to rise—the rise, in his case, which he pointed out unfailingly, being from a grocer's clerk to the ownership of Higginbotham's Cash Store.

Martin Eden looked with a sigh at his unfinished "Pearl-diving" on Monday morning, and took the car down to Oakland to the high school. And when, days later, he applied for the results of his examinations, he learned that he had failed in everything save grammar.

"Your grammar is excellent," Professor Hilton informed him, staring at him through heavy spectacles; "but you know nothing, positively nothing, in the other branches, and your United States history is abominable—there is no other word for it, abominable. I should advise you—"

Professor Hilton paused and glared at him, unsympathetic and unimaginative as one of his own test-tubes. He was professor of physics in the high school, possessor of a large family, a meagre salary, and a select fund of parrot-learned knowledge.

"Yes, sir," Martin said humbly, wishing somehow that the man at the desk in the library was in Professor Hilton's place just then.

"And I should advise you to go back to the grammar school for at least two years. Good day."

Martin was not deeply affected by his failure, though he was surprised at Ruth's shocked expression when he told her Professor Hilton's advice. Her disappointment was so evident that he was sorry he had failed, but chiefly so for her sake.

"You see I was right," she said. "You know far more than any of the students entering high school, and yet you can't pass the examinations. It is because what education you have is fragmentary, sketchy. You need the discipline of study, such as only skilled teachers can give you. You must be thoroughly grounded. Professor Hilton is right, and if I were you, I'd go to night school. A year and a half of it might enable you to catch up that additional six months. Besides, that would leave you your days in which to write, or, if you could not make your living by your pen, you would have your days in which to work in some position."

But if my days are taken up with work and my nights with school, when am I going to see you?—was Martin's first thought, though he refrained from uttering it. Instead, he said:-

"It seems so babyish for me to be going to night school. But I wouldn't mind that if I thought it would pay. But I don't think it will pay. I can do the work quicker than they can teach me. It would be a loss of time—" he thought of her and his desire to have her—"and I can't afford the time. I haven't the time to spare, in fact."

"There is so much that is necessary." She looked at him gently, and he was a brute to oppose her. "Physics and chemistry—you can't do them without laboratory study; and you'll find algebra and geometry almost hopeless with instruction. You need the skilled teachers, the specialists in the art of imparting knowledge."

He was silent for a minute, casting about for the least vainglorious way in which to express himself.

"Please don't think I'm bragging," he began. "I don't intend it that way at all. But I have a feeling that I am what I may call a natural student. I can study by myself. I take to it kindly, like a duck to water. You see yourself what I did with grammar. And I've learned much of other things—you would never dream how much. And I'm only getting started. Wait till I get—" He hesitated and assured himself of the pronunciation before he said "momentum. I'm getting my first real feel of things now. I'm beginning to size up the situation—"

"Please don't say 'size up,'" she interrupted.

"To get a line on things," he hastily amended.

"That doesn't mean anything in correct English," she objected.

He floundered for a fresh start.

"What I'm driving at is that I'm beginning to get the lay of the land."

Out of pity she forebore, and he went on.

"Knowledge seems to me like a chart-room. Whenever I go into the library, I am impressed that way. The part played by teachers is to teach the student the contents of the chart-room in a systematic way. The teachers are guides to the chart-room, that's all. It's not something that they have in their own heads. They don't make it up, don't create it. It's all in the chart-room and they know their way about in it, and it's their business to show the place to strangers who might else get lost. Now I don't get lost easily. I have the bump of location. I usually know where I'm at—What's wrong now?"

"Don't say 'where I'm at.'"

"That's right," he said gratefully, "where I am. But where am I at—I mean, where am I? Oh, yes, in the chart-room. Well, some people—"

"Persons," she corrected.

"Some persons need guides, most persons do; but I think I can get along without them. I've spent a lot of time in the chart-room now, and I'm on the edge of knowing my way about, what charts I want to refer to, what coasts I want to explore. And from the way I line it up, I'll explore a whole lot more quickly by myself. The speed of a fleet, you know, is the speed of the slowest ship, and the speed of the teachers is affected the same way. They can't go any faster than the ruck of their scholars, and I can set a faster pace for myself than they set for a whole schoolroom."

"'He travels the fastest who travels alone,'" she quoted at him.

But I'd travel faster with you just the same, was what he wanted to blurt out, as he caught a vision of a world without end of sunlit spaces and starry voids through which he drifted with her, his arm around her, her pale gold hair blowing about his face. In the same instant he was aware of the pitiful inadequacy of speech. God! If he could so frame words that she could see what he then saw! And he felt the stir in him, like a throe of yearning pain, of the desire to paint these visions that flashed unsummoned on the mirror of his mind. Ah, that was it! He caught at the hem of the secret. It was the very thing that the great writers and master-poets did. That was why they were giants. They knew how to express what they thought, and felt, and saw. Dogs asleep in the sun often whined and barked, but they were unable to tell what they saw that made them whine and bark. He had often wondered what it was. And that was all he was, a dog asleep in the sun. He saw noble and beautiful visions, but he could only whine and bark at Ruth. But he would cease sleeping in the sun. He would stand up, with open eyes, and he would struggle and toil and learn until, with eyes unblinded and tongue untied, he could share with her his visioned wealth. Other men had discovered the trick of expression, of making words obedient servitors, and of making combinations of words mean more than the sum of their separate meanings. He was stirred profoundly by the passing glimpse at the secret, and he was again caught up in the vision of sunlit spaces and starry voids—until it came to him that it was very quiet, and he saw Ruth regarding him with an amused expression and a smile in her eyes.

"I have had a great visioning," he said, and at the sound of his words in his own ears his heart gave a leap. Where had those words come from? They had adequately expressed the pause his vision had put in the conversation. It was a miracle. Never had he so loftily framed a lofty thought. But never had he attempted to frame lofty thoughts in words. That was it. That explained it. He had never tried. But Swinburne had, and Tennyson, and Kipling, and all the other poets. His mind flashed on to his "Pearl-diving." He had never dared the big things, the spirit of the beauty that was a fire in him. That article would be a different thing when he was done with it. He was appalled by the vastness of the beauty that rightfully belonged in it, and again his mind flashed and dared, and he demanded of himself why he could not chant that beauty in noble verse as the great poets did. And there was all the mysterious delight and spiritual wonder of his love for Ruth. Why could he not chant that, too, as the poets did? They had sung of love. So would he. By God!—

And in his frightened ears he heard his exclamation echoing. Carried away, he had breathed it aloud. The blood surged into his face, wave upon wave, mastering the bronze of it till the blush of shame flaunted itself from collar-rim to the roots of his hair.

"I—I—beg your pardon," he stammered. "I was thinking."

"It sounded as if you were praying," she said bravely, but she felt herself inside to be withering and shrinking. It was the first time she had heard an oath from the lips of a man she knew, and she was shocked, not merely as a matter of principle and training, but shocked in spirit by this rough blast of life in the garden of her sheltered maidenhood.

But she forgave, and with surprise at the ease of her forgiveness. Somehow it was not so difficult to forgive him anything. He had not had a chance to be as other men, and he was trying so hard, and succeeding, too. It never entered her head that there could be any other reason for her being kindly disposed toward him. She was tenderly disposed toward him, but she did not know it. She had no way of knowing it. The placid poise of twenty-four years without a single love affair did not fit her with a keen perception of her own feelings, and she who had never warmed to actual love was unaware that she was warming now.

CHAPTER XI

Martin went back to his pearl-diving article, which would have been finished sooner if it had not been broken in upon so frequently by his attempts to write poetry. His poems were love poems, inspired by Ruth, but they were never completed. Not in a day could he learn to chant in noble verse. Rhyme and metre and structure were serious enough in themselves, but there was, over and beyond them, an intangible and evasive something that he caught in all great poetry, but which he could not catch and imprison in his own. It was the elusive spirit of poetry itself that he sensed and sought after but could not capture. It seemed a glow to him, a warm and trailing vapor, ever beyond his reaching, though sometimes he was rewarded by catching at shreds of it and weaving them into phrases that echoed in his brain with haunting notes or drifted across his vision in misty wafture of unseen beauty. It was baffling. He ached with desire to express and could but gibber prosaically as everybody gibbered. He read his fragments aloud. The metre marched along on perfect feet, and the rhyme pounded a longer and equally faultless rhythm, but the glow and high exaltation that he felt within were lacking. He could not understand, and time and again, in despair, defeated and depressed, he returned to his article. Prose was certainly an easier medium.

Following the "Pearl-diving," he wrote an article on the sea as a career, another on turtle-catching, and a third on the northeast trades. Then he tried, as an experiment, a short story, and before he broke his stride he had finished six short stories and despatched them to various magazines. He wrote prolifically, intensely, from morning till night, and late at night, except when he broke off to go to the reading-room, draw books from the library, or to call on Ruth. He was profoundly happy. Life was pitched high. He was in a fever that never broke. The joy of creation that is supposed to belong to the gods was his. All the life about him—the odors of stale vegetables and soapsuds, the slatternly form of his sister, and the jeering face of Mr. Higginbotham—was a dream. The real world was in his mind, and the stories he wrote were so many pieces of reality out of his mind.

The days were too short. There was so much he wanted to study. He cut his sleep down to five hours and found that he could get along upon it. He tried four hours and a half, and regretfully came back to five. He could joyfully have spent all his waking hours upon any one of his pursuits. It was with regret that he ceased from writing to study, that he ceased from study to go to the library, that he tore himself away from that chart-room of knowledge or from the magazines in the reading-room that were filled with the secrets of writers who succeeded in selling their wares. It was like severing heart strings, when he was with Ruth, to stand up and go; and he scorched through the dark streets so as to get home to his books at the least possible expense of time. And hardest of all was it to shut up the algebra or physics, put note-book and pencil aside, and close his tired eyes in sleep. He hated the thought of ceasing to live, even for so short a time, and his sole consolation was that the alarm clock was set five hours ahead. He would lose only five hours anyway, and then the jangling bell would jerk him out of unconsciousness and he would have before him another glorious day of nineteen hours.

In the meantime the weeks were passing, his money was ebbing low, and there was no money coming in. A month after he had mailed it, the adventure serial for boys was returned to him by *The Youth's Companion*. The rejection slip was so tactfully worded that he felt kindly toward the editor. But he did not feel so kindly toward the editor of the *San Francisco Examiner*. After waiting two whole weeks, Martin had written to him. A week later he wrote again. At the end of the month, he went over to San Francisco and personally called upon the editor. But he did not meet that exalted personage, thanks to a Cerberus of an office boy, of tender years and red hair, who guarded the portals. At the end of the fifth week the manuscript came back to him, by mail, without comment. There was no rejection slip, no explanation, nothing. In the same way his other articles were tied up with the other leading San Francisco papers. When he recovered them, he sent them to the magazines in the East, from which they were returned more promptly, accompanied always by the printed rejection slips.

The short stories were returned in similar fashion. He read them over and over, and liked them so much that he could not puzzle out the cause of their rejection, until, one day, he read in a newspaper that manuscripts should always be typewritten. That explained it. Of course editors were so busy that they could not afford the time and strain of reading handwriting. Martin rented a typewriter and spent a day mastering the machine. Each day he typed what he composed, and he typed his earlier manuscripts as fast as they were returned him. He was surprised when the typed ones began to come back. His jaw seemed to become squarer, his chin more aggressive, and he bundled the manuscripts off to new editors.

The thought came to him that he was not a good judge of his own work. He tried it out on Gertrude. He read his stories aloud to her. Her eyes glistened, and she looked at him proudly as she said:-

"Ain't it grand, you writin' those sort of things."

"Yes, yes," he demanded impatiently. "But the story—how did you like it?"

"Just grand," was the reply. "Just grand, an' thrilling, too. I was all worked up."

He could see that her mind was not clear. The perplexity was strong in her good-natured face. So he waited.

"But, say, Mart," after a long pause, "how did it end? Did that young man who spoke so highfalutin' get her?"

And, after he had explained the end, which he thought he had made artistically obvious, she would say:-

"That's what I wanted to know. Why didn't you write that way in the story?"

One thing he learned, after he had read her a number of stories, namely, that she liked happy endings.

"That story was perfectly grand," she announced, straightening up from the wash-tub with a tired sigh and wiping the sweat from her forehead with a red, steamy hand; "but it makes me sad. I want to cry. There is too many sad things in the world anyway. It makes me happy to think about happy things. Now if he'd married her, and—You don't mind, Mart?" she queried apprehensively. "I just happen to feel that way, because I'm tired, I guess. But the story was grand just the same, perfectly grand. Where are you goin' to sell it?"

"That's a horse of another color," he laughed.

"But if you *did* sell it, what do you think you'd get for it?"

"Oh, a hundred dollars. That would be the least, the way prices go."

"My! I do hope you'll sell it!"

"Easy money, eh?" Then he added proudly: "I wrote it in two days. That's fifty dollars a day."

He longed to read his stories to Ruth, but did not dare. He would wait till some were published, he decided, then she would understand what he had been working for. In the meantime he toiled on. Never had the spirit of adventure lured him more strongly than on this amazing exploration of the realm of mind. He bought the text-books on physics and chemistry, and, along with his algebra, worked out problems and demonstrations. He took the laboratory proofs on faith, and his intense power of vision enabled him to see the reactions of chemicals more understandingly than the average student saw them in the laboratory. Martin wandered on through the heavy pages, overwhelmed by the clews he was getting to the nature of things. He had accepted the world as the world, but now he was comprehending the organization of it, the play and interplay of force and matter. Spontaneous explanations of old matters were continually arising in his mind. Levers and purchases fascinated him, and his mind roved backward to hand-spikes and blocks and tackles at sea. The theory of navigation, which enabled the ships to travel unerringly their courses over the pathless ocean, was made clear to him. The mysteries of storm, and rain, and tide were revealed, and the reason for the existence of trade-winds made him wonder whether he had written his article on the northeast trade too soon. At any rate he knew he could write it better now. One afternoon he went out with Arthur to the University of California, and, with bated breath and a feeling of religious awe, went through the laboratories, saw demonstrations, and listened to a physics professor lecturing to his classes.

But he did not neglect his writing. A stream of short stories flowed from his pen, and he branched out into the easier forms of verse—the kind he saw printed in the magazines—though he lost his head and wasted two weeks on a tragedy in blank verse, the swift rejection of which, by half a dozen magazines, dumfounded him. Then he discovered Henley and wrote a series of sea-poems on the model of "Hospital Sketches." They were simple poems, of light and color, and romance and adventure. "Sea Lyrics," he called them, and he judged them to be the best work he had yet done. There were thirty, and he completed them in a month, doing one a day after having done his regular day's work on fiction, which day's work was the equivalent to a week's work of the average successful writer. The toil meant nothing to him. It was not toil. He was finding speech, and all the beauty and wonder that had been pent for years behind his inarticulate lips was now pouring forth in a wild and virile flood.

He showed the "Sea Lyrics" to no one, not even to the editors. He had become distrustful of editors. But it was not distrust that prevented him from submitting the "Lyrics." They were so beautiful to him that he was impelled to save them to share with Ruth in some glorious, far-off time when he would dare to read to her what he had written. Against that time he kept them with him, reading them aloud, going over them until he knew them by heart.

He lived every moment of his waking hours, and he lived in his sleep, his subjective mind rioting through his five hours of surcease and combining the thoughts and events of the day into grotesque and impossible marvels. In reality, he never rested, and a weaker body or a less firmly poised brain would have been prostrated in a general break-down. His late afternoon calls on Ruth were rarer now, for June was approaching, when she would take her degree and finish with the university. Bachelor of Arts!—when he thought of her degree, it seemed she fled beyond him faster than he could pursue.

One afternoon a week she gave to him, and arriving late, he usually stayed for dinner and for music afterward. Those were his red-letter days. The atmosphere of the house, in such contrast with that in which he lived, and the mere nearness to her, sent him forth each time with a firmer grip on his resolve to climb the heights. In spite of the beauty in him, and the aching desire to create, it was for her that he struggled. He was a lover first and always. All other things he subordinated to love.

Greater than his adventure in the world of thought was his love-adventure. The world itself was not so amazing because of the atoms and molecules that composed it according to the propulsions of irresistible force; what made it amazing was the fact that Ruth lived in it. She was the most amazing thing he had ever known, or dreamed, or guessed.

But he was oppressed always by her remoteness. She was so far from him, and he did not know how to approach her. He had been a success with girls and women in his own class; but he had never loved any of them, while he did love her, and besides, she was not merely of another class. His very love elevated her above all classes. She was a being apart, so far apart that he did not know how to draw near to her as a lover should draw near. It was true, as he acquired knowledge and language, that he was drawing nearer, talking her speech, discovering ideas and delights in common; but this did not satisfy his lover's yearning. His lover's imagination had made her holy, too holy, too spiritualized, to have any kinship with him in the flesh. It was his own love that thrust her from him and made her seem impossible for him. Love itself denied him the one thing that it desired.

And then, one day, without warning, the gulf between them was bridged for a moment, and thereafter, though the gulf remained, it was ever narrower. They had been eating cherries—great, luscious, black cherries with a juice of the color of dark wine. And later, as she read aloud to him from "The Princess," he chanced to notice the stain of the cherries on her lips. For the moment her divinity was shattered. She was clay, after all, mere clay, subject to the common law of clay as his clay was subject, or anybody's clay. Her lips were flesh like his, and cherries dyed them as cherries dyed his. And if so with her lips, then was it so with all of her. She was woman, all woman, just like any woman. It came upon him abruptly. It was a revelation that stunned him. It was as if he had seen the sun fall out of the sky, or had seen worshipped purity polluted.

Then he realized the significance of it, and his heart began pounding and challenging him to play the lover with this woman who was not a spirit from other worlds but a mere woman with lips a cherry could stain. He trembled at the audacity of his thought; but all his soul was singing, and reason, in a triumphant paean, assured him he was right. Something of this change in him must have reached her, for she paused from her reading, looked up at him, and smiled. His eyes dropped from her blue eyes to her lips, and the sight of the stain maddened him. His arms all but flashed out to her and around her, in the way of his old careless life. She seemed to lean toward him, to wait, and all his will fought to hold him back.

"You were not following a word," she pouted.

Then she laughed at him, delighting in his confusion, and as he looked into her frank eyes and knew that she had divined nothing of what he felt, he became abashed. He had indeed in thought dared too far. Of all the women he had known there was no woman who would not have guessed—save her. And she had not guessed. There was the difference. She was different. He was appalled by his own grossness, awed by her clear innocence, and he gazed again at her across the gulf. The bridge had broken down.

But still the incident had brought him nearer. The memory of it persisted, and in the moments when he was most cast down, he dwelt upon it eagerly. The gulf was never again so wide. He had accomplished a distance vastly greater than a bachelorship of arts, or a dozen bachelorships. She was pure, it was true, as he had never dreamed of purity; but cherries stained her lips. She was subject to the laws of the universe just as inexorably as he was. She had to eat to live, and when she got her feet wet, she caught cold. But that was not the point. If she could feel hunger and thirst, and heat and cold, then could she feel love—and love for a man. Well, he was a man. And why could he not be the man? "It's up to me to make good," he would murmur fervently. "I will be *the* man. I will make myself *the* man. I will make good."

CHAPTER XII

Early one evening, struggling with a sonnet that twisted all awry the beauty and thought that trailed in glow and vapor through his brain, Martin was called to the telephone.

"It's a lady's voice, a fine lady's," Mr. Higginbotham, who had called him, jeered.

Martin went to the telephone in the corner of the room, and felt a wave of warmth rush through him as he heard Ruth's voice. In his battle with the sonnet he had forgotten her existence, and at the sound of her voice his love for her smote him like a sudden blow. And such a voice!—delicate and sweet, like a strain of music heard far off and faint, or, better, like a bell of silver, a perfect tone, crystal-pure. No mere woman had a voice like that. There was something celestial about it, and it came from other worlds. He could scarcely hear what it said, so ravished was he, though he controlled his face, for he knew that Mr. Higginbotham's ferret eyes were fixed upon him.

It was not much that Ruth wanted to say—merely that Norman had been going to take her to a lecture that night, but that he had a headache, and she was so disappointed, and she had the tickets, and that if he had no other engagement, would he be good enough to take her?

Would he! He fought to suppress the eagerness in his voice. It was amazing. He had always seen her in her own house. And he had never dared to ask her to go anywhere with him. Quite irrelevantly, still at the telephone and talking with her, he felt an overpowering desire to die for her, and visions of heroic sacrifice shaped and dissolved in his whirling brain. He loved her so much, so terribly, so hopelessly. In that moment of mad happiness that she should go out with him, go to a lecture with him—with him, Martin Eden—she soared so far above him that there seemed nothing else for him to do than die for her. It was the only fit way in which he could express the tremendous and lofty emotion he felt for her. It was the sublime abnegation of true love that comes to all lovers, and it came to him there, at the telephone, in a whirlwind of fire and glory; and to die for her, he felt, was to have lived and loved well. And he was only twenty-one, and he had never been in love before.

His hand trembled as he hung up the receiver, and he was weak from the organ which had stirred him. His eyes were shining like an angel's, and his face was transfigured, purged of all earthly dross, and pure and holy.

"Makin' dates outside, eh?" his brother-in-law sneered. "You know what that means. You'll be in the police court yet."

But Martin could not come down from the height. Not even the bestiality of the allusion could bring him back to earth. Anger and hurt were beneath him. He had seen a great vision and was as a god, and he could feel only profound and awful pity for this maggot of a man. He did not look at him, and though his eyes passed over him, he did not see him; and as in a dream he passed out of the room to dress. It was not until he had reached his own room and was tying his necktie that he became aware of a sound that lingered unpleasantly in his ears. On investigating this sound he identified it as the final snort of Bernard Higginbotham, which somehow had not penetrated to his brain before.

As Ruth's front door closed behind them and he came down the steps with her, he found himself greatly perturbed. It was not unalloyed bliss, taking her to the lecture. He did not know what he ought to do. He had seen, on the streets, with persons of her class, that the women took the men's arms. But then, again, he had seen them when they didn't; and he wondered if it was only in the evening that arms were taken, or only between husbands and wives and relatives.

Just before he reached the sidewalk, he remembered Minnie. Minnie had always been a stickler. She had called him down the second time she walked out with him, because he had gone along on the inside, and she had laid the law down to him that a gentleman always walked on the outside—when he was with a lady. And Minnie had made a practice of kicking his heels, whenever they crossed from one side of the street to the other, to remind him to get over on the outside. He wondered where she had got that item of etiquette, and whether it had filtered down from above and was all right.

It wouldn't do any harm to try it, he decided, by the time they had reached the sidewalk; and he swung behind Ruth and took up his station on the outside. Then the other problem presented itself. Should he offer her his arm? He had never offered anybody his arm in his life. The girls he had known never took the fellows' arms. For the first several times they walked freely, side by side, and after that it was arms around the waists, and heads against the fellows' shoulders where the streets were unlighted. But this was different. She wasn't that kind of a girl. He must do something.

He crooked the arm next to her—crooked it very slightly and with secret tentativeness, not invitingly, but just casually, as though he was accustomed to walk that way. And then the wonderful thing happened. He felt her hand upon his arm. Delicious thrills ran through him at the contact, and for a few sweet moments it seemed that he had left the solid earth and was flying with her through the air. But he was soon back again, perturbed by a new complication. They were crossing the street. This would put him on the inside. He should be on the outside. Should he therefore drop her arm and change over? And if he did so, would he have to repeat the manoeuvre the next time? And the next? There was something wrong about it, and he resolved not to caper about and play the fool. Yet he was not satisfied with his conclusion, and when he found himself on the inside, he talked quickly and earnestly, making a show of being carried away by what he was saying, so that, in case he was wrong in not changing sides, his enthusiasm would seem the cause for his carelessness.

As they crossed Broadway, he came face to face with a new problem. In the blaze of the electric lights, he saw Lizzie Connolly and her giggly friend. Only for an instant he hesitated, then his hand went up and his hat came off. He could not be disloyal to his kind, and it was to more than Lizzie Connolly that his hat was lifted. She nodded and looked at him boldly, not with soft and gentle eyes like Ruth's, but with eyes that were handsome and hard, and that swept on past him to Ruth and itemized her face and dress and station. And he was aware that Ruth looked, too, with quick eyes that were timid and mild as a dove's, but which saw, in a look that was a flutter on and past, the working-class girl in her cheap finery and under the strange hat that all working-class girls were wearing just then.

"What a pretty girl!" Ruth said a moment later.

Martin could have blessed her, though he said:-

"I don't know. I guess it's all a matter of personal taste, but she doesn't strike me as being particularly pretty."

"Why, there isn't one woman in ten thousand with features as regular as hers. They are splendid. Her face is as clear-cut as a cameo. And her eyes are beautiful."

"Do you think so?" Martin queried absently, for to him there was only one beautiful woman in the world, and she was beside him, her hand upon his arm.

"Do I think so? If that girl had proper opportunity to dress, Mr. Eden, and if she were taught how to carry herself, you would be fairly dazzled by her, and so would all men."

"She would have to be taught how to speak," he commented, "or else most of the men wouldn't understand her. I'm sure you couldn't understand a quarter of what she said if she just spoke naturally."

"Nonsense! You are as bad as Arthur when you try to make your point."

"You forget how I talked when you first met me. I have learned a new language since then. Before that time I talked as that girl talks. Now I can manage to make myself understood sufficiently in your language to explain that you do not know that other girl's language. And do you know why she carries herself the way she does? I think about such things now, though I never used to think about them, and I am beginning to understand—much."

"But why does she?"

"She has worked long hours for years at machines. When one's body is young, it is very pliable, and hard work will mould it like putty according to the nature of the work. I can tell at a glance the trades of many workingmen I meet on the street. Look at me. Why am I rolling all about the shop? Because of the years I put in on the sea. If I'd put in the same years cow-punching, with my body young and pliable, I wouldn't be rolling now, but I'd be bow-legged. And so with that girl. You noticed that her eyes were what I might call hard. She has never been sheltered. She has had to take care of herself, and a young girl can't take care of herself and keep her eyes soft and gentle like—like yours, for example."

"I think you are right," Ruth said in a low voice. "And it is too bad. She is such a pretty girl."

He looked at her and saw her eyes luminous with pity. And then he remembered that he loved her and was lost in amazement at his fortune that permitted him to love her and to take her on his arm to a lecture.

Who are you, Martin Eden? he demanded of himself in the looking-glass, that night when he got back to his room. He gazed at himself long and curiously. Who are you? What are you? Where do you belong? You belong by rights to girls like Lizzie Connolly. You belong with the legions of toil, with all that is low, and vulgar, and unbeautiful. You belong with the oxen and the drudges, in dirty surroundings among smells and stenches. There are the stale vegetables now. Those potatoes are rotting. Smell them, damn you, smell them. And yet you dare to open the books, to listen to beautiful music, to learn to love beautiful paintings, to speak good English, to think thoughts that none of your own kind thinks, to tear yourself away from the oxen and the Lizzie Connollys and to love a pale spirit of a woman who is a million miles beyond you and who lives in the stars! Who are you? and what are you? damn you! And are you going to make good?

He shook his fist at himself in the glass, and sat down on the edge of the bed to dream for a space with wide eyes. Then he got out note-book and algebra and lost himself in quadratic equations, while the hours slipped by, and the stars dimmed, and the gray of dawn flooded against his window.

CHAPTER XIII

It was the knot of wordy socialists and working-class philosophers that held forth in the City Hall Park on warm afternoons that was responsible for the great discovery. Once or twice in the month, while riding through the park on his way to the library, Martin dismounted from his wheel and listened to the arguments, and each time he tore himself away reluctantly. The tone of discussion was much lower than at Mr. Morse's table. The men were not grave and dignified. They lost their tempers easily and called one another names, while oaths and obscene allusions were frequent on their lips. Once or twice he had seen them come to blows. And yet, he knew not why, there seemed something vital about the stuff of these men's thoughts. Their logomachy was far more stimulating to his intellect than the reserved and quiet dogmatism of Mr. Morse. These men, who slaughtered English, gesticulated like lunatics, and fought one another's ideas with primitive anger, seemed somehow to be more alive than Mr. Morse and his crony, Mr. Butler.

Martin had heard Herbert Spencer quoted several times in the park, but one afternoon a disciple of Spencer's appeared, a seedy tramp with a dirty coat buttoned tightly at the throat to conceal the absence of a shirt. Battle royal was waged, amid the smoking of many cigarettes and the expectoration of much tobacco-juice, wherein the tramp successfully held his own, even when a socialist workman sneered, "There is no god but the Unknowable, and Herbert Spencer is his prophet." Martin was puzzled as to what the discussion was about, but when he rode on to the library he carried with him a new-born interest in Herbert Spencer, and because of the frequency with which the tramp had mentioned "First Principles," Martin drew out that volume.

So the great discovery began. Once before he had tried Spencer, and choosing the "Principles of Psychology" to begin with, he had failed as abjectly as he had failed with Madam Blavatsky. There had been no understanding the book, and he had returned it unread. But this night, after algebra and physics, and an attempt at a sonnet, he got into bed and opened "First Principles." Morning found him still reading. It was impossible for him to sleep. Nor did he write that day. He lay on the bed till his body grew tired, when he tried the hard floor, reading on his back, the book held in the air above him, or changing from side to side. He slept that night, and did his writing next morning, and then the book tempted him and he fell, reading all afternoon, oblivious to everything and oblivious to the fact that that was the afternoon Ruth gave to him. His first consciousness of the immediate world about him was when Bernard Higginbotham jerked open the door and demanded to know if he thought they were running a restaurant.

Martin Eden had been mastered by curiosity all his days. He wanted to know, and it was this desire that had sent him adventuring over the world. But he was now learning from Spencer that he never had known, and that he never could have known had he continued his sailing and wandering forever. He had merely skimmed over the surface of things, observing detached phenomena, accumulating fragments of facts, making superficial little generalizations—and all and everything quite unrelated in a capricious and disorderly world of whim and chance. The mechanism of the flight of birds he had watched and reasoned about with understanding; but it had never entered his head to try to explain the process whereby birds, as organic flying mechanisms, had been developed. He had never dreamed there was such a process. That birds should have come to be, was unguessed. They always had been. They just happened.

And as it was with birds, so had it been with everything. His ignorant and unprepared attempts at philosophy had been fruitless. The medieval metaphysics of Kant had given him the key to nothing, and had served the sole purpose of making him doubt his own intellectual powers. In similar manner his attempt to study evolution had been confined to a hopelessly technical volume by Romanes. He had understood nothing, and the only idea he had gathered was that evolution was a dry-as-dust theory, of a lot of little men possessed of huge and unintelligible vocabularies. And now he learned that evolution was no mere theory but an accepted process of development; that scientists no longer disagreed about it, their only differences being over the method of evolution.

And here was the man Spencer, organizing all knowledge for him, reducing everything to unity, elaborating ultimate realities, and presenting to his startled gaze a universe so concrete of realization that it was like the model of a ship such as sailors make and put into glass bottles. There was no caprice, no chance. All was law. It was in obedience to law that the bird flew, and it was in obedience to the same law that fermenting slime had writhed and squirmed and put out legs and wings and become a bird.

Martin had ascended from pitch to pitch of intellectual living, and here he was at a higher pitch than ever. All the hidden things were laying their secrets bare. He was drunken with comprehension. At night, asleep, he lived with the gods in colossal nightmare; and awake, in the day, he went around like a somnambulist, with absent stare, gazing upon the world he had just discovered. At table he failed to hear the conversation about petty and ignoble things, his eager mind seeking out and following cause and effect in everything before him. In the meat on the platter he saw the shining sun and traced its energy back through all its transformations to its source a hundred million miles away, or traced its energy ahead to the moving muscles in his arms that enabled him to cut the meat, and to the brain wherewith he willed the muscles to move to cut the meat, until, with inward gaze, he saw the same sun shining in his brain. He was entranced by illumination, and did not hear the "Bughouse," whispered by Jim, nor see the anxiety on his sister's face, nor notice the rotary motion of Bernard Higginbotham's finger, whereby he imparted the suggestion of wheels revolving in his brother-in-law's head.

What, in a way, most profoundly impressed Martin, was the correlation of knowledge—of all knowledge. He had been curious to know things, and whatever he acquired he had filed away in separate memory compartments in his brain. Thus, on the subject of sailing he had an immense store. On the subject of woman he had a fairly large store. But these two subjects had been unrelated. Between the two memory compartments there had been no connection. That, in the fabric of knowledge, there should be any connection whatever between a woman with hysterics and a schooner carrying a weather-helm or heaving to in a gale, would have struck him as ridiculous and impossible. But Herbert Spencer had shown him not only that it was not ridiculous, but that it was impossible for there to be no connection. All things were related to all other things from the farthermost star in the wastes of space to the myriads of atoms in the grain of sand under one's foot. This new concept was a perpetual amazement to Martin, and he found himself engaged continually in tracing the relationship between all things under the sun and on the other side of the sun. He drew up lists of the most incongruous things and was unhappy until he succeeded in establishing kinship between them all—kinship between love, poetry, earthquake, fire, rattlesnakes, rainbows, precious gems, monstrosities, sunsets, the roaring of lions, illuminating gas, cannibalism, beauty, murder, lovers, fulcrums, and tobacco. Thus, he unified the universe and held it up and looked at it, or wandered through its byways and alleys and jungles, not as a terrified traveller in the thick of mysteries seeking an unknown goal, but observing and charting and becoming familiar with all there was to know. And the more he knew, the more passionately he admired the universe, and life, and his own life in the midst of it all.

"You fool!" he cried at his image in the looking-glass. "You wanted to write, and you tried to write, and you had nothing in you to write about. What did you have in you?—some childish notions, a few half-baked sentiments, a lot of undigested beauty, a great black mass of ignorance, a heart filled to bursting with love, and an ambition as big as your love and as futile as your ignorance. And you wanted to write! Why, you're just on the edge of beginning to get something in you to write about. You wanted to create beauty, but how could you when you knew nothing about the nature of beauty? You wanted to write about life when you knew nothing of the essential characteristics of life. You wanted to write about the world and the scheme of existence when the world was a Chinese puzzle to you and all that you could have written would have been about what you did not know of the scheme of existence. But cheer up, Martin, my boy. You'll write yet. You know a little, a very little, and you're on the right road now to know more. Some day, if you're lucky, you may come pretty close to knowing all that may be known. Then you will write."

He brought his great discovery to Ruth, sharing with her all his joy and wonder in it. But she did not seem to be so enthusiastic over it. She tacitly accepted it and, in a way, seemed aware of it from her own studies. It did not stir her deeply, as it did him, and he would have been surprised had he not reasoned it out that it was not new and fresh to her as it was to him. Arthur and Norman, he found, believed in evolution and had read Spencer, though it did not seem to have made any vital impression upon them, while the young fellow with the glasses and the mop of hair, Will Olney, sneered disagreeably at Spencer and repeated the epigram, "There is no god but the Unknowable, and Herbert Spencer is his prophet."

But Martin forgave him the sneer, for he had begun to discover that Olney was not in love with Ruth. Later, he was dumfounded to learn from various little happenings not only that Olney did not care for Ruth, but that he had a positive dislike for her. Martin could not understand this. It was a bit of phenomena that he could not correlate with all the rest of the phenomena in the universe. But nevertheless he felt sorry for the young fellow because of the great lack in his nature that prevented him from a proper appreciation of Ruth's fineness and beauty. They rode out into the hills several Sundays on their wheels, and Martin had ample opportunity to observe the armed truce that existed between Ruth and Olney. The latter chummed with Norman, throwing Arthur and Martin into company with Ruth, for which Martin was duly grateful.

Those Sundays were great days for Martin, greatest because he was with Ruth, and great, also, because they were putting him more on a par with the young men of her class. In spite of their long years of disciplined education, he was finding himself their intellectual equal, and the hours spent with them in conversation was so much practice for him in the use of the grammar he had studied so hard. He had abandoned the etiquette books, falling back upon observation to show him the right things to do. Except when carried away by his enthusiasm, he was always on guard, keenly watchful of their actions and learning their little courtesies and refinements of conduct.

The fact that Spencer was very little read was for some time a source of surprise to Martin. "Herbert Spencer," said the man at the desk in the library, "oh, yes, a great mind." But the man did not seem to know anything of the content of that great mind. One evening, at dinner, when Mr. Butler was there, Martin turned the conversation upon Spencer. Mr. Morse bitterly arraigned the English philosopher's agnosticism, but confessed that he had not read "First Principles"; while Mr. Butler stated that he had no patience with Spencer, had never read a line of him, and had managed to get along quite well without him. Doubts arose in Martin's mind, and had he been less strongly individual he would have accepted the general opinion and given Herbert Spencer up. As it was, he found Spencer's explanation of things convincing; and, as he phrased it to himself, to give up Spencer would be equivalent to a navigator throwing the compass and chronometer overboard. So Martin went on into a thorough study of evolution, mastering more and more the subject himself, and being convinced by the corroborative testimony of a thousand independent writers. The more he studied, the more vistas he caught of fields of knowledge yet unexplored, and the regret that days were only twenty-four hours long became a chronic complaint with him.

One day, because the days were so short, he decided to give up algebra and geometry. Trigonometry he had not even attempted. Then he cut chemistry from his study-list, retaining only physics.

"I am not a specialist," he said, in defence, to Ruth. "Nor am I going to try to be a specialist. There are too many special fields for any one man, in a whole lifetime, to master a tithe of them. I must pursue general knowledge. When I need the work of specialists, I shall refer to their books."

"But that is not like having the knowledge yourself," she protested.

"But it is unnecessary to have it. We profit from the work of the specialists. That's what they are for. When I came in, I noticed the chimney-sweeps at work. They're specialists, and when they get done, you will enjoy clean chimneys without knowing anything about the construction of chimneys."

"That's far-fetched, I am afraid."

She looked at him curiously, and he felt a reproach in her gaze and manner. But he was convinced of the rightness of his position.

"All thinkers on general subjects, the greatest minds in the world, in fact, rely on the specialists. Herbert Spencer did that. He generalized upon the findings of thousands of investigators. He would have had to live a thousand lives in order to do it all himself. And so with Darwin. He took advantage of all that had been learned by the florists and cattle-breeders."

"You're right, Martin," Olney said. "You know what you're after, and Ruth doesn't. She doesn't know what she is after for herself even."

"—Oh, yes," Olney rushed on, heading off her objection, "I know you call it general culture. But it doesn't matter what you study if you want general culture. You can study French, or you can study German, or cut them both out and study Esperanto, you'll get the culture tone just the same. You can study Greek or Latin, too, for the same purpose, though it will never be any use to you. It will be culture, though. Why, Ruth studied Saxon, became clever in it,—that was two years ago,—and all that she remembers of it now is 'Whan that sweet Aprile with his schowers soote'—isn't that the way it goes?"

"But it's given you the culture tone just the same," he laughed, again heading her off. "I know. We were in the same classes."

"But you speak of culture as if it should be a means to something," Ruth cried out. Her eyes were flashing, and in her cheeks were two spots of color. "Culture is the end in itself."

"But that is not what Martin wants."

"How do you know?"

"What do you want, Martin?" Olney demanded, turning squarely upon him.

Martin felt very uncomfortable, and looked entreaty at Ruth.

"Yes, what do you want?" Ruth asked. "That will settle it."

"Yes, of course, I want culture," Martin faltered. "I love beauty, and culture will give me a finer and keener appreciation of beauty."

She nodded her head and looked triumph.

"Rot, and you know it," was Olney's comment. "Martin's after career, not culture. It just happens that culture, in his case, is incidental to career. If he wanted to be a chemist, culture would be unnecessary. Martin wants to write, but he's afraid to say so because it will put you in the wrong."

"And why does Martin want to write?" he went on. "Because he isn't rolling in wealth. Why do you fill your head with Saxon and general culture? Because you don't have to make your way in the world. Your father sees to that. He buys your clothes for you, and all the rest. What rotten good is our education, yours and mine and Arthur's and Norman's? We're soaked in general culture, and if our daddies went broke to-day, we'd be falling down to-morrow on teachers' examinations. The best job you could get, Ruth, would be a country school or music teacher in a girls' boarding-school."

"And pray what would you do?" she asked.

"Not a blessed thing. I could earn a dollar and a half a day, common labor, and I might get in as instructor in Hanley's cramming joint—I say might, mind you, and I might be chucked out at the end of the week for sheer inability."

Martin followed the discussion closely, and while he was convinced that Olney was right, he resented the rather cavalier treatment he accorded Ruth. A new conception of love formed in his mind as he listened. Reason had nothing to do with love. It mattered not whether the woman he loved reasoned correctly or incorrectly. Love was above reason. If it just happened that she did not fully appreciate his necessity for a career, that did not make her a bit less lovable. She was all lovable, and what she thought had nothing to do with her lovableness.

"What's that?" he replied to a question from Olney that broke in upon his train of thought.

"I was saying that I hoped you wouldn't be fool enough to tackle Latin."

"But Latin is more than culture," Ruth broke in. "It is equipment."

"Well, are you going to tackle it?" Olney persisted.

Martin was sore beset. He could see that Ruth was hanging eagerly upon his answer.

"I am afraid I won't have time," he said finally. "I'd like to, but I won't have time."

"You see, Martin's not seeking culture," Olney exulted. "He's trying to get somewhere, to do something."

"Oh, but it's mental training. It's mind discipline. It's what makes disciplined minds." Ruth looked expectantly at Martin, as if waiting for him to change his judgment. "You know, the foot-ball players have to train before the big game. And that is what Latin does for the thinker. It trains."

"Rot and bosh! That's what they told us when we were kids. But there is one thing they didn't tell us then. They let us find it out for ourselves afterwards." Olney paused for effect, then added, "And what they didn't tell us was that every gentleman should have studied Latin, but that no gentleman should know Latin."

"Now that's unfair," Ruth cried. "I knew you were turning the conversation just in order to get off something."

"It's clever all right," was the retort, "but it's fair, too. The only men who know their Latin are the apothecaries, the lawyers, and the Latin professors. And if Martin wants to be one of them, I miss my guess. But what's all that got to do with Herbert Spencer anyway? Martin's just discovered Spencer, and he's wild over him. Why? Because Spencer is taking him somewhere. Spencer couldn't take me anywhere, nor you. We haven't got anywhere to go. You'll get married some day, and I'll have nothing to do but keep track of the lawyers and business agents who will take care of the money my father's going to leave me."

Onley got up to go, but turned at the door and delivered a parting shot.

"You leave Martin alone, Ruth. He knows what's best for himself. Look at what he's done already. He makes me sick sometimes, sick and ashamed of myself. He knows more now about the world, and life, and man's place, and all the rest, than Arthur, or Norman, or I, or you, too, for that matter, and in spite of all our Latin, and French, and Saxon, and culture."

"But Ruth is my teacher," Martin answered chivalrously. "She is responsible for what little I have learned."

"Rats!" Olney looked at Ruth, and his expression was malicious. "I suppose you'll be telling me next that you read Spencer on her recommendation—only you didn't. And she doesn't know anything more about Darwin and evolution than I do about King Solomon's mines. What's that jawbreaker definition about something or other, of Spencer's, that you sprang on us the other day—that indefinite, incoherent homogeneity thing? Spring it on her, and see if she understands a word of it. That isn't culture, you see. Well, tra la, and if you tackle Latin, Martin, I won't have any respect for you."

And all the while, interested in the discussion, Martin had been aware of an irk in it as well. It was about studies and lessons, dealing with the rudiments of knowledge, and the schoolboyish tone of it conflicted with the big things that were stirring in him—with the grip upon life that was even then crooking his fingers like eagle's talons, with the cosmic thrills that made him ache, and with the inchoate consciousness of mastery of it all. He likened himself to a poet, wrecked on the shores of a strange land, filled with power of beauty, stumbling and stammering and vainly trying to sing in the rough, barbaric tongue of his brethren in the new land. And so with him. He was alive, painfully alive, to the great universal things, and yet he was compelled to potter and grope among schoolboy topics and debate whether or not he should study Latin.

"What in hell has Latin to do with it?" he demanded before his mirror that night. "I wish dead people would stay dead. Why should I and the beauty in me be ruled by the dead? Beauty is alive and everlasting. Languages come and go. They are the dust of the dead."

And his next thought was that he had been phrasing his ideas very well, and he went to bed wondering why he could not talk in similar fashion when he was with Ruth. He was only a schoolboy, with a schoolboy's tongue, when he was in her presence.

"Give me time," he said aloud. "Only give me time."

Time! Time! Time! was his unending plaint.

CHAPTER XIV

It was not because of Olney, but in spite of Ruth, and his love for Ruth, that he finally decided not to take up Latin. His money meant time. There was so much that was more important than Latin, so many studies that clamored with imperious voices. And he must write. He must earn money. He had had no acceptances. Twoscore of manuscripts were travelling the endless round of the magazines. How did the others do it? He spent long hours in the free reading-room, going over what others had written, studying their work eagerly and critically, comparing it with his own, and wondering, wondering, about the secret trick they had discovered which enabled them to sell their work.

He was amazed at the immense amount of printed stuff that was dead. No light, no life, no color, was shot through it. There was no breath of life in it, and yet it sold, at two cents a word, twenty dollars a thousand—the newspaper clipping had said so. He was puzzled by countless short stories, written lightly and cleverly he confessed, but without vitality or reality. Life was so strange and wonderful, filled with an immensity of problems, of dreams, and of heroic toils, and yet these stories dealt only with the commonplaces of life. He felt the stress and strain of life, its fevers and sweats and wild insurgences—surely this was the stuff to write about! He wanted to glorify the leaders of forlorn hopes, the mad lovers, the giants that fought under stress and strain, amid terror and tragedy, making life crackle with the strength of their endeavor. And yet the magazine short stories seemed intent on glorifying the Mr. Butlers, the sordid dollar-chasers, and the commonplace little love affairs of commonplace little men and women. Was it because the editors of the magazines were commonplace? he demanded. Or were they afraid of life, these writers and editors and readers?

But his chief trouble was that he did not know any editors or writers. And not merely did he not know any writers, but he did not know anybody who had ever attempted to write. There was nobody to tell him, to hint to him, to give him the least word of advice. He began to doubt that editors were real men. They seemed cogs in a machine. That was what it was, a machine. He poured his soul into stories, articles, and poems, and intrusted them to the machine. He folded them just so, put the proper stamps inside the long envelope along with the manuscript, sealed the envelope, put more stamps outside, and dropped it into the mail-box. It travelled across the continent, and after a certain lapse of time the postman returned him the manuscript in another long envelope, on the outside of which were the stamps he had enclosed. There was no human editor at the other end, but a mere cunning arrangement of cogs that changed the manuscript from one envelope to another and stuck on the stamps. It was like the slot machines wherein one dropped pennies, and, with a metallic whirl of machinery had delivered to him a stick of chewing-gum or a tablet of chocolate. It depended upon which slot one dropped the penny in, whether he got chocolate or gum. And so with the editorial machine. One slot brought checks and the other brought rejection slips. So far he had found only the latter slot.

It was the rejection slips that completed the horrible machinelikeness of the process. These slips were printed in stereotyped forms and he had received hundreds of them—as many as a dozen or more on each of his earlier manuscripts. If he had received one line, one personal line, along with one rejection of all his rejections, he would have been cheered. But not one editor had given that proof of existence. And he could conclude only that there were no warm human men at the other end, only mere cogs, well oiled and running beautifully in the machine.

He was a good fighter, whole-souled and stubborn, and he would have been content to continue feeding the machine for years; but he was bleeding to death, and not years but weeks would determine the fight. Each week his board bill brought him nearer destruction, while the postage on forty manuscripts bled him almost as severely. He no longer bought books, and he economized in petty ways and sought to delay the inevitable end; though he did not know how to economize, and brought the end nearer by a week when he gave his sister Marian five dollars for a dress.

He struggled in the dark, without advice, without encouragement, and in the teeth of discouragement. Even Gertrude was beginning to look askance. At first she had tolerated with sisterly fondness what she conceived to be his foolishness; but now, out of sisterly solicitude, she grew anxious. To her it seemed that his foolishness was becoming a madness. Martin knew this and suffered more keenly from it than from the open and nagging contempt of Bernard Higginbotham. Martin had faith in himself, but he was alone in this faith. Not even Ruth had faith. She had wanted him to devote himself to study, and, though she had not openly disapproved of his writing, she had never approved.

He had never offered to show her his work. A fastidious delicacy had prevented him. Besides, she had been studying heavily at the university, and he felt averse to robbing her of her time. But when she had taken her degree, she asked him herself to let her see something of what he had been doing. Martin was elated and diffident. Here was a judge. She was a bachelor of arts. She had studied literature under skilled instructors. Perhaps the editors were capable judges, too. But she would be different from them. She would not hand him a stereotyped rejection slip, nor would she inform him that lack of preference for his work did not necessarily imply lack of merit in his work. She would talk, a warm human being, in her quick, bright way, and, most important of all, she would catch glimpses of the real Martin Eden. In his work she would discern what his heart and soul were like, and she would come to understand something, a little something, of the stuff of his dreams and the strength of his power.

Martin gathered together a number of carbon copies of his short stories, hesitated a moment, then added his "Sea Lyrics." They mounted their wheels on a late June afternoon and rode for the hills. It was the second time he had been out with her alone, and as they rode along through the balmy warmth, just chilled by she sea-breeze to refreshing coolness, he was profoundly impressed by the fact that it was a very beautiful and well-ordered world and that it was good to be alive and to love. They left their wheels by the roadside and climbed to the brown top of an open knoll where the sunburnt grass breathed a harvest breath of dry sweetness and content.

"Its work is done," Martin said, as they seated themselves, she upon his coat, and he sprawling close to the warm earth. He sniffed the sweetness of the tawny grass, which entered his brain and set his thoughts whirling on from the particular to the universal. "It has achieved its reason for existence," he went on, patting the dry grass affectionately. "It quickened with ambition under the dreary downpour of last winter, fought the violent early spring, flowered, and lured the insects and the bees, scattered its seeds, squared itself with its duty and the world, and—"

"Why do you always look at things with such dreadfully practical eyes?" she interrupted.

"Because I've been studying evolution, I guess. It's only recently that I got my eyesight, if the truth were told."

"But it seems to me you lose sight of beauty by being so practical, that you destroy beauty like the boys who catch butterflies and rub the down off their beautiful wings."

He shook his head.

"Beauty has significance, but I never knew its significance before. I just accepted beauty as something meaningless, as something that was just beautiful without rhyme or reason. I did not know anything about beauty. But now I know, or, rather, am just beginning to know. This grass is more beautiful to me now that I know why it is grass, and all the hidden chemistry of sun and rain and earth that makes it become grass. Why, there is romance in the life-history of any grass, yes, and adventure, too. The very thought of it stirs me. When I think of the play of force and matter, and all the tremendous struggle of it, I feel as if I could write an epic on the grass."

"How well you talk," she said absently, and he noted that she was looking at him in a searching way.

He was all confusion and embarrassment on the instant, the blood flushing red on his neck and brow.

"I hope I am learning to talk," he stammered. "There seems to be so much in me I want to say. But it is all so big. I can't find ways to say what is really in me. Sometimes it seems to me that all the world, all life, everything, had taken up residence inside of me and was clamoring for me to be the spokesman. I feel—oh, I can't describe it—I feel the bigness of it, but when I speak, I babble like a little child. It is a great task to transmute feeling and sensation into speech, written or spoken, that will, in turn, in him who reads or listens, transmute itself back into the selfsame feeling and sensation. It is a lordly task. See, I bury my face in the grass, and the breath I draw in through my nostrils sets me quivering with a thousand thoughts and fancies. It is a breath of the universe I have breathed. I know song and laughter, and success and pain, and struggle and death; and I see visions that arise in my brain somehow out of the scent of the grass, and I would like to tell them to you, to the world. But how can I? My tongue is tied. I have tried, by the spoken word, just now, to describe to you the effect on me of the scent of the grass. But I have not succeeded. I have no more than hinted in awkward speech. My words seem gibberish to me. And yet I am stifled with desire to tell. Oh!—" he threw up his hands with a despairing gesture—"it is impossible! It is not understandable! It is incommunicable!"

"But you do talk well," she insisted. "Just think how you have improved in the short time I have known you. Mr. Butler is a noted public speaker. He is always asked by the State Committee to go out on stump during campaign. Yet you talked just as well as he the other night at dinner. Only he was more controlled. You get too excited; but you will get over that with practice. Why, you would make a good public speaker. You can go far—if you want to. You are masterly. You can lead men, I am sure, and there is no reason why you should not succeed at anything you set your hand to, just as you have succeeded with grammar. You would make a good lawyer. You should shine in politics. There is nothing to prevent you from making as great a success as Mr. Butler has made. And minus the dyspepsia," she added with a smile.

They talked on; she, in her gently persistent way, returning always to the need of thorough grounding in education and to the advantages of Latin as part of the foundation for any career. She drew her ideal of the successful man, and it was largely in her father's image, with a few unmistakable lines and touches of color from the image of Mr. Butler. He listened eagerly, with receptive ears, lying on his back and looking up and joying in each movement of her lips as she talked. But his brain was not receptive. There was nothing alluring in the pictures she drew, and he was aware of a dull pain of disappointment and of a sharper ache of love for her. In all she said there was no mention of his writing, and the manuscripts he had brought to read lay neglected on the ground.

At last, in a pause, he glanced at the sun, measured its height above the horizon, and suggested his manuscripts by picking them up.

"I had forgotten," she said quickly. "And I am so anxious to hear."

He read to her a story, one that he flattered himself was among his very best. He called it "The Wine of Life," and the wine of it, that had stolen into his brain when he wrote it, stole into his brain now as he read it. There was a certain magic in the original conception, and he had adorned it with more magic of phrase and touch. All the old fire and passion with which he had written it were reborn in him, and he was swayed and swept away so that he was blind and deaf to the faults of it. But it was not so with Ruth. Her trained ear detected the weaknesses and exaggerations, the overemphasis of the tyro, and she was instantly aware each time the sentence-rhythm tripped and faltered. She scarcely noted the rhythm otherwise, except when it became too pompous, at which moments she was disagreeably impressed with its amateurishness. That was her final judgment on the story as a whole—amateurish, though she did not tell him so. Instead, when he had done, she pointed out the minor flaws and said that she liked the story.

But he was disappointed. Her criticism was just. He acknowledged that, but he had a feeling that he was not sharing his work with her for the purpose of schoolroom correction. The details did not matter. They could take care of themselves. He could mend them, he could learn to mend them. Out of life he had captured something big and attempted to imprison it in the story. It was the big thing out of life he had read to her, not sentence-structure and semicolons. He wanted her to feel with him this big thing that was his, that he had seen with his own eyes, grappled with his own brain, and placed there on the page with his own hands in printed words. Well, he had failed, was his secret decision. Perhaps the editors were right. He had felt the big thing, but he had failed to transmute it. He concealed his disappointment, and joined so easily with her in her criticism that she did not realize that deep down in him was running a strong undercurrent of disagreement.

"This next thing I've called 'The Pot'," he said, unfolding the manuscript. "It has been refused by four or five magazines now, but still I think it is good. In fact, I don't know what to think of it, except that I've caught something there. Maybe it won't affect you as it does me. It's a short thing—only two thousand words."

"How dreadful!" she cried, when he had finished. "It is horrible, unutterably horrible!"

He noted her pale face, her eyes wide and tense, and her clenched hands, with secret satisfaction. He had succeeded. He had communicated the stuff of fancy and feeling from out of his brain. It had struck home. No matter whether she liked it or not, it had gripped her and mastered her, made her sit there and listen and forget details.

"It is life," he said, "and life is not always beautiful. And yet, perhaps because I am strangely made, I find something beautiful there. It seems to me that the beauty is tenfold enhanced because it is there—"

"But why couldn't the poor woman—" she broke in disconnectedly. Then she left the revolt of her thought unexpressed to cry out: "Oh! It is degrading! It is not nice! It is nasty!"

For the moment it seemed to him that his heart stood still. *Nasty*! He had never dreamed it. He had not meant it. The whole sketch stood before him in letters of fire, and in such blaze of illumination he sought vainly for nastiness. Then his heart began to beat again. He was not guilty.

"Why didn't you select a nice subject?" she was saying. "We know there are nasty things in the world, but that is no reason—"

She talked on in her indignant strain, but he was not following her. He was smiling to himself as he looked up into her virginal face, so innocent, so penetratingly innocent, that its purity seemed always to enter into him, driving out of him all dross and bathing him in some ethereal effulgence that was as cool and soft and velvety as starshine. *We know there are nasty things in the world*! He cuddled to him the notion of her knowing, and chuckled over it as a love joke. The next moment, in a flashing vision of multitudinous detail, he sighted the whole sea of life's nastiness that he had known and voyaged over and through, and he forgave her for not understanding the story. It was through no fault of hers that she could not understand. He thanked God that she had been born and sheltered to such innocence. But he knew life, its foulness as well as its fairness, its greatness in spite of the slime that infested it, and by God he was going to have his say on it to the world. Saints in heaven—how could they be anything but fair and pure? No praise to them. But saints in slime—ah, that was the everlasting wonder! That was what made life worth while. To see moral grandeur rising out of cesspools of iniquity; to rise himself and first glimpse beauty, faint and far, through mud-dripping eyes; to see out of weakness, and frailty, and viciousness, and all abysmal brutishness, arising strength, and truth, and high spiritual endowment—

He caught a stray sequence of sentences she was uttering.

"The tone of it all is low. And there is so much that is high. Take 'In Memoriam.'"

He was impelled to suggest "Locksley Hall," and would have done so, had not his vision gripped him again and left him staring at her, the female of his kind, who, out of the primordial ferment, creeping and crawling up the vast ladder of life for a thousand thousand centuries, had emerged on the topmost rung, having become one Ruth, pure, and fair, and divine, and with power to make him know love, and to aspire toward purity, and to desire to taste divinity—him, Martin Eden, who, too, had come up in some amazing fashion from out of the ruck and the mire and the countless mistakes and abortions of unending creation. There was the romance, and the wonder, and the glory. There was the stuff to write, if he could only find speech. Saints in heaven!—They were only saints and could not help themselves. But he was a man.

"You have strength," he could hear her saying, "but it is untutored strength."

"Like a bull in a china shop," he suggested, and won a smile.

"And you must develop discrimination. You must consult taste, and fineness, and tone."

"I dare too much," he muttered.

She smiled approbation, and settled herself to listen to another story.

"I don't know what you'll make of this," he said apologetically. "It's a funny thing. I'm afraid I got beyond my depth in it, but my intentions were good. Don't bother about the little features of it. Just see if you catch the feel of the big thing in it. It is big, and it is true, though the chance is large that I have failed to make it intelligible."

He read, and as he read he watched her. At last he had reached her, he thought. She sat without movement, her eyes steadfast upon him, scarcely breathing, caught up and out of herself, he thought, by the witchery of the thing he had created. He had entitled the story "Adventure," and it was the apotheosis of adventure—not of the adventure of the storybooks, but of real adventure, the savage taskmaster, awful of punishment and awful of reward, faithless and whimsical, demanding terrible patience and heartbreaking days and nights of toil, offering the blazing sunlight glory or dark death at the end of thirst and famine or of the long drag and monstrous delirium of rotting fever, through blood and sweat and stinging insects leading up by long chains of petty and ignoble contacts to royal culminations and lordly achievements.

It was this, all of it, and more, that he had put into his story, and it was this, he believed, that warmed her as she sat and listened. Her eyes were wide, color was in her pale cheeks, and before he finished it seemed to him that she was almost panting. Truly, she was warmed; but she was warmed, not by the story, but by him. She did not think much of the story; it was Martin's intensity of power, the old excess of strength that seemed to pour from his body and on and over her. The paradox of it was that it was the story itself that was freighted with his power, that was the channel, for the time being, through which his strength poured out to her. She was aware only of the strength, and not of the medium, and when she seemed most carried away by what he had written, in reality she had been carried away by something quite foreign to it—by a thought, terrible and perilous, that had formed itself unsummoned in her brain. She had caught herself wondering what marriage was like, and the becoming conscious of the waywardness and ardor of the thought had terrified her. It was unmaidenly. It was not like her. She had never been tormented by womanhood, and she had lived in a dreamland of Tennysonian poesy, dense even to the full significance of that delicate master's delicate allusions to the grossnesses that intrude upon the relations of queens and knights. She had been asleep, always, and now life was thundering imperatively at all her doors. Mentally she was in a panic to shoot the bolts and drop the bars into place, while wanton instincts urged her to throw wide her portals and bid the deliciously strange visitor to enter in.

Martin waited with satisfaction for her verdict. He had no doubt of what it would be, and he was astounded when he heard her say:

"It is beautiful."

"It is beautiful," she repeated, with emphasis, after a pause.

Of course it was beautiful; but there was something more than mere beauty in it, something more stingingly splendid which had made beauty its handmaiden. He sprawled silently on the ground, watching the grisly form of a great doubt rising before him. He had failed. He was inarticulate. He had seen one of the greatest things in the world, and he had not expressed it.

"What did you think of the—" He hesitated, abashed at his first attempt to use a strange word. "Of the *motif*?" he asked.

"It was confused," she answered. "That is my only criticism in the large way. I followed the story, but there seemed so much else. It is too wordy. You clog the action by introducing so much extraneous material."

"That was the major *motif*," he hurriedly explained, "the big underrunning *motif*, the cosmic and universal thing. I tried to make it keep time with the story itself, which was only superficial after all. I was on the right scent, but I guess I did it badly. I did not succeed in suggesting what I was driving at. But I'll learn in time."

She did not follow him. She was a bachelor of arts, but he had gone beyond her limitations. This she did not comprehend, attributing her incomprehension to his incoherence.

"You were too voluble," she said. "But it was beautiful, in places."

He heard her voice as from far off, for he was debating whether he would read her the "Sea Lyrics." He lay in dull despair, while she watched him searchingly, pondering again upon unsummoned and wayward thoughts of marriage.

"You want to be famous?" she asked abruptly.

"Yes, a little bit," he confessed. "That is part of the adventure. It is not the being famous, but the process of becoming so, that counts. And after all, to be famous would be, for me, only a means to something else. I want to be famous very much, for that matter, and for that reason."

"For your sake," he wanted to add, and might have added had she proved enthusiastic over what he had read to her.

But she was too busy in her mind, carving out a career for him that would at least be possible, to ask what the ultimate something was which he had hinted at. There was no career for him in literature. Of that she was convinced. He had proved it to-day, with his amateurish and sophomoric productions. He could talk well, but he was incapable of expressing himself in a literary way. She compared Tennyson, and Browning, and her favorite prose masters with him, and to his hopeless discredit. Yet she did not tell him her whole mind. Her strange interest in him led her to temporize. His desire to write was, after all, a little weakness which he would grow out of in time. Then he would devote himself to the more serious affairs of life. And he would succeed, too. She knew that. He was so strong that he could not fail—if only he would drop writing.

"I wish you would show me all you write, Mr. Eden," she said.

He flushed with pleasure. She was interested, that much was sure. And at least she had not given him a rejection slip. She had called certain portions of his work beautiful, and that was the first encouragement he had ever received from any one.

"I will," he said passionately. "And I promise you, Miss Morse, that I will make good. I have come far, I know that; and I have far to go, and I will cover it if I have to do it on my hands and knees." He held up a bunch of manuscript. "Here are the 'Sea Lyrics.' When you get home, I'll turn them over to you to read at your leisure. And you must be sure to tell me just what you think of them. What I need, you know, above all things, is criticism. And do, please, be frank with me."

"I will be perfectly frank," she promised, with an uneasy conviction that she had not been frank with him and with a doubt if she could be quite frank with him the next time.

CHAPTER XV

"The first battle, fought and finished," Martin said to the looking-glass ten days later. "But there will be a second battle, and a third battle, and battles to the end of time, unless—"

He had not finished the sentence, but looked about the mean little room and let his eyes dwell sadly upon a heap of returned manuscripts, still in their long envelopes, which lay in a corner on the floor. He had no stamps with which to continue them on their travels, and for a week they had been piling up. More of them would come in on the morrow, and on the next day, and the next, till they were all in. And he would be unable to start them out again. He was a month's rent behind on the typewriter, which he could not pay, having barely enough for the week's board which was due and for the employment office fees.

He sat down and regarded the table thoughtfully. There were ink stains upon it, and he suddenly discovered that he was fond of it.

"Dear old table," he said, "I've spent some happy hours with you, and you've been a pretty good friend when all is said and done. You never turned me down, never passed me out a reward-of-unmerit rejection slip, never complained about working overtime."

He dropped his arms upon the table and buried his face in them. His throat was aching, and he wanted to cry. It reminded him of his first fight, when he was six years old, when he punched away with the tears running down his cheeks while the other boy, two years his elder, had beaten and pounded him into exhaustion. He saw the ring of boys, howling like barbarians as he went down at last, writhing in the throes of nausea, the blood streaming from his nose and the tears from his bruised eyes.

"Poor little shaver," he murmured. "And you're just as badly licked now. You're beaten to a pulp. You're down and out."

But the vision of that first fight still lingered under his eyelids, and as he watched he saw it dissolve and reshape into the series of fights which had followed. Six months later Cheese-Face (that was the boy) had whipped him again. But he had blacked Cheese-Face's eye that time. That was going some. He saw them all, fight after fight, himself always whipped and Cheese-Face exulting over him. But he had never run away. He felt strengthened by the memory of that. He had always stayed and taken his medicine. Cheese-Face had been a little fiend at fighting, and had never once shown mercy to him. But he had stayed! He had stayed with it!

Next, he saw a narrow alley, between ramshackle frame buildings. The end of the alley was blocked by a one-story brick building, out of which issued the rhythmic thunder of the presses, running off the first edition of the *Enquirer*. He was eleven, and Cheese-Face was thirteen, and they both carried the *Enquirer*. That was why they were there, waiting for their papers. And, of course, Cheese-Face had picked on him again, and there was another fight that was indeterminate, because at quarter to four the door of the press-room was thrown open and the gang of boys crowded in to fold their papers.

"I'll lick you to-morrow," he heard Cheese-Face promise; and he heard his own voice, piping and trembling with unshed tears, agreeing to be there on the morrow.

And he had come there the next day, hurrying from school to be there first, and beating Cheese-Face by two minutes. The other boys said he was all right, and gave him advice, pointing out his faults as a scrapper and promising him victory if he carried out their instructions. The same boys gave Cheese-Face advice, too. How they had enjoyed the fight! He paused in his recollections long enough to envy them the spectacle he and Cheese-Face had put up. Then the fight was on, and it went on, without rounds, for thirty minutes, until the press-room door was opened.

He watched the youthful apparition of himself, day after day, hurrying from school to the *Enquirer* alley. He could not walk very fast. He was stiff and lame from the incessant fighting. His forearms were black and blue from wrist to elbow, what of the countless blows he had warded off, and here and there the tortured flesh was beginning to fester. His head and arms and shoulders ached, the small of his back ached,—he ached all over, and his brain was heavy and dazed. He did not play at school. Nor did he study. Even to sit still all day at his desk, as he did, was a torment. It seemed centuries since he had begun the round of daily fights, and time stretched away into a nightmare and infinite future of daily fights. Why couldn't Cheese-Face be licked? he often thought; that would put him, Martin, out of his misery. It never entered his head to cease fighting, to allow Cheese-Face to whip him.

And so he dragged himself to the *Enquirer* alley, sick in body and soul, but learning the long patience, to confront his eternal enemy, Cheese-Face, who was just as sick as he, and just a bit willing to quit if it were not for the gang of newsboys that looked on and made pride painful and necessary. One afternoon, after twenty minutes of desperate efforts to annihilate each other according to set rules that did not permit kicking, striking below the belt, nor hitting when one was down, Cheese-Face, panting for breath and reeling, offered to call it quits. And Martin, head on arms, thrilled at the picture he caught of himself, at that moment in the afternoon of long ago, when he reeled and panted and choked with the blood that ran into his mouth and down his throat from his cut lips; when he tottered toward Cheese-Face, spitting out a mouthful of blood so that he could speak, crying out that he would never quit, though Cheese-Face could give in if he wanted to. And Cheese-Face did not give in, and the fight went on.

The next day and the next, days without end, witnessed the afternoon fight. When he put up his arms, each day, to begin, they pained exquisitely, and the first few blows, struck and received, racked his soul; after that things grew numb, and he fought on blindly, seeing as in a dream, dancing and wavering, the large features and burning, animal-like eyes of Cheese-Face. He concentrated upon that face; all else about him was a whirling void. There was nothing else in the world but that face, and he would never know rest, blessed rest, until he had beaten that face into a pulp with his bleeding knuckles, or until the bleeding knuckles that somehow belonged to that face had beaten him into a pulp. And then, one way or the other, he would have rest. But to quit,—for him, Martin, to quit,—that was impossible!

Came the day when he dragged himself into the *Enquirer* alley, and there was no Cheese-Face. Nor did Cheese-Face come. The boys congratulated him, and told him that he had licked Cheese-Face. But Martin was not satisfied. He had not licked Cheese-Face, nor had Cheese-Face licked him. The problem had not been solved. It was not until afterward that they learned that Cheese-Face's father had died suddenly that very day.

Martin skipped on through the years to the night in the nigger heaven at the Auditorium. He was seventeen and just back from sea. A row started. Somebody was bullying somebody, and Martin interfered, to be confronted by Cheese-Face's blazing eyes.

"I'll fix you after de show," his ancient enemy hissed.

Martin nodded. The nigger-heaven bouncer was making his way toward the disturbance.

"I'll meet you outside, after the last act," Martin whispered, the while his face showed undivided interest in the buck-and-wing dancing on the stage.

The bouncer glared and went away.

"Got a gang?" he asked Cheese-Face, at the end of the act.

"Sure."

"Then I got to get one," Martin announced.

Between the acts he mustered his following—three fellows he knew from the nail works, a railroad fireman, and half a dozen of the Boo Gang, along with as many more from the dread Eighteen-and-Market Gang.

When the theatre let out, the two gangs strung along inconspicuously on opposite sides of the street. When they came to a quiet corner, they united and held a council of war.

"Eighth Street Bridge is the place," said a red-headed fellow belonging to Cheese-Face's Gang. "You kin fight in the middle, under the electric light, an' whichever way the bulls come in we kin sneak the other way."

"That's agreeable to me," Martin said, after consulting with the leaders of his own gang.

The Eighth Street Bridge, crossing an arm of San Antonio Estuary, was the length of three city blocks. In the middle of the bridge, and at each end, were electric lights. No policeman could pass those end-lights unseen. It was the safe place for the battle that revived itself under Martin's eyelids. He saw the two gangs, aggressive and sullen, rigidly keeping apart from each other and backing their respective champions; and he saw himself and Cheese-Face stripping. A short distance away lookouts were set, their task being to watch the lighted ends of the bridge. A member of the Boo Gang held Martin's coat, and shirt, and cap, ready to race with them into safety in case the police interfered. Martin watched himself go into the centre, facing Cheese-Face, and he heard himself say, as he held up his hand warningly:-

"They ain't no hand-shakin' in this. Understand? They ain't nothin' but scrap. No throwin' up the sponge. This is a grudge-fight an' it's to a finish. Understand? Somebody's goin' to get licked."

Cheese-Face wanted to demur,—Martin could see that,—but Cheese-Face's old perilous pride was touched before the two gangs.

"Aw, come on," he replied. "Wot's the good of chewin' de rag about it? I'm wit' cheh to de finish."

Then they fell upon each other, like young bulls, in all the glory of youth, with naked fists, with hatred, with desire to hurt, to maim, to destroy. All the painful, thousand years' gains of man in his upward climb through creation were lost. Only the electric light remained, a milestone on the path of the great human adventure. Martin and Cheese-Face were two savages, of the stone age, of the squatting place and the tree refuge. They sank lower and lower into the muddy abyss, back into the dregs of the raw beginnings of life, striving blindly and chemically, as atoms strive, as the star-dust if the heavens strives, colliding, recoiling, and colliding again and eternally again.

"God! We are animals! Brute-beasts!" Martin muttered aloud, as he watched the progress of the fight. It was to him, with his splendid power of vision, like gazing into a kinetoscope. He was both onlooker and participant. His long months of culture and refinement shuddered at the sight; then the present was blotted out of his consciousness and the ghosts of the past possessed him, and he was Martin Eden, just returned from sea and fighting Cheese-Face on the Eighth Street Bridge. He suffered and toiled and sweated and bled, and exulted when his naked knuckles smashed home.

They were twin whirlwinds of hatred, revolving about each other monstrously. The time passed, and the two hostile gangs became very quiet. They had never witnessed such intensity of ferocity, and they were awed by it. The two fighters were greater brutes than they. The first splendid velvet edge of youth and condition wore off, and they fought more cautiously and deliberately. There had been no advantage gained either way. "It's anybody's fight," Martin heard some one saying. Then he followed up a feint, right and left, was fiercely countered, and felt his cheek laid open to the bone. No bare knuckle had done that. He heard mutters of amazement at the ghastly damage wrought, and was drenched with his own blood. But he gave no sign. He became immensely wary, for he was wise with knowledge of the low cunning and foul vileness of his kind. He watched and waited, until he feigned a wild rush, which he stopped midway, for he had seen the glint of metal.

"Hold up yer hand!" he screamed. "Them's brass knuckles, an' you hit me with 'em!"

Both gangs surged forward, growling and snarling. In a second there would be a free-for-all fight, and he would be robbed of his vengeance. He was beside himself.

"You guys keep out!" he screamed hoarsely. "Understand? Say, d'ye understand?"

They shrank away from him. They were brutes, but he was the arch-brute, a thing of terror that towered over them and dominated them.

"This is my scrap, an' they ain't goin' to be no buttin' in. Gimme them knuckles."

Cheese-Face, sobered and a bit frightened, surrendered the foul weapon.

"You passed 'em to him, you red-head sneakin' in behind the push there," Martin went on, as he tossed the knuckles into the water. "I seen you, an' I was wonderin' what you was up to. If you try anything like that again, I'll beat cheh to death. Understand?"

They fought on, through exhaustion and beyond, to exhaustion immeasurable and inconceivable, until the crowd of brutes, its blood-lust sated, terrified by what it saw, begged them impartially to cease. And Cheese-Face, ready to drop and die, or to stay on his legs and die, a grisly monster out of whose features all likeness to Cheese-Face had been beaten, wavered and hesitated; but Martin sprang in and smashed him again and again.

Next, after a seeming century or so, with Cheese-Face weakening fast, in a mix-up of blows there was a loud snap, and Martin's right arm dropped to his side. It was a broken bone. Everybody heard it and knew; and Cheese-Face knew, rushing like a tiger in the other's extremity and raining blow on blow. Martin's gang surged forward to interfere. Dazed by the rapid succession of blows, Martin warned them back with vile and earnest curses sobbed out and groaned in ultimate desolation and despair.

He punched on, with his left hand only, and as he punched, doggedly, only half-conscious, as from a remote distance he heard murmurs of fear in the gangs, and one who said with shaking voice: "This ain't a scrap, fellows. It's murder, an' we ought to stop it."

But no one stopped it, and he was glad, punching on wearily and endlessly with his one arm, battering away at a bloody something before him that was not a face but a horror, an oscillating, hideous, gibbering, nameless thing that persisted before his wavering vision and would not go away. And he punched on and on, slower and slower, as the last shreds of vitality oozed from him, through centuries and aeons and enormous lapses of time, until, in a dim way, he became aware that the nameless thing was sinking, slowly sinking down to the rough board-planking of the bridge. And the next moment he was standing over it, staggering and swaying on shaky legs, clutching at the air for support, and saying in a voice he did not recognize:-

"D'ye want any more? Say, d'ye want any more?"

He was still saying it, over and over,—demanding, entreating, threatening, to know if it wanted any more,—when he felt the fellows of his gang laying hands on him, patting him on the back and trying to put his coat on him. And then came a sudden rush of blackness and oblivion.

The tin alarm-clock on the table ticked on, but Martin Eden, his face buried on his arms, did not hear it. He heard nothing. He did not think. So absolutely had he relived life that he had fainted just as he fainted years before on the Eighth Street Bridge. For a full minute the blackness and the blankness endured. Then, like one from the dead, he sprang upright, eyes flaming, sweat pouring down his face, shouting:-

"I licked you, Cheese-Face! It took me eleven years, but I licked you!"

His knees were trembling under him, he felt faint, and he staggered back to the bed, sinking down and sitting on the edge of it. He was still in the clutch of the past. He looked about the room, perplexed, alarmed, wondering where he was, until he caught sight of the pile of manuscripts in the corner. Then the wheels of memory slipped ahead through four years of time, and he was aware of the present, of the books he had opened and the universe he had won from their pages, of his dreams and ambitions, and of his love for a pale wraith of a girl, sensitive and sheltered and ethereal, who would die of horror did she witness but one moment of what he had just lived through—one moment of all the muck of life through which he had waded.

He arose to his feet and confronted himself in the looking-glass.

"And so you arise from the mud, Martin Eden," he said solemnly. "And you cleanse your eyes in a great brightness, and thrust your shoulders among the stars, doing what all life has done, letting the 'ape and tiger die' and wresting highest heritage from all powers that be."

He looked more closely at himself and laughed.

"A bit of hysteria and melodrama, eh?" he queried. "Well, never mind. You licked Cheese-Face, and you'll lick the editors if it takes twice eleven years to do it in. You can't stop here. You've got to go on. It's to a finish, you know."

CHAPTER XVI

The alarm-clock went off, jerking Martin out of sleep with a suddenness that would have given headache to one with less splendid constitution. Though he slept soundly, he awoke instantly, like a cat, and he awoke eagerly, glad that the five hours of unconsciousness were gone. He hated the oblivion of sleep. There was too much to do, too much of life to live. He grudged every moment of life sleep robbed him of, and before the clock had ceased its clattering he was head and ears in the washbasin and thrilling to the cold bite of the water.

But he did not follow his regular programme. There was no unfinished story waiting his hand, no new story demanding articulation. He had studied late, and it was nearly time for breakfast. He tried to read a chapter in Fiske, but his brain was restless and he closed the book. To-day witnessed the beginning of the new battle, wherein for some time there would be no writing. He was aware of a sadness akin to that with which one leaves home and family. He looked at the manuscripts in the corner. That was it. He was going away from them, his pitiful, dishonored children that were welcome nowhere. He went over and began to rummage among them, reading snatches here and there, his favorite portions. "The Pot" he honored with reading aloud, as he did "Adventure." "Joy," his latest-born, completed the day before and tossed into the corner for lack of stamps, won his keenest approbation.

"I can't understand," he murmured. "Or maybe it's the editors who can't understand. There's nothing wrong with that. They publish worse every month. Everything they publish is worse—nearly everything, anyway."

After breakfast he put the type-writer in its case and carried it down into Oakland.

"I owe a month on it," he told the clerk in the store. "But you tell the manager I'm going to work and that I'll be in in a month or so and straighten up."

He crossed on the ferry to San Francisco and made his way to an employment office. "Any kind of work, no trade," he told the agent; and was interrupted by a new-comer, dressed rather foppishly, as some workingmen dress who have instincts for finer things. The agent shook his head despondently.

"Nothin' doin' eh?" said the other. "Well, I got to get somebody to-day."

He turned and stared at Martin, and Martin, staring back, noted the puffed and discolored face, handsome and weak, and knew that he had been making a night of it.

"Lookin' for a job?" the other queried. "What can you do?"

"Hard labor, sailorizing, run a type-writer, no shorthand, can sit on a horse, willing to do anything and tackle anything," was the answer.

The other nodded.

"Sounds good to me. My name's Dawson, Joe Dawson, an' I'm tryin' to scare up a laundryman."

"Too much for me." Martin caught an amusing glimpse of himself ironing fluffy white things that women wear. But he had taken a liking to the other, and he added: "I might do the plain washing. I learned that much at sea." Joe Dawson thought visibly for a moment.

"Look here, let's get together an' frame it up. Willin' to listen?"

Martin nodded.

"This is a small laundry, up country, belongs to Shelly Hot Springs,—hotel, you know. Two men do the work, boss and assistant. I'm the boss. You don't work for me, but you work under me. Think you'd be willin' to learn?"

Martin paused to think. The prospect was alluring. A few months of it, and he would have time to himself for study. He could work hard and study hard.

"Good grub an' a room to yourself," Joe said.

That settled it. A room to himself where he could burn the midnight oil unmolested.

"But work like hell," the other added.

Martin caressed his swelling shoulder-muscles significantly. "That came from hard work."

"Then let's get to it." Joe held his hand to his head for a moment. "Gee, but it's a stem-winder. Can hardly see. I went down the line last night—everything—everything. Here's the frame-up. The wages for two is a hundred and board. I've ben drawin' down sixty, the second man forty. But he knew the biz. You're green. If I break you in, I'll be doing plenty of your work at first. Suppose you begin at thirty, an' work up to the forty. I'll play fair. Just as soon as you can do your share you get the forty."

"I'll go you," Martin announced, stretching out his hand, which the other shook. "Any advance?—for rail-road ticket and extras?"

"I blew it in," was Joe's sad answer, with another reach at his aching head. "All I got is a return ticket."

"And I'm broke—when I pay my board."

"Jump it," Joe advised.

"Can't. Owe it to my sister."

Joe whistled a long, perplexed whistle, and racked his brains to little purpose.

"I've got the price of the drinks," he said desperately. "Come on, an' mebbe we'll cook up something."

Martin declined.

"Water-wagon?"

This time Martin nodded, and Joe lamented, "Wish I was."

"But I somehow just can't," he said in extenuation. "After I've ben workin' like hell all week I just got to booze up. If I didn't, I'd cut my throat or burn up the premises. But I'm glad you're on the wagon. Stay with it."

Martin knew of the enormous gulf between him and this man—the gulf the books had made; but he found no difficulty in crossing back over that gulf. He had lived all his life in the working-class world, and the *camaraderie* of labor was second nature with him. He solved the difficulty of transportation that was too much for the other's aching head. He would send his trunk up to Shelly Hot Springs on Joe's ticket. As for himself, there was his wheel. It was seventy miles, and he could ride it on Sunday and be ready for work Monday morning. In the meantime he would go home and pack up. There was no one to say good-by to. Ruth and her whole family were spending the long summer in the Sierras, at Lake Tahoe.

He arrived at Shelly Hot Springs, tired and dusty, on Sunday night. Joe greeted him exuberantly. With a wet towel bound about his aching brow, he had been at work all day.

"Part of last week's washin' mounted up, me bein' away to get you," he explained. "Your box arrived all right. It's in your room. But it's a hell of a thing to call a trunk. An' what's in it? Gold bricks?"

Joe sat on the bed while Martin unpacked. The box was a packing-case for breakfast food, and Mr. Higginbotham had charged him half a dollar for it. Two rope handles, nailed on by Martin, had technically transformed it into a trunk eligible for the baggage-car. Joe watched, with bulging eyes, a few shirts and several changes of underclothes come out of the box, followed by books, and more books.

"Books clean to the bottom?" he asked.

Martin nodded, and went on arranging the books on a kitchen table which served in the room in place of a wash-stand.

"Gee!" Joe exploded, then waited in silence for the deduction to arise in his brain. At last it came.

"Say, you don't care for the girls—much?" he queried.

"No," was the answer. "I used to chase a lot before I tackled the books. But since then there's no time."

"And there won't be any time here. All you can do is work an' sleep."

Martin thought of his five hours' sleep a night, and smiled. The room was situated over the laundry and was in the same building with the engine that pumped water, made electricity, and ran the laundry machinery. The engineer, who occupied the adjoining room, dropped in to meet the new hand and helped Martin rig up an electric bulb, on an extension wire, so that it travelled along a stretched cord from over the table to the bed.

The next morning, at quarter-past six, Martin was routed out for a quarter-to-seven breakfast. There happened to be a bath-tub for the servants in the laundry building, and he electrified Joe by taking a cold bath.

"Gee, but you're a hummer!" Joe announced, as they sat down to breakfast in a corner of the hotel kitchen.

With them was the engineer, the gardener, and the assistant gardener, and two or three men from the stable. They ate hurriedly and gloomily, with but little conversation, and as Martin ate and listened he realized how far he had travelled from their status. Their small mental caliber was depressing to him, and he was anxious to get away from them. So he bolted his breakfast, a sickly, sloppy affair, as rapidly as they, and heaved a sigh of relief when he passed out through the kitchen door.

It was a perfectly appointed, small steam laundry, wherein the most modern machinery did everything that was possible for machinery to do. Martin, after a few instructions, sorted the great heaps of soiled clothes, while Joe started the masher and made up fresh supplies of soft-soap, compounded of biting chemicals that compelled him to swathe his mouth and nostrils and eyes in bath-towels till he resembled a mummy. Finished the sorting, Martin lent a hand in wringing the clothes. This was done by dumping them into a spinning receptacle that went at a rate of a few thousand revolutions a minute, tearing the matter from the clothes by centrifugal force. Then Martin began to alternate between the dryer and the wringer, between times "shaking out" socks and stockings. By the afternoon, one feeding and one, stacking up, they were running socks and stockings through the mangle while the irons were heating. Then it was hot irons and underclothes till six o'clock, at which time Joe shook his head dubiously.

"Way behind," he said. "Got to work after supper." And after supper they worked until ten o'clock, under the blazing electric lights, until the last piece of under-clothing was ironed and folded away in the distributing room. It was a hot California night, and though the windows were thrown wide, the room, with its red-hot ironing-stove, was a furnace. Martin and Joe, down to undershirts, bare armed, sweated and panted for air.

"Like trimming cargo in the tropics," Martin said, when they went upstairs.

"You'll do," Joe answered. "You take hold like a good fellow. If you keep up the pace, you'll be on thirty dollars only one month. The second month you'll be gettin' your forty. But don't tell me you never ironed before. I know better."

"Never ironed a rag in my life, honestly, until to-day," Martin protested.

He was surprised at his weariness when he act into his room, forgetful of the fact that he had been on his feet and working without let up for fourteen hours. He set the alarm clock at six, and measured back five hours to one o'clock. He could read until then. Slipping off his shoes, to ease his swollen feet, he sat down at the table with his books. He opened Fiske, where he had left off to read. But he found trouble began to read it through a second time. Then he awoke, in pain from his stiffened muscles and chilled by the mountain wind that had begun to blow in through the window. He looked at the clock. It marked two. He had been asleep four hours. He pulled off his clothes and crawled into bed, where he was asleep the moment after his head touched the pillow.

Tuesday was a day of similar unremitting toil. The speed with which Joe worked won Martin's admiration. Joe was a dozen of demons for work. He was keyed up to concert pitch, and there was never a moment in the long day when he was not fighting for moments. He concentrated himself upon his work and upon how to save time, pointing out to Martin where he did in five motions what could be done in three, or in three motions what could be done in two. "Elimination of waste motion," Martin phrased it as he watched and patterned after. He was a good workman himself, quick and deft, and it had always been a point of pride with him that no man should do any of his work for him or outwork him. As a result, he concentrated with a similar singleness of purpose, greedily snapping up the hints and suggestions thrown out by his working mate. He "rubbed out" collars and cuffs, rubbing the starch out from between the double thicknesses of linen so that there would be no blisters when it came to the ironing, and doing it at a pace that elicited Joe's praise.

There was never an interval when something was not at hand to be done. Joe waited for nothing, waited on nothing, and went on the jump from task to task. They starched two hundred white shirts, with a single gathering movement seizing a shirt so that the wristbands, neckband, yoke, and bosom protruded beyond the circling right hand. At the same moment the left hand held up the body of the shirt so that it would not enter the starch, and at the moment the right hand dipped into the starch—starch so hot that, in order to wring it out, their hands had to thrust, and thrust continually, into a bucket of cold water. And that night they worked till half-past ten, dipping "fancy starch"—all the frilled and airy, delicate wear of ladies.

"Me for the tropics and no clothes," Martin laughed.

"And me out of a job," Joe answered seriously. "I don't know nothin' but laundrying."

"And you know it well."

"I ought to. Began in the Contra Costa in Oakland when I was eleven, shakin' out for the mangle. That was eighteen years ago, an' I've never done a tap of anything else. But this job is the fiercest I ever had. Ought to be one more man on it at least. We work to-morrow night. Always run the mangle Wednesday nights—collars an' cuffs."

Martin set his alarm, drew up to the table, and opened Fiske. He did not finish the first paragraph. The lines blurred and ran together and his head nodded. He walked up and down, batting his head savagely with his fists, but he could not conquer the numbness of sleep. He propped the book before him, and propped his eyelids with his fingers, and fell asleep with his eyes wide open. Then he surrendered, and, scarcely conscious of what he did, got off his clothes and into bed. He slept seven hours of heavy, animal-like sleep, and awoke by the alarm, feeling that he had not had enough.

"Doin' much readin'?" Joe asked.

Martin shook his head.

"Never mind. We got to run the mangle to-night, but Thursday we'll knock off at six. That'll give you a chance."

Martin washed woollens that day, by hand, in a large barrel, with strong soft-soap, by means of a hub from a wagon wheel, mounted on a plunger-pole that was attached to a spring-pole overhead.

"My invention," Joe said proudly. "Beats a washboard an' your knuckles, and, besides, it saves at least fifteen minutes in the week, an' fifteen minutes ain't to be sneezed at in this shebang."

Running the collars and cuffs through the mangle was also Joe's idea. That night, while they toiled on under the electric lights, he explained it.

"Something no laundry ever does, except this one. An' I got to do it if I'm goin' to get done Saturday afternoon at three o'clock. But I know how, an' that's the difference. Got to have right heat, right pressure, and run 'em through three times. Look at that!" He held a cuff aloft. "Couldn't do it better by hand or on a tiler."

Thursday, Joe was in a rage. A bundle of extra "fancy starch" had come in.

"I'm goin' to quit," he announced. "I won't stand for it. I'm goin' to quit it cold. What's the good of me workin' like a slave all week, a-savin' minutes, an' them a-comin' an' ringin' in fancy-starch extras on me? This is a free country, an' I'm to tell that fat Dutchman what I think of him. An' I won't tell 'm in French. Plain United States is good enough for me. Him a-ringin' in fancy starch extras!"

"We got to work to-night," he said the next moment, reversing his judgment and surrendering to fate.

And Martin did no reading that night. He had seen no daily paper all week, and, strangely to him, felt no desire to see one. He was not interested in the news. He was too tired and jaded to be interested in anything, though he planned to leave Saturday afternoon, if they finished at three, and ride on his wheel to Oakland. It was seventy miles, and the same distance back on Sunday afternoon would leave him anything but rested for the second week's work. It would have been easier to go on the train, but the round trip was two dollars and a half, and he was intent on saving money.

CHAPTER XVII

Martin learned to do many things. In the course of the first week, in one afternoon, he and Joe accounted for the two hundred white shirts. Joe ran the tiler, a machine wherein a hot iron was hooked on a steel string which furnished the pressure. By this means he ironed the yoke, wristbands, and neckband, setting the latter at right angles to the shirt, and put the glossy finish on the bosom. As fast as he finished them, he flung the shirts on a rack between him and Martin, who caught them up and "backed" them. This task consisted of ironing all the unstarched portions of the shirts.

It was exhausting work, carried on, hour after hour, at top speed. Out on the broad verandas of the hotel, men and women, in cool white, sipped iced drinks and kept their circulation down. But in the laundry the air was sizzling. The huge stove roared red hot and white hot, while the irons, moving over the damp cloth, sent up clouds of steam. The heat of these irons was different from that used by housewives. An iron that stood the ordinary test of a wet finger was too cold for Joe and Martin, and such test was useless. They went wholly by holding the irons close to their cheeks, gauging the heat by some secret mental process that Martin admired but could not understand. When the fresh irons proved too hot, they hooked them on iron rods and dipped them into cold water. This again required a precise and subtle judgment. A fraction of a second too long in the water and the fine and silken edge of the proper heat was lost, and Martin found time to marvel at the accuracy he developed—an automatic accuracy, founded upon criteria that were machine-like and unerring.

But there was little time in which to marvel. All Martin's consciousness was concentrated in the work. Ceaselessly active, head and hand, an intelligent machine, all that constituted him a man was devoted to furnishing that intelligence. There was no room in his brain for the universe and its mighty problems. All the broad and spacious corridors of his mind were closed and hermetically sealed. The echoing chamber of his soul was a narrow room, a conning tower, whence were directed his arm and shoulder muscles, his ten nimble fingers, and the swift-moving iron along its steaming path in broad, sweeping strokes, just so many strokes and no more, just so far with each stroke and not a fraction of an inch farther, rushing along interminable sleeves, sides, backs, and tails, and tossing the finished shirts, without rumpling, upon the receiving frame. And even as his hurrying soul tossed, it was reaching for another shirt. This went on, hour after hour, while outside all the world swooned under the overhead California sun. But there was no swooning in that superheated room. The cool guests on the verandas needed clean linen.

The sweat poured from Martin. He drank enormous quantities of water, but so great was the heat of the day and of his exertions, that the water sluiced through the interstices of his flesh and out at all his pores. Always, at sea, except at rare intervals, the work he performed had given him ample opportunity to commune with himself. The master of the ship had been lord of Martin's time; but here the manager of the hotel was lord of Martin's thoughts as well. He had no thoughts save for the nerve-racking, body-destroying toil. Outside of that it was impossible to think. He did not know that he loved Ruth. She did not even exist, for his driven soul had no time to remember her. It was only when he crawled to bed at night, or to breakfast in the morning, that she asserted herself to him in fleeting memories.

"This is hell, ain't it?" Joe remarked once.

Martin nodded, but felt a rasp of irritation. The statement had been obvious and unnecessary. They did not talk while they worked. Conversation threw them out of their stride, as it did this time, compelling Martin to miss a stroke of his iron and to make two extra motions before he caught his stride again.

On Friday morning the washer ran. Twice a week they had to put through hotel linen,—the sheets, pillow-slips, spreads, table-cloths, and napkins. This finished, they buckled down to "fancy starch." It was slow work, fastidious and delicate, and Martin did not learn it so readily. Besides, he could not take chances. Mistakes were disastrous.

"See that," Joe said, holding up a filmy corset-cover that he could have crumpled from view in one hand. "Scorch that an' it's twenty dollars out of your wages."

So Martin did not scorch that, and eased down on his muscular tension, though nervous tension rose higher than ever, and he listened sympathetically to the other's blasphemies as he toiled and suffered over the beautiful things that women wear when they do not have to do their own laundrying. "Fancy starch" was Martin's nightmare, and it was Joe's, too. It was "fancy starch" that robbed them of their hard-won minutes. They toiled at it all day. At seven in the evening they broke off to run the hotel linen through the mangle. At ten o'clock, while the hotel guests slept, the two laundrymen sweated on at "fancy starch" till midnight, till one, till two. At half-past two they knocked off.

Saturday morning it was "fancy starch," and odds and ends, and at three in the afternoon the week's work was done.

"You ain't a-goin' to ride them seventy miles into Oakland on top of this?" Joe demanded, as they sat on the stairs and took a triumphant smoke.

"Got to," was the answer.

"What are you goin' for?—a girl?"

"No; to save two and a half on the railroad ticket. I want to renew some books at the library."

"Why don't you send 'em down an' up by express? That'll cost only a quarter each way."

Martin considered it.

"An' take a rest to-morrow," the other urged. "You need it. I know I do. I'm plumb tuckered out."

He looked it. Indomitable, never resting, fighting for seconds and minutes all week, circumventing delays and crushing down obstacles, a fount of resistless energy, a high-driven human motor, a demon for work, now that he had accomplished the week's task he was in a state of collapse. He was worn and haggard, and his handsome face drooped in lean exhaustion. He pulled his cigarette spiritlessly, and his voice was peculiarly dead and monotonous. All the snap and fire had gone out of him. His triumph seemed a sorry one.

"An' next week we got to do it all over again," he said sadly. "An' what's the good of it all, hey? Sometimes I wish I was a hobo. They don't work, an' they get their livin'. Gee! I wish I had a glass of beer; but I can't get up the gumption to go down to the village an' get it. You'll stay over, an' send your books dawn by express, or else you're a damn fool."

"But what can I do here all day Sunday?" Martin asked.

"Rest. You don't know how tired you are. Why, I'm that tired Sunday I can't even read the papers. I was sick once—typhoid. In the hospital two months an' a half. Didn't do a tap of work all that time. It was beautiful."

"It was beautiful," he repeated dreamily, a minute later.

Martin took a bath, after which he found that the head laundryman had disappeared. Most likely he had gone for a glass of beer Martin decided, but the half-mile walk down to the village to find out seemed a long journey to him. He lay on his bed with his shoes off, trying to make up his mind. He did not reach out for a book. He was too tired to feel sleepy, and he lay, scarcely thinking, in a semi-stupor of weariness, until it was time for supper. Joe did not appear for that function, and when Martin heard the gardener remark that most likely he was ripping the slats off the bar, Martin understood. He went to bed immediately afterward, and in the morning decided that he was greatly rested. Joe being still absent, Martin procured a Sunday paper and lay down in a shady nook under the trees. The morning passed, he knew not how. He did not sleep, nobody disturbed him, and he did not finish the paper. He came back to it in the afternoon, after dinner, and fell asleep over it.

So passed Sunday, and Monday morning he was hard at work, sorting clothes, while Joe, a towel bound tightly around his head, with groans and blasphemies, was running the washer and mixing soft-soap.

"I simply can't help it," he explained. "I got to drink when Saturday night comes around."

Another week passed, a great battle that continued under the electric lights each night and that culminated on Saturday afternoon at three o'clock, when Joe tasted his moment of wilted triumph and then drifted down to the village to forget. Martin's Sunday was the same as before. He slept in the shade of the trees, toiled aimlessly through the newspaper, and spent long hours lying on his back, doing nothing, thinking nothing. He was too dazed to think, though he was aware that he did not like himself. He was self-repelled, as though he had undergone some degradation or was intrinsically foul. All that was god-like in him was blotted out. The spur of ambition was blunted; he had no vitality with which to feel the prod of it. He was dead. His soul seemed dead. He was a beast, a work-beast. He saw no beauty in the sunshine sifting down through the green leaves, nor did the azure vault of the sky whisper as of old and hint of cosmic vastness and secrets trembling to disclosure. Life was intolerably dull and stupid, and its taste was bad in his mouth. A black screen was drawn across his mirror of inner vision, and fancy lay in a darkened sick-room where entered no ray of light. He envied Joe, down in the village, rampant, tearing the slats off the bar, his brain gnawing with maggots, exulting in maudlin ways over maudlin things, fantastically and gloriously drunk and forgetful of Monday morning and the week of deadening toil to come.

A third week went by, and Martin loathed himself, and loathed life. He was oppressed by a sense of failure. There was reason for the editors refusing his stuff. He could see that clearly now, and laugh at himself and the dreams he had dreamed. Ruth returned his "Sea Lyrics" by mail. He read her letter apathetically. She did her best to say how much she liked them and that they were beautiful. But she could not lie, and she could not disguise the truth from herself. She knew they were failures, and he read her disapproval in every perfunctory and unenthusiastic line of her letter. And she was right. He was firmly convinced of it as he read the poems over. Beauty and wonder had departed from him, and as he read the poems he caught himself puzzling as to what he had had in mind when he wrote them. His audacities of phrase struck him as grotesque, his felicities of expression were monstrosities, and everything was absurd, unreal, and impossible. He would have burned the "Sea Lyrics" on the spot, had his will been strong enough to set them aflame. There was the engine-room, but the exertion of carrying them to the furnace was not worth while. All his exertion was used in washing other persons' clothes. He did not have any left for private affairs.

He resolved that when Sunday came he would pull himself together and answer Ruth's letter. But Saturday afternoon, after work was finished and he had taken a bath, the desire to forget overpowered him. "I guess I'll go down and see how Joe's getting on," was the way he put it to himself; and in the same moment he knew that he lied. But he did not have the energy to consider the lie. If he had had the energy, he would have refused to consider the lie, because he wanted to forget. He started for the village slowly and casually, increasing his pace in spite of himself as he neared the saloon.

"I thought you was on the water-wagon," was Joe's greeting.

Martin did not deign to offer excuses, but called for whiskey, filling his own glass brimming before he passed the bottle.

"Don't take all night about it," he said roughly.

The other was dawdling with the bottle, and Martin refused to wait for him, tossing the glass off in a gulp and refilling it.

"Now, I can wait for you," he said grimly; "but hurry up."

Joe hurried, and they drank together.

"The work did it, eh?" Joe queried.

Martin refused to discuss the matter.

"It's fair hell, I know," the other went on, "but I kind of hate to see you come off the wagon, Mart. Well, here's how!"

Martin drank on silently, biting out his orders and invitations and awing the barkeeper, an effeminate country youngster with watery blue eyes and hair parted in the middle.

"It's something scandalous the way they work us poor devils," Joe was remarking. "If I didn't bowl up, I'd break loose an' burn down the shebang. My bowlin' up is all that saves 'em, I can tell you that."

But Martin made no answer. A few more drinks, and in his brain he felt the maggots of intoxication beginning to crawl. Ah, it was living, the first breath of life he had breathed in three weeks. His dreams came back to him. Fancy came out of the darkened room and lured him on, a thing of flaming brightness. His mirror of vision was silver-clear, a flashing, dazzling palimpsest of imagery. Wonder and beauty walked with him, hand in hand, and all power was his. He tried to tell it to Joe, but Joe had visions of his own, infallible schemes whereby he would escape the slavery of laundry-work and become himself the owner of a great steam laundry.

"I tell yeh, Mart, they won't be no kids workin' in my laundry—not on yer life. An' they won't be no workin' a livin' soul after six P.M. You hear me talk! They'll be machinery enough an' hands enough to do it all in decent workin' hours, an' Mart, s'help me, I'll make yeh superintendent of the shebang—the whole of it, all of it. Now here's the scheme. I get on the water-wagon an' save my money for two years—save an' then—"

But Martin turned away, leaving him to tell it to the barkeeper, until that worthy was called away to furnish drinks to two farmers who, coming in, accepted Martin's invitation. Martin dispensed royal largess, inviting everybody up, farm-hands, a stableman, and the gardener's assistant from the hotel, the barkeeper, and the furtive hobo who slid in like a shadow and like a shadow hovered at the end of the bar.

CHAPTER XVIII

Monday morning, Joe groaned over the first truck load of clothes to the washer.

"I say," he began.

"Don't talk to me," Martin snarled.

"I'm sorry, Joe," he said at noon, when they knocked off for dinner.

Tears came into the other's eyes.

"That's all right, old man," he said. "We're in hell, an' we can't help ourselves. An', you know, I kind of like you a whole lot. That's what made it—hurt. I cottoned to you from the first."

Martin shook his hand.

"Let's quit," Joe suggested. "Let's chuck it, an' go hoboin'. I ain't never tried it, but it must be dead easy. An' nothin' to do. Just think of it, nothin' to do. I was sick once, typhoid, in the hospital, an' it was beautiful. I wish I'd get sick again."

The week dragged on. The hotel was full, and extra "fancy starch" poured in upon them. They performed prodigies of valor. They fought late each night under the electric lights, bolted their meals, and even got in a half hour's work before breakfast. Martin no longer took his cold baths. Every moment was drive, drive, drive, and Joe was the masterful shepherd of moments, herding them carefully, never losing one, counting them over like a miser counting gold, working on in a frenzy, toil-mad, a feverish machine, aided ably by that other machine that thought of itself as once having been one Martin Eden, a man.

But it was only at rare moments that Martin was able to think. The house of thought was closed, its windows boarded up, and he was its shadowy caretaker. He was a shadow. Joe was right. They were both shadows, and this was the unending limbo of toil. Or was it a dream? Sometimes, in the steaming, sizzling heat, as he swung the heavy irons back and forth over the white garments, it came to him that it was a dream. In a short while, or maybe after a thousand years or so, he would awake, in his little room with the ink-stained table, and take up his writing where he had left off the day before. Or maybe that was a dream, too, and the awakening would be the changing of the watches, when he would drop down out of his bunk in the lurching forecastle and go up on deck, under the tropic stars, and take the wheel and feel the cool tradewind blowing through his flesh.

Came Saturday and its hollow victory at three o'clock.

"Guess I'll go down an' get a glass of beer," Joe said, in the queer, monotonous tones that marked his week-end collapse.

Martin seemed suddenly to wake up. He opened the kit bag and oiled his wheel, putting graphite on the chain and adjusting the bearings. Joe was halfway down to the saloon when Martin passed by, bending low over the handle-bars, his legs driving the ninety-six gear with rhythmic strength, his face set for seventy miles of road and grade and dust. He slept in Oakland that night, and on Sunday covered the seventy miles back. And on Monday morning, weary, he began the new week's work, but he had kept sober.

A fifth week passed, and a sixth, during which he lived and toiled as a machine, with just a spark of something more in him, just a glimmering bit of soul, that compelled him, at each week-end, to scorch off the hundred and forty miles. But this was not rest. It was supermachinelike, and it helped to crush out the glimmering bit of soul that was all that was left him from former life. At the end of the seventh week, without intending it, too weak to resist, he drifted down to the village with Joe and drowned life and found life until Monday morning.

Again, at the week-ends, he ground out the one hundred and forty miles, obliterating the numbness of too great exertion by the numbness of still greater exertion. At the end of three months he went down a third time to the village with Joe. He forgot, and lived again, and, living, he saw, in clear illumination, the beast he was making of himself—not by the drink, but by the work. The drink was an effect, not a cause. It followed inevitably upon the work, as the night follows upon the day. Not by becoming a toil-beast could he win to the heights, was the message the whiskey whispered to him, and he nodded approbation. The whiskey was wise. It told secrets on itself.

He called for paper and pencil, and for drinks all around, and while they drank his very good health, he clung to the bar and scribbled.

"A telegram, Joe," he said. "Read it."

Joe read it with a drunken, quizzical leer. But what he read seemed to sober him. He looked at the other reproachfully, tears oozing into his eyes and down his cheeks.

"You ain't goin' back on me, Mart?" he queried hopelessly.

Martin nodded, and called one of the loungers to him to take the message to the telegraph office.

"Hold on," Joe muttered thickly. "Lemme think."

He held on to the bar, his legs wobbling under him, Martin's arm around him and supporting him, while he thought.

"Make that two laundrymen," he said abruptly. "Here, lemme fix it."

"What are you quitting for?" Martin demanded.

"Same reason as you."

"But I'm going to sea. You can't do that."

"Nope," was the answer, "but I can hobo all right, all right."

Martin looked at him searchingly for a moment, then cried:-

"By God, I think you're right! Better a hobo than a beast of toil. Why, man, you'll live. And that's more than you ever did before."

"I was in hospital, once," Joe corrected. "It was beautiful. Typhoid—did I tell you?"

While Martin changed the telegram to "two laundrymen," Joe went on:-

"I never wanted to drink when I was in hospital. Funny, ain't it? But when I've ben workin' like a slave all week, I just got to bowl up. Ever noticed that cooks drink like hell?—an' bakers, too? It's the work. They've sure got to. Here, lemme pay half of that telegram."

"I'll shake you for it," Martin offered.

"Come on, everybody drink," Joe called, as they rattled the dice and rolled them out on the damp bar.

Monday morning Joe was wild with anticipation. He did not mind his aching head, nor did he take interest in his work. Whole herds of moments stole away and were lost while their careless shepherd gazed out of the window at the sunshine and the trees.

"Just look at it!" he cried. "An' it's all mine! It's free. I can lie down under them trees an' sleep for a thousan' years if I want to. Aw, come on, Mart, let's chuck it. What's the good of waitin' another moment. That's the land of nothin' to do out there, an' I got a ticket for it—an' it ain't no return ticket, b'gosh!"

A few minutes later, filling the truck with soiled clothes for the washer, Joe spied the hotel manager's shirt. He knew its mark, and with a sudden glorious consciousness of freedom he threw it on the floor and stamped on it.

"I wish you was in it, you pig-headed Dutchman!" he shouted. "In it, an' right there where I've got you! Take that! an' that! an' that! damn you! Hold me back, somebody! Hold me back!"

Martin laughed and held him to his work. On Tuesday night the new laundrymen arrived, and the rest of the week was spent breaking them into the routine. Joe sat around and explained his system, but he did no more work.

"Not a tap," he announced. "Not a tap. They can fire me if they want to, but if they do, I'll quit. No more work in mine, thank you kindly. Me for the freight cars an' the shade under the trees. Go to it, you slaves! That's right. Slave an' sweat! Slave an' sweat! An' when you're dead, you'll rot the same as me, an' what's it matter how you live?—eh? Tell me that—what's it matter in the long run?"

On Saturday they drew their pay and came to the parting of the ways.

"They ain't no use in me askin' you to change your mind an' hit the road with me?" Joe asked hopelessly:

Martin shook his head. He was standing by his wheel, ready to start. They shook hands, and Joe held on to his for a moment, as he said:-

"I'm goin' to see you again, Mart, before you an' me die. That's straight dope. I feel it in my bones. Good-by, Mart, an' be good. I like you like hell, you know."

He stood, a forlorn figure, in the middle of the road, watching until Martin turned a bend and was gone from sight.

"He's a good Indian, that boy," he muttered. "A good Indian."

Then he plodded down the road himself, to the water tank, where half a dozen empties lay on a side-track waiting for the up freight.

CHAPTER XIX

Ruth and her family were home again, and Martin, returned to Oakland, saw much of her. Having gained her degree, she was doing no more studying; and he, having worked all vitality out of his mind and body, was doing no writing. This gave them time for each other that they had never had before, and their intimacy ripened fast.

At first, Martin had done nothing but rest. He had slept a great deal, and spent long hours musing and thinking and doing nothing. He was like one recovering from some terrible bout if hardship. The first signs of reawakening came when he discovered more than languid interest in the daily paper. Then he began to read again—light novels, and poetry; and after several days more he was head over heels in his long-neglected Fiske. His splendid body and health made new vitality, and he possessed all the resiliency and rebound of youth.

Ruth showed her disappointment plainly when he announced that he was going to sea for another voyage as soon as he was well rested.

"Why do you want to do that?" she asked.

"Money," was the answer. "I'll have to lay in a supply for my next attack on the editors. Money is the sinews of war, in my case—money and patience."

"But if all you wanted was money, why didn't you stay in the laundry?"

"Because the laundry was making a beast of me. Too much work of that sort drives to drink."

She stared at him with horror in her eyes.

"Do you mean—?" she quavered.

It would have been easy for him to get out of it; but his natural impulse was for frankness, and he remembered his old resolve to be frank, no matter what happened.

"Yes," he answered. "Just that. Several times."

She shivered and drew away from him.

"No man that I have ever known did that—ever did that."

"Then they never worked in the laundry at Shelly Hot Springs," he laughed bitterly. "Toil is a good thing. It is necessary for human health, so all the preachers say, and Heaven knows I've never been afraid of it. But there is such a thing as too much of a good thing, and the laundry up there is one of them. And that's why I'm going to sea one more voyage. It will be my last, I think, for when I come back, I shall break into the magazines. I am certain of it."

She was silent, unsympathetic, and he watched her moodily, realizing how impossible it was for her to understand what he had been through.

"Some day I shall write it up—'The Degradation of Toil' or the 'Psychology of Drink in the Working-class,' or something like that for a title."

Never, since the first meeting, had they seemed so far apart as that day. His confession, told in frankness, with the spirit of revolt behind, had repelled her. But she was more shocked by the repulsion itself than by the cause of it. It pointed out to her how near she had drawn to him, and once accepted, it paved the way for greater intimacy. Pity, too, was aroused, and innocent, idealistic thoughts of reform. She would save this raw young man who had come so far. She would save him from the curse of his early environment, and she would save him from himself in spite of himself. And all this affected her as a very noble state of consciousness; nor did she dream that behind it and underlying it were the jealousy and desire of love.

They rode on their wheels much in the delightful fall weather, and out in the hills they read poetry aloud, now one and now the other, noble, uplifting poetry that turned one's thoughts to higher things. Renunciation, sacrifice, patience, industry, and high endeavor were the principles she thus indirectly preached—such abstractions being objectified in her mind by her father, and Mr. Butler, and by Andrew Carnegie, who, from a poor immigrant boy had arisen to be the book-giver of the world. All of which was appreciated and enjoyed by Martin. He followed her mental processes more clearly now, and her soul was no longer the sealed wonder it had been. He was on terms of intellectual equality with her. But the points of disagreement did not affect his love. His love was more ardent than ever, for he loved her for what she was, and even her physical frailty was an added charm in his eyes. He read of sickly Elizabeth Barrett, who for years had not placed her feet upon the ground, until that day of flame when she eloped with Browning and stood upright, upon the earth, under the open sky; and what Browning had done for her, Martin decided he could do for Ruth. But first, she must love him. The rest would be easy. He would give her strength and health. And he caught glimpses of their life, in the years to come, wherein, against a background of work and comfort and general well-being, he saw himself and Ruth reading and discussing poetry, she propped amid a multitude of cushions on the ground while she read aloud to him. This was the key to the life they would live. And always he saw that particular picture. Sometimes it was she who leaned against him while he read, one arm about her, her head upon his shoulder. Sometimes they pored together over the printed pages of beauty. Then, too, she loved nature, and with generous imagination he changed the scene of their reading—sometimes they read in closed-in valleys with precipitous walls, or in high mountain meadows, and, again, down by the gray sand-dunes with a wreath of billows at their feet, or afar on some volcanic tropic isle where waterfalls descended and became mist, reaching the sea in vapor veils that swayed and shivered to every vagrant wisp of wind. But always, in the foreground, lords of beauty and eternally reading and sharing, lay he and Ruth, and always in the background that was beyond the background of nature, dim and hazy, were work and success and money earned that made them free of the world and all its treasures.

"I should recommend my little girl to be careful," her mother warned her one day.

"I know what you mean. But it is impossible. He if; not—"

Ruth was blushing, but it was the blush of maidenhood called upon for the first time to discuss the sacred things of life with a mother held equally sacred.

"Your kind." Her mother finished the sentence for her.

Ruth nodded.

"I did not want to say it, but he is not. He is rough, brutal, strong—too strong. He has not—"

She hesitated and could not go on. It was a new experience, talking over such matters with her mother. And again her mother completed her thought for her.

"He has not lived a clean life, is what you wanted to say."

Again Ruth nodded, and again a blush mantled her face.

"It is just that," she said. "It has not been his fault, but he has played much with—"

"With pitch?"

"Yes, with pitch. And he frightens me. Sometimes I am positively in terror of him, when he talks in that free and easy way of the things he has done—as if they did not matter. They do matter, don't they?"

They sat with their arms twined around each other, and in the pause her mother patted her hand and waited for her to go on.

"But I am interested in him dreadfully," she continued. "In a way he is my protégé. Then, too, he is my first boy friend—but not exactly friend; rather protégé and friend combined. Sometimes, too, when he frightens me, it seems that he is a bulldog I have taken for a plaything, like some of the 'frat' girls, and he is tugging hard, and showing his teeth, and threatening to break loose."

Again her mother waited.

"He interests me, I suppose, like the bulldog. And there is much good in him, too; but there is much in him that I would not like in—in the other way. You see, I have been thinking. He swears, he smokes, he drinks, he has fought with his fists (he has told me so, and he likes it; he says so). He is all that a man should not be—a man I would want for my—" her voice sank very low—"husband. Then he is too strong. My prince must be tall, and slender, and dark—a graceful, bewitching prince. No, there is no danger of my failing in love with Martin Eden. It would be the worst fate that could befall me."

"But it is not that that I spoke about," her mother equivocated. "Have you thought about him? He is so ineligible in every way, you know, and suppose he should come to love you?"

"But he does—already," she cried.

"It was to be expected," Mrs. Morse said gently. "How could it be otherwise with any one who knew you?"

"Olney hates me!" she exclaimed passionately. "And I hate Olney. I feel always like a cat when he is around. I feel that I must be nasty to him, and even when I don't happen to feel that way, why, he's nasty to me, anyway. But I am happy with Martin Eden. No one ever loved me before—no man, I mean, in that way. And it is sweet to be loved—that way. You know what I mean, mother dear. It is sweet to feel that you are really and truly a woman." She buried her face in her mother's lap, sobbing. "You think I am dreadful, I know, but I am honest, and I tell you just how I feel."

Mrs. Morse was strangely sad and happy. Her child-daughter, who was a bachelor of arts, was gone; but in her place was a woman-daughter. The experiment had succeeded. The strange void in Ruth's nature had been filled, and filled without danger or penalty. This rough sailor-fellow had been the instrument, and, though Ruth did not love him, he had made her conscious of her womanhood.

"His hand trembles," Ruth was confessing, her face, for shame's sake, still buried. "It is most amusing and ridiculous, but I feel sorry for him, too. And when his hands are too trembly, and his eyes too shiny, why, I lecture him about his life and the wrong way he is going about it to mend it. But he worships me, I know. His eyes and his hands do not lie. And it makes me feel grown-up, the thought of it, the very thought of it; and I feel that I am possessed of something that is by rights my own—that makes me like the other girls—and—and young women. And, then, too, I knew that I was not like them before, and I knew that it worried you. You thought you did not let me know that dear worry of yours, but I did, and I wanted to—'to make good,' as Martin Eden says."

It was a holy hour for mother and daughter, and their eyes were wet as they talked on in the twilight, Ruth all white innocence and frankness, her mother sympathetic, receptive, yet calmly explaining and guiding.

"He is four years younger than you," she said. "He has no place in the world. He has neither position nor salary. He is impractical. Loving you, he should, in the name of common sense, be doing something that would give him the right to marry, instead of paltering around with those stories of his and with childish dreams. Martin Eden, I am afraid, will never grow up. He does not take to responsibility and a man's work in the world like your father did, or like all our friends, Mr. Butler for one. Martin Eden, I am afraid, will never be a money-earner. And this world is so ordered that money is necessary to happiness—oh, no, not these swollen fortunes, but enough of money to permit of common comfort and decency. He—he has never spoken?"

"He has not breathed a word. He has not attempted to; but if he did, I would not let him, because, you see, I do not love him."

"I am glad of that. I should not care to see my daughter, my one daughter, who is so clean and pure, love a man like him. There are noble men in the world who are clean and true and manly. Wait for them. You will find one some day, and you will love him and be loved by him, and you will be happy with him as your father and I have been happy with each other. And there is one thing you must always carry in mind—"

"Yes, mother."

Mrs. Morse's voice was low and sweet as she said, "And that is the children."

"I—have thought about them," Ruth confessed, remembering the wanton thoughts that had vexed her in the past, her face again red with maiden shame that she should be telling such things.

"And it is that, the children, that makes Mr. Eden impossible," Mrs. Morse went on incisively. "Their heritage must be clean, and he is, I am afraid, not clean. Your father has told me of sailors' lives, and—and you understand."

Ruth pressed her mother's hand in assent, feeling that she really did understand, though her conception was of something vague, remote, and terrible that was beyond the scope of imagination.

"You know I do nothing without telling you," she began. "—Only, sometimes you must ask me, like this time. I wanted to tell you, but I did not know how. It is false modesty, I know it is that, but you can make it easy for me. Sometimes, like this time, you must ask me, you must give me a chance."

"Why, mother, you are a woman, too!" she cried exultantly, as they stood up, catching her mother's hands and standing erect, facing her in the twilight, conscious of a strangely sweet equality between them. "I should never have thought of you in that way if we had not had this talk. I had to learn that I was a woman to know that you were one, too."

"We are women together," her mother said, drawing her to her and kissing her. "We are women together," she repeated, as they went out of the room, their arms around each other's waists, their hearts swelling with a new sense of companionship.

"Our little girl has become a woman," Mrs. Morse said proudly to her husband an hour later.

"That means," he said, after a long look at his wife, "that means she is in love."

"No, but that she is loved," was the smiling rejoinder. "The experiment has succeeded. She is awakened at last."

"Then we'll have to get rid of him." Mr. Morse spoke briskly, in matter-of-fact, businesslike tones.

But his wife shook her head. "It will not be necessary. Ruth says he is going to sea in a few days. When he comes back, she will not be here. We will send her to Aunt Clara's. And, besides, a year in the East, with the change in climate, people, ideas, and everything, is just the thing she needs."

CHAPTER XX

The desire to write was stirring in Martin once more. Stories and poems were springing into spontaneous creation in his brain, and he made notes of them against the future time when he would give them expression. But he did not write. This was his little vacation; he had resolved to devote it to rest and love, and in both matters he prospered. He was soon spilling over with vitality, and each day he saw Ruth, at the moment of meeting, she experienced the old shock of his strength and health.

"Be careful," her mother warned her once again. "I am afraid you are seeing too much of Martin Eden."

But Ruth laughed from security. She was sure of herself, and in a few days he would be off to sea. Then, by the time he returned, she would be away on her visit East. There was a magic, however, in the strength and health of Martin. He, too, had been told of her contemplated Eastern trip, and he felt the need for haste. Yet he did not know how to make love to a girl like Ruth. Then, too, he was handicapped by the possession of a great fund of experience with girls and women who had been absolutely different from her. They had known about love and life and flirtation, while she knew nothing about such things. Her prodigious innocence appalled him, freezing on his lips all ardors of speech, and convincing him, in spite of himself, of his own unworthiness. Also he was handicapped in another way. He had himself never been in love before. He had liked women in that turgid past of his, and been fascinated by some of them, but he had not known what it was to love them. He had whistled in a masterful, careless way, and they had come to him. They had been diversions, incidents, part of the game men play, but a small part at most. And now, and for the first time, he was a suppliant, tender and timid and doubting. He did not know the way of love, nor its speech, while he was frightened at his loved one's clear innocence.

In the course of getting acquainted with a varied world, whirling on through the ever changing phases of it, he had learned a rule of conduct which was to the effect that when one played a strange game, he should let the other fellow play first. This had stood him in good stead a thousand times and trained him as an observer as well. He knew how to watch the thing that was strange, and to wait for a weakness, for a place of entrance, to divulge itself. It was like sparring for an opening in fist-fighting. And when such an opening came, he knew by long experience to play for it and to play hard.

So he waited with Ruth and watched, desiring to speak his love but not daring. He was afraid of shocking her, and he was not sure of himself. Had he but known it, he was following the right course with her. Love came into the world before articulate speech, and in its own early youth it had learned ways and means that it had never forgotten. It was in this old, primitive way that Martin wooed Ruth. He did not know he was doing it at first, though later he divined it. The touch of his hand on hers was vastly more potent than any word he could utter, the impact of his strength on her imagination was more alluring than the printed poems and spoken passions of a thousand generations of lovers. Whatever his tongue could express would have appealed, in part, to her judgment; but the touch of hand, the fleeting contact, made its way directly to her instinct. Her judgment was as young as she, but her instincts were as old as the race and older. They had been young when love was young, and they were wiser than convention and opinion and all the new-born things. So her judgment did not act. There was no call upon it, and she did not realize the strength of the appeal Martin made from moment to moment to her love-nature. That he loved her, on the other hand, was as clear as day, and she consciously delighted in beholding his love-manifestations—the glowing eyes with their tender lights, the trembling hands, and the never failing swarthy flush that flooded darkly under his sunburn. She even went farther, in a timid way inciting him, but doing it so delicately that he never suspected, and doing it half-consciously, so that she scarcely suspected herself. She thrilled with these proofs of her power that proclaimed her a woman, and she took an Eve-like delight in tormenting him and playing upon him.

Tongue-tied by inexperience and by excess of ardor, wooing unwittingly and awkwardly, Martin continued his approach by contact. The touch of his hand was pleasant to her, and something deliciously more than pleasant. Martin did not know it, but he did know that it was not distasteful to her. Not that they touched hands often, save at meeting and parting; but that in handling the bicycles, in strapping on the books of verse they carried into the hills, and in conning the pages of books side by side, there were opportunities for hand to stray against hand. And there were opportunities, too, for her hair to brush his cheek, and for shoulder to touch shoulder, as they leaned together over the beauty of the books. She smiled to herself at vagrant impulses which arose from nowhere and suggested that she rumple his hair; while he desired greatly, when they tired of reading, to rest his head in her lap and dream with closed eyes about the future that was to be theirs. On Sunday picnics at Shellmound Park and Schuetzen Park, in the past, he had rested his head on many laps, and, usually, he had slept soundly and selfishly while the girls shaded his face from the sun and looked down and loved him and wondered at his lordly carelessness of their love. To rest his head in a girl's lap had been the easiest thing in the world until now, and now he found Ruth's lap inaccessible and impossible. Yet it was right here, in his reticence, that the strength of his wooing lay. It was because of this reticence that he never alarmed her. Herself fastidious and timid, she never awakened to the perilous trend of their intercourse. Subtly and unaware she grew toward him and closer to him, while he, sensing the growing closeness, longed to dare but was afraid.

Once he dared, one afternoon, when he found her in the darkened living room with a blinding headache.

"Nothing can do it any good," she had answered his inquiries. "And besides, I don't take headache powders. Doctor Hall won't permit me."

"I can cure it, I think, and without drugs," was Martin's answer. "I am not sure, of course, but I'd like to try. It's simply massage. I learned the trick first from the Japanese. They are a race of masseurs, you know. Then I learned it all over again with variations from the Hawaiians. They call it *lomi-lomi*. It can accomplish most of the things drugs accomplish and a few things that drugs can't."

Scarcely had his hands touched her head when she sighed deeply.

"That is so good," she said.

She spoke once again, half an hour later, when she asked, "Aren't you tired?"

The question was perfunctory, and she knew what the answer would be. Then she lost herself in drowsy contemplation of the soothing balm of his strength: Life poured from the ends of his fingers, driving the pain before it, or so it seemed to her, until with the easement of pain, she fell asleep and he stole away.

She called him up by telephone that evening to thank him.

"I slept until dinner," she said. "You cured me completely, Mr. Eden, and I don't know how to thank you."

He was warm, and bungling of speech, and very happy, as he replied to her, and there was dancing in his mind, throughout the telephone conversation, the memory of Browning and of sickly Elizabeth Barrett. What had been done could be done again, and he, Martin Eden, could do it and would do it for Ruth Morse. He went back to his room and to the volume of Spencer's "Sociology" lying open on the bed. But he could not read. Love tormented him and overrode his will, so that, despite all determination, he found himself at the little ink-stained table. The sonnet he composed that night was the first of a love-cycle of fifty sonnets which was completed within two months. He had the "Love-sonnets from the Portuguese" in mind as he wrote, and he wrote under the best conditions for great work, at a climacteric of living, in the throes of his own sweet love-madness.

The many hours he was not with Ruth he devoted to the "Love-cycle," to reading at home, or to the public reading-rooms, where he got more closely in touch with the magazines of the day and the nature of their policy and content. The hours he spent with Ruth were maddening alike in promise and in inconclusiveness. It was a week after he cured her headache that a moonlight sail on Lake Merritt was proposed by Norman and seconded by Arthur and Olney. Martin was the only one capable of handling a boat, and he was pressed into service. Ruth sat near him in the stern, while the three young fellows lounged amidships, deep in a wordy wrangle over "frat" affairs.

The moon had not yet risen, and Ruth, gazing into the starry vault of the sky and exchanging no speech with Martin, experienced a sudden feeling of loneliness. She glanced at him. A puff of wind was heeling the boat over till the deck was awash, and he, one hand on tiller and the other on main-sheet, was luffing slightly, at the same time peering ahead to make out the near-lying north shore. He was unaware of her gaze, and she watched him intently, speculating fancifully about the strange warp of soul that led him, a young man with signal powers, to fritter away his time on the writing of stories and poems foredoomed to mediocrity and failure.

Her eyes wandered along the strong throat, dimly seen in the starlight, and over the firm-poised head, and the old desire to lay her hands upon his neck came back to her. The strength she abhorred attracted her. Her feeling of loneliness became more pronounced, and she felt tired. Her position on the heeling boat irked her, and she remembered the headache he had cured and the soothing rest that resided in him. He was sitting beside her, quite beside her, and the boat seemed to tilt her toward him. Then arose in her the impulse to lean against him, to rest herself against his strength—a vague, half-formed impulse, which, even as she considered it, mastered her and made her lean toward him. Or was it the heeling of the boat? She did not know. She never knew. She knew only that she was leaning against him and that the easement and soothing rest were very good. Perhaps it had been the boat's fault, but she made no effort to retrieve it. She leaned lightly against his shoulder, but she leaned, and she continued to lean when he shifted his position to make it more comfortable for her.

It was a madness, but she refused to consider the madness. She was no longer herself but a woman, with a woman's clinging need; and though she leaned ever so lightly, the need seemed satisfied. She was no longer tired. Martin did not speak. Had he, the spell would have been broken. But his reticence of love prolonged it. He was dazed and dizzy. He could not understand what was happening. It was too wonderful to be anything but a delirium. He conquered a mad desire to let go sheet and tiller and to clasp her in his arms. His intuition told him it was the wrong thing to do, and he was glad that sheet and tiller kept his hands occupied and fended off temptation. But he luffed the boat less delicately, spilling the wind shamelessly from the sail so as to prolong the tack to the north shore. The shore would compel him to go about, and the contact would be broken. He sailed with skill, stopping way on the boat without exciting the notice of the wranglers, and mentally forgiving his hardest voyages in that they had made this marvellous night possible, giving him mastery over sea and boat and wind so that he could sail with her beside him, her dear weight against him on his shoulder.

When the first light of the rising moon touched the sail, illuminating the boat with pearly radiance, Ruth moved away from him. And, even as she moved, she felt him move away. The impulse to avoid detection was mutual. The episode was tacitly and secretly intimate. She sat apart from him with burning cheeks, while the full force of it came home to her. She had been guilty of something she would not have her brothers see, nor Olney see. Why had she done it? She had never done anything like it in her life, and yet she had been moonlight-sailing with young men before. She had never desired to do anything like it. She was overcome with shame and with the mystery of her own burgeoning womanhood. She stole a glance at Martin, who was busy putting the boat about on the other tack, and she could have hated him for having made her do an immodest and shameful thing. And he, of all men! Perhaps her mother was right, and she was seeing too much of him. It would never happen again, she resolved, and she would see less of him in the future. She entertained a wild idea of explaining to him the first time they were alone together, of lying to him, of mentioning casually the attack of faintness that had overpowered her just before the moon came up. Then she remembered how they had drawn mutually away before the revealing moon, and she knew he would know it for a lie.

In the days that swiftly followed she was no longer herself but a strange, puzzling creature, wilful over judgment and scornful of self-analysis, refusing to peer into the future or to think about herself and whither she was drifting. She was in a fever of tingling mystery, alternately frightened and charmed, and in constant bewilderment. She had one idea firmly fixed, however, which insured her security. She would not let Martin speak his love. As long as she did this, all would be well. In a few days he would be off to sea. And even if he did speak, all would be well. It could not be otherwise, for she did not love him. Of course, it would be a painful half hour for him, and an embarrassing half hour for her, because it would be her first proposal. She thrilled deliciously at the thought. She was really a woman, with a man ripe to ask for her in marriage. It was a lure to all that was fundamental in her sex. The fabric of her life, of all that constituted her, quivered and grew tremulous. The thought fluttered in her mind like a flame-attracted moth. She went so far as to imagine Martin proposing, herself putting the words into his mouth; and she rehearsed her refusal, tempering it with kindness and exhorting him to true and noble manhood. And especially he must stop smoking cigarettes. She would make a point of that. But no, she must not let him speak at all. She could stop him, and she had told her mother that she would. All flushed and burning, she regretfully dismissed the conjured situation. Her first proposal would have to be deferred to a more propitious time and a more eligible suitor.

CHAPTER XXI

Came a beautiful fall day, warm and languid, palpitant with the hush of the changing season, a California Indian summer day, with hazy sun and wandering wisps of breeze that did not stir the slumber of the air. Filmy purple mists, that were not vapors but fabrics woven of color, hid in the recesses of the hills. San Francisco lay like a blur of smoke upon her heights. The intervening bay was a dull sheen of molten metal, whereon sailing craft lay motionless or drifted with the lazy tide. Far Tamalpais, barely seen in the silver haze, bulked hugely by the Golden Gate, the latter a pale gold pathway under the westering sun. Beyond, the Pacific, dim and vast, was raising on its sky-line tumbled cloud-masses that swept landward, giving warning of the first blustering breath of winter.

The erasure of summer was at hand. Yet summer lingered, fading and fainting among her hills, deepening the purple of her valleys, spinning a shroud of haze from waning powers and sated raptures, dying with the calm content of having lived and lived well. And among the hills, on their favorite knoll, Martin and Ruth sat side by side, their heads bent over the same pages, he reading aloud from the love-sonnets of the woman who had loved Browning as it is given to few men to be loved.

But the reading languished. The spell of passing beauty all about them was too strong. The golden year was dying as it had lived, a beautiful and unrepentant voluptuary, and reminiscent rapture and content freighted heavily the air. It entered into them, dreamy and languorous, weakening the fibres of resolution, suffusing the face of morality, or of judgment, with haze and purple mist. Martin felt tender and melting, and from time to time warm glows passed over him. His head was very near to hers, and when wandering phantoms of breeze stirred her hair so that it touched his face, the printed pages swam before his eyes.

"I don't believe you know a word of what you are reading," she said once when he had lost his place.

He looked at her with burning eyes, and was on the verge of becoming awkward, when a retort came to his lips.

"I don't believe you know either. What was the last sonnet about?"

"I don't know," she laughed frankly. "I've already forgotten. Don't let us read any more. The day is too beautiful."

"It will be our last in the hills for some time," he announced gravely. "There's a storm gathering out there on the sea-rim."

The book slipped from his hands to the ground, and they sat idly and silently, gazing out over the dreamy bay with eyes that dreamed and did not see. Ruth glanced sidewise at his neck. She did not lean toward him. She was drawn by some force outside of herself and stronger than gravitation, strong as destiny. It was only an inch to lean, and it was accomplished without volition on her part. Her shoulder touched his as lightly as a butterfly touches a flower, and just as lightly was the counter-pressure. She felt his shoulder press hers, and a tremor run through him. Then was the time for her to draw back. But she had become an automaton. Her actions had passed beyond the control of her will—she never thought of control or will in the delicious madness that was upon her. His arm began to steal behind her and around her. She waited its slow progress in a torment of delight. She waited, she knew not for what, panting, with dry, burning lips, a leaping pulse, and a fever of expectancy in all her blood. The girdling arm lifted higher and drew her toward him, drew her slowly and caressingly. She could wait no longer. With a tired sigh, and with an impulsive movement all her own, unpremeditated, spasmodic, she rested her head upon his breast. His head bent over swiftly, and, as his lips approached, hers flew to meet them.

This must be love, she thought, in the one rational moment that was vouchsafed her. If it was not love, it was too shameful. It could be nothing else than love. She loved the man whose arms were around her and whose lips were pressed to hers. She pressed more, tightly to him, with a snuggling movement of her body. And a moment later, tearing herself half out of his embrace, suddenly and exultantly she reached up and placed both hands upon Martin Eden's sunburnt neck. So exquisite was the pang of love and desire fulfilled that she uttered a low moan, relaxed her hands, and lay half-swooning in his arms.

Not a word had been spoken, and not a word was spoken for a long time. Twice he bent and kissed her, and each time her lips met his shyly and her body made its happy, nestling movement. She clung to him, unable to release herself, and he sat, half supporting her in his arms, as he gazed with unseeing eyes at the blur of the great city across the bay. For once there were no visions in his brain. Only colors and lights and glows pulsed there, warm as the day and warm as his love. He bent over her. She was speaking.

"When did you love me?" she whispered.

"From the first, the very first, the first moment I laid eye on you. I was mad for love of you then, and in all the time that has passed since then I have only grown the madder. I am maddest, now, dear. I am almost a lunatic, my head is so turned with joy."

"I am glad I am a woman, Martin—dear," she said, after a long sigh.

He crushed her in his arms again and again, and then asked:-

"And you? When did you first know?"

"Oh, I knew it all the time, almost, from the first."

"And I have been as blind as a bat!" he cried, a ring of vexation in his voice. "I never dreamed it until just how, when I—when I kissed you."

"I didn't mean that." She drew herself partly away and looked at him. "I meant I knew you loved almost from the first."

"And you?" he demanded.

"It came to me suddenly." She was speaking very slowly, her eyes warm and fluttery and melting, a soft flush on her cheeks that did not go away. "I never knew until just now when—you put your arms around me. And I never expected to marry you, Martin, not until just now. How did you make me love you?"

"I don't know," he laughed, "unless just by loving you, for I loved you hard enough to melt the heart of a stone, much less the heart of the living, breathing woman you are."

"This is so different from what I thought love would be," she announced irrelevantly.

"What did you think it would be like?"

"I didn't think it would be like this." She was looking into his eyes at the moment, but her own dropped as she continued, "You see, I didn't know what this was like."

He offered to draw her toward him again, but it was no more than a tentative muscular movement of the girdling arm, for he feared that he might be greedy. Then he felt her body yielding, and once again she was close in his arms and lips were pressed on lips.

"What will my people say?" she queried, with sudden apprehension, in one of the pauses.

"I don't know. We can find out very easily any time we are so minded."

"But if mamma objects? I am sure I am afraid to tell her."

"Let me tell her," he volunteered valiantly. "I think your mother does not like me, but I can win her around. A fellow who can win you can win anything. And if we don't—"

"Yes?"

"Why, we'll have each other. But there's no danger not winning your mother to our marriage. She loves you too well."

"I should not like to break her heart," Ruth said pensively.

He felt like assuring her that mothers' hearts were not so easily broken, but instead he said, "And love is the greatest thing in the world."

"Do you know, Martin, you sometimes frighten me. I am frightened now, when I think of you and of what you have been. You must be very, very good to me. Remember, after all, that I am only a child. I never loved before."

"Nor I. We are both children together. And we are fortunate above most, for we have found our first love in each other."

"But that is impossible!" she cried, withdrawing herself from his arms with a swift, passionate movement. "Impossible for you. You have been a sailor, and sailors, I have heard, are—are—"

Her voice faltered and died away.

"Are addicted to having a wife in every port?" he suggested. "Is that what you mean?"

"Yes," she answered in a low voice.

"But that is not love." He spoke authoritatively. "I have been in many ports, but I never knew a passing touch of love until I saw you that first night. Do you know, when I said good night and went away, I was almost arrested."

"Arrested?"

"Yes. The policeman thought I was drunk; and I was, too—with love for you."

"But you said we were children, and I said it was impossible, for you, and we have strayed away from the point."

"I said that I never loved anybody but you," he replied. "You are my first, my very first."

"And yet you have been a sailor," she objected.

"But that doesn't prevent me from loving you the first."

"And there have been women—other women—oh!"

And to Martin Eden's supreme surprise, she burst into a storm of tears that took more kisses than one and many caresses to drive away. And all the while there was running through his head Kipling's line: *"And the Colonel's lady and Judy O'Grady are sisters under their skins."* It was true, he decided; though the novels he had read had led him to believe otherwise. His idea, for which the novels were responsible, had been that only formal proposals obtained in the upper classes. It was all right enough, down whence he had come, for youths and maidens to win each other by contact; but for the exalted personages up above on the heights to make love in similar fashion had seemed unthinkable. Yet the novels were wrong. Here was a proof of it. The same pressures and caresses, unaccompanied by speech, that were efficacious with the girls of the working-class, were equally efficacious with the girls above the working-class. They were all of the same flesh, after all, sisters under their skins; and he might have known as much himself had he remembered his Spencer. As he held Ruth in his arms and soothed her, he took great consolation in the thought that the Colonel's lady and Judy O'Grady were pretty much alike under their skins. It brought Ruth closer to him, made her possible. Her dear flesh was as anybody's flesh, as his flesh. There was no bar to their marriage. Class difference was the only difference, and class was extrinsic. It could be shaken off. A slave, he had read, had risen to the Roman purple. That being so, then he could rise to Ruth. Under her purity, and saintliness, and culture, and ethereal beauty of soul, she was, in things fundamentally human, just like Lizzie Connolly and all Lizzie Connollys. All that was possible of them was possible of her. She could love, and hate, maybe have hysterics; and she could certainly be jealous, as she was jealous now, uttering her last sobs in his arms.

"Besides, I am older than you," she remarked suddenly, opening her eyes and looking up at him, "three years older."

"Hush, you are only a child, and I am forty years older than you, in experience," was his answer.

In truth, they were children together, so far as love was concerned, and they were as naive and immature in the expression of their love as a pair of children, and this despite the fact that she was crammed with a university education and that his head was full of scientific philosophy and the hard facts of life.

They sat on through the passing glory of the day, talking as lovers are prone to talk, marvelling at the wonder of love and at destiny that had flung them so strangely together, and dogmatically believing that they loved to a degree never attained by lovers before. And they returned insistently, again and again, to a rehearsal of their first impressions of each other and to hopeless attempts to analyze just precisely what they felt for each other and how much there was of it.

The cloud-masses on the western horizon received the descending sun, and the circle of the sky turned to rose, while the zenith glowed with the same warm color. The rosy light was all about them, flooding over them, as she sang, "Good-by, Sweet Day." She sang softly, leaning in the cradle of his arm, her hands in his, their hearts in each other's hands.

CHAPTER XXII

Mrs. Morse did not require a mother's intuition to read the advertisement in Ruth's face when she returned home. The flush that would not leave the cheeks told the simple story, and more eloquently did the eyes, large and bright, reflecting an unmistakable inward glory.

"What has happened?" Mrs. Morse asked, having bided her time till Ruth had gone to bed.

"You know?" Ruth queried, with trembling lips.

For reply, her mother's arm went around her, and a hand was softly caressing her hair.

"He did not speak," she blurted out. "I did not intend that it should happen, and I would never have let him speak—only he didn't speak."

"But if he did not speak, then nothing could have happened, could it?"

"But it did, just the same."

"In the name of goodness, child, what are you babbling about?" Mrs. Morse was bewildered. "I don't think I know what happened, after all. What did happen?"

Ruth looked at her mother in surprise.

"I thought you knew. Why, we're engaged, Martin and I."

Mrs. Morse laughed with incredulous vexation.

"No, he didn't speak," Ruth explained. "He just loved me, that was all. I was as surprised as you are. He didn't say a word. He just put his arm around me. And—and I was not myself. And he kissed me, and I kissed him. I couldn't help it. I just had to. And then I knew I loved him."

She paused, waiting with expectancy the benediction of her mother's kiss, but Mrs. Morse was coldly silent.

"It is a dreadful accident, I know," Ruth recommenced with a sinking voice. "And I don't know how you will ever forgive me. But I couldn't help it. I did not dream that I loved him until that moment. And you must tell father for me."

"Would it not be better not to tell your father? Let me see Martin Eden, and talk with him, and explain. He will understand and release you."

"No! no!" Ruth cried, starting up. "I do not want to be released. I love him, and love is very sweet. I am going to marry him—of course, if you will let me."

"We have other plans for you, Ruth, dear, your father and I—oh, no, no; no man picked out for you, or anything like that. Our plans go no farther than your marrying some man in your own station in life, a good and honorable gentleman, whom you will select yourself, when you love him."

"But I love Martin already," was the plaintive protest.

"We would not influence your choice in any way; but you are our daughter, and we could not bear to see you make a marriage such as this. He has nothing but roughness and coarseness to offer you in exchange for all that is refined and delicate in you. He is no match for you in any way. He could not support you. We have no foolish ideas about wealth, but comfort is another matter, and our daughter should at least marry a man who can give her that—and not a penniless adventurer, a sailor, a cowboy, a smuggler, and Heaven knows what else, who, in addition to everything, is hare-brained and irresponsible."

Ruth was silent. Every word she recognized as true.

"He wastes his time over his writing, trying to accomplish what geniuses and rare men with college educations sometimes accomplish. A man thinking of marriage should be preparing for marriage. But not he. As I have said, and I know you agree with me, he is irresponsible. And why should he not be? It is the way of sailors. He has never learned to be economical or temperate. The spendthrift years have marked him. It is not his fault, of course, but that does not alter his nature. And have you thought of the years of licentiousness he inevitably has lived? Have you thought of that, daughter? You know what marriage means."

Ruth shuddered and clung close to her mother.

"I have thought." Ruth waited a long time for the thought to frame itself. "And it is terrible. It sickens me to think of it. I told you it was a dreadful accident, my loving him; but I can't help myself. Could you help loving father? Then it is the same with me. There is something in me, in him—I never knew it was there until to-day—but it is there, and it makes me love him. I never thought to love him, but, you see, I do," she concluded, a certain faint triumph in her voice.

They talked long, and to little purpose, in conclusion agreeing to wait an indeterminate time without doing anything.

The same conclusion was reached, a little later that night, between Mrs. Morse and her husband, after she had made due confession of the miscarriage of her plans.

"It could hardly have come otherwise," was Mr. Morse's judgment. "This sailor-fellow has been the only man she was in touch with. Sooner or later she was going to awaken anyway; and she did awaken, and lo! here was this sailor-fellow, the only accessible man at the moment, and of course she promptly loved him, or thought she did, which amounts to the same thing."

Mrs. Morse took it upon herself to work slowly and indirectly upon Ruth, rather than to combat her. There would be plenty of time for this, for Martin was not in position to marry.

"Let her see all she wants of him," was Mr. Morse's advice. "The more she knows him, the less she'll love him, I wager. And give her plenty of contrast. Make a point of having young people at the house. Young women and young men, all sorts of young men, clever men, men who have done something or who are doing things, men of her own class, gentlemen. She can gauge him by them. They will show him up for what he is. And after all, he is a mere boy of twenty-one. Ruth is no more than a child. It is calf love with the pair of them, and they will grow out of it."

So the matter rested. Within the family it was accepted that Ruth and Martin were engaged, but no announcement was made. The family did not think it would ever be necessary. Also, it was tacitly understood that it was to be a long engagement. They did not ask Martin to go to work, nor to cease writing. They did not intend to encourage him to mend himself. And he aided and abetted them in their unfriendly designs, for going to work was farthest from his thoughts.

"I wonder if you'll like what I have done!" he said to Ruth several days later. "I've decided that boarding with my sister is too expensive, and I am going to board myself. I've rented a little room out in North Oakland, retired neighborhood and all the rest, you know, and I've bought an oil-burner on which to cook."

Ruth was overjoyed. The oil-burner especially pleased her.

"That was the way Mr. Butler began his start," she said.

Martin frowned inwardly at the citation of that worthy gentleman, and went on: "I put stamps on all my manuscripts and started them off to the editors again. Then to-day I moved in, and to-morrow I start to work."

"A position!" she cried, betraying the gladness of her surprise in all her body, nestling closer to him, pressing his hand, smiling. "And you never told me! What is it?"

He shook his head.

"I meant that I was going to work at my writing." Her face fell, and he went on hastily. "Don't misjudge me. I am not going in this time with any iridescent ideas. It is to be a cold, prosaic, matter-of-fact business proposition. It is better than going to sea again, and I shall earn more money than any position in Oakland can bring an unskilled man."

"You see, this vacation I have taken has given me perspective. I haven't been working the life out of my body, and I haven't been writing, at least not for publication. All I've done has been to love you and to think. I've read some, too, but it has been part of my thinking, and I have read principally magazines. I have generalized about myself, and the world, my place in it, and my chance to win to a place that will be fit for you. Also, I've been reading Spencer's 'Philosophy of Style,' and found out a lot of what was the matter with me—or my writing, rather; and for that matter with most of the writing that is published every month in the magazines."

"But the upshot of it all—of my thinking and reading and loving—is that I am going to move to Grub Street. I shall leave masterpieces alone and do hack-work—jokes, paragraphs, feature articles, humorous verse, and society verse—all the rot for which there seems so much demand. Then there are the newspaper syndicates, and the newspaper short-story syndicates, and the syndicates for the Sunday supplements. I can go ahead and hammer out the stuff they want, and earn the equivalent of a good salary by it. There are free-lances, you know, who earn as much as four or five hundred a month. I don't care to become as they; but I'll earn a good living, and have plenty of time to myself, which I wouldn't have in any position."

"Then, I'll have my spare time for study and for real work. In between the grind I'll try my hand at masterpieces, and I'll study and prepare myself for the writing of masterpieces. Why, I am amazed at the distance I have come already. When I first tried to write, I had nothing to write about except a few paltry experiences which I neither understood nor appreciated. But I had no thoughts. I really didn't. I didn't even have the words with which to think. My experiences were so many meaningless pictures. But as I began to add to my knowledge, and to my vocabulary, I saw something more in my experiences than mere pictures. I retained the pictures and I found their interpretation. That was when I began to do good work, when I wrote 'Adventure,' 'Joy,' 'The Pot,' 'The Wine of Life,' 'The Jostling Street,' the 'Love-cycle,' and the 'Sea Lyrics.' I shall write more like them, and better; but I shall do it in my spare time. My feet are on the solid earth, now. Hack-work and income first, masterpieces afterward. Just to show you, I wrote half a dozen jokes last night for the comic weeklies; and just as I was going to bed, the thought struck me to try my hand at a triolet—a humorous one; and inside an hour I had written four. They ought to be worth a dollar apiece. Four dollars right there for a few afterthoughts on the way to bed."

"Of course it's all valueless, just so much dull and sordid plodding; but it is no more dull and sordid than keeping books at sixty dollars a month, adding up endless columns of meaningless figures until one dies. And furthermore, the hack-work keeps me in touch with things literary and gives me time to try bigger things."

"But what good are these bigger-things, these masterpieces?" Ruth demanded. "You can't sell them."

"Oh, yes, I can," he began; but she interrupted.

"All those you named, and which you say yourself are good—you have not sold any of them. We can't get married on masterpieces that won't sell."

"Then we'll get married on triolets that will sell," he asserted stoutly, putting his arm around her and drawing a very unresponsive sweetheart toward him.

"Listen to this," he went on in attempted gayety. "It's not art, but it's a dollar.

"He came in
When I was out,
To borrow some tin
Was why he came in,
And he went without;
So I was in
And he was out."

The merry lilt with which he had invested the jingle was at variance with the dejection that came into his face as he finished. He had drawn no smile from Ruth. She was looking at him in an earnest and troubled way.

"It may be a dollar," she said, "but it is a jester's dollar, the fee of a clown. Don't you see, Martin, the whole thing is lowering. I want the man I love and honor to be something finer and higher than a perpetrator of jokes and doggerel."

"You want him to be like—say Mr. Butler?" he suggested.

"I know you don't like Mr. Butler," she began.

"Mr. Butler's all right," he interrupted. "It's only his indigestion I find fault with. But to save me I can't see any difference between writing jokes or comic verse and running a typewriter, taking dictation, or keeping sets of books. It is all a means to an end. Your theory is for me to begin with keeping books in order to become a successful lawyer or man of business. Mine is to begin with hack-work and develop into an able author."

"There is a difference," she insisted.

"What is it?"

"Why, your good work, what you yourself call good, you can't sell. You have tried, you know that,—but the editors won't buy it."

"Give me time, dear," he pleaded. "The hack-work is only makeshift, and I don't take it seriously. Give me two years. I shall succeed in that time, and the editors will be glad to buy my good work. I know what I am saying; I have faith in myself. I know what I have in me; I know what literature is, now; I know the average rot that is poured out by a lot of little men; and I know that at the end of two years I shall be on the highroad to success. As for business, I shall never succeed at it. I am not in sympathy with it. It strikes me as dull, and stupid, and mercenary, and tricky. Anyway I am not adapted for it. I'd never get beyond a clerkship, and how could you and I be happy on the paltry earnings of a clerk? I want the best of everything in the world for you, and the only time when I won't want it will be when there is something better. And I'm going to get it, going to get all of it. The income of a successful author makes Mr. Butler look cheap. A 'best-seller' will earn anywhere between fifty and a hundred thousand dollars—sometimes more and sometimes less; but, as a rule, pretty close to those figures."

She remained silent; her disappointment was apparent.

"Well?" he asked.

"I had hoped and planned otherwise. I had thought, and I still think, that the best thing for you would be to study shorthand—you already know type-writing—and go into father's office. You have a good mind, and I am confident you would succeed as a lawyer."

CHAPTER XXIII

That Ruth had little faith in his power as a writer, did not alter her nor diminish her in Martin's eyes. In the breathing spell of the vacation he had taken, he had spent many hours in self-analysis, and thereby learned much of himself. He had discovered that he loved beauty more than fame, and that what desire he had for fame was largely for Ruth's sake. It was for this reason that his desire for fame was strong. He wanted to be great in the world's eyes; "to make good," as he expressed it, in order that the woman he loved should be proud of him and deem him worthy.

As for himself, he loved beauty passionately, and the joy of serving her was to him sufficient wage. And more than beauty he loved Ruth. He considered love the finest thing in the world. It was love that had worked the revolution in him, changing him from an uncouth sailor to a student and an artist; therefore, to him, the finest and greatest of the three, greater than learning and artistry, was love. Already he had discovered that his brain went beyond Ruth's, just as it went beyond the brains of her brothers, or the brain of her father. In spite of every advantage of university training, and in the face of her bachelorship of arts, his power of intellect overshadowed hers, and his year or so of self-study and equipment gave him a mastery of the affairs of the world and art and life that she could never hope to possess.

All this he realized, but it did not affect his love for her, nor her love for him. Love was too fine and noble, and he was too loyal a lover for him to besmirch love with criticism. What did love have to do with Ruth's divergent views on art, right conduct, the French Revolution, or equal suffrage? They were mental processes, but love was beyond reason; it was supernatural. He could not belittle love. He worshipped it. Love lay on the mountain-tops beyond the valley-land of reason. It was a sublimates condition of existence, the topmost peak of living, and it came rarely. Thanks to the school of scientific philosophers he favored, he knew the biological significance of love; but by a refined process of the same scientific reasoning he reached the conclusion that the human organism achieved its highest purpose in love, that love must not be questioned, but must be accepted as the highest guerdon of life. Thus, he considered the lover blessed over all creatures, and it was a delight to him to think of "God's own mad lover," rising above the things of earth, above wealth and judgment, public opinion and applause, rising above life itself and "dying on a kiss."

Much of this Martin had already reasoned out, and some of it he reasoned out later. In the meantime he worked, taking no recreation except when he went to see Ruth, and living like a Spartan. He paid two dollars and a half a month rent for the small room he got from his Portuguese landlady, Maria Silva, a virago and a widow, hard working and harsher tempered, rearing her large brood of children somehow, and drowning her sorrow and fatigue at irregular intervals in a gallon of the thin, sour wine that she bought from the corner grocery and saloon for fifteen cents. From detesting her and her foul tongue at first, Martin grew to admire her as he observed the brave fight she made. There were but four rooms in the little house—three, when Martin's was subtracted. One of these, the parlor, gay with an ingrain carpet and dolorous with a funeral card and a death-picture of one of her numerous departed babes, was kept strictly for company. The blinds were always down, and her barefooted tribe was never permitted to enter the sacred precinct save on state occasions. She cooked, and all ate, in the kitchen, where she likewise washed, starched, and ironed clothes on all days of the week except Sunday; for her income came largely from taking in washing from her more prosperous neighbors. Remained the bedroom, small as the one occupied by Martin, into which she and her seven little ones crowded and slept. It was an everlasting miracle to Martin how it was accomplished, and from her side of the thin partition he heard nightly every detail of the going to bed, the squalls and squabbles, the soft chattering, and the sleepy, twittering noises as of birds. Another source of income to Maria were her cows, two of them, which she milked night and morning and which gained a surreptitious livelihood from vacant lots and the grass that grew on either side the public side walks, attended always by one or more of her ragged boys, whose watchful guardianship consisted chiefly in keeping their eyes out for the poundmen.

In his own small room Martin lived, slept, studied, wrote, and kept house. Before the one window, looking out on the tiny front porch, was the kitchen table that served as desk, library, and type-writing stand. The bed, against the rear wall, occupied two-thirds of the total space of the room. The table was flanked on one side by a gaudy bureau, manufactured for profit and not for service, the thin veneer of which was shed day by day. This bureau stood in the corner, and in the opposite corner, on the table's other flank, was the kitchen—the oil-stove on a dry-goods box, inside of which were dishes and cooking utensils, a shelf on the wall for provisions, and a bucket of water on the floor. Martin had to carry his water from the kitchen sink, there being no tap in his room. On days when there was much steam to his cooking, the harvest of veneer from the bureau was unusually generous. Over the bed, hoisted by a tackle to the ceiling, was his bicycle. At first he had tried to keep it in the basement; but the tribe of Silva, loosening the bearings and puncturing the tires, had driven him out. Next he attempted the tiny front porch, until a howling southeaster drenched the wheel a night-long. Then he had retreated with it to his room and slung it aloft.

A small closet contained his clothes and the books he had accumulated and for which there was no room on the table or under the table. Hand in hand with reading, he had developed the habit of making notes, and so copiously did he make them that there would have been no existence for him in the confined quarters had he not rigged several clothes-lines across the room on which the notes were hung. Even so, he was crowded until navigating the room was a difficult task. He could not open the door without first closing the closet door, and *vice versa*. It was impossible for him anywhere to traverse the room in a straight line. To go from the door to the head of the bed was a zigzag course that he was never quite able to accomplish in the dark without collisions. Having settled the difficulty of the conflicting doors, he had to steer sharply to the right to avoid the kitchen. Next, he sheered to the left, to escape the foot of the bed; but this sheer, if too generous, brought him against the corner of the table. With a sudden twitch and lurch, he terminated the sheer and bore off to the right along a sort of canal, one bank of which was the bed, the other the table. When the one chair in the room was at its usual place before the table, the canal was unnavigable. When the chair was not in use, it reposed on top of the bed, though sometimes he sat on the chair when cooking, reading a book while the water boiled, and even becoming skilful enough to manage a paragraph or two while steak was frying. Also, so small was the little corner that constituted the kitchen, he was able, sitting down, to reach anything he needed. In fact, it was expedient to cook sitting down; standing up, he was too often in his own way.

In conjunction with a perfect stomach that could digest anything, he possessed knowledge of the various foods that were at the same time nutritious and cheap. Pea-soup was a common article in his diet, as well as potatoes and beans, the latter large and brown and cooked in Mexican style. Rice, cooked as American housewives never cook it and can never learn to cook it, appeared on Martin's table at least once a day. Dried fruits were less expensive than fresh, and he had usually a pot of them, cooked and ready at hand, for they took the place of butter on his bread. Occasionally he graced his table with a piece of round-steak, or with a soup-bone. Coffee, without cream or milk, he had twice a day, in the evening substituting tea; but both coffee and tea were excellently cooked.

There was need for him to be economical. His vacation had consumed nearly all he had earned in the laundry, and he was so far from his market that weeks must elapse before he could hope for the first returns from his hack-work. Except at such times as he saw Ruth, or dropped in to see his sister Gertude, he lived a recluse, in each day accomplishing at least three days' labor of ordinary men. He slept a scant five hours, and only one with a constitution of iron could have held himself down, as Martin did, day after day, to nineteen consecutive hours of toil. He never lost a moment. On the looking-glass were lists of definitions and pronunciations; when shaving, or dressing, or combing his hair, he conned these lists over. Similar lists were on the wall over the oil-stove, and they were similarly conned while he was engaged in cooking or in washing the dishes. New lists continually displaced the old ones. Every strange or partly familiar word encountered in his reading was immediately jotted down, and later, when a sufficient number had been accumulated, were typed and pinned to the wall or looking-glass. He even carried them in his pockets, and reviewed them at odd moments on the street, or while waiting in butcher shop or grocery to be served.

He went farther in the matter. Reading the works of men who had arrived, he noted every result achieved by them, and worked out the tricks by which they had been achieved—the tricks of narrative, of exposition, of style, the points of view, the contrasts, the epigrams; and of all these he made lists for study. He did not ape. He sought principles. He drew up lists of effective and fetching mannerisms, till out of many such, culled from many writers, he was able to induce the general principle of mannerism, and, thus equipped, to cast about for new and original ones of his own, and to weigh and measure and appraise them properly. In similar manner he collected lists of strong phrases, the phrases of living language, phrases that bit like acid and scorched like flame, or that glowed and were mellow and luscious in the midst of the arid desert of common speech. He sought always for the principle that lay behind and beneath. He wanted to know how the thing was done; after that he could do it for himself. He was not content with the fair face of beauty. He dissected beauty in his crowded little bedroom laboratory, where cooking smells alternated with the outer bedlam of the Silva tribe; and, having dissected and learned the anatomy of beauty, he was nearer being able to create beauty itself.

He was so made that he could work only with understanding. He could not work blindly, in the dark, ignorant of what he was producing and trusting to chance and the star of his genius that the effect produced should be right and fine. He had no patience with chance effects. He wanted to know why and how. His was deliberate creative genius, and, before he began a story or poem, the thing itself was already alive in his brain, with the end in sight and the means of realizing that end in his conscious possession. Otherwise the effort was doomed to failure. On the other hand, he appreciated the chance effects in words and phrases that came lightly and easily into his brain, and that later stood all tests of beauty and power and developed tremendous and incommunicable connotations. Before such he bowed down and marvelled, knowing that they were beyond the deliberate creation of any man. And no matter how much he dissected beauty in search of the principles that underlie beauty and make beauty possible, he was aware, always, of the innermost mystery of beauty to which he did not penetrate and to which no man had ever penetrated. He knew full well, from his Spencer, that man can never attain ultimate knowledge of anything, and that the mystery of beauty was no less than that of life—nay, more that the fibres of beauty and life were intertwisted, and that he himself was but a bit of the same nonunderstandable fabric, twisted of sunshine and star-dust and wonder.

In fact, it was when filled with these thoughts that he wrote his essay entitled "Star-dust," in which he had his fling, not at the principles of criticism, but at the principal critics. It was brilliant, deep, philosophical, and deliciously touched with laughter. Also it was promptly rejected by the magazines as often as it was submitted. But having cleared his mind of it, he went serenely on his way. It was a habit he developed, of incubating and maturing his thought upon a subject, and of then rushing into the type-writer with it. That it did not see print was a matter a small moment with him. The writing of it was the culminating act of a long mental process, the drawing together of scattered threads of thought and the final generalizing upon all the data with which his mind was burdened. To write such an article was the conscious effort by which he freed his mind and made it ready for fresh material and problems. It was in a way akin to that common habit of men and women troubled by real or fancied grievances, who periodically and volubly break their long-suffering silence and "have their say" till the last word is said.

CHAPTER XXIV

The weeks passed. Martin ran out of money, and publishers' checks were far away as ever. All his important manuscripts had come back and been started out again, and his hack-work fared no better. His little kitchen was no longer graced with a variety of foods. Caught in the pinch with a part sack of rice and a few pounds of dried apricots, rice and apricots was his menu three times a day for five days hand-running. Then he startled to realize on his credit. The Portuguese grocer, to whom he had hitherto paid cash, called a halt when Martin's bill reached the magnificent total of three dollars and eighty-five cents.

"For you see," said the grocer, "you no catcha da work, I losa da mon'."

And Martin could reply nothing. There was no way of explaining. It was not true business principle to allow credit to a strong-bodied young fellow of the working-class who was too lazy to work.

"You catcha da job, I let you have mora da grub," the grocer assured Martin. "No job, no grub. Thata da business." And then, to show that it was purely business foresight and not prejudice, "Hava da drink on da house—good friends justa da same."

So Martin drank, in his easy way, to show that he was good friends with the house, and then went supperless to bed.

The fruit store, where Martin had bought his vegetables, was run by an American whose business principles were so weak that he let Martin run a bill of five dollars before stopping his credit. The baker stopped at two dollars, and the butcher at four dollars. Martin added his debts and found that he was possessed of a total credit in all the world of fourteen dollars and eighty-five cents. He was up with his type-writer rent, but he estimated that he could get two months' credit on that, which would be eight dollars. When that occurred, he would have exhausted all possible credit.

The last purchase from the fruit store had been a sack of potatoes, and for a week he had potatoes, and nothing but potatoes, three times a day. An occasional dinner at Ruth's helped to keep strength in his body, though he found it tantalizing enough to refuse further helping when his appetite was raging at sight of so much food spread before it. Now and again, though afflicted with secret shame, he dropped in at his sister's at meal-time and ate as much as he dared—more than he dared at the Morse table.

Day by day he worked on, and day by day the postman delivered to him rejected manuscripts. He had no money for stamps, so the manuscripts accumulated in a heap under the table. Came a day when for forty hours he had not tasted food. He could not hope for a meal at Ruth's, for she was away to San Rafael on a two weeks' visit; and for very shame's sake he could not go to his sister's. To cap misfortune, the postman, in his afternoon round, brought him five returned manuscripts. Then it was that Martin wore his overcoat down into Oakland, and came back without it, but with five dollars tinkling in his pocket. He paid a dollar each on account to the four tradesmen, and in his kitchen fried steak and onions, made coffee, and stewed a large pot of prunes. And having dined, he sat down at his table-desk and completed before midnight an essay which he entitled "The Dignity of Usury." Having typed it out, he flung it under the table, for there had been nothing left from the five dollars with which to buy stamps.

Later on he pawned his watch, and still later his wheel, reducing the amount available for food by putting stamps on all his manuscripts and sending them out. He was disappointed with his hack-work. Nobody cared to buy. He compared it with what he found in the newspapers, weeklies, and cheap magazines, and decided that his was better, far better, than the average; yet it would not sell. Then he discovered that most of the newspapers printed a great deal of what was called "plate" stuff, and he got the address of the association that furnished it. His own work that he sent in was returned, along with a stereotyped slip informing him that the staff supplied all the copy that was needed.

In one of the great juvenile periodicals he noted whole columns of incident and anecdote. Here was a chance. His paragraphs were returned, and though he tried repeatedly he never succeeded in placing one. Later on, when it no longer mattered, he learned that the associate editors and sub-editors augmented their salaries by supplying those paragraphs themselves. The comic weeklies returned his jokes and humorous verse, and the light society verse he wrote for the large magazines found no abiding-place. Then there was the newspaper storiette. He knew that he could write better ones than were published. Managing to obtain the addresses of two newspaper syndicates, he deluged them with storiettes. When he had written twenty and failed to place one of them, he ceased. And yet, from day to day, he read storiettes in the dailies and weeklies, scores and scores of storiettes, not one of which would compare with his. In his despondency, he concluded that he had no judgment whatever, that he was hypnotized by what he wrote, and that he was a self-deluded pretender.

The inhuman editorial machine ran smoothly as ever. He folded the stamps in with his manuscript, dropped it into the letter-box, and from three weeks to a month afterward the postman came up the steps and handed him the manuscript. Surely there were no live, warm editors at the other end. It was all wheels and cogs and oil-cups—a clever mechanism operated by automatons. He reached stages of despair wherein he doubted if editors existed at all. He had never received a sign of the existence of one, and from absence of judgment in rejecting all he wrote it seemed plausible that editors were myths, manufactured and maintained by office boys, typesetters, and pressmen.

The hours he spent with Ruth were the only happy ones he had, and they were not all happy. He was afflicted always with a gnawing restlessness, more tantalizing than in the old days before he possessed her love; for now that he did possess her love, the possession of her was far away as ever. He had asked for two years; time was flying, and he was achieving nothing. Again, he was always conscious of the fact that she did not approve what he was doing. She did not say so directly. Yet indirectly she let him understand it as clearly and definitely as she could have spoken it. It was not resentment with her, but disapproval; though less sweet-natured women might have resented where she was no more than disappointed. Her disappointment lay in that this man she had taken to mould, refused to be moulded. To a certain extent she had found his clay plastic, then it had developed stubbornness, declining to be shaped in the image of her father or of Mr. Butler.

What was great and strong in him, she missed, or, worse yet, misunderstood. This man, whose clay was so plastic that he could live in any number of pigeonholes of human existence, she thought wilful and most obstinate because she could not shape him to live in her pigeonhole, which was the only one she knew. She could not follow the flights of his mind, and when his brain got beyond her, she deemed him erratic. Nobody else's brain ever got beyond her. She could always follow her father and mother, her brothers and Olney; wherefore, when she could not follow Martin, she believed the fault lay with him. It was the old tragedy of insularity trying to serve as mentor to the universal.

"You worship at the shrine of the established," he told her once, in a discussion they had over Praps and Vanderwater. "I grant that as authorities to quote they are most excellent—the two foremost literary critics in the United States. Every school teacher in the land looks up to Vanderwater as the Dean of American criticism. Yet I read his stuff, and it seems to me the perfection of the felicitous expression of the inane. Why, he is no more than a ponderous bromide, thanks to Gelett Burgess. And Praps is no better. His 'Hemlock Mosses,' for instance is beautifully written. Not a comma is out of place; and the tone—ah!—is lofty, so lofty. He is the best-paid critic in the United States. Though, Heaven forbid! he's not a critic at all. They do criticism better in England.

"But the point is, they sound the popular note, and they sound it so beautifully and morally and contentedly. Their reviews remind me of a British Sunday. They are the popular mouthpieces. They back up your professors of English, and your professors of English back them up. And there isn't an original idea in any of their skulls. They know only the established,—in fact, they are the established. They are weak minded, and the established impresses itself upon them as easily as the name of the brewery is impressed on a beer bottle. And their function is to catch all the young fellows attending the university, to drive out of their minds any glimmering originality that may chance to be there, and to put upon them the stamp of the established."

"I think I am nearer the truth," she replied, "when I stand by the established, than you are, raging around like an iconoclastic South Sea Islander."

"It was the missionary who did the image breaking," he laughed. "And unfortunately, all the missionaries are off among the heathen, so there are none left at home to break those old images, Mr. Vanderwater and Mr. Praps."

"And the college professors, as well," she added.

He shook his head emphatically. "No; the science professors should live. They're really great. But it would be a good deed to break the heads of nine-tenths of the English professors—little, microscopic-minded parrots!"

Which was rather severe on the professors, but which to Ruth was blasphemy. She could not help but measure the professors, neat, scholarly, in fitting clothes, speaking in well-modulated voices, breathing of culture and refinement, with this almost indescribable young fellow whom somehow she loved, whose clothes never would fit him, whose heavy muscles told of damning toil, who grew excited when he talked, substituting abuse for calm statement and passionate utterance for cool self-possession. They at least earned good salaries and were—yes, she compelled herself to face it—were gentlemen; while he could not earn a penny, and he was not as they.

She did not weigh Martin's words nor judge his argument by them. Her conclusion that his argument was wrong was reached—unconsciously, it is true—by a comparison of externals. They, the professors, were right in their literary judgments because they were successes. Martin's literary judgments were wrong because he could not sell his wares. To use his own phrase, they made good, and he did not make good. And besides, it did not seem reasonable that he should be right—he who had stood, so short a time before, in that same living room, blushing and awkward, acknowledging his introduction, looking fearfully about him at the bric-a-brac his swinging shoulders threatened to break, asking how long since Swinburne died, and boastfully announcing that he had read "Excelsior" and the "Psalm of Life."

Unwittingly, Ruth herself proved his point that she worshipped the established. Martin followed the processes of her thoughts, but forbore to go farther. He did not love her for what she thought of Praps and Vanderwater and English professors, and he was coming to realize, with increasing conviction, that he possessed brain-areas and stretches of knowledge which she could never comprehend nor know existed.

In music she thought him unreasonable, and in the matter of opera not only unreasonable but wilfully perverse.

"How did you like it?" she asked him one night, on the way home from the opera.

It was a night when he had taken her at the expense of a month's rigid economizing on food. After vainly waiting for him to speak about it, herself still tremulous and stirred by what she had just seen and heard, she had asked the question.

"I liked the overture," was his answer. "It was splendid."

"Yes, but the opera itself?"

"That was splendid too; that is, the orchestra was, though I'd have enjoyed it more if those jumping-jacks had kept quiet or gone off the stage."

Ruth was aghast.

"You don't mean Tetralani or Barillo?" she queried.

"All of them—the whole kit and crew."

"But they are great artists," she protested.

"They spoiled the music just the same, with their antics and unrealities."

"But don't you like Barillo's voice?" Ruth asked. "He is next to Caruso, they say."

"Of course I liked him, and I liked Tetralani even better. Her voice is exquisite—or at least I think so."

"But, but—" Ruth stammered. "I don't know what you mean, then. You admire their voices, yet say they spoiled the music."

"Precisely that. I'd give anything to hear them in concert, and I'd give even a bit more not to hear them when the orchestra is playing. I'm afraid I am a hopeless realist. Great singers are not great actors. To hear Barillo sing a love passage with the voice of an angel, and to hear Tetralani reply like another angel, and to hear it all accompanied by a perfect orgy of glowing and colorful music—is ravishing, most ravishing. I do not admit it. I assert it. But the whole effect is spoiled when I look at them—at Tetralani, five feet ten in her stocking feet and weighing a hundred and ninety pounds, and at Barillo, a scant five feet four, greasy-featured, with the chest of a squat, undersized blacksmith, and at the pair of them, attitudinizing, clasping their breasts, flinging their arms in the air like demented creatures in an asylum; and when I am expected to accept all this as the faithful illusion of a love-scene between a slender and beautiful princess and a handsome, romantic, young prince—why, I can't accept it, that's all. It's rot; it's absurd; it's unreal. That's what's the matter with it. It's not real. Don't tell me that anybody in this world ever made love that way. Why, if I'd made love to you in such fashion, you'd have boxed my ears."

"But you misunderstand," Ruth protested. "Every form of art has its limitations." (She was busy recalling a lecture she had heard at the university on the conventions of the arts.) "In painting there are only two dimensions to the canvas, yet you accept the illusion of three dimensions which the art of a painter enables him to throw into the canvas. In writing, again, the author must be omnipotent. You accept as perfectly legitimate the author's account of the secret thoughts of the heroine, and yet all the time you know that the heroine was alone when thinking these thoughts, and that neither the author nor any one else was capable of hearing them. And so with the stage, with sculpture, with opera, with every art form. Certain irreconcilable things must be accepted."

"Yes, I understood that," Martin answered. "All the arts have their conventions." (Ruth was surprised at his use of the word. It was as if he had studied at the university himself, instead of being ill-equipped from browsing at haphazard through the books in the library.) "But even the conventions must be real. Trees, painted on flat cardboard and stuck up on each side of the stage, we accept as a forest. It is a real enough convention. But, on the other hand, we would not accept a sea scene as a forest. We can't do it. It violates our senses. Nor would you, or, rather, should you, accept the ravings and writhings and agonized contortions of those two lunatics to-night as a convincing portrayal of love."

"But you don't hold yourself superior to all the judges of music?" she protested.

"No, no, not for a moment. I merely maintain my right as an individual. I have just been telling you what I think, in order to explain why the elephantine gambols of Madame Tetralani spoil the orchestra for me. The world's judges of music may all be right. But I am I, and I won't subordinate my taste to the unanimous judgment of mankind. If I don't like a thing, I don't like it, that's all; and there is no reason under the sun why I should ape a liking for it just because the majority of my fellow-creatures like it, or make believe they like it. I can't follow the fashions in the things I like or dislike."

"But music, you know, is a matter of training," Ruth argued; "and opera is even more a matter of training. May it not be—"

"That I am not trained in opera?" he dashed in.

She nodded.

"The very thing," he agreed. "And I consider I am fortunate in not having been caught when I was young. If I had, I could have wept sentimental tears to-night, and the clownish antics of that precious pair would have but enhanced the beauty of their voices and the beauty of the accompanying orchestra. You are right. It's mostly a matter of training. And I am too old, now. I must have the real or nothing. An illusion that won't convince is a palpable lie, and that's what grand opera is to me when little Barillo throws a fit, clutches mighty Tetralani in his arms (also in a fit), and tells her how passionately he adores her."

Again Ruth measured his thoughts by comparison of externals and in accordance with her belief in the established. Who was he that he should be right and all the cultured world wrong? His words and thoughts made no impression upon her. She was too firmly intrenched in the established to have any sympathy with revolutionary ideas. She had always been used to music, and she had enjoyed opera ever since she was a child, and all her world had enjoyed it, too. Then by what right did Martin Eden emerge, as he had so recently emerged, from his rag-time and working-class songs, and pass judgment on the world's music? She was vexed with him, and as she walked beside him she had a vague feeling of outrage. At the best, in her most charitable frame of mind, she considered the statement of his views to be a caprice, an erratic and uncalled-for prank. But when he took her in his arms at the door and kissed her good night in tender lover-fashion, she forgot everything in the outrush of her own love to him. And later, on a sleepless pillow, she puzzled, as she had often puzzled of late, as to how it was that she loved so strange a man, and loved him despite the disapproval of her people.

And next day Martin Eden cast hack-work aside, and at white heat hammered out an essay to which he gave the title, "The Philosophy of Illusion." A stamp started it on its travels, but it was destined to receive many stamps and to be started on many travels in the months that followed.

CHAPTER XXV

Maria Silva was poor, and all the ways of poverty were clear to her. Poverty, to Ruth, was a word signifying a not-nice condition of existence. That was her total knowledge on the subject. She knew Martin was poor, and his condition she associated in her mind with the boyhood of Abraham Lincoln, of Mr. Butler, and of other men who had become successes. Also, while aware that poverty was anything but delectable, she had a comfortable middle-class feeling that poverty was salutary, that it was a sharp spur that urged on to success all men who were not degraded and hopeless drudges. So that her knowledge that Martin was so poor that he had pawned his watch and overcoat did not disturb her. She even considered it the hopeful side of the situation, believing that sooner or later it would arouse him and compel him to abandon his writing.

Ruth never read hunger in Martin's face, which had grown lean and had enlarged the slight hollows in the cheeks. In fact, she marked the change in his face with satisfaction. It seemed to refine him, to remove from him much of the dross of flesh and the too animal-like vigor that lured her while she detested it. Sometimes, when with her, she noted an unusual brightness in his eyes, and she admired it, for it made him appear more the poet and the scholar—the things he would have liked to be and which she would have liked him to be. But Maria Silva read a different tale in the hollow cheeks and the burning eyes, and she noted the changes in them from day to day, by them following the ebb and flow of his fortunes. She saw him leave the house with his overcoat and return without it, though the day was chill and raw, and promptly she saw his cheeks fill out slightly and the fire of hunger leave his eyes. In the same way she had seen his wheel and watch go, and after each event she had seen his vigor bloom again.

Likewise she watched his toils, and knew the measure of the midnight oil he burned. Work! She knew that he outdid her, though his work was of a different order. And she was surprised to behold that the less food he had, the harder he worked. On occasion, in a casual sort of way, when she thought hunger pinched hardest, she would send him in a loaf of new baking, awkwardly covering the act with banter to the effect that it was better than he could bake. And again, she would send one of her toddlers in to him with a great pitcher of hot soup, debating inwardly the while whether she was justified in taking it from the mouths of her own flesh and blood. Nor was Martin ungrateful, knowing as he did the lives of the poor, and that if ever in the world there was charity, this was it.

On a day when she had filled her brood with what was left in the house, Maria invested her last fifteen cents in a gallon of cheap wine. Martin, coming into her kitchen to fetch water, was invited to sit down and drink. He drank her very-good health, and in return she drank his. Then she drank to prosperity in his undertakings, and he drank to the hope that James Grant would show up and pay her for his washing. James Grant was a journeymen carpenter who did not always pay his bills and who owed Maria three dollars.

Both Maria and Martin drank the sour new wine on empty stomachs, and it went swiftly to their heads. Utterly differentiated creatures that they were, they were lonely in their misery, and though the misery was tacitly ignored, it was the bond that drew them together. Maria was amazed to learn that he had been in the Azores, where she had lived until she was eleven. She was doubly amazed that he had been in the Hawaiian Islands, whither she had migrated from the Azores with her people. But her amazement passed all bounds when he told her he had been on Maui, the particular island whereon she had attained womanhood and married. Kahului, where she had first met her husband,—he, Martin, had been there twice! Yes, she remembered the sugar steamers, and he had been on them—well, well, it was a small world. And Wailuku! That place, too! Did he know the head-luna of the plantation? Yes, and had had a couple of drinks with him.

And so they reminiscenced and drowned their hunger in the raw, sour wine. To Martin the future did not seem so dim. Success trembled just before him. He was on the verge of clasping it. Then he studied the deep-lined face of the toil-worn woman before him, remembered her soups and loaves of new baking, and felt spring up in him the warmest gratitude and philanthropy.

"Maria," he exclaimed suddenly. "What would you like to have?"

She looked at him, bepuzzled.

"What would you like to have now, right now, if you could get it?"

"Shoe alla da roun' for da childs—seven pairs da shoe."

"You shall have them," he announced, while she nodded her head gravely. "But I mean a big wish, something big that you want."

Her eyes sparkled good-naturedly. He was choosing to make fun with her, Maria, with whom few made fun these days.

"Think hard," he cautioned, just as she was opening her mouth to speak.

"Alla right," she answered. "I thinka da hard. I lika da house, dis house—all mine, no paya da rent, seven dollar da month."

"You shall have it," he granted, "and in a short time. Now wish the great wish. Make believe I am God, and I say to you anything you want you can have. Then you wish that thing, and I listen."

Maria considered solemnly for a space.

"You no 'fraid?" she asked warningly.

"No, no," he laughed, "I'm not afraid. Go ahead."

"Most verra big," she warned again.

"All right. Fire away."

"Well, den—" She drew a big breath like a child, as she voiced to the uttermost all she cared to demand of life. "I lika da have one milka ranch—good milka ranch. Plenty cow, plenty land, plenty grass. I lika da have near San Le-an; my sister liva dere. I sella da milk in Oakland. I maka da plentee mon. Joe an' Nick no runna da cow. Dey go-a to school. Bimeby maka da good engineer, worka da railroad. Yes, I lika da milka ranch."

She paused and regarded Martin with twinkling eyes.

"You shall have it," he answered promptly.

She nodded her head and touched her lips courteously to the wine-glass and to the giver of the gift she knew would never be given. His heart was right, and in her own heart she appreciated his intention as much as if the gift had gone with it.

"No, Maria," he went on; "Nick and Joe won't have to peddle milk, and all the kids can go to school and wear shoes the whole year round. It will be a first-class milk ranch—everything complete. There will be a house to live in and a stable for the horses, and cow-barns, of course. There will be chickens, pigs, vegetables, fruit trees, and everything like that; and there will be enough cows to pay for a hired man or two. Then you won't have anything to do but take care of the children. For that matter, if you find a good man, you can marry and take it easy while he runs the ranch."

And from such largess, dispensed from his future, Martin turned and took his one good suit of clothes to the pawnshop. His plight was desperate for him to do this, for it cut him off from Ruth. He had no second-best suit that was presentable, and though he could go to the butcher and the baker, and even on occasion to his sister's, it was beyond all daring to dream of entering the Morse home so disreputably apparelled.

He toiled on, miserable and well-nigh hopeless. It began to appear to him that the second battle was lost and that he would have to go to work. In doing this he would satisfy everybody—the grocer, his sister, Ruth, and even Maria, to whom he owed a month's room rent. He was two months behind with his type-writer, and the agency was clamoring for payment or for the return of the machine. In desperation, all but ready to surrender, to make a truce with fate until he could get a fresh start, he took the civil service examinations for the Railway Mail. To his surprise, he passed first. The job was assured, though when the call would come to enter upon his duties nobody knew.

It was at this time, at the lowest ebb, that the smooth-running editorial machine broke down. A cog must have slipped or an oil-cup run dry, for the postman brought him one morning a short, thin envelope. Martin glanced at the upper left-hand corner and read the name and address of the *Transcontinental Monthly*. His heart gave a great leap, and he suddenly felt faint, the sinking feeling accompanied by a strange trembling of the knees. He staggered into his room and sat down on the bed, the envelope still unopened, and in that moment came understanding to him how people suddenly fall dead upon receipt of extraordinarily good news.

Of course this was good news. There was no manuscript in that thin envelope, therefore it was an acceptance. He knew the story in the hands of the *Transcontinental*. It was "The Ring of Bells," one of his horror stories, and it was an even five thousand words. And, since first-class magazines always paid on acceptance, there was a check inside. Two cents a word—twenty dollars a thousand; the check must be a hundred dollars. One hundred dollars! As he tore the envelope open, every item of all his debts surged in his brain—$3.85 to the grocer; butcher $4.00 flat; baker, $2.00; fruit store, $5.00; total, $14.85. Then there was room rent, $2.50; another month in advance, $2.50; two months' type-writer, $8.00; a month in advance, $4.00; total, $31.85. And finally to be added, his pledges, plus interest, with the pawnbroker—watch, $5.50; overcoat, $5.50; wheel, $7.75; suit of clothes, $5.50 (60 % interest, but what did it matter?)—grand total, $56.10. He saw, as if visible in the air before him, in illuminated figures, the whole sum, and the subtraction that followed and that gave a remainder of $43.90. When he had squared every debt, redeemed every pledge, he would still have jingling in his pockets a princely $43.90. And on top of that he would have a month's rent paid in advance on the type-writer and on the room.

By this time he had drawn the single sheet of type-written letter out and spread it open. There was no check. He peered into the envelope, held it to the light, but could not trust his eyes, and in trembling haste tore the envelope apart. There was no check. He read the letter, skimming it line by line, dashing through the editor's praise of his story to the meat of the letter, the statement why the check had not been sent. He found no such statement, but he did find that which made him suddenly wilt. The letter slid from his hand. His eyes went lacklustre, and he lay back on the pillow, pulling the blanket about him and up to his chin.

Five dollars for "The Ring of Bells"—five dollars for five thousand words! Instead of two cents a word, ten words for a cent! And the editor had praised it, too. And he would receive the check when the story was published. Then it was all poppycock, two cents a word for minimum rate and payment upon acceptance. It was a lie, and it had led him astray. He would never have attempted to write had he known that. He would have gone to work—to work for Ruth. He went back to the day he first attempted to write, and was appalled at the enormous waste of time—and all for ten words for a cent. And the other high rewards of writers, that he had read about, must be lies, too. His second-hand ideas of authorship were wrong, for here was the proof of it.

The *Transcontinental* sold for twenty-five cents, and its dignified and artistic cover proclaimed it as among the first-class magazines. It was a staid, respectable magazine, and it had been published continuously since long before he was born. Why, on the outside cover were printed every month the words of one of the world's great writers, words proclaiming the inspired mission of the *Transcontinental* by a star of literature whose first coruscations had appeared inside those self-same covers. And the high and lofty, heaven-inspired *Transcontinental* paid five dollars for five thousand words! The great writer had recently died in a foreign land—in dire poverty, Martin remembered, which was not to be wondered at, considering the magnificent pay authors receive.

Well, he had taken the bait, the newspaper lies about writers and their pay, and he had wasted two years over it. But he would disgorge the bait now. Not another line would he ever write. He would do what Ruth wanted him to do, what everybody wanted him to do—get a job. The thought of going to work reminded him of Joe—Joe, tramping through the land of nothing-to-do. Martin heaved a great sigh of envy. The reaction of nineteen hours a day for many days was strong upon him. But then, Joe was not in love, had none of the responsibilities of love, and he could afford to loaf through the land of nothing-to-do. He, Martin, had something to work for, and go to work he would. He would start out early next morning to hunt a job. And he would let Ruth know, too, that he had mended his ways and was willing to go into her father's office.

Five dollars for five thousand words, ten words for a cent, the market price for art. The disappointment of it, the lie of it, the infamy of it, were uppermost in his thoughts; and under his closed eyelids, in fiery figures, burned the "$3.85" he owed the grocer. He shivered, and was aware of an aching in his bones. The small of his back ached especially. His head ached, the top of it ached, the back of it ached, the brains inside of it ached and seemed to be swelling, while the ache over his brows was intolerable. And beneath the brows, planted under his lids, was the merciless "$3.85." He opened his eyes to escape it, but the white light of the room seemed to sear the balls and forced him to close his eyes, when the "$3.85" confronted him again.

Five dollars for five thousand words, ten words for a cent—that particular thought took up its residence in his brain, and he could no more escape it than he could the "$3.85" under his eyelids. A change seemed to come over the latter, and he watched curiously, till "$2.00" burned in its stead. Ah, he thought, that was the baker. The next sum that appeared was "$2.50." It puzzled him, and he pondered it as if life and death hung on the solution. He owed somebody two dollars and a half, that was certain, but who was it? To find it was the task set him by an imperious and malignant universe, and he wandered through the endless corridors of his mind, opening all manner of lumber rooms and chambers stored with odds and ends of memories and knowledge as he vainly sought the answer. After several centuries it came to him, easily, without effort, that it was Maria. With a great relief he turned his soul to the screen of torment under his lids. He had solved the problem; now he could rest. But no, the "$2.50" faded away, and in its place burned "$8.00." Who was that? He must go the dreary round of his mind again and find out.

How long he was gone on this quest he did not know, but after what seemed an enormous lapse of time, he was called back to himself by a knock at the door, and by Maria's asking if he was sick. He replied in a muffled voice he did not recognize, saying that he was merely taking a nap. He was surprised when he noted the darkness of night in the room. He had received the letter at two in the afternoon, and he realized that he was sick.

Then the "$8.00" began to smoulder under his lids again, and he returned himself to servitude. But he grew cunning. There was no need for him to wander through his mind. He had been a fool. He pulled a lever and made his mind revolve about him, a monstrous wheel of fortune, a merry-go-round of memory, a revolving sphere of wisdom. Faster and faster it revolved, until its vortex sucked him in and he was flung whirling through black chaos.

Quite naturally he found himself at a mangle, feeding starched cuffs. But as he fed he noticed figures printed in the cuffs. It was a new way of marking linen, he thought, until, looking closer, he saw "$3.85" on one of the cuffs. Then it came to him that it was the grocer's bill, and that these were his bills flying around on the drum of the mangle. A crafty idea came to him. He would throw the bills on the floor and so escape paying them. No sooner thought than done, and he crumpled the cuffs spitefully as he flung them upon an unusually dirty floor. Ever the heap grew, and though each bill was duplicated a thousand times, he found only one for two dollars and a half, which was what he owed Maria. That meant that Maria would not press for payment, and he resolved generously that it would be the only one he would pay; so he began searching through the cast-out heap for hers. He sought it desperately, for ages, and was still searching when the manager of the hotel entered, the fat Dutchman. His face blazed with wrath, and he shouted in stentorian tones that echoed down the universe, "I shall deduct the cost of those cuffs from your wages!" The pile of cuffs grew into a mountain, and Martin knew that he was doomed to toil for a thousand years to pay for them. Well, there was nothing left to do but kill the manager and burn down the laundry. But the big Dutchman frustrated him, seizing him by the nape of the neck and dancing him up and down. He danced him over the ironing tables, the stove, and the mangles, and out into the wash-room and over the wringer and washer. Martin was danced until his teeth rattled and his head ached, and he marvelled that the Dutchman was so strong.

And then he found himself before the mangle, this time receiving the cuffs an editor of a magazine was feeding from the other side. Each cuff was a check, and Martin went over them anxiously, in a fever of expectation, but they were all blanks. He stood there and received the blanks for a million years or so, never letting one go by for fear it might be filled out. At last he found it. With trembling fingers he held it to the light. It was for five dollars. "Ha! Ha!" laughed the editor across the mangle. "Well, then, I shall kill you," Martin said. He went out into the wash-room to get the axe, and found Joe starching manuscripts. He tried to make him desist, then swung the axe for him. But the weapon remained poised in mid-air, for Martin found himself back in the ironing room in the midst of a snow-storm. No, it was not snow that was falling, but checks of large denomination, the smallest not less than a thousand dollars. He began to collect them and sort them out, in packages of a hundred, tying each package securely with twine.

He looked up from his task and saw Joe standing before him juggling flat-irons, starched shirts, and manuscripts. Now and again he reached out and added a bundle of checks to the flying miscellany that soared through the roof and out of sight in a tremendous circle. Martin struck at him, but he seized the axe and added it to the flying circle. Then he plucked Martin and added him. Martin went up through the roof, clutching at manuscripts, so that by the time he came down he had a large armful. But no sooner down than up again, and a second and a third time and countless times he flew around the circle. From far off he could hear a childish treble singing: "Waltz me around again, Willie, around, around, around."

He recovered the axe in the midst of the Milky Way of checks, starched shirts, and manuscripts, and prepared, when he came down, to kill Joe. But he did not come down. Instead, at two in the morning, Maria, having heard his groans through the thin partition, came into his room, to put hot flat-irons against his body and damp cloths upon his aching eyes.

CHAPTER XXVI

Martin Eden did not go out to hunt for a job in the morning. It was late afternoon before he came out of his delirium and gazed with aching eyes about the room. Mary, one of the tribe of Silva, eight years old, keeping watch, raised a screech at sight of his returning consciousness. Maria hurried into the room from the kitchen. She put her work-calloused hand upon his hot forehead and felt his pulse.

"You lika da eat?" she asked.

He shook his head. Eating was farthest from his desire, and he wondered that he should ever have been hungry in his life.

"I'm sick, Maria," he said weakly. "What is it? Do you know?"

"Grip," she answered. "Two or three days you alla da right. Better you no eat now. Bimeby plenty can eat, to-morrow can eat maybe."

Martin was not used to sickness, and when Maria and her little girl left him, he essayed to get up and dress. By a supreme exertion of will, with rearing brain and eyes that ached so that he could not keep them open, he managed to get out of bed, only to be left stranded by his senses upon the table. Half an hour later he managed to regain the bed, where he was content to lie with closed eyes and analyze his various pains and weaknesses. Maria came in several times to change the cold cloths on his forehead. Otherwise she left him in peace, too wise to vex him with chatter. This moved him to gratitude, and he murmured to himself, "Maria, you getta da milka ranch, all righta, all right."

Then he remembered his long-buried past of yesterday.

It seemed a life-time since he had received that letter from the *Transcontinental*, a life-time since it was all over and done with and a new page turned. He had shot his bolt, and shot it hard, and now he was down on his back. If he hadn't starved himself, he wouldn't have been caught by La Grippe. He had been run down, and he had not had the strength to throw off the germ of disease which had invaded his system. This was what resulted.

"What does it profit a man to write a whole library and lose his own life?" he demanded aloud. "This is no place for me. No more literature in mine. Me for the counting-house and ledger, the monthly salary, and the little home with Ruth."

Two days later, having eaten an egg and two slices of toast and drunk a cup of tea, he asked for his mail, but found his eyes still hurt too much to permit him to read.

"You read for me, Maria," he said. "Never mind the big, long letters. Throw them under the table. Read me the small letters."

"No can," was the answer. "Teresa, she go to school, she can."

So Teresa Silva, aged nine, opened his letters and read them to him. He listened absently to a long dun from the type-writer people, his mind busy with ways and means of finding a job. Suddenly he was shocked back to himself.

"'We offer you forty dollars for all serial rights in your story,'" Teresa slowly spelled out, "'provided you allow us to make the alterations suggested.'"

"What magazine is that?" Martin shouted. "Here, give it to me!"

He could see to read, now, and he was unaware of the pain of the action. It was the *White Mouse* that was offering him forty dollars, and the story was "The Whirlpool," another of his early horror stories. He read the letter through again and again. The editor told him plainly that he had not handled the idea properly, but that it was the idea they were buying because it was original. If they could cut the story down one-third, they would take it and send him forty dollars on receipt of his answer.

He called for pen and ink, and told the editor he could cut the story down three-thirds if he wanted to, and to send the forty dollars right along.

The letter despatched to the letter-box by Teresa, Martin lay back and thought. It wasn't a lie, after all. The *White Mouse* paid on acceptance. There were three thousand words in "The Whirlpool." Cut down a third, there would be two thousand. At forty dollars that would be two cents a word. Pay on acceptance and two cents a word—the newspapers had told the truth. And he had thought the *White Mouse* a third-rater! It was evident that he did not know the magazines. He had deemed the *Transcontinental* a first-rater, and it paid a cent for ten words. He had classed the *White Mouse* as of no account, and it paid twenty times as much as the *Transcontinental* and also had paid on acceptance.

Well, there was one thing certain: when he got well, he would not go out looking for a job. There were more stories in his head as good as "The Whirlpool," and at forty dollars apiece he could earn far more than in any job or position. Just when he thought the battle lost, it was won. He had proved for his career. The way was clear. Beginning with the *White Mouse* he would add magazine after magazine to his growing list of patrons. Hack-work could be put aside. For that matter, it had been wasted time, for it had not brought him a dollar. He would devote himself to work, good work, and he would pour out the best that was in him. He wished Ruth was there to share in his joy, and when he went over the letters left lying on his bed, he found one from her. It was sweetly reproachful, wondering what had kept him away for so dreadful a length of time. He reread the letter adoringly, dwelling over her handwriting, loving each stroke of her pen, and in the end kissing her signature.

And when he answered, he told her recklessly that he had not been to see her because his best clothes were in pawn. He told her that he had been sick, but was once more nearly well, and that inside ten days or two weeks (as soon as a letter could travel to New York City and return) he would redeem his clothes and be with her.

But Ruth did not care to wait ten days or two weeks. Besides, her lover was sick. The next afternoon, accompanied by Arthur, she arrived in the Morse carriage, to the unqualified delight of the Silva tribe and of all the urchins on the street, and to the consternation of Maria. She boxed the ears of the Silvas who crowded about the visitors on the tiny front porch, and in more than usual atrocious English tried to apologize for her appearance. Sleeves rolled up from soap-flecked arms and a wet gunny-sack around her waist told of the task at which she had been caught. So flustered was she by two such grand young people asking for her lodger, that she forgot to invite them to sit down in the little parlor. To enter Martin's room, they passed through the kitchen, warm and moist and steamy from the big washing in progress. Maria, in her excitement, jammed the bedroom and bedroom-closet doors together, and for five minutes, through the partly open door, clouds of steam, smelling of soap-suds and dirt, poured into the sick chamber.

Ruth succeeded in veering right and left and right again, and in running the narrow passage between table and bed to Martin's side; but Arthur veered too wide and fetched up with clatter and bang of pots and pans in the corner where Martin did his cooking. Arthur did not linger long. Ruth occupied the only chair, and having done his duty, he went outside and stood by the gate, the centre of seven marvelling Silvas, who watched him as they would have watched a curiosity in a side-show. All about the carriage were gathered the children from a dozen blocks, waiting and eager for some tragic and terrible dénouement. Carriages were seen on their street only for weddings and funerals. Here was neither marriage nor death: therefore, it was something transcending experience and well worth waiting for.

Martin had been wild to see Ruth. His was essentially a love-nature, and he possessed more than the average man's need for sympathy. He was starving for sympathy, which, with him, meant intelligent understanding; and he had yet to learn that Ruth's sympathy was largely sentimental and tactful, and that it proceeded from gentleness of nature rather than from understanding of the objects of her sympathy. So it was while Martin held her hand and gladly talked, that her love for him prompted her to press his hand in return, and that her eyes were moist and luminous at sight of his helplessness and of the marks suffering had stamped upon his face.

But while he told her of his two acceptances, of his despair when he received the one from the *Transcontinental*, and of the corresponding delight with which he received the one from the *White Mouse*, she did not follow him. She heard the words he uttered and understood their literal import, but she was not with him in his despair and his delight. She could not get out of herself. She was not interested in selling stories to magazines. What was important to her was matrimony. She was not aware of it, however, any more than she was aware that her desire that Martin take a position was the instinctive and preparative impulse of motherhood. She would have blushed had she been told as much in plain, set terms, and next, she might have grown indignant and asserted that her sole interest lay in the man she loved and her desire for him to make the best of himself. So, while Martin poured out his heart to her, elated with the first success his chosen work in the world had received, she paid heed to his bare words only, gazing now and again about the room, shocked by what she saw.

For the first time Ruth gazed upon the sordid face of poverty. Starving lovers had always seemed romantic to her,—but she had had no idea how starving lovers lived. She had never dreamed it could be like this. Ever her gaze shifted from the room to him and back again. The steamy smell of dirty clothes, which had entered with her from the kitchen, was sickening. Martin must be soaked with it, Ruth concluded, if that awful woman washed frequently. Such was the contagiousness of degradation. When she looked at Martin, she seemed to see the smirch left upon him by his surroundings. She had never seen him unshaven, and the three days' growth of beard on his face was repulsive to her. Not alone did it give him the same dark and murky aspect of the Silva house, inside and out, but it seemed to emphasize that animal-like strength of his which she detested. And here he was, being confirmed in his madness by the two acceptances he took such pride in telling her about. A little longer and he would have surrendered and gone to work. Now he would continue on in this horrible house, writing and starving for a few more months.

"What is that smell?" she asked suddenly.

"Some of Maria's washing smells, I imagine," was the answer. "I am growing quite accustomed to them."

"No, no; not that. It is something else. A stale, sickish smell."

Martin sampled the air before replying.

"I can't smell anything else, except stale tobacco smoke," he announced.

"That's it. It is terrible. Why do you smoke so much, Martin?"

"I don't know, except that I smoke more than usual when I am lonely. And then, too, it's such a long-standing habit. I learned when I was only a youngster."

"It is not a nice habit, you know," she reproved. "It smells to heaven."

"That's the fault of the tobacco. I can afford only the cheapest. But wait until I get that forty-dollar check. I'll use a brand that is not offensive even to the angels. But that wasn't so bad, was it, two acceptances in three days? That forty-five dollars will pay about all my debts."

"For two years' work?" she queried.

"No, for less than a week's work. Please pass me that book over on the far corner of the table, the account book with the gray cover." He opened it and began turning over the pages rapidly. "Yes, I was right. Four days for 'The Ring of Bells,' two days for 'The Whirlpool.' That's forty-five dollars for a week's work, one hundred and eighty dollars a month. That beats any salary I can command. And, besides, I'm just beginning. A thousand dollars a month is not too much to buy for you all I want you to have. A salary of five hundred a month would be too small. That forty-five dollars is just a starter. Wait till I get my stride. Then watch my smoke."

Ruth misunderstood his slang, and reverted to cigarettes.

"You smoke more than enough as it is, and the brand of tobacco will make no difference. It is the smoking itself that is not nice, no matter what the brand may be. You are a chimney, a living volcano, a perambulating smoke-stack, and you are a perfect disgrace, Martin dear, you know you are."

She leaned toward him, entreaty in her eyes, and as he looked at her delicate face and into her pure, limpid eyes, as of old he was struck with his own unworthiness.

"I wish you wouldn't smoke any more," she whispered. "Please, for—my sake."

"All right, I won't," he cried. "I'll do anything you ask, dear love, anything; you know that."

A great temptation assailed her. In an insistent way she had caught glimpses of the large, easy-going side of his nature, and she felt sure, if she asked him to cease attempting to write, that he would grant her wish. In the swift instant that elapsed, the words trembled on her lips. But she did not utter them. She was not quite brave enough; she did not quite dare. Instead, she leaned toward him to meet him, and in his arms murmured:-

"You know, it is really not for my sake, Martin, but for your own. I am sure smoking hurts you; and besides, it is not good to be a slave to anything, to a drug least of all."

"I shall always be your slave," he smiled.

"In which case, I shall begin issuing my commands."

She looked at him mischievously, though deep down she was already regretting that she had not preferred her largest request.

"I live but to obey, your majesty."

"Well, then, my first commandment is, Thou shalt not omit to shave every day. Look how you have scratched my cheek."

And so it ended in caresses and love-laughter. But she had made one point, and she could not expect to make more than one at a time. She felt a woman's pride in that she had made him stop smoking. Another time she would persuade him to take a position, for had he not said he would do anything she asked?

She left his side to explore the room, examining the clothes-lines of notes overhead, learning the mystery of the tackle used for suspending his wheel under the ceiling, and being saddened by the heap of manuscripts under the table which represented to her just so much wasted time. The oil-stove won her admiration, but on investigating the food shelves she found them empty.

"Why, you haven't anything to eat, you poor dear," she said with tender compassion. "You must be starving."

"I store my food in Maria's safe and in her pantry," he lied. "It keeps better there. No danger of my starving. Look at that."

She had come back to his side, and she saw him double his arm at the elbow, the biceps crawling under his shirt-sleeve and swelling into a knot of muscle, heavy and hard. The sight repelled her. Sentimentally, she disliked it. But her pulse, her blood, every fibre of her, loved it and yearned for it, and, in the old, inexplicable way, she leaned toward him, not away from him. And in the moment that followed, when he crushed her in his arms, the brain of her, concerned with the superficial aspects of life, was in revolt; while the heart of her, the woman of her, concerned with life itself, exulted triumphantly. It was in moments like this that she felt to the uttermost the greatness of her love for Martin, for it was almost a swoon of delight to her to feel his strong arms about her, holding her tightly, hurting her with the grip of their fervor. At such moments she found justification for her treason to her standards, for her violation of her own high ideals, and, most of all, for her tacit disobedience to her mother and father. They did not want her to marry this man. It shocked them that she should love him. It shocked her, too, sometimes, when she was apart from him, a cool and reasoning creature. With him, she loved him—in truth, at times a vexed and worried love; but love it was, a love that was stronger than she.

"This La Grippe is nothing," he was saying. "It hurts a bit, and gives one a nasty headache, but it doesn't compare with break-bone fever."

"Have you had that, too?" she queried absently, intent on the heaven-sent justification she was finding in his arms.

And so, with absent queries, she led him on, till suddenly his words startled her.

He had had the fever in a secret colony of thirty lepers on one of the Hawaiian Islands.

"But why did you go there?" she demanded.

Such royal carelessness of body seemed criminal.

"Because I didn't know," he answered. "I never dreamed of lepers. When I deserted the schooner and landed on the beach, I headed inland for some place of hiding. For three days I lived off guavas, *ohia*-apples, and bananas, all of which grew wild in the jungle. On the fourth day I found the trail—a mere foot-trail. It led inland, and it led up. It was the way I wanted to go, and it showed signs of recent travel. At one place it ran along the crest of a ridge that was no more than a knife-edge. The trail wasn't three feet wide on the crest, and on either side the ridge fell away in precipices hundreds of feet deep. One man, with plenty of ammunition, could have held it against a hundred thousand.

"It was the only way in to the hiding-place. Three hours after I found the trail I was there, in a little mountain valley, a pocket in the midst of lava peaks. The whole place was terraced for taro-patches, fruit trees grew there, and there were eight or ten grass huts. But as soon as I saw the inhabitants I knew what I'd struck. One sight of them was enough."

"What did you do?" Ruth demanded breathlessly, listening, like any Desdemona, appalled and fascinated.

"Nothing for me to do. Their leader was a kind old fellow, pretty far gone, but he ruled like a king. He had discovered the little valley and founded the settlement—all of which was against the law. But he had guns, plenty of ammunition, and those Kanakas, trained to the shooting of wild cattle and wild pig, were dead shots. No, there wasn't any running away for Martin Eden. He stayed—for three months."

"But how did you escape?"

"I'd have been there yet, if it hadn't been for a girl there, a half-Chinese, quarter-white, and quarter-Hawaiian. She was a beauty, poor thing, and well educated. Her mother, in Honolulu, was worth a million or so. Well, this girl got me away at last. Her mother financed the settlement, you see, so the girl wasn't afraid of being punished for letting me go. But she made me swear, first, never to reveal the hiding-place; and I never have. This is the first time I have even mentioned it. The girl had just the first signs of leprosy. The fingers of her right hand were slightly twisted, and there was a small spot on her arm. That was all. I guess she is dead, now."

"But weren't you frightened? And weren't you glad to get away without catching that dreadful disease?"

"Well," he confessed, "I was a bit shivery at first; but I got used to it. I used to feel sorry for that poor girl, though. That made me forget to be afraid. She was such a beauty, in spirit as well as in appearance, and she was only slightly touched; yet she was doomed to lie there, living the life of a primitive savage and rotting slowly away. Leprosy is far more terrible than you can imagine it."

"Poor thing," Ruth murmured softly. "It's a wonder she let you get away."

"How do you mean?" Martin asked unwittingly.

"Because she must have loved you," Ruth said, still softly. "Candidly, now, didn't she?"

Martin's sunburn had been bleached by his work in the laundry and by the indoor life he was living, while the hunger and the sickness had made his face even pale; and across this pallor flowed the slow wave of a blush. He was opening his mouth to speak, but Ruth shut him off.

"Never mind, don't answer; it's not necessary," she laughed.

But it seemed to him there was something metallic in her laughter, and that the light in her eyes was cold. On the spur of the moment it reminded him of a gale he had once experienced in the North Pacific. And for the moment the apparition of the gale rose before his eyes—a gale at night, with a clear sky and under a full moon, the huge seas glinting coldly in the moonlight. Next, he saw the girl in the leper refuge and remembered it was for love of him that she had let him go.

"She was noble," he said simply. "She gave me life."

That was all of the incident, but he heard Ruth muffle a dry sob in her throat, and noticed that she turned her face away to gaze out of the window. When she turned it back to him, it was composed, and there was no hint of the gale in her eyes.

"I'm such a silly," she said plaintively. "But I can't help it. I do so love you, Martin, I do, I do. I shall grow more catholic in time, but at present I can't help being jealous of those ghosts of the past, and you know your past is full of ghosts."

"It must be," she silenced his protest. "It could not be otherwise. And there's poor Arthur motioning me to come. He's tired waiting. And now good-by, dear."

"There's some kind of a mixture, put up by the druggists, that helps men to stop the use of tobacco," she called back from the door, "and I am going to send you some."

The door closed, but opened again.

"I do, I do," she whispered to him; and this time she was really gone.

Maria, with worshipful eyes that none the less were keen to note the texture of Ruth's garments and the cut of them (a cut unknown that produced an effect mysteriously beautiful), saw her to the carriage. The crowd of disappointed urchins stared till the carriage disappeared from view, then transferred their stare to Maria, who had abruptly become the most important person on the street. But it was one of her progeny who blasted Maria's reputation by announcing that the grand visitors had been for her lodger. After that Maria dropped back into her old obscurity and Martin began to notice the respectful manner in which he was regarded by the small fry of the neighborhood. As for Maria, Martin rose in her estimation a full hundred per cent, and had the Portuguese grocer witnessed that afternoon carriage-call he would have allowed Martin an additional three-dollars-and-eighty-five-cents' worth of credit.

CHAPTER XXVII

The sun of Martin's good fortune rose. The day after Ruth's visit, he received a check for three dollars from a New York scandal weekly in payment for three of his triolets. Two days later a newspaper published in Chicago accepted his "Treasure Hunters," promising to pay ten dollars for it on publication. The price was small, but it was the first article he had written, his very first attempt to express his thought on the printed page. To cap everything, the adventure serial for boys, his second attempt, was accepted before the end of the week by a juvenile monthly calling itself *Youth and Age*. It was true the serial was twenty-one thousand words, and they offered to pay him sixteen dollars on publication, which was something like seventy-five cents a thousand words; but it was equally true that it was the second thing he had attempted to write and that he was himself thoroughly aware of its clumsy worthlessness.

But even his earliest efforts were not marked with the clumsiness of mediocrity. What characterized them was the clumsiness of too great strength—the clumsiness which the tyro betrays when he crushes butterflies with battering rams and hammers out vignettes with a war-club. So it was that Martin was glad to sell his early efforts for songs. He knew them for what they were, and it had not taken him long to acquire this knowledge. What he pinned his faith to was his later work. He had striven to be something more than a mere writer of magazine fiction. He had sought to equip himself with the tools of artistry. On the other hand, he had not sacrificed strength. His conscious aim had been to increase his strength by avoiding excess of strength. Nor had he departed from his love of reality. His work was realism, though he had endeavored to fuse with it the fancies and beauties of imagination. What he sought was an impassioned realism, shot through with human aspiration and faith. What he wanted was life as it was, with all its spirit-groping and soul-reaching left in.

He had discovered, in the course of his reading, two schools of fiction. One treated of man as a god, ignoring his earthly origin; the other treated of man as a clod, ignoring his heaven-sent dreams and divine possibilities. Both the god and the clod schools erred, in Martin's estimation, and erred through too great singleness of sight and purpose. There was a compromise that approximated the truth, though it flattered not the school of god, while it challenged the brute-savageness of the school of clod. It was his story, "Adventure," which had dragged with Ruth, that Martin believed had achieved his ideal of the true in fiction; and it was in an essay, "God and Clod," that he had expressed his views on the whole general subject.

But "Adventure," and all that he deemed his best work, still went begging among the editors. His early work counted for nothing in his eyes except for the money it brought, and his horror stories, two of which he had sold, he did not consider high work nor his best work. To him they were frankly imaginative and fantastic, though invested with all the glamour of the real, wherein lay their power. This investiture of the grotesque and impossible with reality, he looked upon as a trick—a skilful trick at best. Great literature could not reside in such a field. Their artistry was high, but he denied the worthwhileness of artistry when divorced from humanness. The trick had been to fling over the face of his artistry a mask of humanness, and this he had done in the half-dozen or so stories of the horror brand he had written before he emerged upon the high peaks of "Adventure," "Joy," "The Pot," and "The Wine of Life."

The three dollars he received for the triolets he used to eke out a precarious existence against the arrival of the *White Mouse* check. He cashed the first check with the suspicious Portuguese grocer, paying a dollar on account and dividing the remaining two dollars between the baker and the fruit store. Martin was not yet rich enough to afford meat, and he was on slim allowance when the *White Mouse* check arrived. He was divided on the cashing of it. He had never been in a bank in his life, much less been in one on business, and he had a naive and childlike desire to walk into one of the big banks down in Oakland and fling down his indorsed check for forty dollars. On the other hand, practical common sense ruled that he should cash it with his grocer and thereby make an impression that would later result in an increase of credit. Reluctantly Martin yielded to the claims of the grocer, paying his bill with him in full, and receiving in change a pocketful of jingling coin. Also, he paid the other tradesmen in full, redeemed his suit and his bicycle, paid one month's rent on the type-writer, and paid Maria the overdue month for his room and a month in advance. This left him in his pocket, for emergencies, a balance of nearly three dollars.

In itself, this small sum seemed a fortune. Immediately on recovering his clothes he had gone to see Ruth, and on the way he could not refrain from jingling the little handful of silver in his pocket. He had been so long without money that, like a rescued starving man who cannot let the unconsumed food out of his sight, Martin could not keep his hand off the silver. He was not mean, nor avaricious, but the money meant more than so many dollars and cents. It stood for success, and the eagles stamped upon the coins were to him so many winged victories.

It came to him insensibly that it was a very good world. It certainly appeared more beautiful to him. For weeks it had been a very dull and sombre world; but now, with nearly all debts paid, three dollars jingling in his pocket, and in his mind the consciousness of success, the sun shone bright and warm, and even a rain-squall that soaked unprepared pedestrians seemed a merry happening to him. When he starved, his thoughts had dwelt often upon the thousands he knew were starving the world over; but now that he was feasted full, the fact of the thousands starving was no longer pregnant in his brain. He forgot about them, and, being in love, remembered the countless lovers in the world. Without deliberately thinking about it, *motifs* for love-lyrics began to agitate his brain. Swept away by the creative impulse, he got off the electric car, without vexation, two blocks beyond his crossing.

He found a number of persons in the Morse home. Ruth's two girl-cousins were visiting her from San Rafael, and Mrs. Morse, under pretext of entertaining them, was pursuing her plan of surrounding Ruth with young people. The campaign had begun during Martin's enforced absence, and was already in full swing. She was making a point of having at the house men who were doing things. Thus, in addition to the cousins Dorothy and Florence, Martin encountered two university professors, one of Latin, the other of English; a young army officer just back from the Philippines, one-time school-mate of Ruth's; a young fellow named Melville, private secretary to Joseph Perkins, head of the San Francisco Trust Company; and finally of the men, a live bank cashier, Charles Hapgood, a youngish man of thirty-five, graduate of Stanford University, member of the Nile Club and the Unity Club, and a conservative speaker for the Republican Party during campaigns—in short, a rising young man in every way. Among the women was one who painted portraits, another who was a professional musician, and still another who possessed the degree of Doctor of Sociology and who was locally famous for her social settlement work in the slums of San Francisco. But the women did not count for much in Mrs. Morse's plan. At the best, they were necessary accessories. The men who did things must be drawn to the house somehow.

"Don't get excited when you talk," Ruth admonished Martin, before the ordeal of introduction began.

He bore himself a bit stiffly at first, oppressed by a sense of his own awkwardness, especially of his shoulders, which were up to their old trick of threatening destruction to furniture and ornaments. Also, he was rendered self-conscious by the company. He had never before been in contact with such exalted beings nor with so many of them. Melville, the bank cashier, fascinated him, and he resolved to investigate him at the first opportunity. For underneath Martin's awe lurked his assertive ego, and he felt the urge to measure himself with these men and women and to find out what they had learned from the books and life which he had not learned.

Ruth's eyes roved to him frequently to see how he was getting on, and she was surprised and gladdened by the ease with which he got acquainted with her cousins. He certainly did not grow excited, while being seated removed from him the worry of his shoulders. Ruth knew them for clever girls, superficially brilliant, and she could scarcely understand their praise of Martin later that night at going to bed. But he, on the other hand, a wit in his own class, a gay quizzer and laughter-maker at dances and Sunday picnics, had found the making of fun and the breaking of good-natured lances simple enough in this environment. And on this evening success stood at his back, patting him on the shoulder and telling him that he was making good, so that he could afford to laugh and make laughter and remain unabashed.

Later, Ruth's anxiety found justification. Martin and Professor Caldwell had got together in a conspicuous corner, and though Martin no longer wove the air with his hands, to Ruth's critical eye he permitted his own eyes to flash and glitter too frequently, talked too rapidly and warmly, grew too intense, and allowed his aroused blood to redden his cheeks too much. He lacked decorum and control, and was in decided contrast to the young professor of English with whom he talked.

But Martin was not concerned with appearances! He had been swift to note the other's trained mind and to appreciate his command of knowledge. Furthermore, Professor Caldwell did not realize Martin's concept of the average English professor. Martin wanted him to talk shop, and, though he seemed averse at first, succeeded in making him do it. For Martin did not see why a man should not talk shop.

"It's absurd and unfair," he had told Ruth weeks before, "this objection to talking shop. For what reason under the sun do men and women come together if not for the exchange of the best that is in them? And the best that is in them is what they are interested in, the thing by which they make their living, the thing they've specialized on and sat up days and nights over, and even dreamed about. Imagine Mr. Butler living up to social etiquette and enunciating his views on Paul Verlaine or the German drama or the novels of D'Annunzio. We'd be bored to death. I, for one, if I must listen to Mr. Butler, prefer to hear him talk about his law. It's the best that is in him, and life is so short that I want the best of every man and woman I meet."

"But," Ruth had objected, "there are the topics of general interest to all."

"There, you mistake," he had rushed on. "All persons in society, all cliques in society—or, rather, nearly all persons and cliques—ape their betters. Now, who are the best betters? The idlers, the wealthy idlers. They do not know, as a rule, the things known by the persons who are doing something in the world. To listen to conversation about such things would mean to be bored, wherefore the idlers decree that such things are shop and must not be talked about. Likewise they decree the things that are not shop and which may be talked about, and those things are the latest operas, latest novels, cards, billiards, cocktails, automobiles, horse shows, trout fishing, tuna-fishing, big-game shooting, yacht sailing, and so forth—and mark you, these are the things the idlers know. In all truth, they constitute the shop-talk of the idlers. And the funniest part of it is that many of the clever people, and all the would-be clever people, allow the idlers so to impose upon them. As for me, I want the best a man's got in him, call it shop vulgarity or anything you please."

And Ruth had not understood. This attack of his on the established had seemed to her just so much wilfulness of opinion.

So Martin contaminated Professor Caldwell with his own earnestness, challenging him to speak his mind. As Ruth paused beside them she heard Martin saying:-

"You surely don't pronounce such heresies in the University of California?"

Professor Caldwell shrugged his shoulders. "The honest taxpayer and the politician, you know. Sacramento gives us our appropriations and therefore we kowtow to Sacramento, and to the Board of Regents, and to the party press, or to the press of both parties."

"Yes, that's clear; but how about you?" Martin urged. "You must be a fish out of the water."

"Few like me, I imagine, in the university pond. Sometimes I am fairly sure I am out of water, and that I should belong in Paris, in Grub Street, in a hermit's cave, or in some sadly wild Bohemian crowd, drinking claret,—dago-red they call it in San Francisco,—dining in cheap restaurants in the Latin Quarter, and expressing vociferously radical views upon all creation. Really, I am frequently almost sure that I was cut out to be a radical. But then, there are so many questions on which I am not sure. I grow timid when I am face to face with my human frailty, which ever prevents me from grasping all the factors in any problem—human, vital problems, you know."

And as he talked on, Martin became aware that to his own lips had come the "Song of the Trade Wind":-

"I am strongest at noon,
But under the moon
I stiffen the bunt of the sail."

He was almost humming the words, and it dawned upon him that the other reminded him of the trade wind, of the Northeast Trade, steady, and cool, and strong. He was equable, he was to be relied upon, and withal there was a certain bafflement about him. Martin had the feeling that he never spoke his full mind, just as he had often had the feeling that the trades never blew their strongest but always held reserves of strength that were never used. Martin's trick of visioning was active as ever. His brain was a most accessible storehouse of remembered fact and fancy, and its contents seemed ever ordered and spread for his inspection. Whatever occurred in the instant present, Martin's mind immediately presented associated antithesis or similitude which ordinarily expressed themselves to him in vision. It was sheerly automatic, and his visioning was an unfailing accompaniment to the living present. Just as Ruth's face, in a momentary jealousy had called before his eyes a forgotten moonlight gale, and as Professor

Caldwell made him see again the Northeast Trade herding the white billows across the purple sea, so, from moment to moment, not disconcerting but rather identifying and classifying, new memory-visions rose before him, or spread under his eyelids, or were thrown upon the screen of his consciousness. These visions came out of the actions and sensations of the past, out of things and events and books of yesterday and last week—a countless host of apparitions that, waking or sleeping, forever thronged his mind.

So it was, as he listened to Professor Caldwell's easy flow of speech—the conversation of a clever, cultured man—that Martin kept seeing himself down all his past. He saw himself when he had been quite the hoodlum, wearing a "stiff-rim" Stetson hat and a square-cut, double-breasted coat, with a certain swagger to the shoulders and possessing the ideal of being as tough as the police permitted. He did not disguise it to himself, nor attempt to palliate it. At one time in his life he had been just a common hoodlum, the leader of a gang that worried the police and terrorized honest, working-class householders. But his ideals had changed. He glanced about him at the well-bred, well-dressed men and women, and breathed into his lungs the atmosphere of culture and refinement, and at the same moment the ghost of his early youth, in stiff-rim and square-cut, with swagger and toughness, stalked across the room. This figure, of the corner hoodlum, he saw merge into himself, sitting and talking with an actual university professor.

For, after all, he had never found his permanent abiding place. He had fitted in wherever he found himself, been a favorite always and everywhere by virtue of holding his own at work and at play and by his willingness and ability to fight for his rights and command respect. But he had never taken root. He had fitted in sufficiently to satisfy his fellows but not to satisfy himself. He had been perturbed always by a feeling of unrest, had heard always the call of something from beyond, and had wandered on through life seeking it until he found books and art and love. And here he was, in the midst of all this, the only one of all the comrades he had adventured with who could have made themselves eligible for the inside of the Morse home.

But such thoughts and visions did not prevent him from following Professor Caldwell closely. And as he followed, comprehendingly and critically, he noted the unbroken field of the other's knowledge. As for himself, from moment to moment the conversation showed him gaps and open stretches, whole subjects with which he was unfamiliar. Nevertheless, thanks to his Spencer, he saw that he possessed the outlines of the field of knowledge. It was a matter only of time, when he would fill in the outline. Then watch out, he thought—'ware shoal, everybody! He felt like sitting at the feet of the professor, worshipful and absorbent; but, as he listened, he began to discern a weakness in the other's judgments—a weakness so stray and elusive that he might not have caught it had it not been ever present. And when he did catch it, he leapt to equality at once.

Ruth came up to them a second time, just as Martin began to speak.

"I'll tell you where you are wrong, or, rather, what weakens your judgments," he said. "You lack biology. It has no place in your scheme of things.—Oh, I mean the real interpretative biology, from the ground up, from the laboratory and the test-tube and the vitalized inorganic right on up to the widest aesthetic and sociological generalizations."

Ruth was appalled. She had sat two lecture courses under Professor Caldwell and looked up to him as the living repository of all knowledge.

"I scarcely follow you," he said dubiously.

Martin was not so sure but what he had followed him.

"Then I'll try to explain," he said. "I remember reading in Egyptian history something to the effect that understanding could not be had of Egyptian art without first studying the land question."

"Quite right," the professor nodded.

"And it seems to me," Martin continued, "that knowledge of the land question, in turn, of all questions, for that matter, cannot be had without previous knowledge of the stuff and the constitution of life. How can we understand laws and institutions, religions and customs, without understanding, not merely the nature of the creatures that made them, but the nature of the stuff out of which the creatures are made? Is literature less human than the architecture and sculpture of Egypt? Is there one thing in the known universe that is not subject to the law of evolution?—Oh, I know there is an elaborate evolution of the various arts laid down, but it seems to me to be too mechanical. The human himself is left out. The evolution of the tool, of the harp, of music and song and dance, are all beautifully elaborated; but how about the evolution of the human himself, the development of the basic and intrinsic parts that were in him before he made his first tool or gibbered his first chant? It is that which you do not consider, and which I call biology. It is biology in its largest aspects.

"I know I express myself incoherently, but I've tried to hammer out the idea. It came to me as you were talking, so I was not primed and ready to deliver it. You spoke yourself of the human frailty that prevented one from taking all the factors into consideration. And you, in turn,—or so it seems to me,—leave out the biological factor, the very stuff out of which has been spun the fabric of all the arts, the warp and the woof of all human actions and achievements."

To Ruth's amazement, Martin was not immediately crushed, and that the professor replied in the way he did struck her as forbearance for Martin's youth. Professor Caldwell sat for a full minute, silent and fingering his watch chain.

"Do you know," he said at last, "I've had that same criticism passed on me once before—by a very great man, a scientist and evolutionist, Joseph Le Conte. But he is dead, and I thought to remain undetected; and now you come along and expose me. Seriously, though—and this is confession—I think there is something in your contention—a great deal, in fact. I am too classical, not enough up-to-date in the interpretative branches of science, and I can only plead the disadvantages of my education and a temperamental slothfulness that prevents me from doing the work. I wonder if you'll believe that I've never been inside a physics or chemistry laboratory? It is true, nevertheless. Le Conte was right, and so are you, Mr. Eden, at least to an extent—how much I do not know."

Ruth drew Martin away with her on a pretext; when she had got him aside, whispering:-

"You shouldn't have monopolized Professor Caldwell that way. There may be others who want to talk with him."

"My mistake," Martin admitted contritely. "But I'd got him stirred up, and he was so interesting that I did not think. Do you know, he is the brightest, the most intellectual, man I have ever talked with. And I'll tell you something else. I once thought that everybody who went to universities, or who sat in the high places in society, was just as brilliant and intelligent as he."

"He's an exception," she answered.

"I should say so. Whom do you want me to talk to now?—Oh, say, bring me up against that cashier-fellow."

Martin talked for fifteen minutes with him, nor could Ruth have wished better behavior on her lover's part. Not once did his eyes flash nor his cheeks flush, while the calmness and poise with which he talked surprised her. But in Martin's estimation the whole tribe of bank cashiers fell a few hundred per cent, and for the rest of the evening he labored under the impression that bank cashiers and talkers of platitudes were synonymous phrases. The army officer he found good-natured and simple, a healthy, wholesome young fellow, content to occupy the place in life into which birth and luck had flung him. On learning that he had completed two years in the university, Martin was puzzled to know where he had stored it away. Nevertheless Martin liked him better than the platitudinous bank cashier.

"I really don't object to platitudes," he told Ruth later; "but what worries me into nervousness is the pompous, smugly complacent, superior certitude with which they are uttered and the time taken to do it. Why, I could give that man the whole history of the Reformation in the time he took to tell me that the Union-Labor Party had fused with the Democrats. Do you know, he skins his words as a professional poker-player skins the cards that are dealt out to him. Some day I'll show you what I mean."

"I'm sorry you don't like him," was her reply. "He's a favorite of Mr. Butler's. Mr. Butler says he is safe and honest—calls him the Rock, Peter, and says that upon him any banking institution can well be built."

"I don't doubt it—from the little I saw of him and the less I heard from him; but I don't think so much of banks as I did. You don't mind my speaking my mind this way, dear?"

"No, no; it is most interesting."

"Yes," Martin went on heartily, "I'm no more than a barbarian getting my first impressions of civilization. Such impressions must be entertainingly novel to the civilized person."

"What did you think of my cousins?" Ruth queried.

"I liked them better than the other women. There's plenty of fun in them along with paucity of pretence."

"Then you did like the other women?"

He shook his head.

"That social-settlement woman is no more than a sociological poll-parrot. I swear, if you winnowed her out between the stars, like Tomlinson, there would be found in her not one original thought. As for the portrait-painter, she was a positive bore. She'd make a good wife for the cashier. And the musician woman! I don't care how nimble her fingers are, how perfect her technique, how wonderful her expression—the fact is, she knows nothing about music."

"She plays beautifully," Ruth protested.

"Yes, she's undoubtedly gymnastic in the externals of music, but the intrinsic spirit of music is unguessed by her. I asked her what music meant to her—you know I'm always curious to know that particular thing; and she did not know what it meant to her, except that she adored it, that it was the greatest of the arts, and that it meant more than life to her."

"You were making them talk shop," Ruth charged him.

"I confess it. And if they were failures on shop, imagine my sufferings if they had discoursed on other subjects. Why, I used to think that up here, where all the advantages of culture were enjoyed—" He paused for a moment, and watched the youthful shade of himself, in stiff-rim and square-cut, enter the door and swagger across the room. "As I was saying, up here I thought all men and women were brilliant and radiant. But now, from what little I've seen of them, they strike me as a pack of ninnies, most of them, and ninety percent of the remainder as bores. Now there's Professor Caldwell—he's different. He's a man, every inch of him and every atom of his gray matter."

Ruth's face brightened.

"Tell me about him," she urged. "Not what is large and brilliant—I know those qualities; but whatever you feel is adverse. I am most curious to know."

"Perhaps I'll get myself in a pickle." Martin debated humorously for a moment. "Suppose you tell me first. Or maybe you find in him nothing less than the best."

"I attended two lecture courses under him, and I have known him for two years; that is why I am anxious for your first impression."

"Bad impression, you mean? Well, here goes. He is all the fine things you think about him, I guess. At least, he is the finest specimen of intellectual man I have met; but he is a man with a secret shame."

"Oh, no, no!" he hastened to cry. "Nothing paltry nor vulgar. What I mean is that he strikes me as a man who has gone to the bottom of things, and is so afraid of what he saw that he makes believe to himself that he never saw it. Perhaps that's not the clearest way to express it. Here's another way. A man who has found the path to the hidden temple but has not followed it; who has, perhaps, caught glimpses of the temple and striven afterward to convince himself that it was only a mirage of foliage. Yet another way. A man who could have done things but who placed no value on the doing, and who, all the time, in his innermost heart, is regretting that he has not done them; who has secretly laughed at the rewards for doing, and yet, still more secretly, has yearned for the rewards and for the joy of doing."

"I don't read him that way," she said. "And for that matter, I don't see just what you mean."

"It is only a vague feeling on my part," Martin temporized. "I have no reason for it. It is only a feeling, and most likely it is wrong. You certainly should know him better than I."

From the evening at Ruth's Martin brought away with him strange confusions and conflicting feelings. He was disappointed in his goal, in the persons he had climbed to be with. On the other hand, he was encouraged with his success. The climb had been easier than he expected. He was superior to the climb, and (he did not, with false modesty, hide it from himself) he was superior to the beings among whom he had climbed—with the exception, of course, of Professor Caldwell. About life and the books he knew more than they, and he wondered into what nooks and crannies they had cast aside their educations. He did not know that he was himself possessed of unusual brain vigor; nor did he know that the persons who were given to probing the depths and to thinking ultimate thoughts were not to be found in the drawing rooms of the world's Morses; nor did he dream that such persons were as lonely eagles sailing solitary in the azure sky far above the earth and its swarming freight of gregarious life.

CHAPTER XXVIII

But success had lost Martin's address, and her messengers no longer came to his door. For twenty-five days, working Sundays and holidays, he toiled on "The Shame of the Sun," a long essay of some thirty thousand words. It was a deliberate attack on the mysticism of the Maeterlinck school—an attack from the citadel of positive science upon the wonder-dreamers, but an attack nevertheless that retained much of beauty and wonder of the sort compatible with ascertained fact. It was a little later that he followed up the attack with two short essays, "The Wonder-Dreamers" and "The Yardstick of the Ego." And on essays, long and short, he began to pay the travelling expenses from magazine to magazine.

During the twenty-five days spent on "The Shame of the Sun," he sold hack-work to the extent of six dollars and fifty cents. A joke had brought in fifty cents, and a second one, sold to a high-grade comic weekly, had fetched a dollar. Then two humorous poems had earned two dollars and three dollars respectively. As a result, having exhausted his credit with the tradesmen (though he had increased his credit with the grocer to five dollars), his wheel and suit of clothes went back to the pawnbroker. The type-writer people were again clamoring for money, insistently pointing out that according to the agreement rent was to be paid strictly in advance.

Encouraged by his several small sales, Martin went back to hack-work. Perhaps there was a living in it, after all. Stored away under his table were the twenty storiettes which had been rejected by the newspaper short-story syndicate. He read them over in order to find out how not to write newspaper storiettes, and so doing, reasoned out the perfect formula. He found that the newspaper storiette should never be tragic, should never end unhappily, and should never contain beauty of language, subtlety of thought, nor real delicacy of sentiment. Sentiment it must contain, plenty of it, pure and noble, of the sort that in his own early youth had brought his applause from "nigger heaven"—the "For-God-my-country-and-the-Czar" and "I-may-be-poor-but-I-am-honest" brand of sentiment.

Having learned such precautions, Martin consulted "The Duchess" for tone, and proceeded to mix according to formula. The formula consists of three parts: (1) a pair of lovers are jarred apart; (2) by some deed or event they are reunited; (3) marriage bells. The third part was an unvarying quantity, but the first and second parts could be varied an infinite number of times. Thus, the pair of lovers could be jarred apart by misunderstood motives, by accident of fate, by jealous rivals, by irate parents, by crafty guardians, by scheming relatives, and so forth and so forth; they could be reunited by a brave deed of the man lover, by a similar deed of the woman lover, by change of heart in one lover or the other, by forced confession of crafty guardian, scheming relative, or jealous rival, by voluntary confession of same, by discovery of some unguessed secret, by lover storming girl's heart, by lover making long and noble self-sacrifice, and so on, endlessly. It was very fetching to make the girl propose in the course of being reunited, and Martin discovered, bit by bit, other decidedly piquant and fetching ruses. But marriage bells at the end was the one thing he could take no liberties with; though the heavens rolled up as a scroll and the stars fell, the wedding bells must go on ringing just the same. In quantity, the formula prescribed twelve hundred words minimum dose, fifteen hundred words maximum dose.

Before he got very far along in the art of the storiette, Martin worked out half a dozen stock forms, which he always consulted when constructing storiettes. These forms were like the cunning tables used by mathematicians, which may be entered from top, bottom, right, and left, which entrances consist of scores of lines and dozens of columns, and from which may be drawn, without reasoning or thinking, thousands of different conclusions, all unchallengably precise and true. Thus, in the course of half an hour with his forms, Martin could frame up a dozen or so storiettes, which he put aside and filled in at his convenience. He found that he could fill one in, after a day of serious work, in the hour before going to bed. As he later confessed to Ruth, he could almost do it in his sleep. The real work was in constructing the frames, and that was merely mechanical.

He had no doubt whatever of the efficacy of his formula, and for once he knew the editorial mind when he said positively to himself that the first two he sent off would bring checks. And checks they brought, for four dollars each, at the end of twelve days.

In the meantime he was making fresh and alarming discoveries concerning the magazines. Though the *Transcontinental* had published "The Ring of Bells," no check was forthcoming. Martin needed it, and he wrote for it. An evasive answer and a request for more of his work was all he received. He had gone hungry two days waiting for the reply, and it was then that he put his wheel back in pawn. He wrote regularly, twice a week, to the *Transcontinental* for his five dollars, though it was only semi-occasionally that he elicited a reply. He did not know that the *Transcontinental* had been staggering along precariously for years, that it was a fourth-rater, or tenth-rater, without standing, with a crazy circulation that partly rested on petty bullying and partly on patriotic appealing, and with advertisements that were scarcely more than charitable donations. Nor did he know that the *Transcontinental* was the sole livelihood of the editor and the business manager, and that they could wring their livelihood out of it only by moving to escape paying rent and by never paying any bill they could evade. Nor could he have guessed that the particular five dollars that belonged to him had been appropriated by the business manager for the painting of his house in Alameda, which painting he performed himself, on week-day afternoons, because he could not afford to pay union wages and because the first scab he had employed had had a ladder jerked out from under him and been sent to the hospital with a broken collar-bone.

The ten dollars for which Martin had sold "Treasure Hunters" to the Chicago newspaper did not come to hand. The article had been published, as he had ascertained at the file in the Central Reading-room, but no word could he get from the editor. His letters were ignored. To satisfy himself that they had been received, he registered several of them. It was nothing less than robbery, he concluded—a cold-blooded steal; while he starved, he was pilfered of his merchandise, of his goods, the sale of which was the sole way of getting bread to eat.

Youth and Age was a weekly, and it had published two-thirds of his twenty-one-thousand-word serial when it went out of business. With it went all hopes of getting his sixteen dollars.

To cap the situation, "The Pot," which he looked upon as one of the best things he had written, was lost to him. In despair, casting about frantically among the magazines, he had sent it to *The Billow*, a society weekly in San Francisco. His chief reason for submitting it to that publication was that, having only to travel across the bay from Oakland, a quick decision could be reached. Two weeks later he was overjoyed to see, in the latest number on the news-stand, his story printed in full, illustrated, and in the place of honor. He went home with leaping pulse, wondering how much they would pay him for one of the best things he had done. Also, the celerity with which it had been accepted and published was a pleasant thought to him. That the editor had not informed him of the acceptance made the surprise more complete. After waiting a week, two weeks, and half a week longer, desperation conquered diffidence, and he wrote to the editor of *The Billow*, suggesting that possibly through some negligence of the business manager his little account had been overlooked.

Even if it isn't more than five dollars, Martin thought to himself, it will buy enough beans and pea-soup to enable me to write half a dozen like it, and possibly as good.

Back came a cool letter from the editor that at least elicited Martin's admiration.

"We thank you," it ran, "for your excellent contribution. All of us in the office enjoyed it immensely, and, as you see, it was given the place of honor and immediate publication. We earnestly hope that you liked the illustrations.

"On rereading your letter it seems to us that you are laboring under the misapprehension that we pay for unsolicited manuscripts. This is not our custom, and of course yours was unsolicited. We assumed, naturally, when we received your story, that you understood the situation. We can only deeply regret this unfortunate misunderstanding, and assure you of our unfailing regard. Again, thanking you for your kind contribution, and hoping to receive more from you in the near future, we remain, etc."

There was also a postscript to the effect that though *The Billow* carried no free-list, it took great pleasure in sending him a complimentary subscription for the ensuing year.

After that experience, Martin typed at the top of the first sheet of all his manuscripts: "Submitted at your usual rate."

Some day, he consoled himself, they will be submitted at *my* usual rate.

He discovered in himself, at this period, a passion for perfection, under the sway of which he rewrote and polished "The Jostling Street," "The Wine of Life," "Joy," the "Sea Lyrics," and others of his earlier work. As of old, nineteen hours of labor a day was all too little to suit him. He wrote prodigiously, and he read prodigiously, forgetting in his toil the pangs caused by giving up his tobacco. Ruth's promised cure for the habit, flamboyantly labelled, he stowed away in the most inaccessible corner of his bureau. Especially during his stretches of famine he suffered from lack of the weed; but no matter how often he mastered the craving, it remained with him as strong as ever. He regarded it as the biggest thing he had ever achieved. Ruth's point of view was that he was doing no more than was right. She brought him the anti-tobacco remedy, purchased out of her glove money, and in a few days forgot all about it.

His machine-made storiettes, though he hated them and derided them, were successful. By means of them he redeemed all his pledges, paid most of his bills, and bought a new set of tires for his wheel. The storiettes at least kept the pot a-boiling and gave him time for ambitious work; while the one thing that upheld him was the forty dollars he had received from *The White Mouse*. He anchored his faith to that, and was confident that the really first-class magazines would pay an unknown writer at least an equal rate, if not a better one. But the thing was, how to get into the first-class magazines. His best stories, essays, and poems went begging among them, and yet, each month, he read reams of dull, prosy, inartistic stuff between all their various covers. If only one editor, he sometimes thought, would descend from his high seat of pride to write me one cheering line! No matter if my work is unusual, no matter if it is unfit, for prudential reasons, for their pages, surely there must be some sparks in it, somewhere, a few, to warm them to some sort of appreciation. And thereupon he would get out one or another of his manuscripts, such as "Adventure," and read it over and over in a vain attempt to vindicate the editorial silence.

As the sweet California spring came on, his period of plenty came to an end. For several weeks he had been worried by a strange silence on the part of the newspaper storiette syndicate. Then, one day, came back to him through the mail ten of his immaculate machine-made storiettes. They were accompanied by a brief letter to the effect that the syndicate was overstocked, and that some months would elapse before it would be in the market again for manuscripts. Martin had even been extravagant on the strength of those ten storiettes. Toward the last the syndicate had been paying him five dollars each for them and accepting every one he sent. So he had looked upon the ten as good as sold, and he had lived accordingly, on a basis of fifty dollars in the bank. So it was that he entered abruptly upon a lean period, wherein he continued selling his earlier efforts to publications that would not pay and submitting his later work to magazines that would not buy. Also, he resumed his trips to the pawn-broker down in Oakland. A few jokes and snatches of humorous verse, sold to the New York weeklies, made existence barely possible for him. It was at this time that he wrote letters of inquiry to the several great monthly and quarterly reviews, and learned in reply that they rarely considered unsolicited articles, and that most of their contents were written upon order by well-known specialists who were authorities in their various fields.

CHAPTER XXIX

It was a hard summer for Martin. Manuscript readers and editors were away on vacation, and publications that ordinarily returned a decision in three weeks now retained his manuscript for three months or more. The consolation he drew from it was that a saving in postage was effected by the deadlock. Only the robber-publications seemed to remain actively in business, and to them Martin disposed of all his early efforts, such as "Pearl-diving," "The Sea as a Career," "Turtle-catching," and "The Northeast Trades." For these manuscripts he never received a penny. It is true, after six months' correspondence, he effected a compromise, whereby he received a safety razor for "Turtle-catching," and that *The Acropolis*, having agreed to give him five dollars cash and five yearly subscriptions: for "The Northeast Trades," fulfilled the second part of the agreement.

For a sonnet on Stevenson he managed to wring two dollars out of a Boston editor who was running a magazine with a Matthew Arnold taste and a penny-dreadful purse. "The Peri and the Pearl," a clever skit of a poem of two hundred lines, just finished, white hot from his brain, won the heart of the editor of a San Francisco magazine published in the interest of a great railroad. When the editor wrote, offering him payment in transportation, Martin wrote back to inquire if the transportation was transferable. It was not, and so, being prevented from peddling it, he asked for the return of the poem. Back it came, with the editor's regrets, and Martin sent it to San Francisco again, this time to *The Hornet*, a pretentious monthly that had been fanned into a constellation of the first magnitude by the brilliant journalist who founded it. But *The Hornet's* light had begun to dim long before Martin was born. The editor promised Martin fifteen dollars for the poem, but, when it was published, seemed to forget about it. Several of his letters being ignored, Martin indicted an angry one which drew a reply. It was written by a new editor, who coolly informed Martin that he declined to be held responsible for the old editor's mistakes, and that he did not think much of "The Peri and the Pearl" anyway.

But *The Globe*, a Chicago magazine, gave Martin the most cruel treatment of all. He had refrained from offering his "Sea Lyrics" for publication, until driven to it by starvation. After having been rejected by a dozen magazines, they had come to rest in *The Globe* office. There were thirty poems in the collection, and he was to receive a dollar apiece for them. The first month four were published, and he promptly received a check for four dollars; but when he looked over the magazine, he was appalled at the slaughter. In some cases the titles had been altered: "Finis," for instance, being changed to "The Finish," and "The Song of the Outer Reef" to "The Song of the Coral Reef." In one case, an absolutely different title, a misappropriate title, was substituted. In place of his own, "Medusa Lights," the editor had printed, "The Backward Track." But the slaughter in the body of the poems was terrifying. Martin groaned and sweated and thrust his hands through his hair. Phrases, lines, and stanzas were cut out, interchanged, or juggled about in the most incomprehensible manner. Sometimes lines and stanzas not his own were substituted for his. He could not believe that a sane editor could be guilty of such maltreatment, and his favorite hypothesis was that his poems must have been doctored by the office boy or the stenographer. Martin wrote immediately, begging the editor to cease publishing the lyrics and to return them to him.

He wrote again and again, begging, entreating, threatening, but his letters were ignored. Month by month the slaughter went on till the thirty poems were published, and month by month he received a check for those which had appeared in the current number.

Despite these various misadventures, the memory of the *White Mouse* forty-dollar check sustained him, though he was driven more and more to hack-work. He discovered a bread-and-butter field in the agricultural weeklies and trade journals, though among the religious weeklies he found he could easily starve. At his lowest ebb, when his black suit was in pawn, he made a ten-strike—or so it seemed to him—in a prize contest arranged by the County Committee of the Republican Party. There were three branches of the contest, and he entered them all, laughing at himself bitterly the while in that he was driven to such straits to live. His poem won the first prize of ten dollars, his campaign song the second prize of five dollars, his essay on the principles of the Republican Party the first prize of twenty-five dollars. Which was very gratifying to him until he tried to collect. Something had gone wrong in the County Committee, and, though a rich banker and a state senator were members of it, the money was not forthcoming. While this affair was hanging fire, he proved that he understood the principles of the Democratic Party by winning the first prize for his essay in a similar contest. And, moreover, he received the money, twenty-five dollars. But the forty dollars won in the first contest he never received.

Driven to shifts in order to see Ruth, and deciding that the long walk from north Oakland to her house and back again consumed too much time, he kept his black suit in pawn in place of his bicycle. The latter gave him exercise, saved him hours of time for work, and enabled him to see Ruth just the same. A pair of knee duck trousers and an old sweater made him a presentable wheel costume, so that he could go with Ruth on afternoon rides. Besides, he no longer had opportunity to see much of her in her own home, where Mrs. Morse was thoroughly prosecuting her campaign of entertainment. The exalted beings he met there, and to whom he had looked up but a short time before, now bored him. They were no longer exalted. He was nervous and irritable, what of his hard times, disappointments, and close application to work, and the conversation of such people was maddening. He was not unduly egotistic. He measured the narrowness of their minds by the minds of the thinkers in the books he read. At Ruth's home he never met a large mind, with the exception of Professor Caldwell, and Caldwell he had met there only once. As for the rest, they were numskulls, ninnies, superficial, dogmatic, and ignorant. It was their ignorance that astounded him. What was the matter with them? What had they done with their educations? They had had access to the same books he had. How did it happen that they had drawn nothing from them?

He knew that the great minds, the deep and rational thinkers, existed. He had his proofs from the books, the books that had educated him beyond the Morse standard. And he knew that higher intellects than those of the Morse circle were to be found in the world. He read English society novels, wherein he caught glimpses of men and women talking politics and philosophy. And he read of salons in great cities, even in the United States, where art and intellect congregated. Foolishly, in the past, he had conceived that all well-groomed persons above the working class were persons with power of intellect and vigor of beauty. Culture and collars had gone together, to him, and he had been deceived into believing that college educations and mastery were the same things.

Well, he would fight his way on and up higher. And he would take Ruth with him. Her he dearly loved, and he was confident that she would shine anywhere. As it was clear to him that he had been handicapped by his early environment, so now he perceived that she was similarly handicapped. She had not had a chance to expand. The books on her father's shelves, the paintings on the walls, the music on the piano—all was just so much meretricious display. To real literature, real painting, real music, the Morses and their kind, were dead. And bigger than such things was life, of which they were densely, hopelessly ignorant. In spite of their Unitarian proclivities and their masks of conservative broadmindedness, they were two generations behind interpretative science: their mental processes were mediaeval, while their thinking on the ultimate data of existence and of the universe struck him as the same metaphysical method that was as young as the youngest race, as old as the cave-man, and older—the same that moved the first Pleistocene ape-man to fear the dark; that moved the first hasty Hebrew savage to incarnate Eve from Adam's rib; that moved Descartes to build an idealistic system of the universe out of the projections of his own puny ego; and that moved the famous British ecclesiastic to denounce evolution in satire so scathing as to win immediate applause and leave his name a notorious scrawl on the page of history.

So Martin thought, and he thought further, till it dawned upon him that the difference between these lawyers, officers, business men, and bank cashiers he had met and the members of the working class he had known was on a par with the difference in the food they ate, clothes they wore, neighborhoods in which they lived. Certainly, in all of them was lacking the something more which he found in himself and in the books. The Morses had shown him the best their social position could produce, and he was not impressed by it. A pauper himself, a slave to the money-lender, he knew himself the superior of those he met at the Morses'; and, when his one decent suit of clothes was out of pawn, he moved among them a lord of life, quivering with a sense of outrage akin to what a prince would suffer if condemned to live with goat-herds.

"You hate and fear the socialists," he remarked to Mr. Morse, one evening at dinner; "but why? You know neither them nor their doctrines."

The conversation had been swung in that direction by Mrs. Morse, who had been invidiously singing the praises of Mr. Hapgood. The cashier was Martin's black beast, and his temper was a trifle short where the talker of platitudes was concerned.

"Yes," he had said, "Charley Hapgood is what they call a rising young man—somebody told me as much. And it is true. He'll make the Governor's Chair before he dies, and, who knows? maybe the United States Senate."

"What makes you think so?" Mrs. Morse had inquired.

"I've heard him make a campaign speech. It was so cleverly stupid and unoriginal, and also so convincing, that the leaders cannot help but regard him as safe and sure, while his platitudes are so much like the platitudes of the average voter that—oh, well, you know you flatter any man by dressing up his own thoughts for him and presenting them to him."

"I actually think you are jealous of Mr. Hapgood," Ruth had chimed in.

"Heaven forbid!"

The look of horror on Martin's face stirred Mrs. Morse to belligerence.

"You surely don't mean to say that Mr. Hapgood is stupid?" she demanded icily.

"No more than the average Republican," was the retort, "or average Democrat, either. They are all stupid when they are not crafty, and very few of them are crafty. The only wise Republicans are the millionnaires and their conscious henchmen. They know which side their bread is buttered on, and they know why."

"I am a Republican," Mr. Morse put in lightly. "Pray, how do you classify me?"

"Oh, you are an unconscious henchman."

"Henchman?"

"Why, yes. You do corporation work. You have no working-class nor criminal practice. You don't depend upon wife-beaters and pickpockets for your income. You get your livelihood from the masters of society, and whoever feeds a man is that man's master. Yes, you are a henchman. You are interested in advancing the interests of the aggregations of capital you serve."

Mr. Morse's face was a trifle red.

"I confess, sir," he said, "that you talk like a scoundrelly socialist."

Then it was that Martin made his remark:

"You hate and fear the socialists; but why? You know neither them nor their doctrines."

"Your doctrine certainly sounds like socialism," Mr. Morse replied, while Ruth gazed anxiously from one to the other, and Mrs. Morse beamed happily at the opportunity afforded of rousing her liege lord's antagonism.

"Because I say Republicans are stupid, and hold that liberty, equality, and fraternity are exploded bubbles, does not make me a socialist," Martin said with a smile. "Because I question Jefferson and the unscientific Frenchmen who informed his mind, does not make me a socialist. Believe me, Mr. Morse, you are far nearer socialism than I who am its avowed enemy."

"Now you please to be facetious," was all the other could say.

"Not at all. I speak in all seriousness. You still believe in equality, and yet you do the work of the corporations, and the corporations, from day to day, are busily engaged in burying equality. And you call me a socialist because I deny equality, because I affirm just what you live up to. The Republicans are foes to equality, though most of them fight the battle against equality with the very word itself the slogan on their lips. In the name of equality they destroy equality. That was why I called them stupid. As for myself, I am an individualist. I believe the race is to the swift, the battle to the strong. Such is the lesson I have learned from biology, or at least think I have learned. As I said, I am an individualist, and individualism is the hereditary and eternal foe of socialism."

"But you frequent socialist meetings," Mr. Morse challenged.

"Certainly, just as spies frequent hostile camps. How else are you to learn about the enemy? Besides, I enjoy myself at their meetings. They are good fighters, and, right or wrong, they have read the books. Any one of them knows far more about sociology and all the other ologies than the average captain of industry. Yes, I have been to half a dozen of their meetings, but that doesn't make me a socialist any more than hearing Charley Hapgood orate made me a Republican."

"I can't help it," Mr. Morse said feebly, "but I still believe you incline that way."

Bless me, Martin thought to himself, he doesn't know what I was talking about. He hasn't understood a word of it. What did he do with his education, anyway?

Thus, in his development, Martin found himself face to face with economic morality, or the morality of class; and soon it became to him a grisly monster. Personally, he was an intellectual moralist, and more offending to him than platitudinous pomposity was the morality of those about him, which was a curious hotchpotch of the economic, the metaphysical, the sentimental, and the imitative.

A sample of this curious messy mixture he encountered nearer home. His sister Marian had been keeping company with an industrious young mechanic, of German extraction, who, after thoroughly learning the trade, had set up for himself in a bicycle-repair shop. Also, having got the agency for a low-grade make of wheel, he was prosperous. Marian had called on Martin in his room a short time before to announce her engagement, during which visit she had playfully inspected Martin's palm and told his fortune. On her next visit she brought Hermann von Schmidt along with her. Martin did the honors and congratulated both of them in language so easy and graceful as to affect disagreeably the peasant-mind of his sister's lover. This bad impression was further heightened by Martin's reading aloud the half-dozen stanzas of verse with which he had commemorated Marian's previous visit. It was a bit of society verse, airy and delicate, which he had named "The Palmist." He was surprised, when he finished reading it, to note no enjoyment in his sister's face. Instead, her eyes were fixed anxiously upon her betrothed, and Martin, following her gaze, saw spread on that worthy's asymmetrical features nothing but black and sullen disapproval. The incident passed over, they made an early departure, and Martin forgot all about it, though for the moment he had been puzzled that any woman, even of the working class, should not have been flattered and delighted by having poetry written about her.

Several evenings later Marian again visited him, this time alone. Nor did she waste time in coming to the point, upbraiding him sorrowfully for what he had done.

"Why, Marian," he chided, "you talk as though you were ashamed of your relatives, or of your brother at any rate."

"And I am, too," she blurted out.

Martin was bewildered by the tears of mortification he saw in her eyes. The mood, whatever it was, was genuine.

"But, Marian, why should your Hermann be jealous of my writing poetry about my own sister?"

"He ain't jealous," she sobbed. "He says it was indecent, ob—obscene."

Martin emitted a long, low whistle of incredulity, then proceeded to resurrect and read a carbon copy of "The Palmist."

"I can't see it," he said finally, proffering the manuscript to her. "Read it yourself and show me whatever strikes you as obscene—that was the word, wasn't it?"

"He says so, and he ought to know," was the answer, with a wave aside of the manuscript, accompanied by a look of loathing. "And he says you've got to tear it up. He says he won't have no wife of his with such things written about her which anybody can read. He says it's a disgrace, an' he won't stand for it."

"Now, look here, Marian, this is nothing but nonsense," Martin began; then abruptly changed his mind.

He saw before him an unhappy girl, knew the futility of attempting to convince her husband or her, and, though the whole situation was absurd and preposterous, he resolved to surrender.

"All right," he announced, tearing the manuscript into half a dozen pieces and throwing it into the waste-basket.

He contented himself with the knowledge that even then the original type-written manuscript was reposing in the office of a New York magazine. Marian and her husband would never know, and neither himself nor they nor the world would lose if the pretty, harmless poem ever were published.

Marian, starting to reach into the waste-basket, refrained.

"Can I?" she pleaded.

He nodded his head, regarding her thoughtfully as she gathered the torn pieces of manuscript and tucked them into the pocket of her jacket—ocular evidence of the success of her mission. She reminded him of Lizzie Connolly, though there was less of fire and gorgeous flaunting life in her than in that other girl of the working class whom he had seen twice. But they were on a par, the pair of them, in dress and carriage, and he smiled with inward amusement at the caprice of his fancy which suggested the appearance of either of them in Mrs. Morse's drawing-room. The amusement faded, and he was aware of a great loneliness. This sister of his and the Morse drawing-room were milestones of the road he had travelled. And he had left them behind. He glanced affectionately about him at his few books. They were all the comrades left to him.

"Hello, what's that?" he demanded in startled surprise.

Marian repeated her question.

"Why don't I go to work?" He broke into a laugh that was only half-hearted. "That Hermann of yours has been talking to you."

She shook her head.

"Don't lie," he commanded, and the nod of her head affirmed his charge.

"Well, you tell that Hermann of yours to mind his own business; that when I write poetry about the girl he's keeping company with it's his business, but that outside of that he's got no say so. Understand?

"So you don't think I'll succeed as a writer, eh?" he went on. "You think I'm no good?—that I've fallen down and am a disgrace to the family?"

"I think it would be much better if you got a job," she said firmly, and he saw she was sincere. "Hermann says—"

"Damn Hermann!" he broke out good-naturedly. "What I want to know is when you're going to get married. Also, you find out from your Hermann if he will deign to permit you to accept a wedding present from me."

He mused over the incident after she had gone, and once or twice broke out into laughter that was bitter as he saw his sister and her betrothed, all the members of his own class and the members of Ruth's class, directing their narrow little lives by narrow little formulas—herd-creatures, flocking together and patterning their lives by one another's opinions, failing of being individuals and of really living life because of the childlike formulas by which they were enslaved. He summoned them before him in apparitional procession: Bernard Higginbotham arm in arm with Mr. Butler, Hermann von Schmidt cheek by jowl with Charley Hapgood, and one by one and in pairs he judged them and dismissed them—judged them by the standards of intellect and morality he had learned from the books. Vainly he asked: Where are the great souls, the great men and women? He found them not among the careless, gross, and stupid intelligences that answered the call of vision to his narrow room. He felt a loathing for them such as Circe must have felt for her swine. When he had dismissed the last one and thought himself alone, a late-comer entered, unexpected and unsummoned. Martin watched him and saw the stiff-rim, the square-cut, double-breasted coat and the swaggering shoulders, of the youthful hoodlum who had once been he.

"You were like all the rest, young fellow," Martin sneered. "Your morality and your knowledge were just the same as theirs. You did not think and act for yourself. Your opinions, like your clothes, were ready made; your acts were shaped by popular approval. You were cock of your gang because others acclaimed you the real thing. You fought and ruled the gang, not because you liked to,—you know you really despised it,—but because the other fellows patted you on the shoulder. You licked Cheese-Face because you wouldn't give in, and you wouldn't give in partly because you were an abysmal brute and for the rest because you believed what every one about you believed, that the measure of manhood was the carnivorous ferocity displayed in injuring and marring fellow-creatures' anatomies. Why, you whelp, you even won other fellows' girls away from them, not because you wanted the girls, but because in the marrow of those about you, those who set your moral pace, was the instinct of the wild stallion and the bull-seal. Well, the years have passed, and what do you think about it now?"

As if in reply, the vision underwent a swift metamorphosis. The stiff-rim and the square-cut vanished, being replaced by milder garments; the toughness went out of the face, the hardness out of the eyes; and, the face, chastened and refined, was irradiated from an inner life of communion with beauty and knowledge. The apparition was very like his present self, and, as he regarded it, he noted the student-lamp by which it was illuminated, and the book over which it pored. He glanced at the title and read, "The Science of Æsthetics." Next, he entered into the apparition, trimmed the student-lamp, and himself went on reading "The Science of Æsthetics."

CHAPTER XXX

On a beautiful fall day, a day of similar Indian summer to that which had seen their love declared the year before, Martin read his "Love-cycle" to Ruth. It was in the afternoon, and, as before, they had ridden out to their favorite knoll in the hills. Now and again she had interrupted his reading with exclamations of pleasure, and now, as he laid the last sheet of manuscript with its fellows, he waited her judgment.

She delayed to speak, and at last she spoke haltingly, hesitating to frame in words the harshness of her thought.

"I think they are beautiful, very beautiful," she said; "but you can't sell them, can you? You see what I mean," she said, almost pleaded. "This writing of yours is not practical. Something is the matter—maybe it is with the market—that prevents you from earning a living by it. And please, dear, don't misunderstand me. I am flattered, and made proud, and all that—I could not be a true woman were it otherwise—that you should write these poems to me. But they do not make our marriage possible. Don't you see, Martin? Don't think me mercenary. It is love, the thought of our future, with which I am burdened. A whole year has gone by since we learned we loved each other, and our wedding day is no nearer. Don't think me immodest in thus talking about our wedding, for really I have my heart, all that I am, at stake. Why don't you try to get work on a newspaper, if you are so bound up in your writing? Why not become a reporter?—for a while, at least?"

"It would spoil my style," was his answer, in a low, monotonous voice. "You have no idea how I've worked for style."

"But those storiettes," she argued. "You called them hack-work. You wrote many of them. Didn't they spoil your style?"

"No, the cases are different. The storiettes were ground out, jaded, at the end of a long day of application to style. But a reporter's work is all hack from morning till night, is the one paramount thing of life. And it is a whirlwind life, the life of the moment, with neither past nor future, and certainly without thought of any style but reportorial style, and that certainly is not literature. To become a reporter now, just as my style is taking form, crystallizing, would be to commit literary suicide. As it is, every storiette, every word of every storiette, was a violation of myself, of my self-respect, of my respect for beauty. I tell you it was sickening. I was guilty of sin. And I was secretly glad when the markets failed, even if my clothes did go into pawn. But the joy of writing the 'Love-cycle'! The creative joy in its noblest form! That was compensation for everything."

Martin did not know that Ruth was unsympathetic concerning the creative joy. She used the phrase—it was on her lips he had first heard it. She had read about it, studied about it, in the university in the course of earning her Bachelorship of Arts; but she was not original, not creative, and all manifestations of culture on her part were but harpings of the harpings of others.

"May not the editor have been right in his revision of your 'Sea Lyrics'?" she questioned. "Remember, an editor must have proved qualifications or else he would not be an editor."

"That's in line with the persistence of the established," he rejoined, his heat against the editor-folk getting the better of him. "What is, is not only right, but is the best possible. The existence of anything is sufficient vindication of its fitness to exist—to exist, mark you, as the average person unconsciously believes, not merely in present conditions, but in all conditions. It is their ignorance, of course, that makes them believe such rot—their ignorance, which is nothing more nor less than the henidical mental process described by Weininger. They think they think, and such thinkless creatures are the arbiters of the lives of the few who really think."

He paused, overcome by the consciousness that he had been talking over Ruth's head.

"I'm sure I don't know who this Weininger is," she retorted. "And you are so dreadfully general that I fail to follow you. What I was speaking of was the qualification of editors—"

"And I'll tell you," he interrupted. "The chief qualification of ninety-nine per cent of all editors is failure. They have failed as writers. Don't think they prefer the drudgery of the desk and the slavery to their circulation and to the business manager to the joy of writing. They have tried to write, and they have failed. And right there is the cursed paradox of it. Every portal to success in literature is guarded by those watch-dogs, the failures in literature. The editors, sub-editors, associate editors, most of them, and the manuscript-readers for the magazines and book-publishers, most of them, nearly all of them, are men who wanted to write and who have failed. And yet they, of all creatures under the sun the most unfit, are the very creatures who decide what shall and what shall not find its way into print—they, who have proved themselves not original, who have demonstrated that they lack the divine fire, sit in judgment upon originality and genius. And after them come the reviewers, just so many more failures. Don't tell me that they have not dreamed the dream and attempted to write poetry or fiction; for they have, and they have failed. Why, the average review is more nauseating than cod-liver oil. But you know my opinion on the reviewers and the alleged critics. There are great critics, but they are as rare as comets. If I fail as a writer, I shall have proved for the career of editorship. There's bread and butter and jam, at any rate."

Ruth's mind was quick, and her disapproval of her lover's views was buttressed by the contradiction she found in his contention.

"But, Martin, if that be so, if all the doors are closed as you have shown so conclusively, how is it possible that any of the great writers ever arrived?"

"They arrived by achieving the impossible," he answered. "They did such blazing, glorious work as to burn to ashes those that opposed them. They arrived by course of miracle, by winning a thousand-to-one wager against them. They arrived because they were Carlyle's battle-scarred giants who will not be kept down. And that is what I must do; I must achieve the impossible."

"But if you fail? You must consider me as well, Martin."

"If I fail?" He regarded her for a moment as though the thought she had uttered was unthinkable. Then intelligence illumined his eyes. "If I fail, I shall become an editor, and you will be an editor's wife."

She frowned at his facetiousness—a pretty, adorable frown that made him put his arm around her and kiss it away.

"There, that's enough," she urged, by an effort of will withdrawing herself from the fascination of his strength. "I have talked with father and mother. I never before asserted myself so against them. I demanded to be heard. I was very undutiful. They are against you, you know; but I assured them over and over of my abiding love for you, and at last father agreed that if you wanted to, you could begin right away in his office. And then, of his own accord, he said he would pay you enough at the start so that we could get married and have a little cottage somewhere. Which I think was very fine of him—don't you?"

Martin, with the dull pain of despair at his heart, mechanically reaching for the tobacco and paper (which he no longer carried) to roll a cigarette, muttered something inarticulate, and Ruth went on.

"Frankly, though, and don't let it hurt you—I tell you, to show you precisely how you stand with him—he doesn't like your radical views, and he thinks you are lazy. Of course I know you are not. I know you work hard."

How hard, even she did not know, was the thought in Martin's mind.

"Well, then," he said, "how about my views? Do you think they are so radical?"

He held her eyes and waited the answer.

"I think them, well, very disconcerting," she replied.

The question was answered for him, and so oppressed was he by the grayness of life that he forgot the tentative proposition she had made for him to go to work. And she, having gone as far as she dared, was willing to wait the answer till she should bring the question up again.

She had not long to wait. Martin had a question of his own to propound to her. He wanted to ascertain the measure of her faith in him, and within the week each was answered. Martin precipitated it by reading to her his "The Shame of the Sun."

"Why don't you become a reporter?" she asked when he had finished. "You love writing so, and I am sure you would succeed. You could rise in journalism and make a name for yourself. There are a number of great special correspondents. Their salaries are large, and their field is the world. They are sent everywhere, to the heart of Africa, like Stanley, or to interview the Pope, or to explore unknown Thibet."

"Then you don't like my essay?" he rejoined. "You believe that I have some show in journalism but none in literature?"

"No, no; I do like it. It reads well. But I am afraid it's over the heads of your readers. At least it is over mine. It sounds beautiful, but I don't understand it. Your scientific slang is beyond me. You are an extremist, you know, dear, and what may be intelligible to you may not be intelligible to the rest of us."

"I imagine it's the philosophic slang that bothers you," was all he could say.

He was flaming from the fresh reading of the ripest thought he had expressed, and her verdict stunned him.

"No matter how poorly it is done," he persisted, "don't you see anything in it?—in the thought of it, I mean?"

She shook her head.

"No, it is so different from anything I have read. I read Maeterlinck and understand him—"

"His mysticism, you understand that?" Martin flashed out.

"Yes, but this of yours, which is supposed to be an attack upon him, I don't understand. Of course, if originality counts—"

He stopped her with an impatient gesture that was not followed by speech. He became suddenly aware that she was speaking and that she had been speaking for some time.

"After all, your writing has been a toy to you," she was saying. "Surely you have played with it long enough. It is time to take up life seriously—*our* life, Martin. Hitherto you have lived solely your own."

"You want me to go to work?" he asked.

"Yes. Father has offered—"

"I understand all that," he broke in; "but what I want to know is whether or not you have lost faith in me?"

She pressed his hand mutely, her eyes dim.

"In your writing, dear," she admitted in a half-whisper.

"You've read lots of my stuff," he went on brutally. "What do you think of it? Is it utterly hopeless? How does it compare with other men's work?"

"But they sell theirs, and you—don't."

"That doesn't answer my question. Do you think that literature is not at all my vocation?"

"Then I will answer." She steeled herself to do it. "I don't think you were made to write. Forgive me, dear. You compel me to say it; and you know I know more about literature than you do."

"Yes, you are a Bachelor of Arts," he said meditatively; "and you ought to know."

"But there is more to be said," he continued, after a pause painful to both. "I know what I have in me. No one knows that so well as I. I know I shall succeed. I will not be kept down. I am afire with what I have to say in verse, and fiction, and essay. I do not ask you to have faith in that, though. I do not ask you to have faith in me, nor in my writing. What I do ask of you is to love me and have faith in love."

"A year ago I believed for two years. One of those years is yet to run. And I do believe, upon my honor and my soul, that before that year is run I shall have succeeded. You remember what you told me long ago, that I must serve my apprenticeship to writing. Well, I have served it. I have crammed it and telescoped it. With you at the end awaiting me, I have never shirked. Do you know, I have forgotten what it is to fall peacefully asleep. A few million years ago I knew what it was to sleep my fill and to awake naturally from very glut of sleep. I am awakened always now by an alarm clock. If I fall asleep early or late, I set the alarm accordingly; and this, and the putting out of the lamp, are my last conscious actions."

"When I begin to feel drowsy, I change the heavy book I am reading for a lighter one. And when I doze over that, I beat my head with my knuckles in order to drive sleep away. Somewhere I read of a man who was afraid to sleep. Kipling wrote the story. This man arranged a spur so that when unconsciousness came, his naked body pressed against the iron teeth. Well, I've done the same. I look at the time, and I resolve that not until midnight, or not until one o'clock, or two o'clock, or three o'clock, shall the spur be removed. And so it rowels me awake until the appointed time. That spur has been my bed-mate for months. I have grown so desperate that five and a half hours of sleep is an extravagance. I sleep four hours now. I am starved for sleep. There are times when I am light-headed from want of sleep, times when death, with its rest and sleep, is a positive lure to me, times when I am haunted by Longfellow's lines:

"'The sea is still and deep;
All things within its bosom sleep;

A single step and all is o'er,
A plunge, a bubble, and no more.'

"Of course, this is sheer nonsense. It comes from nervousness, from an overwrought mind. But the point is: Why have I done this? For you. To shorten my apprenticeship. To compel Success to hasten. And my apprenticeship is now served. I know my equipment. I swear that I learn more each month than the average college man learns in a year. I know it, I tell you. But were my need for you to understand not so desperate I should not tell you. It is not boasting. I measure the results by the books. Your brothers, to-day, are ignorant barbarians compared with me and the knowledge I have wrung from the books in the hours they were sleeping. Long ago I wanted to be famous. I care very little for fame now. What I want is you; I am more hungry for you than for food, or clothing, or recognition. I have a dream of laying my head on your breast and sleeping an aeon or so, and the dream will come true ere another year is gone."

His power beat against her, wave upon wave; and in the moment his will opposed hers most she felt herself most strongly drawn toward him. The strength that had always poured out from him to her was now flowering in his impassioned voice, his flashing eyes, and the vigor of life and intellect surging in him. And in that moment, and for the moment, she was aware of a rift that showed in her certitude—a rift through which she caught sight of the real Martin Eden, splendid and invincible; and as animal-trainers have their moments of doubt, so she, for the instant, seemed to doubt her power to tame this wild spirit of a man.

"And another thing," he swept on. "You love me. But why do you love me? The thing in me that compels me to write is the very thing that draws your love. You love me because I am somehow different from the men you have known and might have loved. I was not made for the desk and counting-house, for petty business squabbling, and legal jangling. Make me do such things, make me like those other men, doing the work they do, breathing the air they breathe, developing the point of view they have developed, and you have destroyed the difference, destroyed me, destroyed the thing you love. My desire to write is the most vital thing in me. Had I been a mere clod, neither would I have desired to write, nor would you have desired me for a husband."

"But you forget," she interrupted, the quick surface of her mind glimpsing a parallel. "There have been eccentric inventors, starving their families while they sought such chimeras as perpetual motion. Doubtless their wives loved them, and suffered with them and for them, not because of but in spite of their infatuation for perpetual motion."

"True," was the reply. "But there have been inventors who were not eccentric and who starved while they sought to invent practical things; and sometimes, it is recorded, they succeeded. Certainly I do not seek any impossibilities—"

"You have called it 'achieving the impossible,'" she interpolated.

"I spoke figuratively. I seek to do what men have done before me—to write and to live by my writing."

Her silence spurred him on.

"To you, then, my goal is as much a chimera as perpetual motion?" he demanded.

He read her answer in the pressure of her hand on his—the pitying mother-hand for the hurt child. And to her, just then, he was the hurt child, the infatuated man striving to achieve the impossible.

Toward the close of their talk she warned him again of the antagonism of her father and mother.

"But you love me?" he asked.

"I do! I do!" she cried.

"And I love you, not them, and nothing they do can hurt me." Triumph sounded in his voice. "For I have faith in your love, not fear of their enmity. All things may go astray in this world, but not love. Love cannot go wrong unless it be a weakling that faints and stumbles by the way."

CHAPTER XXXI

Martin had encountered his sister Gertrude by chance on Broadway—as it proved, a most propitious yet disconcerting chance. Waiting on the corner for a car, she had seen him first, and noted the eager, hungry lines of his face and the desperate, worried look of his eyes. In truth, he was desperate and worried. He had just come from a fruitless interview with the pawnbroker, from whom he had tried to wring an additional loan on his wheel. The muddy fall weather having come on, Martin had pledged his wheel some time since and retained his black suit.

"There's the black suit," the pawnbroker, who knew his every asset, had answered. "You needn't tell me you've gone and pledged it with that Jew, Lipka. Because if you have—"

The man had looked the threat, and Martin hastened to cry:-

"No, no; I've got it. But I want to wear it on a matter of business."

"All right," the mollified usurer had replied. "And I want it on a matter of business before I can let you have any more money. You don't think I'm in it for my health?"

"But it's a forty-dollar wheel, in good condition," Martin had argued. "And you've only let me have seven dollars on it. No, not even seven. Six and a quarter; you took the interest in advance."

"If you want some more, bring the suit," had been the reply that sent Martin out of the stuffy little den, so desperate at heart as to reflect it in his face and touch his sister to pity.

Scarcely had they met when the Telegraph Avenue car came along and stopped to take on a crowd of afternoon shoppers. Mrs. Higginbotham divined from the grip on her arm as he helped her on, that he was not going to follow her. She turned on the step and looked down upon him. His haggard face smote her to the heart again.

"Ain't you comin'?" she asked

The next moment she had descended to his side.

"I'm walking—exercise, you know," he explained.

"Then I'll go along for a few blocks," she announced. "Mebbe it'll do me good. I ain't ben feelin' any too spry these last few days."

Martin glanced at her and verified her statement in her general slovenly appearance, in the unhealthy fat, in the drooping shoulders, the tired face with the sagging lines, and in the heavy fall of her feet, without elasticity—a very caricature of the walk that belongs to a free and happy body.

"You'd better stop here," he said, though she had already come to a halt at the first corner, "and take the next car."

"My goodness!—if I ain't all tired a'ready!" she panted. "But I'm just as able to walk as you in them soles. They're that thin they'll bu'st long before you git out to North Oakland."

"I've a better pair at home," was the answer.

"Come out to dinner to-morrow," she invited irrelevantly. "Mr. Higginbotham won't be there. He's goin' to San Leandro on business."

Martin shook his head, but he had failed to keep back the wolfish, hungry look that leapt into his eyes at the suggestion of dinner.

"You haven't a penny, Mart, and that's why you're walkin'. Exercise!" She tried to sniff contemptuously, but succeeded in producing only a sniffle. "Here, lemme see."

And, fumbling in her satchel, she pressed a five-dollar piece into his hand. "I guess I forgot your last birthday, Mart," she mumbled lamely.

Martin's hand instinctively closed on the piece of gold. In the same instant he knew he ought not to accept, and found himself struggling in the throes of indecision. That bit of gold meant food, life, and light in his body and brain, power to go on writing, and—who was to say?—maybe to write something that would bring in many pieces of gold. Clear on his vision burned the manuscripts of two essays he had just completed. He saw them under the table on top of the heap of returned manuscripts for which he had no stamps, and he saw their titles, just as he had typed them—"The High Priests of Mystery," and "The Cradle of Beauty." He had never submitted them anywhere. They were as good as anything he had done in that line. If only he had stamps for them! Then the certitude of his ultimate success rose up in him, an able ally of hunger, and with a quick movement he slipped the coin into his pocket.

"I'll pay you back, Gertrude, a hundred times over," he gulped out, his throat painfully contracted and in his eyes a swift hint of moisture.

"Mark my words!" he cried with abrupt positiveness. "Before the year is out I'll put an even hundred of those little yellow-boys into your hand. I don't ask you to believe me. All you have to do is wait and see."

Nor did she believe. Her incredulity made her uncomfortable, and failing of other expedient, she said:-

"I know you're hungry, Mart. It's sticking out all over you. Come in to meals any time. I'll send one of the children to tell you when Mr. Higginbotham ain't to be there. An' Mart—"

He waited, though he knew in his secret heart what she was about to say, so visible was her thought process to him.

"Don't you think it's about time you got a job?"

"You don't think I'll win out?" he asked.

She shook her head.

"Nobody has faith in me, Gertrude, except myself." His voice was passionately rebellious. "I've done good work already, plenty of it, and sooner or later it will sell."

"How do you know it is good?"

"Because—" He faltered as the whole vast field of literature and the history of literature stirred in his brain and pointed the futility of his attempting to convey to her the reasons for his faith. "Well, because it's better than ninety-nine per cent of what is published in the magazines."

"I wish't you'd listen to reason," she answered feebly, but with unwavering belief in the correctness of her diagnosis of what was ailing him. "I wish't you'd listen to reason," she repeated, "an' come to dinner to-morrow."

After Martin had helped her on the car, he hurried to the post-office and invested three of the five dollars in stamps; and when, later in the day, on the way to the Morse home, he stopped in at the post-office to weigh a large number of long, bulky envelopes, he affixed to them all the stamps save three of the two-cent denomination.

It proved a momentous night for Martin, for after dinner he met Russ Brissenden. How he chanced to come there, whose friend he was or what acquaintance brought him, Martin did not know. Nor had he the curiosity to inquire about him of Ruth. In short, Brissenden struck Martin as anaemic and feather-brained, and was promptly dismissed from his mind. An hour later he decided that Brissenden was a boor as well, what of the way he prowled about from one room to another, staring at the pictures or poking his nose into books and magazines he picked up from the table or drew from the shelves. Though a stranger in the house he finally isolated himself in the midst of the company, huddling into a capacious Morris chair and reading steadily from a thin volume he had drawn from his pocket. As he read, he abstractedly ran his fingers, with a caressing movement, through his hair. Martin noticed him no more that evening, except once when he observed him chaffing with great apparent success with several of the young women.

It chanced that when Martin was leaving, he overtook Brissenden already half down the walk to the street.

"Hello, is that you?" Martin said.

The other replied with an ungracious grunt, but swung alongside. Martin made no further attempt at conversation, and for several blocks unbroken silence lay upon them.

"Pompous old ass!"

The suddenness and the virulence of the exclamation startled Martin. He felt amused, and at the same time was aware of a growing dislike for the other.

"What do you go to such a place for?" was abruptly flung at him after another block of silence.

"Why do you?" Martin countered.

"Bless me, I don't know," came back. "At least this is my first indiscretion. There are twenty-four hours in each day, and I must spend them somehow. Come and have a drink."

"All right," Martin answered.

The next moment he was nonplussed by the readiness of his acceptance. At home was several hours' hack-work waiting for him before he went to bed, and after he went to bed there was a volume of Weismann waiting for him, to say nothing of Herbert Spencer's Autobiography, which was as replete for him with romance as any thrilling novel. Why should he waste any time with this man he did not like? was his thought. And yet, it was not so much the man nor the drink as was it what was associated with the drink—the bright lights, the mirrors and dazzling array of glasses, the warm and glowing faces and the resonant hum of the voices of men. That was it, it was the voices of men, optimistic men, men who breathed success and spent their money for drinks like men. He was lonely, that was what was the matter with him; that was why he had snapped at the invitation as a bonita strikes at a white rag on a hook. Not since with Joe, at Shelly Hot Springs, with the one exception of the wine he took with the Portuguese grocer, had Martin had a drink at a public bar. Mental exhaustion did not produce a craving for liquor such as physical exhaustion did, and he had felt no need for it. But just now he felt desire for the drink, or, rather, for the atmosphere wherein drinks were dispensed and disposed of. Such a place was the Grotto, where Brissenden and he lounged in capacious leather chairs and drank Scotch and soda.

They talked. They talked about many things, and now Brissenden and now Martin took turn in ordering Scotch and soda. Martin, who was extremely strong-headed, marvelled at the other's capacity for liquor, and ever and anon broke off to marvel at the other's conversation. He was not long in assuming that Brissenden knew everything, and in deciding that here was the second intellectual man he had met. But he noted that Brissenden had what Professor Caldwell lacked—namely, fire, the flashing insight and perception, the flaming uncontrol of genius. Living language flowed from him. His thin lips, like the dies of a machine, stamped out phrases that cut and stung; or again, pursing caressingly about the inchoate sound they articulated, the thin lips shaped soft and velvety things, mellow phrases of glow and glory, of haunting beauty, reverberant of the mystery and inscrutableness of life; and yet again the thin lips were like a bugle, from which rang the crash and tumult of cosmic strife, phrases that sounded clear as silver, that were luminous as starry spaces, that epitomized the final word of science and yet said something more—the poet's word, the transcendental truth, elusive and without words which could express, and which none the less found expression in the subtle and all but ungraspable connotations of common words. He, by some wonder of vision, saw beyond the farthest outpost of empiricism, where was no language for narration, and yet, by some golden miracle of speech, investing known words with unknown significances, he conveyed to Martin's consciousness messages that were incommunicable to ordinary souls.

Martin forgot his first impression of dislike. Here was the best the books had to offer coming true. Here was an intelligence, a living man for him to look up to. "I am down in the dirt at your feet," Martin repeated to himself again and again.

"You've studied biology," he said aloud, in significant allusion.

To his surprise Brissenden shook his head.

"But you are stating truths that are substantiated only by biology," Martin insisted, and was rewarded by a blank stare. "Your conclusions are in line with the books which you must have read."

"I am glad to hear it," was the answer. "That my smattering of knowledge should enable me to short-cut my way to truth is most reassuring. As for myself, I never bother to find out if I am right or not. It is all valueless anyway. Man can never know the ultimate verities."

"You are a disciple of Spencer!" Martin cried triumphantly.

"I haven't read him since adolescence, and all I read then was his 'Education.'"

"I wish I could gather knowledge as carelessly," Martin broke out half an hour later. He had been closely analyzing Brissenden's mental equipment. "You are a sheer dogmatist, and that's what makes it so marvellous. You state dogmatically the latest facts which science has been able to establish only by *à posteriori* reasoning. You jump at correct conclusions. You certainly short-cut with a vengeance. You feel your way with the speed of light, by some hyperrational process, to truth."

"Yes, that was what used to bother Father Joseph, and Brother Dutton," Brissenden replied. "Oh, no," he added; "I am not anything. It was a lucky trick of fate that sent me to a Catholic college for my education. Where did you pick up what you know?"

And while Martin told him, he was busy studying Brissenden, ranging from a long, lean, aristocratic face and drooping shoulders to the overcoat on a neighboring chair, its pockets sagged and bulged by the freightage of many books. Brissenden's face and long, slender hands were browned by the sun—excessively browned, Martin thought. This sunburn bothered Martin. It was patent that Brissenden was no outdoor man. Then how had he been ravaged by the sun? Something morbid and significant attached to that sunburn, was Martin's thought as he returned to a study of the face, narrow, with high cheek-bones and cavernous hollows, and graced with as delicate and fine an aquiline nose as Martin had ever seen. There was nothing remarkable about the size of the eyes. They were neither large nor small, while their color was a nondescript brown; but in them smouldered a fire, or, rather, lurked an expression dual and strangely contradictory. Defiant, indomitable, even harsh to excess, they at the same time aroused pity. Martin found himself pitying him he knew not why, though he was soon to learn.

"Oh, I'm a lunger," Brissenden announced, offhand, a little later, having already stated that he came from Arizona. "I've been down there a couple of years living on the climate."

"Aren't you afraid to venture it up in this climate?"

"Afraid?"

There was no special emphasis of his repetition of Martin's word. But Martin saw in that ascetic face the advertisement that there was nothing of which it was afraid. The eyes had narrowed till they were eagle-like, and Martin almost caught his breath as he noted the eagle beak with its dilated nostrils, defiant, assertive, aggressive. Magnificent, was what he commented to himself, his blood thrilling at the sight. Aloud, he quoted:-

"'Under the bludgeoning of Chance My head is bloody but unbowed.'"

"You like Henley," Brissenden said, his expression changing swiftly to large graciousness and tenderness. "Of course, I couldn't have expected anything else of you. Ah, Henley! A brave soul. He stands out among contemporary rhymesters—magazine rhymesters—as a gladiator stands out in the midst of a band of eunuchs."

"You don't like the magazines," Martin softly impeached.

"Do you?" was snarled back at him so savagely as to startle him.

"I—I write, or, rather, try to write, for the magazines," Martin faltered.

"That's better," was the mollified rejoinder. "You try to write, but you don't succeed. I respect and admire your failure. I know what you write. I can see it with half an eye, and there's one ingredient in it that shuts it out of the magazines. It's guts, and magazines have no use for that particular commodity. What they want is wish-wash and slush, and God knows they get it, but not from you."

"I'm not above hack-work," Martin contended.

"On the contrary—" Brissenden paused and ran an insolent eye over Martin's objective poverty, passing from the well-worn tie and the saw-edged collar to the shiny sleeves of the coat and on to the slight fray of one cuff, winding up and dwelling upon Martin's sunken cheeks. "On the contrary, hack-work is above you, so far above you that you can never hope to rise to it. Why, man, I could insult you by asking you to have something to eat."

Martin felt the heat in his face of the involuntary blood, and Brissenden laughed triumphantly.

"A full man is not insulted by such an invitation," he concluded.

"You are a devil," Martin cried irritably.

"Anyway, I didn't ask you."

"You didn't dare."

"Oh, I don't know about that. I invite you now."

Brissenden half rose from his chair as he spoke, as if with the intention of departing to the restaurant forthwith.

Martin's fists were tight-clenched, and his blood was drumming in his temples.

"Bosco! He eats 'em alive! Eats 'em alive!" Brissenden exclaimed, imitating the *spieler* of a locally famous snake-eater.

"I could certainly eat you alive," Martin said, in turn running insolent eyes over the other's disease-ravaged frame.

"Only I'm not worthy of it?"

"On the contrary," Martin considered, "because the incident is not worthy." He broke into a laugh, hearty and wholesome. "I confess you made a fool of me, Brissenden. That I am hungry and you are aware of it are only ordinary phenomena, and there's no disgrace. You see, I laugh at the conventional little moralities of the herd; then you drift by, say a sharp, true word, and immediately I am the slave of the same little moralities."

"You were insulted," Brissenden affirmed.

"I certainly was, a moment ago. The prejudice of early youth, you know. I learned such things then, and they cheapen what I have since learned. They are the skeletons in my particular closet."

"But you've got the door shut on them now?"

"I certainly have."

"Sure?"

"Sure."

"Then let's go and get something to eat."

"I'll go you," Martin answered, attempting to pay for the current Scotch and soda with the last change from his two dollars and seeing the waiter bullied by Brissenden into putting that change back on the table.

Martin pocketed it with a grimace, and felt for a moment the kindly weight of Brissenden's hand upon his shoulder.

CHAPTER XXXII

Promptly, the next afternoon, Maria was excited by Martin's second visitor. But she did not lose her head this time, for she seated Brissenden in her parlor's grandeur of respectability.

"Hope you don't mind my coming?" Brissenden began.

"No, no, not at all," Martin answered, shaking hands and waving him to the solitary chair, himself taking to the bed. "But how did you know where I lived?"

"Called up the Morses. Miss Morse answered the 'phone. And here I am." He tugged at his coat pocket and flung a thin volume on the table. "There's a book, by a poet. Read it and keep it." And then, in reply to Martin's protest: "What have I to do with books? I had another hemorrhage this morning. Got any whiskey? No, of course not. Wait a minute."

He was off and away. Martin watched his long figure go down the outside steps, and, on turning to close the gate, noted with a pang the shoulders, which had once been broad, drawn in now over, the collapsed ruin of the chest. Martin got two tumblers, and fell to reading the book of verse, Henry Vaughn Marlow's latest collection.

"No Scotch," Brissenden announced on his return. "The beggar sells nothing but American whiskey. But here's a quart of it."

"I'll send one of the youngsters for lemons, and we'll make a toddy," Martin offered.

"I wonder what a book like that will earn Marlow?" he went on, holding up the volume in question.

"Possibly fifty dollars," came the answer. "Though he's lucky if he pulls even on it, or if he can inveigle a publisher to risk bringing it out."

"Then one can't make a living out of poetry?"

Martin's tone and face alike showed his dejection.

"Certainly not. What fool expects to? Out of rhyming, yes. There's Bruce, and Virginia Spring, and Sedgwick. They do very nicely. But poetry—do you know how Vaughn Marlow makes his living?—teaching in a boys' cramming-joint down in Pennsylvania, and of all private little hells such a billet is the limit. I wouldn't trade places with him if he had fifty years of life before him. And yet his work stands out from the ruck of the contemporary versifiers as a balas ruby among carrots. And the reviews he gets! Damn them, all of them, the crass manikins!"

"Too much is written by the men who can't write about the men who do write," Martin concurred. "Why, I was appalled at the quantities of rubbish written about Stevenson and his work."

"Ghouls and harpies!" Brissenden snapped out with clicking teeth. "Yes, I know the spawn—complacently pecking at him for his Father Damien letter, analyzing him, weighing him—"

"Measuring him by the yardstick of their own miserable egos," Martin broke in.

"Yes, that's it, a good phrase,—mouthing and besliming the True, and Beautiful, and Good, and finally patting him on the back and saying, 'Good dog, Fido.' Faugh! 'The little chattering daws of men,' Richard Realf called them the night he died."

"Pecking at star-dust," Martin took up the strain warmly; "at the meteoric flight of the master-men. I once wrote a squib on them—the critics, or the reviewers, rather."

360

"Let's see it," Brissenden begged eagerly.

So Martin unearthed a carbon copy of "Star-dust," and during the reading of it Brissenden chuckled, rubbed his hands, and forgot to sip his toddy.

"Strikes me you're a bit of star-dust yourself, flung into a world of cowled gnomes who cannot see," was his comment at the end of it. "Of course it was snapped up by the first magazine?"

Martin ran over the pages of his manuscript book. "It has been refused by twenty-seven of them."

Brissenden essayed a long and hearty laugh, but broke down in a fit of coughing.

"Say, you needn't tell me you haven't tackled poetry," he gasped. "Let me see some of it."

"Don't read it now," Martin pleaded. "I want to talk with you. I'll make up a bundle and you can take it home."

Brissenden departed with the "Love-cycle," and "The Peri and the Pearl," returning next day to greet Martin with:-

"I want more."

Not only did he assure Martin that he was a poet, but Martin learned that Brissenden also was one. He was swept off his feet by the other's work, and astounded that no attempt had been made to publish it.

"A plague on all their houses!" was Brissenden's answer to Martin's volunteering to market his work for him. "Love Beauty for its own sake," was his counsel, "and leave the magazines alone. Back to your ships and your sea—that's my advice to you, Martin Eden. What do you want in these sick and rotten cities of men? You are cutting your throat every day you waste in them trying to prostitute beauty to the needs of magazinedom. What was it you quoted me the other day?—Oh, yes, 'Man, the latest of the ephemera.' Well, what do you, the latest of the ephemera, want with fame? If you got it, it would be poison to you. You are too simple, too elemental, and too rational, by my faith, to prosper on such pap. I hope you never do sell a line to the magazines. Beauty is the only master to serve. Serve her and damn the multitude! Success! What in hell's success if it isn't right there in your Stevenson sonnet, which outranks Henley's 'Apparition,' in that 'Love-cycle,' in those sea-poems?

"It is not in what you succeed in doing that you get your joy, but in the doing of it. You can't tell me. I know it. You know it. Beauty hurts you. It is an everlasting pain in you, a wound that does not heal, a knife of flame. Why should you palter with magazines? Let beauty be your end. Why should you mint beauty into gold? Anyway, you can't; so there's no use in my getting excited over it. You can read the magazines for a thousand years and you won't find the value of one line of Keats. Leave fame and coin alone, sign away on a ship to-morrow, and go back to your sea."

"Not for fame, but for love," Martin laughed. "Love seems to have no place in your Cosmos; in mine, Beauty is the handmaiden of Love."

Brissenden looked at him pityingly and admiringly. "You are so young, Martin boy, so young. You will flutter high, but your wings are of the finest gauze, dusted with the fairest pigments. Do not scorch them. But of course you have scorched them already. It required some glorified petticoat to account for that 'Love-cycle,' and that's the shame of it."

"It glorifies love as well as the petticoat," Martin laughed.

"The philosophy of madness," was the retort. "So have I assured myself when wandering in hasheesh dreams. But beware. These bourgeois cities will kill you. Look at that den of traitors where I met you. Dry rot is no name for it. One can't keep his sanity in such an atmosphere. It's degrading. There's not one of them who is not degrading, man and woman, all of them animated stomachs guided by the high intellectual and artistic impulses of clams—"

He broke off suddenly and regarded Martin. Then, with a flash of divination, he saw the situation. The expression on his face turned to wondering horror.

"And you wrote that tremendous 'Love-cycle' to her—that pale, shrivelled, female thing!"

The next instant Martin's right hand had shot to a throttling clutch on his throat, and he was being shaken till his teeth rattled. But Martin, looking into his eyes, saw no fear there,— naught but a curious and mocking devil. Martin remembered himself, and flung Brissenden, by the neck, sidelong upon the bed, at the same moment releasing his hold.

Brissenden panted and gasped painfully for a moment, then began to chuckle.

"You had made me eternally your debtor had you shaken out the flame," he said.

"My nerves are on a hair-trigger these days," Martin apologized. "Hope I didn't hurt you. Here, let me mix a fresh toddy."

"Ah, you young Greek!" Brissenden went on. "I wonder if you take just pride in that body of yours. You are devilish strong. You are a young panther, a lion cub. Well, well, it is you who must pay for that strength."

"What do you mean?" Martin asked curiously, passing aim a glass. "Here, down this and be good."

"Because—" Brissenden sipped his toddy and smiled appreciation of it. "Because of the women. They will worry you until you die, as they have already worried you, or else I was born yesterday. Now there's no use in your choking me; I'm going to have my say. This is undoubtedly your calf love; but for Beauty's sake show better taste next time. What under heaven do you want with a daughter of the bourgeoisie? Leave them alone. Pick out some great, wanton flame of a woman, who laughs at life and jeers at death and loves one while she may. There are such women, and they will love you just as readily as any pusillanimous product of bourgeois sheltered life."

"Pusillanimous?" Martin protested.

"Just so, pusillanimous; prattling out little moralities that have been prattled into them, and afraid to live life. They will love you, Martin, but they will love their little moralities more. What you want is the magnificent abandon of life, the great free souls, the blazing butterflies and not the little gray moths. Oh, you will grow tired of them, too, of all the female things, if you are unlucky enough to live. But you won't live. You won't go back to your ships and sea; therefore, you'll hang around these pest-holes of cities until your bones are rotten, and then you'll die."

"You can lecture me, but you can't make me talk back," Martin said. "After all, you have but the wisdom of your temperament, and the wisdom of my temperament is just as unimpeachable as yours."

They disagreed about love, and the magazines, and many things, but they liked each other, and on Martin's part it was no less than a profound liking. Day after day they were together, if for no more than the hour Brissenden spent in Martin's stuffy room. Brissenden never arrived without his quart of whiskey, and when they dined together down-town, he drank Scotch and soda throughout the meal. He invariably paid the way for both, and it was through him that Martin learned the refinements of food, drank his first champagne, and made acquaintance with Rhenish wines.

But Brissenden was always an enigma. With the face of an ascetic, he was, in all the failing blood of him, a frank voluptuary. He was unafraid to die, bitter and cynical of all the ways of living; and yet, dying, he loved life, to the last atom of it. He was possessed by a madness to live, to thrill, "to squirm my little space in the cosmic dust whence I came," as he phrased it once himself. He had tampered with drugs and done many strange things in quest of new thrills, new sensations. As he told Martin, he had once gone three days without water, had done so voluntarily, in order to experience the exquisite delight of such a thirst assuaged. Who or what he was, Martin never learned. He was a man without a past, whose future was the imminent grave and whose present was a bitter fever of living.

CHAPTER XXXIII

Martin was steadily losing his battle. Economize as he would, the earnings from hack-work did not balance expenses. Thanksgiving found him with his black suit in pawn and unable to accept the Morses' invitation to dinner. Ruth was not made happy by his reason for not coming, and the corresponding effect on him was one of desperation. He told her that he would come, after all; that he would go over to San Francisco, to the *Transcontinental* office, collect the five dollars due him, and with it redeem his suit of clothes.

In the morning he borrowed ten cents from Maria. He would have borrowed it, by preference, from Brissenden, but that erratic individual had disappeared. Two weeks had passed since Martin had seen him, and he vainly cudgelled his brains for some cause of offence. The ten cents carried Martin across the ferry to San Francisco, and as he walked up Market Street he speculated upon his predicament in case he failed to collect the money. There would then be no way for him to return to Oakland, and he knew no one in San Francisco from whom to borrow another ten cents.

The door to the *Transcontinental* office was ajar, and Martin, in the act of opening it, was brought to a sudden pause by a loud voice from within, which exclaimed:- "But that is not the question, Mr. Ford." (Ford, Martin knew, from his correspondence, to be the editor's name.) "The question is, are you prepared to pay?—cash, and cash down, I mean? I am not interested in the prospects of the *Transcontinental* and what you expect to make it next year. What I want is to be paid for what I do. And I tell you, right now, the Christmas *Transcontinental* don't go to press till I have the money in my hand. Good day. When you get the money, come and see me."

The door jerked open, and the man flung past Martin, with an angry countenance and went down the corridor, muttering curses and clenching his fists. Martin decided not to enter immediately, and lingered in the hallways for a quarter of an hour. Then he shoved the door open and walked in. It was a new experience, the first time he had been inside an editorial office. Cards evidently were not necessary in that office, for the boy carried word to an inner room that there was a man who wanted to see Mr. Ford. Returning, the boy beckoned him from halfway across the room and led him to the private office, the editorial sanctum. Martin's first impression was of the disorder and cluttered confusion of the room. Next he noticed a bewhiskered, youthful-looking man, sitting at a roll-top desk, who regarded him curiously. Martin marvelled at the calm repose of his face. It was evident that the squabble with the printer had not affected his equanimity.

"I—I am Martin Eden," Martin began the conversation. ("And I want my five dollars," was what he would have liked to say.)

But this was his first editor, and under the circumstances he did not desire to scare him too abruptly. To his surprise, Mr. Ford leaped into the air with a "You don't say so!" and the next moment, with both hands, was shaking Martin's hand effusively.

"Can't say how glad I am to see you, Mr. Eden. Often wondered what you were like."

Here he held Martin off at arm's length and ran his beaming eyes over Martin's second-best suit, which was also his worst suit, and which was ragged and past repair, though the trousers showed the careful crease he had put in with Maria's flat-irons.

"I confess, though, I conceived you to be a much older man than you are. Your story, you know, showed such breadth, and vigor, such maturity and depth of thought. A masterpiece, that story—I knew it when I had read the first half-dozen lines. Let me tell you how I first read it. But no; first let me introduce you to the staff."

Still talking, Mr. Ford led him into the general office, where he introduced him to the associate editor, Mr. White, a slender, frail little man whose hand seemed strangely cold, as if he were suffering from a chill, and whose whiskers were sparse and silky.

"And Mr. Ends, Mr. Eden. Mr. Ends is our business manager, you know."

Martin found himself shaking hands with a cranky-eyed, bald-headed man, whose face looked youthful enough from what little could be seen of it, for most of it was covered by a snow-white beard, carefully trimmed—by his wife, who did it on Sundays, at which times she also shaved the back of his neck.

The three men surrounded Martin, all talking admiringly and at once, until it seemed to him that they were talking against time for a wager.

"We often wondered why you didn't call," Mr. White was saying.

"I didn't have the carfare, and I live across the Bay," Martin answered bluntly, with the idea of showing them his imperative need for the money.

Surely, he thought to himself, my glad rags in themselves are eloquent advertisement of my need. Time and again, whenever opportunity offered, he hinted about the purpose of his business. But his admirers' ears were deaf. They sang his praises, told him what they had thought of his story at first sight, what they subsequently thought, what their wives and families thought; but not one hint did they breathe of intention to pay him for it.

"Did I tell you how I first read your story?" Mr. Ford said. "Of course I didn't. I was coming west from New York, and when the train stopped at Ogden, the train-boy on the new run brought aboard the current number of the *Transcontinental*."

My God! Martin thought; you can travel in a Pullman while I starve for the paltry five dollars you owe me. A wave of anger rushed over him. The wrong done him by the *Transcontinental* loomed colossal, for strong upon him were all the dreary months of vain yearning, of hunger and privation, and his present hunger awoke and gnawed at him, reminding him that he had eaten nothing since the day before, and little enough then. For the moment he saw red. These creatures were not even robbers. They were sneak-thieves. By lies and broken promises they had tricked him out of his story. Well, he would show them. And a great resolve surged into his will to the effect that he would not leave the office until he got his money. He remembered, if he did not get it, that there was no way for him to go back to Oakland. He controlled himself with an effort, but not before the wolfish expression of his face had awed and perturbed them.

They became more voluble than ever. Mr. Ford started anew to tell how he had first read "The Ring of Bells," and Mr. Ends at the same time was striving to repeat his niece's appreciation of "The Ring of Bells," said niece being a school-teacher in Alameda.

"I'll tell you what I came for," Martin said finally. "To be paid for that story all of you like so well. Five dollars, I believe, is what you promised me would be paid on publication."

Mr. Ford, with an expression on his mobile features of mediate and happy acquiescence, started to reach for his pocket, then turned suddenly to Mr. Ends, and said that he had left his money home. That Mr. Ends resented this, was patent; and Martin saw the twitch of his arm as if to protect his trousers pocket. Martin knew that the money was there.

"I am sorry," said Mr. Ends, "but I paid the printer not an hour ago, and he took my ready change. It was careless of me to be so short; but the bill was not yet due, and the printer's request, as a favor, to make an immediate advance, was quite unexpected."

Both men looked expectantly at Mr. White, but that gentleman laughed and shrugged his shoulders. His conscience was clean at any rate. He had come into the *Transcontinental* to learn magazine-literature, instead of which he had principally learned finance. The *Transcontinental* owed him four months' salary, and he knew that the printer must be appeased before the associate editor.

"It's rather absurd, Mr. Eden, to have caught us in this shape," Mr. Ford preambled airily. "All carelessness, I assure you. But I'll tell you what we'll do. We'll mail you a check the first thing in the morning. You have Mr. Eden's address, haven't you, Mr. Ends?"

Yes, Mr. Ends had the address, and the check would be mailed the first thing in the morning. Martin's knowledge of banks and checks was hazy, but he could see no reason why they should not give him the check on this day just as well as on the next.

"Then it is understood, Mr. Eden, that we'll mail you the check to-morrow?" Mr. Ford said.

"I need the money to-day," Martin answered stolidly.

"The unfortunate circumstances—if you had chanced here any other day," Mr. Ford began suavely, only to be interrupted by Mr. Ends, whose cranky eyes justified themselves in his shortness of temper.

"Mr. Ford has already explained the situation," he said with asperity. "And so have I. The check will be mailed—"

"I also have explained," Martin broke in, "and I have explained that I want the money to-day."

He had felt his pulse quicken a trifle at the business manager's brusqueness, and upon him he kept an alert eye, for it was in that gentleman's trousers pocket that he divined the *Transcontinental's* ready cash was reposing.

"It is too bad—" Mr. Ford began.

But at that moment, with an impatient movement, Mr. Ends turned as if about to leave the room. At the same instant Martin sprang for him, clutching him by the throat with one hand in such fashion that Mr. Ends' snow-white beard, still maintaining its immaculate trimness, pointed ceilingward at an angle of forty-five degrees. To the horror of Mr. White and Mr. Ford, they saw their business manager shaken like an Astrakhan rug.

"Dig up, you venerable discourager of rising young talent!" Martin exhorted. "Dig up, or I'll shake it out of you, even if it's all in nickels." Then, to the two affrighted onlookers: "Keep away! If you interfere, somebody's liable to get hurt."

Mr. Ends was choking, and it was not until the grip on his throat was eased that he was able to signify his acquiescence in the digging-up programme. All together, after repeated digs, its trousers pocket yielded four dollars and fifteen cents.

"Inside out with it," Martin commanded.

An additional ten cents fell out. Martin counted the result of his raid a second time to make sure.

"You next!" he shouted at Mr. Ford. "I want seventy-five cents more."

Mr. Ford did not wait, but ransacked his pockets, with the result of sixty cents.

"Sure that is all?" Martin demanded menacingly, possessing himself of it. "What have you got in your vest pockets?"

In token of his good faith, Mr. Ford turned two of his pockets inside out. A strip of cardboard fell to the floor from one of them. He recovered it and was in the act of returning it, when Martin cried:-

"What's that?—A ferry ticket? Here, give it to me. It's worth ten cents. I'll credit you with it. I've now got four dollars and ninety-five cents, including the ticket. Five cents is still due me."

He looked fiercely at Mr. White, and found that fragile creature in the act of handing him a nickel.

"Thank you," Martin said, addressing them collectively. "I wish you a good day."

"Robber!" Mr. Ends snarled after him.

"Sneak-thief!" Martin retorted, slamming the door as he passed out.

Martin was elated—so elated that when he recollected that *The Hornet* owed him fifteen dollars for "The Peri and the Pearl," he decided forthwith to go and collect it. But *The Hornet* was run by a set of clean-shaven, strapping young men, frank buccaneers who robbed everything and everybody, not excepting one another. After some breakage of the office furniture, the editor (an ex-college athlete), ably assisted by the business manager, an advertising agent, and the porter, succeeded in removing Martin from the office and in accelerating, by initial impulse, his descent of the first flight of stairs.

"Come again, Mr. Eden; glad to see you any time," they laughed down at him from the landing above.

Martin grinned as he picked himself up.

"Phew!" he murmured back. "The *Transcontinental* crowd were nanny-goats, but you fellows are a lot of prize-fighters."

More laughter greeted this.

"I must say, Mr. Eden," the editor of *The Hornet* called down, "that for a poet you can go some yourself. Where did you learn that right cross—if I may ask?"

"Where you learned that half-Nelson," Martin answered. "Anyway, you're going to have a black eye."

"I hope your neck doesn't stiffen up," the editor wished solicitously: "What do you say we all go out and have a drink on it—not the neck, of course, but the little rough-house?"

"I'll go you if I lose," Martin accepted.

And robbers and robbed drank together, amicably agreeing that the battle was to the strong, and that the fifteen dollars for "The Peri and the Pearl" belonged by right to *The Hornet's* editorial staff.

CHAPTER XXXIV

Arthur remained at the gate while Ruth climbed Maria's front steps. She heard the rapid click of the type-writer, and when Martin let her in, found him on the last page of a manuscript. She had come to make certain whether or not he would be at their table for Thanksgiving dinner; but before she could broach the subject Martin plunged into the one with which he was full.

"Here, let me read you this," he cried, separating the carbon copies and running the pages of manuscript into shape. "It's my latest, and different from anything I've done. It is so altogether different that I am almost afraid of it, and yet I've a sneaking idea it is good. You be judge. It's an Hawaiian story. I've called it 'Wiki-wiki.'"

His face was bright with the creative glow, though she shivered in the cold room and had been struck by the coldness of his hands at greeting. She listened closely while he read, and though he from time to time had seen only disapprobation in her face, at the close he asked:-

"Frankly, what do you think of it?"

"I—I don't know," she, answered. "Will it—do you think it will sell?"

"I'm afraid not," was the confession. "It's too strong for the magazines. But it's true, on my word it's true."

"But why do you persist in writing such things when you know they won't sell?" she went on inexorably. "The reason for your writing is to make a living, isn't it?"

"Yes, that's right; but the miserable story got away with me. I couldn't help writing it. It demanded to be written."

"But that character, that Wiki-Wiki, why do you make him talk so roughly? Surely it will offend your readers, and surely that is why the editors are justified in refusing your work."

"Because the real Wiki-Wiki would have talked that way."

"But it is not good taste."

"It is life," he replied bluntly. "It is real. It is true. And I must write life as I see it."

She made no answer, and for an awkward moment they sat silent. It was because he loved her that he did not quite understand her, and she could not understand him because he was so large that he bulked beyond her horizon.

"Well, I've collected from the *Transcontinental*," he said in an effort to shift the conversation to a more comfortable subject. The picture of the bewhiskered trio, as he had last seen them, mulcted of four dollars and ninety cents and a ferry ticket, made him chuckle.

"Then you'll come!" she cried joyously. "That was what I came to find out."

"Come?" he muttered absently. "Where?"

"Why, to dinner to-morrow. You know you said you'd recover your suit if you got that money."

"I forgot all about it," he said humbly. "You see, this morning the poundman got Maria's two cows and the baby calf, and—well, it happened that Maria didn't have any money, and so I had to recover her cows for her. That's where the *Transcontinental* fiver went—'The Ring of Bells' went into the poundman's pocket."

"Then you won't come?"

He looked down at his clothing.

"I can't."

Tears of disappointment and reproach glistened in her blue eyes, but she said nothing.

"Next Thanksgiving you'll have dinner with me in Delmonico's," he said cheerily; "or in London, or Paris, or anywhere you wish. I know it."

"I saw in the paper a few days ago," she announced abruptly, "that there had been several local appointments to the Railway Mail. You passed first, didn't you?"

He was compelled to admit that the call had come for him, but that he had declined it. "I was so sure—I am so sure—of myself," he concluded. "A year from now I'll be earning more than a dozen men in the Railway Mail. You wait and see."

"Oh," was all she said, when he finished. She stood up, pulling at her gloves. "I must go, Martin. Arthur is waiting for me."

He took her in his arms and kissed her, but she proved a passive sweetheart. There was no tenseness in her body, her arms did not go around him, and her lips met his without their wonted pressure.

She was angry with him, he concluded, as he returned from the gate. But why? It was unfortunate that the poundman had gobbled Maria's cows. But it was only a stroke of fate. Nobody could be blamed for it. Nor did it enter his head that he could have done aught otherwise than what he had done. Well, yes, he was to blame a little, was his next thought, for having refused the call to the Railway Mail. And she had not liked "Wiki-Wiki."

He turned at the head of the steps to meet the letter-carrier on his afternoon round. The ever recurrent fever of expectancy assailed Martin as he took the bundle of long envelopes. One was not long. It was short and thin, and outside was printed the address of *The New York Outview*. He paused in the act of tearing the envelope open. It could not be an acceptance. He had no manuscripts with that publication. Perhaps—his heart almost stood still at the—wild thought—perhaps they were ordering an article from him; but the next instant he dismissed the surmise as hopelessly impossible.

It was a short, formal letter, signed by the office editor, merely informing him that an anonymous letter which they had received was enclosed, and that he could rest assured the *Outview's* staff never under any circumstances gave consideration to anonymous correspondence.

The enclosed letter Martin found to be crudely printed by hand. It was a hotchpotch of illiterate abuse of Martin, and of assertion that the "so-called Martin Eden" who was selling stories to magazines was no writer at all, and that in reality he was stealing stories from old magazines, typing them, and sending them out as his own. The envelope was postmarked "San Leandro." Martin did not require a second thought to discover the author. Higginbotham's grammar, Higginbotham's colloquialisms, Higginbotham's mental quirks and processes, were apparent throughout. Martin saw in every line, not the fine Italian hand, but the coarse grocer's fist, of his brother-in-law.

But why? he vainly questioned. What injury had he done Bernard Higginbotham? The thing was so unreasonable, so wanton. There was no explaining it. In the course of the week a dozen similar letters were forwarded to Martin by the editors of various Eastern magazines. The editors were behaving handsomely, Martin concluded. He was wholly unknown to them, yet some of them had even been sympathetic. It was evident that they detested anonymity. He saw that the malicious attempt to hurt him had failed. In fact, if anything came of it, it was bound to be good, for at least his name had been called to the attention of a number of editors. Sometime, perhaps, reading a submitted manuscript of his, they might remember him as the fellow about whom they had received an anonymous letter. And who was to say that such a remembrance might not sway the balance of their judgment just a trifle in his favor?

It was about this time that Martin took a great slump in Maria's estimation. He found her in the kitchen one morning groaning with pain, tears of weakness running down her cheeks, vainly endeavoring to put through a large ironing. He promptly diagnosed her affliction as La Grippe, dosed her with hot whiskey (the remnants in the bottles for which Brissenden was responsible), and ordered her to bed. But Maria was refractory. The ironing had to be done, she protested, and delivered that night, or else there would be no food on the morrow for the seven small and hungry Silvas.

To her astonishment (and it was something that she never ceased from relating to her dying day), she saw Martin Eden seize an iron from the stove and throw a fancy shirt-waist on the ironing-board. It was Kate Flanagan's best Sunday waist, than whom there was no more exacting and fastidiously dressed woman in Maria's world. Also, Miss Flanagan had sent special instruction that said waist must be delivered by that night. As every one knew, she was keeping company with John Collins, the blacksmith, and, as Maria knew privily, Miss Flanagan and Mr. Collins were going next day to Golden Gate Park. Vain was Maria's attempt to rescue the garment. Martin guided her tottering footsteps to a chair, from where she watched him with bulging eyes. In a quarter of the time it would have taken her she saw the shirt-waist safely ironed, and ironed as well as she could have done it, as Martin made her grant.

"I could work faster," he explained, "if your irons were only hotter."

To her, the irons he swung were much hotter than she ever dared to use.

"Your sprinkling is all wrong," he complained next. "Here, let me teach you how to sprinkle. Pressure is what's wanted. Sprinkle under pressure if you want to iron fast."

He procured a packing-case from the woodpile in the cellar, fitted a cover to it, and raided the scrap-iron the Silva tribe was collecting for the junkman. With fresh-sprinkled garments in the box, covered with the board and pressed by the iron, the device was complete and in operation.

"Now you watch me, Maria," he said, stripping off to his undershirt and gripping an iron that was what he called "really hot."

"An' when he feenish da iron' he washa da wools," as she described it afterward. "He say, 'Maria, you are da greata fool. I showa you how to washa da wools,' an' he shows me, too. Ten minutes he maka da machine—one barrel, one wheel-hub, two poles, justa like dat."

Martin had learned the contrivance from Joe at the Shelly Hot Springs. The old wheel-hub, fixed on the end of the upright pole, constituted the plunger. Making this, in turn, fast to the spring-pole attached to the kitchen rafters, so that the hub played upon the woollens in the barrel, he was able, with one hand, thoroughly to pound them.

"No more Maria washa da wools," her story always ended. "I maka da kids worka da pole an' da hub an' da barrel. Him da smarta man, Mister Eden."

Nevertheless, by his masterly operation and improvement of her kitchen-laundry he fell an immense distance in her regard. The glamour of romance with which her imagination had invested him faded away in the cold light of fact that he was an ex-laundryman. All his books, and his grand friends who visited him in carriages or with countless bottles of whiskey, went for naught. He was, after all, a mere workingman, a member of her own class and caste. He was more human and approachable, but, he was no longer mystery.

Martin's alienation from his family continued. Following upon Mr. Higginbotham's unprovoked attack, Mr. Hermann von Schmidt showed his hand. The fortunate sale of several storiettes, some humorous verse, and a few jokes gave Martin a temporary splurge of prosperity. Not only did he partially pay up his bills, but he had sufficient balance left to redeem his black suit and wheel. The latter, by virtue of a twisted crank-hanger, required repairing, and, as a matter of friendliness with his future brother-in-law, he sent it to Von Schmidt's shop.

The afternoon of the same day Martin was pleased by the wheel being delivered by a small boy. Von Schmidt was also inclined to be friendly, was Martin's conclusion from this unusual favor. Repaired wheels usually had to be called for. But when he examined the wheel, he discovered no repairs had been made. A little later in the day he telephoned his sister's betrothed, and learned that that person didn't want anything to do with him in "any shape, manner, or form."

"Hermann von Schmidt," Martin answered cheerfully, "I've a good mind to come over and punch that Dutch nose of yours."

"You come to my shop," came the reply, "an' I'll send for the police. An' I'll put you through, too. Oh, I know you, but you can't make no rough-house with me. I don't want nothin' to do with the likes of you. You're a loafer, that's what, an' I ain't asleep. You ain't goin' to do no spongin' off me just because I'm marryin' your sister. Why don't you go to work an' earn an honest livin', eh? Answer me that."

Martin's philosophy asserted itself, dissipating his anger, and he hung up the receiver with a long whistle of incredulous amusement. But after the amusement came the reaction, and he was oppressed by his loneliness. Nobody understood him, nobody seemed to have any use for him, except Brissenden, and Brissenden had disappeared, God alone knew where.

Twilight was falling as Martin left the fruit store and turned homeward, his marketing on his arm. At the corner an electric car had stopped, and at sight of a lean, familiar figure alighting, his heart leapt with joy. It was Brissenden, and in the fleeting glimpse, ere the car started up, Martin noted the overcoat pockets, one bulging with books, the other bulging with a quart bottle of whiskey.

CHAPTER XXXV

Brissenden gave no explanation of his long absence, nor did Martin pry into it. He was content to see his friend's cadaverous face opposite him through the steam rising from a tumbler of toddy.

"I, too, have not been idle," Brissenden proclaimed, after hearing Martin's account of the work he had accomplished.

He pulled a manuscript from his inside coat pocket and passed it to Martin, who looked at the title and glanced up curiously.

"Yes, that's it," Brissenden laughed. "Pretty good title, eh? 'Ephemera'—it is the one word. And you're responsible for it, what of your *man*, who is always the erected, the vitalized inorganic, the latest of the ephemera, the creature of temperature strutting his little space on the thermometer. It got into my head and I had to write it to get rid of it. Tell me what you think of it."

Martin's face, flushed at first, paled as he read on. It was perfect art. Form triumphed over substance, if triumph it could be called where the last conceivable atom of substance had found expression in so perfect construction as to make Martin's head swim with delight, to put passionate tears into his eyes, and to send chills creeping up and down his back. It was a long poem of six or seven hundred lines, and it was a fantastic, amazing, unearthly thing. It was terrific, impossible; and yet there it was, scrawled in black ink across the sheets of paper. It dealt with man and his soul-gropings in their ultimate terms, plumbing the abysses of space for the testimony of remotest suns and rainbow spectrums. It was a mad orgy of imagination, wassailing in the skull of a dying man who half sobbed under his breath and was quick with the wild flutter of fading heart-beats. The poem swung in majestic rhythm to the cool tumult of interstellar conflict, to the onset of starry hosts, to the impact of cold suns and the flaming up of nebular in the darkened void; and through it all, unceasing and faint, like a silver shuttle, ran the frail, piping voice of man, a querulous chirp amid the screaming of planets and the crash of systems.

"There is nothing like it in literature," Martin said, when at last he was able to speak. "It's wonderful!—wonderful! It has gone to my head. I am drunken with it. That great, infinitesimal question—I can't shake it out of my thoughts. That questing, eternal, ever recurring, thin little wailing voice of man is still ringing in my ears. It is like the dead-march of a gnat amid the trumpeting of elephants and the roaring of lions. It is insatiable with microscopic desire. I now I'm making a fool of myself, but the thing has obsessed me. You are—I don't know what you are—you are wonderful, that's all. But how do you do it? How do you do it?"

Martin paused from his rhapsody, only to break out afresh.

"I shall never write again. I am a dauber in clay. You have shown me the work of the real artificer-artisan. Genius! This is something more than genius. It transcends genius. It is truth gone mad. It is true, man, every line of it. I wonder if you realize that, you dogmatist. Science cannot give you the lie. It is the truth of the sneer, stamped out from the black iron of the Cosmos and interwoven with mighty rhythms of sound into a fabric of splendor and beauty.

And now I won't say another word. I am overwhelmed, crushed. Yes, I will, too. Let me market it for you."

Brissenden grinned. "There's not a magazine in Christendom that would dare to publish it—you know that."

"I know nothing of the sort. I know there's not a magazine in Christendom that wouldn't jump at it. They don't get things like that every day. That's no mere poem of the year. It's the poem of the century."

"I'd like to take you up on the proposition."

"Now don't get cynical," Martin exhorted. "The magazine editors are not wholly fatuous. I know that. And I'll close with you on the bet. I'll wager anything you want that 'Ephemera' is accepted either on the first or second offering."

"There's just one thing that prevents me from taking you." Brissenden waited a moment. "The thing is big—the biggest I've ever done. I know that. It's my swan song. I am almighty proud of it. I worship it. It's better than whiskey. It is what I dreamed of—the great and perfect thing—when I was a simple young man, with sweet illusions and clean ideals. And I've got it, now, in my last grasp, and I'll not have it pawed over and soiled by a lot of swine. No, I won't take the bet. It's mine. I made it, and I've shared it with you."

"But think of the rest of the world," Martin protested. "The function of beauty is joy-making."

"It's my beauty."

"Don't be selfish."

"I'm not selfish." Brissenden grinned soberly in the way he had when pleased by the thing his thin lips were about to shape. "I'm as unselfish as a famished hog."

In vain Martin strove to shake him from his decision. Martin told him that his hatred of the magazines was rabid, fanatical, and that his conduct was a thousand times more despicable than that of the youth who burned the temple of Diana at Ephesus. Under the storm of denunciation Brissenden complacently sipped his toddy and affirmed that everything the other said was quite true, with the exception of the magazine editors. His hatred of them knew no bounds, and he excelled Martin in denunciation when he turned upon them.

"I wish you'd type it for me," he said. "You know how a thousand times better than any stenographer. And now I want to give you some advice." He drew a bulky manuscript from his outside coat pocket. "Here's your 'Shame of the Sun.' I've read it not once, but twice and three times—the highest compliment I can pay you. After what you've said about 'Ephemera' I must be silent. But this I will say: when 'The Shame of the Sun' is published, it will make a hit. It will start a controversy that will be worth thousands to you just in advertising."

Martin laughed. "I suppose your next advice will be to submit it to the magazines."

"By all means no—that is, if you want to see it in print. Offer it to the first-class houses. Some publisher's reader may be mad enough or drunk enough to report favorably on it. You've read the books. The meat of them has been transmuted in the alembic of Martin Eden's mind and poured into 'The Shame of the Sun,' and one day Martin Eden will be famous, and not the least of his fame will rest upon that work. So you must get a publisher for it—the sooner the better."

Brissenden went home late that night; and just as he mounted the first step of the car, he swung suddenly back on Martin and thrust into his hand a small, tightly crumpled wad of paper.

"Here, take this," he said. "I was out to the races to-day, and I had the right dope."

The bell clanged and the car pulled out, leaving Martin wondering as to the nature of the crinkly, greasy wad he clutched in his hand. Back in his room he unrolled it and found a hundred-dollar bill.

He did not scruple to use it. He knew his friend had always plenty of money, and he knew also, with profound certitude, that his success would enable him to repay it. In the morning he paid every bill, gave Maria three months' advance on the room, and redeemed every pledge at the pawnshop. Next he bought Marian's wedding present, and simpler presents, suitable to Christmas, for Ruth and Gertrude. And finally, on the balance remaining to him, he herded the whole Silva tribe down into Oakland. He was a winter late in redeeming his promise, but redeemed it was, for the last, least Silva got a pair of shoes, as well as Maria herself. Also, there were horns, and dolls, and toys of various sorts, and parcels and bundles of candies and nuts that filled the arms of all the Silvas to overflowing.

It was with this extraordinary procession trooping at his and Maria's heels into a confectioner's in quest if the biggest candy-cane ever made, that he encountered Ruth and her mother. Mrs. Morse was shocked. Even Ruth was hurt, for she had some regard for appearances, and her lover, cheek by jowl with Maria, at the head of that army of Portuguese ragamuffins, was not a pretty sight. But it was not that which hurt so much as what she took to be his lack of pride and self-respect. Further, and keenest of all, she read into the incident the impossibility of his living down his working-class origin. There was stigma enough in the fact of it, but shamelessly to flaunt it in the face of the world—her world—was going too far. Though her engagement to Martin had been kept secret, their long intimacy had not been unproductive of gossip; and in the shop, glancing covertly at her lover and his following, had been several of her acquaintances. She lacked the easy largeness of Martin and could not rise superior to her environment. She had been hurt to the quick, and her sensitive nature was quivering with the shame of it. So it was, when Martin arrived later in the day, that he kept her present in his breast-pocket, deferring the giving of it to a more propitious occasion. Ruth in tears—passionate, angry tears—was a revelation to him. The spectacle of her suffering convinced him that he had been a brute, yet in the soul of him he could not see how nor why. It never entered his head to be ashamed of those he knew, and to take the Silvas out to a Christmas treat could in no way, so it seemed to him, show lack of consideration for Ruth. On the other hand, he did see Ruth's point of view, after she had explained it; and he looked upon it as a feminine weakness, such as afflicted all women and the best of women.

CHAPTER XXXVI

"Come on,—I'll show you the real dirt," Brissenden said to him, one evening in January.

They had dined together in San Francisco, and were at the Ferry Building, returning to Oakland, when the whim came to him to show Martin the "real dirt." He turned and fled across the water-front, a meagre shadow in a flapping overcoat, with Martin straining to keep up with him. At a wholesale liquor store he bought two gallon-demijohns of old port, and with one in each hand boarded a Mission Street car, Martin at his heels burdened with several quart-bottles of whiskey.

If Ruth could see me now, was his thought, while he wondered as to what constituted the real dirt.

"Maybe nobody will be there," Brissenden said, when they dismounted and plunged off to the right into the heart of the working-class ghetto, south of Market Street. "In which case you'll miss what you've been looking for so long."

"And what the deuce is that?" Martin asked.

"Men, intelligent men, and not the gibbering nonentities I found you consorting with in that trader's den. You read the books and you found yourself all alone. Well, I'm going to show you to-night some other men who've read the books, so that you won't be lonely any more."

"Not that I bother my head about their everlasting discussions," he said at the end of a block. "I'm not interested in book philosophy. But you'll find these fellows intelligences and not bourgeois swine. But watch out, they'll talk an arm off of you on any subject under the sun."

"Hope Norton's there," he panted a little later, resisting Martin's effort to relieve him of the two demijohns. "Norton's an idealist—a Harvard man. Prodigious memory. Idealism led him to philosophic anarchy, and his family threw him off. Father's a railroad president and many times millionaire, but the son's starving in 'Frisco, editing an anarchist sheet for twenty-five a month."

Martin was little acquainted in San Francisco, and not at all south of Market; so he had no idea of where he was being led.

"Go ahead," he said; "tell me about them beforehand. What do they do for a living? How do they happen to be here?"

"Hope Hamilton's there." Brissenden paused and rested his hands. "Strawn-Hamilton's his name—hyphenated, you know—comes of old Southern stock. He's a tramp—laziest man I ever knew, though he's clerking, or trying to, in a socialist coöperative store for six dollars a week. But he's a confirmed hobo. Tramped into town. I've seen him sit all day on a bench and never a bite pass his lips, and in the evening, when I invited him to dinner—restaurant two blocks away—have him say, 'Too much trouble, old man. Buy me a package of cigarettes instead.' He was a Spencerian like you till Kreis turned him to materialistic monism. I'll start him on monism if I can. Norton's another monist—only he affirms naught but spirit. He can give Kreis and Hamilton all they want, too."

"Who is Kreis?" Martin asked.

"His rooms we're going to. One time professor—fired from university—usual story. A mind like a steel trap. Makes his living any old way. I know he's been a street fakir when he was down. Unscrupulous. Rob a corpse of a shroud—anything. Difference between him—and the bourgeoisie is that he robs without illusion. He'll talk Nietzsche, or Schopenhauer, or Kant, or anything, but the only thing in this world, not excepting Mary, that he really cares for, is his monism. Haeckel is his little tin god. The only way to insult him is to take a slap at Haeckel."

"Here's the hang-out." Brissenden rested his demijohn at the upstairs entrance, preliminary to the climb. It was the usual two-story corner building, with a saloon and grocery underneath. "The gang lives here—got the whole upstairs to themselves. But Kreis is the only one who has two rooms. Come on."

No lights burned in the upper hall, but Brissenden threaded the utter blackness like a familiar ghost. He stopped to speak to Martin.

"There's one fellow—Stevens—a theosophist. Makes a pretty tangle when he gets going. Just now he's dish-washer in a restaurant. Likes a good cigar. I've seen him eat in a ten-cent hash-house and pay fifty cents for the cigar he smoked afterward. I've got a couple in my pocket for him, if he shows up."

"And there's another fellow—Parry—an Australian, a statistician and a sporting encyclopaedia. Ask him the grain output of Paraguay for 1903, or the English importation of sheetings into China for 1890, or at what weight Jimmy Britt fought Battling Nelson, or who was welter-weight champion of the United States in '68, and you'll get the correct answer with the automatic celerity of a slot-machine. And there's Andy, a stone-mason, has ideas on everything, a good chess-player; and another fellow, Harry, a baker, red hot socialist and strong union man. By the way, you remember Cooks' and Waiters' strike—Hamilton was the chap who organized that union and precipitated the strike—planned it all out in advance, right here in Kreis's rooms. Did it just for the fun of it, but was too lazy to stay by the union. Yet he could have risen high if he wanted to. There's no end to the possibilities in that man—if he weren't so insuperably lazy."

Brissenden advanced through the darkness till a thread of light marked the threshold of a door. A knock and an answer opened it, and Martin found himself shaking hands with Kreis, a handsome brunette man, with dazzling white teeth, a drooping black mustache, and large, flashing black eyes. Mary, a matronly young blonde, was washing dishes in the little back room that served for kitchen and dining room. The front room served as bedchamber and living room. Overhead was the week's washing, hanging in festoons so low that Martin did not see at first the two men talking in a corner. They hailed Brissenden and his demijohns with acclamation, and, on being introduced, Martin learned they were Andy and Parry. He joined them and listened attentively to the description of a prize-fight Parry had seen the night before; while Brissenden, in his glory, plunged into the manufacture of a toddy and the serving of wine and whiskey-and-sodas. At his command, "Bring in the clan," Andy departed to go the round of the rooms for the lodgers.

"We're lucky that most of them are here," Brissenden whispered to Martin. "There's Norton and Hamilton; come on and meet them. Stevens isn't around, I hear. I'm going to get them started on monism if I can. Wait till they get a few jolts in them and they'll warm up."

At first the conversation was desultory. Nevertheless Martin could not fail to appreciate the keen play of their minds. They were men with opinions, though the opinions often clashed, and, though they were witty and clever, they were not superficial. He swiftly saw, no matter upon what they talked, that each man applied the correlation of knowledge and had also a deep-seated and unified conception of society and the Cosmos. Nobody manufactured their opinions for them; they were all rebels of one variety or another, and their lips were strangers to platitudes. Never had Martin, at the Morses', heard so amazing a range of topics discussed. There seemed no limit save time to the things they were alive to. The talk wandered from Mrs. Humphry Ward's new book to Shaw's latest play, through the future of the drama to reminiscences of Mansfield. They appreciated or sneered at the morning editorials, jumped from labor conditions in New Zealand to Henry James and Brander Matthews, passed on to the German designs in the Far East and the economic aspect of the Yellow Peril, wrangled over the German elections and Bebel's last speech, and settled down to local politics, the latest plans and scandals in the union labor party administration, and the wires that were pulled to bring about the Coast Seamen's strike. Martin was struck by the inside knowledge they possessed. They knew what was never printed in the newspapers—the wires and strings and the hidden hands that made the puppets dance. To Martin's surprise, the girl, Mary, joined in the conversation, displaying an intelligence he had never encountered in the few women he had met. They talked together on Swinburne and Rossetti, after which she led him beyond his depth into the by-paths of French literature. His revenge came when she defended Maeterlinck and he brought into action the carefully-thought-out thesis of "The Shame of the Sun."

Several other men had dropped in, and the air was thick with tobacco smoke, when Brissenden waved the red flag.

"Here's fresh meat for your axe, Kreis," he said; "a rose-white youth with the ardor of a lover for Herbert Spencer. Make a Haeckelite of him—if you can."

Kreis seemed to wake up and flash like some metallic, magnetic thing, while Norton looked at Martin sympathetically, with a sweet, girlish smile, as much as to say that he would be amply protected.

Kreis began directly on Martin, but step by step Norton interfered, until he and Kreis were off and away in a personal battle. Martin listened and fain would have rubbed his eyes. It was impossible that this should be, much less in the labor ghetto south of Market. The books were alive in these men. They talked with fire and enthusiasm, the intellectual stimulant stirring them as he had seen drink and anger stir other men. What he heard was no longer the philosophy of the dry, printed word, written by half-mythical demigods like Kant and Spencer. It was living philosophy, with warm, red blood, incarnated in these two men till its very features worked with excitement. Now and again other men joined in, and all followed the discussion with cigarettes going out in their hands and with alert, intent faces.

Idealism had never attracted Martin, but the exposition it now received at the hands of Norton was a revelation. The logical plausibility of it, that made an appeal to his intellect, seemed missed by Kreis and Hamilton, who sneered at Norton as a metaphysician, and who, in turn, sneered back at them as metaphysicians. *Phenomenon* and *noumenon* were bandied back and forth. They charged him with attempting to explain consciousness by itself. He charged them with word-jugglery, with reasoning from words to theory instead of from facts to theory. At this they were aghast. It was the cardinal tenet of their mode of reasoning to start with facts and to give names to the facts.

When Norton wandered into the intricacies of Kant, Kreis reminded him that all good little German philosophies when they died went to Oxford. A little later Norton reminded them of

Hamilton's Law of Parsimony, the application of which they immediately claimed for every reasoning process of theirs. And Martin hugged his knees and exulted in it all. But Norton was no Spencerian, and he, too, strove for Martin's philosophic soul, talking as much at him as to his two opponents.

"You know Berkeley has never been answered," he said, looking directly at Martin. "Herbert Spencer came the nearest, which was not very near. Even the stanchest of Spencer's followers will not go farther. I was reading an essay of Saleeby's the other day, and the best Saleeby could say was that Herbert Spencer *nearly* succeeded in answering Berkeley."

"You know what Hume said?" Hamilton asked. Norton nodded, but Hamilton gave it for the benefit of the rest. "He said that Berkeley's arguments admit of no answer and produce no conviction."

"In his, Hume's, mind," was the reply. "And Hume's mind was the same as yours, with this difference: he was wise enough to admit there was no answering Berkeley."

Norton was sensitive and excitable, though he never lost his head, while Kreis and Hamilton were like a pair of cold-blooded savages, seeking out tender places to prod and poke. As the evening grew late, Norton, smarting under the repeated charges of being a metaphysician, clutching his chair to keep from jumping to his feet, his gray eyes snapping and his girlish face grown harsh and sure, made a grand attack upon their position.

"All right, you Haeckelites, I may reason like a medicine man, but, pray, how do you reason? You have nothing to stand on, you unscientific dogmatists with your positive science which you are always lugging about into places it has no right to be. Long before the school of materialistic monism arose, the ground was removed so that there could be no foundation. Locke was the man, John Locke. Two hundred years ago—more than that, even in his 'Essay concerning the Human Understanding,' he proved the non-existence of innate ideas. The best of it is that that is precisely what you claim. To-night, again and again, you have asserted the non-existence of innate ideas.

"And what does that mean? It means that you can never know ultimate reality. Your brains are empty when you are born. Appearances, or phenomena, are all the content your minds can receive from your five senses. Then noumena, which are not in your minds when you are born, have no way of getting in—"

"I deny—" Kreis started to interrupt.

"You wait till I'm done," Norton shouted. "You can know only that much of the play and interplay of force and matter as impinges in one way or another on our senses. You see, I am willing to admit, for the sake of the argument, that matter exists; and what I am about to do is to efface you by your own argument. I can't do it any other way, for you are both congenitally unable to understand a philosophic abstraction."

"And now, what do you know of matter, according to your own positive science? You know it only by its phenomena, its appearances. You are aware only of its changes, or of such changes in it as cause changes in your consciousness. Positive science deals only with phenomena, yet you are foolish enough to strive to be ontologists and to deal with noumena. Yet, by the very definition of positive science, science is concerned only with appearances. As somebody has said, phenomenal knowledge cannot transcend phenomena."

"You cannot answer Berkeley, even if you have annihilated Kant, and yet, perforce, you assume that Berkeley is wrong when you affirm that science proves the non-existence of God, or, as much to the point, the existence of matter.—You know I granted the reality of matter only in order to make myself intelligible to your understanding. Be positive scientists, if you please; but ontology has no place in positive science, so leave it alone. Spencer is right in his agnosticism, but if Spencer—"

But it was time to catch the last ferry-boat for Oakland, and Brissenden and Martin slipped out, leaving Norton still talking and Kreis and Hamilton waiting to pounce on him like a pair of hounds as soon as he finished.

"You have given me a glimpse of fairyland," Martin said on the ferry-boat. "It makes life worth while to meet people like that. My mind is all worked up. I never appreciated idealism before. Yet I can't accept it. I know that I shall always be a realist. I am so made, I guess. But I'd like to have made a reply to Kreis and Hamilton, and I think I'd have had a word or two for Norton. I didn't see that Spencer was damaged any. I'm as excited as a child on its first visit to the circus. I see I must read up some more. I'm going to get hold of Saleeby. I still think Spencer is unassailable, and next time I'm going to take a hand myself."

But Brissenden, breathing painfully, had dropped off to sleep, his chin buried in a scarf and resting on his sunken chest, his body wrapped in the long overcoat and shaking to the vibration of the propellers.

CHAPTER XXXVII

The first thing Martin did next morning was to go counter both to Brissenden's advice and command. "The Shame of the Sun" he wrapped and mailed to *The Acropolis*. He believed he could find magazine publication for it, and he felt that recognition by the magazines would commend him to the book-publishing houses. "Ephemera" he likewise wrapped and mailed to a magazine. Despite Brissenden's prejudice against the magazines, which was a pronounced mania with him, Martin decided that the great poem should see print. He did not intend, however, to publish it without the other's permission. His plan was to get it accepted by one of the high magazines, and, thus armed, again to wrestle with Brissenden for consent.

Martin began, that morning, a story which he had sketched out a number of weeks before and which ever since had been worrying him with its insistent clamor to be created. Apparently it was to be a rattling sea story, a tale of twentieth-century adventure and romance, handling real characters, in a real world, under real conditions. But beneath the swing and go of the story was to be something else—something that the superficial reader would never discern and which, on the other hand, would not diminish in any way the interest and enjoyment for such a reader. It was this, and not the mere story, that impelled Martin to write it. For that matter, it was always the great, universal motif that suggested plots to him. After having found such a motif, he cast about for the particular persons and particular location in time and space wherewith and wherein to utter the universal thing. "Overdue" was the title he had decided for it, and its length he believed would not be more than sixty thousand words—a bagatelle for him with his splendid vigor of production. On this first day he took hold of it with conscious delight in the mastery of his tools. He no longer worried for fear that the sharp, cutting edges should slip and mar his work. The long months of intense application and study had brought their reward. He could now devote himself with sure hand to the larger phases of the thing he shaped; and as he worked, hour after hour, he felt, as never before, the sure and cosmic grasp with which he held life and the affairs of life. "Overdue" would tell a story that would be true of its particular characters and its particular events; but it would tell, too, he was confident, great vital things that would be true of all time, and all sea, and all life—thanks to Herbert Spencer, he thought, leaning back for a moment from the table. Ay, thanks to Herbert Spencer and to the master-key of life, evolution, which Spencer had placed in his hands.

He was conscious that it was great stuff he was writing. "It will go! It will go!" was the refrain that kept sounding in his ears. Of course it would go. At last he was turning out the thing at which the magazines would jump. The whole story worked out before him in lightning flashes. He broke off from it long enough to write a paragraph in his note-book. This would be the last paragraph in "Overdue"; but so thoroughly was the whole book already composed in his brain that he could write, weeks before he had arrived at the end, the end itself. He compared the tale, as yet unwritten, with the tales of the sea-writers, and he felt it to be immeasurably superior. "There's only one man who could touch it," he murmured aloud, "and that's Conrad. And it ought to make even him sit up and shake hands with me, and say, 'Well done, Martin, my boy.'"

He toiled on all day, recollecting, at the last moment, that he was to have dinner at the Morses'. Thanks to Brissenden, his black suit was out of pawn and he was again eligible for dinner parties. Down town he stopped off long enough to run into the library and search for Saleeby's books. He drew out "The Cycle of Life," and on the car turned to the essay Norton had mentioned on Spencer. As Martin read, he grew angry. His face flushed, his jaw set, and unconsciously his hand clenched, unclenched, and clenched again as if he were taking fresh grips upon some hateful thing out of which he was squeezing the life. When he left the car, he strode along the sidewalk as a wrathful man will stride, and he rang the Morse bell with such viciousness that it roused him to consciousness of his condition, so that he entered in good nature, smiling with amusement at himself. No sooner, however, was he inside than a great depression descended upon him. He fell from the height where he had been up-borne all day on the wings of inspiration. "Bourgeois," "trader's den"—Brissenden's epithets repeated themselves in his mind. But what of that? he demanded angrily. He was marrying Ruth, not her family.

It seemed to him that he had never seen Ruth more beautiful, more spiritual and ethereal and at the same time more healthy. There was color in her cheeks, and her eyes drew him again and again—the eyes in which he had first read immortality. He had forgotten immortality of late, and the trend of his scientific reading had been away from it; but here, in Ruth's eyes, he read an argument without words that transcended all worded arguments. He saw that in her eyes before which all discussion fled away, for he saw love there. And in his own eyes was love; and love was unanswerable. Such was his passionate doctrine.

The half hour he had with her, before they went in to dinner, left him supremely happy and supremely satisfied with life. Nevertheless, at table, the inevitable reaction and exhaustion consequent upon the hard day seized hold of him. He was aware that his eyes were tired and that he was irritable. He remembered it was at this table, at which he now sneered and was so often bored, that he had first eaten with civilized beings in what he had imagined was an atmosphere of high culture and refinement. He caught a glimpse of that pathetic figure of him, so long ago, a self-conscious savage, sprouting sweat at every pore in an agony of apprehension, puzzled by the bewildering minutiae of eating-implements, tortured by the ogre of a servant, striving at a leap to live at such dizzy social altitude, and deciding in the end to be frankly himself, pretending no knowledge and no polish he did not possess.

He glanced at Ruth for reassurance, much in the same manner that a passenger, with sudden panic thought of possible shipwreck, will strive to locate the life preservers. Well, that much had come out of it—love and Ruth. All the rest had failed to stand the test of the books. But Ruth and love had stood the test; for them he found a biological sanction. Love was the most exalted expression of life. Nature had been busy designing him, as she had been busy with all normal men, for the purpose of loving. She had spent ten thousand centuries—ay, a hundred thousand and a million centuries—upon the task, and he was the best she could do. She had made love the strongest thing in him, increased its power a myriad per cent with her gift of imagination, and sent him forth into the ephemera to thrill and melt and mate. His hand sought Ruth's hand beside him hidden by the table, and a warm pressure was given and received. She looked at him a swift instant, and her eyes were radiant and melting. So were his in the thrill that pervaded him; nor did he realize how much that was radiant and melting in her eyes had been aroused by what she had seen in his.

Across the table from him, cater-cornered, at Mr. Morse's right, sat Judge Blount, a local superior court judge. Martin had met him a number of times and had failed to like him. He and Ruth's father were discussing labor union politics, the local situation, and socialism, and Mr. Morse was endeavoring to twit Martin on the latter topic. At last Judge Blount looked across the table with benignant and fatherly pity. Martin smiled to himself.

"You'll grow out of it, young man," he said soothingly. "Time is the best cure for such youthful distempers." He turned to Mr. Morse. "I do not believe discussion is good in such cases. It makes the patient obstinate."

"That is true," the other assented gravely. "But it is well to warn the patient occasionally of his condition."

Martin laughed merrily, but it was with an effort. The day had been too long, the day's effort too intense, and he was deep in the throes of the reaction.

"Undoubtedly you are both excellent doctors," he said; "but if you care a whit for the opinion of the patient, let him tell you that you are poor diagnosticians. In fact, you are both suffering from the disease you think you find in me. As for me, I am immune. The socialist philosophy that riots half-baked in your veins has passed me by."

"Clever, clever," murmured the judge. "An excellent ruse in controversy, to reverse positions."

"Out of your mouth." Martin's eyes were sparkling, but he kept control of himself. "You see, Judge, I've heard your campaign speeches. By some henidical process—henidical, by the way is a favorite word of mine which nobody understands—by some henidical process you persuade yourself that you believe in the competitive system and the survival of the strong, and at the same time you indorse with might and main all sorts of measures to shear the strength from the strong."

"My young man—"

"Remember, I've heard your campaign speeches," Martin warned. "It's on record, your position on interstate commerce regulation, on regulation of the railway trust and Standard Oil, on the conservation of the forests, on a thousand and one restrictive measures that are nothing else than socialistic."

"Do you mean to tell me that you do not believe in regulating these various outrageous exercises of power?"

"That's not the point. I mean to tell you that you are a poor diagnostician. I mean to tell you that I am not suffering from the microbe of socialism. I mean to tell you that it is you who are suffering from the emasculating ravages of that same microbe. As for me, I am an inveterate opponent of socialism just as I am an inveterate opponent of your own mongrel democracy that is nothing else than pseudo-socialism masquerading under a garb of words that will not stand the test of the dictionary."

"I am a reactionary—so complete a reactionary that my position is incomprehensible to you who live in a veiled lie of social organization and whose sight is not keen enough to pierce the veil. You make believe that you believe in the survival of the strong and the rule of the strong. I believe. That is the difference. When I was a trifle younger,—a few months younger,—I believed the same thing. You see, the ideas of you and yours had impressed me. But merchants and traders are cowardly rulers at best; they grunt and grub all their days in the trough of money-getting, and I have swung back to aristocracy, if you please. I am the only individualist in this room. I look to the state for nothing. I look only to the strong man, the man on horseback, to save the state from its own rotten futility."

"Nietzsche was right. I won't take the time to tell you who Nietzsche was, but he was right. The world belongs to the strong—to the strong who are noble as well and who do not wallow in the swine-trough of trade and exchange. The world belongs to the true nobleman, to the great blond beasts, to the noncompromisers, to the 'yes-sayers.' And they will eat you up, you socialists—who are afraid of socialism and who think yourselves individualists. Your slave-morality of the meek and lowly will never save you.—Oh, it's all Greek, I know, and I won't bother you any more with it. But remember one thing. There aren't half a dozen individualists in Oakland, but Martin Eden is one of them."

He signified that he was done with the discussion, and turned to Ruth.

"I'm wrought up to-day," he said in an undertone. "All I want to do is to love, not talk."

He ignored Mr. Morse, who said:-

"I am unconvinced. All socialists are Jesuits. That is the way to tell them."

"We'll make a good Republican out of you yet," said Judge Blount.

"The man on horseback will arrive before that time," Martin retorted with good humor, and returned to Ruth.

But Mr. Morse was not content. He did not like the laziness and the disinclination for sober, legitimate work of this prospective son-in-law of his, for whose ideas he had no respect and of whose nature he had no understanding. So he turned the conversation to Herbert Spencer. Judge Blount ably seconded him, and Martin, whose ears had pricked at the first mention of the philosopher's name, listened to the judge enunciate a grave and complacent diatribe against Spencer. From time to time Mr. Morse glanced at Martin, as much as to say, "There, my boy, you see."

"Chattering daws," Martin muttered under his breath, and went on talking with Ruth and Arthur.

But the long day and the "real dirt" of the night before were telling upon him; and, besides, still in his burnt mind was what had made him angry when he read it on the car.

"What is the matter?" Ruth asked suddenly alarmed by the effort he was making to contain himself.

"There is no god but the Unknowable, and Herbert Spencer is its prophet," Judge Blount was saying at that moment.

Martin turned upon him.

"A cheap judgment," he remarked quietly. "I heard it first in the City Hall Park, on the lips of a workingman who ought to have known better. I have heard it often since, and each time the clap-trap of it nauseates me. You ought to be ashamed of yourself. To hear that great and noble man's name upon your lips is like finding a dew-drop in a cesspool. You are disgusting."

It was like a thunderbolt. Judge Blount glared at him with apoplectic countenance, and silence reigned. Mr. Morse was secretly pleased. He could see that his daughter was shocked. It was what he wanted to do—to bring out the innate ruffianism of this man he did not like.

Ruth's hand sought Martin's beseechingly under the table, but his blood was up. He was inflamed by the intellectual pretence and fraud of those who sat in the high places. A Superior Court Judge! It was only several years before that he had looked up from the mire at such glorious entities and deemed them gods.

Judge Blount recovered himself and attempted to go on, addressing himself to Martin with an assumption of politeness that the latter understood was for the benefit of the ladies. Even this added to his anger. Was there no honesty in the world?

"You can't discuss Spencer with me," he cried. "You do not know any more about Spencer than do his own countrymen. But it is no fault of yours, I grant. It is just a phase of the contemptible ignorance of the times. I ran across a sample of it on my way here this evening. I was reading an essay by Saleeby on Spencer. You should read it. It is accessible to all men. You can buy it in any book-store or draw it from the public library. You would feel ashamed of your paucity of abuse and ignorance of that noble man compared with what Saleeby has collected on the subject. It is a record of shame that would shame your shame."

"'The philosopher of the half-educated,' he was called by an academic Philosopher who was not worthy to pollute the atmosphere he breathed. I don't think you have read ten pages of Spencer, but there have been critics, assumably more intelligent than you, who have read no more than you of Spencer, who publicly challenged his followers to adduce one single idea from all his writings—from Herbert Spencer's writings, the man who has impressed the stamp of his genius over the whole field of scientific research and modern thought; the father of psychology; the man who revolutionized pedagogy, so that to-day the child of the French peasant is taught the three R's according to principles laid down by him. And the little gnats of men sting his memory when they get their very bread and butter from the technical application of his ideas. What little of worth resides in their brains is largely due to him. It is certain that had he never lived, most of what is correct in their parrot-learned knowledge would be absent."

"And yet a man like Principal Fairbanks of Oxford—a man who sits in an even higher place than you, Judge Blount—has said that Spencer will be dismissed by posterity as a poet and dreamer rather than a thinker. Yappers and blatherskites, the whole brood of them! '"First Principles" is not wholly destitute of a certain literary power,' said one of them. And others of them have said that he was an industrious plodder rather than an original thinker. Yappers and blatherskites! Yappers and blatherskites!"

Martin ceased abruptly, in a dead silence. Everybody in Ruth's family looked up to Judge Blount as a man of power and achievement, and they were horrified at Martin's outbreak. The remainder of the dinner passed like a funeral, the judge and Mr. Morse confining their talk to each other, and the rest of the conversation being extremely desultory. Then afterward, when Ruth and Martin were alone, there was a scene.

"You are unbearable," she wept.

But his anger still smouldered, and he kept muttering, "The beasts! The beasts!"

When she averred he had insulted the judge, he retorted:-

"By telling the truth about him?"

"I don't care whether it was true or not," she insisted. "There are certain bounds of decency, and you had no license to insult anybody."

"Then where did Judge Blount get the license to assault truth?" Martin demanded. "Surely to assault truth is a more serious misdemeanor than to insult a pygmy personality such as the judge's. He did worse than that. He blackened the name of a great, noble man who is dead. Oh, the beasts! The beasts!"

His complex anger flamed afresh, and Ruth was in terror of him. Never had she seen him so angry, and it was all mystified and unreasonable to her comprehension. And yet, through her very terror ran the fibres of fascination that had drawn and that still drew her to him—that had compelled her to lean towards him, and, in that mad, culminating moment, lay her hands upon his neck. She was hurt and outraged by what had taken place, and yet she lay in his arms and quivered while he went on muttering, "The beasts! The beasts!" And she still lay there when he said: "I'll not bother your table again, dear. They do not like me, and it is wrong of me to thrust my objectionable presence upon them. Besides, they are just as objectionable to me. Faugh! They are sickening. And to think of it, I dreamed in my innocence that the persons who sat in the high places, who lived in fine houses and had educations and bank accounts, were worth while!"

CHAPTER XXXVIII

"Come on, let's go down to the local."

So spoke Brissenden, faint from a hemorrhage of half an hour before—the second hemorrhage in three days. The perennial whiskey glass was in his hands, and he drained it with shaking fingers.

"What do I want with socialism?" Martin demanded.

"Outsiders are allowed five-minute speeches," the sick man urged. "Get up and spout. Tell them why you don't want socialism. Tell them what you think about them and their ghetto ethics. Slam Nietzsche into them and get walloped for your pains. Make a scrap of it. It will do them good. Discussion is what they want, and what you want, too. You see, I'd like to see you a socialist before I'm gone. It will give you a sanction for your existence. It is the one thing that will save you in the time of disappointment that is coming to you."

"I never can puzzle out why you, of all men, are a socialist," Martin pondered. "You detest the crowd so. Surely there is nothing in the canaille to recommend it to your aesthetic soul." He pointed an accusing finger at the whiskey glass which the other was refilling. "Socialism doesn't seem to save you."

"I'm very sick," was the answer. "With you it is different. You have health and much to live for, and you must be handcuffed to life somehow. As for me, you wonder why I am a socialist. I'll tell you. It is because Socialism is inevitable; because the present rotten and irrational system cannot endure; because the day is past for your man on horseback. The slaves won't stand for it. They are too many, and willy-nilly they'll drag down the would-be equestrian before ever he gets astride. You can't get away from them, and you'll have to swallow the whole slave-morality. It's not a nice mess, I'll allow. But it's been a-brewing and swallow it you must. You are antediluvian anyway, with your Nietzsche ideas. The past is past, and the man who says history repeats itself is a liar. Of course I don't like the crowd, but what's a poor chap to do? We can't have the man on horseback, and anything is preferable to the timid swine that now rule. But come on, anyway. I'm loaded to the guards now, and if I sit here any longer, I'll get drunk. And you know the doctor says—damn the doctor! I'll fool him yet."

It was Sunday night, and they found the small hall packed by the Oakland socialists, chiefly members of the working class. The speaker, a clever Jew, won Martin's admiration at the same time that he aroused his antagonism. The man's stooped and narrow shoulders and weazened chest proclaimed him the true child of the crowded ghetto, and strong on Martin was the age-long struggle of the feeble, wretched slaves against the lordly handful of men who had ruled over them and would rule over them to the end of time. To Martin this withered wisp of a creature was a symbol. He was the figure that stood forth representative of the whole miserable mass of weaklings and inefficients who perished according to biological law on the ragged confines of life. They were the unfit. In spite of their cunning philosophy and of their antlike proclivities for coöperation, Nature rejected them for the exceptional man. Out of the plentiful spawn of life she flung from her prolific hand she selected only the best. It was by the same method that men, aping her, bred race-horses and cucumbers. Doubtless, a creator of a Cosmos could have devised a better method; but creatures of this particular Cosmos must put up with this particular method. Of course, they could squirm as they perished, as the socialists squirmed, as the speaker on the platform and the perspiring crowd were squirming even now as they counselled together for some new device with which to minimize the penalties of living and outwit the Cosmos.

So Martin thought, and so he spoke when Brissenden urged him to give them hell. He obeyed the mandate, walking up to the platform, as was the custom, and addressing the chairman. He began in a low voice, haltingly, forming into order the ideas which had surged in his brain while the Jew was speaking. In such meetings five minutes was the time allotted to each speaker; but when Martin's five minutes were up, he was in full stride, his attack upon their doctrines but half completed. He had caught their interest, and the audience urged the chairman by acclamation to extend Martin's time. They appreciated him as a foeman worthy of their intellect, and they listened intently, following every word. He spoke with fire and conviction, mincing no words in his attack upon the slaves and their morality and tactics and frankly alluding to his hearers as the slaves in question. He quoted Spencer and Malthus, and enunciated the biological law of development.

"And so," he concluded, in a swift résumé, "no state composed of the slave-types can endure. The old law of development still holds. In the struggle for existence, as I have shown, the strong and the progeny of the strong tend to survive, while the weak and the progeny of the weak are crushed and tend to perish. The result is that the strong and the progeny of the strong survive, and, so long as the struggle obtains, the strength of each generation increases. That is development. But you slaves—it is too bad to be slaves, I grant—but you slaves dream of a society where the law of development will be annulled, where no weaklings and inefficients will perish, where every inefficient will have as much as he wants to eat as many times a day as he desires, and where all will marry and have progeny—the weak as well as the strong. What will be the result? No longer will the strength and life-value of each generation increase. On the contrary, it will diminish. There is the Nemesis of your slave philosophy. Your society of slaves—of, by, and for, slaves—must inevitably weaken and go to pieces as the life which composes it weakens and goes to pieces.

"Remember, I am enunciating biology and not sentimental ethics. No state of slaves can stand—"

"How about the United States?" a man yelled from the audience.

"And how about it?" Martin retorted. "The thirteen colonies threw off their rulers and formed the Republic so-called. The slaves were their own masters. There were no more masters of the sword. But you couldn't get along without masters of some sort, and there arose a new set of masters—not the great, virile, noble men, but the shrewd and spidery traders and money-lenders. And they enslaved you over again—but not frankly, as the true, noble men would do with weight of their own right arms, but secretly, by spidery machinations and by wheedling and cajolery and lies. They have purchased your slave judges, they have debauched your slave legislatures, and they have forced to worse horrors than chattel slavery your slave boys and girls. Two million of your children are toiling to-day in this trader-oligarchy of the United States. Ten millions of you slaves are not properly sheltered nor properly fed."

"But to return. I have shown that no society of slaves can endure, because, in its very nature, such society must annul the law of development. No sooner can a slave society be organized than deterioration sets in. It is easy for you to talk of annulling the law of development, but where is the new law of development that will maintain your strength? Formulate it. Is it already formulated? Then state it."

Martin took his seat amidst an uproar of voices. A score of men were on their feet clamoring for recognition from the chair. And one by one, encouraged by vociferous applause, speaking with fire and enthusiasm and excited gestures, they replied to the attack. It was a wild night—but it was wild intellectually, a battle of ideas. Some strayed from the point, but most of the speakers replied directly to Martin. They shook him with lines of thought that were new to him; and gave him insights, not into new biological laws, but into new applications of the old laws. They were too earnest to be always polite, and more than once the chairman rapped and pounded for order.

It chanced that a cub reporter sat in the audience, detailed there on a day dull of news and impressed by the urgent need of journalism for sensation. He was not a bright cub reporter. He was merely facile and glib. He was too dense to follow the discussion. In fact, he had a comfortable feeling that he was vastly superior to these wordy maniacs of the working class. Also, he had a great respect for those who sat in the high places and dictated the policies of nations and newspapers. Further, he had an ideal, namely, of achieving that excellence of the perfect reporter who is able to make something—even a great deal—out of nothing.

He did not know what all the talk was about. It was not necessary. Words like *revolution* gave him his cue. Like a paleontologist, able to reconstruct an entire skeleton from one fossil bone, he was able to reconstruct a whole speech from the one word *revolution*. He did it that night, and he did it well; and since Martin had made the biggest stir, he put it all into his mouth and made him the arch-anarch of the show, transforming his reactionary individualism into the most lurid, red-shirt socialist utterance. The cub reporter was an artist, and it was a large brush with which he laid on the local color—wild-eyed long-haired men, neurasthenia and degenerate types of men, voices shaken with passion, clenched fists raised on high, and all projected against a background of oaths, yells, and the throaty rumbling of angry men.

CHAPTER XXXIX

Over the coffee, in his little room, Martin read next morning's paper. It was a novel experience to find himself head-lined, on the first page at that; and he was surprised to learn that he was the most notorious leader of the Oakland socialists. He ran over the violent speech the cub reporter had constructed for him, and, though at first he was angered by the fabrication, in the end he tossed the paper aside with a laugh.

"Either the man was drunk or criminally malicious," he said that afternoon, from his perch on the bed, when Brissenden had arrived and dropped limply into the one chair.

"But what do you care?" Brissenden asked. "Surely you don't desire the approval of the bourgeois swine that read the newspapers?"

Martin thought for a while, then said:-

"No, I really don't care for their approval, not a whit. On the other hand, it's very likely to make my relations with Ruth's family a trifle awkward. Her father always contended I was a socialist, and this miserable stuff will clinch his belief. Not that I care for his opinion—but what's the odds? I want to read you what I've been doing to-day. It's 'Overdue,' of course, and I'm just about halfway through."

He was reading aloud when Maria thrust open the door and ushered in a young man in a natty suit who glanced briskly about him, noting the oil-burner and the kitchen in the corner before his gaze wandered on to Martin.

"Sit down," Brissenden said.

Martin made room for the young man on the bed and waited for him to broach his business.

"I heard you speak last night, Mr. Eden, and I've come to interview you," he began.

Brissenden burst out in a hearty laugh.

"A brother socialist?" the reporter asked, with a quick glance at Brissenden that appraised the color-value of that cadaverous and dying man.

"And he wrote that report," Martin said softly. "Why, he is only a boy!"

"Why don't you poke him?" Brissenden asked. "I'd give a thousand dollars to have my lungs back for five minutes."

The cub reporter was a trifle perplexed by this talking over him and around him and at him. But he had been commended for his brilliant description of the socialist meeting and had further been detailed to get a personal interview with Martin Eden, the leader of the organized menace to society.

"You do not object to having your picture taken, Mr. Eden?" he said. "I've a staff photographer outside, you see, and he says it will be better to take you right away before the sun gets lower. Then we can have the interview afterward."

"A photographer," Brissenden said meditatively. "Poke him, Martin! Poke him!"

"I guess I'm getting old," was the answer. "I know I ought, but I really haven't the heart. It doesn't seem to matter."

"For his mother's sake," Brissenden urged.

"It's worth considering," Martin replied; "but it doesn't seem worth while enough to rouse sufficient energy in me. You see, it does take energy to give a fellow a poking. Besides, what does it matter?"

"That's right—that's the way to take it," the cub announced airily, though he had already begun to glance anxiously at the door.

"But it wasn't true, not a word of what he wrote," Martin went on, confining his attention to Brissenden.

"It was just in a general way a description, you understand," the cub ventured, "and besides, it's good advertising. That's what counts. It was a favor to you."

"It's good advertising, Martin, old boy," Brissenden repeated solemnly.

"And it was a favor to me—think of that!" was Martin's contribution.

"Let me see—where were you born, Mr. Eden?" the cub asked, assuming an air of expectant attention.

"He doesn't take notes," said Brissenden. "He remembers it all."

"That is sufficient for me." The cub was trying not to look worried. "No decent reporter needs to bother with notes."

"That was sufficient—for last night." But Brissenden was not a disciple of quietism, and he changed his attitude abruptly. "Martin, if you don't poke him, I'll do it myself, if I fall dead on the floor the next moment."

"How will a spanking do?" Martin asked.

Brissenden considered judicially, and nodded his head.

The next instant Martin was seated on the edge of the bed with the cub face downward across his knees.

"Now don't bite," Martin warned, "or else I'll have to punch your face. It would be a pity, for it is such a pretty face."

His uplifted hand descended, and thereafter rose and fell in a swift and steady rhythm. The cub struggled and cursed and squirmed, but did not offer to bite. Brissenden looked on gravely, though once he grew excited and gripped the whiskey bottle, pleading, "Here, just let me swat him once."

"Sorry my hand played out," Martin said, when at last he desisted. "It is quite numb."

He uprighted the cub and perched him on the bed.

"I'll have you arrested for this," he snarled, tears of boyish indignation running down his flushed cheeks. "I'll make you sweat for this. You'll see."

"The pretty thing," Martin remarked. "He doesn't realize that he has entered upon the downward path. It is not honest, it is not square, it is not manly, to tell lies about one's fellow-creatures the way he has done, and he doesn't know it."

"He has to come to us to be told," Brissenden filled in a pause.

"Yes, to me whom he has maligned and injured. My grocery will undoubtedly refuse me credit now. The worst of it is that the poor boy will keep on this way until he deteriorates into a first-class newspaper man and also a first-class scoundrel."

"But there is yet time," quoth Brissenden. "Who knows but what you may prove the humble instrument to save him. Why didn't you let me swat him just once? I'd like to have had a hand in it."

"I'll have you arrested, the pair of you, you b-b-big brutes," sobbed the erring soul.

"No, his mouth is too pretty and too weak." Martin shook his head lugubriously. "I'm afraid I've numbed my hand in vain. The young man cannot reform. He will become eventually a very great and successful newspaper man. He has no conscience. That alone will make him great."

With that the cub passed out the door in trepidation to the last for fear that Brissenden would hit him in the back with the bottle he still clutched.

In the next morning's paper Martin learned a great deal more about himself that was new to him. "We are the sworn enemies of society," he found himself quoted as saying in a column interview. "No, we are not anarchists but socialists." When the reporter pointed out to him that there seemed little difference between the two schools, Martin had shrugged his shoulders in silent affirmation. His face was described as bilaterally asymmetrical, and various other signs of degeneration were described. Especially notable were his thuglike hands and the fiery gleams in his blood-shot eyes.

He learned, also, that he spoke nightly to the workmen in the City Hall Park, and that among the anarchists and agitators that there inflamed the minds of the people he drew the largest audiences and made the most revolutionary speeches. The cub painted a high-light picture of his poor little room, its oil-stove and the one chair, and of the death's-head tramp who kept him company and who looked as if he had just emerged from twenty years of solitary confinement in some fortress dungeon.

The cub had been industrious. He had scurried around and nosed out Martin's family history, and procured a photograph of Higginbotham's Cash Store with Bernard Higginbotham himself standing out in front. That gentleman was depicted as an intelligent, dignified businessman who had no patience with his brother-in-law's socialistic views, and no patience with the brother-in-law, either, whom he was quoted as characterizing as a lazy good-for-nothing who wouldn't take a job when it was offered to him and who would go to jail yet. Hermann Von Schmidt, Marian's husband, had likewise been interviewed. He had called Martin the black sheep of the family and repudiated him. "He tried to sponge off of me, but I put a stop to that good and quick," Von Schmidt had said to the reporter. "He knows better than to come bumming around here. A man who won't work is no good, take that from me."

This time Martin was genuinely angry. Brissenden looked upon the affair as a good joke, but he could not console Martin, who knew that it would be no easy task to explain to Ruth. As for her father, he knew that he must be overjoyed with what had happened and that he would make the most of it to break off the engagement. How much he would make of it he was soon to realize. The afternoon mail brought a letter from Ruth. Martin opened it with a premonition of disaster, and read it standing at the open door when he had received it from the postman. As he read, mechanically his hand sought his pocket for the tobacco and brown paper of his old cigarette days. He was not aware that the pocket was empty or that he had even reached for the materials with which to roll a cigarette.

It was not a passionate letter. There were no touches of anger in it. But all the way through, from the first sentence to the last, was sounded the note of hurt and disappointment. She had expected better of him. She had thought he had got over his youthful wildness, that her love for him had been sufficiently worth while to enable him to live seriously and decently. And now her father and mother had taken a firm stand and commanded that the engagement be broken. That they were justified in this she could not but admit. Their relation could never be a happy one. It had been unfortunate from the first. But one regret she voiced in the whole letter, and it was a bitter one to Martin. "If only you had settled down to some position and attempted to make something of yourself," she wrote. "But it was not to be. Your past life had been too wild and irregular. I can understand that you are not to be blamed. You could act only according to your nature and your early training. So I do not blame you, Martin. Please remember that. It was simply a mistake. As father and mother have contended, we were not made for each other, and we should both be happy because it was discovered not too late.". . "There is no use trying to see me," she said toward the last. "It would be an unhappy meeting for both of us, as well as for my mother. I feel, as it is, that I have caused her great pain and worry. I shall have to do much living to atone for it."

He read it through to the end, carefully, a second time, then sat down and replied. He outlined the remarks he had uttered at the socialist meeting, pointing out that they were in all ways the converse of what the newspaper had put in his mouth. Toward the end of the letter he was God's own lover pleading passionately for love. "Please answer," he said, "and in your answer you have to tell me but one thing. Do you love me? That is all—the answer to that one question."

But no answer came the next day, nor the next. "Overdue" lay untouched upon the table, and each day the heap of returned manuscripts under the table grew larger. For the first time Martin's glorious sleep was interrupted by insomnia, and he tossed through long, restless nights. Three times he called at the Morse home, but was turned away by the servant who answered the bell. Brissenden lay sick in his hotel, too feeble to stir out, and, though Martin was with him often, he did not worry him with his troubles.

For Martin's troubles were many. The aftermath of the cub reporter's deed was even wider than Martin had anticipated. The Portuguese grocer refused him further credit, while the greengrocer, who was an American and proud of it, had called him a traitor to his country and refused further dealings with him—carrying his patriotism to such a degree that he cancelled Martin's account and forbade him ever to attempt to pay it. The talk in the neighborhood reflected the same feeling, and indignation against Martin ran high. No one would have anything to do with a socialist traitor. Poor Maria was dubious and frightened, but she remained loyal. The children of the neighborhood recovered from the awe of the grand carriage which once had visited Martin, and from safe distances they called him "hobo" and "bum." The Silva tribe, however, stanchly defended him, fighting more than one pitched battle for his honor, and black eyes and bloody noses became quite the order of the day and added to Maria's perplexities and troubles.

Once, Martin met Gertrude on the street, down in Oakland, and learned what he knew could not be otherwise—that Bernard Higginbotham was furious with him for having dragged the family into public disgrace, and that he had forbidden him the house.

"Why don't you go away, Martin?" Gertrude had begged. "Go away and get a job somewhere and steady down. Afterwards, when this all blows over, you can come back."

Martin shook his head, but gave no explanations. How could he explain? He was appalled at the awful intellectual chasm that yawned between him and his people. He could never cross it and explain to them his position,—the Nietzschean position, in regard to socialism. There were not words enough in the English language, nor in any language, to make his attitude and conduct intelligible to them. Their highest concept of right conduct, in his case, was to get a job. That was their first word and their last. It constituted their whole lexicon of ideas. Get a job! Go to work! Poor, stupid slaves, he thought, while his sister talked. Small wonder the world belonged to the strong. The slaves were obsessed by their own slavery. A job was to them a golden fetich before which they fell down and worshipped.

He shook his head again, when Gertrude offered him money, though he knew that within the day he would have to make a trip to the pawnbroker.

"Don't come near Bernard now," she admonished him. "After a few months, when he is cooled down, if you want to, you can get the job of drivin' delivery-wagon for him. Any time you want me, just send for me an' I'll come. Don't forget."

She went away weeping audibly, and he felt a pang of sorrow shoot through him at sight of her heavy body and uncouth gait. As he watched her go, the Nietzschean edifice seemed to shake and totter. The slave-class in the abstract was all very well, but it was not wholly satisfactory when it was brought home to his own family. And yet, if there was ever a slave trampled by the strong, that slave was his sister Gertrude. He grinned savagely at the paradox. A fine Nietzsche-man he was, to allow his intellectual concepts to be shaken by the first sentiment or emotion that strayed along—ay, to be shaken by the slave-morality itself, for that was what his pity for his sister really was. The true noble men were above pity and compassion. Pity and compassion had been generated in the subterranean barracoons of the slaves and were no more than the agony and sweat of the crowded miserables and weaklings.

CHAPTER XL

"Overdue" still continued to lie forgotten on the table. Every manuscript that he had had out now lay under the table. Only one manuscript he kept going, and that was Brissenden's "Ephemera." His bicycle and black suit were again in pawn, and the type-writer people were once more worrying about the rent. But such things no longer bothered him. He was seeking a new orientation, and until that was found his life must stand still.

After several weeks, what he had been waiting for happened. He met Ruth on the street. It was true, she was accompanied by her brother, Norman, and it was true that they tried to ignore him and that Norman attempted to wave him aside.

"If you interfere with my sister, I'll call an officer," Norman threatened. "She does not wish to speak with you, and your insistence is insult."

"If you persist, you'll have to call that officer, and then you'll get your name in the papers," Martin answered grimly. "And now, get out of my way and get the officer if you want to. I'm going to talk with Ruth."

"I want to have it from your own lips," he said to her.

She was pale and trembling, but she held up and looked inquiringly.

"The question I asked in my letter," he prompted.

Norman made an impatient movement, but Martin checked him with a swift look.

She shook her head.

"Is all this of your own free will?" he demanded.

"It is." She spoke in a low, firm voice and with deliberation. "It is of my own free will. You have disgraced me so that I am ashamed to meet my friends. They are all talking about me, I know. That is all I can tell you. You have made me very unhappy, and I never wish to see you again."

"Friends! Gossip! Newspaper misreports! Surely such things are not stronger than love! I can only believe that you never loved me."

A blush drove the pallor from her face.

"After what has passed?" she said faintly. "Martin, you do not know what you are saying. I am not common."

"You see, she doesn't want to have anything to do with you," Norman blurted out, starting on with her.

Martin stood aside and let them pass, fumbling unconsciously in his coat pocket for the tobacco and brown papers that were not there.

It was a long walk to North Oakland, but it was not until he went up the steps and entered his room that he knew he had walked it. He found himself sitting on the edge of the bed and staring about him like an awakened somnambulist. He noticed "Overdue" lying on the table and drew up his chair and reached for his pen. There was in his nature a logical compulsion toward completeness. Here was something undone. It had been deferred against the completion of something else. Now that something else had been finished, and he would apply himself to this task until it was finished. What he would do next he did not know. All that he did know was that a climacteric in his life had been attained. A period had been reached, and he was rounding it off in workman-like fashion. He was not curious about the future. He would soon enough find out what it held in store for him. Whatever it was, it did not matter. Nothing seemed to matter.

For five days he toiled on at "Overdue," going nowhere, seeing nobody, and eating meagrely. On the morning of the sixth day the postman brought him a thin letter from the editor of *The Parthenon*. A glance told him that "Ephemera" was accepted. "We have submitted the poem to Mr. Cartwright Bruce," the editor went on to say, "and he has reported so favorably upon it that we cannot let it go. As an earnest of our pleasure in publishing the poem, let me tell you that we have set it for the August number, our July number being already made up. Kindly extend our pleasure and our thanks to Mr. Brissenden. Please send by return mail his photograph and biographical data. If our honorarium is unsatisfactory, kindly telegraph us at once and state what you consider a fair price."

Since the honorarium they had offered was three hundred and fifty dollars, Martin thought it not worth while to telegraph. Then, too, there was Brissenden's consent to be gained. Well, he had been right, after all. Here was one magazine editor who knew real poetry when he saw it. And the price was splendid, even though it was for the poem of a century. As for Cartwright Bruce, Martin knew that he was the one critic for whose opinions Brissenden had any respect.

Martin rode down town on an electric car, and as he watched the houses and cross-streets slipping by he was aware of a regret that he was not more elated over his friend's success and over his own signal victory. The one critic in the United States had pronounced favorably on the poem, while his own contention that good stuff could find its way into the magazines had proved correct. But enthusiasm had lost its spring in him, and he found that he was more anxious to see Brissenden than he was to carry the good news. The acceptance of *The Parthenon* had recalled to him that during his five days' devotion to "Overdue" he had not heard from Brissenden nor even thought about him. For the first time Martin realized the daze he had been in, and he felt shame for having forgotten his friend. But even the shame did not burn very sharply. He was numb to emotions of any sort save the artistic ones concerned in the writing of "Overdue." So far as other affairs were concerned, he had been in a trance. For that matter, he was still in a trance. All this life through which the electric car whirred seemed remote and unreal, and he would have experienced little interest and less shook if the great stone steeple of the church he passed had suddenly crumbled to mortar-dust upon his head.

At the hotel he hurried up to Brissenden's room, and hurried down again. The room was empty. All luggage was gone.

"Did Mr. Brissenden leave any address?" he asked the clerk, who looked at him curiously for a moment.

"Haven't you heard?" he asked.

Martin shook his head.

"Why, the papers were full of it. He was found dead in bed. Suicide. Shot himself through the head."

"Is he buried yet?" Martin seemed to hear his voice, like some one else's voice, from a long way off, asking the question.

"No. The body was shipped East after the inquest. Lawyers engaged by his people saw to the arrangements."

"They were quick about it, I must say," Martin commented.

"Oh, I don't know. It happened five days ago."

"Five days ago?"

"Yes, five days ago."

"Oh," Martin said as he turned and went out.

At the corner he stepped into the Western Union and sent a telegram to *The Parthenon*, advising them to proceed with the publication of the poem. He had in his pocket but five cents with which to pay his carfare home, so he sent the message collect.

Once in his room, he resumed his writing. The days and nights came and went, and he sat at his table and wrote on. He went nowhere, save to the pawnbroker, took no exercise, and ate methodically when he was hungry and had something to cook, and just as methodically went without when he had nothing to cook. Composed as the story was, in advance, chapter by chapter, he nevertheless saw and developed an opening that increased the power of it, though it necessitated twenty thousand additional words. It was not that there was any vital need that the thing should be well done, but that his artistic canons compelled him to do it well. He worked on in the daze, strangely detached from the world around him, feeling like a familiar ghost among these literary trappings of his former life. He remembered that some one had said that a ghost was the spirit of a man who was dead and who did not have sense enough to know it; and he paused for the moment to wonder if he were really dead did unaware of it.

Came the day when "Overdue" was finished. The agent of the type-writer firm had come for the machine, and he sat on the bed while Martin, on the one chair, typed the last pages of the final chapter. "Finis," he wrote, in capitals, at the end, and to him it was indeed finis. He watched the type-writer carried out the door with a feeling of relief, then went over and lay down on the bed. He was faint from hunger. Food had not passed his lips in thirty-six hours, but he did not think about it. He lay on his back, with closed eyes, and did not think at all, while the daze or stupor slowly welled up, saturating his consciousness. Half in delirium, he began muttering aloud the lines of an anonymous poem Brissenden had been fond of quoting to him. Maria, listening anxiously outside his door, was perturbed by his monotonous utterance. The words in themselves were not significant to her, but the fact that he was saying them was. "I have done," was the burden of the poem.

"'I have done—
Put by the lute.
Song and singing soon are over
As the airy shades that hover
In among the purple clover.
I have done—
Put by the lute.
Once I sang as early thrushes
Sing among the dewy bushes;
Now I'm mute.
I am like a weary linnet,
For my throat has no song in it;
I have had my singing minute.
I have done.
Put by the lute.'"

Maria could stand it no longer, and hurried away to the stove, where she filled a quart-bowl with soup, putting into it the lion's share of chopped meat and vegetables which her ladle scraped from the bottom of the pot. Martin roused himself and sat up and began to eat, between spoonfuls reassuring Maria that he had not been talking in his sleep and that he did not have any fever.

After she left him he sat drearily, with drooping shoulders, on the edge of the bed, gazing about him with lack-lustre eyes that saw nothing until the torn wrapper of a magazine, which had come in the morning's mail and which lay unopened, shot a gleam of light into his darkened brain. It is *The Parthenon*, he thought, the August *Parthenon*, and it must contain "Ephemera." If only Brissenden were here to see!

He was turning the pages of the magazine, when suddenly he stopped. "Ephemera" had been featured, with gorgeous head-piece and Beardsley-like margin decorations. On one side of the head-piece was Brissenden's photograph, on the other side was the photograph of Sir John Value, the British Ambassador. A preliminary editorial note quoted Sir John Value as saying that there were no poets in America, and the publication of "Ephemera" was *The Parthenon's*. "There, take that, Sir John Value!" Cartwright Bruce was described as the greatest critic in America, and he was quoted as saying that "Ephemera" was the greatest poem ever written in America. And finally, the editor's foreword ended with: "We have not yet made up our minds entirely as to the merits of "Ephemera"; perhaps we shall never be able to do so. But we have read it often, wondering at the words and their arrangement, wondering where Mr. Brissenden got them, and how he could fasten them together." Then followed the poem.

"Pretty good thing you died, Briss, old man," Martin murmured, letting the magazine slip between his knees to the floor.

The cheapness and vulgarity of it was nauseating, and Martin noted apathetically that he was not nauseated very much. He wished he could get angry, but did not have energy enough to try. He was too numb. His blood was too congealed to accelerate to the swift tidal flow of indignation. After all, what did it matter? It was on a par with all the rest that Brissenden had condemned in bourgeois society.

"Poor Briss," Martin communed; "he would never have forgiven me."

Rousing himself with an effort, he possessed himself of a box which had once contained type-writer paper. Going through its contents, he drew forth eleven poems which his friend had written. These he tore lengthwise and crosswise and dropped into the waste basket. He did it languidly, and, when he had finished, sat on the edge of the bed staring blankly before him.

How long he sat there he did not know, until, suddenly, across his sightless vision he saw form a long horizontal line of white. It was curious. But as he watched it grow in definiteness he saw that it was a coral reef smoking in the white Pacific surges. Next, in the line of breakers he made out a small canoe, an outrigger canoe. In the stern he saw a young bronzed god in scarlet hip-cloth dipping a flashing paddle. He recognized him. He was Moti, the youngest son of Tati, the chief, and this was Tahiti, and beyond that smoking reef lay the sweet land of Papara and the chief's grass house by the river's mouth. It was the end of the day, and Moti was coming home from the fishing. He was waiting for the rush of a big breaker whereon to jump the reef. Then he saw himself, sitting forward in the canoe as he had often sat in the past, dipping a paddle that waited Moti's word to dig in like mad when the turquoise wall of the great breaker rose behind them. Next, he was no longer an onlooker but was himself in the canoe, Moti was crying out, they were both thrusting hard with their paddles, racing on the steep face of the flying turquoise. Under the bow the water was hissing as from a steam jet, the air was filled with driven spray, there was a rush and rumble and long-echoing roar, and the canoe floated on the placid water of the lagoon. Moti laughed and shook the salt water from his eyes, and together they paddled in to the pounded-coral beach where Tati's grass walls through the cocoanut-palms showed golden in the setting sun.

The picture faded, and before his eyes stretched the disorder of his squalid room. He strove in vain to see Tahiti again. He knew there was singing among the trees and that the maidens were dancing in the moonlight, but he could not see them. He could see only the littered writing-table, the empty space where the type-writer had stood, and the unwashed window-pane. He closed his eyes with a groan, and slept.

CHAPTER XLI

He slept heavily all night, and did not stir until aroused by the postman on his morning round. Martin felt tired and passive, and went through his letters aimlessly. One thin envelope, from a robber magazine, contained for twenty-two dollars. He had been dunning for it for a year and a half. He noted its amount apathetically. The old-time thrill at receiving a publisher's check was gone. Unlike his earlier checks, this one was not pregnant with promise of great things to come. To him it was a check for twenty-two dollars, that was all, and it would buy him something to eat.

Another check was in the same mail, sent from a New York weekly in payment for some humorous verse which had been accepted months before. It was for ten dollars. An idea came to him, which he calmly considered. He did not know what he was going to do, and he felt in no hurry to do anything. In the meantime he must live. Also he owed numerous debts. Would it not be a paying investment to put stamps on the huge pile of manuscripts under the table and start them on their travels again? One or two of them might be accepted. That would help him to live. He decided on the investment, and, after he had cashed the checks at the bank down in Oakland, he bought ten dollars' worth of postage stamps. The thought of going home to cook breakfast in his stuffy little room was repulsive to him. For the first time he refused to consider his debts. He knew that in his room he could manufacture a substantial breakfast at a cost of from fifteen to twenty cents. But, instead, he went into the Forum Café and ordered a breakfast that cost two dollars. He tipped the waiter a quarter, and spent fifty cents for a package of Egyptian cigarettes. It was the first time he had smoked since Ruth had asked him to stop. But he could see now no reason why he should not, and besides, he wanted to smoke. And what did the money matter? For five cents he could have bought a package of Durham and brown papers and rolled forty cigarettes—but what of it? Money had no meaning to him now except what it would immediately buy. He was chartless and rudderless, and he had no port to make, while drifting involved the least living, and it was living that hurt.

The days slipped along, and he slept eight hours regularly every night. Though now, while waiting for more checks, he ate in the Japanese restaurants where meals were served for ten cents, his wasted body filled out, as did the hollows in his cheeks. He no longer abused himself with short sleep, overwork, and overstudy. He wrote nothing, and the books were closed. He walked much, out in the hills, and loafed long hours in the quiet parks. He had no friends nor acquaintances, nor did he make any. He had no inclination. He was waiting for some impulse, from he knew not where, to put his stopped life into motion again. In the meantime his life remained run down, planless, and empty and idle.

Once he made a trip to San Francisco to look up the "real dirt." But at the last moment, as he stepped into the upstairs entrance, he recoiled and turned and fled through the swarming ghetto. He was frightened at the thought of hearing philosophy discussed, and he fled furtively, for fear that some one of the "real dirt" might chance along and recognize him.

Sometimes he glanced over the magazines and newspapers to see how "Ephemera" was being maltreated. It had made a hit. But what a hit! Everybody had read it, and everybody was discussing whether or not it was really poetry. The local papers had taken it up, and daily there appeared columns of learned criticisms, facetious editorials, and serious letters from subscribers. Helen Della Delmar (proclaimed with a flourish of trumpets and rolling of tomtoms to be the greatest woman poet in the United States) denied Brissenden a seat beside her on Pegasus and wrote voluminous letters to the public, proving that he was no poet.

The Parthenon came out in its next number patting itself on the back for the stir it had made, sneering at Sir John Value, and exploiting Brissenden's death with ruthless commercialism. A newspaper with a sworn circulation of half a million published an original and spontaneous poem by Helen Della Delmar, in which she gibed and sneered at Brissenden. Also, she was guilty of a second poem, in which she parodied him.

Martin had many times to be glad that Brissenden was dead. He had hated the crowd so, and here all that was finest and most sacred of him had been thrown to the crowd. Daily the vivisection of Beauty went on. Every nincompoop in the land rushed into free print, floating their wizened little egos into the public eye on the surge of Brissenden's greatness. Quoth one paper: "We have received a letter from a gentleman who wrote a poem just like it, only better, some time ago." Another paper, in deadly seriousness, reproving Helen Della Delmar for her parody, said: "But unquestionably Miss Delmar wrote it in a moment of badinage and not quite with the respect that one great poet should show to another and perhaps to the greatest. However, whether Miss Delmar be jealous or not of the man who invented 'Ephemera,' it is certain that she, like thousands of others, is fascinated by his work, and that the day may come when she will try to write lines like his."

Ministers began to preach sermons against "Ephemera," and one, who too stoutly stood for much of its content, was expelled for heresy. The great poem contributed to the gayety of the world. The comic verse-writers and the cartoonists took hold of it with screaming laughter, and in the personal columns of society weeklies jokes were perpetrated on it to the effect that Charley Frensham told Archie Jennings, in confidence, that five lines of "Ephemera" would drive a man to beat a cripple, and that ten lines would send him to the bottom of the river.

Martin did not laugh; nor did he grit his teeth in anger. The effect produced upon him was one of great sadness. In the crash of his whole world, with love on the pinnacle, the crash of magazinedom and the dear public was a small crash indeed. Brissenden had been wholly right in his judgment of the magazines, and he, Martin, had spent arduous and futile years in order to find it out for himself. The magazines were all Brissenden had said they were and more. Well, he was done, he solaced himself. He had hitched his wagon to a star and been landed in a pestiferous marsh. The visions of Tahiti—clean, sweet Tahiti—were coming to him more frequently. And there were the low Paumotus, and the high Marquesas; he saw himself often, now, on board trading schooners or frail little cutters, slipping out at dawn through the reef at Papeete and beginning the long beat through the pearl-atolls to Nukahiva and the Bay of Taiohae, where Tamari, he knew, would kill a pig in honor of his coming, and where Tamari's flower-garlanded daughters would seize his hands and with song and laughter garland him with flowers. The South Seas were calling, and he knew that sooner or later he would answer the call.

In the meantime he drifted, resting and recuperating after the long traverse he had made through the realm of knowledge. When *The Parthenon* check of three hundred and fifty dollars was forwarded to him, he turned it over to the local lawyer who had attended to Brissenden's affairs for his family. Martin took a receipt for the check, and at the same time gave a note for the hundred dollars Brissenden had let him have.

The time was not long when Martin ceased patronizing the Japanese restaurants. At the very moment when he had abandoned the fight, the tide turned. But it had turned too late. Without a thrill he opened a thick envelope from *The Millennium*, scanned the face of a check that represented three hundred dollars, and noted that it was the payment on acceptance for "Adventure." Every debt he owed in the world, including the pawnshop, with its usurious interest, amounted to less than a hundred dollars. And when he had paid everything, and lifted the hundred-dollar note with Brissenden's lawyer, he still had over a hundred dollars in pocket. He ordered a suit of clothes from the tailor and ate his meals in the best cafés in town. He still slept in his little room at Maria's, but the sight of his new clothes caused the neighborhood children to cease from calling him "hobo" and "tramp" from the roofs of woodsheds and over back fences.

"Wiki-Wiki," his Hawaiian short story, was bought by *Warren's Monthly* for two hundred and fifty dollars. *The Northern Review* took his essay, "The Cradle of Beauty," and *Mackintosh's Magazine* took "The Palmist"—the poem he had written to Marian. The editors and readers were back from their summer vacations, and manuscripts were being handled quickly. But Martin could not puzzle out what strange whim animated them to this general acceptance of the things they had persistently rejected for two years. Nothing of his had been published. He was not known anywhere outside of Oakland, and in Oakland, with the few who thought they knew him, he was notorious as a red-shirt and a socialist. So there was no explaining this sudden acceptability of his wares. It was sheer jugglery of fate.

After it had been refused by a number of magazines, he had taken Brissenden's rejected advice and started, "The Shame of the Sun" on the round of publishers. After several refusals, Singletree, Darnley & Co. accepted it, promising fall publication. When Martin asked for an advance on royalties, they wrote that such was not their custom, that books of that nature rarely paid for themselves, and that they doubted if his book would sell a thousand copies. Martin figured what the book would earn him on such a sale. Retailed at a dollar, on a royalty of fifteen per cent, it would bring him one hundred and fifty dollars. He decided that if he had it to do over again he would confine himself to fiction. "Adventure," one-fourth as long, had brought him twice as much from *The Millennium*. That newspaper paragraph he had read so long ago had been true, after all. The first-class magazines did not pay on acceptance, and they paid well. Not two cents a word, but four cents a word, had *The Millennium* paid him. And, furthermore, they bought good stuff, too, for were they not buying his? This last thought he accompanied with a grin.

He wrote to Singletree, Darnley & Co., offering to sell out his rights in "The Shame of the Sun" for a hundred dollars, but they did not care to take the risk. In the meantime he was not in need of money, for several of his later stories had been accepted and paid for. He actually opened a bank account, where, without a debt in the world, he had several hundred dollars to his credit. "Overdue," after having been declined by a number of magazines, came to rest at the Meredith-Lowell Company. Martin remembered the five dollars Gertrude had given him, and his resolve to return it to her a hundred times over; so he wrote for an advance on royalties of five hundred dollars. To his surprise a check for that amount, accompanied by a contract, came by return mail. He cashed the check into five-dollar gold pieces and telephoned Gertrude that he wanted to see her.

She arrived at the house panting and short of breath from the haste she had made. Apprehensive of trouble, she had stuffed the few dollars she possessed into her hand-satchel; and so sure was she that disaster had overtaken her brother, that she stumbled forward, sobbing, into his arms, at the same time thrusting the satchel mutely at him.

"I'd have come myself," he said. "But I didn't want a row with Mr. Higginbotham, and that is what would have surely happened."

"He'll be all right after a time," she assured him, while she wondered what the trouble was that Martin was in. "But you'd best get a job first an' steady down. Bernard does like to see a man at honest work. That stuff in the newspapers broke 'm all up. I never saw 'm so mad before."

"I'm not going to get a job," Martin said with a smile. "And you can tell him so from me. I don't need a job, and there's the proof of it."

He emptied the hundred gold pieces into her lap in a glinting, tinkling stream.

"You remember that fiver you gave me the time I didn't have carfare? Well, there it is, with ninety-nine brothers of different ages but all of the same size."

If Gertrude had been frightened when she arrived, she was now in a panic of fear. Her fear was such that it was certitude. She was not suspicious. She was convinced. She looked at Martin in horror, and her heavy limbs shrank under the golden stream as though it were burning her.

"It's yours," he laughed.

She burst into tears, and began to moan, "My poor boy, my poor boy!"

He was puzzled for a moment. Then he divined the cause of her agitation and handed her the Meredith-Lowell letter which had accompanied the check. She stumbled through it, pausing now and again to wipe her eyes, and when she had finished, said:-

"An' does it mean that you come by the money honestly?"

"More honestly than if I'd won it in a lottery. I earned it."

Slowly faith came back to her, and she reread the letter carefully. It took him long to explain to her the nature of the transaction which had put the money into his possession, and longer still to get her to understand that the money was really hers and that he did not need it.

"I'll put it in the bank for you," she said finally.

"You'll do nothing of the sort. It's yours, to do with as you please, and if you won't take it, I'll give it to Maria. She'll know what to do with it. I'd suggest, though, that you hire a servant and take a good long rest."

"I'm goin' to tell Bernard all about it," she announced, when she was leaving.

Martin winced, then grinned.

"Yes, do," he said. "And then, maybe, he'll invite me to dinner again."

"Yes, he will—I'm sure he will!" she exclaimed fervently, as she drew him to her and kissed and hugged him.

CHAPTER XLII

One day Martin became aware that he was lonely. He was healthy and strong, and had nothing to do. The cessation from writing and studying, the death of Brissenden, and the estrangement from Ruth had made a big hole in his life; and his life refused to be pinned down to good living in cafés and the smoking of Egyptian cigarettes. It was true the South Seas were calling to him, but he had a feeling that the game was not yet played out in the United States. Two books were soon to be published, and he had more books that might find publication. Money could be made out of them, and he would wait and take a sackful of it into the South Seas. He knew a valley and a bay in the Marquesas that he could buy for a thousand Chili dollars. The valley ran from the horseshoe, land-locked bay to the tops of the dizzy, cloud-capped peaks and contained perhaps ten thousand acres. It was filled with tropical fruits, wild chickens, and wild pigs, with an occasional herd of wild cattle, while high up among the peaks were herds of wild goats harried by packs of wild dogs. The whole place was wild. Not a human lived in it. And he could buy it and the bay for a thousand Chili dollars.

The bay, as he remembered it, was magnificent, with water deep enough to accommodate the largest vessel afloat, and so safe that the South Pacific Directory recommended it to the best careening place for ships for hundreds of miles around. He would buy a schooner—one of those yacht-like, coppered crafts that sailed like witches—and go trading copra and pearling among the islands. He would make the valley and the bay his headquarters. He would build a patriarchal grass house like Tati's, and have it and the valley and the schooner filled with dark-skinned servitors. He would entertain there the factor of Taiohae, captains of wandering traders, and all the best of the South Pacific riffraff. He would keep open house and entertain like a prince. And he would forget the books he had opened and the world that had proved an illusion.

To do all this he must wait in California to fill the sack with money. Already it was beginning to flow in. If one of the books made a strike, it might enable him to sell the whole heap of manuscripts. Also he could collect the stories and the poems into books, and make sure of the valley and the bay and the schooner. He would never write again. Upon that he was resolved. But in the meantime, awaiting the publication of the books, he must do something more than live dazed and stupid in the sort of uncaring trance into which he had fallen.

He noted, one Sunday morning, that the Bricklayers' Picnic took place that day at Shell Mound Park, and to Shell Mound Park he went. He had been to the working-class picnics too often in his earlier life not to know what they were like, and as he entered the park he experienced a recrudescence of all the old sensations. After all, they were his kind, these working people. He had been born among them, he had lived among them, and though he had strayed for a time, it was well to come back among them.

"If it ain't Mart!" he heard some one say, and the next moment a hearty hand was on his shoulder. "Where you ben all the time? Off to sea? Come on an' have a drink."

It was the old crowd in which he found himself—the old crowd, with here and there a gap, and here and there a new face. The fellows were not bricklayers, but, as in the old days, they attended all Sunday picnics for the dancing, and the fighting, and the fun. Martin drank with them, and began to feel really human once more. He was a fool to have ever left them, he thought; and he was very certain that his sum of happiness would have been greater had he remained with them and let alone the books and the people who sat in the high places. Yet the beer seemed not so good as of yore. It didn't taste as it used to taste. Brissenden had spoiled him for steam beer, he concluded, and wondered if, after all, the books had spoiled him for companionship with these friends of his youth. He resolved that he would not be so spoiled, and he went on to the dancing pavilion. Jimmy, the plumber, he met there, in the company of a tall, blond girl who promptly forsook him for Martin.

"Gee, it's like old times," Jimmy explained to the gang that gave him the laugh as Martin and the blonde whirled away in a waltz. "An' I don't give a rap. I'm too damned glad to see 'm back. Watch 'm waltz, eh? It's like silk. Who'd blame any girl?"

But Martin restored the blonde to Jimmy, and the three of them, with half a dozen friends, watched the revolving couples and laughed and joked with one another. Everybody was glad to see Martin back. No book of his been published; he carried no fictitious value in their eyes. They liked him for himself. He felt like a prince returned from excile, and his lonely heart burgeoned in the geniality in which it bathed. He made a mad day of it, and was at his best. Also, he had money in his pockets, and, as in the old days when he returned from sea with a pay-day, he made the money fly.

Once, on the dancing-floor, he saw Lizzie Connolly go by in the arms of a young workingman; and, later, when he made the round of the pavilion, he came upon her sitting by a refreshment table. Surprise and greetings over, he led her away into the grounds, where they could talk without shouting down the music. From the instant he spoke to her, she was his. He knew it. She showed it in the proud humility of her eyes, in every caressing movement of her proudly carried body, and in the way she hung upon his speech. She was not the young girl as he had known her. She was a woman, now, and Martin noted that her wild, defiant beauty had improved, losing none of its wildness, while the defiance and the fire seemed more in control. "A beauty, a perfect beauty," he murmured admiringly under his breath. And he knew she was his, that all he had to do was to say "Come," and she would go with him over the world wherever he led.

Even as the thought flashed through his brain he received a heavy blow on the side of his head that nearly knocked him down. It was a man's fist, directed by a man so angry and in such haste that the fist had missed the jaw for which it was aimed. Martin turned as he staggered, and saw the fist coming at him in a wild swing. Quite as a matter of course he ducked, and the fist flew harmlessly past, pivoting the man who had driven it. Martin hooked with his left, landing on the pivoting man with the weight of his body behind the blow. The man went to the ground sidewise, leaped to his feet, and made a mad rush. Martin saw his passion-distorted face and wondered what could be the cause of the fellow's anger. But while he wondered, he shot in a straight left, the weight of his body behind the blow. The man went over backward and fell in a crumpled heap. Jimmy and others of the gang were running toward them.

Martin was thrilling all over. This was the old days with a vengeance, with their dancing, and their fighting, and their fun. While he kept a wary eye on his antagonist, he glanced at Lizzie. Usually the girls screamed when the fellows got to scrapping, but she had not screamed. She was looking on with bated breath, leaning slightly forward, so keen was her interest, one hand pressed to her breast, her cheek flushed, and in her eyes a great and amazed admiration.

The man had gained his feet and was struggling to escape the restraining arms that were laid on him.

"She was waitin' for me to come back!" he was proclaiming to all and sundry. "She was waitin' for me to come back, an' then that fresh guy comes buttin' in. Let go o' me, I tell yeh. I'm goin' to fix 'm."

"What's eatin' yer?" Jimmy was demanding, as he helped hold the young fellow back. "That guy's Mart Eden. He's nifty with his mits, lemme tell you that, an' he'll eat you alive if you monkey with 'm."

"He can't steal her on me that way," the other interjected.

"He licked the Flyin' Dutchman, an' you know *him*," Jimmy went on expostulating. "An' he did it in five rounds. You couldn't last a minute against him. See?"

This information seemed to have a mollifying effect, and the irate young man favored Martin with a measuring stare.

"He don't look it," he sneered; but the sneer was without passion.

"That's what the Flyin' Dutchman thought," Jimmy assured him. "Come on, now, let's get outa this. There's lots of other girls. Come on."

The young fellow allowed himself to be led away toward the pavilion, and the gang followed after him.

"Who is he?" Martin asked Lizzie. "And what's it all about, anyway?"

Already the zest of combat, which of old had been so keen and lasting, had died down, and he discovered that he was self-analytical, too much so to live, single heart and single hand, so primitive an existence.

Lizzie tossed her head.

"Oh, he's nobody," she said. "He's just ben keepin' company with me."

"I had to, you see," she explained after a pause. "I was gettin' pretty lonesome. But I never forgot." Her voice sank lower, and she looked straight before her. "I'd throw 'm down for you any time."

Martin looking at her averted face, knowing that all he had to do was to reach out his hand and pluck her, fell to pondering whether, after all, there was any real worth in refined, grammatical English, and, so, forgot to reply to her.

"You put it all over him," she said tentatively, with a laugh.

"He's a husky young fellow, though," he admitted generously. "If they hadn't taken him away, he might have given me my hands full."

"Who was that lady friend I seen you with that night?" she asked abruptly.

"Oh, just a lady friend," was his answer.

"It was a long time ago," she murmured contemplatively. "It seems like a thousand years."

But Martin went no further into the matter. He led the conversation off into other channels. They had lunch in the restaurant, where he ordered wine and expensive delicacies and afterward he danced with her and with no one but her, till she was tired. He was a good dancer, and she whirled around and around with him in a heaven of delight, her head against his shoulder, wishing that it could last forever. Later in the afternoon they strayed off among the trees, where, in the good old fashion, she sat down while he sprawled on his back, his head in her lap. He lay and dozed, while she fondled his hair, looked down on his closed eyes, and loved him without reserve. Looking up suddenly, he read the tender advertisement in her face. Her eyes fluttered down, then they opened and looked into his with soft defiance.

"I've kept straight all these years," she said, her voice so low that it was almost a whisper.

In his heart Martin knew that it was the miraculous truth. And at his heart pleaded a great temptation. It was in his power to make her happy. Denied happiness himself, why should he deny happiness to her? He could marry her and take her down with him to dwell in the grass-walled castle in the Marquesas. The desire to do it was strong, but stronger still was the imperative command of his nature not to do it. In spite of himself he was still faithful to Love. The old days of license and easy living were gone. He could not bring them back, nor could he go back to them. He was changed—how changed he had not realized until now.

"I am not a marrying man, Lizzie," he said lightly.

The hand caressing his hair paused perceptibly, then went on with the same gentle stroke. He noticed her face harden, but it was with the hardness of resolution, for still the soft color was in her cheeks and she was all glowing and melting.

"I did not mean that—" she began, then faltered. "Or anyway I don't care."

"I don't care," she repeated. "I'm proud to be your friend. I'd do anything for you. I'm made that way, I guess."

Martin sat up. He took her hand in his. He did it deliberately, with warmth but without passion; and such warmth chilled her.

"Don't let's talk about it," she said.

"You are a great and noble woman," he said. "And it is I who should be proud to know you. And I am, I am. You are a ray of light to me in a very dark world, and I've got to be straight with you, just as straight as you have been."

"I don't care whether you're straight with me or not. You could do anything with me. You could throw me in the dirt an' walk on me. An' you're the only man in the world that can," she added with a defiant flash. "I ain't taken care of myself ever since I was a kid for nothin'."

"And it's just because of that that I'm not going to," he said gently. "You are so big and generous that you challenge me to equal generousness. I'm not marrying, and I'm not—well, loving without marrying, though I've done my share of that in the past. I'm sorry I came here to-day and met you. But it can't be helped now, and I never expected it would turn out this way."

"But look here, Lizzie. I can't begin to tell you how much I like you. I do more than like you. I admire and respect you. You are magnificent, and you are magnificently good. But what's the use of words? Yet there's something I'd like to do. You've had a hard life; let me make it easy for you." (A joyous light welled into her eyes, then faded out again.) "I'm pretty sure of getting hold of some money soon—lots of it."

In that moment he abandoned the idea of the valley and the bay, the grass-walled castle and the trim, white schooner. After all, what did it matter? He could go away, as he had done so often, before the mast, on any ship bound anywhere.

"I'd like to turn it over to you. There must be something you want—to go to school or business college. You might like to study and be a stenographer. I could fix it for you. Or maybe your father and mother are living—I could set them up in a grocery store or something. Anything you want, just name it, and I can fix it for you."

She made no reply, but sat, gazing straight before her, dry-eyed and motionless, but with an ache in the throat which Martin divined so strongly that it made his own throat ache. He regretted that he had spoken. It seemed so tawdry what he had offered her—mere money—compared with what she offered him. He offered her an extraneous thing with which he could part without a pang, while she offered him herself, along with disgrace and shame, and sin, and all her hopes of heaven.

"Don't let's talk about it," she said with a catch in her voice that she changed to a cough. She stood up. "Come on, let's go home. I'm all tired out."

The day was done, and the merrymakers had nearly all departed. But as Martin and Lizzie emerged from the trees they found the gang waiting for them. Martin knew immediately the meaning of it. Trouble was brewing. The gang was his body-guard. They passed out through the gates of the park with, straggling in the rear, a second gang, the friends that Lizzie's young man had collected to avenge the loss of his lady. Several constables and special police officers, anticipating trouble, trailed along to prevent it, and herded the two gangs separately aboard the train for San Francisco. Martin told Jimmy that he would get off at Sixteenth Street Station and catch the electric car into Oakland. Lizzie was very quiet and without interest in what was impending. The train pulled in to Sixteenth Street Station, and the waiting electric car could be seen, the conductor of which was impatiently clanging the gong.

"There she is," Jimmy counselled. "Make a run for it, an' we'll hold 'em back. Now you go! Hit her up!"

The hostile gang was temporarily disconcerted by the manoeuvre, then it dashed from the train in pursuit. The staid and sober Oakland folk who sat upon the car scarcely noted the young fellow and the girl who ran for it and found a seat in front on the outside. They did not connect the couple with Jimmy, who sprang on the steps, crying to the motorman:-

"Slam on the juice, old man, and beat it outa here!"

The next moment Jimmy whirled about, and the passengers saw him land his fist on the face of a running man who was trying to board the car. But fists were landing on faces the whole length of the car. Thus, Jimmy and his gang, strung out on the long, lower steps, met the attacking gang. The car started with a great clanging of its gong, and, as Jimmy's gang drove off the last assailants, they, too, jumped off to finish the job. The car dashed on, leaving the flurry of combat far behind, and its dumfounded passengers never dreamed that the quiet young man and the pretty working-girl sitting in the corner on the outside seat had been the cause of the row.

Martin had enjoyed the fight, with a recrudescence of the old fighting thrills. But they quickly died away, and he was oppressed by a great sadness. He felt very old—centuries older than those careless, care-free young companions of his others days. He had travelled far, too far to go back. Their mode of life, which had once been his, was now distasteful to him. He was disappointed in it all. He had developed into an alien. As the steam beer had tasted raw, so their companionship seemed raw to him. He was too far removed. Too many thousands of opened books yawned between them and him. He had exiled himself. He had travelled in the vast realm of intellect until he could no longer return home. On the other hand, he was human, and his gregarious need for companionship remained unsatisfied. He had found no new home. As the gang could not understand him, as his own family could not understand him, as the bourgeoisie could not understand him, so this girl beside him, whom he honored high, could not understand him nor the honor he paid her. His sadness was not untouched with bitterness as he thought it over.

"Make it up with him," he advised Lizzie, at parting, as they stood in front of the workingman's shack in which she lived, near Sixth and Market. He referred to the young fellow whose place he had usurped that day.

"I can't—now," she said.

"Oh, go on," he said jovially. "All you have to do is whistle and he'll come running."

"I didn't mean that," she said simply.

And he knew what she had meant.

She leaned toward him as he was about to say good night. But she leaned not imperatively, not seductively, but wistfully and humbly. He was touched to the heart. His large tolerance rose up in him. He put his arms around her, and kissed her, and knew that upon his own lips rested as true a kiss as man ever received.

"My God!" she sobbed. "I could die for you. I could die for you."

She tore herself from him suddenly and ran up the steps. He felt a quick moisture in his eyes.

"Martin Eden," he communed. "You're not a brute, and you're a damn poor Nietzscheman. You'd marry her if you could and fill her quivering heart full with happiness. But you can't, you can't. And it's a damn shame."

"'A poor old tramp explains his poor old ulcers,'" he muttered, remembering his Henly. "'Life is, I think, a blunder and a shame.' It is—a blunder and a shame."

CHAPTER XLIII

"The Shame of the Sun" was published in October. As Martin cut the cords of the express package and the half-dozen complimentary copies from the publishers spilled out on the table, a heavy sadness fell upon him. He thought of the wild delight that would have been his had this happened a few short months before, and he contrasted that delight that should have been with his present uncaring coldness. His book, his first book, and his pulse had not gone up a fraction of a beat, and he was only sad. It meant little to him now. The most it meant was that it might bring some money, and little enough did he care for money.

He carried a copy out into the kitchen and presented it to Maria.

"I did it," he explained, in order to clear up her bewilderment. "I wrote it in the room there, and I guess some few quarts of your vegetable soup went into the making of it. Keep it. It's yours. Just to remember me by, you know."

He was not bragging, not showing off. His sole motive was to make her happy, to make her proud of him, to justify her long faith in him. She put the book in the front room on top of the family Bible. A sacred thing was this book her lodger had made, a fetich of friendship. It softened the blow of his having been a laundryman, and though she could not understand a line of it, she knew that every line of it was great. She was a simple, practical, hard-working woman, but she possessed faith in large endowment.

Just as emotionlessly as he had received "The Shame of the Sun" did he read the reviews of it that came in weekly from the clipping bureau. The book was making a hit, that was evident. It meant more gold in the money sack. He could fix up Lizzie, redeem all his promises, and still have enough left to build his grass-walled castle.

Singletree, Darnley & Co. had cautiously brought out an edition of fifteen hundred copies, but the first reviews had started a second edition of twice the size through the presses; and ere this was delivered a third edition of five thousand had been ordered. A London firm made arrangements by cable for an English edition, and hot-footed upon this came the news of French, German, and Scandinavian translations in progress. The attack upon the Maeterlinck school could not have been made at a more opportune moment. A fierce controversy was precipitated. Saleeby and Haeckel indorsed and defended "The Shame of the Sun," for once finding themselves on the same side of a question. Crookes and Wallace ranged up on the opposing side, while Sir Oliver Lodge attempted to formulate a compromise that would jibe with his particular cosmic theories. Maeterlinck's followers rallied around the standard of mysticism. Chesterton set the whole world laughing with a series of alleged non-partisan essays on the subject, and the whole affair, controversy and controversialists, was well-nigh swept into the pit by a thundering broadside from George Bernard Shaw. Needless to say the arena was crowded with hosts of lesser lights, and the dust and sweat and din became terrific.

"It is a most marvellous happening," Singletree, Darnley & Co. wrote Martin, "a critical philosophic essay selling like a novel. You could not have chosen your subject better, and all contributory factors have been unwarrantedly propitious. We need scarcely to assure you that we are making hay while the sun shines. Over forty thousand copies have already been sold in the United States and Canada, and a new edition of twenty thousand is on the presses. We are overworked, trying to supply the demand. Nevertheless we have helped to create that demand.

We have already spent five thousand dollars in advertising. The book is bound to be a record-breaker."

"Please find herewith a contract in duplicate for your next book which we have taken the liberty of forwarding to you. You will please note that we have increased your royalties to twenty per cent, which is about as high as a conservative publishing house dares go. If our offer is agreeable to you, please fill in the proper blank space with the title of your book. We make no stipulations concerning its nature. Any book on any subject. If you have one already written, so much the better. Now is the time to strike. The iron could not be hotter."

"On receipt of signed contract we shall be pleased to make you an advance on royalties of five thousand dollars. You see, we have faith in you, and we are going in on this thing big. We should like, also, to discuss with you the drawing up of a contract for a term of years, say ten, during which we shall have the exclusive right of publishing in book-form all that you produce. But more of this anon."

Martin laid down the letter and worked a problem in mental arithmetic, finding the product of fifteen cents times sixty thousand to be nine thousand dollars. He signed the new contract, inserting "The Smoke of Joy" in the blank space, and mailed it back to the publishers along with the twenty storiettes he had written in the days before he discovered the formula for the newspaper storiette. And promptly as the United States mail could deliver and return, came Singletree, Darnley & Co.'s check for five thousand dollars.

"I want you to come down town with me, Maria, this afternoon about two o'clock," Martin said, the morning the check arrived. "Or, better, meet me at Fourteenth and Broadway at two o'clock. I'll be looking out for you."

At the appointed time she was there; but *shoes* was the only clew to the mystery her mind had been capable of evolving, and she suffered a distinct shock of disappointment when Martin walked her right by a shoe-store and dived into a real estate office. What happened thereupon resided forever after in her memory as a dream. Fine gentlemen smiled at her benevolently as they talked with Martin and one another; a type-writer clicked; signatures were affixed to an imposing document; her own landlord was there, too, and affixed his signature; and when all was over and she was outside on the sidewalk, her landlord spoke to her, saying, "Well, Maria, you won't have to pay me no seven dollars and a half this month."

Maria was too stunned for speech.

"Or next month, or the next, or the next," her landlord said.

She thanked him incoherently, as if for a favor. And it was not until she had returned home to North Oakland and conferred with her own kind, and had the Portuguese grocer investigate, that she really knew that she was the owner of the little house in which she had lived and for which she had paid rent so long.

"Why don't you trade with me no more?" the Portuguese grocer asked Martin that evening, stepping out to hail him when he got off the car; and Martin explained that he wasn't doing his own cooking any more, and then went in and had a drink of wine on the house. He noted it was the best wine the grocer had in stock.

"Maria," Martin announced that night, "I'm going to leave you. And you're going to leave here yourself soon. Then you can rent the house and be a landlord yourself. You've a brother in San Leandro or Haywards, and he's in the milk business. I want you to send all your washing back unwashed—understand?—unwashed, and to go out to San Leandro to-morrow, or Haywards, or wherever it is, and see that brother of yours. Tell him to come to see me. I'll be stopping at the Metropole down in Oakland. He'll know a good milk-ranch when he sees one."

And so it was that Maria became a landlord and the sole owner of a dairy, with two hired men to do the work for her and a bank account that steadily increased despite the fact that her whole brood wore shoes and went to school. Few persons ever meet the fairy princes they dream about; but Maria, who worked hard and whose head was hard, never dreaming about fairy princes, entertained hers in the guise of an ex-laundryman.

In the meantime the world had begun to ask: "Who is this Martin Eden?" He had declined to give any biographical data to his publishers, but the newspapers were not to be denied. Oakland was his own town, and the reporters nosed out scores of individuals who could supply information. All that he was and was not, all that he had done and most of what he had not done, was spread out for the delectation of the public, accompanied by snapshots and photographs—the latter procured from the local photographer who had once taken Martin's picture and who promptly copyrighted it and put it on the market. At first, so great was his disgust with the magazines and all bourgeois society, Martin fought against publicity; but in the end, because it was easier than not to, he surrendered. He found that he could not refuse himself to the special writers who travelled long distances to see him. Then again, each day was so many hours long, and, since he no longer was occupied with writing and studying, those hours had to be occupied somehow; so he yielded to what was to him a whim, permitted interviews, gave his opinions on literature and philosophy, and even accepted invitations of the bourgeoisie. He had settled down into a strange and comfortable state of mind. He no longer cared. He forgave everybody, even the cub reporter who had painted him red and to whom he now granted a full page with specially posed photographs.

He saw Lizzie occasionally, and it was patent that she regretted the greatness that had come to him. It widened the space between them. Perhaps it was with the hope of narrowing it that she yielded to his persuasions to go to night school and business college and to have herself gowned by a wonderful dressmaker who charged outrageous prices. She improved visibly from day to day, until Martin wondered if he was doing right, for he knew that all her compliance and endeavor was for his sake. She was trying to make herself of worth in his eyes—of the sort of worth he seemed to value. Yet he gave her no hope, treating her in brotherly fashion and rarely seeing her.

"Overdue" was rushed upon the market by the Meredith-Lowell Company in the height of his popularity, and being fiction, in point of sales it made even a bigger strike than "The Shame of the Sun." Week after week his was the credit of the unprecedented performance of having two books at the head of the list of best-sellers. Not only did the story take with the fiction-readers, but those who read "The Shame of the Sun" with avidity were likewise attracted to the sea-story by the cosmic grasp of mastery with which he had handled it. First he had attacked the literature of mysticism, and had done it exceeding well; and, next, he had successfully supplied the very literature he had exposited, thus proving himself to be that rare genius, a critic and a creator in one.

Money poured in on him, fame poured in on him; he flashed, comet-like, through the world of literature, and he was more amused than interested by the stir he was making. One thing was puzzling him, a little thing that would have puzzled the world had it known. But the world would have puzzled over his bepuzzlement rather than over the little thing that to him loomed gigantic. Judge Blount invited him to dinner. That was the little thing, or the beginning of the little thing, that was soon to become the big thing. He had insulted Judge Blount, treated him abominably, and Judge Blount, meeting him on the street, invited him to dinner. Martin bethought himself of the numerous occasions on which he had met Judge Blount at the Morses' and when Judge Blount had not invited him to dinner. Why had he not invited him to dinner then? he asked himself. He had not changed. He was the same Martin Eden. What made the difference? The fact that the stuff he had written had appeared inside the covers of books? But it was work performed. It was not something he had done since. It was achievement accomplished at the very time Judge Blount was sharing this general view and sneering at his Spencer and his intellect. Therefore it was not for any real value, but for a purely fictitious value that Judge Blount invited him to dinner.

Martin grinned and accepted the invitation, marvelling the while at his complacence. And at the dinner, where, with their womankind, were half a dozen of those that sat in high places, and where Martin found himself quite the lion, Judge Blount, warmly seconded by Judge Hanwell, urged privately that Martin should permit his name to be put up for the Styx—the ultra-select club to which belonged, not the mere men of wealth, but the men of attainment. And Martin declined, and was more puzzled than ever.

He was kept busy disposing of his heap of manuscripts. He was overwhelmed by requests from editors. It had been discovered that he was a stylist, with meat under his style. *The Northern Review*, after publishing "The Cradle of Beauty," had written him for half a dozen similar essays, which would have been supplied out of the heap, had not *Burton's Magazine*, in a speculative mood, offered him five hundred dollars each for five essays. He wrote back that he would supply the demand, but at a thousand dollars an essay. He remembered that all these manuscripts had been refused by the very magazines that were now clamoring for them. And their refusals had been cold-blooded, automatic, stereotyped. They had made him sweat, and now he intended to make them sweat. *Burton's Magazine* paid his price for five essays, and the remaining four, at the same rate, were snapped up by *Mackintosh's Monthly, The Northern Review* being too poor to stand the pace. Thus went out to the world "The High Priests of Mystery," "The Wonder-Dreamers," "The Yardstick of the Ego," "Philosophy of Illusion," "God and Clod," "Art and Biology," "Critics and Test-tubes," "Star-dust," and "The Dignity of Usury,"—to raise storms and rumblings and mutterings that were many a day in dying down.

Editors wrote to him telling him to name his own terms, which he did, but it was always for work performed. He refused resolutely to pledge himself to any new thing. The thought of again setting pen to paper maddened him. He had seen Brissenden torn to pieces by the crowd, and despite the fact that him the crowd acclaimed, he could not get over the shock nor gather any respect for the crowd. His very popularity seemed a disgrace and a treason to Brissenden. It made him wince, but he made up his mind to go on and fill the money-bag.

He received letters from editors like the following: "About a year ago we were unfortunate enough to refuse your collection of love-poems. We were greatly impressed by them at the time, but certain arrangements already entered into prevented our taking them. If you still have them, and if you will be kind enough to forward them, we shall be glad to publish the entire collection on your own terms. We are also prepared to make a most advantageous offer for bringing them out in book-form."

Martin recollected his blank-verse tragedy, and sent it instead. He read it over before mailing, and was particularly impressed by its sophomoric amateurishness and general worthlessness. But he sent it; and it was published, to the everlasting regret of the editor. The public was indignant and incredulous. It was too far a cry from Martin Eden's high standard to that serious bosh. It was asserted that he had never written it, that the magazine had faked it very clumsily, or that Martin Eden was emulating the elder Dumas and at the height of success was hiring his writing done for him. But when he explained that the tragedy was an early effort of his literary childhood, and that the magazine had refused to be happy unless it got it, a great laugh went up at the magazine's expense and a change in the editorship followed. The tragedy was never brought out in book-form, though Martin pocketed the advance royalties that had been paid.

Coleman's Weekly sent Martin a lengthy telegram, costing nearly three hundred dollars, offering him a thousand dollars an article for twenty articles. He was to travel over the United States, with all expenses paid, and select whatever topics interested him. The body of the telegram was devoted to hypothetical topics in order to show him the freedom of range that was to be his. The only restriction placed upon him was that he must confine himself to the United States. Martin sent his inability to accept and his regrets by wire "collect."

"Wiki-Wiki," published in *Warren's Monthly*, was an instantaneous success. It was brought out forward in a wide-margined, beautifully decorated volume that struck the holiday trade and sold like wildfire. The critics were unanimous in the belief that it would take its place with those two classics by two great writers, "The Bottle Imp" and "The Magic Skin."

The public, however, received the "Smoke of Joy" collection rather dubiously and coldly. The audacity and unconventionality of the storiettes was a shock to bourgeois morality and prejudice; but when Paris went mad over the immediate translation that was made, the American and English reading public followed suit and bought so many copies that Martin compelled the conservative house of Singletree, Darnley & Co. to pay a flat royalty of twenty-five per cent for a third book, and thirty per cent flat for a fourth. These two volumes comprised all the short stories he had written and which had received, or were receiving, serial publication. "The Ring of Bells" and his horror stories constituted one collection; the other collection was composed of "Adventure," "The Pot," "The Wine of Life," "The Whirlpool," "The Jostling Street," and four other stories. The Lowell-Meredith Company captured the collection of all his essays, and the Maxmillian Company got his "Sea Lyrics" and the "Love-cycle," the latter receiving serial publication in the *Ladies' Home Companion* after the payment of an extortionate price.

Martin heaved a sigh of relief when he had disposed of the last manuscript. The grass-walled castle and the white, coppered schooner were very near to him. Well, at any rate he had discovered Brissenden's contention that nothing of merit found its way into the magazines. His own success demonstrated that Brissenden had been wrong.

And yet, somehow, he had a feeling that Brissenden had been right, after all. "The Shame of the Sun" had been the cause of his success more than the stuff he had written. That stuff had been merely incidental. It had been rejected right and left by the magazines. The publication of "The Shame of the Sun" had started a controversy and precipitated the landslide in his favor. Had there been no "Shame of the Sun" there would have been no landslide, and had there been no miracle in the go of "The Shame of the Sun" there would have been no landslide. Singletree, Darnley & Co. attested that miracle. They had brought out a first edition of fifteen hundred copies and been dubious of selling it. They were experienced publishers and no one had been more astounded than they at the success which had followed. To them it had been in truth a miracle. They never got over it, and every letter they wrote him reflected their reverent awe of that first mysterious happening. They did not attempt to explain it. There was no explaining it. It had happened. In the face of all experience to the contrary, it had happened.

So it was, reasoning thus, that Martin questioned the validity of his popularity. It was the bourgeoisie that bought his books and poured its gold into his money-sack, and from what little he knew of the bourgeoisie it was not clear to him how it could possibly appreciate or comprehend what he had written. His intrinsic beauty and power meant nothing to the hundreds of thousands who were acclaiming him and buying his books. He was the fad of the hour, the adventurer who had stormed Parnassus while the gods nodded. The hundreds of thousands read him and acclaimed him with the same brute non-understanding with which they had flung themselves on Brissenden's "Ephemera" and torn it to pieces—a wolf-rabble that fawned on him instead of fanging him. Fawn or fang, it was all a matter of chance. One thing he knew with absolute certitude: "Ephemera" was infinitely greater than anything he had done. It was infinitely greater than anything he had in him. It was a poem of centuries. Then the tribute the mob paid him was a sorry tribute indeed, for that same mob had wallowed "Ephemera" into the mire. He sighed heavily and with satisfaction. He was glad the last manuscript was sold and that he would soon be done with it all.

CHAPTER XLIV

Mr. Morse met Martin in the office of the Hotel Metropole. Whether he had happened there just casually, intent on other affairs, or whether he had come there for the direct purpose of inviting him to dinner, Martin never could quite make up his mind, though he inclined toward the second hypothesis. At any rate, invited to dinner he was by Mr. Morse—Ruth's father, who had forbidden him the house and broken off the engagement.

Martin was not angry. He was not even on his dignity. He tolerated Mr. Morse, wondering the while how it felt to eat such humble pie. He did not decline the invitation. Instead, he put it off with vagueness and indefiniteness and inquired after the family, particularly after Mrs. Morse and Ruth. He spoke her name without hesitancy, naturally, though secretly surprised that he had had no inward quiver, no old, familiar increase of pulse and warm surge of blood.

He had many invitations to dinner, some of which he accepted. Persons got themselves introduced to him in order to invite him to dinner. And he went on puzzling over the little thing that was becoming a great thing. Bernard Higginbotham invited him to dinner. He puzzled the harder. He remembered the days of his desperate starvation when no one invited him to dinner. That was the time he needed dinners, and went weak and faint for lack of them and lost weight from sheer famine. That was the paradox of it. When he wanted dinners, no one gave them to him, and now that he could buy a hundred thousand dinners and was losing his appetite, dinners were thrust upon him right and left. But why? There was no justice in it, no merit on his part. He was no different. All the work he had done was even at that time work performed. Mr. and Mrs. Morse had condemned him for an idler and a shirk and through Ruth had urged that he take a clerk's position in an office. Furthermore, they had been aware of his work performed. Manuscript after manuscript of his had been turned over to them by Ruth. They had read them. It was the very same work that had put his name in all the papers, and, it was his name being in all the papers that led them to invite him.

One thing was certain: the Morses had not cared to have him for himself or for his work. Therefore they could not want him now for himself or for his work, but for the fame that was his, because he was somebody amongst men, and—why not?—because he had a hundred thousand dollars or so. That was the way bourgeois society valued a man, and who was he to expect it otherwise? But he was proud. He disdained such valuation. He desired to be valued for himself, or for his work, which, after all, was an expression of himself. That was the way Lizzie valued him. The work, with her, did not even count. She valued him, himself. That was the way Jimmy, the plumber, and all the old gang valued him. That had been proved often enough in the days when he ran with them; it had been proved that Sunday at Shell Mound Park. His work could go hang. What they liked, and were willing to scrap for, was just Mart Eden, one of the bunch and a pretty good guy.

Then there was Ruth. She had liked him for himself, that was indisputable. And yet, much as she had liked him she had liked the bourgeois standard of valuation more. She had opposed his writing, and principally, it seemed to him, because it did not earn money. That had been her criticism of his "Love-cycle." She, too, had urged him to get a job. It was true, she refined it to "position," but it meant the same thing, and in his own mind the old nomenclature stuck. He had read her all that he wrote—poems, stories, essays—"Wiki-Wiki," "The Shame of the

Sun," everything. And she had always and consistently urged him to get a job, to go to work—good God!—as if he hadn't been working, robbing sleep, exhausting life, in order to be worthy of her.

So the little thing grew bigger. He was healthy and normal, ate regularly, slept long hours, and yet the growing little thing was becoming an obsession. *Work performed*. The phrase haunted his brain. He sat opposite Bernard Higginbotham at a heavy Sunday dinner over Higginbotham's Cash Store, and it was all he could do to restrain himself from shouting out:-

"It was work performed! And now you feed me, when then you let me starve, forbade me your house, and damned me because I wouldn't get a job. And the work was already done, all done. And now, when I speak, you check the thought unuttered on your lips and hang on my lips and pay respectful attention to whatever I choose to say. I tell you your party is rotten and filled with grafters, and instead of flying into a rage you hum and haw and admit there is a great deal in what I say. And why? Because I'm famous; because I've a lot of money. Not because I'm Martin Eden, a pretty good fellow and not particularly a fool. I could tell you the moon is made of green cheese and you would subscribe to the notion, at least you would not repudiate it, because I've got dollars, mountains of them. And it was all done long ago; it was work performed, I tell you, when you spat upon me as the dirt under your feet."

But Martin did not shout out. The thought gnawed in his brain, an unceasing torment, while he smiled and succeeded in being tolerant. As he grew silent, Bernard Higginbotham got the reins and did the talking. He was a success himself, and proud of it. He was self-made. No one had helped him. He owed no man. He was fulfilling his duty as a citizen and bringing up a large family. And there was Higginbotham's Cash Store, that monument of his own industry and ability. He loved Higginbotham's Cash Store as some men loved their wives. He opened up his heart to Martin, showed with what keenness and with what enormous planning he had made the store. And he had plans for it, ambitious plans. The neighborhood was growing up fast. The store was really too small. If he had more room, he would be able to put in a score of labor-saving and money-saving improvements. And he would do it yet. He was straining every effort for the day when he could buy the adjoining lot and put up another two-story frame building. The upstairs he could rent, and the whole ground-floor of both buildings would be Higginbotham's Cash Store. His eyes glistened when he spoke of the new sign that would stretch clear across both buildings.

Martin forgot to listen. The refrain of "Work performed," in his own brain, was drowning the other's clatter. The refrain maddened him, and he tried to escape from it.

"How much did you say it would cost?" he asked suddenly.

His brother-in-law paused in the middle of an expatiation on the business opportunities of the neighborhood. He hadn't said how much it would cost. But he knew. He had figured it out a score of times.

"At the way lumber is now," he said, "four thousand could do it."

"Including the sign?"

"I didn't count on that. It'd just have to come, onc't the buildin' was there."

"And the ground?"

"Three thousand more."

He leaned forward, licking his lips, nervously spreading and closing his fingers, while he watched Martin write a check. When it was passed over to him, he glanced at the amount-seven thousand dollars.

"I—I can't afford to pay more than six per cent," he said huskily.

Martin wanted to laugh, but, instead, demanded:-

"How much would that be?"

"Lemme see. Six per cent—six times seven—four hundred an' twenty."

"That would be thirty-five dollars a month, wouldn't it?"

Higginbotham nodded.

"Then, if you've no objection, well arrange it this way." Martin glanced at Gertrude. "You can have the principal to keep for yourself, if you'll use the thirty-five dollars a month for cooking and washing and scrubbing. The seven thousand is yours if you'll guarantee that Gertrude does no more drudgery. Is it a go?"

Mr. Higginbotham swallowed hard. That his wife should do no more housework was an affront to his thrifty soul. The magnificent present was the coating of a pill, a bitter pill. That his wife should not work! It gagged him.

"All right, then," Martin said. "I'll pay the thirty-five a month, and—"

He reached across the table for the check. But Bernard Higginbotham got his hand on it first, crying:

"I accept! I accept!"

When Martin got on the electric car, he was very sick and tired. He looked up at the assertive sign.

"The swine," he groaned. "The swine, the swine."

When *Mackintosh's Magazine* published "The Palmist," featuring it with decorations by Berthier and with two pictures by Wenn, Hermann von Schmidt forgot that he had called the verses obscene. He announced that his wife had inspired the poem, saw to it that the news reached the ears of a reporter, and submitted to an interview by a staff writer who was accompanied by a staff photographer and a staff artist. The result was a full page in a Sunday supplement, filled with photographs and idealized drawings of Marian, with many intimate details of Martin Eden and his family, and with the full text of "The Palmist" in large type, and republished by special permission of *Mackintosh's Magazine*. It caused quite a stir in the neighborhood, and good housewives were proud to have the acquaintances of the great writer's sister, while those who had not made haste to cultivate it. Hermann von Schmidt chuckled in his little repair shop and decided to order a new lathe. "Better than advertising," he told Marian, "and it costs nothing."

"We'd better have him to dinner," she suggested.

And to dinner Martin came, making himself agreeable with the fat wholesale butcher and his fatter wife—important folk, they, likely to be of use to a rising young man like Hermann Von Schmidt. No less a bait, however, had been required to draw them to his house than his great brother-in-law. Another man at table who had swallowed the same bait was the superintendent of the Pacific Coast agencies for the Asa Bicycle Company. Him Von Schmidt desired to please and propitiate because from him could be obtained the Oakland agency for the bicycle. So Hermann von Schmidt found it a goodly asset to have Martin for a brother-in-law, but in his heart of hearts he couldn't understand where it all came in. In the silent watches of the night, while his wife slept, he had floundered through Martin's books and poems, and decided that the world was a fool to buy them.

And in his heart of hearts Martin understood the situation only too well, as he leaned back and gloated at Von Schmidt's head, in fancy punching it well-nigh off of him, sending blow after blow home just right—the chuckle-headed Dutchman! One thing he did like about him, however. Poor as he was, and determined to rise as he was, he nevertheless hired one servant to take the heavy work off of Marian's hands. Martin talked with the superintendent of the Asa agencies, and after dinner he drew him aside with Hermann, whom he backed financially for the best bicycle store with fittings in Oakland. He went further, and in a private talk with Hermann told him to keep his eyes open for an automobile agency and garage, for there was no reason that he should not be able to run both establishments successfully.

With tears in her eyes and her arms around his neck, Marian, at parting, told Martin how much she loved him and always had loved him. It was true, there was a perceptible halt midway in her assertion, which she glossed over with more tears and kisses and incoherent stammerings, and which Martin inferred to be her appeal for forgiveness for the time she had lacked faith in him and insisted on his getting a job.

"He can't never keep his money, that's sure," Hermann von Schmidt confided to his wife. "He got mad when I spoke of interest, an' he said damn the principal and if I mentioned it again, he'd punch my Dutch head off. That's what he said—my Dutch head. But he's all right, even if he ain't no business man. He's given me my chance, an' he's all right."

Invitations to dinner poured in on Martin; and the more they poured, the more he puzzled. He sat, the guest of honor, at an Arden Club banquet, with men of note whom he had heard about and read about all his life; and they told him how, when they had read "The Ring of Bells" in the *Transcontinental*, and "The Peri and the Pearl" in *The Hornet*, they had immediately picked him for a winner. My God! and I was hungry and in rags, he thought to himself. Why didn't you give me a dinner then? Then was the time. It was work performed. If you are feeding me now for work performed, why did you not feed me then when I needed it? Not one word in "The Ring of Bells," nor in "The Peri and the Pearl" has been changed. No; you're not feeding me now for work performed. You are feeding me because everybody else is feeding me and because it is an honor to feed me. You are feeding me now because you are herd animals; because you are part of the mob; because the one blind, automatic thought in the mob-mind just now is to feed me. And where does Martin Eden and the work Martin Eden performed come in in all this? he asked himself plaintively, then arose to respond cleverly and wittily to a clever and witty toast.

So it went. Wherever he happened to be—at the Press Club, at the Redwood Club, at pink teas and literary gatherings—always were remembered "The Ring of Bells" and "The Peri and the Pearl" when they were first published. And always was Martin's maddening and unuttered demand: Why didn't you feed me then? It was work performed. "The Ring of Bells" and "The Peri and the Pearl" are not changed one iota. They were just as artistic, just as worth while, then as now. But you are not feeding me for their sake, nor for the sake of anything else I have written. You're feeding me because it is the style of feeding just now, because the whole mob is crazy with the idea of feeding Martin Eden.

And often, at such times, he would abruptly see slouch in among the company a young hoodlum in square-cut coat and under a stiff-rim Stetson hat. It happened to him at the Gallina

Society in Oakland one afternoon. As he rose from his chair and stepped forward across the platform, he saw stalk through the wide door at the rear of the great room the young hoodlum with the square-cut coat and stiff-rim hat. Five hundred fashionably gowned women turned their heads, so intent and steadfast was Martin's gaze, to see what he was seeing. But they saw only the empty centre aisle. He saw the young tough lurching down that aisle and wondered if he would remove the stiff-rim which never yet had he seen him without. Straight down the aisle he came, and up the platform. Martin could have wept over that youthful shade of himself, when he thought of all that lay before him. Across the platform he swaggered, right up to Martin, and into the foreground of Martin's consciousness disappeared. The five hundred women applauded softly with gloved hands, seeking to encourage the bashful great man who was their guest. And Martin shook the vision from his brain, smiled, and began to speak.

The Superintendent of Schools, good old man, stopped Martin on the street and remembered him, recalling seances in his office when Martin was expelled from school for fighting.

"I read your 'Ring of Bells' in one of the magazines quite a time ago," he said. "It was as good as Poe. Splendid, I said at the time, splendid!"

Yes, and twice in the months that followed you passed me on the street and did not know me, Martin almost said aloud. Each time I was hungry and heading for the pawnbroker. Yet it was work performed. You did not know me then. Why do you know me now?

"I was remarking to my wife only the other day," the other was saying, "wouldn't it be a good idea to have you out to dinner some time? And she quite agreed with me. Yes, she quite agreed with me."

"Dinner?" Martin said so sharply that it was almost a snarl.

"Why, yes, yes, dinner, you know—just pot luck with us, with your old superintendent, you rascal," he uttered nervously, poking Martin in an attempt at jocular fellowship.

Martin went down the street in a daze. He stopped at the corner and looked about him vacantly.

"Well, I'll be damned!" he murmured at last. "The old fellow was afraid of me."

CHAPTER XLV

Kreis came to Martin one day—Kreis, of the "real dirt"; and Martin turned to him with relief, to receive the glowing details of a scheme sufficiently wild-catty to interest him as a fictionist rather than an investor. Kreis paused long enough in the midst of his exposition to tell him that in most of his "Shame of the Sun" he had been a chump.

"But I didn't come here to spout philosophy," Kreis went on. "What I want to know is whether or not you will put a thousand dollars in on this deal?"

"No, I'm not chump enough for that, at any rate," Martin answered. "But I'll tell you what I will do. You gave me the greatest night of my life. You gave me what money cannot buy. Now I've got money, and it means nothing to me. I'd like to turn over to you a thousand dollars of what I don't value for what you gave me that night and which was beyond price. You need the money. I've got more than I need. You want it. You came for it. There's no use scheming it out of me. Take it."

Kreis betrayed no surprise. He folded the check away in his pocket.

"At that rate I'd like the contract of providing you with many such nights," he said.

"Too late." Martin shook his head. "That night was the one night for me. I was in paradise. It's commonplace with you, I know. But it wasn't to me. I shall never live at such a pitch again. I'm done with philosophy. I want never to hear another word of it."

"The first dollar I ever made in my life out of my philosophy," Kreis remarked, as he paused in the doorway. "And then the market broke."

Mrs. Morse drove by Martin on the street one day, and smiled and nodded. He smiled back and lifted his hat. The episode did not affect him. A month before it might have disgusted him, or made him curious and set him to speculating about her state of consciousness at that moment. But now it was not provocative of a second thought. He forgot about it the next moment. He forgot about it as he would have forgotten the Central Bank Building or the City Hall after having walked past them. Yet his mind was preternaturally active. His thoughts went ever around and around in a circle. The centre of that circle was "work performed"; it ate at his brain like a deathless maggot. He awoke to it in the morning. It tormented his dreams at night. Every affair of life around him that penetrated through his senses immediately related itself to "work performed." He drove along the path of relentless logic to the conclusion that he was nobody, nothing. Mart Eden, the hoodlum, and Mart Eden, the sailor, had been real, had been he; but Martin Eden! the famous writer, did not exist. Martin Eden, the famous writer, was a vapor that had arisen in the mob-mind and by the mob-mind had been thrust into the corporeal being of Mart Eden, the hoodlum and sailor. But it couldn't fool him. He was not that sun-myth that the mob was worshipping and sacrificing dinners to. He knew better.

He read the magazines about himself, and pored over portraits of himself published therein until he was unable to associate his identity with those portraits. He was the fellow who had lived and thrilled and loved; who had been easy-going and tolerant of the frailties of life; who had served in the forecastle, wandered in strange lands, and led his gang in the old fighting days. He was the fellow who had been stunned at first by the thousands of books in the free library, and who had afterward learned his way among them and mastered them; he was the fellow who had burned the midnight oil and bedded with a spur and written books himself. But the one thing he was not was that colossal appetite that all the mob was bent upon feeding.

There were things, however, in the magazines that amused him. All the magazines were claiming him. *Warren's Monthly* advertised to its subscribers that it was always on the quest after new writers, and that, among others, it had introduced Martin Eden to the reading public. *The White Mouse* claimed him; so did *The Northern Review* and *Mackintosh's Magazine*, until silenced by *The Globe*, which pointed triumphantly to its files where the mangled "Sea Lyrics" lay buried. *Youth and Age*, which had come to life again after having escaped paying its bills, put in a prior claim, which nobody but farmers' children ever read. The *Transcontinental* made a dignified and convincing statement of how it first discovered Martin Eden, which was warmly disputed by *The Hornet*, with the exhibit of "The Peri and the Pearl." The modest claim of Singletree, Darnley & Co. was lost in the din. Besides, that publishing firm did not own a magazine wherewith to make its claim less modest.

The newspapers calculated Martin's royalties. In some way the magnificent offers certain magazines had made him leaked out, and Oakland ministers called upon him in a friendly way, while professional begging letters began to clutter his mail. But worse than all this were the women. His photographs were published broadcast, and special writers exploited his strong, bronzed face, his scars, his heavy shoulders, his clear, quiet eyes, and the slight hollows in his cheeks like an ascetic's. At this last he remembered his wild youth and smiled. Often, among the women he met, he would see now one, now another, looking at him, appraising him, selecting him. He laughed to himself. He remembered Brissenden's warning and laughed again. The women would never destroy him, that much was certain. He had gone past that stage.

Once, walking with Lizzie toward night school, she caught a glance directed toward him by a well-gowned, handsome woman of the bourgeoisie. The glance was a trifle too long, a shade too considerate. Lizzie knew it for what it was, and her body tensed angrily. Martin noticed, noticed the cause of it, told her how used he was becoming to it and that he did not care anyway.

"You ought to care," she answered with blazing eyes. "You're sick. That's what's the matter."

"Never healthier in my life. I weigh five pounds more than I ever did."

"It ain't your body. It's your head. Something's wrong with your think-machine. Even I can see that, an' I ain't nobody."

He walked on beside her, reflecting.

"I'd give anything to see you get over it," she broke out impulsively. "You ought to care when women look at you that way, a man like you. It's not natural. It's all right enough for sissy-boys. But you ain't made that way. So help me, I'd be willing an' glad if the right woman came along an' made you care."

When he left Lizzie at night school, he returned to the Metropole.

Once in his rooms, he dropped into a Morris chair and sat staring straight before him. He did not doze. Nor did he think. His mind was a blank, save for the intervals when unsummoned memory pictures took form and color and radiance just under his eyelids. He saw these pictures, but he was scarcely conscious of them—no more so than if they had been dreams. Yet he was not asleep. Once, he roused himself and glanced at his watch. It was just eight o'clock. He had nothing to do, and it was too early for bed. Then his mind went blank again, and the pictures began to form and vanish under his eyelids. There was nothing distinctive about the pictures. They were always masses of leaves and shrub-like branches shot through with hot sunshine.

A knock at the door aroused him. He was not asleep, and his mind immediately connected the knock with a telegram, or letter, or perhaps one of the servants bringing back clean clothes from the laundry. He was thinking about Joe and wondering where he was, as he said, "Come in."

He was still thinking about Joe, and did not turn toward the door. He heard it close softly. There was a long silence. He forgot that there had been a knock at the door, and was still staring blankly before him when he heard a woman's sob. It was involuntary, spasmodic, checked, and stifled—he noted that as he turned about. The next instant he was on his feet.

"Ruth!" he said, amazed and bewildered.

Her face was white and strained. She stood just inside the door, one hand against it for support, the other pressed to her side. She extended both hands toward him piteously, and started forward to meet him. As he caught her hands and led her to the Morris chair he noticed how cold they were. He drew up another chair and sat down on the broad arm of it. He was too confused to speak. In his own mind his affair with Ruth was closed and sealed. He felt much in the same way that he would have felt had the Shelly Hot Springs Laundry suddenly invaded the Hotel Metropole with a whole week's washing ready for him to pitch into. Several times he was about to speak, and each time he hesitated.

"No one knows I am here," Ruth said in a faint voice, with an appealing smile.

"What did you say?"

He was surprised at the sound of his own voice.

She repeated her words.

"Oh," he said, then wondered what more he could possibly say.

"I saw you come in, and I waited a few minutes."

"Oh," he said again.

He had never been so tongue-tied in his life. Positively he did not have an idea in his head. He felt stupid and awkward, but for the life of him he could think of nothing to say. It would have been easier had the intrusion been the Shelly Hot Springs laundry. He could have rolled up his sleeves and gone to work.

"And then you came in," he said finally.

She nodded, with a slightly arch expression, and loosened the scarf at her throat.

"I saw you first from across the street when you were with that girl."

"Oh, yes," he said simply. "I took her down to night school."

"Well, aren't you glad to see me?" she said at the end of another silence.

"Yes, yes." He spoke hastily. "But wasn't it rash of you to come here?"

"I slipped in. Nobody knows I am here. I wanted to see you. I came to tell you I have been very foolish. I came because I could no longer stay away, because my heart compelled me to come, because—because I wanted to come."

She came forward, out of her chair and over to him. She rested her hand on his shoulder a moment, breathing quickly, and then slipped into his arms. And in his large, easy way, desirous of not inflicting hurt, knowing that to repulse this proffer of herself was to inflict the most grievous hurt a woman could receive, he folded his arms around her and held her close. But there was no warmth in the embrace, no caress in the contact. She had come into his arms, and he held her, that was all. She nestled against him, and then, with a change of position, her hands crept up and rested upon his neck. But his flesh was not fire beneath those hands, and he felt awkward and uncomfortable.

"What makes you tremble so?" he asked. "Is it a chill? Shall I light the grate?"

He made a movement to disengage himself, but she clung more closely to him, shivering violently.

"It is merely nervousness," she said with chattering teeth. "I'll control myself in a minute. There, I am better already."

Slowly her shivering died away. He continued to hold her, but he was no longer puzzled. He knew now for what she had come.

"My mother wanted me to marry Charley Hapgood," she announced.

"Charley Hapgood, that fellow who speaks always in platitudes?" Martin groaned. Then he added, "And now, I suppose, your mother wants you to marry me."

He did not put it in the form of a question. He stated it as a certitude, and before his eyes began to dance the rows of figures of his royalties.

"She will not object, I know that much," Ruth said.

"She considers me quite eligible?"

Ruth nodded.

"And yet I am not a bit more eligible now than I was when she broke our engagement," he meditated. "I haven't changed any. I'm the same Martin Eden, though for that matter I'm a bit worse—I smoke now. Don't you smell my breath?"

In reply she pressed her open fingers against his lips, placed them graciously and playfully, and in expectancy of the kiss that of old had always been a consequence. But there was no caressing answer of Martin's lips. He waited until the fingers were removed and then went on.

"I am not changed. I haven't got a job. I'm not looking for a job. Furthermore, I am not going to look for a job. And I still believe that Herbert Spencer is a great and noble man and that Judge Blount is an unmitigated ass. I had dinner with him the other night, so I ought to know."

"But you didn't accept father's invitation," she chided.

"So you know about that? Who sent him? Your mother?"

She remained silent.

"Then she did send him. I thought so. And now I suppose she has sent you."

"No one knows that I am here," she protested. "Do you think my mother would permit this?"

"She'd permit you to marry me, that's certain."

She gave a sharp cry. "Oh, Martin, don't be cruel. You have not kissed me once. You are as unresponsive as a stone. And think what I have dared to do." She looked about her with a shiver, though half the look was curiosity. "Just think of where I am."

"*I could die for you! I could die for you!*"—Lizzie's words were ringing in his ears.

"Why didn't you dare it before?" he asked harshly. "When I hadn't a job? When I was starving? When I was just as I am now, as a man, as an artist, the same Martin Eden? That's the question I've been propounding to myself for many a day—not concerning you merely, but concerning everybody. You see I have not changed, though my sudden apparent appreciation in value compels me constantly to reassure myself on that point. I've got the same flesh on my bones, the same ten fingers and toes. I am the same. I have not developed any new strength nor virtue. My brain is the same old brain. I haven't made even one new generalization on literature or philosophy. I am personally of the same value that I was when nobody wanted me. And what is puzzling me is why they want me now. Surely they don't want me for myself, for myself is the same old self they did not want. Then they must want me for something else, for something that is outside of me, for something that is not I! Shall I tell you what that something is? It is for the recognition I have received. That recognition is not I. It resides in the minds of others. Then again for the money I have earned and am earning. But that money is not I. It resides in banks and in the pockets of Tom, Dick, and Harry. And is it for that, for the recognition and the money, that you now want me?"

"You are breaking my heart," she sobbed. "You know I love you, that I am here because I love you."

"I am afraid you don't see my point," he said gently. "What I mean is: if you love me, how does it happen that you love me now so much more than you did when your love was weak enough to deny me?"

"Forget and forgive," she cried passionately. "I loved you all the time, remember that, and I am here, now, in your arms."

"I'm afraid I am a shrewd merchant, peering into the scales, trying to weigh your love and find out what manner of thing it is."

She withdrew herself from his arms, sat upright, and looked at him long and searchingly. She was about to speak, then faltered and changed her mind.

"You see, it appears this way to me," he went on. "When I was all that I am now, nobody out of my own class seemed to care for me. When my books were all written, no one who had read the manuscripts seemed to care for them. In point of fact, because of the stuff I had written they seemed to care even less for me. In writing the stuff it seemed that I had committed acts that were, to say the least, derogatory. 'Get a job,' everybody said."

She made a movement of dissent.

"Yes, yes," he said; "except in your case you told me to get a position. The homely word *job*, like much that I have written, offends you. It is brutal. But I assure you it was no less brutal to me when everybody I knew recommended it to me as they would recommend right conduct to an immoral creature. But to return. The publication of what I had written, and the public notice I received, wrought a change in the fibre of your love. Martin Eden, with his work all performed, you would not marry. Your love for him was not strong enough to enable you to marry him. But your love is now strong enough, and I cannot avoid the conclusion that its strength arises from the publication and the public notice. In your case I do not mention royalties, though I am certain that they apply to the change wrought in your mother and father. Of course, all this is not flattering to me. But worst of all, it makes me question love, sacred love. Is love so gross a thing that it must feed upon publication and public notice? It would seem so. I have sat and thought upon it till my head went around."

"Poor, dear head." She reached up a hand and passed the fingers soothingly through his hair. "Let it go around no more. Let us begin anew, now. I loved you all the time. I know that I was weak in yielding to my mother's will. I should not have done so. Yet I have heard you speak so often with broad charity of the fallibility and frailty of humankind. Extend that charity to me. I acted mistakenly. Forgive me."

"Oh, I do forgive," he said impatiently. "It is easy to forgive where there is really nothing to forgive. Nothing that you have done requires forgiveness. One acts according to one's lights, and more than that one cannot do. As well might I ask you to forgive me for my not getting a job."

"I meant well," she protested. "You know that I could not have loved you and not meant well."

"True; but you would have destroyed me out of your well-meaning."

"Yes, yes," he shut off her attempted objection. "You would have destroyed my writing and my career. Realism is imperative to my nature, and the bourgeois spirit hates realism. The bourgeoisie is cowardly. It is afraid of life. And all your effort was to make me afraid of life. You would have formalized me. You would have compressed me into a two-by-four pigeonhole of life, where all life's values are unreal, and false, and vulgar." He felt her stir protestingly. "Vulgarity—a hearty vulgarity, I'll admit—is the basis of bourgeois refinement and culture. As I say, you wanted to formalize me, to make me over into one of your own class, with your class-ideals, class-values, and class-prejudices." He shook his head sadly. "And you do not understand, even now, what I am saying. My words do not mean to you what I endeavor to make them mean. What I say is so much fantasy to you. Yet to me it is vital reality. At the best you are a trifle puzzled and amused that this raw boy, crawling up out of the mire of the abyss, should pass judgment upon your class and call it vulgar."

She leaned her head wearily against his shoulder, and her body shivered with recurrent nervousness. He waited for a time for her to speak, and then went on.

"And now you want to renew our love. You want us to be married. You want me. And yet, listen—if my books had not been noticed, I'd nevertheless have been just what I am now. And you would have stayed away. It is all those damned books—"

"Don't swear," she interrupted.

Her reproof startled him. He broke into a harsh laugh.

"That's it," he said, "at a high moment, when what seems your life's happiness is at stake, you are afraid of life in the same old way—afraid of life and a healthy oath."

She was stung by his words into realization of the puerility of her act, and yet she felt that he had magnified it unduly and was consequently resentful. They sat in silence for a long time, she thinking desperately and he pondering upon his love which had departed. He knew, now, that he had not really loved her. It was an idealized Ruth he had loved, an ethereal creature of his own creating, the bright and luminous spirit of his love-poems. The real bourgeois Ruth, with all the bourgeois failings and with the hopeless cramp of the bourgeois psychology in her mind, he had never loved.

She suddenly began to speak.

"I know that much you have said is so. I have been afraid of life. I did not love you well enough. I have learned to love better. I love you for what you are, for what you were, for the ways even by which you have become. I love you for the ways wherein you differ from what you call my class, for your beliefs which I do not understand but which I know I can come to understand. I shall devote myself to understanding them. And even your smoking and your swearing—they are part of you and I will love you for them, too. I can still learn. In the last ten minutes I have learned much. That I have dared to come here is a token of what I have already learned. Oh, Martin!—"

She was sobbing and nestling close against him.

For the first time his arms folded her gently and with sympathy, and she acknowledged it with a happy movement and a brightening face.

"It is too late," he said. He remembered Lizzie's words. "I am a sick man—oh, not my body. It is my soul, my brain. I seem to have lost all values. I care for nothing. If you had been this way a few months ago, it would have been different. It is too late, now."

"It is not too late," she cried. "I will show you. I will prove to you that my love has grown, that it is greater to me than my class and all that is dearest to me. All that is dearest to the bourgeoisie I will flout. I am no longer afraid of life. I will leave my father and mother, and let my name become a by-word with my friends. I will come to you here and now, in free love if you will, and I will be proud and glad to be with you. If I have been a traitor to love, I will now, for love's sake, be a traitor to all that made that earlier treason."

She stood before him, with shining eyes.

"I am waiting, Martin," she whispered, "waiting for you to accept me. Look at me."

It was splendid, he thought, looking at her. She had redeemed herself for all that she had lacked, rising up at last, true woman, superior to the iron rule of bourgeois convention. It was splendid, magnificent, desperate. And yet, what was the matter with him? He was not thrilled nor stirred by what she had done. It was splendid and magnificent only intellectually. In what should have been a moment of fire, he coldly appraised her. His heart was untouched. He was unaware of any desire for her. Again he remembered Lizzie's words.

"I am sick, very sick," he said with a despairing gesture. "How sick I did not know till now. Something has gone out of me. I have always been unafraid of life, but I never dreamed of being sated with life. Life has so filled me that I am empty of any desire for anything. If there were room, I should want you, now. You see how sick I am."

He leaned his head back and closed his eyes; and like a child, crying, that forgets its grief in watching the sunlight percolate through the tear-dimmed films over the pupils, so Martin forgot his sickness, the presence of Ruth, everything, in watching the masses of vegetation, shot through hotly with sunshine that took form and blazed against this background of his eyelids. It was not restful, that green foliage. The sunlight was too raw and glaring. It hurt him to look at it, and yet he looked, he knew not why.

He was brought back to himself by the rattle of the door-knob. Ruth was at the door.

"How shall I get out?" she questioned tearfully. "I am afraid."

"Oh, forgive me," he cried, springing to his feet. "I'm not myself, you know. I forgot you were here." He put his hand to his head. "You see, I'm not just right. I'll take you home. We can go out by the servants' entrance. No one will see us. Pull down that veil and everything will be all right."

She clung to his arm through the dim-lighted passages and down the narrow stairs.

"I am safe now," she said, when they emerged on the sidewalk, at the same time starting to take her hand from his arm.

"No, no, I'll see you home," he answered.

"No, please don't," she objected. "It is unnecessary."

Again she started to remove her hand. He felt a momentary curiosity. Now that she was out of danger she was afraid. She was in almost a panic to be quit of him. He could see no reason for it and attributed it to her nervousness. So he restrained her withdrawing hand and started to walk on with her. Halfway down the block, he saw a man in a long overcoat shrink back into a doorway. He shot a glance in as he passed by, and, despite the high turned-up collar, he was certain that he recognized Ruth's brother, Norman.

During the walk Ruth and Martin held little conversation. She was stunned. He was apathetic. Once, he mentioned that he was going away, back to the South Seas, and, once, she asked him to forgive her having come to him. And that was all. The parting at her door was conventional. They shook hands, said good night, and he lifted his hat. The door swung shut, and he lighted a cigarette and turned back for his hotel. When he came to the doorway into which he had seen Norman shrink, he stopped and looked in in a speculative humor.

"She lied," he said aloud. "She made believe to me that she had dared greatly, and all the while she knew the brother that brought her was waiting to take her back." He burst into laughter. "Oh, these bourgeois! When I was broke, I was not fit to be seen with his sister. When I have a bank account, he brings her to me."

As he swung on his heel to go on, a tramp, going in the same direction, begged him over his shoulder.

"Say, mister, can you give me a quarter to get a bed?" were the words.

But it was the voice that made Martin turn around. The next instant he had Joe by the hand.

"D'ye remember that time we parted at the Hot Springs?" the other was saying. "I said then we'd meet again. I felt it in my bones. An' here we are."

"You're looking good," Martin said admiringly, "and you've put on weight."

"I sure have." Joe's face was beaming. "I never knew what it was to live till I hit hoboin'. I'm thirty pounds heavier an' feel tiptop all the time. Why, I was worked to skin an' bone in them old days. Hoboin' sure agrees with me."

"But you're looking for a bed just the same," Martin chided, "and it's a cold night."

"Huh? Lookin' for a bed?" Joe shot a hand into his hip pocket and brought it out filled with small change. "That beats hard graft," he exulted. "You just looked good; that's why I battered you."

Martin laughed and gave in.

"You've several full-sized drunks right there," he insinuated.

Joe slid the money back into his pocket.

"Not in mine," he announced. "No gettin' oryide for me, though there ain't nothin' to stop me except I don't want to. I've ben drunk once since I seen you last, an' then it was unexpected, bein' on an empty stomach. When I work like a beast, I drink like a beast. When I live like a man, I drink like a man—a jolt now an' again when I feel like it, an' that's all."

Martin arranged to meet him next day, and went on to the hotel. He paused in the office to look up steamer sailings. The *Mariposa* sailed for Tahiti in five days.

"Telephone over to-morrow and reserve a stateroom for me," he told the clerk. "No deck-stateroom, but down below, on the weather-side,—the port-side, remember that, the port-side. You'd better write it down."

Once in his room he got into bed and slipped off to sleep as gently as a child. The occurrences of the evening had made no impression on him. His mind was dead to impressions. The glow of warmth with which he met Joe had been most fleeting. The succeeding minute he had been bothered by the ex-laundryman's presence and by the compulsion of conversation. That in five more days he sailed for his loved South Seas meant nothing to him. So he closed his eyes and slept normally and comfortably for eight uninterrupted hours. He was not restless. He did not change his position, nor did he dream. Sleep had become to him oblivion, and each day that he awoke, he awoke with regret. Life worried and bored him, and time was a vexation.

CHAPTER XLVI

"Say, Joe," was his greeting to his old-time working-mate next morning, "there's a Frenchman out on Twenty-eighth Street. He's made a pot of money, and he's going back to France. It's a dandy, well-appointed, small steam laundry. There's a start for you if you want to settle down. Here, take this; buy some clothes with it and be at this man's office by ten o'clock. He looked up the laundry for me, and he'll take you out and show you around. If you like it, and think it is worth the price—twelve thousand—let me know and it is yours. Now run along. I'm busy. I'll see you later."

"Now look here, Mart," the other said slowly, with kindling anger, "I come here this mornin' to see you. Savve? I didn't come here to get no laundry. I come a here for a talk for old friends' sake, and you shove a laundry at me. I tell you, what you can do. You can take that laundry an' go to hell."

He was out of the room when Martin caught him and whirled him around.

"Now look here, Joe," he said; "if you act that way, I'll punch your head. An for old friends' sake I'll punch it hard. Savve?—you will, will you?"

Joe had clinched and attempted to throw him, and he was twisting and writhing out of the advantage of the other's hold. They reeled about the room, locked in each other's arms, and came down with a crash across the splintered wreckage of a wicker chair. Joe was underneath, with arms spread out and held and with Martin's knee on his chest. He was panting and gasping for breath when Martin released him.

"Now we'll talk a moment," Martin said. "You can't get fresh with me. I want that laundry business finished first of all. Then you can come back and we'll talk for old sake's sake. I told you I was busy. Look at that."

A servant had just come in with the morning mail, a great mass of letters and magazines.

"How can I wade through that and talk with you? You go and fix up that laundry, and then we'll get together."

"All right," Joe admitted reluctantly. "I thought you was turnin' me down, but I guess I was mistaken. But you can't lick me, Mart, in a stand-up fight. I've got the reach on you."

"We'll put on the gloves sometime and see," Martin said with a smile.

"Sure; as soon as I get that laundry going." Joe extended his arm. "You see that reach? It'll make you go a few."

Martin heaved a sigh of relief when the door closed behind the laundryman. He was becoming anti-social. Daily he found it a severer strain to be decent with people. Their presence perturbed him, and the effort of conversation irritated him. They made him restless, and no sooner was he in contact with them than he was casting about for excuses to get rid of them.

He did not proceed to attack his mail, and for a half hour he lolled in his chair, doing nothing, while no more than vague, half-formed thoughts occasionally filtered through his intelligence, or rather, at wide intervals, themselves constituted the flickering of his intelligence.

He roused himself and began glancing through his mail. There were a dozen requests for autographs—he knew them at sight; there were professional begging letters; and there were letters from cranks, ranging from the man with a working model of perpetual motion, and the man who demonstrated that the surface of the earth was the inside of a hollow sphere, to the man seeking financial aid to purchase the Peninsula of Lower California for the purpose of communist colonization. There were letters from women seeking to know him, and over one such he smiled, for enclosed was her receipt for pew-rent, sent as evidence of her good faith and as proof of her respectability.

Editors and publishers contributed to the daily heap of letters, the former on their knees for his manuscripts, the latter on their knees for his books—his poor disdained manuscripts that had kept all he possessed in pawn for so many dreary months in order to find them in postage. There were unexpected checks for English serial rights and for advance payments on foreign translations. His English agent announced the sale of German translation rights in three of his books, and informed him that Swedish editions, from which he could expect nothing because Sweden was not a party to the Berne Convention, were already on the market. Then there was a nominal request for his permission for a Russian translation, that country being likewise outside the Berne Convention.

He turned to the huge bundle of clippings which had come in from his press bureau, and read about himself and his vogue, which had become a furore. All his creative output had been flung to the public in one magnificent sweep. That seemed to account for it. He had taken the public off its feet, the way Kipling had, that time when he lay near to death and all the mob, animated by a mob-mind thought, began suddenly to read him. Martin remembered how that same world-mob, having read him and acclaimed him and not understood him in the least, had, abruptly, a few months later, flung itself upon him and torn him to pieces. Martin grinned at the thought. Who was he that he should not be similarly treated in a few more months? Well, he would fool the mob. He would be away, in the South Seas, building his grass house, trading for pearls and copra, jumping reefs in frail outriggers, catching sharks and bonitas, hunting wild goats among the cliffs of the valley that lay next to the valley of Taiohae.

In the moment of that thought the desperateness of his situation dawned upon him. He saw, cleared eyed, that he was in the Valley of the Shadow. All the life that was in him was fading, fainting, making toward death.

He realized how much he slept, and how much he desired to sleep. Of old, he had hated sleep. It had robbed him of precious moments of living. Four hours of sleep in the twenty-four had meant being robbed of four hours of life. How he had grudged sleep! Now it was life he grudged. Life was not good; its taste in his mouth was without tang, and bitter. This was his peril. Life that did not yearn toward life was in fair way toward ceasing. Some remote instinct for preservation stirred in him, and he knew he must get away. He glanced about the room, and the thought of packing was burdensome. Perhaps it would be better to leave that to the last. In the meantime he might be getting an outfit.

He put on his hat and went out, stopping in at a gun-store, where he spent the remainder of the morning buying automatic rifles, ammunition, and fishing tackle. Fashions changed in trading, and he knew he would have to wait till he reached Tahiti before ordering his trade-goods. They could come up from Australia, anyway. This solution was a source of pleasure. He had avoided doing something, and the doing of anything just now was unpleasant. He went back to the hotel gladly, with a feeling of satisfaction in that the comfortable Morris chair was waiting for him; and he groaned inwardly, on entering his room, at sight of Joe in the Morris chair.

Joe was delighted with the laundry. Everything was settled, and he would enter into possession next day. Martin lay on the bed, with closed eyes, while the other talked on. Martin's thoughts were far away—so far away that he was rarely aware that he was thinking. It was only by an effort that he occasionally responded. And yet this was Joe, whom he had always liked. But Joe was too keen with life. The boisterous impact of it on Martin's jaded mind was a hurt. It was an aching probe to his tired sensitiveness. When Joe reminded him that sometime in the future they were going to put on the gloves together, he could almost have screamed.

"Remember, Joe, you're to run the laundry according to those old rules you used to lay down at Shelly Hot Springs," he said. "No overworking. No working at night. And no children at the mangles. No children anywhere. And a fair wage."

Joe nodded and pulled out a note-book.

"Look at here. I was workin' out them rules before breakfast this A.M. What d'ye think of them?"

He read them aloud, and Martin approved, worrying at the same time as to when Joe would take himself off.

It was late afternoon when he awoke. Slowly the fact of life came back to him. He glanced about the room. Joe had evidently stolen away after he had dozed off. That was considerate of Joe, he thought. Then he closed his eyes and slept again.

In the days that followed Joe was too busy organizing and taking hold of the laundry to bother him much; and it was not until the day before sailing that the newspapers made the announcement that he had taken passage on the *Mariposa*. Once, when the instinct of preservation fluttered, he went to a doctor and underwent a searching physical examination. Nothing could be found the matter with him. His heart and lungs were pronounced magnificent. Every organ, so far as the doctor could know, was normal and was working normally.

"There is nothing the matter with you, Mr. Eden," he said, "positively nothing the matter with you. You are in the pink of condition. Candidly, I envy you your health. It is superb. Look at that chest. There, and in your stomach, lies the secret of your remarkable constitution. Physically, you are a man in a thousand—in ten thousand. Barring accidents, you should live to be a hundred."

And Martin knew that Lizzie's diagnosis had been correct. Physically he was all right. It was his "think-machine" that had gone wrong, and there was no cure for that except to get away to the South Seas. The trouble was that now, on the verge of departure, he had no desire to go. The South Seas charmed him no more than did bourgeois civilization. There was no zest in the thought of departure, while the act of departure appalled him as a weariness of the flesh. He would have felt better if he were already on board and gone.

The last day was a sore trial. Having read of his sailing in the morning papers, Bernard Higginbotham, Gertrude, and all the family came to say good-by, as did Hermann von Schmidt and Marian. Then there was business to be transacted, bills to be paid, and everlasting reporters to be endured. He said good-by to Lizzie Connolly, abruptly, at the entrance to night school, and hurried away. At the hotel he found Joe, too busy all day with the laundry to have come to him earlier. It was the last straw, but Martin gripped the arms of his chair and talked and listened for half an hour.

"You know, Joe," he said, "that you are not tied down to that laundry. There are no strings on it. You can sell it any time and blow the money. Any time you get sick of it and want to hit the road, just pull out. Do what will make you the happiest."

Joe shook his head.

"No more road in mine, thank you kindly. Hoboin's all right, exceptin' for one thing—the girls. I can't help it, but I'm a ladies' man. I can't get along without 'em, and you've got to get along without 'em when you're hoboin'. The times I've passed by houses where dances an' parties was goin' on, an' heard the women laugh, an' saw their white dresses and smiling faces through the windows—Gee! I tell you them moments was plain hell. I like dancin' an' picnics, an' walking in the moonlight, an' all the rest too well. Me for the laundry, and a good front, with big iron dollars clinkin' in my jeans. I seen a girl already, just yesterday, and, d'ye know, I'm feelin' already I'd just as soon marry her as not. I've ben whistlin' all day at the thought of it. She's a beaut, with the kindest eyes and softest voice you ever heard. Me for her, you can stack on that. Say, why don't you get married with all this money to burn? You could get the finest girl in the land."

Martin shook his head with a smile, but in his secret heart he was wondering why any man wanted to marry. It seemed an amazing and incomprehensible thing.

From the deck of the *Mariposa*, at the sailing hour, he saw Lizzie Connolly hiding in the skirts of the crowd on the wharf. Take her with you, came the thought. It is easy to be kind. She will be supremely happy. It was almost a temptation one moment, and the succeeding moment it became a terror. He was in a panic at the thought of it. His tired soul cried out in protest. He turned away from the rail with a groan, muttering, "Man, you are too sick, you are too sick."

He fled to his stateroom, where he lurked until the steamer was clear of the dock. In the dining saloon, at luncheon, he found himself in the place of honor, at the captain's right; and he was not long in discovering that he was the great man on board. But no more unsatisfactory great man ever sailed on a ship. He spent the afternoon in a deck-chair, with closed eyes, dozing brokenly most of the time, and in the evening went early to bed.

After the second day, recovered from seasickness, the full passenger list was in evidence, and the more he saw of the passengers the more he disliked them. Yet he knew that he did them injustice. They were good and kindly people, he forced himself to acknowledge, and in the moment of acknowledgment he qualified—good and kindly like all the bourgeoisie, with all the psychological cramp and intellectual futility of their kind, they bored him when they talked with him, their little superficial minds were so filled with emptiness; while the boisterous high spirits and the excessive energy of the younger people shocked him. They were never quiet, ceaselessly playing deck-quoits, tossing rings, promenading, or rushing to the rail with loud cries to watch the leaping porpoises and the first schools of flying fish.

He slept much. After breakfast he sought his deck-chair with a magazine he never finished. The printed pages tired him. He puzzled that men found so much to write about, and, puzzling, dozed in his chair. When the gong awoke him for luncheon, he was irritated that he must awaken. There was no satisfaction in being awake.

Once, he tried to arouse himself from his lethargy, and went forward into the forecastle with the sailors. But the breed of sailors seemed to have changed since the days he had lived in the forecastle. He could find no kinship with these stolid-faced, ox-minded bestial creatures. He was in despair. Up above nobody had wanted Martin Eden for his own sake, and he could not go back to those of his own class who had wanted him in the past. He did not want them. He could not stand them any more than he could stand the stupid first-cabin passengers and the riotous young people.

Life was to him like strong, white light that hurts the tired eyes of a sick person. During every conscious moment life blazed in a raw glare around him and upon him. It hurt. It hurt intolerably. It was the first time in his life that Martin had travelled first class. On ships at sea he had always been in the forecastle, the steerage, or in the black depths of the coal-hold, passing coal. In those days, climbing up the iron ladders out the pit of stifling heat, he had often caught glimpses of the passengers, in cool white, doing nothing but enjoy themselves, under awnings spread to keep the sun and wind away from them, with subservient stewards taking care of their every want and whim, and it had seemed to him that the realm in which they moved and had their being was nothing else than paradise. Well, here he was, the great man on board, in the midmost centre of it, sitting at the captain's right hand, and yet vainly harking back to forecastle and stoke-hole in quest of the Paradise he had lost. He had found no new one, and now he could not find the old one.

He strove to stir himself and find something to interest him. He ventured the petty officers' mess, and was glad to get away. He talked with a quartermaster off duty, an intelligent man who promptly prodded him with the socialist propaganda and forced into his hands a bunch of leaflets and pamphlets. He listened to the man expounding the slave-morality, and as he listened, he thought languidly of his own Nietzsche philosophy. But what was it worth, after all? He remembered one of Nietzsche's mad utterances wherein that madman had doubted truth. And who was to say? Perhaps Nietzsche had been right. Perhaps there was no truth in anything, no truth in truth—no such thing as truth. But his mind wearied quickly, and he was content to go back to his chair and doze.

Miserable as he was on the steamer, a new misery came upon him. What when the steamer reached Tahiti? He would have to go ashore. He would have to order his trade-goods, to find a passage on a schooner to the Marquesas, to do a thousand and one things that were awful to contemplate. Whenever he steeled himself deliberately to think, he could see the desperate peril in which he stood. In all truth, he was in the Valley of the Shadow, and his danger lay in that he was not afraid. If he were only afraid, he would make toward life. Being unafraid, he was drifting deeper into the shadow. He found no delight in the old familiar things of life. The *Mariposa* was now in the northeast trades, and this wine of wind, surging against him, irritated him. He had his chair moved to escape the embrace of this lusty comrade of old days and nights.

The day the *Mariposa* entered the doldrums, Martin was more miserable than ever. He could no longer sleep. He was soaked with sleep, and perforce he must now stay awake and endure the white glare of life. He moved about restlessly. The air was sticky and humid, and the rain-squalls were unrefreshing. He ached with life. He walked around the deck until that hurt too much, then sat in his chair until he was compelled to walk again. He forced himself at last to finish the magazine, and from the steamer library he culled several volumes of poetry. But they could not hold him, and once more he took to walking.

He stayed late on deck, after dinner, but that did not help him, for when he went below, he could not sleep. This surcease from life had failed him. It was too much. He turned on the electric light and tried to read. One of the volumes was a Swinburne. He lay in bed, glancing through its pages, until suddenly he became aware that he was reading with interest. He finished the stanza, attempted to read on, then came back to it. He rested the book face downward on his breast and fell to thinking. That was it. The very thing. Strange that it had never come to him before. That was the meaning of it all; he had been drifting that way all the time, and now Swinburne showed him that it was the happy way out. He wanted rest, and here was rest awaiting him. He glanced at the open port-hole. Yes, it was large enough. For the first time in weeks he felt happy. At last he had discovered the cure of his ill. He picked up the book and read the stanza slowly aloud:-

"'From too much love of living,
From hope and fear set free,
We thank with brief thanksgiving
Whatever gods may be
That no life lives forever;
That dead men rise up never;
That even the weariest river
Winds somewhere safe to sea.'"

He looked again at the open port. Swinburne had furnished the key. Life was ill, or, rather, it had become ill—an unbearable thing. "That dead men rise up never!" That line stirred him with a profound feeling of gratitude. It was the one beneficent thing in the universe. When life became an aching weariness, death was ready to soothe away to everlasting sleep. But what was he waiting for? It was time to go.

He arose and thrust his head out the port-hole, looking down into the milky wash. The *Mariposa* was deeply loaded, and, hanging by his hands, his feet would be in the water. He could slip in noiselessly. No one would hear. A smother of spray dashed up, wetting his face. It tasted salt on his lips, and the taste was good. He wondered if he ought to write a swan-song, but laughed the thought away. There was no time. He was too impatient to be gone.

Turning off the light in his room so that it might not betray him, he went out the port-hole feet first. His shoulders stuck, and he forced himself back so as to try it with one arm down by his side. A roll of the steamer aided him, and he was through, hanging by his hands. When his feet touched the sea, he let go. He was in a milky froth of water. The side of the *Mariposa* rushed past him like a dark wall, broken here and there by lighted ports. She was certainly making time. Almost before he knew it, he was astern, swimming gently on the foam-crackling surface.

A bonita struck at his white body, and he laughed aloud. It had taken a piece out, and the sting of it reminded him of why he was there. In the work to do he had forgotten the purpose of it. The lights of the *Mariposa* were growing dim in the distance, and there he was, swimming confidently, as though it were his intention to make for the nearest land a thousand miles or so away.

It was the automatic instinct to live. He ceased swimming, but the moment he felt the water rising above his mouth the hands struck out sharply with a lifting movement. The will to live, was his thought, and the thought was accompanied by a sneer. Well, he had will,—ay, will strong enough that with one last exertion it could destroy itself and cease to be.

He changed his position to a vertical one. He glanced up at the quiet stars, at the same time emptying his lungs of air. With swift, vigorous propulsion of hands and feet, he lifted his shoulders and half his chest out of water. This was to gain impetus for the descent. Then he let himself go and sank without movement, a white statue, into the sea. He breathed in the water deeply, deliberately, after the manner of a man taking an anaesthetic. When he strangled, quite involuntarily his arms and legs clawed the water and drove him up to the surface and into the clear sight of the stars.

The will to live, he thought disdainfully, vainly endeavoring not to breathe the air into his bursting lungs. Well, he would have to try a new way. He filled his lungs with air, filled them full. This supply would take him far down. He turned over and went down head first, swimming with all his strength and all his will. Deeper and deeper he went. His eyes were open, and he watched the ghostly, phosphorescent trails of the darting bonita. As he swam, he hoped that they would not strike at him, for it might snap the tension of his will. But they did not strike, and he found time to be grateful for this last kindness of life.

Down, down, he swam till his arms and leg grew tired and hardly moved. He knew that he was deep. The pressure on his ear-drums was a pain, and there was a buzzing in his head. His endurance was faltering, but he compelled his arms and legs to drive him deeper until his will snapped and the air drove from his lungs in a great explosive rush. The bubbles rubbed and bounded like tiny balloons against his cheeks and eyes as they took their upward flight. Then came pain and strangulation. This hurt was not death, was the thought that oscillated through his reeling consciousness. Death did not hurt. It was life, the pangs of life, this awful, suffocating feeling; it was the last blow life could deal him.

His wilful hands and feet began to beat and churn about, spasmodically and feebly. But he had fooled them and the will to live that made them beat and churn. He was too deep down. They could never bring him to the surface. He seemed floating languidly in a sea of dreamy vision. Colors and radiances surrounded him and bathed him and pervaded him. What was that? It seemed a lighthouse; but it was inside his brain—a flashing, bright white light. It flashed swifter and swifter. There was a long rumble of sound, and it seemed to him that he was falling down a vast and interminable stairway. And somewhere at the bottom he fell into darkness. That much he knew. He had fallen into darkness. And at the instant he knew, he ceased to know.

BURNING DAYLIGHT

PART I

CHAPTER I

It was a quiet night in the Shovel. At the bar, which ranged along one side of the large chinked-log room, leaned half a dozen men, two of whom were discussing the relative merits of spruce-tea and lime-juice as remedies for scurvy. They argued with an air of depression and with intervals of morose silence. The other men scarcely heeded them. In a row, against the opposite wall, were the gambling games. The crap-table was deserted. One lone man was playing at the faro-table. The roulette-ball was not even spinning, and the gamekeeper stood by the roaring, red-hot stove, talking with the young, dark-eyed woman, comely of face and figure, who was known from Juneau to Fort Yukon as the Virgin. Three men sat in at stud-poker, but they played with small chips and without enthusiasm, while there were no onlookers. On the floor of the dancing-room, which opened out at the rear, three couples were waltzing drearily to the strains of a violin and a piano.

Circle City was not deserted, nor was money tight. The miners were in from Moseyed Creek and the other diggings to the west, the summer washing had been good, and the men's pouches were heavy with dust and nuggets. The Klondike had not yet been discovered, nor had the miners of the Yukon learned the possibilities of deep digging and wood-firing. No work was done in the winter, and they made a practice of hibernating in the large camps like Circle City during the long Arctic night. Time was heavy on their hands, their pouches were well filled, and the only social diversion to be found was in the saloons. Yet the Shovel was practically deserted, and the Virgin, standing by the stove, yawned with uncovered mouth and said to Charley Bates:—

"If something don't happen soon, I'm gin' to bed. What's the matter with the camp, anyway? Everybody dead?"

Bates did not even trouble to reply, but went on moodily rolling a cigarette. Dan MacDonald, pioneer saloonman and gambler on the upper Yukon, owner and proprietor of the Tivoli and all its games, wandered forlornly across the great vacant space of floor and joined the two at the stove.

"Anybody dead?" the Virgin asked him.

"Looks like it," was the answer.

"Then it must be the whole camp," she said with an air of finality and with another yawn.

MacDonald grinned and nodded, and opened his mouth to speak, when the front door swung wide and a man appeared in the light. A rush of frost, turned to vapor by the heat of the room, swirled about him to his knees and poured on across the floor, growing thinner and thinner, and perishing a dozen feet from the stove. Taking the wisp broom from its nail inside the door, the newcomer brushed the snow from his moccasins and high German socks. He would have appeared a large man had not a huge French-Canadian stepped up to him from the bar and gripped his hand.

"Hello, Daylight!" was his greeting. "By Gar, you good for sore eyes!"

"Hello, Louis, when did you-all blow in?" returned the newcomer. "Come up and have a drink and tell us all about Bone Creek. Why, dog-gone you-all, shake again. Where's that pardner of yours? I'm looking for him."

Another huge man detached himself from the bar to shake hands. Olaf Henderson and French Louis, partners together on Bone Creek, were the two largest men in the country, and though they were but half a head taller than the newcomer, between them he was dwarfed completely.

"Hello, Olaf, you're my meat, savvee that," said the one called Daylight. "To-morrow's my birthday, and I'm going to put you-all on your back—savvee? And you, too, Louis. I can put you-all on your back on my birthday—savvee? Come up and drink, Olaf, and I'll tell you-all about it."

The arrival of the newcomer seemed to send a flood of warmth through the place. "It's Burning Daylight," the Virgin cried, the first to recognize him as he came into the light. Charley Bates' tight features relaxed at the sight, and MacDonald went over and joined the three at the bar. With the advent of Burning Daylight the whole place became suddenly brighter and cheerier. The barkeepers were active. Voices were raised. Somebody laughed. And when the fiddler, peering into the front room, remarked to the pianist, "It's Burning Daylight," the waltz-time perceptibly quickened, and the dancers, catching the contagion, began to whirl about as if they really enjoyed it. It was known to them of old time that nothing languished when Burning Daylight was around.

He turned from the bar and saw the woman by the stove and the eager look of welcome she extended him.

"Hello, Virgin, old girl," he called. "Hello, Charley. What's the matter with you-all? Why wear faces like that when coffins cost only three ounces? Come up, you-all, and drink. Come up, you unburied dead, and name your poison. Come up, everybody. This is my night, and I'm going to ride it. To-morrow I'm thirty, and then I'll be an old man. It's the last fling of youth. Are you-all with me? Surge along, then. Surge along.

"Hold on there, Davis," he called to the faro-dealer, who had shoved his chair back from the table. "I'm going you one flutter to see whether you-all drink with me or we-all drink with you."

Pulling a heavy sack of gold-dust from his coat pocket, he dropped it on the HIGH CARD.

"Fifty," he said.

The faro-dealer slipped two cards. The high card won. He scribbled the amount on a pad, and the weigher at the bar balanced fifty dollars' worth of dust in the gold-scales and poured it into Burning Daylight's sack. The waltz in the back room being finished, the three couples, followed by the fiddler and the pianist and heading for the bar, caught Daylight's eye.

"Surge along, you-all" he cried. "Surge along and name it. This is my night, and it ain't a night that comes frequent. Surge up, you Siwashes and Salmon-eaters. It's my night, I tell you-all—"

"A blame mangy night," Charley Bates interpolated.

"You're right, my son," Burning Daylight went on gaily.

"A mangy night, but it's MY night, you see. I'm the mangy old he-wolf. Listen to me howl."

And howl he did, like a lone gray timber wolf, till the Virgin thrust her pretty fingers in her ears and shivered. A minute later she was whirled away in his arms to the dancing-floor, where, along with the other three women and their partners, a rollicking Virginia reel was soon in progress. Men and women danced in moccasins, and the place was soon a-roar, Burning Daylight the centre of it and the animating spark, with quip and jest and rough merriment rousing them out of the slough of despond in which he had found them.

The atmosphere of the place changed with his coming. He seemed to fill it with his tremendous vitality. Men who entered from the street felt it immediately, and in response to their queries the barkeepers nodded at the back room, and said comprehensively, "Burning Daylight's on the tear." And the men who entered remained, and kept the barkeepers busy. The gamblers took heart of life, and soon the tables were filled, the click of chips and whir of the roulette-ball rising monotonously and imperiously above the hoarse rumble of men's voices and their oaths and heavy laughs.

Few men knew Elam Harnish by any other name than Burning Daylight, the name which had been given him in the early days in the land because of his habit of routing his comrades out of their blankets with the complaint that daylight was burning. Of the pioneers in that far Arctic wilderness, where all men were pioneers, he was reckoned among the oldest. Men like Al Mayo and Jack McQuestion antedated him; but they had entered the land by crossing the Rockies from the Hudson Bay country to the east. He, however, had been the pioneer over the Chilcoot and Chilcat passes. In the spring of 1883, twelve years before, a stripling of eighteen, he had crossed over the Chilcoot with five comrades.

In the fall he had crossed back with one. Four had perished by mischance in the bleak, uncharted vastness. And for twelve years Elam Harnish had continued to grope for gold among the shadows of the Circle.

And no man had groped so obstinately nor so enduringly. He had grown up with the land. He knew no other land. Civilization was a dream of some previous life. Camps like Forty Mile and Circle City were to him metropolises. And not alone had he grown up with the land, for, raw as it was, he had helped to make it. He had made history and geography, and those that followed wrote of his traverses and charted the trails his feet had broken.

Heroes are seldom given to hero-worship, but among those of that young land, young as he was, he was accounted an elder hero. In point of time he was before them. In point of deed he was beyond them. In point of endurance it was acknowledged that he could kill the hardiest of them. Furthermore, he was accounted a nervy man, a square man, and a white man.

In all lands where life is a hazard lightly played with and lightly flung aside, men turn, almost automatically, to gambling for diversion and relaxation. In the Yukon men gambled their lives for gold, and those that won gold from the ground gambled for it with one another. Nor was Elam Harnish an exception. He was a man's man primarily, and the instinct in him to play the game of life was strong. Environment had determined what form that game should take. He was born on an Iowa farm, and his father had emigrated to eastern Oregon, in which mining country Elam's boyhood was lived. He had known nothing but hard knocks for big stakes. Pluck and endurance counted in the game, but the great god Chance dealt the cards. Honest work for sure but meagre returns did not count. A man played big. He risked everything for everything, and anything less than everything meant that he was a loser. So for twelve Yukon years, Elam Harnish had been a loser. True, on Moosehide Creek the past summer he had taken out twenty thousand dollars, and what was left in the ground was twenty thousand more. But, as he himself proclaimed, that was no more than getting his ante back. He had ante'd his life for a dozen years, and forty thousand was a small pot for such a stake—the price of a drink and a dance at the Tivoli, of a winter's flutter at Circle City, and a grubstake for the year to come.

The men of the Yukon reversed the old maxim till it read: hard come, easy go. At the end of the reel, Elam Harnish called the house up to drink again. Drinks were a dollar apiece, gold rated at sixteen dollars an ounce; there were thirty in the house that accepted his invitation, and between every dance the house was Elam's guest. This was his night, and nobody was to be allowed to pay for anything.

Not that Elam Harnish was a drinking man. Whiskey meant little to him. He was too vital and robust, too untroubled in mind and body, to incline to the slavery of alcohol. He spent months at a time on trail and river when he drank nothing stronger than coffee, while he had gone a year at a time without even coffee. But he was gregarious, and since the sole social expression of the Yukon was the saloon, he expressed himself that way. When he was a lad in the mining camps of the West, men had always done that. To him it was the proper way for a man to express himself socially. He knew no other way.

He was a striking figure of a man, despite his garb being similar to that of all the men in the Tivoli. Soft-tanned moccasins of moose-hide, beaded in Indian designs, covered his feet. His trousers were ordinary overalls, his coat was made from a blanket. Long-gauntleted leather mittens, lined with wool, hung by his side. They were connected in the Yukon fashion, by a leather thong passed around the neck and across the shoulders. On his head was a fur cap, the ear-flaps raised and the tying-cords dangling. His face, lean and slightly long, with the suggestion of hollows under the cheek-bones, seemed almost Indian. The burnt skin and keen dark eyes contributed to this effect, though the bronze of the skin and the eyes themselves were essentially those of a white man. He looked older than thirty, and yet, smooth-shaven and without wrinkles, he was almost boyish. This impression of age was based on no tangible evidence. It came from the abstracter facts of the man, from what he had endured and survived, which was far beyond that of ordinary men. He had lived life naked and tensely, and something of all this smouldered in his eyes, vibrated in his voice, and seemed forever a-whisper on his lips.

The lips themselves were thin, and prone to close tightly over the even, white teeth. But their harshness was retrieved by the upward curl at the corners of his mouth. This curl gave to him sweetness, as the minute puckers at the corners of the eyes gave him laughter. These necessary graces saved him from a nature that was essentially savage and that otherwise would have been cruel and bitter. The nose was lean, full-nostrilled, and delicate, and of a size to fit the face; while the high forehead, as if to atone for its narrowness, was splendidly domed and symmetrical. In line with the Indian effect was his hair, very straight and very black, with a gloss to it that only health could give.

"Burning Daylight's burning candlelight," laughed Dan MacDonald, as an outburst of exclamations and merriment came from the dancers.

"An' he is der boy to do it, eh, Louis?" said Olaf Henderson.

"Yes, by Gar! you bet on dat," said French Louis. "Dat boy is all gold—"

"And when God Almighty washes Daylight's soul out on the last big slucin' day," MacDonald interrupted, "why, God Almighty'll have to shovel gravel along with him into the sluice-boxes."

"Dot iss goot," Olaf Henderson muttered, regarding the gambler with profound admiration.

"Ver' good," affirmed French Louis. "I t'ink we take a drink on dat one time, eh?"

CHAPTER II

It was two in the morning when the dancers, bent on getting something to eat, adjourned the dancing for half an hour. And it was at this moment that Jack Kearns suggested poker. Jack Kearns was a big, bluff-featured man, who, along with Bettles, had made the disastrous attempt to found a post on the head-reaches of the Koyokuk, far inside the Arctic Circle. After that, Kearns had fallen back on his posts at Forty Mile and Sixty Mile and changed the direction of his ventures by sending out to the States for a small sawmill and a river steamer. The former was even then being sledded across Chilcoot Pass by Indians and dogs, and would come down the Yukon in the early summer after the ice-run. Later in the summer, when Bering Sea and the mouth of the Yukon cleared of ice, the steamer, put together at St. Michaels, was to be expected up the river loaded to the guards with supplies.

Jack Kearns suggested poker. French Louis, Dan MacDonald, and Hal Campbell (who had make a strike on Moosehide), all three of whom were not dancing because there were not girls enough to go around, inclined to the suggestion. They were looking for a fifth man when Burning Daylight emerged from the rear room, the Virgin on his arm, the train of dancers in his wake. In response to the hail of the poker-players, he came over to their table in the corner.

"Want you to sit in," said Campbell. "How's your luck?"

"I sure got it to-night," Burning Daylight answered with enthusiasm, and at the same time felt the Virgin press his arm warningly. She wanted him for the dancing. "I sure got my luck with me, but I'd sooner dance. I ain't hankerin' to take the money away from you-all."

Nobody urged. They took his refusal as final, and the Virgin was pressing his arm to turn him away in pursuit of the supper-seekers, when he experienced a change of heart. It was not that he did not want to dance, nor that he wanted to hurt her; but that insistent pressure on his arm put his free man-nature in revolt. The thought in his mind was that he did not want any woman running him. Himself a favorite with women, nevertheless they did not bulk big with him. They were toys, playthings, part of the relaxation from the bigger game of life. He met women along with the whiskey and gambling, and from observation he had found that it was far easier to break away from the drink and the cards than from a woman once the man was properly entangled.

He was a slave to himself, which was natural in one with a healthy ego, but he rebelled in ways either murderous or panicky at being a slave to anybody else. Love's sweet servitude was a thing of which he had no comprehension. Men he had seen in love impressed him as lunatics, and lunacy was a thing he had never considered worth analyzing. But comradeship with men was different from love with women. There was no servitude in comradeship. It was a business proposition, a square deal between men who did not pursue each other, but who shared the risks of trail and river and mountain in the pursuit of life and treasure. Men and women pursued each other, and one must needs bend the other to his will or hers. Comradeship was different. There was no slavery about it; and though he, a strong man beyond strength's seeming, gave far more than he received, he gave not something due but in royal largess, his gifts of toil or heroic effort falling generously from his hands. To pack for days over the gale-swept passes or across the mosquito-ridden marshes, and to pack double the weight his comrade packed, did not involve unfairness or compulsion. Each did his best. That was the business essence of it. Some men were stronger than others—true; but so long as each man did his best it was fair exchange, the business spirit was observed, and the square deal obtained.

But with women—no. Women gave little and wanted all. Women had apron-strings and were prone to tie them about any man who looked twice in their direction. There was the Virgin, yawning her head off when he came in and mightily pleased that he asked her to dance. One dance was all very well, but because he danced twice and thrice with her and several times more, she squeezed his arm when they asked him to sit in at poker. It was the obnoxious apron-string, the first of the many compulsions she would exert upon him if he gave in. Not that she was not a nice bit of a woman, healthy and strapping and good to look upon, also a very excellent dancer, but that she was a woman with all a woman's desire to rope him with her apron-strings and tie him hand and foot for the branding. Better poker. Besides, he liked poker as well as he did dancing.

He resisted the pull on his arm by the mere negative mass of him, and said:—

"I sort of feel a hankering to give you-all a flutter."

Again came the pull on his arm. She was trying to pass the apron-string around him. For the fraction of an instant he was a savage, dominated by the wave of fear and murder that rose up in him. For that infinitesimal space of time he was to all purposes a frightened tiger filled with rage and terror at the apprehension of the trap. Had he been no more than a savage, he would have leapt wildly from the place or else sprung upon her and destroyed her. But in that same instant there stirred in him the generations of discipline by which man had become an inadequate social animal. Tact and sympathy strove with him, and he smiled with his eyes into the Virgin's eyes as he said:—

"You-all go and get some grub. I ain't hungry. And we'll dance some more by and by. The night's young yet. Go to it, old girl."

He released his arm and thrust her playfully on the shoulder, at the same time turning to the poker-players.

"Take off the limit and I'll go you-all."

"Limit's the roof," said Jack Kearns.

"Take off the roof."

The players glanced at one another, and Kearns announced, "The roof's off."

Elam Harnish dropped into the waiting chair, started to pull out his gold-sack, and changed his mind. The Virgin pouted a moment, then followed in the wake of the other dancers.

"I'll bring you a sandwich, Daylight," she called back over her shoulder.

He nodded. She was smiling her forgiveness. He had escaped the apron-string, and without hurting her feelings too severely.

"Let's play markers," he suggested. "Chips do everlastingly clutter up the table....If it's agreeable to you-all?"

"I'm willing," answered Hal Campbell. "Let mine run at five hundred."

"Mine, too," answered Harnish, while the others stated the values they put on their own markers, French Louis, the most modest, issuing his at a hundred dollars each.

In Alaska, at that time, there were no rascals and no tin-horn gamblers. Games were conducted honestly, and men trusted one another. A man's word was as good as his gold in the blower. A marker was a flat, oblong composition chip worth, perhaps, a cent. But when a man betted a marker in a game and said it was worth five hundred dollars, it was accepted as worth five hundred dollars. Whoever won it knew that the man who issued it would redeem it with five hundred dollars' worth of dust weighed out on the scales. The markers being of different colors, there was no difficulty in identifying the owners. Also, in that early Yukon day, no one dreamed of playing table-stakes. A man was good in a game for all that he possessed, no matter where his possessions were or what was their nature.

Harnish cut and got the deal. At this good augury, and while shuffling the deck, he called to the barkeepers to set up the drinks for the house. As he dealt the first card to Dan MacDonald, on his left, he called out:

"Get down to the ground, you-all, Malemutes, huskies, and Siwash purps! Get down and dig in! Tighten up them traces! Put your weight into the harness and bust the breast-bands! Whoop-la! Yow! We're off and bound for Helen Breakfast! And I tell you-all clear and plain there's goin' to be stiff grades and fast goin' to-night before we win to that same lady. And somebody's goin' to bump...hard."

Once started, it was a quiet game, with little or no conversation, though all about the players the place was a-roar. Elam Harnish had ignited the spark. More and more miners dropped in to the Tivoli and remained. When Burning Daylight went on the tear, no man cared to miss it. The dancing-floor was full. Owing to the shortage of women, many of the men tied bandanna handkerchiefs around their arms in token of femininity and danced with other men. All the games were crowded, and the voices of the men talking at the long bar and grouped about the stove were accompanied by the steady click of chips and the sharp whir, rising and falling, of the roulette-ball. All the materials of a proper Yukon night were at hand and mixing.

The luck at the table varied monotonously, no big hands being out. As a result, high play went on with small hands though no play lasted long. A filled straight belonging to French Louis gave him a pot of five thousand against two sets of threes held by Campbell and Kearns. One pot of eight hundred dollars was won by a pair of treys on a showdown. And once Harnish called Kearns for two thousand dollars on a cold steal. When Kearns laid down his hand it showed a bobtail flush, while Harnish's hand proved that he had had the nerve to call on a pair of tens.

But at three in the morning the big combination of hands arrived.

It was the moment of moments that men wait weeks for in a poker game. The news of it tingled over the Tivoli. The onlookers became quiet. The men farther away ceased talking and moved over to the table. The players deserted the other games, and the dancing-floor was forsaken, so that all stood at last, fivescore and more, in a compact and silent group, around the poker-table. The high betting had begun before the draw, and still the high betting went on, with the draw not in sight. Kearns had dealt, and French Louis had opened the pot with one marker—in his case one hundred dollars. Campbell had merely "seen" it, but Elam Harnish, corning next, had tossed in five hundred dollars, with the remark to MacDonald that he was letting him in easy.

MacDonald, glancing again at his hand, put in a thousand in markers. Kearns, debating a long time over his hand, finally "saw." It then cost French Louis nine hundred to remain in the game, which he contributed after a similar debate. It cost Campbell likewise nine hundred to remain and draw cards, but to the surprise of all he saw the nine hundred and raised another thousand.

"You-all are on the grade at last," Harnish remarked, as he saw the fifteen hundred and raised a thousand in turn. "Helen Breakfast's sure on top this divide, and you-all had best look out for bustin' harness."

"Me for that same lady," accompanied MacDonald's markers for two thousand and for an additional thousand-dollar raise.

It was at this stage that the players sat up and knew beyond peradventure that big hands were out. Though their features showed nothing, each man was beginning unconsciously to tense. Each man strove to appear his natural self, and each natural self was different. Hal Campbell affected his customary cautiousness.

French Louis betrayed interest. MacDonald retained his whole-souled benevolence, though it seemed to take on a slightly exaggerated tone. Kearns was coolly dispassionate and noncommittal, while Elam Harnish appeared as quizzical and jocular as ever. Eleven thousand dollars were already in the pot, and the markers were heaped in a confused pile in the centre of the table.

"I ain't go no more markers," Kearns remarked plaintively. "We'd best begin I.O.U.'s."

"Glad you're going to stay," was MacDonald's cordial response.

"I ain't stayed yet. I've got a thousand in already. How's it stand now?"

"It'll cost you three thousand for a look in, but nobody will stop you from raising."

"Raise—hell. You must think I got a pat like yourself." Kearns looked at his hand. "But I'll tell you what I'll do, Mac.

"I've got a hunch, and I'll just see that three thousand."

He wrote the sum on a slip of paper, signed his name, and consigned it to the centre of the table.

French Louis became the focus of all eyes. He fingered his cards nervously for a space. Then, with a "By Gar! Ah got not one leetle beet hunch," he regretfully tossed his hand into the discards.

The next moment the hundred and odd pairs of eyes shifted to Campbell.

"I won't hump you, Jack," he said, contenting himself with calling the requisite two thousand.

The eyes shifted to Harnish, who scribbled on a piece of paper and shoved it forward.

"I'll just let you-all know this ain't no Sunday-school society of philanthropy," he said. "I see you, Jack, and I raise you a thousand. Here's where you-all get action on your pat, Mac."

"Action's what I fatten on, and I lift another thousand," was MacDonald's rejoinder. "Still got that hunch, Jack?"

"I still got the hunch." Kearns fingered his cards a long time. "And I'll play it, but you've got to know how I stand. There's my steamer, the Bella—worth twenty thousand if she's worth an ounce. There's Sixty Mile with five thousand in stock on the shelves. And you know I got a sawmill coming in. It's at Linderman now, and the scow is building. Am I good?"

"Dig in; you're sure good," was Daylight's answer. "And while we're about it, I may mention casual that I got twenty thousand in Mac's safe, there, and there's twenty thousand more in the ground on Moosehide. You know the ground, Campbell. Is they that-all in the dirt?"

"There sure is, Daylight."

"How much does it cost now?" Kearns asked.

"Two thousand to see."

"We'll sure hump you if you-all come in," Daylight warned him.

"It's an almighty good hunch," Kearns said, adding his slip for two thousand to the growing heap. "I can feel her crawlin' up and down my back."

"I ain't got a hunch, but I got a tolerable likeable hand," Campbell announced, as he slid in his slip; "but it's not a raising hand."

"Mine is," Daylight paused and wrote. "I see that thousand and raise her the same old thousand."

The Virgin, standing behind him, then did what a man's best friend was not privileged to do. Reaching over Daylight's shoulder, she picked up his hand and read it, at the same time shielding the faces of the five cards close to his chest. What she saw were three queens and a pair of eights, but nobody guessed what she saw. Every player's eyes were on her face as she scanned the cards, but no sign did she give. Her features might have been carved from ice, for her expression was precisely the same before, during, and after. Not a muscle quivered; nor was there the slightest dilation of a nostril, nor the slightest increase of light in the eyes. She laid the hand face down again on the table, and slowly the lingering eyes withdrew from her, having learned nothing.

MacDonald smiled benevolently. "I see you, Daylight, and I hump this time for two thousand. How's that hunch, Jack?"

"Still a-crawling, Mac. You got me now, but that hunch is a rip-snorter persuadin' sort of a critter, and it's my plain duty to ride it. I call for three thousand. And I got another hunch: Daylight's going to call, too."

"He sure is," Daylight agreed, after Campbell had thrown up his hand. "He knows when he's up against it, and he plays accordin'. I see that two thousand, and then I'll see the draw."

In a dead silence, save for the low voices of the three players, the draw was made. Thirty-four thousand dollars were already in the pot, and the play possibly not half over. To the Virgin's amazement, Daylight held up his three queens, discarding his eights and calling for two cards. And this time not even she dared look at what he had drawn. She knew her limit of control. Nor did he look. The two new cards lay face down on the table where they had been dealt to him.

"Cards?" Kearns asked of MacDonald.

"Got enough," was the reply.

"You can draw if you want to, you know," Kearns warned him.

"Nope; this'll do me."

Kearns himself drew two cards, but did not look at them.

Still Harnish let his cards lie.

"I never bet in the teeth of a pat hand," he said slowly, looking at the saloon-keeper. "You-all start her rolling, Mac."

MacDonald counted his cards carefully, to make double sure it was not a foul hand, wrote a sum on a paper slip, and slid it into the pot, with the simple utterance:—

"Five thousand."

Kearns, with every eye upon him, looked at his two-card draw, counted the other three to dispel any doubt of holding more than five cards, and wrote on a betting slip.

"I see you, Mac," he said, "and I raise her a little thousand just so as not to keep Daylight out."

The concentrated gaze shifted to Daylight. He likewise examined his draw and counted his five cards.

"I see that six thousand, and I raise her five thousand...just to try and keep you out, Jack."

"And I raise you five thousand just to lend a hand at keeping Jack out," MacDonald said, in turn.

His voice was slightly husky and strained, and a nervous twitch in the corner of his mouth followed speech.

Kearns was pale, and those who looked on noted that his hand trembled as he wrote his slip. But his voice was unchanged.

"I lift her along for five thousand," he said.

Daylight was now the centre. The kerosene lamps above flung high lights from the rash of sweat on his forehead. The bronze of his cheeks was darkened by the accession of blood. His black eyes glittered, and his nostrils were distended and eager. They were large nostrils, tokening his descent from savage ancestors who had survived by virtue of deep lungs and generous air-passages. Yet, unlike MacDonald, his voice was firm and customary, and, unlike Kearns, his hand did not tremble when he wrote.

"I call, for ten thousand," he said. "Not that I'm afraid of you-all, Mac. It's that hunch of Jack's."

"I hump his hunch for five thousand just the same," said MacDonald. "I had the best hand before the draw, and I still guess I got it."

"Mebbe this is a case where a hunch after the draw is better'n the hunch before," Kearns remarked; "wherefore duty says, 'Lift her, Jack, lift her,' and so I lift her another five thousand."

Daylight leaned back in his chair and gazed up at the kerosene lamps while he computed aloud.

"I was in nine thousand before the draw, and I saw and raised eleven thousand—that makes thirty. I'm only good for ten more."

He leaned forward and looked at Kearns. "So I call that ten thousand."

"You can raise if you want," Kearns answered. "Your dogs are good for five thousand in this game."

"Nary dawg. You-all can win my dust and dirt, but nary one of my dawgs. I just call."

MacDonald considered for a long time. No one moved or whispered.

Not a muscle was relaxed on the part of the onlookers. Not the weight of a body shifted from one leg to the other. It was a sacred silence. Only could be heard the roaring draft of the huge stove, and from without, muffled by the log-walls, the howling of dogs. It was not every night that high stakes were played on the Yukon, and for that matter, this was the highest in the history of the country. The saloon-keeper finally spoke.

"If anybody else wins, they'll have to take a mortgage on the Tivoli."

The two other players nodded.

"So I call, too." MacDonald added his slip for five thousand.

Not one of them claimed the pot, and not one of them called the size of his hand. Simultaneously and in silence they faced their cards on the table, while a general tiptoeing and craning of necks took place among the onlookers. Daylight showed four queens and an ace; MacDonald four jacks and an ace; and Kearns four kings and a trey. Kearns reached forward with an encircling movement of his arm and drew the pot in to him, his arm shaking as he did so.

Daylight picked the ace from his hand and tossed it over alongside MacDonald's ace, saying:—

"That's what cheered me along, Mac. I knowed it was only kings that could beat me, and he had them.

"What did you-all have?" he asked, all interest, turning to Campbell.

"Straight flush of four, open at both ends—a good drawing hand."

"You bet! You could a' made a straight, a straight flush, or a flush out of it."

"That's what I thought," Campbell said sadly. "It cost me six thousand before I quit."

"I wisht you-all'd drawn," Daylight laughed. "Then I wouldn't a' caught that fourth queen. Now I've got to take Billy Rawlins' mail contract and mush for Dyea. What's the size of the killing, Jack?"

Kearns attempted to count the pot, but was too excited. Daylight drew it across to him, with firm fingers separating and stacking the markers and I.O.U.'s and with clear brain adding the sum.

"One hundred and twenty-seven thousand," he announced. "You-all can sell out now, Jack, and head for home."

The winner smiled and nodded, but seemed incapable of speech.

"I'd shout the drinks," MacDonald said, "only the house don't belong to me any more."

"Yes, it does," Kearns replied, first wetting his lips with his tongue. "Your note's good for any length of time. But the drinks are on me."

"Name your snake-juice, you-all—the winner pays!" Daylight called out loudly to all about him, at the same time rising from his chair and catching the Virgin by the arm. "Come on for a reel, you-all dancers. The night's young yet, and it's Helen Breakfast and the mail contract for me in the morning. Here, you-all Rawlins, you—I hereby do take over that same contract, and I start for salt water at nine A.M.—savvee? Come on, you-all! Where's that fiddler?"

CHAPTER III

It was Daylight's night. He was the centre and the head of the revel, unquenchably joyous, a contagion of fun. He multiplied himself, and in so doing multiplied the excitement. No prank he suggested was too wild for his followers, and all followed save those that developed into singing imbeciles and fell warbling by the wayside. Yet never did trouble intrude. It was known on the Yukon that when Burning Daylight made a night of it, wrath and evil were forbidden. On his nights men dared not quarrel. In the younger days such things had happened, and then men had known what real wrath was, and been man-handled as only Burning Daylight could man-handle. On his nights men must laugh and be happy or go home. Daylight was inexhaustible. In between dances he paid over to Kearns the twenty thousand in dust and transferred to him his Moosehide claim. Likewise he arranged the taking over of Billy Rawlins' mail contract, and made his preparations for the start. He despatched a messenger to rout out Kama, his dog-driver—a Tananaw Indian, far-wandered from his tribal home in the service of the invading whites. Kama entered the Tivoli, tall, lean, muscular, and fur-clad, the pick of his barbaric race and barbaric still, unshaken and unabashed by the revellers that rioted about him while Daylight gave his orders. "Um," said Kama, tabling his instructions on his fingers. "Get um letters from Rawlins. Load um on sled. Grub for Selkirk—you think um plenty dog-grub stop Selkirk?"

"Plenty dog-grub, Kama."

"Um, bring sled this place nine um clock. Bring um snowshoes. No bring um tent. Mebbe bring um fly? um little fly?"

"No fly," Daylight answered decisively.

"Um much cold."

"We travel light—savvee? We carry plenty letters out, plenty letters back. You are strong man. Plenty cold, plenty travel, all right."

"Sure all right," Kama muttered, with resignation.

"Much cold, no care a damn. Um ready nine um clock."

He turned on his moccasined heel and walked out, imperturbable, sphinx-like, neither giving nor receiving greetings nor looking to right or left. The Virgin led Daylight away into a corner.

"Look here, Daylight," she said, in a low voice, "you're busted."

"Higher'n a kite."

"I've eight thousand in Mac's safe—" she began.

But Daylight interrupted. The apron-string loomed near and he shied like an unbroken colt.

"It don't matter," he said. "Busted I came into the world, busted I go out, and I've been busted most of the time since I arrived. Come on; let's waltz."

"But listen," she urged. "My money's doing nothing. I could lend it to you—a grub-stake," she added hurriedly, at sight of the alarm in his face.

"Nobody grub-stakes me," was the answer. "I stake myself, and when I make a killing it's sure all mine. No thank you, old girl. Much obliged. I'll get my stake by running the mail out and in."

"Daylight," she murmured, in tender protest.

But with a sudden well-assumed ebullition of spirits he drew her toward the dancing-floor, and as they swung around and around in a waltz she pondered on the iron heart of the man who held her in his arms and resisted all her wiles.

At six the next morning, scorching with whiskey, yet ever himself, he stood at the bar putting every man's hand down. The way of it was that two men faced each other across a corner, their right elbows resting on the bar, their right hands gripped together, while each strove to press the other's hand down. Man after man came against him, but no man put his hand down, even Olaf Henderson and French Louis failing despite their hugeness. When they contended it was a trick, a trained muscular knack, he challenged them to another test.

"Look here, you-all" he cried. "I'm going to do two things: first, weigh my sack; and second, bet it that after you-all have lifted clean from the floor all the sacks of flour you-all are able, I'll put on two more sacks and lift the whole caboodle clean."

"By Gar! Ah take dat!" French Louis rumbled above the cheers.

"Hold on!" Olaf Henderson cried. "I ban yust as good as you, Louis. I yump half that bet."

Put on the scales, Daylight's sack was found to balance an even four hundred dollars, and Louis and Olaf divided the bet between them. Fifty-pound sacks of flour were brought in from MacDonald's cache. Other men tested their strength first. They straddled on two chairs, the flour sacks beneath them on the floor and held together by rope-lashings. Many of the men were able, in this manner, to lift four or five hundred pounds, while some succeeded with as high as six hundred. Then the two giants took a hand, tying at seven hundred. French Louis then added another sack, and swung seven hundred and fifty clear. Olaf duplicated the performance, whereupon both failed to clear eight hundred. Again and again they strove, their foreheads beaded with sweat, their frames crackling with the effort. Both were able to shift the weight and to bump it, but clear the floor with it they could not.

"By Gar! Daylight, dis tam you mek one beeg meestake," French Louis said, straightening up and stepping down from the chairs. "Only one damn iron man can do dat. One hundred pun' more—my frien', not ten poun' more." The sacks were unlashed, but when two sacks were added, Kearns interfered. "Only one sack more."

"Two!" some one cried. "Two was the bet."

"They didn't lift that last sack," Kearns protested.

"They only lifted seven hundred and fifty."

But Daylight grandly brushed aside the confusion.

"What's the good of you-all botherin' around that way? What's one more sack? If I can't lift three more, I sure can't lift two. Put 'em in."

He stood upon the chairs, squatted, and bent his shoulders down till his hands closed on the rope. He shifted his feet slightly, tautened his muscles with a tentative pull, then relaxed again, questing for a perfect adjustment of all the levers of his body.

French Louis, looking on sceptically, cried out,

"Pool lak hell, Daylight! Pool lak hell!"

Daylight's muscles tautened a second time, and this time in earnest, until steadily all the energy of his splendid body was applied, and quite imperceptibly, without jerk or strain, the bulky nine hundred pounds rose from the door and swung back and forth, pendulum like, between his legs.

Olaf Henderson sighed a vast audible sigh. The Virgin, who had tensed unconsciously till her muscles hurt her, relaxed. While French Louis murmured reverently:—

"M'sieu Daylight, salut! Ay am one beeg baby. You are one beeg man."

Daylight dropped his burden, leaped to the floor, and headed for the bar.

"Weigh in!" he cried, tossing his sack to the weigher, who transferred to it four hundred dollars from the sacks of the two losers.

"Surge up, everybody!" Daylight went on. "Name your snake-juice! The winner pays!"

"This is my night!" he was shouting, ten minutes later. "I'm the lone he-wolf, and I've seen thirty winters. This is my birthday, my one day in the year, and I can put any man on his back. Come on, you-all! I'm going to put you-all in the snow. Come on, you chechaquos [1] and sourdoughs[2], and get your baptism!"

The rout streamed out of doors, all save the barkeepers and the singing Bacchuses. Some fleeting thought of saving his own dignity entered MacDonald's head, for he approached Daylight with outstretched hand.

"What? You first?" Daylight laughed, clasping the other's hand as if in greeting.

"No, no," the other hurriedly disclaimed. "Just congratulations on your birthday. Of course you can put me in the snow. What chance have I against a man that lifts nine hundred pounds?"

MacDonald weighed one hundred and eighty pounds, and Daylight had him gripped solely by his hand; yet, by a sheer abrupt jerk, he took the saloon-keeper off his feet and flung him face downward in the snow. In quick succession, seizing the men nearest him, he threw half a dozen more. Resistance was useless. They flew helter-skelter out of his grips, landing in all manner of attitudes, grotesquely and harmlessly, in the soft snow. It soon became difficult, in the dim starlight, to distinguish between those thrown and those waiting their turn, and he began feeling their backs and shoulders, determining their status by whether or not he found them powdered with snow.

"Baptized yet?" became his stereotyped question, as he reached out his terrible hands.

Several score lay down in the snow in a long row, while many others knelt in mock humility, scooping snow upon their heads and claiming the rite accomplished. But a group of five stood upright, backwoodsmen and frontiersmen, they, eager to contest any man's birthday.

Graduates of the hardest of man-handling schools, veterans of multitudes of rough-and-tumble battles, men of blood and sweat and endurance, they nevertheless lacked one thing that Daylight possessed in high degree—namely, an almost perfect brain and muscular coordination. It was simple, in its way, and no virtue of his. He had been born with this endowment. His nerves carried messages more quickly than theirs; his mental processes, culminating in acts of will, were quicker than theirs; his muscles themselves, by some immediacy of chemistry, obeyed the messages of his will quicker than theirs. He was so made, his muscles were high-power explosives. The levers of his body snapped into play like the jaws of steel traps. And in addition to all this, his was that super-strength that is the dower of but one human in millions—a strength depending not on size but on degree, a supreme organic excellence residing in the stuff of the muscles themselves. Thus, so swiftly could he apply a stress, that, before an opponent could become aware and resist, the aim of the stress had been accomplished. In turn, so swiftly did he become aware of a stress applied to him, that he saved himself by resistance or by delivering a lightning counter-stress.

"It ain't no use you-all standing there," Daylight addressed the waiting group. "You-all might as well get right down and take your baptizing. You-all might down me any other day in the year, but on my birthday I want you-all to know I'm the best man. Is that Pat Hanrahan's mug looking hungry and willing? Come on, Pat." Pat Hanrahan, ex-bare-knuckle-prize fighter and roughhouse-expert, stepped forth. The two men came against each other in grips, and almost before he had exerted himself the Irishman found himself in the merciless vise of a half-Nelson that buried him head and shoulders in the snow. Joe Hines, ex-lumber-jack, came down with an impact equal to a fall from a two-story building—his overthrow accomplished by a cross-buttock, delivered, he claimed, before he was ready.

There was nothing exhausting in all this to Daylight. He did not heave and strain through long minutes. No time, practically, was occupied. His body exploded abruptly and terrifically in one instant, and on the next instant was relaxed. Thus, Doc Watson, the gray-bearded, iron bodied man without a past, a fighting terror himself, was overthrown in the fraction of a second preceding his own onslaught. As he was in the act of gathering himself for a spring, Daylight was upon him, and with such fearful suddenness as to crush him backward and down. Olaf Henderson, receiving his cue from this, attempted to take Daylight unaware, rushing upon him from one side as he stooped with extended hand to help Doc Watson up. Daylight dropped on his hands and knees, receiving in his side Olaf's knees. Olaf's momentum carried him clear over the obstruction in a long, flying fall. Before he could rise, Daylight had whirled him over on his back and was rubbing his face and ears with snow and shoving handfuls down his neck. "Ay ban yust as good a man as you ban, Daylight," Olaf spluttered, as he pulled himself to his feet; "but by Yupiter, I ban navver see a grip like that." French Louis was the last of the five, and he had seen enough to make him cautious. He circled and baffled for a full minute before coming to grips; and for another full minute they strained and reeled without either winning the advantage. And then, just as the contest was becoming interesting, Daylight effected one of his lightning shifts, changing all stresses and leverages and at the same time delivering one of his muscular explosions. French Louis resisted till his huge frame crackled, and then, slowly, was forced over and under and downward.

"The winner pays!" Daylight cried; as he sprang to his feet and led the way back into the Tivoli. "Surge along you-all! This way to the snake-room!"

They lined up against the long bar, in places two or three deep, stamping the frost from their moccasined feet, for outside the temperature was sixty below. Bettles, himself one of the gamest of the old-timers in deeds and daring ceased from his drunken lay of the "Sassafras Root," and titubated over to congratulate Daylight. But in the midst of it he felt impelled to make a speech, and raised his voice oratorically.

"I tell you fellers I'm plum proud to call Daylight my friend. We've hit the trail together afore now, and he's eighteen carat from his moccasins up, damn his mangy old hide, anyway. He was a shaver when he first hit this country. When you fellers was his age, you wa'n't dry behind the ears yet. He never was no kid. He was born a full-grown man. An' I tell you a man had to be a man in them days. This wa'n't no effete civilization like it's come to be now." Bettles paused long enough to put his arm in a proper bear-hug around Daylight's neck. "When you an' me mushed into the Yukon in the good ole days, it didn't rain soup and they wa'n't no free-lunch joints. Our camp fires was lit where we killed our game, and most of the time we lived on salmon-tracks and rabbit-bellies—ain't I right?"

But at the roar of laughter that greeted his inversion, Bettles released the bear-hug and turned fiercely on them. "Laugh, you mangy short-horns, laugh! But I tell you plain and simple, the best of you ain't knee-high fit to tie Daylight's moccasin strings.

"Ain't I right, Campbell? Ain't I right, Mac? Daylight's one of the old guard, one of the real sour-doughs. And in them days they wa'n't ary a steamboat or ary a trading-post, and we cusses had to live offen salmon-bellies and rabbit-tracks."

He gazed triumphantly around, and in the applause that followed arose cries for a speech from Daylight. He signified his consent. A chair was brought, and he was helped to stand upon it. He was no more sober than the crowd above which he now towered—a wild crowd, uncouthly garmented, every foot moccasined or muc-lucked[3], with mittens dangling from necks and with furry ear-flaps raised so that they took on the seeming of the winged helmets of the Norsemen. Daylight's black eyes were flashing, and the flush of strong drink flooded darkly under the bronze of his cheeks. He was greeted with round on round of affectionate cheers, which brought a suspicious moisture to his eyes, albeit many of the voices were inarticulate and inebriate. And yet, men have so behaved since the world began, feasting, fighting, and carousing, whether in the dark cave-mouth or by the fire of the squatting-place, in the palaces of imperial Rome and the rock strongholds of robber barons, or in the sky-aspiring hotels of modern times and in the boozing-kens of sailor-town. Just so were these men, empire-builders in the Arctic Light, boastful and drunken and clamorous, winning surcease for a few wild moments from the grim reality of their heroic toil. Modern heroes they, and in nowise different from the heroes of old time. "Well, fellows, I don't know what to say to you-all," Daylight began lamely, striving still to control his whirling brain. "I think I'll tell you-all a story. I had a pardner wunst, down in Juneau. He come from North Caroliney, and he used to tell this same story to me. It was down in the mountains in his country, and it was a wedding. There they was, the family and all the friends. The parson was just puttin' on the last touches, and he says, 'They as the Lord have joined let no man put asunder.'

"'Parson,' says the bridegroom, 'I rises to question your grammar in that there sentence. I want this weddin' done right.'

"When the smoke clears away, the bride she looks around and sees a dead parson, a dead bridegroom, a dead brother, two dead uncles, and five dead wedding-guests.

"So she heaves a mighty strong sigh and says, 'Them new-fangled, self-cocking revolvers sure has played hell with my prospects.'

"And so I say to you-all," Daylight added, as the roar of laughter died down, "that them four kings of Jack Kearns sure has played hell with my prospects. I'm busted higher'n a kite, and I'm hittin' the trail for Dyea—"

"Goin' out?" some one called. A spasm of anger wrought on his face for a flashing instant, but in the next his good-humor was back again.

"I know you-all are only pokin' fun asking such a question," he said, with a smile. "Of course I ain't going out."

"Take the oath again, Daylight," the same voice cried.

"I sure will. I first come over Chilcoot in '83. I went out over the Pass in a fall blizzard, with a rag of a shirt and a cup of raw flour. I got my grub-stake in Juneau that winter, and in the spring I went over the Pass once more. And once more the famine drew me out. Next spring I went in again, and I swore then that I'd never come out till I made my stake. Well, I ain't made it, and here I am. And I ain't going out now. I get the mail and I come right back. I won't stop the night at Dyea. I'll hit up Chilcoot soon as I change the dogs and get the mail and grub. And so I swear once more, by the mill-tails of hell and the head of John the Baptist, I'll never hit for the Outside till I make my pile. And I tell you-all, here and now, it's got to be an almighty big pile."

"How much might you call a pile?" Bettles demanded from beneath, his arms clutched lovingly around Daylight's legs.

"Yes, how much? What do you call a pile?" others cried.

Daylight steadied himself for a moment and debated. "Four or five millions," he said slowly, and held up his hand for silence as his statement was received with derisive yells. "I'll be real conservative, and put the bottom notch at a million. And for not an ounce less'n that will I go out of the country."

Again his statement was received with an outburst of derision. Not only had the total gold output of the Yukon up to date been below five millions, but no man had ever made a strike of a hundred thousand, much less of a million.

"You-all listen to me. You seen Jack Kearns get a hunch to-night. We had him sure beat before the draw. His ornery three kings was no good. But he just knew there was another king coming—that was his hunch—and he got it. And I tell you-all I got a hunch. There's a big strike coming on the Yukon, and it's just about due. I don't mean no ornery Moosehide, Birch-Creek kind of a strike. I mean a real rip-snorter hair-raiser. I tell you-all she's in the air and hell-bent for election. Nothing can stop her, and she'll come up river. There's where you-all track my moccasins in the near future if you-all want to find me—somewhere in the country around Stewart River, Indian River, and Klondike River. When I get back with the mail, I'll head that way so fast you-all won't see my trail for smoke. She's a-coming, fellows, gold from the grass roots down, a hundred dollars to the pan, and a stampede in from the Outside fifty thousand strong. You-all'll think all hell's busted loose when that strike is made."

He raised his glass to his lips. "Here's kindness, and hoping you-all will be in on it."

He drank and stepped down from the chair, falling into another one of Bettles' bear-hugs.

"If I was you, Daylight, I wouldn't mush to-day," Joe Hines counselled, coming in from consulting the spirit thermometer outside the door. "We're in for a good cold snap. It's sixty-two below now, and still goin' down. Better wait till she breaks."

Daylight laughed, and the old sour-doughs around him laughed.

"Just like you short-horns," Bettles cried, "afeard of a little frost. And blamed little you know Daylight, if you think frost kin stop 'm."

"Freeze his lungs if he travels in it," was the reply.

"Freeze pap and lollypop! Look here, Hines, you only ben in this here country three years. You ain't seasoned yet. I've seen Daylight do fifty miles up on the Koyokuk on a day when the thermometer busted at seventy-two."

Hines shook his head dolefully.

"Them's the kind that does freeze their lungs," he lamented. "If Daylight pulls out before this snap breaks, he'll never get through—an' him travelin' without tent or fly."

"It's a thousand miles to Dyea," Bettles announced, climbing on the chair and supporting his swaying body by an arm passed around Daylight's neck. "It's a thousand miles, I'm sayin' an' most of the trail unbroke, but I bet any chechaquo—anything he wants—that Daylight makes Dyea in thirty days."

"That's an average of over thirty-three miles a day," Doc Watson warned, "and I've travelled some myself. A blizzard on Chilcoot would tie him up for a week."

"Yep," Bettles retorted, "an' Daylight'll do the second thousand back again on end in thirty days more, and I got five hundred dollars that says so, and damn the blizzards."

To emphasize his remarks, he pulled out a gold-sack the size of a bologna sausage and thumped it down on the bar. Doc Watson thumped his own sack alongside.

"Hold on!" Daylight cried. "Bettles's right, and I want in on this. I bet five hundred that sixty days from now I pull up at the Tivoli door with the Dyea mail."

A sceptical roar went up, and a dozen men pulled out their sacks.

Jack Kearns crowded in close and caught Daylight's attention.

"I take you, Daylight," he cried. "Two to one you don't—not in seventy-five days."

"No charity, Jack," was the reply. "The bettin's even, and the time is sixty days."

"Seventy-five days, and two to one you don't," Kearns insisted. "Fifty Mile'll be wide open and the rim-ice rotten."

"What you win from me is yours," Daylight went on. "And, by thunder, Jack, you can't give it back that way. I won't bet with you. You're trying to give me money. But I tell you-all one thing, Jack, I got another hunch. I'm goin' to win it back some one of these days. You-all just wait till the big strike up river. Then you and me'll take the roof off and sit in a game that'll be full man's size. Is it a go?"

They shook hands.

"Of course he'll make it," Kearns whispered in Bettles' ear. "And there's five hundred Daylight's back in sixty days," he added aloud.

Billy Rawlins closed with the wager, and Bettles hugged Kearns ecstatically.

"By Yupiter, I ban take that bet," Olaf Henderson said, dragging Daylight away from Bettles and Kearns.

"Winner pays!" Daylight shouted, closing the wager.

"And I'm sure going to win, and sixty days is a long time between drinks, so I pay now. Name your brand, you hoochinoos! Name your brand!"

Bettles, a glass of whiskey in hand, climbed back on his chair, and swaying back and forth, sang the one song he knew:—

"O, it's Henry Ward Beecher
And Sunday-school teachers
All sing of the sassafras-root;
But you bet all the same,
If it had its right name
It's the juice of the forbidden fruit."

The crowd roared out the chorus:—

"But you bet all the same
If it had its right name
It's the juice of the forbidden fruit."

Somebody opened the outer door. A vague gray light filtered in.

"Burning daylight, burning daylight," some one called warningly.

Daylight paused for nothing, heading for the door and pulling down his ear-flaps. Kama stood outside by the sled, a long, narrow affair, sixteen inches wide and seven and a half feet in length, its slatted bottom raised six inches above the steel-shod runners. On it, lashed with thongs of moose-hide, were the light canvas bags that contained the mail, and the food and gear for dogs and men. In front of it, in a single line, lay curled five frost-rimed dogs. They were huskies, matched in size and color, all unusually large and all gray. From their cruel jaws to their bushy tails they were as like as peas in their likeness to timber-wolves. Wolves they were, domesticated, it was true, but wolves in appearance and in all their characteristics. On top the sled load, thrust under the lashings and ready for immediate use, were two pairs of snowshoes.

Bettles pointed to a robe of Arctic hare skins, the end of which showed in the mouth of a bag.

"That's his bed," he said. "Six pounds of rabbit skins. Warmest thing he ever slept under, but I'm damned if it could keep me warm, and I can go some myself. Daylight's a hell-fire furnace, that's what he is."

"I'd hate to be that Indian," Doc Watson remarked.

"He'll kill'm, he'll kill'm sure," Bettles chanted exultantly. "I know. I've ben with Daylight on trail. That man ain't never ben tired in his life. Don't know what it means. I seen him travel all day with wet socks at forty-five below. There ain't another man living can do that."

While this talk went on, Daylight was saying good-by to those that clustered around him. The Virgin wanted to kiss him, and, fuddled slightly though he was with the whiskey, he saw his way out without compromising with the apron-string. He kissed the Virgin, but he kissed the other three women with equal partiality. He pulled on his long mittens, roused the dogs to their feet, and took his Place at the gee-pole.[4]

"Mush, you beauties!" he cried.

The animals threw their weights against their breastbands on the instant, crouching low to the snow, and digging in their claws. They whined eagerly, and before the sled had gone half a dozen lengths both Daylight and Kama (in the rear) were running to keep up. And so, running, man and dogs dipped over the bank and down to the frozen bed of the Yukon, and in the gray light were gone.

[1] Tenderfeet.

[2] Old-timers.

[3] Muc-luc: a water-tight, Eskimo boot, made from walrus-hide and trimmed with fur.

[4] A gee-pole: stout pole projecting forward from one side of the front end of the sled, by which the sled is steered.

CHAPTER IV

On the river, where was a packed trail and where snowshoes were unnecessary, the dogs averaged six miles an hour. To keep up with them, the two men were compelled to run. Daylight and Kama relieved each other regularly at the gee-pole, for here was the hard work of steering the flying sled and of keeping in advance of it. The man relieved dropped behind the sled, occasionally leaping upon it and resting.

It was severe work, but of the sort that was exhilarating.

They were flying, getting over the ground, making the most of the packed trail. Later on they would come to the unbroken trail, where three miles an hour would constitute good going. Then there would be no riding and resting, and no running. Then the gee-pole would be the easier task, and a man would come back to it to rest after having completed his spell to the fore, breaking trail with the snowshoes for the dogs. Such work was far from exhilarating also, they must expect places where for miles at a time they must toil over chaotic ice-jams, where they would be fortunate if they made two miles an hour. And there would be the inevitable bad jams, short ones, it was true, but so bad that a mile an hour would require terrific effort. Kama and Daylight did not talk. In the nature of the work they could not, nor in their own natures were they given to talking while they worked. At rare intervals, when necessary, they addressed each other in monosyllables, Kama, for the most part, contenting himself with grunts. Occasionally a dog whined or snarled, but in the main the team kept silent. Only could be heard the sharp, jarring grate of the steel runners over the hard surface and the creak of the straining sled.

As if through a wall, Daylight had passed from the hum and roar of the Tivoli into another world—a world of silence and immobility. Nothing stirred. The Yukon slept under a coat of ice three feet thick. No breath of wind blew. Nor did the sap move in the hearts of the spruce trees that forested the river banks on either hand. The trees, burdened with the last infinitesimal pennyweight of snow their branches could hold, stood in absolute petrifaction. The slightest tremor would have dislodged the snow, and no snow was dislodged. The sled was the one point of life and motion in the midst of the solemn quietude, and the harsh churn of its runners but emphasized the silence through which it moved.

It was a dead world, and furthermore, a gray world. The weather was sharp and clear; there was no moisture in the atmosphere, no fog nor haze; yet the sky was a gray pall. The reason for this was that, though there was no cloud in the sky to dim the brightness of day, there was no sun to give brightness. Far to the south the sun climbed steadily to meridian, but between it and the frozen Yukon intervened the bulge of the earth. The Yukon lay in a night shadow, and the day itself was in reality a long twilight-light. At a quarter before twelve, where a wide bend of the river gave a long vista south, the sun showed its upper rim above the sky-line. But it did not rise perpendicularly. Instead, it rose on a slant, so that by high noon it had barely lifted its lower rim clear of the horizon. It was a dim, wan sun. There was no heat to its rays, and a man could gaze squarely into the full orb of it without hurt to his eyes. No sooner had it reached meridian than it began its slant back beneath the horizon, and at quarter past twelve the earth threw its shadow again over the land.

The men and dogs raced on. Daylight and Kama were both savages so far as their stomachs were concerned. They could eat irregularly in time and quantity, gorging hugely on occasion, and on occasion going long stretches without eating at all. As for the dogs, they ate but once a day, and then rarely did they receive more than a pound each of dried fish. They were ravenously hungry and at the same time splendidly in condition. Like the wolves, their forebears, their nutritive processes were rigidly economical and perfect. There was no waste. The last least particle of what they consumed was transformed into energy.

And Kama and Daylight were like them. Descended themselves from the generations that had endured, they, too, endured. Theirs was the simple, elemental economy. A little food equipped them with prodigious energy. Nothing was lost. A man of soft civilization, sitting at a desk, would have grown lean and woe-begone on the fare that kept Kama and Daylight at the top-notch of physical efficiency. They knew, as the man at the desk never knows, what it is to be normally hungry all the time, so that they could eat any time. Their appetites were always with them and on edge, so that they bit voraciously into whatever offered and with an entire innocence of indigestion.

By three in the afternoon the long twilight faded into night. The stars came out, very near and sharp and bright, and by their light dogs and men still kept the trail. They were indefatigable. And this was no record run of a single day, but the first day of sixty such days. Though Daylight had passed a night without sleep, a night of dancing and carouse, it seemed to have left no effect. For this there were two explanations first, his remarkable vitality; and next, the fact that such nights were rare in his experience. Again enters the man at the desk, whose physical efficiency would be more hurt by a cup of coffee at bedtime than could Daylight's by a whole night long of strong drink and excitement.

Daylight travelled without a watch, feeling the passage of time and largely estimating it by subconscious processes. By what he considered must be six o'clock, he began looking for a camping-place. The trail, at a bend, plunged out across the river. Not having found a likely spot, they held on for the opposite bank a mile away. But midway they encountered an ice-jam which took an hour of heavy work to cross. At last Daylight glimpsed what he was looking for, a dead tree close by the bank. The sled was run in and up. Kama grunted with satisfaction, and the work of making camp was begun.

The division of labor was excellent. Each knew what he must do. With one ax Daylight chopped down the dead pine. Kama, with a snowshoe and the other ax, cleared away the two feet of snow above the Yukon ice and chopped a supply of ice for cooking purposes. A piece of dry birch bark started the fire, and Daylight went ahead with the cooking while the Indian unloaded the sled and fed the dogs their ration of dried fish. The food sacks he slung high in the trees beyond leaping-reach of the huskies. Next, he chopped down a young spruce tree and trimmed off the boughs. Close to the fire he trampled down the soft snow and covered the packed space with the boughs. On this flooring he tossed his own and Daylight's gear-bags, containing dry socks and underwear and their sleeping-robes. Kama, however, had two robes of rabbit skin to Daylight's one.

They worked on steadily, without speaking, losing no time. Each did whatever was needed, without thought of leaving to the other the least task that presented itself to hand. Thus, Kama saw when more ice was needed and went and got it, while a snowshoe, pushed over by the lunge of a dog, was stuck on end again by Daylight. While coffee was boiling, bacon frying, and flapjacks were being mixed, Daylight found time to put on a big pot of beans. Kama came back, sat down on the edge of the spruce boughs, and in the interval of waiting, mended harness.

"I t'ink dat Skookum and Booga make um plenty fight maybe," Kama remarked, as they sat down to eat.

"Keep an eye on them," was Daylight's answer.

And this was their sole conversation throughout the meal. Once, with a muttered imprecation, Kama leaped away, a stick of firewood in hand, and clubbed apart a tangle of fighting dogs. Daylight, between mouthfuls, fed chunks of ice into the tin pot, where it thawed into water. The meal finished, Kama replenished the fire, cut more wood for the morning, and returned to the spruce bough bed and his harness-mending. Daylight cut up generous chunks of bacon and dropped them in the pot of bubbling beans. The moccasins of both men were wet, and this in spite of the intense cold; so when there was no further need for them to leave the oasis of spruce boughs, they took off their moccasins and hung them on short sticks to dry before the fire, turning them about from time to time. When the beans were finally cooked, Daylight ran part of them into a bag of flour-sacking a foot and a half long and three inches in diameter. This he then laid on the snow to freeze. The remainder of the beans were left in the pot for breakfast.

It was past nine o'clock, and they were ready for bed. The squabbling and bickering among the dogs had long since died down, and the weary animals were curled in the snow, each with his feet and nose bunched together and covered by his wolf's brush of a tail. Kama spread his sleeping-furs and lighted his pipe. Daylight rolled a brown-paper cigarette, and the second conversation of the evening took place.

"I think we come near sixty miles," said Daylight.

"Um, I t'ink so," said Kama.

They rolled into their robes, all-standing, each with a woolen Mackinaw jacket on in place of the parkas[5] they had worn all day. Swiftly, almost on the instant they closed their eyes, they were asleep. The stars leaped and danced in the frosty air, and overhead the colored bars of the aurora borealis were shooting like great searchlights.

In the darkness Daylight awoke and roused Kama. Though the aurora still flamed, another day had begun. Warmed-over flapjacks, warmed-over beans, fried bacon, and coffee composed the breakfast. The dogs got nothing, though they watched with wistful mien from a distance, sitting up in the snow, their tails curled around their paws. Occasionally they lifted one fore paw or the other, with a restless movement, as if the frost tingled in their feet. It was bitter cold, at least sixty-five below zero, and when Kama harnessed the dogs with naked hands he was compelled several times to go over to the fire and warm the numbing finger-tips. Together the two men loaded and lashed the sled. They warmed their hands for the last time, pulled on their mittens, and mushed the dogs over the bank and down to the river-trail. According to Daylight's estimate, it was around seven o'clock; but the stars danced just as brilliantly, and faint, luminous streaks of greenish aurora still pulsed overhead.

Two hours later it became suddenly dark—so dark that they kept to the trail largely by instinct; and Daylight knew that his time-estimate had been right. It was the darkness before dawn, never anywhere more conspicuous than on the Alaskan winter-trail.

Slowly the gray light came stealing through the gloom, imperceptibly at first, so that it was almost with surprise that they noticed the vague loom of the trail underfoot. Next, they were able to see the wheel-dog, and then the whole string of running dogs and snow-stretches on either side. Then the near bank loomed for a moment and was gone, loomed a second time and remained. In a few minutes the far bank, a mile away, unobtrusively came into view, and ahead and behind, the whole frozen river could be seen, with off to the left a wide-extending range of sharp-cut, snow-covered mountains. And that was all. No sun arose. The gray light remained gray.

Once, during the day, a lynx leaped lightly across the trail, under the very nose of the lead-dog, and vanished in the white woods. The dogs' wild impulses roused. They raised the hunting-cry of the pack, surged against their collars, and swerved aside in pursuit. Daylight, yelling "Whoa!" struggled with the gee-pole and managed to overturn the sled into the soft snow. The dogs gave up, the sled was righted, and five minutes later they were flying along the hard-packed trail again. The lynx was the only sign of life they had seen in two days, and it, leaping velvet-footed and vanishing, had been more like an apparition.

At twelve o'clock, when the sun peeped over the earth-bulge, they stopped and built a small fire on the ice. Daylight, with the ax, chopped chunks off the frozen sausage of beans. These, thawed and warmed in the frying-pan, constituted their meal. They had no coffee. He did not believe in the burning of daylight for such a luxury. The dogs stopped wrangling with one another, and looked on wistfully. Only at night did they get their pound of fish. In the meantime they worked.

The cold snap continued. Only men of iron kept the trail at such low temperatures, and Kama and Daylight were picked men of their races. But Kama knew the other was the better man, and thus, at the start, he was himself foredoomed to defeat. Not that he slackened his effort or willingness by the slightest conscious degree, but that he was beaten by the burden he carried in his mind. His attitude toward Daylight was worshipful. Stoical, taciturn, proud of his physical prowess, he found all these qualities incarnated in his white companion. Here was one that excelled in the things worth excelling in, a man-god ready to hand, and Kama could not but worship—withal he gave no signs of it. No wonder the race of white men conquered, was his thought, when it bred men like this man. What chance had the Indian against such a dogged, enduring breed? Even the Indians did not travel at such low temperatures, and theirs was the wisdom of thousands of generations; yet here was this Daylight, from the soft Southland, harder than they, laughing at their fears, and swinging along the trail ten and twelve hours a day. And this Daylight thought that he could keep up a day's pace of thirty-three miles for sixty days! Wait till a fresh fall of snow came down, or they struck the unbroken trail or the rotten rim-ice that fringed open water.

In the meantime Kama kept the pace, never grumbling, never shirking. Sixty-five degrees below zero is very cold. Since water freezes at thirty-two above, sixty-five below meant ninety-seven degrees below freezing-point. Some idea of the significance of this may be gained by conceiving of an equal difference of temperature in the opposite direction. One hundred and twenty-nine on the thermometer constitutes a very hot day, yet such a temperature is but ninety-seven degrees above freezing. Double this difference, and possibly some slight conception may be gained of the cold through which Kama and Daylight travelled between dark and dark and through the dark.

Kama froze the skin on his cheek-bones, despite frequent rubbings, and the flesh turned black and sore. Also he slightly froze the edges of his lung-tissues—a dangerous thing, and the basic reason why a man should not unduly exert himself in the open at sixty-five below. But Kama never complained, and Daylight was a furnace of heat, sleeping as warmly under his six pounds of rabbit skins as the other did under twelve pounds.

On the second night, fifty more miles to the good, they camped in the vicinity of the boundary between Alaska and the Northwest Territory. The rest of the journey, save the last short stretch to Dyea, would be travelled on Canadian territory. With the hard trail, and in the absence of fresh snow, Daylight planned to make the camp of Forty Mile on the fourth night. He told Kama as much, but on the third day the temperature began to rise, and they knew snow was not far off; for on the Yukon it must get warm in order to snow. Also, on this day, they encountered ten miles of chaotic ice-jams, where, a thousand times, they lifted the loaded sled over the huge cakes by the strength of their arms and lowered it down again. Here the dogs were well-nigh useless, and both they and the men were tried excessively by the roughness of the way. An hour's extra running that night caught up only part of the lost time.

In the morning they awoke to find ten inches of snow on their robes. The dogs were buried under it and were loath to leave their comfortable nests. This new snow meant hard going. The sled runners would not slide over it so well, while one of the men must go in advance of the dogs and pack it down with snowshoes so that they should not wallow. Quite different was it from the ordinary snow known to those of the Southland. It was hard, and fine, and dry. It was more like sugar. Kick it, and it flew with a hissing noise like sand. There was no cohesion among the particles, and it could not be moulded into snowballs. It was not composed of flakes, but of crystals—tiny, geometrical frost-crystals. In truth, it was not snow, but frost.

The weather was warm, as well, barely twenty below zero, and the two men, with raised ear-flaps and dangling mittens, sweated as they toiled. They failed to make Forty Mile that night, and when they passed that camp next day Daylight paused only long enough to get the mail and additional grub. On the afternoon of the following day they camped at the mouth of the Klondike River. Not a soul had they encountered since Forty Mile, and they had made their own trail. As yet, that winter, no one had travelled the river south of Forty Mile, and, for that matter, the whole winter through they might be the only ones to travel it. In that day the Yukon was a lonely land. Between the Klondike River and Salt Water at Dyea intervened six hundred miles of snow-covered wilderness, and in all that distance there were but two places where Daylight might look forward to meeting men. Both were isolated trading-posts, Sixty Mile and Fort Selkirk. In the summer-time Indians might be met with at the mouths of the Stewart and White rivers, at the Big and Little Salmons, and on Lake Le Barge; but in the winter, as he well knew, they would be on the trail of the moose-herds, following them back into the mountains.

That night, camped at the mouth of the Klondike, Daylight did not turn in when the evening's work was done. Had a white man been present, Daylight would have remarked that he felt his "hunch" working. As it was, he tied on his snowshoes, left the dogs curled in the snow and Kama breathing heavily under his rabbit skins, and climbed up to the big flat above the high earth-bank. But the spruce trees were too thick for an outlook, and he threaded his way across the flat and up the first steep slopes of the mountain at the back. Here, flowing in from the east at right angles, he could see the Klondike, and, bending grandly from the south, the Yukon. To the left, and downstream, toward Moosehide Mountain, the huge splash of white, from which it took its name, showing clearly in the starlight. Lieutenant Schwatka had given it its name, but he, Daylight, had first seen it long before that intrepid explorer had crossed the Chilcoot and rafted down the Yukon.

But the mountain received only passing notice. Daylight's interest was centered in the big flat itself, with deep water all along its edge for steamboat landings.

"A sure enough likely town site," he muttered. "Room for a camp of forty thousand men. All that's needed is the gold-strike." He meditated for a space. "Ten dollars to the pan'll do it, and it'd be the all-firedest stampede Alaska ever seen. And if it don't come here, it'll come somewhere hereabouts. It's a sure good idea to keep an eye out for town sites all the way up."

He stood a while longer, gazing out over the lonely flat and visioning with constructive imagination the scene if the stampede did come. In fancy, he placed the sawmills, the big trading stores, the saloons, and dance-halls, and the long streets of miners' cabins. And along those streets he saw thousands of men passing up and down, while before the stores were the heavy freighting-sleds, with long strings of dogs attached. Also he saw the heavy freighters pulling down the main street and heading up the frozen Klondike toward the imagined somewhere where the diggings must be located.

He laughed and shook the vision from his eyes, descended to the level, and crossed the flat to camp. Five minutes after he had rolled up in his robe, he opened his eyes and sat up, amazed that he was not already asleep. He glanced at the Indian sleeping beside him, at the embers of the dying fire, at the five dogs beyond, with their wolf's brushes curled over their noses, and at the four snowshoes standing upright in the snow.

"It's sure hell the way that hunch works on me" he murmured. His mind reverted to the poker game. "Four kings!" He grinned reminiscently. "That WAS a hunch!"

He lay down again, pulled the edge of the robe around his neck and over his ear-flaps, closed his eyes, and this time fell asleep.

[5] Parka: a light, hooded, smock-like garment made of cotton drill.

CHAPTER V

At Sixty Mile they restocked provisions, added a few pounds of letters to their load, and held steadily on. From Forty Mile they had had unbroken trail, and they could look forward only to unbroken trail clear to Dyea. Daylight stood it magnificently, but the killing pace was beginning to tell on Kama. His pride kept his mouth shut, but the result of the chilling of his lungs in the cold snap could not be concealed. Microscopically small had been the edges of the lung-tissue touched by the frost, but they now began to slough off, giving rise to a dry, hacking cough. Any unusually severe exertion precipitated spells of coughing, during which he was almost like a man in a fit. The blood congested in his eyes till they bulged, while the tears ran down his cheeks. A whiff of the smoke from frying bacon would start him off for a half-hour's paroxysm, and he kept carefully to windward when Daylight was cooking.

They plodded days upon days and without end over the soft, unpacked snow. It was hard, monotonous work, with none of the joy and blood-stir that went with flying over hard surface. Now one man to the fore in the snowshoes, and now the other, it was a case of stubborn, unmitigated plod. A yard of powdery snow had to be pressed down, and the wide-webbed shoe, under a man's weight, sank a full dozen inches into the soft surface. Snowshoe work, under such conditions, called for the use of muscles other than those used in ordinary walking. From step to step the rising foot could not come up and forward on a slant. It had to be raised perpendicularly. When the snowshoe was pressed into the snow, its nose was confronted by a vertical wall of snow twelve inches high. If the foot, in rising, slanted forward the slightest bit, the nose of the shoe penetrated the obstructing wall and tipped downward till the heel of the shoe struck the man's leg behind. Thus up, straight up, twelve inches, each foot must be raised every time and all the time, ere the forward swing from the knee could begin.

On this partially packed surface followed the dogs, the man at the gee-pole, and the sled. At the best, toiling as only picked men could toil, they made no more than three miles an hour. This meant longer hours of travel, and Daylight, for good measure and for a margin against accidents, hit the trail for twelve hours a day. Since three hours were consumed by making camp at night and cooking beans, by getting breakfast in the morning and breaking camp, and by thawing beans at the midday halt, nine hours were left for sleep and recuperation, and neither men nor dogs wasted many minutes of those nine hours.

At Selkirk, the trading post near Pelly River, Daylight suggested that Kama lay over, rejoining him on the back trip from Dyea. A strayed Indian from Lake Le Barge was willing to take his place; but Kama was obdurate. He grunted with a slight intonation of resentment, and that was all. The dogs, however, Daylight changed, leaving his own exhausted team to rest up against his return, while he went on with six fresh dogs.

They travelled till ten o'clock the night they reached Selkirk, and at six next morning they plunged ahead into the next stretch of wilderness of nearly five hundred miles that lay between Selkirk and Dyea. A second cold snap came on, but cold or warm it was all the same, an unbroken trail. When the thermometer went down to fifty below, it was even harder to travel, for at that low temperature the hard frost-crystals were more like sand-grains in the resistance they offered to the sled runners. The dogs had to pull harder than over the same snow at twenty or thirty below zero. Daylight increased the day's travel to thirteen hours. He jealously guarded the margin he had gained, for he knew there were difficult stretches to come.

It was not yet quite midwinter, and the turbulent Fifty Mile River vindicated his judgment. In many places it ran wide open, with precarious rim-ice fringing it on either side. In numerous places, where the water dashed against the steep-sided bluffs, rim-ice was unable to form. They turned and twisted, now crossing the river, now coming back again, sometimes making half a dozen attempts before they found a way over a particularly bad stretch. It was slow work. The ice-bridges had to be tested, and either Daylight or Kama went in advance, snowshoes on their feet, and long poles carried crosswise in their hands. Thus, if they broke through, they could cling to the pole that bridged the hole made by their bodies. Several such accidents were the share of each. At fifty below zero, a man wet to the waist cannot travel without freezing; so each ducking meant delay. As soon as rescued, the wet man ran up and down to keep up his circulation, while his dry companion built a fire. Thus protected, a change of garments could be made and the wet ones dried against the next misadventure.

To make matters worse, this dangerous river travel could not be done in the dark, and their working day was reduced to the six hours of twilight. Every moment was precious, and they strove never to lose one. Thus, before the first hint of the coming of gray day, camp was broken, sled loaded, dogs harnessed, and the two men crouched waiting over the fire. Nor did they make the midday halt to eat. As it was, they were running far behind their schedule, each day eating into the margin they had run up. There were days when they made fifteen miles, and days when they made a dozen. And there was one bad stretch where in two days they covered nine miles, being compelled to turn their backs three times on the river and to portage sled and outfit over the mountains.

At last they cleared the dread Fifty Mile River and came out on Lake Le Barge. Here was no open water nor jammed ice. For thirty miles or more the snow lay level as a table; withal it lay three feet deep and was soft as flour. Three miles an hour was the best they could make, but Daylight celebrated the passing of the Fifty Mile by traveling late. At eleven in the morning they emerged at the foot of the lake. At three in the afternoon, as the Arctic night closed down, he caught his first sight of the head of the lake, and with the first stars took his bearings. At eight in the evening they left the lake behind and entered the mouth of the Lewes River. Here a halt of half an hour was made, while chunks of frozen boiled beans were thawed and the dogs were given an extra ration of fish. Then they pulled on up the river till one in the morning, when they made their regular camp.

They had hit the trail sixteen hours on end that day, the dogs had come in too tired to fight among themselves or even snarl, and Kama had perceptibly limped the last several miles; yet Daylight was on trail next morning at six o'clock. By eleven he was at the foot of White Horse, and that night saw him camped beyond the Box Canon, the last bad river-stretch behind him, the string of lakes before him.

There was no let up in his pace. Twelve hours a day, six in the twilight, and six in the dark, they toiled on the trail. Three hours were consumed in cooking, repairing harnesses, and making and breaking camp, and the remaining nine hours dogs and men slept as if dead. The iron strength of Kama broke. Day by day the terrific toil sapped him. Day by day he consumed more of his reserves of strength. He became slower of movement, the resiliency went out of his muscles, and his limp became permanent. Yet he labored stoically on, never shirking, never grunting a hint of complaint. Daylight was thin-faced and tired.

He looked tired; yet somehow, with that marvelous mechanism of a body that was his, he drove on, ever on, remorselessly on. Never was he more a god in Kama's mind than in the last days of the south-bound traverse, as the failing Indian watched him, ever to the fore, pressing onward with urgency of endurance such as Kama had never seen nor dreamed could thrive in human form.

The time came when Kama was unable to go in the lead and break trail, and it was a proof that he was far gone when he permitted Daylight to toil all day at the heavy snowshoe work. Lake by lake they crossed the string of lakes from Marsh to Linderman, and began the ascent of Chilcoot. By all rights, Daylight should have camped below the last pitch of the pass at the dim end of day; but he kept on and over and down to Sheep Camp, while behind him raged a snow-storm that would have delayed him twenty-four hours.

This last excessive strain broke Kama completely. In the morning he could not travel. At five, when called, he sat up after a struggle, groaned, and sank back again. Daylight did the camp work of both, harnessed the dogs, and, when ready for the start, rolled the helpless Indian in all three sleeping robes and lashed him on top of the sled. The going was good; they were on the last lap; and he raced the dogs down through Dyea Canon and along the hard-packed trail that led to Dyea Post. And running still, Kama groaning on top the load, and Daylight leaping at the gee-pole to avoid going under the runners of the flying sled, they arrived at Dyea by the sea.

True to his promise, Daylight did not stop. An hour's time saw the sled loaded with the ingoing mail and grub, fresh dogs harnessed, and a fresh Indian engaged. Kama never spoke from the time of his arrival till the moment Daylight, ready to depart, stood beside him to say good-by. They shook hands.

"You kill um dat damn Indian," Kama said. "Sawee, Daylight? You kill um."

"He'll sure last as far as Pelly," Daylight grinned.

Kama shook his head doubtfully, and rolled over on his side, turning his back in token of farewell.

Daylight won across Chilcoot that same day, dropping down five hundred feet in the darkness and the flurrying snow to Crater Lake, where he camped. It was a 'cold' camp, far above the timber-line, and he had not burdened his sled with firewood. That night three feet of snow covered them, and in the black morning, when they dug themselves out, the Indian tried to desert. He had had enough of traveling with what he considered a madman. But Daylight persuaded him in grim ways to stay by the outfit, and they pulled on across Deep Lake and Long Lake and dropped down to the level-going of Lake Linderman. It was the same killing pace going in as coming out, and the Indian did not stand it as well as Kama. He, too, never complained. Nor did he try again to desert. He toiled on and did his best, while he renewed his resolve to steer clear of Daylight in the future. The days slipped into days, nights and twilight's alternating, cold snaps gave way to snow-falls, and cold snaps came on again, and all the while, through the long hours, the miles piled up behind them.

But on the Fifty Mile accident befell them. Crossing an ice-bridge, the dogs broke through and were swept under the down-stream ice. The traces that connected the team with the wheel-dog parted, and the team was never seen again. Only the one wheel-dog remained, and

Daylight harnessed the Indian and himself to the sled. But a man cannot take the place of a dog at such work, and the two men were attempting to do the work of five dogs. At the end of the first hour, Daylight lightened up. Dog-food, extra gear, and the spare ax were thrown away. Under the extraordinary exertion the dog snapped a tendon the following day, and was hopelessly disabled. Daylight shot it, and abandoned the sled. On his back he took one hundred and sixty pounds of mail and grub, and on the Indian's put one hundred and twenty-five pounds. The stripping of gear was remorseless. The Indian was appalled when he saw every pound of worthless mail matter retained, while beans, cups, pails, plates, and extra clothing were thrown by the board. One robe each was kept, one ax, one tin pail, and a scant supply of bacon and flour. Bacon could be eaten raw on a pinch, and flour, stirred in hot water, could keep men going. Even the rifle and the score of rounds of ammunition were left behind.

And in this fashion they covered the two hundred miles to Selkirk. Daylight travelled late and early, the hours formerly used by camp-making and dog-tending being now devoted to the trail. At night they crouched over a small fire, wrapped in their robes, drinking flour broth and thawing bacon on the ends of sticks; and in the morning darkness, without a word, they arose, slipped on their packs, adjusted head-straps, and hit the trail. The last miles into Selkirk, Daylight drove the Indian before him, a hollow-cheeked, gaunt-eyed wraith of a man who else would have lain down and slept or abandoned his burden of mail.

At Selkirk, the old team of dogs, fresh and in condition, were harnessed, and the same day saw Daylight plodding on, alternating places at the gee-pole, as a matter of course, with the Le Barge Indian who had volunteered on the way out. Daylight was two days behind his schedule, and falling snow and unpacked trail kept him two days behind all the way to Forty Mile. And here the weather favored. It was time for a big cold snap, and he gambled on it, cutting down the weight of grub for dogs and men. The men of Forty Mile shook their heads ominously, and demanded to know what he would do if the snow still fell.

"That cold snap's sure got to come," he laughed, and mushed out on the trail.

A number of sleds had passed back and forth already that winter between Forty Mile and Circle City, and the trail was well packed. And the cold snap came and remained, and Circle City was only two hundred miles away. The Le Barge Indian was a young man, unlearned yet in his own limitations, and filled with pride.

He took Daylight's pace with joy, and even dreamed, at first, that he would play the white man out. The first hundred miles he looked for signs of weakening, and marveled that he saw them not.

Throughout the second hundred miles he observed signs in himself, and gritted his teeth and kept up. And ever Daylight flew on and on, running at the gee-pole or resting his spell on top the flying sled. The last day, clearer and colder than ever, gave perfect going, and they covered seventy miles. It was ten at night when they pulled up the earth-bank and flew along the main street of Circle City; and the young Indian, though it was his spell to ride, leaped off and ran behind the sled. It was honorable braggadocio, and despite the fact that he had found his limitations and was pressing desperately against them, he ran gamely on.

CHAPTER VI

A crowd filled the Tivoli—the old crowd that had seen Daylight depart two months before; for this was the night of the sixtieth day, and opinion was divided as ever as to whether or not he would compass the achievement. At ten o'clock bets were still being made, though the odds rose, bet by bet, against his success. Down in her heart the Virgin believed he had failed, yet she made a bet of twenty ounces with Charley Bates, against forty ounces, that Daylight would arrive before midnight.

She it was who heard the first yelps of the dogs.

"Listen!" she cried. "It's Daylight!"

There was a general stampede for the door; but where the double storm-doors were thrown wide open, the crowd fell back. They heard the eager whining of dogs, the snap of a dog-whip, and the voice of Daylight crying encouragement as the weary animals capped all they had done by dragging the sled in over the wooden floor. They came in with a rush, and with them rushed in the frost, a visible vapor of smoking white, through which their heads and backs showed, as they strained in the harness, till they had all the seeming of swimming in a river. Behind them, at the gee-pole, came Daylight, hidden to the knees by the swirling frost through which he appeared to wade.

He was the same old Daylight, withal lean and tired-looking, and his black eyes were sparkling and flashing brighter than ever. His parka of cotton drill hooded him like a monk, and fell in straight lines to his knees. Grimed and scorched by camp-smoke and fire, the garment in itself told the story of his trip. A two-months' beard covered his face; and the beard, in turn, was matted with the ice of his breathing through the long seventy-mile run.

His entry was spectacular, melodramatic; and he knew it. It was his life, and he was living it at the top of his bent. Among his fellows he was a great man, an Arctic hero. He was proud of the fact, and it was a high moment for him, fresh from two thousand miles of trail, to come surging into that bar-room, dogs, sled, mail, Indian, paraphernalia, and all. He had performed one more exploit that would make the Yukon ring with his name—he, Burning Daylight, the king of travelers and dog-mushers.

He experienced a thrill of surprise as the roar of welcome went up and as every familiar detail of the Tivoli greeted his vision—the long bar and the array of bottles, the gambling games, the big stove, the weigher at the gold-scales, the musicians, the men and women, the Virgin, Celia, and Nellie, Dan MacDonald, Bettles, Billy Rawlins, Olaf Henderson, Doc Watson,—all of them.

It was just as he had left it, and in all seeming it might well be the very day he had left. The sixty days of incessant travel through the white wilderness suddenly telescoped, and had no existence in time. They were a moment, an incident. He had plunged out and into them through the wall of silence, and back through the wall of silence he had plunged, apparently the next instant, and into the roar and turmoil of the Tivoli.

A glance down at the sled with its canvas mail-bags was necessary to reassure him of the reality of those sixty days and the two thousand miles over the ice. As in a dream, he shook the hands that were thrust out to him. He felt a vast exaltation. Life was magnificent. He loved it all. A great sense of humanness and comradeship swept over him. These were all his, his own kind. It was immense, tremendous. He felt melting in the heart of him, and he would have liked to shake hands with them all at once, to gather them to his breast in one mighty embrace.

He drew a deep breath and cried: "The winner pays, and I'm the winner, ain't I? Surge up, you-all Malemutes and Siwashes, and name your poison! There's your Dyea mail, straight from Salt Water, and no hornswogglin about it! Cast the lashings adrift, you-all, and wade into it!"

A dozen pairs of hands were at the sled-lashings, when the young Le Barge Indian, bending at the same task, suddenly and limply straightened up. In his eyes was a great surprise. He stared about him wildly, for the thing he was undergoing was new to him.

He was profoundly struck by an unguessed limitation. He shook as with a palsy, and he gave at the knees, slowly sinking down to fall suddenly across the sled and to know the smashing blow of darkness across his consciousness.

"Exhaustion," said Daylight. "Take him off and put him to bed, some of you-all. He's sure a good Indian."

"Daylight's right," was Doc Watson's verdict, a moment later. "The man's plumb tuckered out."

The mail was taken charge of, the dogs driven away to quarters and fed, and Bettles struck up the paean of the sassafras root as they lined up against the long bar to drink and talk and collect their debts.

A few minutes later, Daylight was whirling around the dance-floor, waltzing with the Virgin. He had replaced his parka with his fur cap and blanket-cloth coat, kicked off his frozen moccasins, and was dancing in his stocking feet. After wetting himself to the knees late that afternoon, he had run on without changing his foot-gear, and to the knees his long German socks were matted with ice. In the warmth of the room it began to thaw and to break apart in clinging chunks. These chunks rattled together as his legs flew around, and every little while they fell clattering to the floor and were slipped upon by the other dancers. But everybody forgave Daylight. He, who was one of the few that made the Law in that far land, who set the ethical pace, and by conduct gave the standard of right and wrong, was nevertheless above the Law. He was one of those rare and favored mortals who can do no wrong. What he did had to be right, whether others were permitted or not to do the same things. Of course, such mortals are so favored by virtue of the fact that they almost always do the right and do it in finer and higher ways than other men. So Daylight, an elder hero in that young land and at the same time younger than most of them, moved as a creature apart, as a man above men, as a man who was greatly man and all man. And small wonder it was that the Virgin yielded herself to his arms, as they danced dance after dance, and was sick at heart at the knowledge that he found nothing in her more than a good friend and an excellent dancer. Small consolation it was to know that he had never loved any woman. She was sick with love of him, and he danced with her as he would dance with any woman, as he would dance with a man who was a good dancer and upon whose arm was tied a handkerchief to conventionalize him into a woman.

One such man Daylight danced with that night. Among frontiersmen it has always been a test of endurance for one man to whirl another down; and when Ben Davis, the faro-dealer, a gaudy bandanna on his arm, got Daylight in a Virginia reel, the fun began. The reel broke up and all fell back to watch. Around and around the two men whirled, always in the one direction. Word was passed on into the big bar-room, and bar and gambling tables were deserted. Everybody wanted to see, and they packed and jammed the dance-room. The musicians played on and on, and on and on the two men whirled. Davis was skilled at the trick, and on the Yukon he had put many a strong man on his back. But after a few minutes it was clear that he, and not Daylight, was going.

For a while longer they spun around, and then Daylight suddenly stood still, released his partner, and stepped back, reeling himself, and fluttering his hands aimlessly, as if to support himself against the air. But Davis, a giddy smile of consternation on his face, gave sideways, turned in an attempt to recover balance, and pitched headlong to the floor. Still reeling and staggering and clutching at the air with his hands, Daylight caught the nearest girl and started on in a waltz. Again he had done the big thing. Weary from two thousand miles over the ice and a run that day of seventy miles, he had whirled a fresh man down, and that man Ben Davis.

Daylight loved the high places, and though few high places there were in his narrow experience, he had made a point of sitting in the highest he had ever glimpsed. The great world had never heard his name, but it was known far and wide in the vast silent North, by whites and Indians and Eskimos, from Bering Sea to the Passes, from the head reaches of remotest rivers to the tundra shore of Point Barrow. Desire for mastery was strong in him, and it was all one whether wrestling with the elements themselves, with men, or with luck in a gambling game. It was all a game, life and its affairs. And he was a gambler to the core. Risk and chance were meat and drink. True, it was not altogether blind, for he applied wit and skill and strength; but behind it all was the everlasting Luck, the thing that at times turned on its votaries and crushed the wise while it blessed the fools—Luck, the thing all men sought and dreamed to conquer. And so he. Deep in his life-processes Life itself sang the siren song of its own majesty, ever a-whisper and urgent, counseling him that he could achieve more than other men, win out where they failed, ride to success where they perished. It was the urge of Life healthy and strong, unaware of frailty and decay, drunken with sublime complacence, ego-mad, enchanted by its own mighty optimism.

And ever in vaguest whisperings and clearest trumpet-calls came the message that sometime, somewhere, somehow, he would run Luck down, make himself the master of Luck, and tie it and brand it as his own. When he played poker, the whisper was of four aces and royal flushes. When he prospected, it was of gold in the grass-roots, gold on bed-rock, and gold all the way down. At the sharpest hazards of trail and river and famine, the message was that other men might die, but that he would pull through triumphant. It was the old, old lie of Life fooling itself, believing itself—immortal and indestructible, bound to achieve over other lives and win to its heart's desire.

And so, reversing at times, Daylight waltzed off his dizziness and led the way to the bar. But a united protest went up. His theory that the winner paid was no longer to be tolerated. It was contrary to custom and common sense, and while it emphasized good-fellowship, nevertheless, in the name of good-fellowship it must cease. The drinks were rightfully on Ben Davis, and Ben Davis must buy them. Furthermore, all drinks and general treats that Daylight was guilty of ought to be paid by the house, for Daylight brought much custom to it whenever he made a night. Bettles was the spokesman, and his argument, tersely and offensively vernacular, was unanimously applauded.

Daylight grinned, stepped aside to the roulette-table, and bought a stack of yellow chips. At the end of ten minutes he weighed in at the scales, and two thousand dollars in gold-dust was poured into his own and an extra sack. Luck, a mere flutter of luck, but it was his. Elation was added to elation. He was living, and the night was his. He turned upon his well-wishing critics.

"Now the winner sure does pay," he said.

And they surrendered. There was no withstanding Daylight when he vaulted on the back of life, and rode it bitted and spurred.

At one in the morning he saw Elijah Davis herding Henry Finn and Joe Hines, the lumberjack, toward the door. Daylight interfered.

"Where are you-all going?" he demanded, attempting to draw them to the bar.

"Bed," Elijah Davis answered.

He was a lean tobacco-chewing New Englander, the one daring spirit in his family that had heard and answered the call of the West shouting through the Mount Desert back odd-lots. "Got to," Joe Hines added apologetically. "We're mushing out in the mornin'."

Daylight still detained them. "Where to? What's the excitement?"

"No excitement," Elijah explained. "We're just a-goin' to play your hunch, an' tackle the Upper Country. Don't you want to come along?"

"I sure do," Daylight affirmed.

But the question had been put in fun, and Elijah ignored the acceptance.

"We're tacklin' the Stewart," he went on. "Al Mayo told me he seen some likely lookin' bars first time he come down the Stewart, and we're goin' to sample 'em while the river's froze. You listen, Daylight, an' mark my words, the time's comin' when winter diggin's'll be all the go. There'll be men in them days that'll laugh at our summer stratchin' an' ground-wallerin'."

At that time, winter mining was undreamed of on the Yukon. From the moss and grass the land was frozen to bed-rock, and frozen gravel, hard as granite, defied pick and shovel. In the summer the men stripped the earth down as fast as the sun thawed it. Then was the time they did their mining. During the winter they freighted their provisions, went moose-hunting, got all ready for the summer's work, and then loafed the bleak, dark months through in the big central camps such as Circle City and Forty Mile.

"Winter diggin's sure comin'," Daylight agreed. "Wait till that big strike is made up river. Then you-all'll see a new kind of mining. What's to prevent wood-burning and sinking shafts and drifting along bed-rock? Won't need to timber. That frozen muck and gravel'll stand till hell is froze and its mill-tails is turned to ice-cream. Why, they'll be working pay-streaks a hundred feet deep in them days that's comin'. I'm sure going along with you-all, Elijah."

Elijah laughed, gathered his two partners up, and was making a second attempt to reach the door.

"Hold on," Daylight called. "I sure mean it."

The three men turned back suddenly upon him, in their faces surprise, delight, and incredulity.

"G'wan, you're foolin'," said Finn, the other lumberjack, a quiet, steady, Wisconsin man.

"There's my dawgs and sled," Daylight answered. "That'll make two teams and halve the loads—though we-all'll have to travel easy for a spell, for them dawgs is sure tired."

The three men were overjoyed, but still a trifle incredulous.

"Now look here," Joe Hines blurted out, "none of your foolin, Daylight. We mean business. Will you come?"

Daylight extended his hand and shook.

"Then you'd best be gettin' to bed," Elijah advised. "We're mushin' out at six, and four hours' sleep is none so long."

"Mebbe we ought to lay over a day and let him rest up," Finn suggested.

Daylight's pride was touched.

"No you don't," he cried. "We all start at six. What time do you-all want to be called? Five? All right, I'll rouse you-all out."

"You oughter have some sleep," Elijah counselled gravely. "You can't go on forever."

Daylight was tired, profoundly tired. Even his iron body acknowledged weariness. Every muscle was clamoring for bed and rest, was appalled at continuance of exertion and at thought of the trail again. All this physical protest welled up into his brain in a wave of revolt. But deeper down, scornful and defiant, was Life itself, the essential fire of it, whispering that all Daylight's fellows were looking on, that now was the time to pile deed upon deed, to flaunt his strength in the face of strength. It was merely Life, whispering its ancient lies. And in league with it was whiskey, with all its consummate effrontery and vain-glory.

"Mebbe you-all think I ain't weaned yet?" Daylight demanded. "Why, I ain't had a drink, or a dance, or seen a soul in two months. You-all get to bed. I'll call you-all at five."

And for the rest of the night he danced on in his stocking feet, and at five in the morning, rapping thunderously on the door of his new partners' cabin, he could be heard singing the song that had given him his name:—

"Burning daylight, you-all Stewart River hunchers! Burning daylight! Burning daylight! Burning daylight!"

CHAPTER VII

This time the trail was easier. It was better packed, and they were not carrying mail against time. The day's run was shorter, and likewise the hours on trail. On his mail run Daylight had played out three Indians; but his present partners knew that they must not be played out when they arrived at the Stewart bars, so they set the slower pace. And under this milder toil, where his companions nevertheless grew weary, Daylight recuperated and rested up. At Forty Mile they laid over two days for the sake of the dogs, and at Sixty Mile Daylight's team was left with the trader. Unlike Daylight, after the terrible run from Selkirk to Circle City, they had been unable to recuperate on the back trail. So the four men pulled on from Sixty Mile with a fresh team of dogs on Daylight's sled.

The following night they camped in the cluster of islands at the mouth of the Stewart. Daylight talked town sites, and, though the others laughed at him, he staked the whole maze of high, wooded islands.

"Just supposing the big strike does come on the Stewart," he argued. "Mebbe you-all'll be in on it, and then again mebbe you-all won't. But I sure will. You-all'd better reconsider and go in with me on it."

But they were stubborn.

"You're as bad as Harper and Joe Ladue," said Joe Hines. "They're always at that game. You know that big flat jest below the Klondike and under Moosehide Mountain? Well, the recorder at Forty Mile was tellin' me they staked that not a month ago—The Harper & Ladue Town Site. Ha! Ha! Ha!"

Elijah and Finn joined him in his laughter; but Daylight was gravely in earnest.

"There she is!" he cried. "The hunch is working! It's in the air, I tell you-all! What'd they-all stake the big flat for if they-all didn't get the hunch? Wish I'd staked it."

The regret in his voice was provocative of a second burst of laughter.

"Laugh, you-all, laugh! That's what's the trouble with you-all. You-all think gold-hunting is the only way to make a stake. But let me tell you-all that when the big strike sure does come, you-all'll do a little surface-scratchin' and muck-raking, but danged little you-all'll have to show for it. You-all laugh at quicksilver in the riffles and think flour gold was manufactured by God Almighty for the express purpose of fooling suckers and chechaquos. Nothing but coarse gold for you-all, that's your way, not getting half of it out of the ground and losing into the tailings half of what you-all do get.

"But the men that land big will be them that stake the town sites, organize the tradin' companies, start the banks—"

Here the explosion of mirth drowned him out. Banks in Alaska! The idea of it was excruciating.

"Yep, and start the stock exchanges—"

Again they were convulsed. Joe Hines rolled over on his sleeping-robe, holding his sides.

"And after them will come the big mining sharks that buy whole creeks where you-all have been scratching like a lot of picayune hens, and they-all will go to hydraulicking in summer and steam-thawing in winter—"

Steam-thawing! That was the limit. Daylight was certainly exceeding himself in his consummate fun-making. Steam-thawing—when even wood-burning was an untried experiment, a dream in the air!

"Laugh, dang you, laugh! Why your eyes ain't open yet. You-all are a bunch of little mewing kittens. I tell you-all if that strike comes on Klondike, Harper and Ladue will be millionaires. And if it comes on Stewart, you-all watch the Elam Harnish town site boom. In them days, when you-all come around makin' poor mouths..." He heaved a sigh of resignation. "Well, I suppose I'll have to give you-all a grub-stake or soup, or something or other."

Daylight had vision. His scope had been rigidly limited, yet whatever he saw, he saw big. His mind was orderly, his imagination practical, and he never dreamed idly. When he superimposed a feverish metropolis on a waste of timbered, snow-covered flat, he predicated first the gold-strike that made the city possible, and next he had an eye for steamboat landings, sawmill and warehouse locations, and all the needs of a far-northern mining city. But this, in turn, was the mere setting for something bigger, namely, the play of temperament. Opportunities swarmed in the streets and buildings and human and economic relations of the city of his dream. It was a larger table for gambling. The limit was the sky, with the Southland on one side and the aurora borealis on the other. The play would be big, bigger than any Yukoner had ever imagined, and he, Burning Daylight, would see that he got in on that play.

In the meantime there was naught to show for it but the hunch. But it was coming. As he would stake his last ounce on a good poker hand, so he staked his life and effort on the hunch that the future held in store a big strike on the Upper River. So he and his three companions, with dogs, and sleds, and snowshoes, toiled up the frozen breast of the Stewart, toiled on and on through the white wilderness where the unending stillness was never broken by the voices of men, the stroke of an ax, or the distant crack of a rifle. They alone moved through the vast and frozen quiet, little mites of earth-men, crawling their score of miles a day, melting the ice that they might have water to drink, camping in the snow at night, their wolf-dogs curled in frost-rimed, hairy bunches, their eight snowshoes stuck on end in the snow beside the sleds.

No signs of other men did they see, though once they passed a rude poling-boat, cached on a platform by the river bank. Whoever had cached it had never come back for it; and they wondered and mushed on. Another time they chanced upon the site of an Indian village, but the Indians had disappeared; undoubtedly they were on the higher reaches of the Stewart in pursuit of the moose-herds. Two hundred miles up from the Yukon, they came upon what Elijah decided were the bars mentioned by Al Mayo. A permanent camp was made, their outfit of food cached on a high platform to keep it from the dogs, and they started work on the bars, cutting their way down to gravel through the rim of ice.

It was a hard and simple life. Breakfast over, and they were at work by the first gray light; and when night descended, they did their cooking and camp-chores, smoked and yarned for a while, then rolled up in their sleeping-robes, and slept while the aurora borealis flamed overhead and the stars leaped and danced in the great cold. Their fare was monotonous: sourdough bread, bacon, beans, and an occasional dish of rice cooked along with a handful of prunes. Fresh meat they failed to obtain. There was an unwonted absence of animal life. At rare intervals they chanced upon the trail of a snowshoe rabbit or an ermine; but in the main it seemed that all life had fled the land. It was a condition not unknown to them, for in all their experience, at one time or another, they had travelled one year through a region teeming with game, where, a year or two or three years later, no game at all would be found.

Gold they found on the bars, but not in paying quantities. Elijah, while on a hunt for moose fifty miles away, had panned the surface gravel of a large creek and found good colors. They harnessed their dogs, and with light outfits sledded to the place. Here, and possibly for the first time in the history of the Yukon, wood-burning, in sinking a shaft, was tried. It was Daylight's initiative. After clearing away the moss and grass, a fire of dry spruce was built. Six hours of burning thawed eight inches of muck. Their picks drove full depth into it, and, when they had shoveled out, another fire was started. They worked early and late, excited over the success of the experiment. Six feet of frozen muck brought them to gravel, likewise frozen. Here progress was slower. But they learned to handle their fires better, and were soon able to thaw five and six inches at a burning. Flour gold was in this gravel, and after two feet it gave away again to muck. At seventeen feet they struck a thin streak of gravel, and in it coarse gold, testpans running as high as six and eight dollars. Unfortunately, this streak of gravel was not more than an inch thick. Beneath it was more muck, tangled with the trunks of ancient trees and containing fossil bones of forgotten monsters. But gold they had found—coarse gold; and what more likely than that the big deposit would be found on bed-rock? Down to bed-rock they would go, if it were forty feet away. They divided into two shifts, working day and night, on two shafts, and the smoke of their burning rose continually.

It was at this time that they ran short of beans and that Elijah was despatched to the main camp to bring up more grub. Elijah was one of the hard-bitten old-time travelers himself. The round trip was a hundred miles, but he promised to be back on the third day, one day going light, two days returning heavy. Instead, he arrived on the night of the second day. They had just gone to bed when they heard him coming.

"What in hell's the matter now?" Henry Finn demanded, as the empty sled came into the circle of firelight and as he noted that Elijah's long, serious face was longer and even more serious.

Joe Hines threw wood on the fire, and the three men, wrapped in their robes, huddled up close to the warmth. Elijah's whiskered face was matted with ice, as were his eyebrows, so that, what of his fur garb, he looked like a New England caricature of Father Christmas.

"You recollect that big spruce that held up the corner of the cache next to the river?" Elijah began.

The disaster was quickly told. The big tree, with all the seeming of hardihood, promising to stand for centuries to come, had suffered from a hidden decay. In some way its rooted grip on the earth had weakened. The added burden of the cache and the winter snow had been too much for it; the balance it had so long maintained with the forces of its environment had been overthrown; it had toppled and crashed to the ground, wrecking the cache and, in turn, overthrowing the balance with environment that the four men and eleven dogs had been maintaining. Their supply of grub was gone. The wolverines had got into the wrecked cache, and what they had not eaten they had destroyed.

"They plumb e't all the bacon and prunes and sugar and dog-food," Elijah reported, "and gosh darn my buttons, if they didn't gnaw open the sacks and scatter the flour and beans and rice from Dan to Beersheba. I found empty sacks where they'd dragged them a quarter of a mile away."

Nobody spoke for a long minute. It was nothing less than a catastrophe, in the dead of an Arctic winter and in a game-abandoned land, to lose their grub. They were not panic-stricken, but they were busy looking the situation squarely in the face and considering. Joe Hines was the first to speak.

"We can pan the snow for the beans and rice... though there wa'n't more'n eight or ten pounds of rice left."

"And somebody will have to take a team and pull for Sixty Mile," Daylight said next.

"I'll go," said Finn.

They considered a while longer.

"But how are we going to feed the other team and three men till he gets back?" Hines demanded.

"Only one thing to it," was Elijah's contribution. "You'll have to take the other team, Joe, and pull up the Stewart till you find them Indians. Then you come back with a load of meat. You'll get here long before Henry can make it from Sixty Mile, and while you're gone there'll only be Daylight and me to feed, and we'll feed good and small."

"And in the morning we-all'll pull for the cache and pan snow to find what grub we've got." Daylight lay back, as he spoke, and rolled in his robe to sleep, then added: "Better turn in for an early start. Two of you can take the dogs down. Elijah and me'll skin out on both sides and see if we-all can scare up a moose on the way down."

CHAPTER VIII

No time was lost. Hines and Finn, with the dogs, already on short rations, were two days in pulling down. At noon of the third day Elijah arrived, reporting no moose sign. That night Daylight came in with a similar report. As fast as they arrived, the men had started careful panning of the snow all around the cache. It was a large task, for they found stray beans fully a hundred yards from the cache. One more day all the men toiled. The result was pitiful, and the four showed their caliber in the division of the few pounds of food that had been recovered. Little as it was, the lion's share was left with Daylight and Elijah. The men who pulled on with the dogs, one up the Stewart and one down, would come more quickly to grub. The two who remained would have to last out till the others returned. Furthermore, while the dogs, on several ounces each of beans a day, would travel slowly, nevertheless, the men who travelled with them, on a pinch, would have the dogs themselves to eat. But the men who remained, when the pinch came, would have no dogs. It was for this reason that Daylight and Elijah took the more desperate chance. They could not do less, nor did they care to do less. The days passed, and the winter began merging imperceptibly into the Northland spring that comes like a thunderbolt of suddenness. It was the spring of 1896 that was preparing. Each day the sun rose farther east of south, remained longer in the sky, and set farther to the west. March ended and April began, and Daylight and Elijah, lean and hungry, wondered what had become of their two comrades. Granting every delay, and throwing in generous margins for good measure, the time was long since passed when they should have returned. Without doubt they had met with disaster. The party had considered the possibility of disaster for one man, and that had been the principal reason for despatching the two in different directions. But that disaster should have come to both of them was the final blow.

In the meantime, hoping against hope, Daylight and Elija eked out a meagre existence. The thaw had not yet begun, so they were able to gather the snow about the ruined cache and melt it in pots and pails and gold pans. Allowed to stand for a while, when poured off, a thin deposit of slime was found on the bottoms of the vessels. This was the flour, the infinitesimal trace of it scattered through thousands of cubic yards of snow. Also, in this slime occurred at intervals a water-soaked tea-leaf or coffee-ground, and there were in it fragments of earth and litter. But the farther they worked away from the site of the cache, the thinner became the trace of flour, the smaller the deposit of slime.

Elijah was the older man, and he weakened first, so that he came to lie up most of the time in his furs. An occasional tree-squirrel kept them alive. The hunting fell upon Daylight, and it was hard work. With but thirty rounds of ammunition, he dared not risk a miss; and, since his rifle was a 45-90, he was compelled to shoot the small creatures through the head. There were very few of them, and days went by without seeing one. When he did see one, he took infinite precautions. He would stalk it for hours. A score of times, with arms that shook from weakness, he would draw a sight on the animal and refrain from pulling the trigger. His inhibition was a thing of iron. He was the master. Not til absolute certitude was his did he shoot. No matter how sharp the pangs of hunger and desire for that palpitating morsel of chattering life, he refused to take the slightest risk of a miss. He, born gambler, was gambling in the bigger way. His life was the stake, his cards were the cartridges, and he played as only a big gambler could play, with infinite precaution, with infinite consideration. Each shot meant a squirrel, and though days elapsed between shots, it never changed his method of play.

Of the squirrels, nothing was lost. Even the skins were boiled to make broth, the bones pounded into fragments that could be chewed and swallowed. Daylight prospected through the snow, and found occasional patches of mossberries. At the best, mossberries were composed practically of seeds and water, with a tough rind of skin about them; but the berries he found were of the preceding year, dry and shrivelled, and the nourishment they contained verged on the minus quality. Scarcely better was the bark of young saplings, stewed for an hour and swallowed after prodigious chewing.

April drew toward its close, and spring smote the land. The days stretched out their length. Under the heat of the sun, the snow began to melt, while from down under the snow arose the trickling of tiny streams. For twenty-four hours the Chinook wind blew, and in that twenty-four hours the snow was diminished fully a foot in depth. In the late afternoons the melting snow froze again, so that its surface became ice capable of supporting a man's weight. Tiny white snow-birds appeared from the south, lingered a day, and resumed their journey into the north. Once, high in the air, looking for open water and ahead of the season, a wedged squadron of wild geese honked northwards. And down by the river bank a clump of dwarf willows burst into bud. These young buds, stewed, seemed to posess an encouraging nutrition. Elijah took heart of hope, though he was cast down again when Daylight failed to find another clump of willows.

The sap was rising in the trees, and daily the trickle of unseen streamlets became louder as the frozen land came back to life. But the river held in its bonds of frost. Winter had been long months in riveting them, and not in a day were they to be broken, not even by the thunderbolt of spring. May came, and stray last-year's mosquitoes, full-grown but harmless, crawled out of rock crevices and rotten logs. Crickets began to chirp, and more geese and ducks flew overhead. And still the river held. By May tenth, the ice of the Stewart, with a great rending and snapping, tore loose from the banks and rose three feet. But it did not go down-stream. The lower Yukon, up to where the Stewart flowed into it, must first break and move on. Until then the ice of the Stewart could only rise higher and higher on the increasing flood beneath. When the Yukon would break was problematical. Two thousand miles away it flowed into Bering Sea, and it was the ice conditions of Bering Sea that would determine when the Yukon could rid itself of the millions of tons of ice that cluttered its breast.

On the twelfth of May, carrying their sleeping-robes, a pail, an ax, and the precious rifle, the two men started down the river on the ice. Their plan was to gain to the cached poling-boat they had seen, so that at the first open water they could launch it and drift with the stream to Sixty Mile. In their weak condition, without food, the going was slow and difficult. Elijah developed a habit of falling down and being unable to rise. Daylight gave of his own strength to lift him to his feet, whereupon the older man would stagger automatically on until he stumbled and fell again.

On the day they should have reached the boat, Elijah collapsed utterly. When Daylight raised him, he fell again. Daylight essayed to walk with him, supporting him, but such was Daylight's own weakness that they fell together.

Dragging Elijah to the bank, a rude camp was made, and Daylight started out in search of squirrels. It was at this time that he likewise developed the falling habit. In the evening he found his first squirrel, but darkness came on without his getting a certain shot. With primitive patience he waited till next day, and then, within the hour, the squirrel was his.

The major portion he fed to Elijah, reserving for himself the tougher parts and the bones. But such is the chemistry of life, that this small creature, this trifle of meat that moved, by being eaten, transmuted to the meat of the men the same power to move. No longer did the squirrel run up spruce trees, leap from branch to branch, or cling chattering to giddy perches. Instead, the same energy that had done these things flowed into the wasted muscles and reeling wills of the men, making them move—nay, moving them—till they tottered the several intervening miles to the cached boat, underneath which they fell together and lay motionless a long time.

Light as the task would have been for a strong man to lower the small boat to the ground, it took Daylight hours. And many hours more, day by day, he dragged himself around it, lying on his side to calk the gaping seams with moss. Yet, when this was done, the river still held. Its ice had risen many feet, but would not start down-stream. And one more task waited, the launching of the boat when the river ran water to receive it. Vainly Daylight staggered and stumbled and fell and crept through the snow that was wet with thaw, or across it when the night's frost still crusted it beyond the weight of a man, searching for one more squirrel, striving to achieve one more transmutation of furry leap and scolding chatter into the lifts and tugs of a man's body that would hoist the boat over the rim of shore-ice and slide it down into the stream.

Not till the twentieth of May did the river break. The down-stream movement began at five in the morning, and already were the days so long that Daylight sat up and watched the ice-run. Elijah was too far gone to be interested in the spectacle. Though vaguely conscious, he lay without movement while the ice tore by, great cakes of it caroming against the bank, uprooting trees, and gouging out earth by hundreds of tons.

All about them the land shook and reeled from the shock of these tremendous collisions. At the end of an hour the run stopped. Somewhere below it was blocked by a jam. Then the river began to rise, lifting the ice on its breast till it was higher than the bank. From behind ever more water bore down, and ever more millions of tons of ice added their weight to the congestion. The pressures and stresses became terrific. Huge cakes of ice were squeezed out till they popped into the air like melon seeds squeezed from between the thumb and forefinger of a child, while all along the banks a wall of ice was forced up. When the jam broke, the noise of grinding and smashing redoubled. For another hour the run continued. The river fell rapidly. But the wall of ice on top the bank, and extending down into the falling water, remained.

The tail of the ice-run passed, and for the first time in six months Daylight saw open water. He knew that the ice had not yet passed out from the upper reaches of the Stewart, that it lay in packs and jams in those upper reaches, and that it might break loose and come down in a second run any time; but the need was too desperate for him to linger. Elijah was so far gone that he might pass at any moment. As for himself, he was not sure that enough strength remained in his wasted muscles to launch the boat. It was all a gamble. If he waited for the second ice-run, Elijah would surely die, and most probably himself. If he succeeded in launching the boat, if he kept ahead of the second ice-run, if he did not get caught by some of the runs from the upper Yukon; if luck favored in all these essential particulars, as well as in a score of minor ones, they would reach Sixty Mile and be saved, if—and again the if—he had strength enough to land the boat at Sixty Mile and not go by.

He set to work. The wall of ice was five feet above the ground on which the boat rested. First prospecting for the best launching-place, he found where a huge cake of ice shelved upward from the river that ran fifteen feet below to the top of the wall. This was a score of feet away, and at the end of an hour he had managed to get the boat that far. He was sick with nausea from his exertions, and at times it seemed that blindness smote him, for he could not see, his eyes vexed with spots and points of light that were as excruciating as diamond-dust, his heart pounding up in his throat and suffocating him. Elijah betrayed no interest, did not move nor open his eyes; and Daylight fought out his battle alone. At last, falling on his knees from the shock of exertion, he got the boat poised on a secure balance on top the wall. Crawling on hands and knees, he placed in the boat his rabbit-skin robe, the rifle, and the pail. He did not bother with the ax. It meant an additional crawl of twenty feet and back, and if the need for it should arise he well knew he would be past all need.

Elijah proved a bigger task than he had anticipated. A few inches at a time, resting in between, he dragged him over the ground and up a broken rubble of ice to the side of the boat. But into the boat he could not get him. Elijah's limp body was far more difficult to lift and handle than an equal weight of like dimensions but rigid. Daylight failed to hoist him, for the body collapsed at the middle like a part-empty sack of corn. Getting into the boat, Daylight tried vainly to drag his comrade in after him. The best he could do was to get Elijah's head and shoulders on top the gunwale. When he released his hold, to heave from farther down the body, Elijah promptly gave at the middle and came down on the ice.

In despair, Daylight changed his tactics. He struck the other in the face.

"God Almighty, ain't you-all a man?" he cried. "There! damn you-all! there!"

At each curse he struck him on the cheeks, the nose, the mouth, striving, by the shock of the hurt, to bring back the sinking soul and far-wandering will of the man. The eyes fluttered open.

"Now listen!" he shouted hoarsely. "When I get your head to the gunwale, hang on! Hear me? Hang on! Bite into it with your teeth, but HANG ON!"

The eyes fluttered down, but Daylight knew the message had been received. Again he got the helpless man's head and shoulders on the gunwale.

"Hang on, damn you! Bite in!" he shouted, as he shifted his grip lower down.

One weak hand slipped off the gunwale, the fingers of the other hand relaxed, but Elijah obeyed, and his teeth held on. When the lift came, his face ground forward, and the splintery wood tore and crushed the skin from nose, lips, and chin; and, face downward, he slipped on and down to the bottom of the boat till his limp middle collapsed across the gunwale and his legs hung down outside. But they were only his legs, and Daylight shoved them in; after him. Breathing heavily, he turned Elijah over on his back, and covered him with his robes.

The final task remained—the launching of the boat. This, of necessity, was the severest of all, for he had been compelled to load his comrade in aft of the balance. It meant a supreme effort at lifting. Daylight steeled himself and began. Something must have snapped, for, though he was unaware of it, the next he knew he was lying doubled on his stomach across the sharp stern of the boat. Evidently, and for the first time in his life, he had fainted. Furthermore, it seemed to him that he was finished, that he had not one more movement left in him, and that, strangest of all, he did not care. Visions came to him, clear-cut and real, and concepts sharp as steel cutting-edges. He, who all his days had looked on naked Life, had never seen so much of Life's nakedness before. For the first time he experienced a doubt of his own glorious personality. For the moment Life faltered and forgot to lie. After all, he was a little earth-maggot, just like all the other earth-maggots, like the squirrel he had eaten, like the other men he had seen fail and die, like Joe Hines and Henry Finn, who had already failed and were surely dead, like Elijah lying there uncaring, with his skinned face, in the bottom of the boat. Daylight's position was such that from where he lay he could look up river to the bend, around which, sooner or later, the next ice-run would come. And as he looked he seemed to see back through the past to a time when neither white man nor Indian was in the land, and ever he saw the same Stewart River, winter upon winter, breasted with ice, and spring upon spring bursting that ice asunder and running free. And he saw also into an illimitable future, when the last generations of men were gone from off the face of Alaska, when he, too, would be gone, and he saw, ever remaining, that river, freezing and fresheting, and running on and on.

Life was a liar and a cheat. It fooled all creatures. It had fooled him, Burning Daylight, one of its chiefest and most joyous exponents. He was nothing—a mere bunch of flesh and nerves and sensitiveness that crawled in the muck for gold, that dreamed and aspired and gambled, and that passed and was gone. Only the dead things remained, the things that were not flesh and nerves and sensitiveness, the sand and muck and gravel, the stretching flats, the mountains, the river itself, freezing and breaking, year by year, down all the years. When all was said and done, it was a scurvy game. The dice were loaded. Those that died did not win, and all died. Who won? Not even Life, the stool-pigeon, the arch-capper for the game—Life, the ever flourishing graveyard, the everlasting funeral procession.

He drifted back to the immediate present for a moment and noted that the river still ran wide open, and that a moose-bird, perched on the bow of the boat, was surveying him impudently. Then he drifted dreamily back to his meditations.

There was no escaping the end of the game. He was doomed surely to be out of it all. And what of it? He pondered that question again and again.

Conventional religion had passed Daylight by. He had lived a sort of religion in his square dealing and right playing with other men, and he had not indulged in vain metaphysics about future life. Death ended all. He had always believed that, and been unafraid. And at this moment, the boat fifteen feet above the water and immovable, himself fainting with weakness and without a particle of strength left in him, he still believed that death ended all, and he was still unafraid. His views were too simply and solidly based to be overthrown by the first squirm, or the last, of death-fearing life.

He had seen men and animals die, and into the field of his vision, by scores, came such deaths. He saw them over again, just as he had seen them at the time, and they did not shake him.

What of it? They were dead, and dead long since. They weren't bothering about it. They weren't lying on their bellies across a boat and waiting to die. Death was easy—easier than he had ever imagined; and, now that it was near, the thought of it made him glad.

A new vision came to him. He saw the feverish city of his dream—the gold metropolis of the North, perched above the Yukon on a high earth-bank and far-spreading across the flat. He saw the river steamers tied to the bank and lined against it three deep; he saw the sawmills working and the long dog-teams, with double sleds behind, freighting supplies to the diggings.

And he saw, further, the gambling-houses, banks, stock-exchanges, and all the gear and chips and markers, the chances and opportunities, of a vastly bigger gambling game than any he had ever seen. It was sure hell, he thought, with the hunch a-working and that big strike coming, to be out of it all. Life thrilled and stirred at the thought and once more began uttering his ancient lies.

Daylight rolled over and off the boat, leaning against it as he sat on the ice. He wanted to be in on that strike. And why shouldn't he? Somewhere in all those wasted muscles of his was enough strength, if he could gather it all at once, to up-end the boat and launch it. Quite irrelevantly the idea suggested itself of buying a share in the Klondike town site from Harper and Joe Ladue. They would surely sell a third interest cheap. Then, if the strike came on the Stewart, he would be well in on it with the Elam Harnish town site; if on the Klondike, he would not be quite out of it.

In the meantime, he would gather strength. He stretched out on the ice full length, face downward, and for half an hour he lay and rested. Then he arose, shook the flashing blindness from his eyes, and took hold of the boat. He knew his condition accurately. If the first effort failed, the following efforts were doomed to fail. He must pull all his rallied strength into the one effort, and so thoroughly must he put all of it in that there would be none left for other attempts.

He lifted, and he lifted with the soul of him as well as with the body, consuming himself, body and spirit, in the effort. The boat rose. He thought he was going to faint, but he continued to lift. He felt the boat give, as it started on its downward slide. With the last shred of his strength he precipitated himself into it, landing in a sick heap on Elijah's legs. He was beyond attempting to rise, and as he lay he heard and felt the boat take the water. By watching the tree-tops he knew it was whirling. A smashing shock and flying fragments of ice told him that it had struck the bank. A dozen times it whirled and struck, and then it floated easily and free.

Daylight came to, and decided he had been asleep. The sun denoted that several hours had passed. It was early afternoon. He dragged himself into the stern and sat up. The boat was in the middle of the stream. The wooded banks, with their base-lines of flashing ice, were slipping by. Near him floated a huge, uprooted pine. A freak of the current brought the boat against it. Crawling forward, he fastened the painter to a root.

The tree, deeper in the water, was travelling faster, and the painter tautened as the boat took the tow. Then, with a last giddy look around, wherein he saw the banks tilting and swaying and the sun swinging in pendulum-sweep across the sky, Daylight wrapped himself in his rabbit-skin robe, lay down in the bottom, and fell asleep.

When he awoke, it was dark night. He was lying on his back, and he could see the stars shining. A subdued murmur of swollen waters could be heard. A sharp jerk informed him that the boat, swerving slack into the painter, had been straightened out by the swifter-moving pine tree. A piece of stray drift-ice thumped against the boat and grated along its side. Well, the following jam hadn't caught him yet, was his thought, as he closed his eyes and slept again.

It was bright day when next he opened his eyes. The sun showed it to be midday. A glance around at the far-away banks, and he knew that he was on the mighty Yukon. Sixty Mile could not be far away. He was abominably weak. His movements were slow, fumbling, and inaccurate, accompanied by panting and head-swimming, as he dragged himself into a sitting-up position in the stern, his rifle beside him. He looked a long time at Elijah, but could not see whether he breathed or not, and he was too immeasurably far away to make an investigation.

He fell to dreaming and meditating again, dreams and thoughts being often broken by sketches of blankness, wherein he neither slept, nor was unconscious, nor was aware of anything. It seemed to him more like cogs slipping in his brain. And in this intermittent way he reviewed the situation. He was still alive, and most likely would be saved, but how came it that he was not lying dead across the boat on top the ice-rim? Then he recollected the great final effort he had made. But why had he made it? he asked himself. It had not been fear of death. He had not been afraid, that was sure. Then he remembered the hunch and the big strike he believed was coming, and he knew that the spur had been his desire to sit in for a hand at that big game. And again why? What if he made his million? He would die, just the same as those that never won more than grub-stakes. Then again why? But the blank stretches in his thinking process began to come more frequently, and he surrendered to the delightful lassitude that was creeping over him.

He roused with a start. Something had whispered in him that he must awake. Abruptly he saw Sixty Mile, not a hundred feet away.

The current had brought him to the very door. But the same current was now sweeping him past and on into the down-river wilderness. No one was in sight. The place might have been deserted, save for the smoke he saw rising from the kitchen chimney. He tried to call, but found he had no voice left. An unearthly guttural hiss alternately rattled and wheezed in his throat. He fumbled for the rifle, got it to his shoulder, and pulled the trigger. The recoil of the discharge tore through his frame, racking it with a thousand agonies. The rifle had fallen across his knees, and an attempt to lift it to his shoulder failed. He knew he must be quick, and felt that he was fainting, so he pulled the trigger of the gun where it lay. This time it kicked off and overboard. But just before darkness rushed over him, he saw the kitchen door open, and a woman look out of the big log house that was dancing a monstrous jig among the trees.

CHAPTER IX

Ten days later, Harper and Joe Ladue arrived at Sixty Mile, and Daylight, still a trifle weak, but strong enough to obey the hunch that had come to him, traded a third interest in his Stewart town site for a third interest in theirs on the Klondike.

They had faith in the Upper Country, and Harper left down-stream, with a raft-load of supplies, to start a small post at the mouth of the Klondike.

"Why don't you tackle Indian River, Daylight?" Harper advised, at parting. "There's whole slathers of creeks and draws draining in up there, and somewhere gold just crying to be found. That's my hunch. There's a big strike coming, and Indian River ain't going to be a million miles away."

"And the place is swarming with moose," Joe Ladue added. "Bob Henderson's up there somewhere, been there three years now, swearing something big is going to happen, living off'n straight moose and prospecting around like a crazy man."

Daylight decided to go Indian River a flutter, as he expressed it; but Elijah could not be persuaded into accompanying him. Elijah's soul had been seared by famine, and he was obsessed by fear of repeating the experience.

"I jest can't bear to separate from grub," he explained. "I know it's downright foolishness, but I jest can't help it. It's all I can do to tear myself away from the table when I know I'm full to bustin' and ain't got storage for another bite. I'm going back to Circle to camp by a cache until I get cured."

Daylight lingered a few days longer, gathering strength and arranging his meagre outfit. He planned to go in light, carrying a pack of seventy-five pounds and making his five dogs pack as well, Indian fashion, loading them with thirty pounds each. Depending on the report of Ladue, he intended to follow Bob Henderson's example and live practically on straight meat. When Jack Kearns' scow, laden with the sawmill from Lake Linderman, tied up at Sixty Mile, Daylight bundled his outfit and dogs on board, turned his town-site application over to Elijah to be filed, and the same day was landed at the mouth of Indian River.

Forty miles up the river, at what had been described to him as Quartz Creek, he came upon signs of Bob Henderson's work, and also at Australia Creek, thirty miles farther on. The weeks came and went, but Daylight never encountered the other man. However, he found moose plentiful, and he and his dogs prospered on the meat diet. He found "pay" that was no more than "wages" on a dozen surface bars, and from the generous spread of flour gold in the muck and gravel of a score of creeks, he was more confident than ever that coarse gold in quantity was waiting to be unearthed. Often he turned his eyes to the northward ridge of hills, and pondered if the gold came from them. In the end, he ascended Dominion Creek to its head, crossed the divide, and came down on the tributary to the Klondike that was later to be called Hunker Creek. While on the divide, had he kept the big dome on his right, he would have come down on the Gold Bottom, so named by Bob Henderson, whom he would have found at work on it, taking out the first pay-gold ever panned on the Klondike. Instead, Daylight continued down Hunker to the Klondike, and on to the summer fishing camp of the Indians on the Yukon.

Here for a day he camped with Carmack, a squaw-man, and his Indian brother-in-law, Skookum Jim, bought a boat, and, with his dogs on board, drifted down the Yukon to Forty Mile. August was drawing to a close, the days were growing shorter, and winter was coming on. Still with unbounded faith in his hunch that a strike was coming in the Upper Country, his plan was to get together a party of four or five, and, if that was impossible, at least a partner, and to pole back up the river before the freeze-up to do winter prospecting. But the men of Forty Mile were without faith. The diggings to the westward were good enough for them.

Then it was that Carmack, his brother-in-law, Skookum Jim, and Cultus Charlie, another Indian, arrived in a canoe at Forty Mile, went straight to the gold commissioner, and recorded three claims and a discovery claim on Bonanza Creek. After that, in the Sourdough Saloon, that night, they exhibited coarse gold to the sceptical crowd. Men grinned and shook their heads. They had seen the motions of a gold strike gone through before. This was too patently a scheme of Harper's and Joe Ladue's, trying to entice prospecting in the vicinity of their town site and trading post. And who was Carmack? A squaw-man. And who ever heard of a squaw-man striking anything? And what was Bonanza Creek? Merely a moose pasture, entering the Klondike just above its mouth, and known to old-timers as Rabbit Creek. Now if Daylight or Bob Henderson had recorded claims and shown coarse gold, they'd known there was something in it. But Carmack, the squaw-man! And Skookum Jim! And Cultus Charlie! No, no; that was asking too much.

Daylight, too, was sceptical, and this despite his faith in the Upper Country. Had he not, only a few days before, seen Carmack loafing with his Indians and with never a thought of prospecting?

But at eleven that night, sitting on the edge of his bunk and unlacing his moccasins, a thought came to him. He put on his coat and hat and went back to the Sourdough. Carmack was still there, flashing his coarse gold in the eyes of an unbelieving generation. Daylight ranged alongside of him and emptied Carmack's sack into a blower. This he studied for a long time. Then, from his own sack, into another blower, he emptied several ounces of Circle City and Forty Mile gold. Again, for a long time, he studied and compared. Finally, he pocketed his own gold, returned Carmack's, and held up his hand for silence.

"Boys, I want to tell you-all something," he said. "She's sure come—the up-river strike. And I tell you-all, clear and forcible, this is it. There ain't never been gold like that in a blower in this country before. It's new gold. It's got more silver in it. You-all can see it by the color. Carmack's sure made a strike. Who-all's got faith to come along with me?"

There were no volunteers. Instead, laughter and jeers went up.

"Mebbe you got a town site up there," some one suggested.

"I sure have," was the retort, "and a third interest in Harper and Ladue's. And I can see my corner lots selling out for more than your hen-scratching ever turned up on Birch Creek."

"That's all right, Daylight," one Curly Parson interposed soothingly. "You've got a reputation, and we know you're dead sure on the square. But you're as likely as any to be mistook on a flimflam game, such as these loafers is putting up. I ask you straight: When did Carmack do this here prospecting? You said yourself he was lying in camp, fishing salmon along with his Siwash relations, and that was only the other day."

"And Daylight told the truth," Carmack interrupted excitedly. "And I'm telling the truth, the gospel truth. I wasn't prospecting. Hadn't no idea of it. But when Daylight pulls out, the very same day, who drifts in, down river, on a raft-load of supplies, but Bob Henderson. He'd come out to Sixty Mile, planning to go back up Indian River and portage the grub across the divide between Quartz Creek and Gold Bottom—"

"Where in hell's Gold Bottom?" Curly Parsons demanded.

"Over beyond Bonanza that was Rabbit Creek," the squaw-man went on. "It's a draw of a big creek that runs into the Klondike. That's the way I went up, but I come back by crossing the divide, keeping along the crest several miles, and dropping down into Bonanza. 'Come along with me, Carmack, and get staked,' says Bob Henderson to me. 'I've hit it this time, on Gold Bottom. I've took out forty-five ounces already.' And I went along, Skookum Jim and Cultus Charlie, too. And we all staked on Gold Bottom. I come back by Bonanza on the chance of finding a moose. Along down Bonanza we stopped and cooked grub. I went to sleep, and what does Skookum Jim do but try his hand at prospecting. He'd been watching Henderson, you see. He goes right slap up to the foot of a birch tree, first pan, fills it with dirt, and washes out more'n a dollar coarse gold. Then he wakes me up, and I goes at it. I got two and a half the first lick. Then I named the creek 'Bonanza,' staked Discovery, and we come here and recorded."

He looked about him anxiously for signs of belief, but found himself in a circle of incredulous faces—all save Daylight, who had studied his countenance while he told his story.

"How much is Harper and Ladue givin' you for manufacturing a stampede?" some one asked.

"They don't know nothing about it," Carmack answered. "I tell you it's the God Almighty's truth. I washed out three ounces in an hour."

"And there's the gold," Daylight said. "I tell you-all boys they ain't never been gold like that in the blower before. Look at the color of it."

"A trifle darker," Curly Parson said. "Most likely Carmack's been carrying a couple of silver dollars along in the same sack. And what's more, if there's anything in it, why ain't Bob Henderson smoking along to record?"

"He's up on Gold Bottom," Carmack explained. "We made the strike coming back."

A burst of laughter was his reward.

"Who-all'll go pardners with me and pull out in a poling-boat to-morrow for this here Bonanza?" Daylight asked.

No one volunteered.

"Then who-all'll take a job from me, cash wages in advance, to pole up a thousand pounds of grub?"

Curly Parsons and another, Pat Monahan, accepted, and, with his customary speed, Daylight paid them their wages in advance and arranged the purchase of the supplies, though he emptied his sack in doing so. He was leaving the Sourdough, when he suddenly turned back to the bar from the door.

"Got another hunch?" was the query.

"I sure have," he answered. "Flour's sure going to be worth what a man will pay for it this winter up on the Klondike. Who'll lend me some money?"

On the instant a score of the men who had declined to accompany him on the wild-goose chase were crowding about him with proffered gold-sacks.

"How much flour do you want?" asked the Alaska Commercial Company's storekeeper.

"About two ton."

The proffered gold-sacks were not withdrawn, though their owners were guilty of an outrageous burst of merriment.

"What are you going to do with two tons?" the store-keeper demanded.

"Son," Daylight made reply, "you-all ain't been in this country long enough to know all its curves. I'm going to start a sauerkraut factory and combined dandruff remedy."

He borrowed money right and left, engaging and paying six other men to bring up the flour in half as many more poling-boats. Again his sack was empty, and he was heavily in debt.

Curly Parsons bowed his head on the bar with a gesture of despair.

"What gets me," he moaned, "is what you're going to do with it all."

"I'll tell you-all in simple A, B, C and one, two, three." Daylight held up one finger and began checking off. "Hunch number one: a big strike coming in Upper Country. Hunch number two: Carmack's made it. Hunch number three: ain't no hunch at all. It's a cinch. If one and two is right, then flour just has to go sky-high. If I'm riding hunches one and two, I just got to ride this cinch, which is number three. If I'm right, flour'll balance gold on the scales this winter. I tell you-all boys, when you-all got a hunch, play it for all it's worth. What's luck good for, if you-all ain't to ride it? And when you-all ride it, ride like hell. I've been years in this country, just waiting for the right hunch to come along. And here she is. Well, I'm going to play her, that's all. Good night, you-all; good night."

CHAPTER X

Still men were without faith in the strike. When Daylight, with his heavy outfit of flour, arrived at the mouth of the Klondike, he found the big flat as desolate and tenantless as ever. Down close by the river, Chief Isaac and his Indians were camped beside the frames on which they were drying salmon. Several old-timers were also in camp there. Having finished their summer work on Ten Mile Creek, they had come down the Yukon, bound for Circle City. But at Sixty Mile they had learned of the strike, and stopped off to look over the ground. They had just returned to their boat when Daylight landed his flour, and their report was pessimistic.

"Damned moose-pasture," quoth one, Long Jim Harney, pausing to blow into his tin mug of tea. "Don't you have nothin' to do with it, Daylight. It's a blamed rotten sell. They're just going through the motions of a strike. Harper and Ladue's behind it, and Carmack's the stool-pigeon. Whoever heard of mining a moose-pasture half a mile between rim-rock and God alone knows how far to bed-rock!"

Daylight nodded sympathetically, and considered for a space.

"Did you-all pan any?" he asked finally.

"Pan hell!" was the indignant answer. "Think I was born yesterday! Only a chechaquo'd fool around that pasture long enough to fill a pan of dirt. You don't catch me at any such foolishness. One look was enough for me. We're pulling on in the morning for Circle City. I ain't never had faith in this Upper Country. Head-reaches of the Tanana is good enough for me from now on, and mark my words, when the big strike comes, she'll come down river. Johnny, here, staked a couple of miles below Discovery, but he don't know no better." Johnny looked shamefaced.

"I just did it for fun," he explained. "I'd give my chance in the creek for a pound of Star plug."

"I'll go you," Daylight said promptly. "But don't you-all come squealing if I take twenty or thirty thousand out of it."

Johnny grinned cheerfully.

"Gimme the tobacco," he said.

"Wish I'd staked alongside," Long Jim murmured plaintively.

"It ain't too late," Daylight replied.

"But it's a twenty-mile walk there and back."

"I'll stake it for you to-morrow when I go up," Daylight offered.

"Then you do the same as Johnny. Get the fees from Tim Logan. He's tending bar in the Sourdough, and he'll lend it to me. Then fill in your own name, transfer to me, and turn the papers over to Tim."

"Me, too," chimed in the third old-timer.

And for three pounds of Star plug chewing tobacco, Daylight bought outright three five-hundred-foot claims on Bonanza. He could still stake another claim in his own name, the others being merely transfers.

"Must say you're almighty brash with your chewin' tobacco," Long Jim grinned. "Got a factory somewheres?"

"Nope, but I got a hunch," was the retort, "and I tell you-all it's cheaper than dirt to ride her at the rate of three plugs for three claims."

But an hour later, at his own camp, Joe Ladue strode in, fresh from Bonanza Creek. At first, non-committal over Carmack's strike, then, later, dubious, he finally offered Daylight a hundred dollars for his share in the town site.

"Cash?" Daylight queried.

"Sure. There she is."

So saying, Ladue pulled out his gold-sack. Daylight hefted it absent-mindedly, and, still absent-mindedly, untied the strings and ran some of the gold-dust out on his palm. It showed darker than any dust he had ever seen, with the exception of Carmack's. He ran the gold back tied the mouth of the sack, and returned it to Ladue.

"I guess you-all need it more'n I do," was Daylight's comment.

"Nope; got plenty more," the other assured him.

"Where that come from?"

Daylight was all innocence as he asked the question, and Ladue received the question as stolidly as an Indian. Yet for a swift instant they looked into each other's eyes, and in that instant an intangible something seemed to flash out from all the body and spirit of Joe Ladue. And it seemed to Daylight that he had caught this flash, sensed a secret something in the knowledge and plans behind the other's eyes.

"You-all know the creek better'n me," Daylight went on. "And if my share in the town site's worth a hundred to you-all with what you-all know, it's worth a hundred to me whether I know it or not."

"I'll give you three hundred," Ladue offered desperately.

"Still the same reasoning. No matter what I don't know, it's worth to me whatever you-all are willing to pay for it."

Then it was that Joe Ladue shamelessly gave over. He led Daylight away from the camp and men and told him things in confidence.

"She's sure there," he said in conclusion. "I didn't sluice it, or cradle it. I panned it, all in that sack, yesterday, on the rim-rock. I tell you, you can shake it out of the grassroots. And what's on bed-rock down in the bottom of the creek they ain't no way of tellin'. But she's big, I tell you, big. Keep it quiet, and locate all you can. It's in spots, but I wouldn't be none surprised if some of them claims yielded as high as fifty thousand. The only trouble is that it's spotted."

A month passed by, and Bonanza Creek remained quiet. A sprinkling of men had staked; but most of them, after staking, had gone on down to Forty Mile and Circle City. The few that possessed sufficient faith to remain were busy building log cabins against the coming of winter. Carmack and his Indian relatives were occupied in building a sluice box and getting a head of water. The work was slow, for they had to saw their lumber by hand from the standing forest. But farther down Bonanza were four men who had drifted in from up river, Dan McGilvary, Dave McKay, Dave Edwards, and Harry Waugh. They were a quiet party, neither asking nor giving confidences, and they herded by themselves. But Daylight, who had panned the spotted rim of Carmack's claim and shaken coarse gold from the grass-roots, and who had panned the rim at a hundred other places up and down the length of the creek and found nothing, was curious to know what lay on bed-rock. He had noted the four quiet men sinking a shaft close by the stream, and he had heard their whip-saw going as they made lumber for the sluice boxes. He did not wait for an invitation, but he was present the first day they sluiced. And at the end of five hours' shovelling for one man, he saw them take out thirteen ounces and a half of gold.

It was coarse gold, running from pinheads to a twelve-dollar nugget, and it had come from off bed-rock. The first fall snow was flying that day, and the Arctic winter was closing down; but Daylight had no eyes for the bleak-gray sadness of the dying, short-lived summer. He saw his vision coming true, and on the big flat was upreared anew his golden city of the snows. Gold had been found on bed-rock. That was the big thing. Carmack's strike was assured. Daylight staked a claim in his own name adjoining the three he had purchased with his plug tobacco. This gave him a block of property two thousand feet long and extending in width from rim-rock to rim-rock.

Returning that night to his camp at the mouth of Klondike, he found in it Kama, the Indian he had left at Dyea. Kama was travelling by canoe, bringing in the last mail of the year. In his possession was some two hundred dollars in gold-dust, which Daylight immediately borrowed. In return, he arranged to stake a claim for him, which he was to record when he passed through Forty Mile. When Kama departed next morning, he carried a number of letters for Daylight, addressed to all the old-timers down river, in which they were urged to come up immediately and stake.

Also Kama carried letters of similar import, given him by the other men on Bonanza.

"It will sure be the gosh-dangdest stampede that ever was," Daylight chuckled, as he tried to vision the excited populations of Forty Mile and Circle City tumbling into poling-boats and racing the hundreds of miles up the Yukon; for he knew that his word would be unquestioningly accepted.

With the arrival of the first stampeders, Bonanza Creek woke up, and thereupon began a long-distance race between unveracity and truth, wherein, lie no matter how fast, men were continually overtaken and passed by truth. When men who doubted Carmack's report of two and a half to the pan, themselves panned two and a half, they lied and said that they were getting an ounce. And long ere the lie was fairly on its way, they were getting not one ounce but five ounces. This they claimed was ten ounces; but when they filled a pan of dirt to prove the lie, they washed out twelve ounces. And so it went. They continued valiantly to lie, but the truth continued to outrun them.

One day in December Daylight filled a pan from bed rock on his own claim and carried it into his cabin. Here a fire burned and enabled him to keep water unfrozen in a canvas tank. He squatted over the tank and began to wash. Earth and gravel seemed to fill the pan. As he imparted to it a circular movement, the lighter, coarser particles washed out over the edge. At times he combed the surface with his fingers, raking out handfuls of gravel. The contents of the pan diminished. As it drew near to the bottom, for the purpose of fleeting and tentative examination, he gave the pan a sudden sloshing movement, emptying it of water. And the whole bottom showed as if covered with butter. Thus the yellow gold flashed up as the muddy water was flirted away. It was gold—gold-dust, coarse gold, nuggets, large nuggets. He was all alone. He set the pan down for a moment and thought long thoughts. Then he finished the washing, and weighed the result in his scales. At the rate of sixteen dollars to the ounce, the pan had contained seven hundred and odd dollars. It was beyond anything that even he had dreamed. His fondest anticipation's had gone no farther than twenty or thirty thousand dollars to a claim; but here were claims worth half a million each at the least, even if they were spotted.

He did not go back to work in the shaft that day, nor the next, nor the next. Instead, capped and mittened, a light stampeding outfit, including his rabbit skin robe, strapped on his back, he was out and away on a many-days' tramp over creeks and divides, inspecting the whole neighboring territory. On each creek he was entitled to locate one claim, but he was chary in thus surrendering up his chances. On Hunker Creek only did he stake a claim. Bonanza Creek he found staked from mouth to source, while every little draw and pup and gulch that drained into it was like-wise staked. Little faith was had in these side-streams. They had been staked by the hundreds of men who had failed to get in on Bonanza. The most popular of these creeks was Adams. The one least fancied was Eldorado, which flowed into Bonanza, just above Karmack's Discovery claim. Even Daylight disliked the looks of Eldorado; but, still riding his hunch, he bought a half share in one claim on it for half a sack of flour. A month later he paid eight hundred dollars for the adjoining claim. Three months later, enlarging this block of property, he paid forty thousand for a third claim; and, though it was concealed in the future, he was destined, not long after, to pay one hundred and fifty thousand for a fourth claim on the creek that had been the least liked of all the creeks.

In the meantime, and from the day he washed seven hundred dollars from a single pan and squatted over it and thought a long thought, he never again touched hand to pick and shovel. As he said to Joe Ladue the night of that wonderful washing:—

"Joe, I ain't never going to work hard again. Here's where I begin to use my brains. I'm going to farm gold. Gold will grow gold if you-all have the savvee and can get hold of some for seed. When I seen them seven hundred dollars in the bottom of the pan, I knew I had the seed at last."

"Where are you going to plant it?" Joe Ladue had asked.

And Daylight, with a wave of his hand, definitely indicated the whole landscape and the creeks that lay beyond the divides.

"There she is," he said, "and you-all just watch my smoke. There's millions here for the man who can see them. And I seen all them millions this afternoon when them seven hundred dollars peeped up at me from the bottom of the pan and chirruped, 'Well, if here ain't Burning Daylight come at last.'"

CHAPTER XI

The hero of the Yukon in the younger days before the Carmack strike, Burning Daylight now became the hero of the strike. The story of his hunch and how he rode it was told up and down the land. Certainly he had ridden it far and away beyond the boldest, for no five of the luckiest held the value in claims that he held. And, furthermore, he was still riding the hunch, and with no diminution of daring. The wise ones shook their heads and prophesied that he would lose every ounce he had won. He was speculating, they contended, as if the whole country was made of gold, and no man could win who played a placer strike in that fashion.

On the other hand, his holdings were reckoned as worth millions, and there were men so sanguine that they held the man a fool who coppered[6] any bet Daylight laid. Behind his magnificent free-handedness and careless disregard for money were hard, practical judgment, imagination and vision, and the daring of the big gambler. He foresaw what with his own eyes he had never seen, and he played to win much or lose all.

"There's too much gold here in Bonanza to be just a pocket," he argued. "It's sure come from a mother-lode somewhere, and other creeks will show up. You-all keep your eyes on Indian River. The creeks that drain that side the Klondike watershed are just as likely to have gold as the creeks that drain this side."

And he backed this opinion to the extent of grub-staking half a dozen parties of prospectors across the big divide into the Indian River region. Other men, themselves failing to stake on lucky creeks, he put to work on his Bonanza claims. And he paid them well—sixteen dollars a day for an eight-hour shift, and he ran three shifts. He had grub to start them on, and when, on the last water, the Bella arrived loaded with provisions, he traded a warehouse site to Jack Kearns for a supply of grub that lasted all his men through the winter of 1896. And that winter, when famine pinched, and flour sold for two dollars a pound, he kept three shifts of men at work on all four of the Bonanza claims. Other mine-owners paid fifteen dollars a day to their men; but he had been the first to put men to work, and from the first he paid them a full ounce a day. One result was that his were picked men, and they more than earned their higher pay.

One of his wildest plays took place in the early winter after the freeze-up. Hundreds of stampeders, after staking on other creeks than Bonanza, had gone on disgruntled down river to Forty Mile and Circle City. Daylight mortgaged one of his Bonanza dumps with the Alaska Commercial Company, and tucked a letter of credit into his pouch. Then he harnessed his dogs and went down on the ice at a pace that only he could travel. One Indian down, another Indian back, and four teams of dogs was his record. And at Forty Mile and Circle City he bought claims by the score. Many of these were to prove utterly worthless, but some few of them were to show up more astoundingly than any on Bonanza. He bought right and left, paying as low as fifty dollars and as high as five thousand. This highest one he bought in the Tivoli Saloon. It was an upper claim on Eldorado, and when he agreed to the price, Jacob Wilkins, an old-timer just returned from a look at the moose-pasture, got up and left the room, saying:—

"Daylight, I've known you seven year, and you've always seemed sensible till now. And now you're just letting them rob you right and left. That's what it is—robbery. Five thousand for a claim on that damned moose-pasture is bunco. I just can't stay in the room and see you buncoed that way."

"I tell you-all," Daylight answered, "Wilkins, Carmack's strike's so big that we-all can't see it all. It's a lottery. Every claim I buy is a ticket. And there's sure going to be some capital prizes."

Jacob Wilkins, standing in the open door, sniffed incredulously.

"Now supposing, Wilkins," Daylight went on, "supposing you-all knew it was going to rain soup. What'd you-all do? Buy spoons, of course. Well, I'm sure buying spoons. She's going to rain soup up there on the Klondike, and them that has forks won't be catching none of it."

But Wilkins here slammed the door behind him, and Daylight broke off to finish the purchase of the claim.

Back in Dawson, though he remained true to his word and never touched hand to pick and shovel, he worked as hard as ever in his life. He had a thousand irons in the fire, and they kept him busy. Representation work was expensive, and he was compelled to travel often over the various creeks in order to decide which claims should lapse and which should be retained. A quartz miner himself in his early youth, before coming to Alaska, he dreamed of finding the mother-lode. A placer camp he knew was ephemeral, while a quartz camp abided, and he kept a score of men in the quest for months. The mother-lode was never found, and, years afterward, he estimated that the search for it had cost him fifty thousand dollars.

But he was playing big. Heavy as were his expenses, he won more heavily. He took lays, bought half shares, shared with the men he grub-staked, and made personal locations. Day and night his dogs were ready, and he owned the fastest teams; so that when a stampede to a new discovery was on, it was Burning Daylight to the fore through the longest, coldest nights till he blazed his stakes next to Discovery. In one way or another (to say nothing of the many worthless creeks) he came into possession of properties on the good creeks, such as Sulphur, Dominion, Excelsis, Siwash, Cristo, Alhambra, and Doolittle. The thousands he poured out flowed back in tens of thousands. Forty Mile men told the story of his two tons of flour, and made calculations of what it had returned him that ranged from half a million to a million. One thing was known beyond all doubt, namely, that the half share in the first Eldorado claim, bought by him for a half sack of flour, was worth five hundred thousand. On the other hand, it was told that when Freda, the dancer, arrived from over the passes in a Peterborough canoe in the midst of a drive of mush-ice on the Yukon, and when she offered a thousand dollars for ten sacks and could find no sellers, he sent the flour to her as a present without ever seeing her. In the same way ten sacks were sent to the lone Catholic priest who was starting the first hospital.

His generosity was lavish. Others called it insane. At a time when, riding his hunch, he was getting half a million for half a sack of flour, it was nothing less than insanity to give twenty whole sacks to a dancing-girl and a priest. But it was his way. Money was only a marker. It was the game that counted with him. The possession of millions made little change in him, except that he played the game more passionately. Temperate as he had always been, save on rare occasions, now that he had the wherewithal for unlimited drinks and had daily access to them, he drank even less. The most radical change lay in that, except when on trail, he no longer did his own cooking. A broken-down miner lived in his log cabin with him and now cooked for him. But it was the same food: bacon, beans, flour, prunes, dried fruits, and rice. He still dressed as formerly: overalls, German socks, moccasins, flannel shirt, fur cap, and blanket coat. He did not take up with cigars, which cost, the cheapest, from half a dollar to a dollar each. The same Bull Durham and brown-paper cigarette, hand-rolled, contented him. It was true that he kept more dogs, and paid enormous prices for them. They were not a luxury, but a matter of business. He needed speed in his travelling and stampeding. And by the same token, he hired a cook. He was too busy to cook for himself, that was all. It was poor business, playing for millions, to spend time building fires and boiling water.

Dawson grew rapidly that winter of 1896. Money poured in on Daylight from the sale of town lots. He promptly invested it where it would gather more. In fact, he played the dangerous game of pyramiding, and no more perilous pyramiding than in a placer camp could be imagined. But he played with his eyes wide open.

"You-all just wait till the news of this strike reaches the Outside," he told his old-timer cronies in the Moosehorn Saloon. "The news won't get out till next spring. Then there's going to be three rushes. A summer rush of men coming in light; a fall rush of men with outfits; and a spring rush, the next year after that, of fifty thousand. You-all won't be able to see the landscape for chechaquos. Well, there's the summer and fall rush of 1897 to commence with. What are you-all going to do about it?"

"What are you going to do about it?" a friend demanded.

"Nothing," he answered. "I've sure already done it. I've got a dozen gangs strung out up the Yukon getting out logs. You-all'll see their rafts coming down after the river breaks. Cabins! They sure will be worth what a man can pay for them next fall. Lumber! It will sure go to top-notch. I've got two sawmills freighting in over the passes. They'll come down as soon as the lakes open up. And if you-all are thinking of needing lumber, I'll make you-all contracts right now—three hundred dollars a thousand, undressed."

Corner lots in desirable locations sold that winter for from ten to thirty thousand dollars. Daylight sent word out over the trails and passes for the newcomers to bring down log-rafts, and, as a result, the summer of 1897 saw his sawmills working day and night, on three shifts, and still he had logs left over with which to build cabins. These cabins, land included, sold at from one to several thousand dollars. Two-story log buildings, in the business part of town, brought him from forty to fifty thousand dollars apiece. These fresh accretions of capital were immediately invested in other ventures. He turned gold over and over, until everything that he touched seemed to turn to gold.

But that first wild winter of Carmack's strike taught Daylight many things. Despite the prodigality of his nature, he had poise. He watched the lavish waste of the mushroom millionaires, and failed quite to understand it. According to his nature and outlook, it was all very well to toss an ante away in a night's frolic. That was what he had done the night of the poker-game in Circle City when he lost fifty thousand—all that he possessed. But he had looked on that fifty thousand as a mere ante. When it came to millions, it was different. Such a fortune was a stake, and was not to be sown on bar-room floors, literally sown, flung broadcast out of the moosehide sacks by drunken millionaires who had lost all sense of proportion. There was McMann, who ran up a single bar-room bill of thirty-eight thousand dollars; and Jimmie the Rough, who spent one hundred thousand a month for four months in riotous living, and then fell down drunk in the snow one March night and was frozen to death; and Swiftwater Bill, who, after spending three valuable claims in an extravagance of debauchery, borrowed three thousand dollars with which to leave the country, and who, out of this sum, because the lady-love that had jilted him liked eggs, cornered the one hundred and ten dozen eggs on the Dawson market, paying twenty-four dollars a dozen for them and promptly feeding them to the wolf-dogs.

Champagne sold at from forty to fifty dollars a quart, and canned oyster stew at fifteen dollars. Daylight indulged in no such luxuries. He did not mind treating a bar-room of men to whiskey at fifty cents a drink, but there was somewhere in his own extravagant nature a sense of fitness and arithmetic that revolted against paying fifteen dollars for the contents of an oyster can. On the other hand, he possibly spent more money in relieving hard-luck cases than did the wildest of the new millionaires on insane debauchery. Father Judge, of the hospital, could have told of far more important donations than that first ten sacks of flour. And old-timers who came to Daylight invariably went away relieved according to their need. But fifty dollars for a quart of fizzy champagne! That was appalling.

And yet he still, on occasion, made one of his old-time hell-roaring nights. But he did so for different reasons. First, it was expected of him because it had been his way in the old days. And second, he could afford it. But he no longer cared quite so much for that form of diversion. He had developed, in a new way, the taste for power. It had become a lust with him. By far the wealthiest miner in Alaska, he wanted to be still wealthier. It was a big game he was playing in, and he liked it better than any other game. In a way, the part he played was creative. He was doing something. And at no time, striking another chord of his nature, could he take the joy in a million-dollar Eldorado dump that was at all equivalent to the joy he took in watching his two sawmills working and the big down river log-rafts swinging into the bank in the big eddy just above Moosehide Mountain. Gold, even on the scales, was, after all, an abstraction. It represented things and the power to do. But the sawmills were the things themselves, concrete and tangible, and they were things that were a means to the doing of more things. They were dreams come true, hard and indubitable realizations of fairy gossamers.

With the summer rush from the Outside came special correspondents for the big newspapers and magazines, and one and all, using unlimited space, they wrote Daylight up; so that, so far as the world was concerned, Daylight loomed the largest figure in Alaska. Of course, after several months, the world became interested in the Spanish War, and forgot all about him; but in the Klondike itself Daylight still remained the most prominent figure. Passing along the streets of Dawson, all heads turned to follow him, and in the saloons chechaquos watched him awesomely, scarcely taking their eyes from him as long as he remained in their range of vision. Not alone was he the richest man in the country, but he was Burning Daylight, the pioneer, the man who, almost in the midst of antiquity of that young land, had crossed the Chilcoot and drifted down the Yukon to meet those elder giants, Al Mayo and Jack McQuestion. He was the Burning Daylight of scores of wild adventures, the man who carried word to the ice-bound whaling fleet across the tundra wilderness to the Arctic Sea, who raced the mail from Circle to Salt Water and back again in sixty days, who saved the whole Tanana tribe from perishing in the winter of '91—in short, the man who smote the chechaquos' imaginations more violently than any other dozen men rolled into one.

He had the fatal facility for self-advertisement. Things he did, no matter how adventitious or spontaneous, struck the popular imagination as remarkable. And the latest thing he had done was always on men's lips, whether it was being first in the heartbreaking stampede to Danish Creek, in killing the record baldface grizzly over on Sulphur Creek, or in winning the single-paddle canoe race on the Queen's Birthday, after being forced to participate at the last moment by the failure of the sourdough representative to appear. Thus, one night in the Moosehorn, he locked horns with Jack Kearns in the long-promised return game of poker. The sky and eight o'clock in the morning were made the limits, and at the close of the game Daylight's winnings were two hundred and thirty thousand dollars. To Jack Kearns, already a several-times millionaire, this loss was not vital. But the whole community was thrilled by the size of the stakes, and each one of the dozen correspondents in the field sent out a sensational article.

[6] To copper: a term in faro, meaning to play a card to lose.

CHAPTER XII

Despite his many sources of revenue, Daylight's pyramiding kept him pinched for cash throughout the first winter. The pay-gravel, thawed on bed-rock and hoisted to the surface, immediately froze again. Thus his dumps, containing several millions of gold, were inaccessible. Not until the returning sun thawed the dumps and melted the water to wash them was he able to handle the gold they contained. And then he found himself with a surplus of gold, deposited in the two newly organized banks; and he was promptly besieged by men and groups of men to enlist his capital in their enterprises.

But he elected to play his own game, and he entered combinations only when they were generally defensive or offensive. Thus, though he had paid the highest wages, he joined the Mine-owners' Association, engineered the fight, and effectually curbed the growing insubordination of the wage-earners. Times had changed. The old days were gone forever. This was a new era, and Daylight, the wealthy mine-owner, was loyal to his class affiliations. It was true, the old-timers who worked for him, in order to be saved from the club of the organized owners, were made foremen over the gang of chechaquos; but this, with Daylight, was a matter of heart, not head. In his heart he could not forget the old days, while with his head he played the economic game according to the latest and most practical methods.

But outside of such group-combinations of exploiters, he refused to bind himself to any man's game. He was playing a great lone hand, and he needed all his money for his own backing. The newly founded stock-exchange interested him keenly. He had never before seen such an institution, but he was quick to see its virtues and to utilize it. Most of all, it was gambling, and on many an occasion not necessary for the advancement of his own schemes, he, as he called it, went the stock-exchange a flutter, out of sheer wantonness and fun.

"It sure beats faro," was his comment one day, when, after keeping the Dawson speculators in a fever for a week by alternate bulling and bearing, he showed his hand and cleaned up what would have been a fortune to any other man.

Other men, having made their strike, had headed south for the States, taking a furlough from the grim Arctic battle. But, asked when he was going Outside, Daylight always laughed and said when he had finished playing his hand. He also added that a man was a fool to quit a game just when a winning hand had been dealt him.

It was held by the thousands of hero-worshipping chechaquos that Daylight was a man absolutely without fear. But Bettles and Dan MacDonald and other sourdoughs shook their heads and laughed as they mentioned women. And they were right. He had always been afraid of them from the time, himself a lad of seventeen, when Queen Anne, of Juneau, made open and ridiculous love to him. For that matter, he never had known women. Born in a mining-camp where they were rare and mysterious, having no sisters, his mother dying while he was an infant, he had never been in contact with them. True, running away from Queen Anne, he had later encountered them on the Yukon and cultivated an acquaintance with them—the pioneer ones who crossed the passes on the trail of the men who had opened up the first diggings. But no lamb had ever walked with a wolf in greater fear and trembling than had he walked with them. It was a matter of masculine pride that he should walk with them, and he had done so in fair seeming; but women had remained to him a closed book, and he preferred a game of solo or seven-up any time.

And now, known as the King of the Klondike, carrying several other royal titles, such as Eldorado King, Bonanza King, the Lumber Baron, and the Prince of the Stampeders, not to omit the proudest appellation of all, namely, the Father of the Sourdoughs, he was more afraid of women than ever. As never before they held out their arms to him, and more women were flocking into the country day by day. It mattered not whether he sat at dinner in the gold commissioner's house, called for the drinks in a dancehall, or submitted to an interview from the woman representative of the New York Sun, one and all of them held out their arms.

There was one exception, and that was Freda, the girl that danced, and to whom he had given the flour. She was the only woman in whose company he felt at ease, for she alone never reached out her arms. And yet it was from her that he was destined to receive next to his severest fright. It came about in the fall of 1897. He was returning from one of his dashes, this time to inspect Henderson, a creek that entered the Yukon just below the Stewart. Winter had come on with a rush, and he fought his way down the Yukon seventy miles in a frail Peterborough canoe in the midst of a run of mush-ice. Hugging the rim-ice that had already solidly formed, he shot across the ice-spewing mouth of the Klondike just in time to see a lone man dancing excitedly on the rim and pointing into the water. Next, he saw the fur-clad body of a woman, face under, sinking in the midst of the driving mush-ice. A lane opening in the swirl of the current, it was a matter of seconds to drive the canoe to the spot, reach to the shoulder in the water, and draw the woman gingerly to the canoe's side. It was Freda. And all might yet have been well with him, had she not, later, when brought back to consciousness, blazed at him with angry blue eyes and demanded: "Why did you? Oh, why did you?"

This worried him. In the nights that followed, instead of sinking immediately to sleep as was his wont, he lay awake, visioning her face and that blue blaze of wrath, and conning her words over and over. They rang with sincerity. The reproach was genuine. She had meant just what she said. And still he pondered.

The next time he encountered her she had turned away from him angrily and contemptuously. And yet again, she came to him to beg his pardon, and she dropped a hint of a man somewhere, sometime,—she said not how,—who had left her with no desire to live. Her speech was frank, but incoherent, and all he gleaned from it was that the event, whatever it was, had happened years before. Also, he gleaned that she had loved the man.

That was the thing—love. It caused the trouble. It was more terrible than frost or famine. Women were all very well, in themselves good to look upon and likable; but along came this thing called love, and they were seared to the bone by it, made so irrational that one could never guess what they would do next.

This Freda-woman was a splendid creature, full-bodied, beautiful, and nobody's fool; but love had come along and soured her on the world, driving her to the Klondike and to suicide so compellingly that she was made to hate the man that saved her life.

Well, he had escaped love so far, just as he had escaped smallpox; yet there it was, as contagious as smallpox, and a whole lot worse in running its course. It made men and women do such fearful and unreasonable things. It was like delirium tremens, only worse. And if he, Daylight, caught it, he might have it as badly as any of them. It was lunacy, stark lunacy, and contagious on top of it all. A half dozen young fellows were crazy over Freda. They all wanted to marry her. Yet she, in turn, was crazy over that some other fellow on the other side of the world, and would have nothing to do with them.

But it was left to the Virgin to give him his final fright. She was found one morning dead in her cabin. A shot through the head had done it, and she had left no message, no explanation. Then came the talk. Some wit, voicing public opinion, called it a case of too much Daylight. She had killed herself because of him. Everybody knew this, and said so. The correspondents wrote it up, and once more Burning Daylight, King of the Klondike, was sensationally featured in the Sunday supplements of the United States. The Virgin had straightened up, so the feature-stories ran, and correctly so. Never had she entered a Dawson City dance-hall. When she first arrived from Circle City, she had earned her living by washing clothes. Next, she had bought a sewing-machine and made men's drill parkas, fur caps, and moosehide mittens. Then she had gone as a clerk into the First Yukon Bank. All this, and more, was known and told, though one and all were agreed that Daylight, while the cause, had been the innocent cause of her untimely end.

And the worst of it was that Daylight knew it was true. Always would he remember that last night he had seen her. He had thought nothing of it at the time; but, looking back, he was haunted by every little thing that had happened. In the light of the tragic event, he could understand everything—her quietness, that calm certitude as if all vexing questions of living had been smoothed out and were gone, and that certain ethereal sweetness about all that she had said and done that had been almost maternal. He remembered the way she had looked at him, how she had laughed when he narrated Mickey Dolan's mistake in staking the fraction on Skookum Gulch. Her laughter had been lightly joyous, while at the same time it had lacked its oldtime robustness. Not that she had been grave or subdued. On the contrary, she had been so patently content, so filled with peace.

She had fooled him, fool that he was. He had even thought that night that her feeling for him had passed, and he had taken delight in the thought, and caught visions of the satisfying future friendship that would be theirs with this perturbing love out of the way.

And then, when he stood at the door, cap in hand, and said good night. It had struck him at the time as a funny and embarrassing thing, her bending over his hand and kissing it. He had felt like a fool, but he shivered now when he looked back on it and felt again the touch of her lips on his hand. She was saying good-by, an eternal good-by, and he had never guessed. At that very moment, and for all the moments of the evening, coolly and deliberately, as he well knew her way, she had been resolved to die. If he had only known it! Untouched by the contagious malady himself, nevertheless he would have married her if he had had the slightest inkling of what she contemplated. And yet he knew, furthermore, that hers was a certain stiff-kneed pride that would not have permitted her to accept marriage as an act of philanthropy. There had really been no saving her, after all. The love-disease had fastened upon her, and she had been doomed from the first to perish of it.

Her one possible chance had been that he, too, should have caught it. And he had failed to catch it. Most likely, if he had, it would have been from Freda or some other woman. There was Dartworthy, the college man who had staked the rich fraction on Bonanza above Discovery. Everybody knew that old Doolittle's daughter, Bertha, was madly in love with him. Yet, when he contracted the disease, of all women, it had been with the wife of Colonel Walthstone, the great Guggenhammer mining expert. Result, three lunacy cases: Dartworthy selling out his mine for one-tenth its value; the poor woman sacrificing her respectability and sheltered nook in society to flee with him in an open boat down the Yukon; and Colonel Walthstone, breathing murder and destruction, taking out after them in another open boat. The whole impending tragedy had moved on down the muddy Yukon, passing Forty Mile and Circle and losing itself in the wilderness beyond. But there it was, love, disorganizing men's and women's lives, driving toward destruction and death, turning topsy-turvy everything that was sensible and considerate, making bawds or suicides out of virtuous women, and scoundrels and murderers out of men who had always been clean and square.

For the first time in his life Daylight lost his nerve. He was badly and avowedly frightened. Women were terrible creatures, and the love-germ was especially plentiful in their neighborhood.

And they were so reckless, so devoid of fear. THEY were not frightened by what had happened to the Virgin. They held out their arms to him more seductively than ever. Even without his fortune, reckoned as a mere man, just past thirty, magnificently strong and equally good-looking and good-natured, he was a prize for most normal women. But when to his natural excellences were added the romance that linked with his name and the enormous wealth that was his, practically every free woman he encountered measured him with an appraising and delighted eye, to say nothing of more than one woman who was not free. Other men might have been spoiled by this and led to lose their heads; but the only effect on him was to increase his fright. As a result he refused most invitations to houses where women might be met, and frequented bachelor boards and the Moosehorn Saloon, which had no dance-hall attached.

CHAPTER XIII

Six thousand spent the winter of 1897 in Dawson, work on the creeks went on apace, while beyond the passes it was reported that one hundred thousand more were waiting for the spring. Late one brief afternoon, Daylight, on the benches between French Hill and Skookum Hill, caught a wider vision of things. Beneath him lay the richest part of Eldorado Creek, while up and down Bonanza he could see for miles. It was a scene of a vast devastation. The hills, to their tops, had been shorn of trees, and their naked sides showed signs of goring and perforating that even the mantle of snow could not hide. Beneath him, in every direction were the cabins of men. But not many men were visible. A blanket of smoke filled the valleys and turned the gray day to melancholy twilight. Smoke arose from a thousand holes in the snow, where, deep down on bed-rock, in the frozen muck and gravel, men crept and scratched and dug, and ever built more fires to break the grip of the frost. Here and there, where new shafts were starting, these fires flamed redly. Figures of men crawled out of the holes, or disappeared into them, or, on raised platforms of hand-hewn timber, windlassed the thawed gravel to the surface, where it immediately froze. The wreckage of the spring washing appeared everywhere—piles of sluice-boxes, sections of elevated flumes, huge water-wheels,—all the debris of an army of gold-mad men.

"It-all's plain gophering," Daylight muttered aloud.

He looked at the naked hills and realized the enormous wastage of wood that had taken place. From this bird's-eye view he realized the monstrous confusion of their excited workings. It was a gigantic inadequacy. Each worked for himself, and the result was chaos. In this richest of diggings it cost out by their feverish, unthinking methods another dollar was left hopelessly in the earth. Given another year, and most of the claims would be worked out, and the sum of the gold taken out would no more than equal what was left behind.

Organization was what was needed, he decided; and his quick imagination sketched Eldorado Creek, from mouth to source, and from mountain top to mountain top, in the hands of one capable management. Even steam-thawing, as yet untried, but bound to come, he saw would be a makeshift. What should be done was to hydraulic the valley sides and benches, and then, on the creek bottom, to use gold-dredges such as he had heard described as operating in California.

There was the very chance for another big killing. He had wondered just what was precisely the reason for the Guggenhammers and the big English concerns sending in their high-salaried experts. That was their scheme. That was why they had approached him for the sale of worked-out claims and tailings. They were content to let the small mine-owners gopher out what they could, for there would be millions in the leavings.

And, gazing down on the smoky inferno of crude effort, Daylight outlined the new game he would play, a game in which the Guggenhammers and the rest would have to reckon with him. Cut along with the delight in the new conception came a weariness. He was tired of the long Arctic years, and he was curious about the Outside—the great world of which he had heard other men talk and of which he was as ignorant as a child. There were games out there to play. It was a larger table, and there was no reason why he with his millions should not sit in and take a hand. So it was, that afternoon on Skookum Hill, that he resolved to play this last best Klondike hand and pull for the Outside.

It took time, however. He put trusted agents to work on the heels of great experts, and on the creeks where they began to buy he likewise bought. Wherever they tried to corner a worked-out creek, they found him standing in the way, owning blocks of claims or artfully scattered claims that put all their plans to naught.

"I play you-all wide open to win—am I right" he told them once, in a heated conference.

Followed wars, truces, compromises, victories, and defeats. By 1898, sixty thousand men were on the Klondike and all their fortunes and affairs rocked back and forth and were affected by the battles Daylight fought. And more and more the taste for the larger game urged in Daylight's mouth. Here he was already locked in grapples with the great Guggenhammers, and winning, fiercely winning. Possibly the severest struggle was waged on Ophir, the veriest of moose-pastures, whose low-grade dirt was valuable only because of its vastness. The ownership of a block of seven claims in the heart of it gave Daylight his grip and they could not come to terms. The Guggenhammer experts concluded that it was too big for him to handle, and when they gave him an ultimatum to that effect he accepted and bought them out.

The plan was his own, but he sent down to the States for competent engineers to carry it out. In the Rinkabilly watershed, eighty miles away, he built his reservoir, and for eighty miles the huge wooden conduit carried the water across country to Ophir. Estimated at three millions, the reservoir and conduit cost nearer four. Nor did he stop with this. Electric power plants were installed, and his workings were lighted as well as run by electricity. Other sourdoughs, who had struck it rich in excess of all their dreams, shook their heads gloomily, warned him that he would go broke, and declined to invest in so extravagant a venture.

But Daylight smiled, and sold out the remainder of his town-site holdings. He sold at the right time, at the height of the placer boom. When he prophesied to his old cronies, in the Moosehorn Saloon, that within five years town lots in Dawson could not be given away, while the cabins would be chopped up for firewood, he was laughed at roundly, and assured that the mother-lode would be found ere that time. But he went ahead, when his need for lumber was finished, selling out his sawmills as well. Likewise, he began to get rid of his scattered holdings on the various creeks, and without thanks to any one he finished his conduit, built his dredges, imported his machinery, and made the gold of Ophir immediately accessible. And he, who five years before had crossed over the divide from Indian River and threaded the silent wilderness, his dogs packing Indian fashion, himself living Indian fashion on straight moose meat, now heard the hoarse whistles calling his hundreds of laborers to work, and watched them toil under the white glare of the arc-lamps.

But having done the thing, he was ready to depart. And when he let the word go out, the Guggenhammers vied with the English concerns and with a new French company in bidding for Ophir and all its plant. The Guggenhammers bid highest, and the price they paid netted Daylight a clean million. It was current rumor that he was worth anywhere from twenty to thirty millions. But he alone knew just how he stood, and that, with his last claim sold and the table swept clean of his winnings, he had ridden his hunch to the tune of just a trifle over eleven millions.

His departure was a thing that passed into the history of the Yukon along with his other deeds. All the Yukon was his guest, Dawson the seat of the festivity. On that one last night no man's dust save his own was good. Drinks were not to be purchased. Every saloon ran open, with extra relays of exhausted bartenders, and the drinks were given away. A man who refused this hospitality, and persisted in paying, found a dozen fights on his hands. The veriest chechaquos rose up to defend the name of Daylight from such insult. And through it all, on moccasined feet, moved Daylight, hell-roaring Burning Daylight, over-spilling with good nature and camaraderie, howling his he-wolf howl and claiming the night as his, bending men's arms down on the bars, performing feats of strength, his bronzed face flushed with drink, his black eyes flashing, clad in overalls and blanket coat, his ear-flaps dangling and his gauntleted mittens swinging from the cord across the shoulders. But this time it was neither an ante nor a stake that he threw away, but a mere marker in the game that he who held so many markers would not miss.

As a night, it eclipsed anything that Dawson had ever seen. It was Daylight's desire to make it memorable, and his attempt was a success. A goodly portion of Dawson got drunk that night. The fall weather was on, and, though the freeze-up of the Yukon still delayed, the thermometer was down to twenty-five below zero and falling. Wherefore, it was necessary to organize gangs of life-savers, who patrolled the streets to pick up drunken men from where they fell in the snow and where an hour's sleep would be fatal. Daylight, whose whim it was to make them drunk by hundreds and by thousands, was the one who initiated this life saving. He wanted Dawson to have its night, but, in his deeper processes never careless nor wanton, he saw to it that it was a night without accident. And, like his olden nights, his ukase went forth that there should be no quarrelling nor fighting, offenders to be dealt with by him personally. Nor did he have to deal with any. Hundreds of devoted followers saw to it that the evilly disposed were rolled in the snow and hustled off to bed. In the great world, where great captains of industry die, all wheels under their erstwhile management are stopped for a minute.

But in the Klondike, such was its hilarious sorrow at the departure of its captain, that for twenty-four hours no wheels revolved. Even great Ophir, with its thousand men on the pay-roll, closed down. On the day after the night there were no men present or fit to go to work.

Next morning, at break of day, Dawson said good-by. The thousands that lined the bank wore mittens and their ear-flaps pulled down and tied. It was thirty below zero, the rim-ice was thickening, and the Yukon carried a run of mush-ice. From the deck of the Seattle, Daylight waved and called his farewells. As the lines were cast off and the steamer swung out into the current, those near him saw the moisture well up in Daylight's eyes. In a way, it was to him departure from his native land, this grim Arctic region which was practically the only land he had known. He tore off his cap and waved it.

"Good-by, you-all!" he called. "Good-by, you-all!"

PART II

CHAPTER I

In no blaze of glory did Burning Daylight descend upon San Francisco. Not only had he been forgotten, but the Klondike along with him. The world was interested in other things, and the Alaskan adventure, like the Spanish War, was an old story. Many things had happened since then. Exciting things were happening every day, and the sensation-space of newspapers was limited. The effect of being ignored, however, was an exhilaration. Big man as he had been in the Arctic game, it merely showed how much bigger was this new game, when a man worth eleven millions, and with a history such as his, passed unnoticed.

He settled down in St. Francis Hotel, was interviewed by the cub-reporters on the hotel-run, and received brief paragraphs of notice for twenty-four hours. He grinned to himself, and began to look around and get acquainted with the new order of beings and things. He was very awkward and very self-possessed. In addition to the stiffening afforded his backbone by the conscious ownership of eleven millions, he possessed an enormous certitude.

Nothing abashed him, nor was he appalled by the display and culture and power around him. It was another kind of wilderness, that was all; and it was for him to learn the ways of it, the signs and trails and water-holes where good hunting lay, and the bad stretches of field and flood to be avoided. As usual, he fought shy of the women. He was still too badly scared to come to close quarters with the dazzling and resplendent creatures his own millions made accessible.

They looked and longed, but he so concealed his timidity that he had all the seeming of moving boldly among them. Nor was it his wealth alone that attracted them. He was too much a man, and too much an unusual type of man. Young yet, barely thirty-six, eminently handsome, magnificently strong, almost bursting with a splendid virility, his free trail-stride, never learned on pavements, and his black eyes, hinting of great spaces and unwearied with the close perspective of the city dwellers, drew many a curious and wayward feminine glance. He saw, grinned knowingly to himself, and faced them as so many dangers, with a cool demeanor that was a far greater personal achievement than had they been famine, frost, or flood.

He had come down to the States to play the man's game, not the woman's game; and the men he had not yet learned. They struck him as soft—soft physically; yet he divined them hard in their dealings, but hard under an exterior of supple softness. It struck him that there was something cat-like about them. He met them in the clubs, and wondered how real was the good-fellowship they displayed and how quickly they would unsheathe their claws and gouge and rend. "That's the proposition," he repeated to himself; "what will they-all do when the play is close and down to brass tacks?" He felt unwarrantably suspicious of them. "They're sure slick," was his secret judgment; and from bits of gossip dropped now and again he felt his judgment well buttressed. On the other hand, they radiated an atmosphere of manliness and the fair play that goes with manliness. They might gouge and rend in a fight—which was no more than natural; but he felt, somehow, that they would gouge and rend according to rule. This was the impression he got of them—a generalization tempered by knowledge that there was bound to be a certain percentage of scoundrels among them.

Several months passed in San Francisco during which time he studied the game and its rules, and prepared himself to take a hand. He even took private instruction in English, and succeeded in eliminating his worst faults, though in moments of excitement he was prone to lapse into "you-all," "knowed," "sure," and similar solecisms. He learned to eat and dress and generally comport himself after the manner of civilized man; but through it all he remained himself, not unduly reverential nor considerative, and never hesitating to stride rough-shod over any soft-faced convention if it got in his way and the provocation were great enough. Also, and unlike the average run of weaker men coming from back countries and far places, he failed to reverence the particular tin gods worshipped variously by the civilized tribes of men. He had seen totems before, and knew them for what they were.

Tiring of being merely an onlooker, he ran up to Nevada, where the new gold-mining boom was fairly started—"just to try a flutter," as he phrased it to himself. The flutter on the Tonopah Stock Exchange lasted just ten days, during which time his smashing, wild-bull game played ducks and drakes with the more stereotyped gamblers, and at the end of which time, having gambled Floridel into his fist, he let go for a net profit of half a million. Whereupon, smacking his lips, he departed for San Francisco and the St. Francis Hotel. It tasted good, and his hunger for the game became more acute.

And once more the papers sensationalized him. BURNING DAYLIGHT was a big-letter headline again. Interviewers flocked about him.

Old files of magazines and newspapers were searched through, and the romantic and historic Elam Harnish, Adventurer of the Frost, King of the Klondike, and father of the Sourdoughs, strode upon the breakfast table of a million homes along with the toast and breakfast foods. Even before his elected time, he was forcibly launched into the game. Financiers and promoters, and all the flotsam and jetsam of the sea of speculation surged upon the shores of his eleven millions. In self-defence he was compelled to open offices. He had made them sit up and take notice, and now, willy-nilly, they were dealing him hands and clamoring for him to play. Well, play he would; he'd show 'em; even despite the elated prophesies made of how swiftly he would be trimmed—prophesies coupled with descriptions of the bucolic game he would play and of his wild and woolly appearance.

He dabbled in little things at first—"stalling for time," as he explained it to Holdsworthy, a friend he had made at the Alta-Pacific Club. Daylight himself was a member of the club, and Holdsworthy had proposed him. And it was well that Daylight played closely at first, for he was astounded by the multitudes of sharks—"ground-sharks," he called them—that flocked about him.

He saw through their schemes readily enough, and even marveled that such numbers of them could find sufficient prey to keep them going. Their rascality and general dubiousness was so transparent that he could not understand how any one could be taken in by them.

And then he found that there were sharks and sharks. Holdsworthy treated him more like a brother than a mere fellow-clubman, watching over him, advising him, and introducing him to the magnates of the local financial world. Holdsworthy's family lived in a delightful bungalow near Menlo Park, and here Daylight spent a number of weekends, seeing a fineness and kindness of home life of which he had never dreamed. Holdsworthy was an enthusiast over flowers, and a half lunatic over raising prize poultry; and these engrossing madnesses were a source of perpetual joy to Daylight, who looked on in tolerant good humor. Such amiable weaknesses tokened the healthfulness of the man, and drew Daylight closer to him. A prosperous, successful business man without great ambition, was Daylight's estimate of him—a man too easily satisfied with the small stakes of the game ever to launch out in big play.

On one such week-end visit, Holdsworthy let him in on a good thing, a good little thing, a brickyard at Glen Ellen. Daylight listened closely to the other's description of the situation. It was a most reasonable venture, and Daylight's one objection was that it was so small a matter and so far out of his line; and he went into it only as a matter of friendship, Holdsworthy explaining that he was himself already in a bit, and that while it was a good thing, he would be compelled to make sacrifices in other directions in order to develop it. Daylight advanced the capital, fifty thousand dollars, and, as he laughingly explained afterward, "I was stung, all right, but it wasn't Holdsworthy that did it half as much as those blamed chickens and fruit-trees of his."

It was a good lesson, however, for he learned that there were few faiths in the business world, and that even the simple, homely faith of breaking bread and eating salt counted for little in the face of a worthless brickyard and fifty thousand dollars in cash.

But the sharks and sharks of various orders and degrees, he concluded, were on the surface. Deep down, he divined, were the integrities and the stabilities. These big captains of industry and masters of finance, he decided, were the men to work with. By the very nature of their huge deals and enterprises they had to play fair. No room there for little sharpers' tricks and bunco games. It was to be expected that little men should salt gold-mines with a shotgun and work off worthless brick-yards on their friends, but in high finance such methods were not worth while. There the men were engaged in developing the country, organizing its railroads, opening up its mines, making accessible its vast natural resources. Their play was bound to be big and stable. "They sure can't afford tin-horn tactics," was his summing up.

So it was that he resolved to leave the little men, the Holdsworthys, alone; and, while he met them in good-fellowship, he chummed with none, and formed no deep friendships. He did not dislike the little men, the men of the Alta-Pacific, for instance. He merely did not elect to choose them for partners in the big game in which he intended to play. What that big game was, even he did not know. He was waiting to find it. And in the meantime he played small hands, investing in several arid-lands reclamation projects and keeping his eyes open for the big chance when it should come along.

And then he met John Dowsett, the great John Dowsett. The whole thing was fortuitous. This cannot be doubted, as Daylight himself knew, it was by the merest chance, when in Los Angeles, that he heard the tuna were running strong at Santa Catalina, and went over to the island instead of returning directly to San Francisco as he had planned. There he met John Dowsett, resting off for several days in the middle of a flying western trip. Dowsett had of course heard of the spectacular Klondike King and his rumored thirty millions, and he certainly found himself interested by the man in the acquaintance that was formed. Somewhere along in this acquaintanceship the idea must have popped into his brain. But he did not broach it, preferring to mature it carefully. So he talked in large general ways, and did his best to be agreeable and win Daylight's friendship.

It was the first big magnate Daylight had met face to face, and he was pleased and charmed. There was such a kindly humanness about the man, such a genial democraticness, that Daylight found it hard to realize that this was THE John Dowsett, president of a string of banks, insurance manipulator, reputed ally of the lieutenants of Standard Oil, and known ally of the Guggenhammers.

Nor did his looks belie his reputation and his manner.

Physically, he guaranteed all that Daylight knew of him. Despite his sixty years and snow-white hair, his hand-shake was firmly hearty, and he showed no signs of decrepitude, walking with a quick, snappy step, making all movements definitely and decisively. His skin was a healthy pink, and his thin, clean lips knew the way to writhe heartily over a joke. He had honest blue eyes of palest blue; they looked out at one keenly and frankly from under shaggy gray brows. His mind showed itself disciplined and orderly, and its workings struck Daylight as having all the certitude of a steel trap. He was a man who KNEW and who never decorated his knowledge with foolish frills of sentiment or emotion. That he was accustomed to command was patent, and every word and gesture tingled with power. Combined with this was his sympathy and tact, and Daylight could note easily enough all the earmarks that distinguished him from a little man of the Holdsworthy caliber. Daylight knew also his history, the prime old American stock from which he had descended, his own war record, the John Dowsett before him who had been one of the banking buttresses of the Cause of the Union, the Commodore Dowsett of the War of 1812 the General Dowsett of Revolutionary fame, and that first far Dowsett, owner of lands and slaves in early New England.

"He's sure the real thing," he told one of his fellow-clubmen afterwards, in the smoking-room of the Alta-Pacific. "I tell you, Gallon, he was a genuine surprise to me. I knew the big ones had to be like that, but I had to see him to really know it. He's one of the fellows that does things. You can see it sticking out all over him. He's one in a thousand, that's straight, a man to tie to. There's no limit to any game he plays, and you can stack on it that he plays right up to the handle. I bet he can lose or win half a dozen million without batting an eye."

Gallon puffed at his cigar, and at the conclusion of the panegyric regarded the other curiously; but Daylight, ordering cocktails, failed to note this curious stare.

"Going in with him on some deal, I suppose," Gallon remarked.

"Nope, not the slightest idea. Here's kindness. I was just explaining that I'd come to understand how these big fellows do big things. Why, d'ye know, he gave me such a feeling that he knew everything, that I was plumb ashamed of myself."

"I guess I could give him cards and spades when it comes to driving a dog-team, though," Daylight observed, after a meditative pause. "And I really believe I could put him on to a few wrinkles in poker and placer mining, and maybe in paddling a birch canoe. And maybe I stand a better chance to learn the game he's been playing all his life than he would stand of learning the game I played up North."

CHAPTER II

It was not long afterward that Daylight came on to New York. A letter from John Dowsett had been the cause—a simple little typewritten letter of several lines. But Daylight had thrilled as he read it. He remembered the thrill that was his, a callow youth of fifteen, when, in Tempas Butte, through lack of a fourth man, Tom Galsworthy, the gambler, had said, "Get in, Kid; take a hand." That thrill was his now. The bald, typewritten sentences seemed gorged with mystery. "Our Mr. Howison will call upon you at your hotel. He is to be trusted. We must not be seen together. You will understand after we have had our talk." Daylight conned the words over and over. That was it. The big game had arrived, and it looked as if he were being invited to sit in and take a hand. Surely, for no other reason would one man so peremptorily invite another man to make a journey across the continent.

They met—thanks to "our" Mr. Howison,—up the Hudson, in a magnificent country home. Daylight, according to instructions, arrived in a private motor-car which had been furnished him. Whose car it was he did not know any more than did he know the owner of the house, with its generous, rolling, tree-studded lawns. Dowsett was already there, and another man whom Daylight recognized before the introduction was begun. It was Nathaniel Letton, and none other. Daylight had seen his face a score of times in the magazines and newspapers, and read about his standing in the financial world and about his endowed University of Daratona. He, likewise, struck Daylight as a man of power, though he was puzzled in that he could find no likeness to Dowsett. Except in the matter of cleanness,—a cleanness that seemed to go down to the deepest fibers of him,—Nathaniel Letton was unlike the other in every particular. Thin to emaciation, he seemed a cold flame of a man, a man of a mysterious, chemic sort of flame, who, under a glacier-like exterior, conveyed, somehow, the impression of the ardent heat of a thousand suns. His large gray eyes were mainly responsible for this feeling, and they blazed out feverishly from what was almost a death's-head, so thin was the face, the skin of which was a ghastly, dull, dead white. Not more than fifty, thatched with a sparse growth of iron-gray hair, he looked several times the age of Dowsett. Yet Nathaniel Letton possessed control—Daylight could see that plainly. He was a thin-faced ascetic, living in a state of high, attenuated calm—a molten planet under a transcontinental ice sheet. And yet, above all most of all, Daylight was impressed by the terrific and almost awful cleanness of the man. There was no dross in him. He had all the seeming of having been purged by fire. Daylight had the feeling that a healthy man-oath would be a deadly offence to his ears, a sacrilege and a blasphemy.

They drank—that is, Nathaniel Letton took mineral water served by the smoothly operating machine of a lackey who inhabited the place, while Dowsett took Scotch and soda and Daylight a cocktail. Nobody seemed to notice the unusualness of a Martini at midnight, though Daylight looked sharply for that very thing; for he had long since learned that Martinis had their strictly appointed times and places. But he liked Martinis, and, being a natural man, he chose deliberately to drink when and how he pleased. Others had noticed this peculiar habit of his, but not so Dowsett and Letton; and Daylight's secret thought was: "They sure wouldn't bat an eye if I called for a glass of corrosive sublimate."

Leon Guggenhammer arrived in the midst of the drink, and ordered Scotch. Daylight studied him curiously. This was one of the great Guggenhammer family; a younger one, but nevertheless one of the crowd with which he had locked grapples in the North. Nor did Leon Guggenhammer fail to mention cognizance of that old affair. He complimented Daylight on his prowess—"The echoes of Ophir came down to us, you know. And I must say, Mr. Daylight—er, Mr. Harnish, that you whipped us roundly in that affair."

Echoes! Daylight could not escape the shock of the phrase—echoes had come down to them of the fight into which he had flung all his strength and the strength of his Klondike millions. The Guggenhammers sure must go some when a fight of that dimension was no more than a skirmish of which they deigned to hear echoes.

"They sure play an almighty big game down here," was his conclusion, accompanied by a corresponding elation that it was just precisely that almighty big game in which he was about to be invited to play a hand. For the moment he poignantly regretted that rumor was not true, and that his eleven millions were not in reality thirty millions. Well, that much he would be frank about; he would let them know exactly how many stacks of chips he could buy.

Leon Guggenhammer was young and fat. Not a day more than thirty, his face, save for the adumbrated puff sacks under the eyes, was as smooth and lineless as a boy's. He, too, gave the impression of cleanness. He showed in the pink of health; his unblemished, smooth-shaven skin shouted advertisement of his splendid physical condition. In the face of that perfect skin, his very fatness and mature, rotund paunch could be nothing other than normal. He was constituted to be prone to fatness, that was all.

The talk soon centred down to business, though Guggenhammer had first to say his say about the forthcoming international yacht race and about his own palatial steam yacht, the Electra, whose recent engines were already antiquated. Dowsett broached the plan, aided by an occasional remark from the other two, while Daylight asked questions. Whatever the proposition was, he was going into it with his eyes open. And they filled his eyes with the practical vision of what they had in mind.

"They will never dream you are with us," Guggenhammer interjected, as the outlining of the matter drew to a close, his handsome Jewish eyes flashing enthusiastically. "They'll think you are raiding on your own in proper buccaneer style."

"Of course, you understand, Mr. Harnish, the absolute need for keeping our alliance in the dark," Nathaniel Letton warned gravely.

Daylight nodded his head. "And you also understand," Letton went on, "that the result can only be productive of good. The thing is legitimate and right, and the only ones who may be hurt are the stock gamblers themselves. It is not an attempt to smash the market. As you see yourself, you are to bull the market. The honest investor will be the gainer."

"Yes, that's the very thing," Dowsett said. "The commercial need for copper is continually increasing. Ward Valley Copper, and all that it stands for,—practically one-quarter of the world's supply, as I have shown you,—is a big thing, how big, even we can scarcely estimate. Our arrangements are made. We have plenty of capital ourselves, and yet we want more. Also, there is too much Ward Valley out to suit our present plans. Thus we kill both birds with one stone—"

"And I am the stone," Daylight broke in with a smile.

"Yes, just that. Not only will you bull Ward Valley, but you will at the same time gather Ward Valley in. This will be of inestimable advantage to us, while you and all of us will profit by it as well. And as Mr. Letton has pointed out, the thing is legitimate and square. On the eighteenth the directors meet, and, instead of the customary dividend, a double dividend will be declared."

"And where will the shorts be then?" Leon Guggenhammer cried excitedly.

"The shorts will be the speculators," Nathaniel Letton explained, "the gamblers, the froth of Wall Street—you understand. The genuine investors will not be hurt. Furthermore, they will have learned for the thousandth time to have confidence in Ward Valley. And with their confidence we can carry through the large developments we have outlined to you."

"There will be all sorts of rumors on the street," Dowsett warned Daylight, "but do not let them frighten you. These rumors may even originate with us. You can see how and why clearly. But rumors are to be no concern of yours. You are on the inside. All you have to do is buy, buy, buy, and keep on buying to the last stroke, when the directors declare the double dividend. Ward Valley will jump so that it won't be feasible to buy after that."

"What we want," Letton took up the strain, pausing significantly to sip his mineral water, "what we want is to take large blocks of Ward Valley off the hands of the public. We could do this easily enough by depressing the market and frightening the holders. And we could do it more cheaply in such fashion. But we are absolute masters of the situation, and we are fair enough to buy Ward Valley on a rising market. Not that we are philanthropists, but that we need the investors in our big development scheme. Nor do we lose directly by the transaction. The instant the action of the directors becomes known, Ward Valley will rush heavenward. In addition, and outside the legitimate field of the transaction, we will pinch the shorts for a very large sum. But that is only incidental, you understand, and in a way, unavoidable. On the other hand, we shall not turn up our noses at that phase of it. The shorts shall be the veriest gamblers, of course, and they will get no more than they deserve."

"And one other thing, Mr. Harnish," Guggenhammer said, "if you exceed your available cash, or the amount you care to invest in the venture, don't fail immediately to call on us. Remember, we are behind you."

"Yes, we are behind you," Dowsett repeated.

Nathaniel Letton nodded his head in affirmation.

"Now about that double dividend on the eighteenth—" John Dowsett drew a slip of paper from his note-book and adjusted his glasses.

"Let me show you the figures. Here, you see..."

And thereupon he entered into a long technical and historical explanation of the earnings and dividends of Ward Valley from the day of its organization.

The whole conference lasted not more than an hour, during which time Daylight lived at the topmost of the highest peak of life that he had ever scaled. These men were big players. They were powers. True, as he knew himself, they were not the real inner circle. They did not rank with the Morgans and Harrimans. And yet they were in touch with those giants and were themselves lesser giants. He was pleased, too, with their attitude toward him. They met him deferentially, but not patronizingly. It was the deference of equality, and Daylight could not escape the subtle flattery of it; for he was fully aware that in experience as well as wealth they were far and away beyond him.

"We'll shake up the speculating crowd," Leon Guggenhammer proclaimed jubilantly, as they rose to go. "And you are the man to do it, Mr. Harnish. They are bound to think you are on your own, and their shears are all sharpened for the trimming of newcomers like you."

"They will certainly be misled," Letton agreed, his eerie gray eyes blazing out from the voluminous folds of the huge Mueller with which he was swathing his neck to the ears. "Their minds run in ruts. It is the unexpected that upsets their stereotyped calculations—any new combination, any strange factor, any fresh variant. And you will be all that to them, Mr. Harnish. And I repeat, they are gamblers, and they will deserve all that befalls them. They clog and cumber all legitimate enterprise. You have no idea of the trouble they cause men like us—sometimes, by their gambling tactics, upsetting the soundest plans, even overturning the stablest institutions."

Dowsett and young Guggenhammer went away in one motor-car, and Letton by himself in another. Daylight, with still in the forefront of his consciousness all that had occurred in the preceding hour, was deeply impressed by the scene at the moment of departure. The three machines stood like weird night monsters at the gravelled foot of the wide stairway under the unlighted porte-cochere. It was a dark night, and the lights of the motor-cars cut as sharply through the blackness as knives would cut through solid substance. The obsequious lackey—the automatic genie of the house which belonged to none of the three men,—stood like a graven statue after having helped them in. The fur-coated chauffeurs bulked dimly in their seats. One after the other, like spurred steeds, the cars leaped into the blackness, took the curve of the driveway, and were gone.

Daylight's car was the last, and, peering out, he caught a glimpse of the unlighted house that loomed hugely through the darkness like a mountain. Whose was it? he wondered. How came they to use it for their secret conference? Would the lackey talk? How about the chauffeurs? Were they trusted men like "our" Mr. Howison? Mystery? The affair was alive with it. And hand in hand with mystery walked Power. He leaned back and inhaled his cigarette. Big things were afoot. The cards were shuffled even the for a mighty deal, and he was in on it. He remembered back to his poker games with Jack Kearns, and laughed aloud. He had played for thousands in those days on the turn of a card; but now he was playing for millions. And on the eighteenth, when that dividend was declared, he chuckled at the confusion that would inevitably descend upon the men with the sharpened shears waiting to trim him—him, Burning Daylight.

CHAPTER III

Back at his hotel, though nearly two in the morning, he found the reporters waiting to interview him. Next morning there were more. And thus, with blare of paper trumpet, was he received by New York. Once more, with beating of toms-toms and wild hullaballoo, his picturesque figure strode across the printed sheet. The King of the Klondike, the hero of the Arctic, the thirty-million-dollar millionaire of the North, had come to New York. What had he come for? To trim the New Yorkers as he had trimmed the Tonopah crowd in Nevada? Wall Street had best watch out, for the wild man of Klondike had just come to town. Or, perchance, would Wall Street trim him? Wall Street had trimmed many wild men; would this be Burning Daylight's fate? Daylight grinned to himself, and gave out ambiguous interviews. It helped the game, and he grinned again, as he meditated that Wall Street would sure have to go some before it trimmed him.

They were prepared for him to play, and, when heavy buying of Ward Valley began, it was quickly decided that he was the operator. Financial gossip buzzed and hummed. He was after the Guggenhammers once more. The story of Ophir was told over again and sensationalized until even Daylight scarcely recognized it. Still, it was all grist to his mill. The stock gamblers were clearly befooled. Each day he increased his buying, and so eager were the sellers that Ward Valley rose but slowly. "It sure beats poker," Daylight whispered gleefully to himself, as he noted the perturbation he was causing. The newspapers hazarded countless guesses and surmises, and Daylight was constantly dogged by a small battalion of reporters. His own interviews were gems. Discovering the delight the newspapers took in his vernacular, in his "you-alls," and "sures," and "surge-ups," he even exaggerated these particularities of speech, exploiting the phrases he had heard other frontiersmen use, and inventing occasionally a new one of his own.

A wildly exciting time was his during the week preceding Thursday the eighteenth. Not only was he gambling as he had never gambled before, but he was gambling at the biggest table in the world and for stakes so large that even the case-hardened habitues of that table were compelled to sit up. In spite of the unlimited selling, his persistent buying compelled Ward Valley steadily to rise, and as Thursday approached, the situation became acute. Something had to smash. How much Ward Valley was this Klondike gambler going to buy? How much could he buy? What was the Ward Valley crowd doing all this time? Daylight appreciated the interviews with them that appeared—interviews delightfully placid and non-committal. Leon Guggenhammer even hazarded the opinion that this Northland Croesus might possibly be making a mistake. But not that they cared, John Dowsett explained. Nor did they object. While in the dark regarding his intentions, of one thing they were certain; namely, that he was bulling Ward Valley. And they did not mind that. No matter what happened to him and his spectacular operations, Ward Valley was all right, and would remain all right, as firm as the Rock of Gibraltar. No; they had no Ward Valley to sell, thank you. This purely fictitious state of the market was bound shortly to pass, and Ward Valley was not to be induced to change the even tenor of its way by any insane stock exchange flurry. "It is purely gambling from beginning to end," were Nathaniel Letton's words; "and we refuse to have anything to do with it or to take notice of it in any way."

During this time Daylight had several secret meetings with his partners—one with Leon Guggenhammer, one with John Dowsett, and two with Mr. Howison. Beyond congratulations, they really amounted to nothing; for, as he was informed, everything was going satisfactorily.

But on Tuesday morning a rumor that was disconcerting came to Daylight's ears. It was also published in the Wall Street Journal, and it was to the effect, on apparently straight inside information, that on Thursday, when the directors of Ward Valley met, instead of the customary dividend being declared, an assessment would be levied. It was the first check Daylight had received. It came to him with a shock that if the thing were so he was a broken man. And it also came to him that all this colossal operating of his was being done on his own money. Dowsett, Guggenhammer, and Letton were risking nothing. It was a panic, short-lived, it was true, but sharp enough while it lasted to make him remember Holdsworthy and the brickyard, and to impel him to cancel all buying orders while he rushed to a telephone.

"Nothing in it—only a rumor," came Leon Guggenhammer's throaty voice in the receiver. "As you know," said Nathaniel Letton, "I am one of the directors, and I should certainly be aware of it were such action contemplated." And John Dowsett: "I warned you against just such rumors. There is not an iota of truth in it—certainly not. I tell you on my honor as a gentleman."

Heartily ashamed of himself for his temporary loss of nerve, Daylight returned to his task. The cessation of buying had turned the Stock Exchange into a bedlam, and down all the line of stocks the bears were smashing. Ward Valley, as the ape, received the brunt of the shock, and was already beginning to tumble. Daylight calmly doubled his buying orders. And all through Tuesday and Wednesday, and Thursday morning, he went on buying, while Ward Valley rose triumphantly higher. Still they sold, and still he bought, exceeding his power to buy many times over, when delivery was taken into account. What of that? On this day the double dividend would be declared, he assured himself. The pinch of delivery would be on the shorts. They would be making terms with him.

And then the thunderbolt struck. True to the rumor, Ward Valley levied the assessment. Daylight threw up his arms. He verified the report and quit. Not alone Ward Valley, but all securities were being hammered down by the triumphant bears. As for Ward Valley, Daylight did not even trouble to learn if it had fetched bottom or was still tumbling. Not stunned, not even bewildered, while Wall Street went mad, Daylight withdrew from the field to think it over. After a short conference with his brokers, he proceeded to his hotel, on the way picking up the evening papers and glancing at the head-lines. BURNING DAYLIGHT CLEANED OUT, he read; DAYLIGHT GETS HIS; ANOTHER WESTERNER FAILS TO FIND EASY MONEY. As he entered his hotel, a later edition announced the suicide of a young man, a lamb, who had followed Daylight's play.

What in hell did he want to kill himself for? was Daylight's muttered comment.

He passed up to his rooms, ordered a Martini cocktail, took off his shoes, and sat down to think. After half an hour he roused himself to take the drink, and as he felt the liquor pass warmingly through his body, his features relaxed into a slow, deliberate, yet genuine grin. He was laughing at himself.

"Buncoed, by gosh!" he muttered.

Then the grin died away, and his face grew bleak and serious. Leaving out his interests in the several Western reclamation projects (which were still assessing heavily), he was a ruined man. But harder hit than this was his pride. He had been so easy. They had gold-bricked him, and he had nothing to show for it. The simplest farmer would have had documents, while he had nothing but a gentleman's agreement, and a verbal one at that. Gentleman's agreement. He snorted over it. John Dowsett's voice, just as he had heard it in the telephone receiver, sounded in his ears the words, "On my honor as a gentleman." They were sneak-thieves and swindlers, that was what they were, and they had given him the double-cross. The newspapers were right. He had come to New York to be trimmed, and Messrs. Dowsett, Letton, and Guggenhammer had done it. He was a little fish, and they had played with him ten days—ample time in which to swallow him, along with his eleven millions. Of course, they had been unloading on him all the time, and now they were buying Ward Valley back for a song ere the market righted itself. Most probably, out of his share of the swag, Nathaniel Letton would erect a couple of new buildings for that university of his. Leon Guggenhammer would buy new engines for that yacht, or a whole fleet of yachts. But what the devil Dowsett would do with his whack, was beyond him—most likely start another string of banks.

And Daylight sat and consumed cocktails and saw back in his life to Alaska, and lived over the grim years in which he had battled for his eleven millions. For a while murder ate at his heart, and wild ideas and sketchy plans of killing his betrayers flashed through his mind. That was what that young man should have done instead of killing himself. He should have gone gunning. Daylight unlocked his grip and took out his automatic pistol—a big Colt's .44. He released the safety catch with his thumb, and operating the sliding outer barrel, ran the contents of the clip through the mechanism. The eight cartridges slid out in a stream. He refilled the clip, threw a cartridge into the chamber, and, with the trigger at full cock, thrust up the safety ratchet. He shoved the weapon into the side pocket of his coat, ordered another Martini, and resumed his seat.

He thought steadily for an hour, but he grinned no more. Lines formed in his face, and in those lines were the travail of the North, the bite of the frost, all that he had achieved and suffered—the long, unending weeks of trail, the bleak tundra shore of Point Barrow, the smashing ice-jam of the Yukon, the battles with animals and men, the lean-dragged days of famine, the long months of stinging hell among the mosquitoes of the Koyokuk, the toil of pick and shovel, the scars and mars of pack-strap and tump-line, the straight meat diet with the dogs, and all the long procession of twenty full years of toil and sweat and endeavor.

At ten o'clock he arose and pored over the city directory. Then he put on his shoes, took a cab, and departed into the night. Twice he changed cabs, and finally fetched up at the night office of a detective agency. He superintended the thing himself, laid down money in advance in profuse quantities, selected the six men he needed, and gave them their instructions. Never, for so simple a task, had they been so well paid; for, to each, in addition to office charges, he gave a five-hundred-dollar bill, with the promise of another if he succeeded. Some time next day, he was convinced, if not sooner, his three silent partners would come together. To each one two of his detectives were to be attached. Time and place was all he wanted to learn.

"Stop at nothing, boys," were his final instructions. "I must have this information. Whatever you do, whatever happens, I'll sure see you through."

Returning to his hotel, he changed cabs as before, went up to his room, and with one more cocktail for a nightcap, went to bed and to sleep. In the morning he dressed and shaved, ordered breakfast and the newspapers sent up, and waited. But he did not drink. By nine o'clock his telephone began to ring and the reports to come in. Nathaniel Letton was taking the train at Tarrytown. John Dowsett was coming down by the subway. Leon Guggenhammer had not stirred out yet, though he was assuredly within. And in this fashion, with a map of the city spread out before him, Daylight followed the movements of his three men as they drew together. Nathaniel Letton was at his offices in the Mutual-Solander Building. Next arrived Guggenhammer. Dowsett was still in his own offices. But at eleven came the word that he also had arrived, and several minutes later Daylight was in a hired motor-car and speeding for the Mutual-Solander Building.

CHAPTER IV

Nathaniel Letton was talking when the door opened; he ceased, and with his two companions gazed with controlled perturbation at Burning Daylight striding into the room. The free, swinging movements of the trail-traveler were unconsciously exaggerated in that stride of his. In truth, it seemed to him that he felt the trail beneath his feet.

"Howdy, gentlemen, howdy," he remarked, ignoring the unnatural calm with which they greeted his entrance. He shook hands with them in turn, striding from one to another and gripping their hands so heartily that Nathaniel Letton could not forbear to wince. Daylight flung himself into a massive chair and sprawled lazily, with an appearance of fatigue. The leather grip he had brought into the room he dropped carelessly beside him on the floor.

"Goddle mighty, but I've sure been going some," he sighed. "We sure trimmed them beautiful. It was real slick. And the beauty of the play never dawned on me till the very end. It was pure and simple knock down and drag out. And the way they fell for it was amazin'."

The geniality in his lazy Western drawl reassured them. He was not so formidable, after all. Despite the act that he had effected an entrance in the face of Letton's instructions to the outer office, he showed no indication of making a scene or playing rough.

"Well," Daylight demanded good-humoredly, "ain't you-all got a good word for your pardner? Or has his sure enough brilliance plumb dazzled you-all?"

Letton made a dry sound in his throat. Dowsett sat quietly and waited, while Leon Guggenhammer struggled into articulation.

"You have certainly raised Cain," he said.

Daylight's black eyes flashed in a pleased way.

"Didn't I, though!" he proclaimed jubilantly. "And didn't we fool'em! I was totally surprised. I never dreamed they would be that easy.

"And now," he went on, not permitting the pause to grow awkward, "we-all might as well have an accounting. I'm pullin' West this afternoon on that blamed Twentieth Century." He tugged at his grip, got it open, and dipped into it with both his hands. "But don't forget, boys, when you-all want me to hornswoggle Wall Street another flutter, all you-all have to do is whisper the word. I'll sure be right there with the goods."

His hands emerged, clutching a great mass of stubs, check-books, and broker's receipts. These he deposited in a heap on the big table, and dipping again, he fished out the stragglers and added them to the pile. He consulted a slip of paper, drawn from his coat pocket, and read aloud:—

"Ten million twenty-seven thousand and forty-two dollars and sixty-eight cents is my figurin' on my expenses. Of course that-all's taken from the winnings before we-all get to figurin' on the whack-up. Where's your figures? It must a' been a Goddle mighty big clean-up."

The three men looked their bepuzzlement at one another. The man was a bigger fool than they had imagined, or else he was playing a game which they could not divine.

Nathaniel Letton moistened his lips and spoke up.

"It will take some hours yet, Mr. Harnish, before the full accounting can be made. Mr. Howison is at work upon it now. We—ah—as you say, it has been a gratifying clean-up.

Suppose we have lunch together and talk it over. I'll have the clerks work through the noon hour, so that you will have ample time to catch your train."

Dowsett and Guggenhammer manifested a relief that was almost obvious. The situation was clearing. It was disconcerting, under the circumstances, to be pent in the same room with this heavy-muscled, Indian-like man whom they had robbed. They remembered unpleasantly the many stories of his strength and recklessness. If Letton could only put him off long enough for them to escape into the policed world outside the office door, all would be well; and Daylight showed all the signs of being put off.

"I'm real glad to hear that," he said. "I don't want to miss that train, and you-all have done me proud, gentlemen, letting me in on this deal. I just do appreciate it without being able to express my feelings. But I am sure almighty curious, and I'd like terrible to know, Mr. Letton, what your figures of our winning is. Can you-all give me a rough estimate?"

Nathaniel Letton did not look appealingly at his two friends, but in the brief pause they felt that appeal pass out from him. Dowsett, of sterner mould than the others, began to divine that the Klondiker was playing. But the other two were still older the blandishment of his child-like innocence.

"It is extremely—er—difficult," Leon Guggenhammer began. "You see, Ward Valley has fluctuated so, er—"

"That no estimate can possibly be made in advance," Letton supplemented.

"Approximate it, approximate it," Daylight counselled cheerfully.

"It don't hurt if you-all are a million or so out one side or the other. The figures'll straighten that up. But I'm that curious I'm just itching all over. What d'ye say?"

"Why continue to play at cross purposes?" Dowsett demanded abruptly and coldly. "Let us have the explanation here and now. Mr. Harnish is laboring under a false impression, and he should be set straight. In this deal—"

But Daylight interrupted. He had played too much poker to be unaware or unappreciative of the psychological factor, and he headed Dowsett off in order to play the denouncement of the present game in his own way.

"Speaking of deals," he said, "reminds me of a poker game I once seen in Reno, Nevada. It wa'n't what you-all would call a square game. They-all was tin-horns that sat in. But they was a tenderfoot—short-horns they-all are called out there. He stands behind the dealer and sees that same dealer give hisself four aces offen the bottom of the deck. The tenderfoot is sure shocked. He slides around to the player facin' the dealer across the table.

"'Say,' he whispers, 'I seen the dealer deal hisself four aces.'

"'Well, an' what of it?" says the player.

"'I'm tryin' to tell you-all because I thought you-all ought to know,' says the tenderfoot. 'I tell you-all I seen him deal hisself four aces.'

"'Say, mister,' says the player, 'you-all'd better get outa here. You-all don't understand the game. It's his deal, ain't it?'"

The laughter that greeted his story was hollow and perfunctory, but Daylight appeared not to notice it.

"Your story has some meaning, I suppose," Dowsett said pointedly.

Daylight looked at him innocently and did not reply. He turned jovially to Nathaniel Letton.

"Fire away," he said. "Give us an approximation of our winning. As I said before, a million out one way or the other won't matter, it's bound to be such an almighty big winning." By this time Letton was stiffened by the attitude Dowsett had taken, and his answer was prompt and definite.

"I fear you are under a misapprehension, Mr. Harnish. There are no winnings to be divided with you. Now don't get excited, I beg of you. I have but to press this button..."

Far from excited, Daylight had all the seeming of being stunned. He felt absently in his vest pocket for a match, lighted it, and discovered that he had no cigarette. The three men watched him with the tense closeness of cats. Now that it had come, they knew that they had a nasty few minutes before them.

"Do you-all mind saying that over again?" Daylight said. "Seems to me I ain't got it just exactly right. You-all said...?"

He hung with painful expectancy on Nathaniel Letton's utterance.

"I said you were under a misapprehension, Mr. Harnish, that was all. You have been stock gambling, and you have been hard hit. But neither Ward Valley, nor I, nor my associates, feel that we owe you anything."

Daylight pointed at the heap of receipts and stubs on the table.

"That-all represents ten million twenty-seven thousand and forty-two dollars and sixty-eight cents, hard cash. Ain't it good for anything here?"

Letton smiled and shrugged his shoulders.

Daylight looked at Dowsett and murmured:—

"I guess that story of mine had some meaning, after all." He laughed in a sickly fashion. "It was your deal all right, and you-all dole them right, too. Well, I ain't kicking. I'm like the player in that poker game. It was your deal, and you-all had a right to do your best. And you done it—cleaned me out slicker'n a whistle."

He gazed at the heap on the table with an air of stupefaction.

"And that-all ain't worth the paper it's written on. Gol dast it, you-all can sure deal 'em 'round when you get a chance. Oh, no, I ain't a-kicking. It was your deal, and you-all certainly done me, and a man ain't half a man that squeals on another man's deal. And now the hand is played out, and the cards are on the table, and the deal's over, but..."

His hand, dipping swiftly into his inside breast pocket, appeared with the big Colt's automatic.

"As I was saying, the old deal's finished. Now it's MY deal, and I'm a-going to see if I can hold them four aces—

"Take your hand away, you whited sepulchre!" he cried sharply.

Nathaniel Letton's hand, creeping toward the push-button on the desk, was abruptly arrested.

"Change chairs," Daylight commanded. "Take that chair over there, you gangrene-livered skunk. Jump! By God! or I'll make you leak till folks'll think your father was a water hydrant and your mother a sprinkling-cart. You-all move your chair alongside, Guggenhammer; and you-all Dowsett, sit right there, while I just irrelevantly explain the virtues of this here automatic. She's loaded for big game and she goes off eight times. She's a sure hummer when she gets started.

"Preliminary remarks being over, I now proceed to deal. Remember, I ain't making no remarks about your deal. You done your darndest, and it was all right. But this is my deal, and it's up to me to do my darndest. In the first place, you-all know me. I'm Burning Daylight—savvee? Ain't afraid of God, devil, death, nor destruction. Them's my four aces, and they sure copper your bets. Look at that there living skeleton. Letton, you're sure afraid to die. Your bones is all rattling together you're that scared. And look at that fat Jew there. This little weapon's sure put the fear of God in his heart. He's yellow as a sick persimmon. Dowsett, you're a cool one. You-all ain't batted an eye nor turned a hair. That's because you're great on arithmetic. And that makes you-all dead easy in this deal of mine. You're sitting there and adding two and two together, and you-all know I sure got you skinned. You know me, and that I ain't afraid of nothing. And you-all adds up all your money and knows you ain't a-going to die if you can help it."

"I'll see you hanged," was Dowsett's retort.

"Not by a damned sight. When the fun starts, you're the first I plug. I'll hang all right, but you-all won't live to see it. You-all die here and now while I'll die subject to the law's delay—savvee? Being dead, with grass growing out of your carcasses, you won't know when I hang, but I'll sure have the pleasure a long time of knowing you-all beat me to it."

Daylight paused.

"You surely wouldn't kill us?" Letton asked in a queer, thin voice.

Daylight shook his head.

"It's sure too expensive. You-all ain't worth it. I'd sooner have my chips back. And I guess you-all'd sooner give my chips back than go to the dead-house."

A long silence followed.

"Well, I've done dealt. It's up to you-all to play. But while you're deliberating, I want to give you-all a warning: if that door opens and any one of you cusses lets on there's anything unusual, right here and then I sure start plugging. They ain't a soul'll get out the room except feet first."

A long session of three hours followed. The deciding factor was not the big automatic pistol, but the certitude that Daylight would use it. Not alone were the three men convinced of this, but Daylight himself was convinced. He was firmly resolved to kill the men if his money was not forthcoming. It was not an easy matter, on the spur of the moment, to raise ten millions in paper currency, and there were vexatious delays. A dozen times Mr. Howison and the head clerk were summoned into the room. On these occasions the pistol lay on Daylight's lap, covered carelessly by a newspaper, while he was usually engaged in rolling or lighting his brown-paper cigarettes. But in the end, the thing was accomplished. A suit-case was brought up by one of the clerks from the waiting motor-car, and Daylight snapped it shut on the last package of bills. He paused at the door to make his final remarks.

"There's three several things I sure want to tell you-all. When I get outside this door, you-all'll be set free to act, and I just want to warn you-all about what to do. In the first place, no warrants for my arrest—savvee? This money's mine, and I ain't robbed you of it. If it gets out how you gave me the double-cross and how I done you back again, the laugh'll be on you, and it'll sure be an almighty big laugh. You-all can't afford that laugh. Besides, having got back my stake that you-all robbed me of, if you arrest me and try to rob me a second time, I'll go gunning for you-all, and I'll sure get you. No little fraid-cat shrimps like you-all can skin

Burning Daylight. If you win you lose, and there'll sure be some several unexpected funerals around this burg.

"Just look me in the eye, and you-all'll savvee I mean business. Them stubs and receipts on the table is all yourn. Good day."

As the door shut behind him, Nathaniel Letton sprang for the telephone, and Dowsett intercepted him.

"What are you going to do?" Dowsett demanded.

"The police. It's downright robbery. I won't stand it. I tell you I won't stand it."

Dowsett smiled grimly, but at the same time bore the slender financier back and down into his chair.

"We'll talk it over," he said; and in Leon Guggenhammer he found an anxious ally.

And nothing ever came of it. The thing remained a secret with the three men. Nor did Daylight ever give the secret away, though that afternoon, leaning back in his stateroom on the Twentieth Century, his shoes off, and feet on a chair, he chuckled long and heartily. New York remained forever puzzled over the affair; nor could it hit upon a rational explanation. By all rights, Burning Daylight should have gone broke, yet it was known that he immediately reappeared in San Francisco possessing an apparently unimpaired capital. This was evidenced by the magnitude of the enterprises he engaged in, such as, for instance, Panama Mail, by sheer weight of money and fighting power wresting the control away from Shiftily and selling out in two months to the Harriman interests at a rumored enormous advance.

CHAPTER V

Back in San Francisco, Daylight quickly added to his reputation In ways it was not an enviable reputation. Men were afraid of him. He became known as a fighter, a fiend, a tiger. His play was a ripping and smashing one, and no one knew where or how his next blow would fall. The element of surprise was large. He balked on the unexpected, and, fresh from the wild North, his mind not operating in stereotyped channels, he was able in unusual degree to devise new tricks and stratagems. And once he won the advantage, he pressed it remorselessly. "As relentless as a Red Indian," was said of him, and it was said truly.

On the other hand, he was known as "square." His word was as good as his bond, and this despite the fact that he accepted nobody's word. He always shied at propositions based on gentlemen's agreements, and a man who ventured his honor as a gentleman, in dealing with Daylight, inevitably was treated to an unpleasant time. Daylight never gave his own word unless he held the whip-hand. It was a case with the other fellow taking it or nothing.

Legitimate investment had no place in Daylight's play. It tied up his money, and reduced the element of risk. It was the gambling side of business that fascinated him, and to play in his slashing manner required that his money must be ready to hand. It was never tied up save for short intervals, for he was principally engaged in turning it over and over, raiding here, there, and everywhere, a veritable pirate of the financial main. A five-per cent safe investment had no attraction for him; but to risk millions in sharp, harsh skirmish, standing to lose everything or to win fifty or a hundred per cent, was the savor of life to him. He played according to the rules of the game, but he played mercilessly. When he got a man or a corporation down and they squealed, he gouged no less hard. Appeals for financial mercy fell on deaf ears. He was a free lance, and had no friendly business associations. Such alliances as were formed from time to time were purely affairs of expediency, and he regarded his allies as men who would give him the double-cross or ruin him if a profitable chance presented. In spite of this point of view, he was faithful to his allies. But he was faithful just as long as they were and no longer. The treason had to come from them, and then it was 'Ware Daylight.

The business men and financiers of the Pacific coast never forgot the lesson of Charles Klinkner and the California & Altamont Trust Company. Klinkner was the president. In partnership with Daylight, the pair raided the San Jose Interurban. The powerful Lake Power & Electric Lighting corporation came to the rescue, and Klinkner, seeing what he thought was the opportunity, went over to the enemy in the thick of the pitched battle. Daylight lost three millions before he was done with it, and before he was done with it he saw the California & Altamont Trust Company hopelessly wrecked, and Charles Klinkner a suicide in a felon's cell. Not only did Daylight lose his grip on San Jose Interurban, but in the crash of his battle front he lost heavily all along the line. It was conceded by those competent to judge that he could have compromised and saved much. But, instead, he deliberately threw up the battle with San Jose Interurban and Lake Power, and, apparently defeated, with Napoleonic suddenness struck at Klinkner. It was the last unexpected thing Klinkner would have dreamed of, and Daylight knew it. He knew, further, that the California & Altamont Trust Company has an intrinsically sound institution, but that just then it was in a precarious condition due to Klinkner's speculations with its money. He knew, also, that in a few months the Trust Company would be more firmly on its feet than ever, thanks to those same speculations, and that if he were to strike he must strike immediately. "It's just that much money in pocket and a whole lot more," he was reported to have said in connection with his heavy losses. "It's just so much insurance against the future. Henceforth, men who go in with me on deals will think twice before they try to double-cross me, and then some."

The reason for his savageness was that he despised the men with whom he played. He had a conviction that not one in a hundred of them was intrinsically square; and as for the square ones, he prophesied that, playing in a crooked game, they were sure to lose and in the long run go broke. His New York experience had opened his eyes. He tore the veils of illusion from the business game, and saw its nakedness. He generalized upon industry and society somewhat as follows:—

Society, as organized, was a vast bunco game. There were many hereditary inefficients—men and women who were not weak enough to be confined in feeble-minded homes, but who were not strong enough to be ought else than hewers of wood and drawers of water.

Then there were the fools who took the organized bunco game seriously, honoring and respecting it. They were easy game for the others, who saw clearly and knew the bunco game for what it was.

Work, legitimate work, was the source of all wealth. That was to say, whether it was a sack of potatoes, a grand piano, or a seven-passenger touring car, it came into being only by the performance of work. Where the bunco came in was in the distribution of these things after labor had created them. He failed to see the horny-handed sons of toil enjoying grand pianos or riding in automobiles. How this came about was explained by the bunco. By tens of thousands and hundreds of thousands men sat up nights and schemed how they could get between the workers and the things the workers produced. These schemers were the business men. When they got between the worker and his product, they took a whack out of it for themselves The size of the whack was determined by no rule of equity; but by their own strength and swinishness. It was always a case of "all the traffic can bear." He saw all men in the business game doing this.

One day, in a mellow mood (induced by a string of cocktails and a hearty lunch), he started a conversation with Jones, the elevator boy. Jones was a slender, mop-headed, man-grown, truculent flame of an individual who seemed to go out of his way to insult his passengers. It was this that attracted Daylight's interest, and he was not long in finding out what was the matter with Jones. He was a proletarian, according to his own aggressive classification, and he had wanted to write for a living. Failing to win with the magazines, and compelled to find himself in food and shelter, he had gone to the little valley of Petacha, not a hundred miles from Los Angeles. Here, toiling in the day-time, he planned to write and study at night. But the railroad charged all the traffic would bear. Petacha was a desert valley, and produced only three things: cattle, fire-wood, and charcoal. For freight to Los Angeles on a carload of cattle the railroad charged eight dollars. This, Jones explained, was due to the fact that the cattle had legs and could be driven to Los Angeles at a cost equivalent to the charge per car load. But firewood had no legs, and the railroad charged just precisely twenty-four dollars a carload.

This was a fine adjustment, for by working hammer-and-tongs through a twelve-hour day, after freight had been deducted from the selling price of the wood in Los Angeles, the woodchopper received one dollar and sixty cents. Jones had thought to get ahead of the game by turning his wood into charcoal. His estimates were satisfactory. But the railroad also made estimates. It issued a rate of forty-two dollars a car on charcoal. At the end of three months, Jones went over his figures, and found that he was still making one dollar and sixty cents a day.

"So I quit," Jones concluded. "I went hobbling for a year, and I got back at the railroads. Leaving out the little things, I came across the Sierras in the summer and touched a match to the snow-sheds. They only had a little thirty-thousand-dollar fire. I guess that squared up all balances due on Petacha."

"Son, ain't you afraid to be turning loose such information?" Daylight gravely demanded.

"Not on your life," quoth Jones. "They can't prove it. You could say I said so, and I could say I didn't say so, and a hell of a lot that evidence would amount to with a jury."

Daylight went into his office and meditated awhile. That was it: all the traffic would bear. From top to bottom, that was the rule of the game; and what kept the game going was the fact that a sucker was born every minute. If a Jones were born every minute, the game wouldn't last very long. Lucky for the players that the workers weren't Joneses.

But there were other and larger phases of the game. Little business men, shopkeepers, and such ilk took what whack they could out of the product of the worker; but, after all, it was the large business men who formed the workers through the little business men. When all was said and done, the latter, like Jones in Petacha Valley, got no more than wages out of their whack. In truth, they were hired men for the large business men. Still again, higher up, were the big fellows. They used vast and complicated paraphernalia for the purpose, on a large scale of getting between hundreds of thousands of workers and their products. These men were not so much mere robbers as gamblers. And, not content with their direct winnings, being essentially gamblers, they raided one another. They called this feature of the game HIGH FINANCE. They were all engaged primarily in robbing the worker, but every little while they formed combinations and robbed one another of the accumulated loot. This explained the fifty-thousand-dollar raid on him by Holdsworthy and the ten-million-dollar raid on him by Dowsett, Letton, and Guggenhammer. And when he raided Panama Mail he had done exactly the same thing. Well, he concluded, it was finer sport robbing the robbers than robbing the poor stupid workers.

Thus, all unread in philosophy, Daylight preempted for himself the position and vocation of a twentieth-century superman. He found, with rare and mythical exceptions, that there was no noblesse oblige among the business and financial supermen. As a clever traveler had announced in an after-dinner speech at the Alta-Pacific, "There was honor amongst thieves, and this was what distinguished thieves from honest men." That was it. It hit the nail on the head. These modern supermen were a lot of sordid banditti who had the successful effrontery to preach a code of right and wrong to their victims which they themselves did not practise. With them, a man's word was good just as long as he was compelled to keep it. THOU SHALT NOT STEAL was only applicable to the honest worker. They, the supermen, were above such commandments. They certainly stole and were honored by their fellows according to the magnitude of their stealings.

The more Daylight played the game, the clearer the situation grew. Despite the fact that every robber was keen to rob every other robber, the band was well organized. It practically controlled the political machinery of society, from the ward politician up to the Senate of the

United States. It passed laws that gave it privilege to rob. It enforced these laws by means of the police, the marshals, the militia and regular army, and the courts. And it was a snap. A superman's chiefest danger was his fellow-superman. The great stupid mass of the people did not count. They were constituted of such inferior clay that the veriest chicanery fooled them. The superman manipulated the strings, and when robbery of the workers became too slow or monotonous, they turned loose and robbed one another.

Daylight was philosophical, but not a philosopher. He had never read the books. He was a hard-headed, practical man, and farthest from him was any intention of ever reading the books. He had lived life in the simple, where books were not necessary for an understanding of life, and now life in the complex appeared just as simple. He saw through its frauds and fictions, and found it as elemental as on the Yukon. Men were made of the same stuff. They had the same passions and desires. Finance was poker on a larger scale. The men who played were the men who had stakes. The workers were the fellows toiling for grubstakes. He saw the game played out according to the everlasting rules, and he played a hand himself. The gigantic futility of humanity organized and befuddled by the bandits did not shock him. It was the natural order. Practically all human endeavors were futile. He had seen so much of it. His partners had starved and died on the Stewart. Hundreds of old-timers had failed to locate on Bonanza and Eldorado, while Swedes and chechaquos had come in on the moose-pasture and blindly staked millions. It was life, and life was a savage proposition at best. Men in civilization robbed because they were so made. They robbed just as cats scratched, famine pinched, and frost bit.

So it was that Daylight became a successful financier. He did not go in for swindling the workers. Not only did he not have the heart for it, but it did not strike him as a sporting proposition. The workers were so easy, so stupid. It was more like slaughtering fat hand-reared pheasants on the English preserves he had heard about. The sport to him, was in waylaying the successful robbers and taking their spoils from them. There was fun and excitement in that, and sometimes they put up the very devil of a fight. Like Robin Hood of old, Daylight proceeded to rob the rich; and, in a small way, to distribute to the needy.

But he was charitable after his own fashion. The great mass of human misery meant nothing to him. That was part of the everlasting order. He had no patience with the organized charities and the professional charity mongers. Nor, on the other hand, was what he gave a conscience dole. He owed no man, and restitution was unthinkable. What he gave was a largess, a free, spontaneous gift; and it was for those about him. He never contributed to an earthquake fund in Japan nor to an open-air fund in New York City. Instead, he financed Jones, the elevator boy, for a year that he might write a book. When he learned that the wife of his waiter at the St. Francis was suffering from tuberculosis, he sent her to Arizona, and later, when her case was declared hopeless, he sent the husband, too, to be with her to the end. Likewise, he bought a string of horse-hair bridles from a convict in a Western penitentiary, who spread the good news until it seemed to Daylight that half the convicts in that institution were making bridles for him. He bought them all, paying from twenty to fifty dollars each for them. They were beautiful and honest things, and he decorated all the available wall-space of his bedroom with them.

The grim Yukon life had failed to make Daylight hard. It required civilization to produce this result. In the fierce, savage game he now played, his habitual geniality imperceptibly slipped away from him, as did his lazy Western drawl. As his speech became sharp and nervous, so did his mental processes. In the swift rush of the game he found less and less time to spend on being merely good-natured. The change marked his face itself.

The lines grew sterner. Less often appeared the playful curl of his lips, the smile in the wrinkling corners of his eyes. The eyes themselves, black and flashing, like an Indian's, betrayed glints of cruelty and brutal consciousness of power. His tremendous vitality remained, and radiated from all his being, but it was vitality under the new aspect of the man-trampling man-conqueror. His battles with elemental nature had been, in a way, impersonal; his present battles were wholly with the males of his species, and the hardships of the trail, the river, and the frost marred him far less than the bitter keenness of the struggle with his fellows.

He still had recrudescence of geniality, but they were largely periodical and forced, and they were usually due to the cocktails he took prior to meal-time. In the North, he had drunk deeply and at irregular intervals; but now his drinking became systematic and disciplined. It was an unconscious development, but it was based upon physical and mental condition. The cocktails served as an inhibition. Without reasoning or thinking about it, the strain of the office, which was essentially due to the daring and audacity of his ventures, required check or cessation; and he found, through the weeks and months, that the cocktails supplied this very thing. They constituted a stone wall. He never drank during the morning, nor in office hours; but the instant he left the office he proceeded to rear this wall of alcoholic inhibition athwart his consciousness. The office became immediately a closed affair. It ceased to exist. In the afternoon, after lunch, it lived again for one or two hours, when, leaving it, he rebuilt the wall of inhibition. Of course, there were exceptions to this; and, such was the rigor of his discipline, that if he had a dinner or a conference before him in which, in a business way, he encountered enemies or allies and planned or prosecuted campaigns, he abstained from drinking. But the instant the business was settled, his everlasting call went out for a Martini, and for a double-Martini at that, served in a long glass so as not to excite comment.

CHAPTER VI

Into Daylight's life came Dede Mason. She came rather imperceptibly. He had accepted her impersonally along with the office furnishing, the office boy, Morrison, the chief, confidential, and only clerk, and all the rest of the accessories of a superman's gambling place of business. Had he been asked any time during the first months she was in his employ, he would have been unable to tell the color of her eyes. From the fact that she was a demiblonde, there resided dimly in his subconsciousness a conception that she was a brunette. Likewise he had an idea that she was not thin, while there was an absence in his mind of any idea that she was fat. As to how she dressed, he had no ideas at all. He had no trained eye in such matters, nor was he interested. He took it for granted, in the lack of any impression to the contrary, that she was dressed some how. He knew her as "Miss Mason," and that was all, though he was aware that as a stenographer she seemed quick and accurate. This impression, however, was quite vague, for he had had no experience with other stenographers, and naturally believed that they were all quick and accurate.

One morning, signing up letters, he came upon an I shall. Glancing quickly over the page for similar constructions, he found a number of I wills. The I shall was alone. It stood out conspicuously. He pressed the call-bell twice, and a moment later Dede Mason entered. "Did I say that, Miss Mason?" he asked, extending the letter to her and pointing out the criminal phrase. A shade of annoyance crossed her face. She stood convicted.

"My mistake," she said. "I am sorry. But it's not a mistake, you know," she added quickly.

"How do you make that out?" challenged Daylight. "It sure don't sound right, in my way of thinking."

She had reached the door by this time, and now turned the offending letter in her hand. "It's right just the same."

"But that would make all those I wills wrong, then," he argued.

"It does," was her audacious answer. "Shall I change them?"

"I shall be over to look that affair up on Monday." Daylight repeated the sentence from the letter aloud. He did it with a grave, serious air, listening intently to the sound of his own voice. He shook his head. "It don't sound right, Miss Mason. It just don't sound right. Why, nobody writes to me that way. They all say I will—educated men, too, some of them. Ain't that so?"

"Yes," she acknowledged, and passed out to her machine to make the correction.

It chanced that day that among the several men with whom he sat at luncheon was a young Englishman, a mining engineer. Had it happened any other time it would have passed unnoticed, but, fresh from the tilt with his stenographer, Daylight was struck immediately by the Englishman's I shall. Several times, in the course of the meal, the phrase was repeated, and Daylight was certain there was no mistake about it.

After luncheon he cornered Macintosh, one of the members whom he knew to have been a college man, because of his football reputation.

"Look here, Bunny," Daylight demanded, "which is right, I shall be over to look that affair up on Monday, or I will be over to look that affair up on Monday?"

The ex-football captain debated painfully for a minute. "Blessed if I know," he confessed. "Which way do I say it?"

"Oh, I will, of course."

"Then the other is right, depend upon it. I always was rotten on grammar."

On the way back to the office, Daylight dropped into a bookstore and bought a grammar; and for a solid hour, his feet up on the desk, he toiled through its pages. "Knock off my head with little apples if the girl ain't right," he communed aloud at the end of the session. For the first time it struck him that there was something about his stenographer. He had accepted her up to then, as a female creature and a bit of office furnishing. But now, having demonstrated that she knew more grammar than did business men and college graduates, she became an individual. She seemed to stand out in his consciousness as conspicuously as the I shall had stood out on the typed page, and he began to take notice.

He managed to watch her leaving that afternoon, and he was aware for the first time that she was well-formed, and that her manner of dress was satisfying. He knew none of the details of women's dress, and he saw none of the details of her neat shirt-waist and well-cut tailor suit. He saw only the effect in a general, sketchy way. She looked right. This was in the absence of anything wrong or out of the way.

"She's a trim little good-looker," was his verdict, when the outer office door closed on her.

The next morning, dictating, he concluded that he liked the way she did her hair, though for the life of him he could have given no description of it. The impression was pleasing, that was all.

She sat between him and the window, and he noted that her hair was light brown, with hints of golden bronze. A pale sun, shining in, touched the golden bronze into smouldering fires that were very pleasing to behold. Funny, he thought, that he had never observed this phenomenon before.

In the midst of the letter he came to the construction which had caused the trouble the day before. He remembered his wrestle with the grammar, and dictated.

"I shall meet you halfway this proposition—"

Miss Mason gave a quick look up at him. The action was purely involuntary, and, in fact, had been half a startle of surprise. The next instant her eyes had dropped again, and she sat waiting to go on with the dictation. But in that moment of her glance Daylight had noted that her eyes were gray. He was later to learn that at times there were golden lights in those same gray eyes; but he had seen enough, as it was, to surprise him, for he became suddenly aware that he had always taken her for a brunette with brown eyes, as a matter of course.

"You were right, after all," he confessed, with a sheepish grin that sat incongruously on his stern, Indian-like features.

Again he was rewarded by an upward glance and an acknowledging smile, and this time he verified the fact that her eyes were gray.

"But it don't sound right, just the same," he complained. At this she laughed outright.

"I beg your pardon," she hastened to make amends, and then spoiled it by adding, "but you are so funny."

Daylight began to feel a slight awkwardness, and the sun would persist in setting her hair a-smouldering.

"I didn't mean to be funny," he said.

"That was why I laughed. But it is right, and perfectly good grammar."

"All right," he sighed—"I shall meet you halfway in this proposition—got that?" And the dictation went on. He discovered that in the intervals, when she had nothing to do, she read books and magazines, or worked on some sort of feminine fancy work.

Passing her desk, once, he picked up a volume of Kipling's poems and glanced bepuzzled through the pages. "You like reading, Miss Mason?" he said, laying the book down.

"Oh, yes," was her answer; "very much."

Another time it was a book of Wells', The Wheels of Change. "What's it all about?" Daylight asked.

"Oh, it's just a novel, a love-story." She stopped, but he still stood waiting, and she felt it incumbent to go on.

"It's about a little Cockney draper's assistant, who takes a vacation on his bicycle, and falls in with a young girl very much above him. Her mother is a popular writer and all that. And the situation is very curious, and sad, too, and tragic. Would you care to read it?"

"Does he get her?" Daylight demanded.

"No; that's the point of it. He wasn't—"

"And he doesn't get her, and you've read all them pages, hundreds of them, to find that out?" Daylight muttered in amazement.

Miss Mason was nettled as well as amused.

"But you read the mining and financial news by the hour," she retorted.

"But I sure get something out of that. It's business, and it's different. I get money out of it. What do you get out of books?"

"Points of view, new ideas, life."

"Not worth a cent cash."

"But life's worth more than cash," she argued.

"Oh, well," he said, with easy masculine tolerance, "so long as you enjoy it. That's what counts, I suppose; and there's no accounting for taste."

Despite his own superior point of view, he had an idea that she knew a lot, and he experienced a fleeting feeling like that of a barbarian face to face with the evidence of some tremendous culture. To Daylight culture was a worthless thing, and yet, somehow, he was vaguely troubled by a sense that there was more in culture than he imagined.

Again, on her desk, in passing, he noticed a book with which he was familiar. This time he did not stop, for he had recognized the cover. It was a magazine correspondent's book on the Klondike, and he knew that he and his photograph figured in it and he knew, also, of a certain sensational chapter concerned with a woman's suicide, and with one "Too much Daylight."

After that he did not talk with her again about books. He imagined what erroneous conclusions she had drawn from that particular chapter, and it stung him the more in that they were undeserved. Of all unlikely things, to have the reputation of being a lady-killer,—he, Burning Daylight,—and to have a woman kill herself out of love for him. He felt that he was a most unfortunate man and wondered by what luck that one book of all the thousands of books should have fallen into his stenographer's hands. For some days afterward he had an uncomfortable sensation of guiltiness whenever he was in Miss Mason's presence; and once he was positive that he caught her looking at him with a curious, intent gaze, as if studying what manner of man he was.

He pumped Morrison, the clerk, who had first to vent his personal grievance against Miss Mason before he could tell what little he knew of her.

"She comes from Siskiyou County. She's very nice to work with in the office, of course, but she's rather stuck on herself—exclusive, you know."

"How do you make that out?" Daylight queried.

"Well, she thinks too much of herself to associate with those she works with, in the office here, for instance. She won't have anything to do with a fellow, you see. I've asked her out repeatedly, to the theatre and the chutes and such things. But nothing doing. Says she likes plenty of sleep, and can't stay up late, and has to go all the way to Berkeley—that's where she lives."

This phase of the report gave Daylight a distinct satisfaction. She was a bit above the ordinary, and no doubt about it. But Morrison's next words carried a hurt.

"But that's all hot air. She's running with the University boys, that's what she's doing. She needs lots of sleep and can't go to the theatre with me, but she can dance all hours with them. I've heard it pretty straight that she goes to all their hops and such things. Rather stylish and high-toned for a stenographer, I'd say. And she keeps a horse, too. She rides astride all over those hills out there. I saw her one Sunday myself. Oh, she's a high-flyer, and I wonder how she does it. Sixty-five a month don't go far. Then she has a sick brother, too."

"Live with her people?" Daylight asked.

"No; hasn't got any. They were well to do, I've heard. They must have been, or that brother of hers couldn't have gone to the University of California. Her father had a big cattle-ranch, but he got to fooling with mines or something, and went broke before he died. Her mother died long before that. Her brother must cost a lot of money. He was a husky once, played football, was great on hunting and being out in the mountains and such things. He got his accident breaking horses, and then rheumatism or something got into him. One leg is shorter than the other and withered up some. He has to walk on crutches. I saw her out with him once—crossing the ferry. The doctors have been experimenting on him for years, and he's in the French Hospital now, I think."

All of which side-lights on Miss Mason went to increase Daylight's interest in her. Yet, much as he desired, he failed to get acquainted with her. He had thoughts of asking her to luncheon, but his was the innate chivalry of the frontiersman, and the thoughts never came to anything. He knew a self-respecting, square-dealing man was not supposed to take his stenographer to luncheon. Such things did happen, he knew, for he heard the chaffing gossip of the club; but he did not think much of such men and felt sorry for the girls. He had a strange notion that a man had less rights over those he employed than over mere acquaintances or strangers. Thus, had Miss Mason not been his employee, he was confident that he would have had her to luncheon or the theatre in no time. But he felt that it was an imposition for an employer, because he bought the time of an employee in working hours, to presume in any way upon any of the rest of that employee's time. To do so was to act like a bully. The situation was unfair. It was taking advantage of the fact that the employee was dependent on one for a livelihood. The employee might permit the imposition through fear of angering the employer and not through any personal inclination at all.

In his own case he felt that such an imposition would be peculiarly obnoxious, for had she not read that cursed Klondike correspondent's book? A pretty idea she must have of him, a girl that was too high-toned to have anything to do with a good-looking, gentlemanly fellow like Morrison. Also, and down under all his other reasons, Daylight was timid. The only thing he had ever been afraid of in his life was woman, and he had been afraid all his life. Nor was that timidity to be put easily to flight now that he felt the first glimmering need and desire for woman. The specter of the apron-string still haunted him, and helped him to find excuses for getting on no forwarder with Dede Mason.

CHAPTER VII

Not being favored by chance in getting acquainted with Dede Mason, Daylight's interest in her slowly waned. This was but natural, for he was plunged deep in hazardous operations, and the fascinations of the game and the magnitude of it accounted for all the energy that even his magnificent organism could generate.

Such was his absorption that the pretty stenographer slowly and imperceptibly faded from the forefront of his consciousness. Thus, the first faint spur, in the best sense, of his need for woman ceased to prod. So far as Dede Mason was concerned, he possessed no more than a complacent feeling of satisfaction in that he had a very nice stenographer. And, completely to put the quietus on any last lingering hopes he might have had of her, he was in the thick of his spectacular and intensely bitter fight with the Coastwise Steam Navigation Company, and the Hawaiian, Nicaraguan, and Pacific-Mexican Steamship-Company. He stirred up a bigger muss than he had anticipated, and even he was astounded at the wide ramifications of the struggle and at the unexpected and incongruous interests that were drawn into it. Every newspaper in San Francisco turned upon him. It was true, one or two of them had first intimated that they were open to subsidization, but Daylight's judgment was that the situation did not warrant such expenditure. Up to this time the press had been amusingly tolerant and good-naturedly sensational about him, but now he was to learn what virulent scrupulousness an antagonized press was capable of. Every episode of his life was resurrected to serve as foundations for malicious fabrications. Daylight was frankly amazed at the new interpretation put upon all he had accomplished and the deeds he had done. From an Alaskan hero he was metamorphosed into an Alaskan bully, liar, desperado, and all around "bad Man." Not content with this, lies upon lies, out of whole cloth, were manufactured about him. He never replied, though once he went to the extent of disburdening his mind to half a dozen reporters. "Do your damnedest," he told them. "Burning Daylight's bucked bigger things than your dirty, lying sheets. And I don't blame you, boys... that is, not much. You can't help it. You've got to live. There's a mighty lot of women in this world that make their living in similar fashion to yours, because they're not able to do anything better. Somebody's got to do the dirty work, and it might as well be you. You're paid for it, and you ain't got the backbone to rustle cleaner jobs."

The socialist press of the city jubilantly exploited this utterance, scattering it broadcast over San Francisco in tens of thousands of paper dodgers. And the journalists, stung to the quick, retaliated with the only means in their power-printer's ink abuse. The attack became bitterer than ever. The whole affair sank to the deeper deeps of rancor and savageness. The poor woman who had killed herself was dragged out of her grave and paraded on thousands of reams of paper as a martyr and a victim to Daylight's ferocious brutality. Staid, statistical articles were published, proving that he had made his start by robbing poor miners of their claims, and that the capstone to his fortune had been put in place by his treacherous violation of faith with the Guggenhammers in the deal on Ophir. And there were editorials written in which he was called an enemy of society, possessed of the manners and culture of a caveman, a fomenter of wasteful business troubles, the destroyer of the city's prosperity in commerce and trade, an anarchist of dire menace; and one editorial gravely recommended that hanging would be a lesson to him and his ilk, and concluded with the fervent hope that some day his big motor-car would smash up and smash him with it.

He was like a big bear raiding a bee-hive and, regardless of the stings, he obstinately persisted in pawing for the honey. He gritted his teeth and struck back. Beginning with a raid on two steamship companies, it developed into a pitched battle with a city, a state, and a continental coastline. Very well; they wanted fight, and they would get it. It was what he wanted, and he felt justified in having come down from the Klondike, for here he was gambling at a bigger table than ever the Yukon had supplied. Allied with him, on a splendid salary, with princely pickings thrown in, was a lawyer, Larry Hegan, a young Irishman with a reputation to make, and whose peculiar genius had been unrecognized until Daylight picked up with him. Hegan had Celtic imagination and daring, and to such degree that Daylight's cooler head was necessary as a check on his wilder visions. Hegan's was a Napoleonic legal mind, without balance, and it was just this balance that Daylight supplied. Alone, the Irishman was doomed to failure, but directed by Daylight, he was on the highroad to fortune and recognition. Also, he was possessed of no more personal or civic conscience than Napoleon.

It was Hegan who guided Daylight through the intricacies of modern politics, labor organization, and commercial and corporation law. It was Hegan, prolific of resource and suggestion, who opened Daylight's eyes to undreamed possibilities in twentieth-century warfare; and it was Daylight, rejecting, accepting, and elaborating, who planned the campaigns and prosecuted them. With the Pacific coast from Peugeot Sound to Panama, buzzing and humming, and with San Francisco furiously about his ears, the two big steamship companies had all the appearance of winning. It looked as if Burning Daylight was being beaten slowly to his knees. And then he struck—at the steamship companies, at San Francisco, at the whole Pacific coast.

It was not much of a blow at first. A Christian Endeavor convention being held in San Francisco, a row was started by Express Drivers' Union No. 927 over the handling of a small heap of baggage at the Ferry Building. A few heads were broken, a score of arrests made, and the baggage was delivered. No one would have guessed that behind this petty wrangle was the fine Irish hand of Hegan, made potent by the Klondike gold of Burning Daylight. It was an insignificant affair at best—or so it seemed. But the Teamsters' Union took up the quarrel, backed by the whole Water Front Federation. Step by step, the strike became involved. A refusal of cooks and waiters to serve scab teamsters or teamsters' employers brought out the cooks and waiters. The butchers and meat-cutters refused to handle meat destined for unfair restaurants. The combined Employers' Associations put up a solid front, and found facing them the 40,000 organized laborers of San Francisco. The restaurant bakers and the bakery wagon drivers struck, followed by the milkers, milk drivers, and chicken pickers. The building trades asserted its position in unambiguous terms, and all San Francisco was in turmoil.

But still, it was only San Francisco. Hegan's intrigues were masterly, and Daylight's campaign steadily developed. The powerful fighting organization known as the Pacific Slope Seaman's Union refused to work vessels the cargoes of which were to be handled by scab longshoremen and freight-handlers. The union presented its ultimatum, and then called a strike. This had been Daylight's objective all the time. Every incoming coastwise vessel was boarded by the union officials and its crew sent ashore. And with the Seamen went the firemen, the engineers, and the sea cooks and waiters. Daily the number of idle steamers increased. It was impossible to get scab crews, for the men of the Seaman's Union were fighters trained in the hard school of the sea, and when they went out it meant blood and death to scabs. This phase of the strike spread up and down the entire Pacific coast, until all the ports were filled with idle ships, and sea transportation was at a standstill. The days and weeks dragged out, and the strike held. The Coastwise Steam Navigation Company, and the Hawaiian, Nicaraguan, and Pacific-Mexican Steamship Company were tied up completely. The expenses of combating the strike were tremendous, and they were earning nothing, while daily the situation went from bad to worse, until "peace at any price" became the cry. And still there was no peace, until Daylight and his allies played out their hand, raked in the winnings, and allowed a goodly portion of a continent to resume business.

It was noted, in following years, that several leaders of workmen built themselves houses and blocks of renting flats and took trips to the old countries, while, more immediately, other leaders and "dark horses" came to political preferment and the control of the municipal government and the municipal moneys. In fact, San Francisco's boss-ridden condition was due in greater degree to Daylight's widespreading battle than even San Francisco ever dreamed. For the part he had played, the details of which were practically all rumor and guesswork, quickly leaked out, and in consequence he became a much-execrated and well-hated man. Nor had Daylight himself dreamed that his raid on the steamship companies would have grown to such colossal proportions.

But he had got what he was after. He had played an exciting hand and won, beating the steamship companies down into the dust and mercilessly robbing the stockholders by perfectly legal methods before he let go. Of course, in addition to the large sums of money he had paid over, his allies had rewarded themselves by gobbling the advantages which later enabled them to loot the city. His alliance with a gang of cutthroats had brought about a lot of cutthroating. But his conscience suffered no twinges. He remembered what he had once heard an old preacher utter, namely, that they who rose by the sword perished by the sword. One took his chances when he played with cutting throats, and his, Daylight's, throat was still intact. That was it! And he had won. It was all gamble and war between the strong men. The fools did not count. They were always getting hurt; and that they always had been getting hurt was the conclusion he drew from what little he knew of history. San Francisco had wanted war, and he had given it war. It was the game. All the big fellows did the same, and they did much worse, too.

"Don't talk to me about morality and civic duty," he replied to a persistent interviewer. "If you quit your job tomorrow and went to work on another paper, you would write just what you were told to write. It's morality and civic duty now with you; on the new job it would be backing up a thieving railroad with... morality and civic duty, I suppose. Your price, my son, is just about thirty per week. That's what you sell for. But your paper would sell for a bit more. Pay its price to-day, and it would shift its present rotten policy to some other rotten policy; but it would never let up on morality and civic duty.

"And all because a sucker is born every minute. So long as the people stand for it, they'll get it good and plenty, my son. And the shareholders and business interests might as well shut up squawking about how much they've been hurt. You never hear ary squeal out of them when they've got the other fellow down and are gouging him. This is the time THEY got gouged, and that's all there is to it. Talk about mollycoddles! Son, those same fellows would steal crusts from starving men and pull gold fillings from the mouths of corpses, yep, and squawk like Sam Scratch if some blamed corpse hit back. They're all tarred with the same brush, little and big. Look at your Sugar Trust—with all its millions stealing water like a common thief from New York City, and short-weighing the government on its phoney scales. Morality and civic duty! Son, forget it."

CHAPTER VIII

Daylight's coming to civilization had not improved him. True, he wore better clothes, had learned slightly better manners, and spoke better English. As a gambler and a man-trampler he had developed remarkable efficiency. Also, he had become used to a higher standard of living, and he had whetted his wits to razor sharpness in the fierce, complicated struggle of fighting males. But he had hardened, and at the expense of his old-time, whole-souled geniality. Of the essential refinements of civilization he knew nothing. He did not know they existed. He had become cynical, bitter, and brutal. Power had its effect on him that it had on all men. Suspicious of the big exploiters, despising the fools of the exploited herd, he had faith only in himself. This led to an undue and erroneous exaltation of his ego, while kindly consideration of others—nay, even simple respect—was destroyed, until naught was left for him but to worship at the shrine of self. Physically, he was not the man of iron muscles who had come down out of the Arctic. He did not exercise sufficiently, ate more than was good for him, and drank altogether too much. His muscles were getting flabby, and his tailor called attention to his increasing waistband. In fact, Daylight was developing a definite paunch. This physical deterioration was manifest likewise in his face. The lean Indian visage was suffering a city change. The slight hollows in the cheeks under the high cheek-bones had filled out. The beginning of puff-sacks under the eyes was faintly visible. The girth of the neck had increased, and the first crease and fold of a double chin were becoming plainly discernible. The old effect of asceticism, bred of terrific hardships and toil, had vanished; the features had become broader and heavier, betraying all the stigmata of the life he lived, advertising the man's self-indulgence, harshness, and brutality.

Even his human affiliations were descending. Playing a lone hand, contemptuous of most of the men with whom he played, lacking in sympathy or understanding of them, and certainly independent of them, he found little in common with those to be encountered, say at the Alta-Pacific. In point of fact, when the battle with the steamship companies was at its height and his raid was inflicting incalculable damage on all business interests, he had been asked to resign from the Alta-Pacific. The idea had been rather to his liking, and he had found new quarters in clubs like the Riverside, organized and practically maintained by the city bosses. He found that he really liked such men better. They were more primitive and simple, and they did not put on airs. They were honest buccaneers, frankly in the game for what they could get out of it, on the surface more raw and savage, but at least not glossed over with oily or graceful hypocrisy. The Alta-Pacific had suggested that his resignation be kept a private matter, and then had privily informed the newspapers. The latter had made great capital out of the forced resignation, but Daylight had grinned and silently gone his way, though registering a black mark against more than one club member who was destined to feel, in the days to come, the crushing weight of the Klondiker's financial paw.

The storm-centre of a combined newspaper attack lasting for months, Daylight's character had been torn to shreds. There was no fact in his history that had not been distorted into a criminality or a vice. This public making of him over into an iniquitous monster had pretty well crushed any lingering hope he had of getting acquainted with Dede Mason. He felt that there was no chance for her ever to look kindly on a man of his caliber, and, beyond increasing her salary to seventy-five dollars a month, he proceeded gradually to forget about her. The increase was made known to her through Morrison, and later she thanked Daylight, and that was the end of it.

One week-end, feeling heavy and depressed and tired of the city and its ways, he obeyed the impulse of a whim that was later to play an important part in his life. The desire to get out of the city for a whiff of country air and for a change of scene was the cause. Yet, to himself, he made the excuse of going to Glen Ellen for the purpose of inspecting the brickyard with which Holdsworthy had goldbricked him.

He spent the night in the little country hotel, and on Sunday morning, astride a saddle-horse rented from the Glen Ellen butcher, rode out of the village. The brickyard was close at hand on the flat beside the Sonoma Creek. The kilns were visible among the trees, when he glanced to the left and caught sight of a cluster of wooded knolls half a mile away, perched on the rolling slopes of Sonoma Mountain. The mountain, itself wooded, towered behind. The trees on the knolls seemed to beckon to him.

The dry, early-summer air, shot through with sunshine, was wine to him. Unconsciously he drank it in deep breaths. The prospect of the brickyard was uninviting. He was jaded with all things business, and the wooded knolls were calling to him. A horse was between his legs—a good horse, he decided; one that sent him back to the cayuses he had ridden during his eastern Oregon boyhood. He had been somewhat of a rider in those early days, and the champ of bit and creak of saddle-leather sounded good to him now.

Resolving to have his fun first, and to look over the brickyard afterward, he rode on up the hill, prospecting for a way across country to get to the knolls. He left the country road at the first gate he came to and cantered through a hayfield. The grain was waist-high on either side the wagon road, and he sniffed the warm aroma of it with delighted nostrils. Larks flew up before him, and from everywhere came mellow notes. From the appearance of the road it was patent that it had been used for hauling clay to the now idle brickyard. Salving his conscience with the idea that this was part of the inspection, he rode on to the clay-pit—a huge scar in a hillside. But he did not linger long, swinging off again to the left and leaving the road. Not a farm-house was in sight, and the change from the city crowding was essentially satisfying. He rode now through open woods, across little flower-scattered glades, till he came upon a spring. Flat on the ground, he drank deeply of the clear water, and, looking about him, felt with a shock the beauty of the world. It came to him like a discovery; he had never realized it before, he concluded, and also, he had forgotten much. One could not sit in at high finance and keep track of such things. As he drank in the air, the scene, and the distant song of larks, he felt like a poker-player rising from a night-long table and coming forth from the pent atmosphere to taste the freshness of the morn.

At the base of the knolls he encountered a tumble-down stake-and-rider fence. From the look of it he judged it must be forty years old at least—the work of some first pioneer who had taken up the land when the days of gold had ended. The woods were very thick here, yet fairly clear of underbrush, so that, while the blue sky was screened by the arched branches, he was able to ride beneath. He now found himself in a nook of several acres, where the oak and manzanita and madrono gave way to clusters of stately redwoods. Against the foot of a steep-sloped knoll he came upon a magnificent group of redwoods that seemed to have gathered about a tiny gurgling spring.

He halted his horse, for beside the spring uprose a wild California lily. It was a wonderful flower, growing there in the cathedral nave of lofty trees. At least eight feet in height, its stem rose straight and slender, green and bare for two-thirds its length, and then burst into a shower of snow-white waxen bells. There were hundreds of these blossoms, all from the one stem, delicately poised and ethereally frail. Daylight had never seen anything like it. Slowly his gaze wandered from it to all that was about him. He took off his hat, with almost a vague religious feeling. This was different. No room for contempt and evil here. This was clean and fresh and beautiful-something he could respect. It was like a church. The atmosphere was one of holy calm. Here man felt the prompting of nobler things. Much of this and more was in Daylight's heart as he looked about him. But it was not a concept of his mind. He merely felt it without thinking about it at all.

On the steep incline above the spring grew tiny maidenhair ferns, while higher up were larger ferns and brakes. Great, moss-covered trunks of fallen trees lay here and there, slowly sinking back and merging into the level of the forest mould. Beyond, in a slightly clearer space, wild grape and honeysuckle swung in green riot from gnarled old oak trees. A gray Douglas squirrel crept out on a branch and watched him. From somewhere came the distant knocking of a woodpecker. This sound did not disturb the hush and awe of the place. Quiet woods, noises belonged there and made the solitude complete. The tiny bubbling ripple of the spring and the gray flash of tree-squirrel were as yardsticks with which to measure the silence and motionless repose.

"Might be a million miles from anywhere," Daylight whispered to himself.

But ever his gaze returned to the wonderful lily beside the bubbling spring.

He tethered the horse and wandered on foot among the knolls. Their tops were crowned with century-old spruce trees, and their sides clothed with oaks and madronos and native holly. But to the perfect redwoods belonged the small but deep canon that threaded its way among the knolls. Here he found no passage out for his horse, and he returned to the lily beside the spring. On foot, tripping, stumbling, leading the animal, he forced his way up the hillside. And ever the ferns carpeted the way of his feet, ever the forest climbed with him and arched overhead, and ever the clean joy and sweetness stole in upon his senses.

On the crest he came through an amazing thicket of velvet-trunked young madronos, and emerged on an open hillside that led down into a tiny valley. The sunshine was at first dazzling in its brightness, and he paused and rested, for he was panting from the exertion. Not of old had he known shortness of breath such as this, and muscles that so easily tired at a stiff climb. A tiny stream ran down the tiny valley through a tiny meadow that was carpeted knee-high with grass and blue and white nemophila. The hillside was covered with Mariposa lilies and wild hyacinth, down through which his horse dropped slowly, with circumspect feet and reluctant gait.

Crossing the stream, Daylight followed a faint cattle trail over a low, rocky hill and through a wine-wooded forest of manzanita, and emerged upon another tiny valley, down which filtered another spring-fed, meadow-bordered streamlet. A jack-rabbit bounded from a bush under his horse's nose, leaped the stream, and vanished up the opposite hillside of scrub-oak. Daylight watched it admiringly as he rode on to the head of the meadow. Here he startled up a many-pronged buck, that seemed to soar across the meadow, and to soar over the stake-and-rider fence, and, still soaring, disappeared in a friendly copse beyond.

Daylight's delight was unbounded. It seemed to him that he had never been so happy. His old woods' training was aroused, and he was keenly interested in everything in the moss on the trees and branches; in the bunches of mistletoe hanging in the oaks; in the nest of a wood-rat; in the water-cress growing in the sheltered eddies of the little stream; in the butterflies drifting through the rifted sunshine and shadow; in the blue jays that flashed in splashes of gorgeous color across the forest aisles; in the tiny birds, like wrens, that hopped among the bushes and imitated certain minor quail-calls; and in the crimson-crested woodpecker that ceased its knocking and cocked its head on one side to survey him. Crossing the stream, he struck faint vestiges of a wood-road, used, evidently, a generation back, when the meadow had been cleared of its oaks. He found a hawk's nest on the lightning-shattered tipmost top of a six-foot redwood. And to complete it all his horse stumbled upon several large broods of half-grown quail, and the air was filled with the thrum of their flight. He halted and watched the young ones "petrifying" and disappearing on the ground before his eyes, and listening to the anxious calls of the old ones hidden in the thickets.

"It sure beats country places and bungalows at Menlo Park," he communed aloud; "and if ever I get the hankering for country life, it's me for this every time."

The old wood-road led him to a clearing, where a dozen acres of grapes grew on wine-red soil. A cow-path, more trees and thickets, and he dropped down a hillside to the southeast exposure. Here, poised above a big forested canon, and looking out upon Sonoma Valley, was a small farm-house. With its barn and outhouses it snuggled into a nook in the hillside, which protected it from west and north. It was the erosion from this hillside, he judged, that had formed the little level stretch of vegetable garden. The soil was fat and black, and there was water in plenty, for he saw several faucets running wide open.

Forgotten was the brickyard. Nobody was at home, but Daylight dismounted and ranged the vegetable garden, eating strawberries and green peas, inspecting the old adobe barn and the rusty plough and harrow, and rolling and smoking cigarettes while he watched the antics of several broods of young chickens and the mother hens. A foottrail that led down the wall of the big canyon invited him, and he proceeded to follow it. A water-pipe, usually above ground, paralleled the trail, which he concluded led upstream to the bed of the creek. The wall of the canon was several hundred feet from top to bottom, and magnificent were the untouched trees that the place was plunged in perpetual shade. He measured with his eye spruces five and six feet in diameter and redwoods even larger. One such he passed, a twister that was at least ten or eleven feet through. The trail led straight to a small dam where was the intake for the pipe that watered the vegetable garden. Here, beside the stream, were alders and laurel trees, and he walked through fern-brakes higher than his head. Velvety moss was everywhere, out of which grew maiden-hair and gold-back ferns.

Save for the dam, it was a virgin wild. No ax had invaded, and the trees died only of old age and stress of winter storm. The huge trunks of those that had fallen lay moss-covered, slowly resolving back into the soil from which they sprang. Some had lain so long that they were quite gone, though their faint outlines, level with the mould, could still be seen. Others bridged the stream, and from beneath the bulk of one monster half a dozen younger trees, overthrown and crushed by the fall, growing out along the ground, still lived and prospered, their roots bathed by the stream, their upshooting branches catching the sunlight through the gap that had been made in the forest roof.

Back at the farm-house, Daylight mounted and rode on away from the ranch and into the wilder canons and steeper steeps beyond. Nothing could satisfy his holiday spirit now but the ascent of Sonoma Mountain. And here on the crest, three hours afterward, he emerged, tired and sweaty, garments torn and face and hands scratched, but with sparkling eyes and an unwonted zestfulness of expression. He felt the illicit pleasure of a schoolboy playing truant. The big gambling table of San Francisco seemed very far away. But there was more than illicit pleasure in his mood. It was as though he were going through a sort of cleansing bath. No room here for all the sordidness, meanness, and viciousness that filled the dirty pool of city existence. Without pondering in detail upon the matter at all, his sensations were of purification and uplift. Had he been asked to state how he felt, he would merely have said that he was having a good time; for he was unaware in his self-consciousness of the potent charm of nature that was percolating through his city-rotted body and brain—potent, in that he came of an abysmal past of wilderness dwellers, while he was himself coated with but the thinnest rind of crowded civilization.

There were no houses in the summit of Sonoma Mountain, and, all alone under the azure California sky, he reined in on the southern edge of the peak. He saw open pasture country, intersected with wooded canons, descending to the south and west from his feet, crease on crease and roll on roll, from lower level to lower level, to the floor of Petaluma Valley, flat as a billiard-table, a cardboard affair, all patches and squares of geometrical regularity where the fat freeholds were farmed. Beyond, to the west, rose range on range of mountains cuddling purple mists of atmosphere in their valleys; and still beyond, over the last range of all, he saw the silver sheen of the Pacific. Swinging his horse, he surveyed the west and north, from Santa Rosa to St. Helena, and on to the east, across Sonoma to the chaparral-covered range that shut off the view of Napa Valley. Here, part way up the eastern wall of Sonoma Valley, in range of a line intersecting the little village of Glen Ellen, he made out a scar upon a hillside. His first thought was that it was the dump of a mine tunnel, but remembering that he was not in gold-bearing country, he dismissed the scar from his mind and continued the circle of his survey to the southeast, where, across the waters of San Pablo Bay, he could see, sharp and distant, the twin peaks of Mount Diablo. To the south was Mount Tamalpais, and, yes, he was right, fifty miles away, where the draughty winds of the Pacific blew in the Golden Gate, the smoke of San Francisco made a low-lying haze against the sky.

"I ain't seen so much country all at once in many a day," he thought aloud.

He was loath to depart, and it was not for an hour that he was able to tear himself away and take the descent of the mountain. Working out a new route just for the fun of it, late afternoon was upon him when he arrived back at the wooded knolls. Here, on the top of one of them, his keen eyes caught a glimpse of a shade of green sharply differentiated from any he had seen all day. Studying it for a minute, he concluded that it was composed of three cypress trees, and he knew that nothing else than the hand of man could have planted them there. Impelled by curiosity purely boyish, he made up his mind to investigate. So densely wooded was the knoll, and so steep, that he had to dismount and go up on foot, at times even on hands and knees struggling hard to force a way through the thicker underbrush. He came out abruptly upon the cypresses. They were enclosed in a small square of ancient fence; the pickets he could plainly see had been hewn and sharpened by hand. Inside were the mounds of two children's graves. Two wooden headboards, likewise hand-hewn, told the state Little David, born 1855, died 1859; and Little Roy, born 1853, died 1860.

"The poor little kids," Daylight muttered. The graves showed signs of recent care. Withered bouquets of wild flowers were on the mounds, and the lettering on the headboards was freshly painted. Guided by these clews, Daylight cast about for a trail, and found one leading down the side opposite to his ascent. Circling the base of the knoll, he picked up with his horse and rode on to the farm-house. Smoke was rising from the chimney and he was quickly in conversation with a nervous, slender young man, who, he learned, was only a tenant on the ranch. How large was it? A matter of one hundred and eighty acres, though it seemed much larger. This was because it was so irregularly shaped. Yes, it included the clay-pit and all the knolls, and its boundary that ran along the big canon was over a mile long.

"You see," the young man said, "it was so rough and broken that when they began to farm this country the farmers bought in the good land to the edge of it. That's why its boundaries are all gouged and jagged.

"Oh, yes, he and his wife managed to scratch a living without working too hard. They didn't have to pay much rent. Hillard, the owner, depended on the income from the clay-pit. Hillard was well off, and had big ranches and vineyards down on the flat of the valley. The brickyard paid ten cents a cubic yard for the clay. As for the rest of the ranch, the land was good in patches, where it was cleared, like the vegetable garden and the vineyard, but the rest of it was too much up-and-down."

"You're not a farmer," Daylight said. The young man laughed and shook his head. "No; I'm a telegraph operator. But the wife and I decided to take a two years' vacation, and ... here we are. But the time's about up. I'm going back into the office this fall after I get the grapes off."

Yes, there were about eleven acres in the vineyard—wine grapes. The price was usually good. He grew most of what they ate. If he owned the place, he'd clear a patch of land on the side-hill above the vineyard and plant a small home orchard. The soil was good. There was plenty of pasturage all over the ranch, and there were several cleared patches, amounting to about fifteen acres in all, where he grew as much mountain hay as could be found. It sold for three to five dollars more a ton than the rank-stalked valley hay.

Daylight listened, there came to him a sudden envy of this young fellow living right in the midst of all this which Daylight had travelled through the last few hours.

"What in thunder are you going back to the telegraph office for?" he demanded.

The young man smiled with a certain wistfulness. "Because we can't get ahead here..." (he hesitated an instant), "and because there are added expenses coming. The rent, small as it is, counts; and besides, I'm not strong enough to effectually farm the place. If I owned it, or if I were a real husky like you, I'd ask nothing better. Nor would the wife." Again the wistful smile hovered on his face. "You see, we're country born, and after bucking with cities for a few years, we kind of feel we like the country best. We've planned to get ahead, though, and then some day we'll buy a patch of land and stay with it."

The graves of the children? Yes, he had relettered them and hoed the weeds out. It had become the custom. Whoever lived on the ranch did that. For years, the story ran, the father and mother had returned each summer to the graves. But there had come a time when they came no more, and then old Hillard started the custom. The scar across the valley? An old mine. It had never paid. The men had worked on it, off and on, for years, for the indications had been good. But that was years and years ago. No paying mine had ever been struck in the valley, though there had been no end of prospect-holes put down and there had been a sort of rush there thirty years back.

A frail-looking young woman came to the door to call the young man to supper. Daylight's first thought was that city living had not agreed with her. And then he noted the slight tan and healthy glow that seemed added to her face, and he decided that the country was the place for her. Declining an invitation to supper, he rode on for Glen Ellen sitting slack-kneed in the saddle and softly humming forgotten songs. He dropped down the rough, winding road through covered pasture, with here and there thickets of manzanita and vistas of open glades. He listened greedily to the quail calling, and laughed outright, once, in sheer joy, at a tiny chipmunk that fled scolding up a bank, slipping on the crumbly surface and falling down, then dashing across the road under his horse's nose and, still scolding, scrabbling up a protecting oak.

Daylight could not persuade himself to keep to the travelled roads that day, and another cut across country to Glen Ellen brought him upon a canon that so blocked his way that he was glad to follow a friendly cow-path. This led him to a small frame cabin. The doors and windows were open, and a cat was nursing a litter of kittens in the doorway, but no one seemed at home. He descended the trail that evidently crossed the canon. Part way down, he met an old man coming up through the sunset. In his hand he carried a pail of foamy milk. He wore no hat, and in his face, framed with snow-white hair and beard, was the ruddy glow and content of the passing summer day. Daylight thought that he had never seen so contented-looking a being.

"How old are you, daddy?" he queried.

"Eighty-four," was the reply. "Yes, sirree, eighty-four, and spryer than most."

"You must a' taken good care of yourself," Daylight suggested.

"I don't know about that. I ain't loafed none. I walked across the Plains with an ox-team and fit Injuns in '51, and I was a family man then with seven youngsters. I reckon I was as old then as you are now, or pretty nigh on to it."

"Don't you find it lonely here?"

The old man shifted the pail of milk and reflected. "That all depends," he said oracularly. "I ain't never been lonely except when the old wife died. Some fellers are lonely in a crowd, and I'm one of them. That's the only time I'm lonely, is when I go to 'Frisco. But I don't go no more, thank you 'most to death. This is good enough for me. I've ben right here in this valley since '54—one of the first settlers after the Spaniards."

Daylight started his horse, saying:—

"Well, good night, daddy. Stick with it. You got all the young bloods skinned, and I guess you've sure buried a mighty sight of them."

The old man chuckled, and Daylight rode on, singularly at peace with himself and all the world. It seemed that the old contentment of trail and camp he had known on the Yukon had come back to him. He could not shake from his eyes the picture of the old pioneer coming up the trail through the sunset light. He was certainly going some for eighty-four. The thought of following his example entered Daylight's mind, but the big game of San Francisco vetoed the idea.

"Well, anyway," he decided, "when I get old and quit the game, I'll settle down in a place something like this, and the city can go to hell."

CHAPTER IX

Instead of returning to the city on Monday, Daylight rented the butcher's horse for another day and crossed the bed of the valley to its eastern hills to look at the mine. It was dryer and rockier here than where he had been the day before, and the ascending slopes supported mainly chaparral, scrubby and dense and impossible to penetrate on horseback. But in the canyons water was plentiful and also a luxuriant forest growth. The mine was an abandoned affair, but he enjoyed the half-hour's scramble around. He had had experience in quartz-mining before he went to Alaska, and he enjoyed the recrudescence of his old wisdom in such matters. The story was simple to him: good prospects that warranted the starting of the tunnel into the sidehill; the three months' work and the getting short of money; the lay-off while the men went away and got jobs; then the return and a new stretch of work, with the "pay" ever luring and ever receding into the mountain, until, after years of hope, the men had given up and vanished. Most likely they were dead by now, Daylight thought, as he turned in the saddle and looked back across the canyon at the ancient dump and dark mouth of the tunnel.

As on the previous day, just for the joy of it, he followed cattle-trails at haphazard and worked his way up toward the summits. Coming out on a wagon road that led upward, he followed it for several miles, emerging in a small, mountain-encircled valley, where half a dozen poor ranchers farmed the wine-grapes on the steep slopes. Beyond, the road pitched upward. Dense chaparral covered the exposed hillsides but in the creases of the canons huge spruce trees grew, and wild oats and flowers.

Half an hour later, sheltering under the summits themselves, he came out on a clearing. Here and there, in irregular patches where the steep and the soil favored, wine grapes were growing. Daylight could see that it had been a stiff struggle, and that wild nature showed fresh signs of winning—chaparral that had invaded the clearings; patches and parts of patches of vineyard, unpruned, grassgrown, and abandoned; and everywhere old stake-and-rider fences vainly striving to remain intact. Here, at a small farm-house surrounded by large outbuildings, the road ended. Beyond, the chaparral blocked the way.

He came upon an old woman forking manure in the barnyard, and reined in by the fence.

"Hello, mother," was his greeting; "ain't you got any men-folk around to do that for you?"

She leaned on her pitchfork, hitched her skirt in at the waist, and regarded him cheerfully. He saw that her toil-worn, weather-exposed hands were like a man's, callused, large-knuckled, and gnarled, and that her stockingless feet were thrust into heavy man's brogans.

"Nary a man," she answered. "And where be you from, and all the way up here? Won't you stop and hitch and have a glass of wine?"

Striding clumsily but efficiently, like a laboring-man, she led him into the largest building, where Daylight saw a hand-press and all the paraphernalia on a small scale for the making of wine. It was too far and too bad a road to haul the grapes to the valley wineries, she explained, and so they were compelled to do it themselves. "They," he learned, were she and her daughter, the latter a widow of forty-odd. It had been easier before the grandson died and before he went away to fight savages in the Philippines. He had died out there in battle.

Daylight drank a full tumbler of excellent Riesling, talked a few minutes, and accounted for a second tumbler. Yes, they just managed not to starve. Her husband and she had taken up this government land in '57 and cleared it and farmed it ever since, until he died, when she had carried it on. It actually didn't pay for the toil, but what were they to do? There was the wine trust, and wine was down. That Riesling? She delivered it to the railroad down in the valley for twenty-two cents a gallon. And it was a long haul. It took a day for the round trip. Her daughter was gone now with a load.

Daylight knew that in the hotels, Riesling, not quite so good even, was charged for at from a dollar and a half to two dollars a quart. And she got twenty-two cents a gallon. That was the game. She was one of the stupid lowly, she and her people before her—the ones that did the work, drove their oxen across the Plains, cleared and broke the virgin land, toiled all days and all hours, paid their taxes, and sent their sons and grandsons out to fight and die for the flag that gave them such ample protection that they were able to sell their wine for twenty-two cents. The same wine was served to him at the St. Francis for two dollars a quart, or eight dollars a short gallon. That was it.

Between her and her hand-press on the mountain clearing and him ordering his wine in the hotel was a difference of seven dollars and seventy-eight cents. A clique of sleek men in the city got between her and him to just about that amount. And, besides them, there was a horde of others that took their whack. They called it railroading, high finance, banking, wholesaling, real estate, and such things, but the point was that they got it, while she got what was left,— twenty-two cents. Oh, well, a sucker was born every minute, he sighed to himself, and nobody was to blame; it was all a game, and only a few could win, but it was damned hard on the suckers.

"How old are you, mother?" he asked.

"Seventy-nine come next January."

"Worked pretty hard, I suppose?"

"Sense I was seven. I was bound out in Michigan state until I was woman-grown. Then I married, and I reckon the work got harder and harder."

"When are you going to take a rest?"

She looked at him, as though she chose to think his question facetious, and did not reply.

"Do you believe in God?"

She nodded her head.

"Then you get it all back," he assured her; but in his heart he was wondering about God, that allowed so many suckers to be born and that did not break up the gambling game by which they were robbed from the cradle to the grave.

"How much of that Riesling you got?"

She ran her eyes over the casks and calculated. "Just short of eight hundred gallons."

He wondered what he could do with all of it, and speculated as to whom he could give it away.

"What would you do if you got a dollar a gallon for it?" he asked.

"Drop dead, I suppose."

"No; speaking seriously."

"Get me some false teeth, shingle the house, and buy a new wagon. The road's mighty hard on wagons."

"And after that?"

"Buy me a coffin."

"Well, they're yours, mother, coffin and all."

She looked her incredulity.

"No; I mean it. And there's fifty to bind the bargain. Never mind the receipt. It's the rich ones that need watching, their memories being so infernal short, you know. Here's my address. You've got to deliver it to the railroad. And now, show me the way out of here. I want to get up to the top."

On through the chaparral he went, following faint cattle trails and working slowly upward till he came out on the divide and gazed down into Napa Valley and back across to Sonoma Mountain... "A sweet land," he muttered, "an almighty sweet land."

Circling around to the right and dropping down along the cattle-trails, he quested for another way back to Sonoma Valley; but the cattle-trails seemed to fade out, and the chaparral to grow thicker with a deliberate viciousness and even when he won through in places, the canon and small feeders were too precipitous for his horse, and turned him back. But there was no irritation about it. He enjoyed it all, for he was back at his old game of bucking nature. Late in the afternoon he broke through, and followed a well-defined trail down a dry canon. Here he got a fresh thrill. He had heard the baying of the hound some minutes before, and suddenly, across the bare face of the hill above him, he saw a large buck in flight. And not far behind came the deer-hound, a magnificent animal. Daylight sat tense in his saddle and watched until they disappeared, his breath just a trifle shorter, as if he, too, were in the chase, his nostrils distended, and in his bones the old hunting ache and memories of the days before he came to live in cities.

The dry canon gave place to one with a slender ribbon of running water. The trail ran into a wood-road, and the wood-road emerged across a small flat upon a slightly travelled county road. There were no farms in this immediate section, and no houses. The soil was meagre, the bed-rock either close to the surface or constituting the surface itself. Manzanita and scrub-oak, however, flourished and walled the road on either side with a jungle growth. And out a runway through this growth a man suddenly scuttled in a way that reminded Daylight of a rabbit.

He was a little man, in patched overalls; bareheaded, with a cotton shirt open at the throat and down the chest. The sun was ruddy-brown in his face, and by it his sandy hair was bleached on the ends to peroxide blond. He signed to Daylight to halt, and held up a letter. "If you're going to town, I'd be obliged if you mail this."

"I sure will." Daylight put it into his coat pocket.

"Do you live hereabouts, stranger?"

But the little man did not answer. He was gazing at Daylight in a surprised and steadfast fashion.

"I know you," the little man announced. "You're Elam Harnish—Burning Daylight, the papers call you. Am I right?"

Daylight nodded.

"But what under the sun are you doing here in the chaparral?"

Daylight grinned as he answered, "Drumming up trade for a free rural delivery route."

"Well, I'm glad I wrote that letter this afternoon," the little man went on, "or else I'd have missed seeing you. I've seen your photo in the papers many a time, and I've a good memory for faces. I recognized you at once. My name's Ferguson."

"Do you live hereabouts?" Daylight repeated his query.

"Oh, yes. I've got a little shack back here in the bush a hundred yards, and a pretty spring, and a few fruit trees and berry bushes. Come in and take a look. And that spring is a dandy. You never tasted water like it. Come in and try it."

Walking and leading his horse, Daylight followed the quick-stepping eager little man through the green tunnel and emerged abruptly upon the clearing, if clearing it might be called, where wild nature and man's earth-scratching were inextricably blended. It was a tiny nook in the hills, protected by the steep walls of a canon mouth. Here were several large oaks, evidencing a richer soil. The erosion of ages from the hillside had slowly formed this deposit of fat earth. Under the oaks, almost buried in them, stood a rough, unpainted cabin, the wide verandah of which, with chairs and hammocks, advertised an out-of doors bedchamber. Daylight's keen eyes took in every thing. The clearing was irregular, following the patches of the best soil, and every fruit tree and berry bush, and even each vegetable plant, had the water personally conducted to it. The tiny irrigation channels were every where, and along some of them the water was running.

Ferguson looked eagerly into his visitor's face for signs of approbation.

"What do you think of it, eh?"

"Hand-reared and manicured, every blessed tree," Daylight laughed, but the joy and satisfaction that shone in his eyes contented the little man.

"Why, d'ye know, I know every one of those trees as if they were sons of mine. I planted them, nursed them, fed them, and brought them up. Come on and peep at the spring."

"It's sure a hummer," was Daylight's verdict, after due inspection and sampling, as they turned back for the house.

The interior was a surprise. The cooking being done in the small, lean-to kitchen, the whole cabin formed a large living room. A great table in the middle was comfortably littered with books and magazines. All the available wall space, from floor to ceiling, was occupied by filled bookshelves. It seemed to Daylight that he had never seen so many books assembled in one place. Skins of wildcat, 'coon, and deer lay about on the pine-board floor.

"Shot them myself, and tanned them, too," Ferguson proudly asserted.

The crowning feature of the room was a huge fireplace of rough stones and boulders.

"Built it myself," Ferguson proclaimed, "and, by God, she drew! Never a wisp of smoke anywhere save in the pointed channel, and that during the big southeasters."

Daylight found himself charmed and made curious by the little man. Why was he hiding away here in the chaparral, he and his books? He was nobody's fool, anybody could see that. Then why? The whole affair had a tinge of adventure, and Daylight accepted an invitation to supper, half prepared to find his host a raw-fruit-and-nut-eater or some similar sort of health faddest. At table, while eating rice and jack-rabbit curry (the latter shot by Ferguson), they talked it over, and Daylight found the little man had no food "views." He ate whatever he liked, and all he wanted, avoiding only such combinations that experience had taught him disagreed with his digestion.

Next, Daylight surmised that he might be touched with religion; but, quest about as he would, in a conversation covering the most divergent topics, he could find no hint of queerness or unusualness. So it was, when between them they had washed and wiped the dishes and put them away, and had settled down to a comfortable smoke, that Daylight put his question.

"Look here, Ferguson. Ever since we got together, I've been casting about to find out what's wrong with you, to locate a screw loose somewhere, but I'll be danged if I've succeeded. What are you doing here, anyway? What made you come here? What were you doing for a living before you came here? Go ahead and elucidate yourself."

Ferguson frankly showed his pleasure at the questions.

"First of all," he began, "the doctors wound up by losing all hope for me. Gave me a few months at best, and that, after a course in sanatoriums and a trip to Europe and another to Hawaii. They tried electricity, and forced feeding, and fasting. I was a graduate of about everything in the curriculum. They kept me poor with their bills while I went from bad to worse. The trouble with me was two fold: first, I was a born weakling; and next, I was living unnaturally—too much work, and responsibility, and strain. I was managing editor of the Times-Tribune—"

Daylight gasped mentally, for the Times-Tribune was the biggest and most influential paper in San Francisco, and always had been so.

"—and I wasn't strong enough for the strain. Of course my body went back on me, and my mind, too, for that matter. It had to be bolstered up with whiskey, which wasn't good for it any more than was the living in clubs and hotels good for my stomach and the rest of me. That was what ailed me; I was living all wrong."

He shrugged his shoulders and drew at his pipe.

"When the doctors gave me up, I wound up my affairs and gave the doctors up. That was fifteen years ago. I'd been hunting through here when I was a boy, on vacations from college, and when I was all down and out it seemed a yearning came to me to go back to the country. So I quit, quit everything, absolutely, and came to live in the Valley of the Moon—that's the Indian name, you know, for Sonoma Valley. I lived in the lean-to the first year; then I built the cabin and sent for my books. I never knew what happiness was before, nor health. Look at me now and dare to tell me that I look forty-seven."

"I wouldn't give a day over forty," Daylight confessed.

"Yet the day I came here I looked nearer sixty, and that was fifteen years ago."

They talked along, and Daylight looked at the world from new angles. Here was a man, neither bitter nor cynical, who laughed at the city-dwellers and called them lunatics; a man who did not care for money, and in whom the lust for power had long since died. As for the friendship of the city-dwellers, his host spoke in no uncertain terms.

"What did they do, all the chaps I knew, the chaps in the clubs with whom I'd been cheek by jowl for heaven knows how long? I was not beholden to them for anything, and when I slipped out there was not one of them to drop me a line and say, 'How are you, old man? Anything I can do for you?' For several weeks it was: 'What's become of Ferguson?' After that I became a reminiscence and a memory. Yet every last one of them knew I had nothing but my salary and that I'd always lived a lap ahead of it."

"But what do you do now?" was Daylight's query. "You must need cash to buy clothes and magazines?"

"A week's work or a month's work, now and again, ploughing in the winter, or picking grapes in the fall, and there's always odd jobs with the farmers through the summer. I don't need much, so I don't have to work much. Most of my time I spend fooling around the place. I could do hack work for the magazines and newspapers; but I prefer the ploughing and the grape picking. Just look at me and you can see why. I'm hard as rocks. And I like the work. But I tell you a chap's got to break in to it. It's a great thing when he's learned to pick grapes a whole long day and come home at the end of it with that tired happy feeling, instead of being in a state of physical collapse. That fireplace—those big stones—I was soft, then, a little, anemic, alcoholic degenerate, with the spunk of a rabbit and about one per cent as much stamina, and some of those big stones nearly broke my back and my heart. But I persevered, and used my body in the way Nature intended it should be used—not bending over a desk and swilling whiskey... and, well, here I am, a better man for it, and there's the fireplace, fine and dandy, eh?

"And now tell me about the Klondike, and how you turned San Francisco upside down with that last raid of yours. You're a bonny fighter, you know, and you touch my imagination, though my cooler reason tells me that you are a lunatic like the rest. The lust for power! It's a dreadful affliction. Why didn't you stay in your Klondike? Or why don't you clear out and live a natural life, for instance, like mine? You see, I can ask questions, too. Now you talk and let me listen for a while."

It was not until ten o'clock that Daylight parted from Ferguson. As he rode along through the starlight, the idea came to him of buying the ranch on the other side of the valley. There was no thought in his mind of ever intending to live on it. His game was in San Francisco. But he liked the ranch, and as soon as he got back to the office he would open up negotiations with Hillard. Besides, the ranch included the clay-pit, and it would give him the whip-hand over Holdsworthy if he ever tried to cut up any didoes.

CHAPTER X

The time passed, and Daylight played on at the game. But the game had entered upon a new phase. The lust for power in the mere gambling and winning was metamorphosing into the lust for power in order to revenge. There were many men in San Francisco against whom he had registered black marks, and now and again, with one of his lightning strokes, he erased such a mark. He asked no quarter; he gave no quarter. Men feared and hated him, and no one loved him, except Larry Hegan, his lawyer, who would have laid down his life for him. But he was the only man with whom Daylight was really intimate, though he was on terms of friendliest camaraderie with the rough and unprincipled following of the bosses who ruled the Riverside Club.

On the other hand, San Francisco's attitude toward Daylight had undergone a change. While he, with his slashing buccaneer methods, was a distinct menace to the more orthodox financial gamblers, he was nevertheless so grave a menace that they were glad enough to leave him alone. He had already taught them the excellence of letting a sleeping dog lie. Many of the men, who knew that they were in danger of his big bear-paw when it reached out for the honey vats, even made efforts to placate him, to get on the friendly side of him. The Alta-Pacific approached him confidentially with an offer of reinstatement, which he promptly declined. He was after a number of men in that club, and, whenever opportunity offered, he reached out for them and mangled them. Even the newspapers, with one or two blackmailing exceptions, ceased abusing him and became respectful. In short, he was looked upon as a bald-faced grizzly from the Arctic wilds to whom it was considered expedient to give the trail. At the time he raided the steamship companies, they had yapped at him and worried him, the whole pack of them, only to have him whirl around and whip them in the fiercest pitched battle San Francisco had ever known. Not easily forgotten was the Pacific Slope Seaman's strike and the giving over of the municipal government to the labor bosses and grafters. The destruction of Charles Klinkner and the California and Altamont Trust Company had been a warning. But it was an isolated case; they had been confident in strength in numbers—until he taught them better.

Daylight still engaged in daring speculations, as, for instance, at the impending outbreak of the Japanese-Russian War, when, in the face of the experience and power of the shipping gamblers, he reached out and clutched practically a monopoly of available steamer-charters. There was scarcely a battered tramp on the Seven Seas that was not his on time charter. As usual, his position was, "You've got to come and see me"; which they did, and, to use another of his phrases, they "paid through the nose" for the privilege. And all his venturing and fighting had now but one motive. Some day, as he confided to Hegan, when he'd made a sufficient stake, he was going back to New York and knock the spots out of Messrs. Dowsett, Letton, and Guggenhammer. He'd show them what an all-around general buzz-saw he was and what a mistake they'd made ever to monkey with him. But he never lost his head, and he knew that he was not yet strong enough to go into death-grapples with those three early enemies. In the meantime the black marks against them remained for a future easement day.

Dede Mason was still in the office. He had made no more overtures, discussed no more books and no more grammar. He had no active interest in her, and she was to him a pleasant memory of what had never happened, a joy, which, by his essential nature, he was barred from ever knowing. Yet, while his interest had gone to sleep and his energy was consumed in the endless battles he waged, he knew every trick of the light on her hair, every quick denote mannerism of movement, every line of her figure as expounded by her tailor-made gowns. Several times, six months or so apart, he had increased her salary, until now she was receiving ninety dollars a month. Beyond this he dared not go, though he had got around it by making the work easier. This he had accomplished after her return from a vacation, by retaining her substitute as an assistant. Also, he had changed his office suite, so that now the two girls had a room by themselves.

His eye had become quite critical wherever Dede Mason was concerned. He had long since noted her pride of carriage. It was unobtrusive, yet it was there. He decided, from the way she carried it, that she deemed her body a thing to be proud of, to be cared for as a beautiful and valued possession. In this, and in the way she carried her clothes, he compared her with her assistant, with the stenographers he encountered in other offices, with the women he saw on the sidewalks. "She's sure well put up," he communed with himself; "and she sure knows how to dress and carry it off without being stuck on herself and without laying it on thick."

The more he saw of her, and the more he thought he knew of her, the more unapproachable did she seem to him. But since he had no intention of approaching her, this was anything but an unsatisfactory fact. He was glad he had her in his office, and hoped she'd stay, and that was about all.

Daylight did not improve with the passing years. The life was not good for him. He was growing stout and soft, and there was unwonted flabbiness in his muscles. The more he drank cocktails, the more he was compelled to drink in order to get the desired result, the inhibitions that eased him down from the concert pitch of his operations. And with this went wine, too, at meals, and the long drinks after dinner of Scotch and soda at the Riverside. Then, too, his body suffered from lack of exercise; and, from lack of decent human associations, his moral fibres were weakening. Never a man to hide anything, some of his escapades became public, such as speeding, and of joy-rides in his big red motor-car down to San Jose with companions distinctly sporty—incidents that were narrated as good fun and comically in the newspapers.

Nor was there anything to save him. Religion had passed him by. "A long time dead" was his epitome of that phase of speculation. He was not interested in humanity. According to his rough-hewn sociology, it was all a gamble. God was a whimsical, abstract, mad thing called Luck. As to how one happened to be born—whether a sucker or a robber—was a gamble to begin with; Luck dealt out the cards, and the little babies picked up the hands allotted them. Protest was vain. Those were their cards and they had to play them, willy-nilly, hunchbacked or straight backed, crippled or clean-limbed, addle-pated or clear-headed. There was no fairness in it. The cards most picked up put them into the sucker class; the cards of a few enabled them to become robbers. The playing of the cards was life—the crowd of players, society.

The table was the earth, and the earth, in lumps and chunks, from loaves of bread to big red motor-cars, was the stake. And in the end, lucky and unlucky, they were all a long time dead.

It was hard on the stupid lowly, for they were coppered to lose from the start; but the more he saw of the others, the apparent winners, the less it seemed to him that they had anything to brag about. They, too, were a long time dead, and their living did not amount to much. It was a wild animal fight; the strong trampled the weak, and the strong, he had already discovered,—men like Dowsett, and Letton, and Guggenhammer,—were not necessarily the best. He remembered his miner comrades of the Arctic. They were the stupid lowly, they did the hard work and were robbed of the fruit of their toil just as was the old woman making wine in the Sonoma hills; and yet they had finer qualities of truth, and loyalty, and square-dealing than did the men who robbed them. The winners seemed to be the crooked ones, the unfaithful ones, the wicked ones. And even they had no say in the matter. They played the cards that were given them; and Luck, the monstrous, mad-god thing, the owner of the whole shebang, looked on and grinned. It was he who stacked the universal card-deck of existence.

There was no justice in the deal. The little men that came, the little pulpy babies, were not even asked if they wanted to try a flutter at the game. They had no choice. Luck jerked them into life, slammed them up against the jostling table, and told them: "Now play, damn you, play!" And they did their best, poor little devils. The play of some led to steam yachts and mansions; of others, to the asylum or the pauper's ward. Some played the one same card, over and over, and made wine all their days in the chaparral, hoping, at the end, to pull down a set of false teeth and a coffin. Others quit the game early, having drawn cards that called for violent death, or famine in the Barrens, or loathsome and lingering disease. The hands of some called for kingship and irresponsible and numerated power; other hands called for ambition, for wealth in untold sums, for disgrace and shame, or for women and wine.

As for himself, he had drawn a lucky hand, though he could not see all the cards. Somebody or something might get him yet. The mad god, Luck, might be tricking him along to some such end. An unfortunate set of circumstances, and in a month's time the robber gang might be wardancing around his financial carcass. This very day a street-car might run him down, or a sign fall from a building and smash in his skull. Or there was disease, ever rampant, one of Luck's grimmest whims. Who could say? To-morrow, or some other day, a ptomaine bug, or some other of a thousand bugs, might jump out upon him and drag him down. There was Doctor Bascom, Lee Bascom who had stood beside him a week ago and talked and argued, a picture of magnificent youth, and strength, and health. And in three days he was dead—pneumonia, rheumatism of the heart, and heaven knew what else—at the end screaming in agony that could be heard a block away. That had been terrible. It was a fresh, raw stroke in Daylight's consciousness. And when would his own turn come? Who could say?

In the meantime there was nothing to do but play the cards he could see in his hand, and they were BATTLE, REVENGE, AND COCKTAILS. And Luck sat over all and grinned.

CHAPTER XI

One Sunday, late in the afternoon, found Daylight across the bay in the Piedmont hills back of Oakland. As usual, he was in a big motor-car, though not his own, the guest of Swiftwater Bill, Luck's own darling, who had come down to spend the clean-up of the seventh fortune wrung from the frozen Arctic gravel. A notorious spender, his latest pile was already on the fair road to follow the previous six. He it was, in the first year of Dawson, who had cracked an ocean of champagne at fifty dollars a quart; who, with the bottom of his gold-sack in sight, had cornered the egg-market, at twenty-four dollars per dozen, to the tune of one hundred and ten dozen, in order to pique the lady-love who had jilted him; and he it was, paying like a prince for speed, who had chartered special trains and broken all records between San Francisco and New York. And here he was once more, the "luck-pup of hell," as Daylight called him, throwing his latest fortune away with the same old-time facility.

It was a merry party, and they had made a merry day of it, circling the bay from San Francisco around by San Jose and up to Oakland, having been thrice arrested for speeding, the third time, however, on the Haywards stretch, running away with their captor. Fearing that a telephone message to arrest them had been flashed ahead, they had turned into the back-road through the hills, and now, rushing in upon Oakland by a new route, were boisterously discussing what disposition they should make of the constable.

"We'll come out at Blair Park in ten minutes," one of the men announced. "Look here, Swiftwater, there's a crossroads right ahead, with lots of gates, but it'll take us backcountry clear into Berkeley. Then we can come back into Oakland from the other side, sneak across on the ferry, and send the machine back around to-night with the chauffeur."

But Swiftwater Bill failed to see why he should not go into Oakland by way of Blair Park, and so decided.

The next moment, flying around a bend, the back-road they were not going to take appeared. Inside the gate leaning out from her saddle and just closing it, was a young woman on a chestnut sorrel. With his first glimpse, Daylight felt there was something strangely familiar about her. The next moment, straightening up in the saddle with a movement he could not fail to identify, she put the horse into a gallop, riding away with her back toward them. It was Dede Mason—he remembered what Morrison had told him about her keeping a riding horse, and he was glad she had not seen him in this riotous company. Swiftwater Bill stood up, clinging with one hand to the back of the front seat and waving the other to attract her attention. His lips were pursed for the piercing whistle for which he was famous and which Daylight knew of old, when Daylight, with a hook of his leg and a yank on the shoulder, slammed the startled Bill down into his seat.

"You m-m-must know the lady," Swiftwater Bill spluttered.

"I sure do," Daylight answered, "so shut up."

"Well, I congratulate your good taste, Daylight. She's a peach, and she rides like one, too."

Intervening trees at that moment shut her from view, and Swiftwater Bill plunged into the problem of disposing of their constable, while Daylight, leaning back with closed eyes, was still seeing Dede Mason gallop off down the country road. Swiftwater Bill was right. She certainly could ride. And, sitting astride, her seat was perfect. Good for Dede! That was an added point, her having the courage to ride in the only natural and logical manner. Her head as screwed on right, that was one thing sure.

On Monday morning, coming in for dictation, he looked at her with new interest, though he gave no sign of it; and the stereotyped business passed off in the stereotyped way. But the following Sunday found him on a horse himself, across the bay and riding through the Piedmont hills. He made a long day of it, but no glimpse did he catch of Dede Mason, though he even took the back-road of many gates and rode on into Berkeley. Here, along the lines of multitudinous houses, up one street and down another, he wondered which of them might be occupied by her. Morrison had said long ago that she lived in Berkeley, and she had been headed that way in the late afternoon of the previous Sunday—evidently returning home.

It had been a fruitless day, so far as she was concerned; and yet not entirely fruitless, for he had enjoyed the open air and the horse under him to such purpose that, on Monday, his instructions were out to the dealers to look for the best chestnut sorrel that money could buy. At odd times during the week he examined numbers of chestnut sorrels, tried several, and was unsatisfied. It was not till Saturday that he came upon Bob. Daylight knew him for what he wanted the moment he laid eyes on him. A large horse for a riding animal, he was none too large for a big man like Daylight. In splendid condition, Bob's coat in the sunlight was a flame of fire, his arched neck a jeweled conflagration.

"He's a sure winner," was Daylight's comment; but the dealer was not so sanguine. He was selling the horse on commission, and its owner had insisted on Bob's true character being given. The dealer gave it.

"Not what you'd call a real vicious horse, but a dangerous one. Full of vinegar and all-round cussedness, but without malice. Just as soon kill you as not, but in a playful sort of way, you understand, without meaning to at all. Personally, I wouldn't think of riding him. But he's a stayer. Look at them lungs. And look at them legs. Not a blemish. He's never been hurt or worked. Nobody ever succeeded in taking it out of him. Mountain horse, too, trail-broke and all that, being raised in rough country. Sure-footed as a goat, so long as he don't get it into his head to cut up. Don't shy. Ain't really afraid, but makes believe. Don't buck, but rears. Got to ride him with a martingale. Has a bad trick of whirling around without cause It's his idea of a joke on his rider. It's all just how he feels One day he'll ride along peaceable and pleasant for twenty miles. Next day, before you get started, he's well-nigh unmanageable. Knows automobiles so he can lay down alongside of one and sleep or eat hay out of it. He'll let nineteen go by without batting an eye, and mebbe the twentieth, just because he's feeling frisky, he'll cut up over like a range cayuse. Generally speaking, too lively for a gentleman, and too unexpected. Present owner nicknamed him Judas Iscariot, and refuses to sell without the buyer knowing all about him first. There, that's about all I know, except look at that mane and tail. Ever see anything like it? Hair as fine as a baby's."

The dealer was right. Daylight examined the mane and found it finer than any horse's hair he had ever seen. Also, its color was unusual in that it was almost auburn. While he ran his fingers through it, Bob turned his head and playfully nuzzled Daylight's shoulder.

"Saddle him up, and I'll try him," he told the dealer. "I wonder if he's used to spurs. No English saddle, mind. Give me a good Mexican and a curb bit—not too severe, seeing as he likes to rear."

Daylight superintended the preparations, adjusting the curb strap and the stirrup length, and doing the cinching. He shook his head at the martingale, but yielded to the dealer's advice and allowed it to go on. And Bob, beyond spirited restlessness and a few playful attempts, gave no trouble. Nor in the hour's ride that followed, save for some permissible curveting and prancing, did he misbehave. Daylight was delighted; the purchase was immediately made; and Bob, with riding gear and personal equipment, was despatched across the bay forthwith to take up his quarters in the stables of the Oakland Riding Academy.

The next day being Sunday, Daylight was away early, crossing on the ferry and taking with him Wolf, the leader of his sled team, the one dog which he had selected to bring with him when he left Alaska. Quest as he would through the Piedmont hills and along the many-gated back-road to Berkeley, Daylight saw nothing of Dede Mason and her chestnut sorrel. But he had little time for disappointment, for his own chestnut sorrel kept him busy. Bob proved a handful of impishness and contrariety, and he tried out his rider as much as his rider tried him out. All of Daylight's horse knowledge and horse sense was called into play, while Bob, in turn, worked every trick in his lexicon. Discovering that his martingale had more slack in it than usual, he proceeded to give an exhibition of rearing and hind-leg walking. After ten hopeless minutes of it, Daylight slipped off and tightened the martingale, whereupon Bob gave an exhibition of angelic goodness.

He fooled Daylight completely. At the end of half an hour of goodness, Daylight, lured into confidence, was riding along at a walk and rolling a cigarette, with slack knees and relaxed seat, the reins lying on the animal's neck. Bob whirled abruptly and with lightning swiftness, pivoting on his hind legs, his fore legs just lifted clear of the ground. Daylight found himself with his right foot out of the stirrup and his arms around the animal's neck; and Bob took advantage of the situation to bolt down the road. With a hope that he should not encounter Dede Mason at that moment, Daylight regained his seat and checked in the horse.

Arrived back at the same spot, Bob whirled again. This time Daylight kept his seat, but, beyond a futile rein across the neck, did nothing to prevent the evolution. He noted that Bob whirled to the right, and resolved to keep him straightened out by a spur on the left. But so abrupt and swift was the whirl that warning and accomplishment were practically simultaneous.

"Well, Bob," he addressed the animal, at the same time wiping the sweat from his own eyes, "I'm free to confess that you're sure the blamedest all-fired quickest creature I ever saw. I guess the way to fix you is to keep the spur just a-touching—ah! you brute!"

For, the moment the spur touched him, his left hind leg had reached forward in a kick that struck the stirrup a smart blow. Several times, out of curiosity, Daylight attempted the spur, and each time Bob's hoof landed the stirrup. Then Daylight, following the horse's example of the unexpected, suddenly drove both spurs into him and reached him underneath with the quirt.

"You ain't never had a real licking before," he muttered as Bob, thus rudely jerked out of the circle of his own impish mental processes, shot ahead.

Half a dozen times spurs and quirt bit into him, and then Daylight settled down to enjoy the mad magnificent gallop. No longer punished, at the end of a half mile Bob eased down into a fast canter. Wolf, toiling in the rear, was catching up, and everything was going nicely.

"I'll give you a few pointers on this whirling game, my boy," Daylight was saying to him, when Bob whirled.

He did it on a gallop, breaking the gallop off short by fore legs stiffly planted. Daylight fetched up against his steed's neck with clasped arms, and at the same instant, with fore feet clear of the ground, Bob whirled around. Only an excellent rider could have escaped being unhorsed, and as it was, Daylight was nastily near to it. By the time he recovered his seat, Bob was in full career, bolting the way he had come, and making Wolf side-jump to the bushes.

"All right, darn you!" Daylight grunted, driving in spurs and quirt again and again. "Back-track you want to go, and back-track you sure will go till you're dead sick of it."

When, after a time, Bob attempted to ease down the mad pace, spurs and quirt went into him again with undiminished vim and put him to renewed effort. And when, at last, Daylight decided that the horse had had enough, he turned him around abruptly and put him into a gentle canter on the forward track. After a time he reined him in to a stop to see if he were breathing painfully.

Standing for a minute, Bob turned his head and nuzzled his rider's stirrup in a roguish, impatient way, as much as to intimate that it was time they were going on.

"Well, I'll be plumb gosh darned!" was Daylight's comment. "No ill-will, no grudge, no nothing-and after that lambasting! You're sure a hummer, Bob."

Once again Daylight was lulled into fancied security. For an hour Bob was all that could be desired of a spirited mount, when, and as usual without warning, he took to whirling and bolting. Daylight put a stop to this with spurs and quirt, running him several punishing miles in the direction of his bolt. But when he turned him around and started forward, Bob proceeded to feign fright at trees, cows, bushes, Wolf, his own shadow—in short, at every ridiculously conceivable object. At such times, Wolf lay down in the shade and looked on, while Daylight wrestled it out.

So the day passed. Among other things, Bob developed a trick of making believe to whirl and not whirling. This was as exasperating as the real thing, for each time Daylight was fooled into tightening his leg grip and into a general muscular tensing of all his body. And then, after a few make-believe attempts, Bob actually did whirl and caught Daylight napping again and landed him in the old position with clasped arms around the neck.

And to the end of the day, Bob continued to be up to one trick or another; after passing a dozen automobiles on the way into Oakland, suddenly electing to go mad with fright at a most ordinary little runabout. And just before he arrived back at the stable he capped the day with a combined whirling and rearing that broke the martingale and enabled him to gain a perpendicular position on his hind legs. At this juncture a rotten stirrup leather parted, and Daylight was all but unhorsed.

But he had taken a liking to the animal, and repented not of his bargain. He realized that Bob was not vicious nor mean, the trouble being that he was bursting with high spirits and was endowed with more than the average horse's intelligence. It was the spirits and the intelligence, combined with inordinate roguishness, that made him what he was. What was required to control him was a strong hand, with tempered sternness and yet with the requisite touch of brutal dominance.

"It's you or me, Bob," Daylight told him more than once that day.

And to the stableman, that night:—

"My, but ain't he a looker! Ever see anything like him? Best piece of horseflesh I ever straddled, and I've seen a few in my time."

And to Bob, who had turned his head and was up to his playful nuzzling:—

"Good-by, you little bit of all right. See you again next Sunday A.M., and just you bring along your whole basket of tricks, you old son-of-a-gun."

CHAPTER XII

Throughout the week Daylight found himself almost as much interested in Bob as in Dede; and, not being in the thick of any big deals, he was probably more interested in both of them than in the business game. Bob's trick of whirling was of especial moment to him. How to overcome it,—that was the thing. Suppose he did meet with Dede out in the hills; and suppose, by some lucky stroke of fate, he should manage to be riding alongside of her; then that whirl of Bob's would be most disconcerting and embarrassing. He was not particularly anxious for her to see him thrown forward on Bob's neck. On the other hand, suddenly to leave her and go dashing down the back-track, plying quirt and spurs, wouldn't do, either.

What was wanted was a method wherewith to prevent that lightning whirl. He must stop the animal before it got around. The reins would not do this. Neither would the spurs. Remained the quirt.

But how to accomplish it? Absent-minded moments were many that week, when, sitting in his office chair, in fancy he was astride the wonderful chestnut sorrel and trying to prevent an anticipated whirl. One such moment, toward the end of the week, occurred in the middle of a conference with Hegan. Hegan, elaborating a new and dazzling legal vision, became aware that Daylight was not listening. His eyes had gone lack-lustre, and he, too, was seeing with inner vision.

"Got it" he cried suddenly. "Hegan, congratulate me. It's as simple as rolling off a log. All I've got to do is hit him on the nose, and hit him hard."

Then he explained to the startled Hegan, and became a good listener again, though he could not refrain now and again from making audible chuckles of satisfaction and delight. That was the scheme. Bob always whirled to the right. Very well. He would double the quirt in his hand and, the instant of the whirl, that doubled quirt would rap Bob on the nose. The horse didn't live, after it had once learned the lesson, that would whirl in the face of the doubled quirt.

More keenly than ever, during that week in the office did Daylight realize that he had no social, nor even human contacts with Dede. The situation was such that he could not ask her the simple question whether or not she was going riding next Sunday. It was a hardship of a new sort, this being the employer of a pretty girl. He looked at her often, when the routine work of the day was going on, the question he could not ask her tickling at the founts of speech—Was she going riding next Sunday? And as he looked, he wondered how old she was, and what love passages she had had, must have had, with those college whippersnappers with whom, according to Morrison, she herded and danced. His mind was very full of her, those six days between the Sundays, and one thing he came to know thoroughly well; he wanted her. And so much did he want her that his old timidity of the apron-string was put to rout. He, who had run away from women most of his life, had now grown so courageous as to pursue. Some Sunday, sooner or later, he would meet her outside the office, somewhere in the hills, and then, if they did not get acquainted, it would be because she did not care to get acquainted.

Thus he found another card in the hand the mad god had dealt him.

How important that card was to become he did not dream, yet he decided that it was a pretty good card. In turn, he doubted. Maybe it was a trick of Luck to bring calamity and disaster upon him. Suppose Dede wouldn't have him, and suppose he went on loving her more and more, harder and harder? All his old generalized terrors of love revived. He remembered the disastrous love affairs of men and women he had known in the past. There was Bertha Doolittle, old Doolittle's daughter, who had been madly in love with Dartworthy, the rich Bonanza fraction owner; and Dartworthy, in turn, not loving Bertha at all, but madly loving Colonel Walthstone's wife and eloping down the Yukon with her; and Colonel Walthstone himself, madly loving his own wife and lighting out in pursuit of the fleeing couple. And what had been the outcome? Certainly Bertha's love had been unfortunate and tragic, and so had the love of the other three. Down below Minook, Colonel Walthstone and Dartworthy had fought it out. Dartworthy had been killed. A bullet through the Colonel's lungs had so weakened him that he died of pneumonia the following spring. And the Colonel's wife had no one left alive on earth to love.

And then there was Freda, drowning herself in the running mush-ice because of some man on the other side of the world, and hating him, Daylight, because he had happened along and pulled her out of the mush-ice and back to life. And the Virgin.... The old memories frightened him. If this love-germ gripped him good and hard, and if Dede wouldn't have him, it might be almost as bad as being gouged out of all he had by Dowsett, Letton, and Guggenhammer. Had his nascent desire for Dede been less, he might well have been frightened out of all thought of her. As it was, he found consolation in the thought that some love affairs did come out right. And for all he knew, maybe Luck had stacked the cards for him to win. Some men were born lucky, lived lucky all their days, and died lucky. Perhaps, too, he was such a man, a born luck-pup who could not lose.

Sunday came, and Bob, out in the Piedmont hills, behaved like an angel. His goodness, at times, was of the spirited prancing order, but otherwise he was a lamb. Daylight, with doubled quirt ready in his right hand, ached for a whirl, just one whirl, which Bob, with an excellence of conduct that was tantalizing, refused to perform. But no Dede did Daylight encounter. He vainly circled about among the hill roads and in the afternoon took the steep grade over the divide of the second range and dropped into Maraga Valley. Just after passing the foot of the descent, he heard the hoof beats of a cantering horse. It was from ahead and coming toward him. What if it were Dede? He turned Bob around and started to return at a walk. If it were Dede, he was born to luck, he decided; for the meeting couldn't have occurred under better circumstances. Here they were, both going in the same direction, and the canter would bring her up to him just where the stiff grade would compel a walk. There would be nothing else for her to do than ride with him to the top of the divide; and, once there, the equally stiff descent on the other side would compel more walking.

The canter came nearer, but he faced straight ahead until he heard the horse behind check to a walk. Then he glanced over his shoulder. It was Dede. The recognition was quick, and, with her, accompanied by surprise. What more natural thing than that, partly turning his horse, he should wait till she caught up with him; and that, when abreast they should continue abreast on up the grade? He could have sighed with relief. The thing was accomplished, and so easily. Greetings had been exchanged; here they were side by side and going in the same direction with miles and miles ahead of them.

He noted that her eye was first for the horse and next for him.

"Oh, what a beauty" she had cried at sight of Bob. From the shining light in her eyes, and the face filled with delight, he would scarcely have believed that it belonged to a young woman he had known in the office, the young woman with the controlled, subdued office face.

"I didn't know you rode," was one of her first remarks. "I imagined you were wedded to get-there-quick machines."

"I've just taken it up lately," was his answer. "Beginning to get stout; you know, and had to take it off somehow."

She gave a quick sidewise glance that embraced him from head to heel, including seat and saddle, and said:—

"But you've ridden before."

She certainly had an eye for horses and things connected with horses was his thought, as he replied:—

"Not for many years. But I used to think I was a regular rip-snorter when I was a youngster up in Eastern Oregon, sneaking away from camp to ride with the cattle and break cayuses and that sort of thing."

Thus, and to his great relief, were they launched on a topic of mutual interest. He told her about Bob's tricks, and of the whirl and his scheme to overcome it; and she agreed that horses had to be handled with a certain rational severity, no matter how much one loved them. There was her Mab, which she had for eight years and which she had had break of stall-kicking. The process had been painful for Mab, but it had cured her.

"You've ridden a lot," Daylight said.

"I really can't remember the first time I was on a horse," she told him. "I was born on a ranch, you know, and they couldn't keep me away from the horses. I must have been born with the love for them. I had my first pony, all my own, when I was six. When I was eight I knew what it was to be all day in the saddle along with Daddy. By the time I was eleven he was taking me on my first deer hunts. I'd be lost without a horse. I hate indoors, and without Mab here I suppose I'd have been sick and dead long ago."

"You like the country?" he queried, at the same moment catching his first glimpse of a light in her eyes other than gray. "As much as I detest the city," she answered. "But a woman can't earn a living in the country. So I make the best of it—along with Mab."

And thereat she told him more of her ranch life in the days before her father died. And Daylight was hugely pleased with himself. They were getting acquainted. The conversation had not lagged in the full half hour they had been together.

"We come pretty close from the same part of the country," he said. "I was raised in Eastern Oregon, and that's none so far from Siskiyou."

The next moment he could have bitten out his tongue for her quick question was:—

"How did you know I came from Siskiyou? I'm sure I never mentioned it."

"I don't know," he floundered temporarily. "I heard somewhere that you were from thereabouts."

Wolf, sliding up at that moment, sleek-footed and like a shadow, caused her horse to shy and passed the awkwardness off, for they talked Alaskan dogs until the conversation drifted back to horses. And horses it was, all up the grade and down the other side.

When she talked, he listened and followed her, and yet all the while he was following his own thoughts and impressions as well. It was a nervy thing for her to do, this riding astride, and he didn't know, after all, whether he liked it or not. His ideas of women were prone to be old-fashioned; they were the ones he had imbibed in the early-day, frontier life of his youth, when no woman was seen on anything but a side-saddle. He had grown up to the tacit fiction that women on horseback were not bipeds. It came to him with a shock, this sight of her so manlike in her saddle. But he had to confess that the sight looked good to him just then.

Two other immediate things about her struck him. First, there were the golden spots in her eyes. Queer that he had never noticed them before. Perhaps the light in the office had not been right, and perhaps they came and went. No; they were glows of color—a sort of diffused, golden light. Nor was it golden, either, but it was nearer that than any color he knew. It certainly was not any shade of yellow. A lover's thoughts are ever colored, and it is to be doubted if any one else in the world would have called Dede's eyes golden. But Daylight's mood verged on the tender and melting, and he preferred to think of them as golden, and therefore they were golden.

And then she was so natural. He had been prepared to find her a most difficult young woman to get acquainted with. Yet here it was proving so simple. There was nothing highfalutin about her company manners—it was by this homely phrase that he differentiated this Dede on horseback from the Dede with the office manners whom he had always known. And yet, while he was delighted with the smoothness with which everything was going, and with the fact that they had found plenty to talk about, he was aware of an irk under it all. After all, this talk was empty and idle. He was a man of action, and he wanted her, Dede Mason, the woman; he wanted her to love him and to be loved by him; and he wanted all this glorious consummation then and there. Used to forcing issues used to gripping men and things and bending them to his will, he felt, now, the same compulsive prod of mastery. He wanted to tell her that he loved her and that there was nothing else for her to do but marry him. And yet he did not obey the prod. Women were fluttery creatures, and here mere mastery would prove a bungle. He remembered all his hunting guile, the long patience of shooting meat in famine when a hit or a miss meant life or death. Truly, though this girl did not yet mean quite that, nevertheless she meant much to him—more, now, than ever, as he rode beside her, glancing at her as often as he dared, she in her corduroy riding-habit, so bravely manlike, yet so essentially and revealingly woman, smiling, laughing, talking, her eyes sparkling, the flush of a day of sun and summer breeze warm in her cheeks.

CHAPTER XIII

Another Sunday man and horse and dog roved the Piedmont hills. And again Daylight and Dede rode together. But this time her surprise at meeting him was tinctured with suspicion; or rather, her surprise was of another order. The previous Sunday had been quite accidental, but his appearing a second time among her favorite haunts hinted of more than the fortuitous. Daylight was made to feel that she suspected him, and he, remembering that he had seen a big rock quarry near Blair Park, stated offhand that he was thinking of buying it. His one-time investment in a brickyard had put the idea into his head—an idea that he decided was a good one, for it enabled him to suggest that she ride along with him to inspect the quarry.

So several hours he spent in her company, in which she was much the same girl as before, natural, unaffected, lighthearted, smiling and laughing, a good fellow, talking horses with unflagging enthusiasm, making friends with the crusty-tempered Wolf, and expressing the desire to ride Bob, whom she declared she was more in love with than ever. At this last Daylight demurred. Bob was full of dangerous tricks, and he wouldn't trust any one on him except his worst enemy.

"You think, because I'm a girl, that I don't know anything about horses," she flashed back. "But I've been thrown off and bucked off enough not to be over-confident. And I'm not a fool. I wouldn't get on a bucking horse. I've learned better. And I'm not afraid of any other kind. And you say yourself that Bob doesn't buck."

"But you've never seen him cutting up didoes," Daylight said.

"But you must remember I've seen a few others, and I've been on several of them myself. I brought Mab here to electric cars, locomotives, and automobiles. She was a raw range colt when she came to me. Broken to saddle that was all. Besides, I won't hurt your horse."

Against his better judgment, Daylight gave in, and, on an unfrequented stretch of road, changed saddles and bridles.

"Remember, he's greased lightning," he warned, as he helped her to mount.

She nodded, while Bob pricked up his ears to the knowledge that he had a strange rider on his back. The fun came quickly enough—too quickly for Dede, who found herself against Bob's neck as he pivoted around and bolted the other way. Daylight followed on her horse and watched. He saw her check the animal quickly to a standstill, and immediately, with rein across neck and a decisive prod of the left spur, whirl him back the way he had come and almost as swiftly.

"Get ready to give him the quirt on the nose," Daylight called.

But, too quickly for her, Bob whirled again, though this time, by a severe effort, she saved herself from the undignified position against his neck. His bolt was more determined, but she pulled him into a prancing walk, and turned him roughly back with her spurred heel. There was nothing feminine in the way she handled him; her method was imperative and masculine. Had this not been so, Daylight would have expected her to say she had had enough. But that little preliminary exhibition had taught him something of Dede's quality. And if it had not, a glance at her gray eyes, just perceptibly angry with herself, and at her firm-set mouth, would have told him the same thing. Daylight did not suggest anything, while he hung almost gleefully upon her actions in anticipation of what the fractious Bob was going to get. And Bob got it, on his next whirl, or attempt, rather, for he was no more than halfway around when the quirt met him smack on his tender nose. There and then, in his bewilderment, surprise, and pain, his fore feet, just skimming above the road, dropped down.

"Great!" Daylight applauded. "A couple more will fix him. He's too smart not to know when he's beaten."

Again Bob tried. But this time he was barely quarter around when the doubled quirt on his nose compelled him to drop his fore feet to the road. Then, with neither rein nor spur, but by the mere threat of the quirt, she straightened him out.

Dede looked triumphantly at Daylight.

"Let me give him a run?" she asked.

Daylight nodded, and she shot down the road. He watched her out of sight around the bend, and watched till she came into sight returning. She certainly could sit her horse, was his thought, and she was a sure enough hummer. God, she was the wife for a man! Made most of them look pretty slim. And to think of her hammering all week at a typewriter. That was no place for her. She should be a man's wife, taking it easy, with silks and satins and diamonds (his frontier notion of what befitted a wife beloved), and dogs, and horses, and such things—"And we'll see, Mr. Burning Daylight, what you and me can do about it," he murmured to himself! and aloud to her:—

"You'll do, Miss Mason; you'll do. There's nothing too good in horseflesh you don't deserve, a woman who can ride like that. No; stay with him, and we'll jog along to the quarry." He chuckled. "Say, he actually gave just the least mite of a groan that last time you fetched him. Did you hear it? And did you see the way he dropped his feet to the road—just like he'd struck a stone wall. And he's got savvee enough to know from now on that that same stone wall will be always there ready for him to lam into."

When he parted from her that afternoon, at the gate of the road that led to Berkeley, he drew off to the edge of the intervening clump of trees, where, unobserved, he watched her out of sight. Then, turning to ride back into Oakland, a thought came to him that made him grin ruefully as he muttered: "And now it's up to me to make good and buy that blamed quarry. Nothing less than that can give me an excuse for snooping around these hills."

But the quarry was doomed to pass out of his plans for a time, for on the following Sunday he rode alone. No Dede on a chestnut sorrel came across the back-road from Berkeley that day, nor the day a week later. Daylight was beside himself with impatience and apprehension, though in the office he contained himself. He noted no change in her, and strove to let none show in himself. The same old monotonous routine went on, though now it was irritating and maddening. Daylight found a big quarrel on his hands with a world that wouldn't let a man behave toward his stenographer after the way of all men and women. What was the good of owning millions anyway? he demanded one day of the desk-calendar, as she passed out after receiving his dictation.

As the third week drew to a close and another desolate Sunday confronted him, Daylight resolved to speak, office or no office. And as was his nature, he went simply and directly to the point She had finished her work with him, and was gathering her note pad and pencils together to depart, when he said:—

"Oh, one thing more, Miss Mason, and I hope you won't mind my being frank and straight out. You've struck me right along as a sensible-minded girl, and I don't think you'll take offence at what I'm going to say. You know how long you've been in the office—it's years, now, several of them, anyway; and you know I've always been straight and aboveboard with you. I've never what you call—presumed. Because you were in my office I've tried to be more careful than if—if you wasn't in my office—you understand. But just the same, it don't make me any the less human. I'm a lonely sort of a fellow—don't take that as a bid for kindness. What I mean by it is to try and tell you just how much those two rides with you have meant. And now I hope you won't mind my just asking why you haven't been out riding the last two Sundays?"

He came to a stop and waited, feeling very warm and awkward, the perspiration starting in tiny beads on his forehead. She did not speak immediately, and he stepped across the room and raised the window higher.

"I have been riding," she answered; "in other directions."

"But why...?" He failed somehow to complete the question. "Go ahead and be frank with me," he urged. "Just as frank as I am with you. Why didn't you ride in the Piedmont hills? I hunted for you everywhere.

"And that is just why." She smiled, and looked him straight in the eyes for a moment, then dropped her own. "Surely, you understand, Mr. Harnish."

He shook his head glumly.

"I do, and I don't. I ain't used to city ways by a long shot. There's things one mustn't do, which I don't mind as long as I don't want to do them."

"But when you do?" she asked quickly.

"Then I do them." His lips had drawn firmly with this affirmation of will, but the next instant he was amending the statement "That is, I mostly do. But what gets me is the things you mustn't do when they're not wrong and they won't hurt anybody—this riding, for instance."

She played nervously with a pencil for a time, as if debating her reply, while he waited patiently.

"This riding," she began; "it's not what they call the right thing. I leave it to you. You know the world. You are Mr. Harnish, the millionaire—"

"Gambler," he broke in harshly

She nodded acceptance of his term and went on.

"And I'm a stenographer in your office—"

"You're a thousand times better than me—" he attempted to interpolate, but was in turn interrupted.

"It isn't a question of such things. It's a simple and fairly common situation that must be considered. I work for you. And it isn't what you or I might think, but what other persons will think. And you don't need to be told any more about that. You know yourself."

Her cool, matter-of-fact speech belied her—or so Daylight thought, looking at her perturbed feminineness, at the rounded lines of her figure, the breast that deeply rose and fell, and at the color that was now excited in her cheeks.

"I'm sorry I frightened you out of your favorite stamping ground," he said rather aimlessly.

"You didn't frighten me," she retorted, with a touch of fire. "I'm not a silly seminary girl. I've taken care of myself for a long time now, and I've done it without being frightened. We were together two Sundays, and I'm sure I wasn't frightened of Bob, or you. It isn't that. I have no fears of taking care of myself, but the world insists on taking care of one as well. That's the trouble. It's what the world would have to say about me and my employer meeting regularly and riding in the hills on Sundays. It's funny, but it's so. I could ride with one of the clerks without remark, but with you—no."

"But the world don't know and don't need to know," he cried.

"Which makes it worse, in a way, feeling guilty of nothing and yet sneaking around back-roads with all the feeling of doing something wrong. It would be finer and braver for me publicly..."

"To go to lunch with me on a week-day," Daylight said, divining the drift of her uncompleted argument.

She nodded.

"I didn't have that quite in mind, but it will do. I'd prefer doing the brazen thing and having everybody know it, to doing the furtive thing and being found out. Not that I'm asking to be invited to lunch," she added, with a smile; "but I'm sure you understand my position."

"Then why not ride open and aboveboard with me in the hills?" he urged.

She shook her head with what he imagined was just the faintest hint of regret, and he went suddenly and almost maddeningly hungry for her.

"Look here, Miss Mason, I know you don't like this talking over of things in the office. Neither do I. It's part of the whole thing, I guess; a man ain't supposed to talk anything but business with his stenographer. Will you ride with me next Sunday, and we can talk it over thoroughly then and reach some sort of a conclusion. Out in the hills is the place where you can talk something besides business. I guess you've seen enough of me to know I'm pretty square. I—I do honor and respect you, and ... and all that, and I..." He was beginning to flounder, and the hand that rested on the desk blotter was visibly trembling. He strove to pull himself together. "I just want to harder than anything ever in my life before. I—I—I can't explain myself, but I do, that's all. Will you?—Just next Sunday? To-morrow?"

Nor did he dream that her low acquiescence was due, as much as anything else, to the beads of sweat on his forehead, his trembling hand, and his all too-evident general distress.

CHAPTER XIV

"Of course, there's no way of telling what anybody wants from what they say." Daylight rubbed Bob's rebellious ear with his quirt and pondered with dissatisfaction the words he had just uttered. They did not say what he had meant them to say. "What I'm driving at is that you say flatfooted that you won't meet me again, and you give your reasons, but how am I to know they are your real reasons? Mebbe you just don't want to get acquainted with me, and won't say so for fear of hurting my feelings. Don't you see? I'm the last man in the world to shove in where I'm not wanted. And if I thought you didn't care a whoop to see anything more of me, why, I'd clear out so blamed quick you couldn't see me for smoke."

Dede smiled at him in acknowledgment of his words, but rode on silently. And that smile, he thought, was the most sweetly wonderful smile he had ever seen. There was a difference in it, he assured himself, from any smile she had ever given him before.

It was the smile of one who knew him just a little bit, of one who was just the least mite acquainted with him. Of course, he checked himself up the next moment, it was unconscious on her part. It was sure to come in the intercourse of any two persons.

Any stranger, a business man, a clerk, anybody after a few casual meetings would show similar signs of friendliness. It was bound to happen, but in her case it made more impression on him; and, besides, it was such a sweet and wonderful smile. Other women he had known had never smiled like that; he was sure of it.

It had been a happy day. Daylight had met her on the back-road from Berkeley, and they had had hours together. It was only now, with the day drawing to a close and with them approaching the gate of the road to Berkeley, that he had broached the important subject.

She began her answer to his last contention, and he listened gratefully.

"But suppose, just suppose, that the reasons I have given are the only ones?—that there is no question of my not wanting to know you?"

"Then I'd go on urging like Sam Scratch," he said quickly. "Because, you see, I've always noticed that folks that incline to anything are much more open to hearing the case stated. But if you did have that other reason up your sleeve, if you didn't want to know me, if—if, well, if you thought my feelings oughtn't to be hurt just because you had a good job with me..." Here, his calm consideration of a possibility was swamped by the fear that it was an actuality, and he lost the thread of his reasoning. "Well, anyway, all you have to do is to say the word and I'll clear out.

"And with no hard feelings; it would be just a case of bad luck for me. So be honest, Miss Mason, please, and tell me if that's the reason—I almost got a hunch that it is."

She glanced up at him, her eyes abruptly and slightly moist, half with hurt, half with anger.

"Oh, but that isn't fair," she cried. "You give me the choice of lying to you and hurting you in order to protect myself by getting rid of you, or of throwing away my protection by telling you the truth, for then you, as you said yourself, would stay and urge."

Her cheeks were flushed, her lips tremulous, but she continued to look him frankly in the eyes.

Daylight smiled grimly with satisfaction.

"I'm real glad, Miss Mason, real glad for those words."

"But they won't serve you," she went on hastily. "They can't serve you. I refuse to let them. This is our last ride, and... here is the gate."

Ranging her mare alongside, she bent, slid the catch, and followed the opening gate.

"No; please, no," she said, as Daylight started to follow.

Humbly acquiescent, he pulled Bob back, and the gate swung shut between them. But there was more to say, and she did not ride on.

"Listen, Miss Mason," he said, in a low voice that shook with sincerity; "I want to assure you of one thing. I'm not just trying to fool around with you. I like you, I want you, and I was never more in earnest in my life. There's nothing wrong in my intentions or anything like that. What I mean is strictly honorable—"

But the expression of her face made him stop. She was angry, and she was laughing at the same time.

"The last thing you should have said," she cried. "It's like a—a matrimonial bureau: intentions strictly honorable; object, matrimony. But it's no more than I deserved. This is what I suppose you call urging like Sam Scratch."

The tan had bleached out of Daylight's skin since the time he came to live under city roofs, so that the flush of blood showed readily as it crept up his neck past the collar and overspread his face. Nor in his exceeding discomfort did he dream that she was looking upon him at that moment with more kindness than at any time that day. It was not in her experience to behold big grown-up men who blushed like boys, and already she repented the sharpness into which she had been surprised.

"Now, look here, Miss Mason," he began, slowly and stumblingly at first, but accelerating into a rapidity of utterance that was almost incoherent; "I'm a rough sort of a man, I know that, and I know I don't know much of anything. I've never had any training in nice things. I've never made love before, and I've never been in love before either—and I don't know how to go about it any more than a thundering idiot. What you want to do is get behind my tomfool words and get a feel of the man that's behind them. That's me, and I mean all right, if I don't know how to go about it."

Dede Mason had quick, birdlike ways, almost flitting from mood to mood; and she was all contrition on the instant.

"Forgive me for laughing," she said across the gate. "It wasn't really laughter. I was surprised off my guard, and hurt, too. You see, Mr. Harnish, I've not been..."

She paused, in sudden fear of completing the thought into which her birdlike precipitancy had betrayed her.

"What you mean is that you've not been used to such sort of proposing," Daylight said; "a sort of on-the-run, 'Howdy, glad-to-make-your-acquaintance, won't-you-be-mine' proposition."

She nodded and broke into laughter, in which he joined, and which served to pass the awkwardness away. He gathered heart at this, and went on in greater confidence, with cooler head and tongue.

"There, you see, you prove my case. You've had experience in such matters. I don't doubt you've had slathers of proposals. Well, I haven't, and I'm like a fish out of water. Besides, this ain't a proposal. It's a peculiar situation, that's all, and I'm in a corner. I've got enough plain horse-sense to know a man ain't supposed to argue marriage with a girl as a reason for getting acquainted with her. And right there was where I was in the hole. Number one, I can't get acquainted with you in the office. Number two, you say you won't see me out of the office to give me a chance. Number three, your reason is that folks will talk because you work for me. Number four, I just got to get acquainted with you, and I just got to get you to see that I mean fair and all right. Number five, there you are on one side the gate getting ready to go, and me here on the other side the gate pretty desperate and bound to say something to make you reconsider. Number six, I said it. And now and finally, I just do want you to reconsider."

And, listening to him, pleasuring in the sight of his earnest, perturbed face and in the simple, homely phrases that but emphasized his earnestness and marked the difference between him and the average run of men she had known, she forgot to listen and lost herself in her own thoughts. The love of a strong man is ever a lure to a normal woman, and never more strongly did Dede feel the lure than now, looking across the closed gate at Burning Daylight. Not that she would ever dream of marrying him—she had a score of reasons against it; but why not at least see more of him? He was certainly not repulsive to her. On the contrary, she liked him, had always liked him from the day she had first seen him and looked upon his lean Indian face and into his flashing Indian eyes. He was a figure of a man in more ways than his mere magnificent muscles. Besides, Romance had gilded him, this doughty, rough-hewn adventurer of the North, this man of many deeds and many millions, who had come down out of the Arctic to wrestle and fight so masterfully with the men of the South.

Savage as a Red Indian, gambler and profligate, a man without morals, whose vengeance was never glutted and who stamped on the faces of all who opposed him—oh, yes, she knew all the hard names he had been called. Yet she was not afraid of him. There was more than that in the connotation of his name. Burning Daylight called up other things as well. They were there in the newspapers, the magazines, and the books on the Klondike. When all was said, Burning Daylight had a mighty connotation—one to touch any woman's imagination, as it touched hers, the gate between them, listening to the wistful and impassioned simplicity of his speech. Dede was after all a woman, with a woman's sex-vanity, and it was this vanity that was pleased by the fact that such a man turned in his need to her.

And there was more that passed through her mind—sensations of tiredness and loneliness; trampling squadrons and shadowy armies of vague feelings and vaguer prompting; and deeper and dimmer whisperings and echoings, the flutterings of forgotten generations crystallized into being and fluttering anew and always, undreamed and unguessed, subtle and potent, the spirit and essence of life that under a thousand deceits and masks forever makes for life. It was a strong temptation, just to ride with this man in the hills. It would be that only and nothing more, for she was firmly convinced that his way of life could never be her way. On the other hand, she was vexed by none of the ordinary feminine fears and timidities. That she could take care of herself under any and all circumstances she never doubted. Then why not? It was such a little thing, after all.

She led an ordinary, humdrum life at best. She ate and slept and worked, and that was about all. As if in review, her anchorite existence passed before her: six days of the week spent in the office and in journeying back and forth on the ferry; the hours stolen before bedtime for snatches of song at the piano, for doing her own special laundering, for sewing and mending and casting up of meagre accounts; the two evenings a week of social diversion she permitted herself; the other stolen hours and Saturday afternoons spent with her brother at the hospital;

and the seventh day, Sunday, her day of solace, on Mab's back, out among the blessed hills. But it was lonely, this solitary riding. Nobody of her acquaintance rode. Several girls at the University had been persuaded into trying it, but after a Sunday or two on hired livery hacks they had lost interest. There was Madeline, who bought her own horse and rode enthusiastically for several months, only to get married and go away to live in Southern California. After years of it, one did get tired of this eternal riding alone.

He was such a boy, this big giant of a millionaire who had half the rich men of San Francisco afraid of him. Such a boy! She had never imagined this side of his nature.

"How do folks get married?" he was saying. "Why, number one, they meet; number two, like each other's looks; number three, get acquainted; and number four, get married or not, according to how they like each other after getting acquainted. But how in thunder we're to have a chance to find out whether we like each other enough is beyond my savvee, unless we make that chance ourselves. I'd come to see you, call on you, only I know you're just rooming or boarding, and that won't do."

Suddenly, with a change of mood, the situation appeared to Dede ridiculously absurd. She felt a desire to laugh—not angrily, not hysterically, but just jolly. It was so funny. Herself, the stenographer, he, the notorious and powerful gambling millionaire, and the gate between them across which poured his argument of people getting acquainted and married. Also, it was an impossible situation. On the face of it, she could not go on with it. This program of furtive meetings in the hills would have to discontinue. There would never be another meeting. And if, denied this, he tried to woo her in the office, she would be compelled to lose a very good position, and that would be an end of the episode. It was not nice to contemplate; but the world of men, especially in the cities, she had not found particularly nice. She had not worked for her living for years without losing a great many of her illusions.

"We won't do any sneaking or hiding around about it," Daylight was explaining. "We'll ride around as bold if you please, and if anybody sees us, why, let them. If they talk—well, so long as our consciences are straight we needn't worry. Say the word, and Bob will have on his back the happiest man alive."

She shook her head, pulled in the mare, who was impatient to be off for home, and glanced significantly at the lengthening shadows.

"It's getting late now, anyway," Daylight hurried on, "and we've settled nothing after all. Just one more Sunday, anyway—that's not asking much—to settle it in."

"We've had all day," she said.

"But we started to talk it over too late. We'll tackle it earlier next time. This is a big serious proposition with me, I can tell you. Say next Sunday?"

"Are men ever fair?" she asked. "You know thoroughly well that by 'next Sunday' you mean many Sundays."

"Then let it be many Sundays," he cried recklessly, while she thought that she had never seen him looking handsomer. "Say the word. Only say the word. Next Sunday at the quarry..."

She gathered the reins into her hand preliminary to starting.

"Good night," she said, "and—"

"Yes," he whispered, with just the faintest touch of impressiveness.

"Yes," she said, her voice low but distinct.

At the same moment she put the mare into a canter and went down the road without a backward glance, intent on an analysis of her own feelings. With her mind made up to say no—and to the last instant she had been so resolved—her lips nevertheless had said yes. Or at least it seemed the lips. She had not intended to consent. Then why had she? Her first surprise and bewilderment at so wholly unpremeditated an act gave way to consternation as she considered its consequences. She knew that Burning Daylight was not a man to be trifled with, that under his simplicity and boyishness he was essentially a dominant male creature, and that she had pledged herself to a future of inevitable stress and storm. And again she demanded of herself why she had said yes at the very moment when it had been farthest from her intention.

CHAPTER XV

Life at the office went on much the way it had always gone. Never, by word or look, did they acknowledge that the situation was in any wise different from what it had always been. Each Sunday saw the arrangement made for the following Sunday's ride; nor was this ever referred to in the office. Daylight was fastidiously chivalrous on this point. He did not want to lose her from the office. The sight of her at her work was to him an undiminishing joy. Nor did he abuse this by lingering over dictation or by devising extra work that would detain her longer before his eyes. But over and beyond such sheer selfishness of conduct was his love of fair play. He scorned to utilize the accidental advantages of the situation. Somewhere within him was a higher appeasement of love than mere possession. He wanted to be loved for himself, with a fair field for both sides.

On the other hand, had he been the most artful of schemers he could not have pursued a wiser policy. Bird-like in her love of individual freedom, the last woman in the world to be bullied in her affections, she keenly appreciated the niceness of his attitude. She did this consciously, but deeper than all consciousness, and intangible as gossamer, were the effects of this. All unrealizable, save for some supreme moment, did the web of Daylight's personality creep out and around her. Filament by filament, these secret and undreamable bonds were being established. They it was that could have given the cue to her saying yes when she had meant to say no. And in some such fashion, in some future crisis of greater moment, might she not, in violation of all dictates of sober judgment, give another unintentional consent?

Among other good things resulting from his growing intimacy with Dede, was Daylight's not caring to drink so much as formerly. There was a lessening in desire for alcohol of which even he at last became aware. In a way she herself was the needed inhibition. The thought of her was like a cocktail. Or, at any rate, she substituted for a certain percentage of cocktails. From the strain of his unnatural city existence and of his intense gambling operations, he had drifted on to the cocktail route. A wall must forever be built to give him easement from the high pitch, and Dede became a part of this wall. Her personality, her laughter, the intonations of her voice, the impossible golden glow of her eyes, the light on her hair, her form, her dress, her actions on horseback, her merest physical mannerisms—all, pictured over and over in his mind and dwelt upon, served to take the place of many a cocktail or long Scotch and soda.

In spite of their high resolve, there was a very measurable degree of the furtive in their meetings. In essence, these meetings were stolen. They did not ride out brazenly together in the face of the world. On the contrary, they met always unobserved, she riding across the many-gated backroad from Berkeley to meet him halfway. Nor did they ride on any save unfrequented roads, preferring to cross the second range of hills and travel among a church-going farmer folk who would scarcely have recognized even Daylight from his newspaper photographs.

He found Dede a good horsewoman—good not merely in riding but in endurance. There were days when they covered sixty, seventy, and even eighty miles; nor did Dede ever claim any day too long, nor—another strong recommendation to Daylight—did the hardest day ever the slightest chafe of the chestnut sorrel's back. "A sure enough hummer," was Daylight's stereotyped but ever enthusiastic verdict to himself.

They learned much of each other on these long, uninterrupted rides. They had nothing much to talk about but themselves, and, while she received a liberal education concerning Arctic travel and gold-mining, he, in turn, touch by touch, painted an ever clearer portrait of her. She amplified the ranch life of her girlhood, prattling on about horses and dogs and persons and things until it was as if he saw the whole process of her growth and her becoming. All this he was able to trace on through the period of her father's failure and death, when she had been compelled to leave the university and go into office work. The brother, too, she spoke of, and of her long struggle to have him cured and of her now fading hopes. Daylight decided that it was easier to come to an understanding of her than he had anticipated, though he was always aware that behind and under all he knew of her was the mysterious and baffling woman and sex. There, he was humble enough to confess to himself, was a chartless, shoreless sea, about which he knew nothing and which he must nevertheless somehow navigate.

His lifelong fear of woman had originated out of non-understanding and had also prevented him from reaching any understanding. Dede on horseback, Dede gathering poppies on a summer hillside, Dede taking down dictation in her swift shorthand strokes—all this was comprehensible to him. But he did not know the Dede who so quickly changed from mood to mood, the Dede who refused steadfastly to ride with him and then suddenly consented, the Dede in whose eyes the golden glow forever waxed and waned and whispered hints and messages that were not for his ears. In all such things he saw the glimmering profundities of sex, acknowledged their lure, and accepted them as incomprehensible.

There was another side of her, too, of which he was consciously ignorant. She knew the books, was possessed of that mysterious and awful thing called "culture." And yet, what continually surprised him was that this culture was never obtruded on their intercourse. She did not talk books, nor art, nor similar folderols. Homely minded as he was himself, he found her almost equally homely minded. She liked the simple and the out-of-doors, the horses and the hills, the sunlight and the flowers. He found himself in a partly new flora, to which she was the guide, pointing out to him all the varieties of the oaks, making him acquainted with the madrono and the manzanita, teaching him the names, habits, and habitats of unending series of wild flowers, shrubs, and ferns. Her keen woods eye was another delight to him. It had been trained in the open, and little escaped it. One day, as a test, they strove to see which could discover the greater number of birds' nests. And he, who had always prided himself on his own acutely trained observation, found himself hard put to keep his score ahead. At the end of the day he was but three nests in the lead, one of which she challenged stoutly and of which even he confessed serious doubt. He complimented her and told her that her success must be due to the fact that she was a bird herself, with all a bird's keen vision and quick-flashing ways.

The more he knew her the more he became convinced of this birdlike quality in her. That was why she liked to ride, he argued. It was the nearest approach to flying. A field of poppies, a glen of ferns, a row of poplars on a country lane, the tawny brown of a hillside, the shaft of sunlight on a distant peak—all such were provocative of quick joys which seemed to him like so many outbursts of song. Her joys were in little things, and she seemed always singing. Even in sterner things it was the same. When she rode Bob and fought with that magnificent brute for mastery, the qualities of an eagle were uppermost in her.

These quick little joys of hers were sources of joy to him. He joyed in her joy, his eyes as excitedly fixed on her as bears were fixed on the object of her attention. Also through her he came to a closer discernment and keener appreciation of nature. She showed him colors in the landscape that he would never have dreamed were there. He had known only the primary colors. All colors of red were red. Black was black, and brown was just plain brown until it became yellow, when it was no longer brown. Purple he had always imagined was red, something like blood, until she taught him better. Once they rode out on a high hill brow where wind-blown poppies blazed about their horses' knees, and she was in an ecstasy over the lines of the many distances. Seven, she counted, and he, who had gazed on landscapes all his life, for the first time learned what a "distance" was. After that, and always, he looked upon the face of nature with a more seeing eye, learning a delight of his own in surveying the serried ranks of the upstanding ranges, and in slow contemplation of the purple summer mists that haunted the languid creases of the distant hills.

But through it all ran the golden thread of love. At first he had been content just to ride with Dede and to be on comradely terms with her; but the desire and the need for her increased. The more he knew of her, the higher was his appraisal. Had she been reserved and haughty with him, or been merely a giggling, simpering creature of a woman, it would have been different. Instead, she amazed him with her simplicity and wholesomeness, with her great store of comradeliness. This latter was the unexpected. He had never looked upon woman in that way. Woman, the toy; woman, the harpy; woman, the necessary wife and mother of the race's offspring,—all this had been his expectation and understanding of woman. But woman, the comrade and playfellow and joyfellow—this was what Dede had surprised him in. And the more she became worth while, the more ardently his love burned, unconsciously shading his voice with caresses, and with equal unconsciousness flaring up signal fires in his eyes. Nor was she blind to it yet, like many women before her, she thought to play with the pretty fire and escape the consequent conflagration.

"Winter will soon be coming on," she said regretfully, and with provocation, one day, "and then there won't be any more riding."

"But I must see you in the winter just the same," he cried hastily.

She shook her head.

"We have been very happy and all that," she said, looking at him with steady frankness. "I remember your foolish argument for getting acquainted, too; but it won't lead to anything; it can't. I know myself too well to be mistaken."

Her face was serious, even solicitous with desire not to hurt, and her eyes were unwavering, but in them was the light, golden and glowing—the abyss of sex into which he was now unafraid to gaze.

"I've been pretty good," he declared. "I leave it to you if I haven't. It's been pretty hard, too, I can tell you. You just think it over. Not once have I said a word about love to you, and me loving you all the time. That's going some for a man that's used to having his own way. I'm somewhat of a rusher when it comes to travelling. I reckon I'd rush God Almighty if it came to a race over the ice. And yet I didn't rush you. I guess this fact is an indication of how much I do love you. Of course I want you to marry me. Have I said a word about it, though? Nary a chirp, nary a flutter. I've been quiet and good, though it's almost made me sick at times, this keeping quiet. I haven't asked you to marry me. I'm not asking you now. Oh, not but what you satisfy me. I sure know you're the wife for me. But how about myself? Do you know me well enough know your own mind?" He shrugged his shoulders. "I don't know, and I ain't going to take chances on it now. You've got to know for sure whether you think you could get along with me or not, and I'm playing a slow conservative game. I ain't a-going to lose for overlooking my hand."

This was love-making of a sort beyond Dede's experience. Nor had she ever heard of anything like it. Furthermore, its lack of ardor carried with it a shock which she could overcome only by remembering the way his hand had trembled in the past, and by remembering the passion she had seen that very day and every day in his eyes, or heard in his voice. Then, too, she recollected what he had said to her weeks before: "Maybe you don't know what patience is," he had said, and threat told her of shooting squirrels with a big rifle the time he and Elijah Davis had starved on the Stewart River.

"So you see," he urged, "just for a square deal we've got to see some more of each other this winter. Most likely your mind ain't made up yet—"

"But it is," she interrupted. "I wouldn't dare permit myself to care for you. Happiness, for me, would not lie that way. I like you, Mr. Harnish, and all that, but it can never be more than that."

"It's because you don't like my way of living," he charged, thinking in his own mind of the sensational joyrides and general profligacy with which the newspapers had credited him—thinking this, and wondering whether or not, in maiden modesty, she would disclaim knowledge of it.

To his surprise, her answer was flat and uncompromising.

"No; I don't."

"I know I've been brash on some of those rides that got into the papers," he began his defense, "and that I've been travelling with a lively crowd."

"I don't mean that," she said, "though I know about it too, and can't say that I like it. But it is your life in general, your business. There are women in the world who could marry a man like you and be happy, but I couldn't. And the more I cared for such a man, the more unhappy I should be. You see, my unhappiness, in turn, would tend to make him unhappy. I should make a mistake, and he would make an equal mistake, though his would not be so hard on him because he would still have his business."

"Business!" Daylight gasped. "What's wrong with my business? I play fair and square. There's nothing under hand about it, which can't be said of most businesses, whether of the big corporations or of the cheating, lying, little corner-grocerymen. I play the straight rules of the game, and I don't have to lie or cheat or break my word."

Dede hailed with relief the change in the conversation and at the same time the opportunity to speak her mind.

"In ancient Greece," she began pedantically, "a man was judged a good citizen who built houses, planted trees—" She did not complete the quotation, but drew the conclusion hurriedly. "How many houses have you built? How many trees have you planted?"

He shook his head noncommittally, for he had not grasped the drift of the argument.

"Well," she went on, "two winters ago you cornered coal—"

"Just locally," he grinned reminiscently, "just locally. And I took advantage of the car shortage and the strike in British Columbia."

"But you didn't dig any of that coal yourself. Yet you forced it up four dollars a ton and made a lot of money. That was your business. You made the poor people pay more for their coal. You played fair, as you said, but you put your hands down into all their pockets and took their money away from them. I know. I burn a grate fire in my sitting-room at Berkeley. And instead of eleven dollars a ton for Rock Wells, I paid fifteen dollars that winter. You robbed me of four dollars. I could stand it. But there were thousands of the very poor who could not stand it. You might call it legal gambling, but to me it was downright robbery."

Daylight was not abashed. This was no revelation to him. He remembered the old woman who made wine in the Sonoma hills and the millions like her who were made to be robbed.

"Now look here, Miss Mason, you've got me there slightly, I grant. But you've seen me in business a long time now, and you know I don't make a practice of raiding the poor people. I go after the big fellows. They're my meat. They rob the poor, and I rob them. That coal deal was an accident. I wasn't after the poor people in that, but after the big fellows, and I got them, too. The poor people happened to get in the way and got hurt, that was all.

"Don't you see," he went on, "the whole game is a gamble. Everybody gambles in one way or another. The farmer gambles against the weather and the market on his crops. So does the United States Steel Corporation. The business of lots of men is straight robbery of the poor people. But I've never made that my business. You know that. I've always gone after the robbers."

"I missed my point," she admitted. "Wait a minute."

And for a space they rode in silence.

"I see it more clearly than I can state it, but it's something like this. There is legitimate work, and there's work that—well, that isn't legitimate. The farmer works the soil and produces grain. He's making something that is good for humanity. He actually, in a way, creates something, the grain that will fill the mouths of the hungry."

"And then the railroads and market-riggers and the rest proceed to rob him of that same grain,"—Daylight broke in Dede smiled and held up her hand.

"Wait a minute. You'll make me lose my point. It doesn't hurt if they rob him of all of it so that he starves to death. The point is that the wheat he grew is still in the world. It exists. Don't you see? The farmer created something, say ten tons of wheat, and those ten tons exist. The railroads haul the wheat to market, to the mouths that will eat it. This also is legitimate. It's like some one bringing you a glass of water, or taking a cinder out of your eye. Something has been done, in a way been created, just like the wheat."

"But the railroads rob like Sam Scratch," Daylight objected.

"Then the work they do is partly legitimate and partly not. Now we come to you. You don't create anything. Nothing new exists when you're done with your business. Just like the coal. You didn't dig it. You didn't haul it to market. You didn't deliver it. Don't you see? that's what I meant by planting the trees and building the houses. You haven't planted one tree nor built a single house."

"I never guessed there was a woman in the world who could talk business like that," he murmured admiringly. "And you've got me on that point. But there's a lot to be said on my side just the same. Now you listen to me. I'm going to talk under three heads. Number one: We live a short time, the best of us, and we're a long time dead. Life is a big gambling game. Some are born lucky and some are born unlucky. Everybody sits in at the table, and everybody tries to rob everybody else. Most of them get robbed. They're born suckers.

"Fellow like me comes along and sizes up the proposition. I've got two choices. I can herd with the suckers, or I can herd with the robbers. As a sucker, I win nothing. Even the crusts of bread are snatched out of my mouth by the robbers. I work hard all my days, and die working. And I ain't never had a flutter. I've had nothing but work, work, work. They talk about the dignity of labor. I tell you there ain't no dignity in that sort of labor. My other choice is to herd with the robbers, and I herd with them. I play that choice wide open to win. I get the automobiles, and the porterhouse steaks, and the soft beds.

"Number two: There ain't much difference between playing halfway robber like the railroad hauling that farmer's wheat to market, and playing all robber and robbing the robbers like I do. And, besides, halfway robbery is too slow a game for me to sit in. You don't win quick enough for me."

"But what do you want to win for?" Dede demanded. "You have millions and millions, already. You can't ride in more than one automobile at a time, sleep in more than one bed at a time."

"Number three answers that," he said, "and here it is: Men and things are so made that they have different likes. A rabbit likes a vegetarian diet. A lynx likes meat. Ducks swim; chickens are scairt of water. One man collects postage stamps, another man collects butterflies. This man goes in for paintings, that man goes in for yachts, and some other fellow for hunting big game. One man thinks horse-racing is It, with a big I, and another man finds the biggest satisfaction in actresses. They can't help these likes. They have them, and what are they going to do about it? Now I like gambling. I like to play the game. I want to play it big and play it quick. I'm just made that way. And I play it."

"But why can't you do good with all your money?"

Daylight laughed.

"Doing good with your money! It's like slapping God in the face, as much as to tell him that he don't know how to run his world and that you'll be much obliged if he'll stand out of the way and give you a chance. Thinking about God doesn't keep me sitting up nights, so I've got another way of looking at it. Ain't it funny, to go around with brass knuckles and a big club breaking folks' heads and taking their money away from them until I've got a pile, and then, repenting of my ways, going around and bandaging up the heads the other robbers are breaking? I leave it to you. That's what doing good with money amounts to. Every once in a while some robber turns soft-hearted and takes to driving an ambulance. That's what Carnegie did. He smashed heads in pitched battles at Homestead, regular wholesale head-breaker he was, held up the suckers for a few hundred million, and now he goes around dribbling it back to them. Funny? I leave it to you."

He rolled a cigarette and watched her half curiously, half amusedly. His replies and harsh generalizations of a harsh school were disconcerting, and she came back to her earlier position.

"I can't argue with you, and you know that. No matter how right a woman is, men have such a way about them well, what they say sounds most convincing, and yet the woman is still certain they are wrong. But there is one thing—the creative joy. Call it gambling if you will, but just the same it seems to me more satisfying to create something, make something, than just to roll dice out of a dice-box all day long. Why, sometimes, for exercise, or when I've got to pay fifteen dollars for coal, I curry Mab and give her a whole half hour's brushing. And when I see her coat clean and shining and satiny, I feel a satisfaction in what I've done. So it must be with the man who builds a house or plants a tree. He can look at it. He made it. It's his handiwork. Even if somebody like you comes along and takes his tree away from him, still it is there, and still did he make it. You can't rob him of that, Mr. Harnish, with all your millions. It's the creative joy, and it's a higher joy than mere gambling. Haven't you ever made things yourself—a log cabin up in the Yukon, or a canoe, or raft, or something? And don't you remember how satisfied you were, how good you felt, while you were doing it and after you had it done?"

While she spoke his memory was busy with the associations she recalled. He saw the deserted flat on the river bank by the Klondike, and he saw the log cabins and warehouses spring up, and all the log structures he had built, and his sawmills working night and day on three shifts.

"Why, dog-gone it, Miss Mason, you're right—in a way. I've built hundreds of houses up there, and I remember I was proud and glad to see them go up. I'm proud now, when I remember them. And there was Ophir—the most God-forsaken moose-pasture of a creek you ever laid eyes on. I made that into the big Ophir. Why, I ran the water in there from the Rinkabilly, eighty miles away. They all said I couldn't, but I did it, and I did it by myself. The dam and the flume cost me four million. But you should have seen that Ophir—power plants, electric lights, and hundreds of men on the pay-roll, working night and day. I guess I do get an inkling of what you mean by making a thing. I made Ophir, and by God, she was a sure hummer—I beg your pardon. I didn't mean to cuss. But that Ophir!—I sure am proud of her now, just as the last time I laid eyes on her."

"And you won something there that was more than mere money," Dede encouraged. "Now do you know what I would do if I had lots of money and simply had to go on playing at business? Take all the southerly and westerly slopes of these bare hills. I'd buy them in and plant eucalyptus on them. I'd do it for the joy of doing it anyway; but suppose I had that gambling twist in me which you talk about, why, I'd do it just the same and make money out of the trees. And there's my other point again. Instead of raising the price of coal without adding an ounce of coal to the market supply, I'd be making thousands and thousands of cords of firewood—making something where nothing was before. And everybody who ever crossed on the ferries would look up at these forested hills and be made glad. Who was made glad by your adding four dollars a ton to Rock Wells?"

It was Daylight's turn to be silent for a time while she waited an answer.

"Would you rather I did things like that?" he asked at last.

"It would be better for the world, and better for you," she answered noncommittally.

CHAPTER XVI

All week every one in the office knew that something new and big was afoot in Daylight's mind. Beyond some deals of no importance, he had not been interested in anything for several months. But now he went about in an almost unbroken brown study, made unexpected and lengthy trips across the bay to Oakland, or sat at his desk silent and motionless for hours. He seemed particularly happy with what occupied his mind. At times men came in and conferred with him—and with new faces and differing in type from those that usually came to see him.

On Sunday Dede learned all about it. "I've been thinking a lot of our talk," he began, "and I've got an idea I'd like to give it a flutter. And I've got a proposition to make your hair stand up. It's what you call legitimate, and at the same time it's the gosh-dangdest gamble a man ever went into. How about planting minutes wholesale, and making two minutes grow where one minute grew before? Oh, yes, and planting a few trees, too—say several million of them. You remember the quarry I made believe I was looking at? Well, I'm going to buy it. I'm going to buy these hills, too, clear from here around to Berkeley and down the other way to San Leandro. I own a lot of them already, for that matter. But mum is the word. I'll be buying a long time to come before anything much is guessed about it, and I don't want the market to jump up out of sight. You see that hill over there. It's my hill running clear down its slopes through Piedmont and halfway along those rolling hills into Oakland. And it's nothing to all the things I'm going to buy."

He paused triumphantly. "And all to make two minutes grow where one grew before?" Dede queried, at the same time laughing heartily at his affectation of mystery.

He stared at her fascinated. She had such a frank, boyish way of throwing her head back when she laughed. And her teeth were an unending delight to him. Not small, yet regular and firm, without a blemish, he considered then the healthiest, whitest, prettiest teeth he had ever seen. And for months he had been comparing them with the teeth of every woman he met.

It was not until her laughter was over that he was able to continue.

"The ferry system between Oakland and San Francisco is the worst one-horse concern in the United States. You cross on it every day, six days in the week. That's say, twenty-five days a month, or three hundred a year. Now long does it take you one way? Forty minutes, if you're lucky. I'm going to put you across in twenty minutes. If that ain't making two minutes grow where one grew before, knock off my head with little apples. I'll save you twenty minutes each way. That's forty minutes a day, times three hundred, equals twelve thousand minutes a year, just for you, just for one person. Let's see: that's two hundred whole hours. Suppose I save two hundred hours a year for thousands of other folks,—that's farming some, ain't it?"

Dede could only nod breathlessly. She had caught the contagion of his enthusiasm, though she had no clew as to how this great time-saving was to be accomplished.

"Come on," he said. "Let's ride up that hill, and when I get you out on top where you can see something, I'll talk sense."

A small footpath dropped down to the dry bed of the canon, which they crossed before they began the climb. The slope was steep and covered with matted brush and bushes, through which the horses slipped and lunged. Bob, growing disgusted, turned back suddenly and attempted to pass Mab. The mare was thrust sidewise into the denser bush, where she nearly fell. Recovering, she flung her weight against Bob. Both riders' legs were caught in the consequent squeeze, and, as Bob plunged ahead down hill, Dede was nearly scraped off. Daylight threw his horse on to its haunches and at the same time dragged Dede back into the saddle. Showers of twigs and leaves fell upon them, and predicament followed predicament, until they emerged on the hilltop the worse for wear but happy and excited. Here no trees obstructed the view. The particular hill on which they were, out-jutted from the regular line of the range, so that the sweep of their vision extended over three-quarters of the circle. Below, on the flat land bordering the bay, lay Oakland, and across the bay was San Francisco. Between the two cities they could see the white ferry-boats on the water. Around to their right was Berkeley, and to their left the scattered villages between Oakland and San Leandro. Directly in the foreground was Piedmont, with its desultory dwellings and patches of farming land, and from Piedmont the land rolled down in successive waves upon Oakland.

"Look at it," said Daylight, extending his arm in a sweeping gesture. "A hundred thousand people there, and no reason there shouldn't be half a million. There's the chance to make five people grow where one grows now. Here's the scheme in a nutshell. Why don't more people live in Oakland? No good service with San Francisco, and, besides, Oakland is asleep. It's a whole lot better place to live in than San Francisco. Now, suppose I buy in all the street railways of Oakland, Berkeley, Alameda, San Leandro, and the rest,—bring them under one head with a competent management? Suppose I cut the time to San Francisco one-half by building a big pier out there almost to Goat Island and establishing a ferry system with modern up-to-date boats? Why, folks will want to live over on this side. Very good. They'll need land on which to build. So, first I buy up the land. But the land's cheap now. Why? Because it's in the country, no electric roads, no quick communication, nobody guessing that the electric roads are coming. I'll build the roads. That will make the land jump up. Then I'll sell the land as fast as the folks will want to buy because of the improved ferry system and transportation facilities.

"You see, I give the value to the land by building the roads. Then I sell the land and get that value back, and after that, there's the roads, all carrying folks back and forth and earning big money. Can't lose. And there's all sorts of millions in it.

"I'm going to get my hands on some of that water front and the tide-lands. Take between where I'm going to build my pier and the old pier. It's shallow water. I can fill and dredge and put in a system of docks that will handle hundreds of ships. San Francisco's water front is congested. No more room for ships. With hundreds of ships loading and unloading on this side right into the freight cars of three big railroads, factories will start up over here instead of crossing to San Francisco. That means factory sites. That means me buying in the factory sites before anybody guesses the cat is going to jump, much less, which way. Factories mean tens of thousands of workingmen and their families. That means more houses and more land, and that means me, for I'll be there to sell them the land. And tens of thousands of families means tens of thousands of nickels every day for my electric cars. The growing population will mean more stores, more banks, more everything. And that'll mean me, for I'll be right there with business property as well as home property. What do you think of it?"

Therefore she could answer, he was off again, his mind's eye filled with this new city of his dream which he built on the Alameda hills by the gateway to the Orient.

"Do you know—I've been looking it up—the Firth Of Clyde, where all the steel ships are built, isn't half as wide as Oakland Creek down there, where all those old hulks lie? Why ain't it a Firth of Clyde? Because the Oakland City Council spends its time debating about prunes and raisins. What is needed is somebody to see things, and, after that, organization. That's me. I didn't make Ophir for nothing. And once things begin to hum, outside capital will pour in. All I do is start it going. 'Gentlemen,' I say, 'here's all the natural advantages for a great metropolis. God Almighty put them advantages here, and he put me here to see them. Do you want to land your tea and silk from Asia and ship it straight East? Here's the docks for your steamers, and here's the railroads. Do you want factories from which you can ship direct by land or water? Here's the site, and here's the modern, up-to-date city, with the latest improvements for yourselves and your workmen, to live in.'"

"Then there's the water. I'll come pretty close to owning the watershed. Why not the waterworks too? There's two water companies in Oakland now, fighting like cats and dogs and both about broke. What a metropolis needs is a good water system. They can't give it. They're stick-in-the-muds. I'll gobble them up and deliver the right article to the city. There's money there, too—money everywhere. Everything works in with everything else. Each improvement makes the value of everything else pump up. It's people that are behind the value. The bigger the crowd that herds in one place, the more valuable is the real estate. And this is the very place for a crowd to herd. Look at it. Just look at it! You could never find a finer site for a great city. All it needs is the herd, and I'll stampede a couple of hundred thousand people in here inside two years. And what's more it won't be one of these wild cat land booms. It will be legitimate. Twenty years for now there'll be a million people on this side the bay. Another thing is hotels. There isn't a decent one in the town. I'll build a couple of up-to-date ones that'll make them sit up and take notice. I won't care if they don't pay for years. Their effect will more than give me my money back out of the other holdings. And, oh, yes, I'm going to plant eucalyptus, millions of them, on these hills."

"But how are you going to do it?" Dede asked. "You haven't enough money for all that you've planned."

"I've thirty million, and if I need more I can borrow on the land and other things. Interest on mortgages won't anywhere near eat up the increase in land values, and I'll be selling land right along."

In the weeks that followed, Daylight was a busy man. He spent most of his time in Oakland, rarely coming to the office. He planned to move the office to Oakland, but, as he told Dede, the secret preliminary campaign of buying had to be put through first. Sunday by Sunday, now from this hilltop and now from that, they looked down upon the city and its farming suburbs, and he pointed out to her his latest acquisitions. At first it was patches and sections of land here and there; but as the weeks passed it was the unowned portions that became rare, until at last they stood as islands surrounded by Daylight's land.

It meant quick work on a colossal scale, for Oakland and the adjacent country was not slow to feel the tremendous buying. But Daylight had the ready cash, and it had always been his policy to strike quickly. Before the others could get the warning of the boom, he quietly accomplished many things. At the same time that his agents were purchasing corner lots and entire blocks in the heart of the business section and the waste lands for factory sites, Day was rushing franchises through the city council, capturing the two exhausted water companies and the eight or nine independent street railways, and getting his grip on the Oakland Creek and the bay tide-lands for his dock system. The tide-lands had been in litigation for years, and he took the bull by the horns—buying out the private owners and at the same time leasing from the city fathers.

By the time that Oakland was aroused by this unprecedented activity in every direction and was questioning excitedly the meaning of it, Daylight secretly bought the chief Republican newspaper and the chief Democratic organ, and moved boldly into his new offices. Of necessity, they were on a large scale, occupying four floors of the only modern office building in the town—the only building that wouldn't have to be torn down later on, as Daylight put it. There was department after department, a score of them, and hundreds of clerks and stenographers. As he told Dede: "I've got more companies than you can shake a stick at. There's the Alameda & Contra Costa Land Syndicate, the Consolidated Street Railways, the Yerba Buena Ferry Company, the United Water Company, the Piedmont Realty Company, the Fairview and Portola Hotel Company, and half a dozen more that I've got to refer to a notebook to remember. There's the Piedmont Laundry Farm, and Redwood Consolidated Quarries. Starting in with our quarry, I just kept a-going till I got them all. And there's the ship-building company I ain't got a name for yet. Seeing as I had to have ferry-boats, I decided to build them myself. They'll be done by the time the pier is ready for them. Phew! It all sure beats poker. And I've had the fun of gouging the robber gangs as well. The water company bunches are squealing yet. I sure got them where the hair was short. They were just about all in when I came along and finished them off."

"But why do you hate them so?" Dede asked.

"Because they're such cowardly skunks."

"But you play the same game they do."

"Yes; but not in the same way." Daylight regarded her thoughtfully. "When I say cowardly skunks, I mean just that,—cowardly skunks. They set up for a lot of gamblers, and there ain't one in a thousand of them that's got the nerve to be a gambler. They're four-flushers, if you know what that means. They're a lot of little cottontail rabbits making believe they're big rip-snorting timber wolves. They set out to everlastingly eat up some proposition but at the first sign of trouble they turn tail and stampede for the brush. Look how it works. When the big fellows wanted to unload Little Copper, they sent Jakey Fallow into the New York Stock Exchange to yell out: 'I'll buy all or any part of Little Copper at fifty five,' Little Copper being at fifty-four. And in thirty minutes them cottontails—financiers, some folks call them—bid up Little Copper to sixty. And an hour after that, stampeding for the brush, they were throwing Little Copper overboard at forty-five and even forty.

"They're catspaws for the big fellows. Almost as fast as they rob the suckers, the big fellows come along and hold them up. Or else the big fellows use them in order to rob each other. That's the way the Chattanooga Coal and Iron Company was swallowed up by the trust in the last panic. The trust made that panic. It had to break a couple of big banking companies and squeeze half a dozen big fellows, too, and it did it by stampeding the cottontails. The cottontails did the rest all right, and the trust gathered in Chattanooga Coal and Iron. Why, any man, with nerve and savvee, can start them cottontails jumping for the brush. I don't exactly hate them myself, but I haven't any regard for chicken-hearted four-flushers."

CHAPTER XVII

For months Daylight was buried in work. The outlay was terrific, and there was nothing coming in. Beyond a general rise in land values, Oakland had not acknowledged his irruption on the financial scene. The city was waiting for him to show what he was going to do, and he lost no time about it. The best skilled brains on the market were hired by him for the different branches of the work. Initial mistakes he had no patience with, and he was determined to start right, as when he engaged Wilkinson, almost doubling his big salary, and brought him out from Chicago to take charge of the street railway organization. Night and day the road gangs toiled on the streets. And night and day the pile-drivers hammered the big piles down into the mud of San Francisco Bay. The pier was to be three miles long, and the Berkeley hills were denuded of whole groves of mature eucalyptus for the piling.

At the same time that his electric roads were building out through the hills, the hay-fields were being surveyed and broken up into city squares, with here and there, according to best modern methods, winding boulevards and strips of park. Broad streets, well graded, were made, with sewers and water-pipes ready laid, and macadamized from his own quarries. Cement sidewalks were also laid, so that all the purchaser had to do was to select his lot and architect and start building. The quick service of Daylight's new electric roads into Oakland made this big district immediately accessible, and long before the ferry system was in operation hundreds of residences were going up.

The profit on this land was enormous. In a day, his onslaught of wealth had turned open farming country into one of the best residential districts of the city.

But this money that flowed in upon him was immediately poured back into his other investments. The need for electric cars was so great that he installed his own shops for building them. And even on the rising land market, he continued to buy choice factory sites and building properties. On the advice of Wilkinson, practically every electric road already in operation was rebuilt. The light, old fashioned rails were torn out and replaced by the heaviest that were manufactured. Corner lots, on the sharp turns of narrow streets, were bought and ruthlessly presented to the city in order to make wide curves for his tracks and high speed for his cars. Then, too, there were the main-line feeders for his ferry system, tapping every portion of Oakland, Alameda, and Berkeley, and running fast expresses to the pier end. The same large-scale methods were employed in the water system. Service of the best was needed, if his huge land investment was to succeed. Oakland had to be made into a worth-while city, and that was what he intended to do. In addition to his big hotels, he built amusement parks for the common people, and art galleries and club-house country inns for the more finicky classes. Even before there was any increase in population, a marked increase in street-railway traffic took place. There was nothing fanciful about his schemes. They were sound investments.

"What Oakland wants is a first class theatre," he said, and, after vainly trying to interest local capital, he started the building of the theatre himself; for he alone had vision for the two hundred thousand new people that were coming to the town.

But no matter what pressure was on Daylight, his Sundays he reserved for his riding in the hills. It was not the winter weather, however, that brought these rides with Dede to an end. One

Saturday afternoon in the office she told him not to expect to meet her next day, and, when he pressed for an explanation:

"I've sold Mab."

Daylight was speechless for the moment. Her act meant one of so many serious things that he couldn't classify it. It smacked almost of treachery. She might have met with financial disaster.

It might be her way of letting him know she had seen enough of him. Or...

"What's the matter?" he managed to ask.

"I couldn't afford to keep her with hay forty-five dollars a ton," Dede answered.

"Was that your only reason?" he demanded, looking at her steadily; for he remembered her once telling him how she had brought the mare through one winter, five years before, when hay had gone as high as sixty dollars a ton.

"No. My brother's expenses have been higher, as well, and I was driven to the conclusion that since I could not afford both, I'd better let the mare go and keep the brother."

Daylight felt inexpressibly saddened. He was suddenly aware of a great emptiness. What would a Sunday be without Dede? And Sundays without end without her? He drummed perplexedly on the desk with his fingers.

"Who bought her?" he asked. Dede's eyes flashed in the way long since familiar to him when she was angry.

"Don't you dare buy her back for me," she cried. "And don't deny that that was what you had in mind."

"I won't deny it. It was my idea to a tee. But I wouldn't have done it without asking you first, and seeing how you feel about it, I won't even ask you. But you thought a heap of that mare, and it's pretty hard on you to lose her. I'm sure sorry. And I'm sorry, too, that you won't be riding with me tomorrow. I'll be plumb lost. I won't know what to do with myself."

"Neither shall I," Dede confessed mournfully, "except that I shall be able to catch up with my sewing."

"But I haven't any sewing."

Daylight's tone was whimsically plaintive, but secretly he was delighted with her confession of loneliness. It was almost worth the loss of the mare to get that out of her. At any rate, he meant something to her. He was not utterly unliked.

"I wish you would reconsider, Miss Mason," he said softly. "Not alone for the mare's sake, but for my sake. Money don't cut any ice in this. For me to buy that mare wouldn't mean as it does to most men to send a bouquet of flowers or a box of candy to a young lady. And I've never sent you flowers or candy." He observed the warning flash of her eyes, and hurried on to escape refusal. "I'll tell you what we'll do. Suppose I buy the mare and own her myself, and lend her to you when you want to ride. There's nothing wrong in that. Anybody borrows a horse from anybody, you know."

Agin he saw refusal, and headed her off.

"Lots of men take women buggy-riding. There's nothing wrong in that. And the man always furnishes the horse and buggy. Well, now, what's the difference between my taking you buggy-riding and furnishing the horse and buggy, and taking you horse-back-riding and furnishing the horses?"

She shook her head, and declined to answer, at the same time looking at the door as if to intimate that it was time for this unbusinesslike conversation to end. He made one more effort.

"Do you know, Miss Mason, I haven't a friend in the world outside you? I mean a real friend, man or woman, the kind you chum with, you know, and that you're glad to be with and sorry to be away from. Hegan is the nearest man I get to, and he's a million miles away from me. Outside business, we don't hitch. He's got a big library of books, and some crazy kind of culture, and he spends all his off times reading things in French and German and other outlandish lingoes—when he ain't writing plays and poetry. There's nobody I feel chummy with except you, and you know how little we've chummed—once a week, if it didn't rain, on Sunday. I've grown kind of to depend on you. You're a sort of—of—of—"

"A sort of habit," she said with a smile.

"That's about it. And that mare, and you astride of her, coming along the road under the trees or through the sunshine—why, with both you and the mare missing, there won't be anything worth waiting through the week for. If you'd just let me buy her back—"

"No, no; I tell you no." Dede rose impatiently, but her eyes were moist with the memory of her pet. "Please don't mention her to me again. If you think it was easy to part with her, you are mistaken. But I've seen the last of her, and I want to forget her."

Daylight made no answer, and the door closed behind him.

Half an hour later he was conferring with Jones, the erstwhile elevator boy and rabid proletarian whom Daylight long before had grubstaked to literature for a year. The resulting novel had been a failure. Editors and publishers would not look at it, and now Daylight was using the disgruntled author in a little private secret service system he had been compelled to establish for himself. Jones, who affected to be surprised at nothing after his crushing experience with railroad freight rates on firewood and charcoal, betrayed no surprise now when the task was given to him to locate the purchaser of a certain sorrel mare.

"How high shall I pay for her?" he asked.

"Any price. You've got to get her, that's the point. Drive a sharp bargain so as not to excite suspicion, but buy her. Then you deliver her to that address up in Sonoma County. The man's the caretaker on a little ranch I have there. Tell him he's to take whacking good care of her. And after that forget all about it. Don't tell me the name of the man you buy her from. Don't tell me anything about it except that you've got her and delivered her. Savvee?"

But the week had not passed, when Daylight noted the flash in Dede's eyes that boded trouble.

"Something's gone wrong—what is it?" he asked boldly.

"Mab," she said. "The man who bought her has sold her already. If I thought you had anything to do with it—"

"I don't even know who you sold her to," was Daylight's answer. "And what's more, I'm not bothering my head about her. She was your mare, and it's none of my business what you did with her. You haven't got her, that's sure and worse luck. And now, while we're on touchy subjects, I'm going to open another one with you. And you needn't get touchy about it, for it's not really your business at all."

She waited in the pause that followed, eyeing him almost suspiciously.

"It's about that brother of yours. He needs more than you can do for him. Selling that mare of yours won't send him to Germany. And that's what his own doctors say he needs—that crack

German specialist who rips a man's bones and muscles into pulp and then molds them all over again. Well, I want to send him to Germany and give that crack a flutter, that's all."

"If it were only possible" she said, half breathlessly, and wholly without anger. "Only it isn't, and you know it isn't. I can't accept money from you—"

"Hold on, now," he interrupted. "Wouldn't you accept a drink of water from one of the Twelve Apostles if you was dying of thirst? Or would you be afraid of his evil intentions"—she made a gesture of dissent "—or of what folks might say about it?"

"But that's different," she began.

"Now look here, Miss Mason. You've got to get some foolish notions out of your head. This money notion is one of the funniest things I've seen. Suppose you was falling over a cliff, wouldn't it be all right for me to reach out and hold you by the arm? Sure it would. But suppose you ended another sort of help—instead of the strength of arm, the strength of my pocket? That would be all and that's what they all say. But why do they say it. Because the robber gangs want all the suckers to be honest and respect money. If the suckers weren't honest and didn't respect money, where would the robbers be? Don't you see? The robbers don't deal in arm-holds; they deal in dollars. Therefore arm-holds are just common and ordinary, while dollars are sacred—so sacred that you didn't let me lend you a hand with a few.

"Or here's another way," he continued, spurred on by her mute protest. "It's all right for me to give the strength of my arm when you're falling over a cliff. But if I take that same strength of arm and use it at pick-and-shovel work for a day and earn two dollars, you won't have anything to do with the two dollars. Yet it's the same old strength of arm in a new form, that's all. Besides, in this proposition it won't be a claim on you. It ain't even a loan to you. It's an arm-hold I'm giving your brother—just the same sort of arm-hold as if he was falling over a cliff. And a nice one you are, to come running out and yell 'Stop!' at me, and let your brother go on over the cliff. What he needs to save his legs is that crack in Germany, and that's the arm-hold I'm offering.

"Wish you could see my rooms. Walls all decorated with horsehair bridles—scores of them—hundreds of them. They're no use to me, and they cost like Sam Scratch. But there's a lot of convicts making them, and I go on buying. Why, I've spent more money in a single night on whiskey than would get the best specialists and pay all the expenses of a dozen cases like your brother's. And remember, you've got nothing to do with this. If your brother wants to look on it as a loan, all right. It's up to him, and you've got to stand out of the way while I pull him back from that cliff."

Still Dede refused, and Daylight's argument took a more painful turn.

"I can only guess that you're standing in your brother's way on account of some mistaken idea in your head that this is my idea of courting. Well, it ain't. You might as well think I'm courting all those convicts I buy bridles from. I haven't asked you to marry me, and if I do I won't come trying to buy you into consenting. And there won't be anything underhand when I come a-asking."

Dede's face was flushed and angry. "If you knew how ridiculous you are, you'd stop," she blurted out. "You can make me more uncomfortable than any man I ever knew. Every little while you give me to understand that you haven't asked me to marry you yet. I'm not waiting to be asked, and I warned you from the first that you had no chance. And yet you hold it over my head that some time, some day, you're going to ask me to marry you. Go ahead and ask me now, and get your answer and get it over and done with."

He looked at her in honest and pondering admiration. "I want you so bad, Miss Mason, that I don't dast to ask you now," he said, with such whimsicality and earnestness as to make her throw her head back in a frank boyish laugh. "Besides, as I told you, I'm green at it. I never went a-courting before, and I don't want to make any mistakes."

"But you're making them all the time," she cried impulsively. "No man ever courted a woman by holding a threatened proposal over her head like a club."

"I won't do it any more," he said humbly. "And anyway, we're off the argument. My straight talk a minute ago still holds. You're standing in your brother's way. No matter what notions you've got in your head, you've got to get out of the way and give him a chance. Will you let me go and see him and talk it over with him? I'll make it a hard and fast business proposition. I'll stake him to get well, that's all, and charge him interest."

She visibly hesitated.

"And just remember one thing, Miss Mason: it's HIS leg, not yours."

Still she refrained from giving her answer, and Daylight went on strengthening his position.

"And remember, I go over to see him alone. He's a man, and I can deal with him better without womenfolks around. I'll go over to-morrow afternoon."

CHAPTER XVIII

Daylight had been wholly truthful when he told Dede that he had no real friends. On speaking terms with thousands, on fellowship and drinking terms with hundreds, he was a lonely man. He failed to find the one man, or group of several men, with whom he could be really intimate. Cities did not make for comradeship as did the Alaskan trail. Besides, the types of men were different. Scornful and contemptuous of business men on the one hand, on the other his relations with the San Francisco bosses had been more an alliance of expediency than anything else. He had felt more of kinship for the franker brutality of the bosses and their captains, but they had failed to claim any deep respect. They were too prone to crookedness. Bonds were better than men's word in this modern world, and one had to look carefully to the bonds.

In the old Yukon days it had been different. Bonds didn't go. A man said he had so much, and even in a poker game his appeasement was accepted.

Larry Hegan, who rose ably to the largest demands of Daylight's operations and who had few illusions and less hypocrisy, might have proved a chum had it not been for his temperamental twist. Strange genius that he was, a Napoleon of the law, with a power of visioning that far exceeded Daylight's, he had nothing in common with Daylight outside the office. He spent his time with books, a thing Daylight could not abide. Also, he devoted himself to the endless writing of plays which never got beyond manuscript form, and, though Daylight only sensed the secret taint of it, was a confirmed but temperate eater of hasheesh. Hegan lived all his life cloistered with books in a world of agitation. With the out-of-door world he had no understanding nor tolerance. In food and drink he was abstemious as a monk, while exercise was a thing abhorrent. Daylight's friendships, in lieu of anything closer, were drinking friendships and roistering friendships. And with the passing of the Sunday rides with Dede, he fell back more and more upon these for diversion. The cocktail wall of inhibition he reared more assiduously than ever.

The big red motor-car was out more frequently now, while a stable hand was hired to give Bob exercise. In his early San Francisco days, there had been intervals of easement between his deals, but in this present biggest deal of all the strain was unremitting. Not in a month, or two, or three, could his huge land investment be carried to a successful consummation. And so complete and wide-reaching was it that complications and knotty situations constantly arose. Every day brought its problems, and when he had solved them in his masterful way, he left the office in his big car, almost sighing with relief at anticipation of the approaching double Martini. Rarely was he made tipsy. His constitution was too strong for that. Instead, he was that direst of all drinkers, the steady drinker, deliberate and controlled, who averaged a far higher quantity of alcohol than the irregular and violent drinker. For six weeks hard-running he had seen nothing of Dede except in the office, and there he resolutely refrained from making approaches. But by the seventh Sunday his hunger for her overmastered him. It was a stormy day.

A heavy southeast gale was blowing, and squall after squall of rain and wind swept over the city. He could not take his mind off of her, and a persistent picture came to him of her sitting by a window and sewing feminine fripperies of some sort. When the time came for his first pre-luncheon cocktail to be served to him in his rooms, he did not take it.

Filled with a daring determination, he glanced at his note book for Dede's telephone number, and called for the switch.

At first it was her landlady's daughter who was raised, but in a minute he heard the voice he had been hungry to hear.

"I just wanted to tell you that I'm coming out to see you," he said. "I didn't want to break in on you without warning, that was all."

"Has something happened?" came her voice.

"I'll tell you when I get there," he evaded.

He left the red car two blocks away and arrived on foot at the pretty, three-storied, shingled Berkeley house. For an instant only, he was aware of an inward hesitancy, but the next moment he rang the bell. He knew that what he was doing was in direct violation of her wishes, and that he was setting her a difficult task to receive as a Sunday caller the multimillionaire and notorious Elam Harnish of newspaper fame. On the other hand, the one thing he did not expect of her was what he would have termed "silly female capers."

And in this he was not disappointed.

She came herself to the door to receive him and shake hands with him. He hung his mackintosh and hat on the rack in the comfortable square hall and turned to her for direction.

"They are busy in there," she said, indicating the parlor from which came the boisterous voices of young people, and through the open door of which he could see several college youths. "So you will have to come into my rooms."

She led the way through the door opening out of the hall to the right, and, once inside, he stood awkwardly rooted to the floor, gazing about him and at her and all the time trying not to gaze. In his perturbation he failed to hear and see her invitation to a seat. So these were her quarters. The intimacy of it and her making no fuss about it was startling, but it was no more than he would have expected of her. It was almost two rooms in one, the one he was in evidently the sitting-room, and the one he could see into, the bedroom. Beyond an oaken dressing-table, with an orderly litter of combs and brushes and dainty feminine knickknacks, there was no sign of its being used as a bedroom. The broad couch, with a cover of old rose and banked high with cushions, he decided must be the bed, but it was farthest from any experience of a civilized bed he had ever had.

Not that he saw much of detail in that awkward moment of standing. His general impression was one of warmth and comfort and beauty. There were no carpets, and on the hardwood floor he caught a glimpse of several wolf and coyote skins. What captured and perceptibly held his eye for a moment was a Crouched Venus that stood on a Steinway upright against a background of mountain-lion skin on the wall.

But it was Dede herself that smote most sharply upon sense and perception. He had always cherished the idea that she was very much a woman—the lines of her figure, her hair, her eyes, her voice, and birdlike laughing ways had all contributed to this; but here, in her own rooms, clad in some flowing, clinging gown, the emphasis of sex was startling. He had been accustomed to her only in trim tailor suits and shirtwaists, or in riding costume of velvet corduroy, and he was not prepared for this new revelation. She seemed so much softer, so much more pliant, and tender, and lissome. She was a part of this atmosphere of quietude and beauty. She fitted into it just as she had fitted in with the sober office furnishings.

"Won't you sit down?" she repeated.

He felt like an animal long denied food. His hunger for her welled up in him, and he proceeded to "wolf" the dainty morsel before him. Here was no patience, no diplomacy. The straightest, direct way was none too quick for him and, had he known it, the least unsuccessful way he could have chosen.

"Look here," he said, in a voice that shook with passion, "there's one thing I won't do, and that's propose to you in the office. That's why I'm here. Dede Mason, I want you. I just want you."

While he spoke he advanced upon her, his black eyes burning with bright fire, his aroused blood swarthy in his cheek.

So precipitate was he, that she had barely time to cry out her involuntary alarm and to step back, at the same time catching one of his hands as he attempted to gather her into his arms.

In contrast to him, the blood had suddenly left her cheeks. The hand that had warded his off and that still held it, was trembling. She relaxed her fingers, and his arm dropped to his side. She wanted to say something, do something, to pass on from the awkwardness of the situation, but no intelligent thought nor action came into her mind. She was aware only of a desire to laugh. This impulse was party hysterical and partly spontaneous humor—the latter growing from instant to instant. Amazing as the affair was, the ridiculous side of it was not veiled to her. She felt like one who had suffered the terror of the onslaught of a murderous footpad only to find out that it was an innocent pedestrian asking the time.

Daylight was the quicker to achieve action. "Oh, I know I'm a sure enough fool," he said. "I—I guess I'll sit down. Don't be scairt, Miss Mason. I'm not real dangerous."

"I'm not afraid," she answered, with a smile, slipping down herself into a chair, beside which, on the floor, stood a sewing-basket from which, Daylight noted, some white fluffy thing of lace and muslin overflowed. Again she smiled. "Though I confess you did startle me for the moment."

"It's funny," Daylight sighed, almost with regret; "here I am, strong enough to bend you around and tie knots in you. Here I am, used to having my will with man and beast and anything. And here I am sitting in this chair, as weak and helpless as a little lamb. You sure take the starch out of me."

Dede vainly cudgeled her brains in quest of a reply to these remarks. Instead, her thought dwelt insistently upon the significance of his stepping aside, in the middle of a violent proposal, in order to make irrelevant remarks. What struck her was the man's certitude. So little did he doubt that he would have her, that he could afford to pause and generalize upon love and the effects of love.

She noted his hand unconsciously slipping in the familiar way into the side coat pocket where she knew he carried his tobacco and brown papers.

"You may smoke, if you want to," she said. He withdrew his hand with a jerk, as if something in the pocket had stung him.

"No, I wasn't thinking of smoking. I was thinking of you. What's a man to do when he wants a woman but ask her to marry him? That's all that I'm doing. I can't do it in style. I know that. But I can use straight English, and that's good enough for me. I sure want you mighty bad,

Miss Mason. You're in my mind 'most all the time, now. And what I want to know is—well, do you want me? That's all."

"I—I wish you hadn't asked," she said softly.

"Mebbe it's best you should know a few things before you give me an answer," he went on, ignoring the fact that the answer had already been given. "I never went after a woman before in my life, all reports to the contrary not withstanding. The stuff you read about me in the papers and books, about me being a lady-killer, is all wrong. There's not an iota of truth in it. I guess I've done more than my share of card-playing and whiskey-drinking, but women I've let alone. There was a woman that killed herself, but I didn't know she wanted me that bad or else I'd have married her—not for love, but to keep her from killing herself. She was the best of the boiling, but I never gave her any encouragement. I'm telling you all this because you've read about it, and I want you to get it straight from me.

"Lady-killer!" he snorted. "Why, Miss Mason, I don't mind telling you that I've sure been scairt of women all my life. You're the first one I've not been afraid of. That's the strange thing about it. I just plumb worship you, and yet I'm not afraid of you. Mebbe it's because you're different from the women I know. You've never chased me. Lady-killer! Why, I've been running away from ladies ever since I can remember, and I guess all that saved me was that I was strong in the wind and that I never fell down and broke a leg or anything.

"I didn't ever want to get married until after I met you, and until a long time after I met you. I cottoned to you from the start; but I never thought it would get as bad as marriage. Why, I can't get to sleep nights, thinking of you and wanting you."

He came to a stop and waited. She had taken the lace and muslin from the basket, possibly to settle her nerves and wits, and was sewing upon it. As she was not looking at him, he devoured her with his eyes. He noted the firm, efficient hands—hands that could control a horse like Bob, that could run a typewriter almost as fast as a man could talk, that could sew on dainty garments, and that, doubtlessly, could play on the piano over there in the corner. Another ultra-feminine detail he noticed—her slippers. They were small and bronze. He had never imagined she had such a small foot. Street shoes and riding boots were all that he had ever seen on her feet, and they had given no advertisement of this. The bronze slippers fascinated him, and to them his eyes repeatedly turned.

A knock came at the door, which she answered. Daylight could not help hearing the conversation. She was wanted at the telephone.

"Tell him to call up again in ten minutes," he heard her say, and the masculine pronoun caused in him a flashing twinge of jealousy. Well, he decided, whoever it was, Burning Daylight would give him a run for his money. The marvel to him was that a girl like Dede hadn't been married long since.

She came back, smiling to him, and resumed her sewing. His eyes wandered from the efficient hands to the bronze slippers and back again, and he swore to himself that there were mighty few stenographers like her in existence. That was because she must have come of pretty good stock, and had a pretty good raising. Nothing else could explain these rooms of hers and the clothes she wore and the way she wore them.

"Those ten minutes are flying," he suggested.

"I can't marry you," she said.

"You don't love me?"

She shook her head.

"Do you like me—the littlest bit?"

This time she nodded, at the same time allowing the smile of amusement to play on her lips. But it was amusement without contempt. The humorous side of a situation rarely appealed in vain to her.

"Well, that's something to go on," he announced. "You've got to make a start to get started. I just liked you at first, and look what it's grown into. You recollect, you said you didn't like my way of life. Well, I've changed it a heap. I ain't gambling like I used to. I've gone into what you called the legitimate, making two minutes grow where one grew before, three hundred thousand folks where only a hundred thousand grew before. And this time next year there'll be two million eucalyptus growing on the hills. Say do you like me more than the littlest bit?"

She raised her eyes from her work and looked at him as she answered:

"I like you a great deal, but—"

He waited a moment for her to complete the sentence, failing which, he went on himself.

"I haven't an exaggerated opinion of myself, so I know I ain't bragging when I say I'll make a pretty good husband. You'd find I was no hand at nagging and fault-finding. I can guess what it must be for a woman like you to be independent. Well, you'd be independent as my wife. No strings on you. You could follow your own sweet will, and nothing would be too good for you. I'd give you everything your heart desired—"

"Except yourself," she interrupted suddenly, almost sharply.

Daylight's astonishment was momentary.

"I don't know about that. I'd be straight and square, and live true. I don't hanker after divided affections."

"I don't mean that," she said. "Instead of giving yourself to your wife, you would give yourself to the three hundred thousand people of Oakland, to your street railways and ferry-routes, to the two million trees on the hills to everything business—and—and to all that that means."

"I'd see that I didn't," he declared stoutly. "I'd be yours to command."

"You think so, but it would turn out differently." She suddenly became nervous. "We must stop this talk. It is too much like attempting to drive a bargain. 'How much will you give?' 'I'll give so much.' 'I want more,' and all that. I like you, but not enough to marry you, and I'll never like you enough to marry you."

"How do you know that?" he demanded.

"Because I like you less and less."

Daylight sat dumfounded. The hurt showed itself plainly in his face.

"Oh, you don't understand," she cried wildly, beginning to lose self-control—"It's not that way I mean. I do like you; the more I've known you the more I've liked you. And at the same time the more I've known you the less would I care to marry you."

This enigmatic utterance completed Daylight's perplexity.

"Don't you see?" she hurried on. "I could have far easier married the Elam Harnish fresh from Klondike, when I first laid eyes on him long ago, than marry you sitting before me now."

He shook his head slowly. "That's one too many for me. The more you know and like a man the less you want to marry him. Familiarity breeds contempt—I guess that's what you mean."

"No, no," she cried, but before she could continue, a knock came on the door.

"The ten minutes is up," Daylight said.

His eyes, quick with observation like an Indian's, darted about the room while she was out. The impression of warmth and comfort and beauty predominated, though he was unable to analyze it; while the simplicity delighted him—expensive simplicity, he decided, and most of it leftovers from the time her father went broke and died. He had never before appreciated a plain hardwood floor with a couple of wolfskins; it sure beat all the carpets in creation. He stared solemnly at a bookcase containing a couple of hundred books. There was mystery. He could not understand what people found so much to write about.

Writing things and reading things were not the same as doing things, and himself primarily a man of action, doing things was alone comprehensible.

His gaze passed on from the Crouched Venus to a little tea-table with all its fragile and exquisite accessories, and to a shining copper kettle and copper chafing-dish. Chafing dishes were not unknown to him, and he wondered if she concocted suppers on this one for some of those University young men he had heard whispers about. One or two water-colors on the wall made him conjecture that she had painted them herself. There were photographs of horses and of old masters, and the trailing purple of a Burial of Christ held him for a time. But ever his gaze returned to that Crouched Venus on the piano. To his homely, frontier-trained mind, it seemed curious that a nice young woman should have such a bold, if not sinful, object on display in her own room. But he reconciled himself to it by an act of faith. Since it was Dede, it must be eminently all right. Evidently such things went along with culture. Larry Hegan had similar casts and photographs in his book-cluttered quarters. But then, Larry Hegan was different. There was that hint of unhealth about him that Daylight invariably sensed in his presence, while Dede, on the contrary, seemed always so robustly wholesome, radiating an atmosphere compounded of the sun and wind and dust of the open road. And yet, if such a clean, healthy woman as she went in for naked women crouching on her piano, it must be all right. Dede made it all right. She could come pretty close to making anything all right. Besides, he didn't understand culture anyway.

She reentered the room, and as she crossed it to her chair, he admired the way she walked, while the bronze slippers were maddening.

"I'd like to ask you several questions," he began immediately "Are you thinking of marrying somebody?"

She laughed merrily and shook her head.

"Do you like anybody else more than you like me?—that man at the 'phone just now, for instance?"

"There isn't anybody else. I don't know anybody I like well enough to marry. For that matter, I don't think I am a marrying woman. Office work seems to spoil one for that."

Daylight ran his eyes over her, from her face to the tip of a bronze slipper, in a way that made the color mantle in her cheeks. At the same time he shook his head sceptically.

"It strikes me that you're the most marryingest woman that ever made a man sit up and take notice. And now another question. You see, I've just got to locate the lay of the land. Is there anybody you like as much as you like me?"

But Dede had herself well in hand.

"That's unfair," she said. "And if you stop and consider, you will find that you are doing the very thing you disclaimed—namely, nagging. I refuse to answer any more of your questions. Let us talk about other things. How is Bob?"

Half an hour later, whirling along through the rain on Telegraph Avenue toward Oakland, Daylight smoked one of his brown-paper cigarettes and reviewed what had taken place. It was not at all bad, was his summing up, though there was much about it that was baffling. There was that liking him the more she knew him and at the same time wanting to marry him less. That was a puzzler.

But the fact that she had refused him carried with it a certain elation. In refusing him she had refused his thirty million dollars. That was going some for a ninety dollar-a-month stenographer who had known better ties. She wasn't after money, that was patent. Every woman he had encountered had seemed willing to swallow him down for the sake of his money. Why, he had doubled his fortune, made fifteen millions, since the day she first came to work for him, and behold, any willingness to marry him she might have possessed had diminished as his money had increased.

"Gosh!" he muttered. "If I clean up a hundred million on this land deal she won't even be on speaking terms with me."

But he could not smile the thing away. It remained to baffle him, that enigmatic statement of hers that she could more easily have married the Elam Harnish fresh from the Klondike than the present Elam Harnish. Well, he concluded, the thing to do was for him to become more like that old-time Daylight who had come down out of the North to try his luck at the bigger game. But that was impossible. He could not set back the flight of time. Wishing wouldn't do it, and there was no other way. He might as well wish himself a boy again.

Another satisfaction he cuddled to himself from their interview. He had heard of stenographers before, who refused their employers, and who invariably quit their positions immediately afterward. But Dede had not even hinted at such a thing. No matter how baffling she was, there was no nonsensical silliness about her. She was level headed. But, also, he had been level-headed and was partly responsible for this. He hadn't taken advantage of her in the office. True, he had twice overstepped the bounds, but he had not followed it up and made a practice of it. She knew she could trust him. But in spite of all this he was confident that most young women would have been silly enough to resign a position with a man they had turned down. And besides, after he had put it to her in the right light, she had not been silly over his sending her brother to Germany.

"Gee!" he concluded, as the car drew up before his hotel. "If I'd only known it as I do now, I'd have popped the question the first day she came to work. According to her say-so, that would have been the proper moment. She likes me more and more, and the more she likes me the less she'd care to marry me! Now what do you think of that? She sure must be fooling."

CHAPTER XIX

Once again, on a rainy Sunday, weeks afterward, Daylight proposed to Dede. As on the first time, he restrained himself until his hunger for her overwhelmed him and swept him away in his red automobile to Berkeley. He left the machine several blocks away and proceeded to the house on foot. But Dede was out, the landlady's daughter told him, and added, on second thought, that she was out walking in the hills. Furthermore, the young lady directed him where Dede's walk was most likely to extend.

Daylight obeyed the girl's instructions, and soon the street he followed passed the last house and itself ceased where began the first steep slopes of the open hills. The air was damp with the on-coming of rain, for the storm had not yet burst, though the rising wind proclaimed its imminence. As far as he could see, there was no sign of Dede on the smooth, grassy hills. To the right, dipping down into a hollow and rising again, was a large, full-grown eucalyptus grove. Here all was noise and movement, the lofty, slender trunked trees swaying back and forth in the wind and clashing their branches together. In the squalls, above all the minor noises of creaking and groaning, arose a deep thrumming note as of a mighty harp. Knowing Dede as he did, Daylight was confident that he would find her somewhere in this grove where the storm effects were so pronounced. And find her he did, across the hollow and on the exposed crest of the opposing slope where the gale smote its fiercest blows.

There was something monotonous, though not tiresome, about the way Daylight proposed. Guiltless of diplomacy subterfuge, he was as direct and gusty as the gale itself. He had time neither for greeting nor apology.

"It's the same old thing," he said. "I want you and I've come for you. You've just got to have me, Dede, for the more I think about it the more certain I am that you've got a Sneaking liking for me that's something more than just Ordinary liking. And you don't dast say that it isn't; now dast you?"

He had shaken hands with her at the moment he began speaking, and he had continued to hold her hand. Now, when she did not answer, she felt a light but firmly insistent pressure as of his drawing her to him. Involuntarily, she half-yielded to him, her desire for the moment stronger than her will. Then suddenly she drew herself away, though permitting her hand still to remain in his.

"You sure ain't afraid of me?" he asked, with quick compunction.

"No." She smiled woefully. "Not of you, but of myself."

"You haven't taken my dare," he urged under this encouragement.

"Please, please," she begged. "We can never marry, so don't let us discuss it."

"Then I copper your bet to lose." He was almost gay, now, for success was coming faster than his fondest imagining. She liked him, without a doubt; and without a doubt she liked him well enough to let him hold her hand, well enough to be not repelled by the nearness of him.

She shook her head. "No, it is impossible. You would lose your bet."

For the first time a dark suspicion crossed Daylight's mind—a clew that explained everything.

"Say, you ain't been let in for some one of these secret marriages have you?"

The consternation in his voice and on his face was too much for her, and her laugh rang out, merry and spontaneous as a burst of joy from the throat of a bird.

Daylight knew his answer, and, vexed with himself decided that action was more efficient than speech. So he stepped between her and the wind and drew her so that she stood close in the shelter of him. An unusually stiff squall blew about them and thrummed overhead in the tree-tops and both paused to listen. A shower of flying leaves enveloped them, and hard on the heel of the wind came driving drops of rain. He looked down on her and on her hair wind-blown about her face; and because of her closeness to him and of a fresher and more poignant realization of what she meant to him, he trembled so that she was aware of it in the hand that held hers.

She suddenly leaned against him, bowing her head until it rested lightly upon his breast. And so they stood while another squall, with flying leaves and scattered drops of rain, rattled past. With equal suddenness she lifted her head and looked at him.

"Do you know," she said, "I prayed last night about you. I prayed that you would fail, that you would lose everything everything."

Daylight stared his amazement at this cryptic utterance. "That sure beats me. I always said I got out of my depth with women, and you've got me out of my depth now. Why you want me to lose everything, seeing as you like me—"

"I never said so."

"You didn't dast say you didn't. So, as I was saying: liking me, why you'd want me to go broke is clean beyond my simple understanding. It's right in line with that other puzzler of yours, the more-you-like-me-the-less-you-want-to-marry-me one. Well, you've just got to explain, that's all."

His arms went around her and held her closely, and this time she did not resist. Her head was bowed, and he had not see her face, yet he had a premonition that she was crying. He had learned the virtue of silence, and he waited her will in the matter. Things had come to such a pass that she was bound to tell him something now. Of that he was confident.

"I am not romantic," she began, again looking at him as he spoke.

"It might be better for me if I were. Then I could make a fool of myself and be unhappy for the rest of my life. But my abominable common sense prevents. And that doesn't make me a bit happier, either."

"I'm still out of my depth and swimming feeble," Daylight said, after waiting vainly for her to go on. "You've got to show me, and you ain't shown me yet. Your common sense and praying that I'd go broke is all up in the air to me. Little woman, I just love you mighty hard, and I want you to marry me. That's straight and simple and right off the bat. Will you marry me?"

She shook her head slowly, and then, as she talked, seemed to grow angry, sadly angry; and Daylight knew that this anger was against him.

"Then let me explain, and just as straight and simply as you have asked." She paused, as if casting about for a beginning. "You are honest and straightforward. Do you want me to be honest and straightforward as a woman is not supposed to be?—to tell you things that will hurt you?—to make confessions that ought to shame me? to behave in what many men would think was an unwomanly manner?"

The arm around her shoulder pressed encouragement, but he did not speak.

"I would dearly like to marry you, but I am afraid. I am proud and humble at the same time that a man like you should care for me. But you have too much money. There's where my abominable common sense steps in. Even if we did marry, you could never be my man—my lover and my husband. You would be your money's man. I know I am a foolish woman, but I want my man for myself. You would not be free for me. Your money possesses you, taking your time, your thoughts, your energy, everything, bidding you go here and go there, do this and do that. Don't you see? Perhaps it's pure silliness, but I feel that I can love much, give much—give all, and in return, though I don't want all, I want much—and I want much more than your money would permit you to give me.

"And your money destroys you; it makes you less and less nice. I am not ashamed to say that I love you, because I shall never marry you. And I loved you much when I did not know you at all, when you first came down from Alaska and I first went into the office. You were my hero. You were the Burning Daylight of the gold-diggings, the daring traveler and miner. And you looked it. I don't see how any woman could have looked at you without loving you—then. But you don't look it now.

"Please, please, forgive me for hurting you. You wanted straight talk, and I am giving it to you. All these last years you have been living unnaturally. You, a man of the open, have been cooping yourself up in the cities with all that that means. You are not the same man at all, and your money is destroying you. You are becoming something different, something not so healthy, not so clean, not so nice. Your money and your way of life are doing it. You know it. You haven't the same body now that you had then. You are putting on flesh, and it is not healthy flesh. You are kind and genial with me, I know, but you are not kind and genial to all the world as you were then. You have become harsh and cruel. And I know. Remember, I have studied you six days a week, month after month, year after year; and I know more about the most insignificant parts of you than you know of all of me. The cruelty is not only in your heart and thoughts, but it is there in face. It has put its lines there. I have watched them come and grow. Your money, and the life it compels you to lead have done all this. You are being brutalized and degraded. And this process can only go on and on until you are hopelessly destroyed—"

He attempted to interrupt, but she stopped him, herself breathless and her voice trembling.

"No, no; let me finish utterly. I have done nothing but think, think, think, all these months, ever since you came riding with me, and now that I have begun to speak I am going to speak all that I have in me. I do love you, but I cannot marry you and destroy love. You are growing into a thing that I must in the end despise. You can't help it. More than you can possibly love me, do you love this business game. This business—and it's all perfectly useless, so far as you are concerned—claims all of you. I sometimes think it would be easier to share you equitably with another woman than to share you with this business. I might have half of you, at any rate. But this business would claim, not half of you, but nine-tenths of you, or ninety-nine hundredths.

"Remember, the meaning of marriage to me is not to get a man's money to spend. I want the man. You say you want ME. And suppose I consented, but gave you only one-hundredth part of me. Suppose there was something else in my life that took the other ninety-nine parts, and, furthermore, that ruined my figure, that put pouches under my eyes and crows-feet in the corners, that made me unbeautiful to look upon and that made my spirit unbeautiful. Would you be satisfied with that one-hundredth part of me? Yet that is all you are offering me of yourself. Do you wonder that I won't marry you?—that I can't?"

Daylight waited to see if she were quite done, and she went on again.

"It isn't that I am selfish. After all, love is giving, not receiving. But I see so clearly that all my giving could not do you any good. You are like a sick man. You don't play business like other men. You play it heart and and all of you. No matter what you believed and intended a wife would be only a brief diversion. There is that magnificent Bob, eating his head off in the stable. You would buy me a beautiful mansion and leave me in it to yawn my head off, or cry my eyes out because of my helplessness and inability to save you. This disease of business would be corroding you and marring you all the time. You play it as you have played everything else, as in Alaska you played the life of the trail. Nobody could be permitted to travel as fast and as far as you, to work as hard or endure as much. You hold back nothing; you put all you've got into whatever you are doing."

"Limit is the sky," he grunted grim affirmation.

"But if you would only play the lover-husband that way—"

Her voice faltered and stopped, and a blush showed in her wet cheeks as her eyes fell before his.

"And now I won't say another word," she added. "I've delivered a whole sermon."

She rested now, frankly and fairly, in the shelter of his arms, and both were oblivious to the gale that rushed past them in quicker and stronger blasts. The big downpour of rain had not yet come, but the mist-like squalls were more frequent. Daylight was openly perplexed, and he was still perplexed when he began to speak.

"I'm stumped. I'm up a tree. I'm clean flabbergasted, Miss Mason—or Dede, because I love to call you that name. I'm free to confess there's a mighty big heap in what you say. As I understand it, your conclusion is that you'd marry me if I hadn't a cent and if I wasn't getting fat. No, no; I'm not joking. I acknowledge the corn, and that's just my way of boiling the matter down and summing it up. If I hadn't a cent, and if I was living a healthy life with all the time in the world to love you and be your husband instead of being awash to my back teeth in business and all the rest—why, you'd marry me.

"That's all as clear as print, and you're correcter than I ever guessed before. You've sure opened my eyes a few. But I'm stuck. What can I do? My business has sure roped, thrown, and branded me. I'm tied hand and foot, and I can't get up and meander over green pastures. I'm like the man that got the bear by the tail. I can't let go; and I want you, and I've got to let go to get you.

"I don't know what to do, but something's sure got to happen—I can't lose you. I just can't. And I'm not going to. Why, you're running business a close second right now. Business never kept me awake nights.

"You've left me no argument. I know I'm not the same man that came from Alaska. I couldn't hit the trail with the dogs as I did in them days. I'm soft in my muscles, and my mind's gone hard. I used to respect men. I despise them now. You see, I spent all my life in the open, and I reckon I'm an open-air man. Why, I've got the prettiest little ranch you ever laid eyes on, up in Glen Ellen. That's where I got stuck for that brick-yard. You recollect handling the correspondence. I only laid eyes on the ranch that one time, and I so fell in love with it that I bought it there and then. I just rode around the hills, and was happy as a kid out of school. I'd

596

be a better man living in the country. The city doesn't make me better. You're plumb right there. I know it. But suppose your prayer should be answered and I'd go clean broke and have to work for day's wages?"

She did not answer, though all the body of her seemed to urge consent.

"Suppose I had nothing left but that little ranch, and was satisfied to grow a few chickens and scratch a living somehow—would you marry me then, Dede?"

"Why, we'd be together all the time!" she cried.

"But I'd have to be out ploughing once in a while," he warned, "or driving to town to get the grub."

"But there wouldn't be the office, at any rate, and no man to see, and men to see without end. But it is all foolish and impossible, and we'll have to be starting back now if we're to escape the rain."

Then was the moment, among the trees, where they began the descent of the hill, that Daylight might have drawn her closely to him and kissed her once. But he was too perplexed with the new thoughts she had put into his head to take advantage of the situation. He merely caught her by the arm and helped her over the rougher footing.

"It's darn pretty country up there at Glen Ellen," he said meditatively. "I wish you could see it."

At the edge of the grove he suggested that it might be better for them to part there.

"It's your neighborhood, and folks is liable to talk."

But she insisted that he accompany her as far as the house.

"I can't ask you in," she said, extending her hand at the foot of the steps.

The wind was humming wildly in sharply recurrent gusts, but still the rain held off.

"Do you know," he said, "taking it by and large, it's the happiest day of my life." He took off his hat, and the wind rippled and twisted his black hair as he went on solemnly, "And I'm sure grateful to God, or whoever or whatever is responsible for your being on this earth. For you do like me heaps. It's been my joy to hear you say so to-day. It's—" He left the thought arrested, and his face assumed the familiar whimsical expression as he murmured: "Dede, Dede, we've just got to get married. It's the only way, and trust to luck for it's coming out all right—".

But the tears were threatening to rise in her eyes again, as she shook her head and turned and went up the steps.

CHAPTER XX

When the ferry system began to run, and the time between Oakland and San Francisco was demonstrated to be cut in half, the tide of Daylight's terrific expenditure started to turn. Not that it really did turn, for he promptly went into further investments. Thousands of lots in his residence tracts were sold, and thousands of homes were being built. Factory sites also were selling, and business properties in the heart of Oakland. All this tended to a steady appreciation in value of Daylight's huge holdings. But, as of old, he had his hunch and was riding it. Already he had begun borrowing from the banks. The magnificent profits he made on the land he sold were turned into more land, into more development; and instead of paying off old loans, he contracted new ones. As he had pyramided in Dawson City, he now pyramided in Oakland; but he did it with the knowledge that it was a stable enterprise rather than a risky placer-mining boom.

In a small way, other men were following his lead, buying and selling land and profiting by the improvement work he was doing. But this was to be expected, and the small fortunes they were making at his expense did not irritate him. There was an exception, however. One Simon Dolliver, with money to go in with, and with cunning and courage to back it up, bade fair to become a several times millionaire at Daylight's expense. Dolliver, too, pyramided, playing quickly and accurately, and keeping his money turning over and over. More than once Daylight found him in the way, as he himself had got in the way of the Guggenhammers when they first set their eyes on Ophir Creek.

Work on Daylight's dock system went on apace, yet was one of those enterprises that consumed money dreadfully and that could not be accomplished as quickly as a ferry system. The engineering difficulties were great, the dredging and filling a cyclopean task. The mere item of piling was anything but small. A good average pile, by the time it was delivered on the ground, cost a twenty-dollar gold piece, and these piles were used in unending thousands. All accessible groves of mature eucalyptus were used, and as well, great rafts of pine piles were towed down the coast from Peugeot Sound.

Not content with manufacturing the electricity for his street railways in the old-fashioned way, in power-houses, Daylight organized the Sierra and Salvador Power Company. This immediately assumed large proportions. Crossing the San Joaquin Valley on the way from the mountains, and plunging through the Contra Costa hills, there were many towns, and even a robust city, that could be supplied with power, also with light; and it became a street- and house-lighting project as well. As soon as the purchase of power sites in the Sierras was rushed through, the survey parties were out and building operations begun.

And so it went. There were a thousand maws into which he poured unceasing streams of money. But it was all so sound and legitimate, that Daylight, born gambler that he was, and with his clear, wide vision, could not play softly and safely. It was a big opportunity, and to him there was only one way to play it, and that was the big way. Nor did his one confidential adviser, Larry Hegan, aid him to caution. On the contrary, it was Daylight who was compelled to veto the wilder visions of that able hasheesh dreamer. Not only did Daylight borrow heavily from the banks and trust companies, but on several of his corporations he was compelled to issue stock. He did this grudgingly however, and retained most of his big enterprises of his own. Among the companies in which he reluctantly allowed the investing public to join were the Golden Gate Dock Company, and Recreation Parks Company, the United Water Company, the Uncial Shipbuilding Company, and the Sierra and Salvador Power Company. Nevertheless, between himself and Hegan, he retained the controlling share in each of these enterprises.

His affair with Dede Mason only seemed to languish. While delaying to grapple with the strange problem it presented, his desire for her continued to grow. In his gambling simile, his conclusion was that Luck had dealt him the most remarkable card in the deck, and that for years he had overlooked it. Love was the card, and it beat them all. Love was the king card of trumps, the fifth ace, the joker in a game of tenderfoot poker. It was the card of cards, and play it he would, to the limit, when the opening came. He could not see that opening yet. The present game would have to play to some sort of a conclusion first.

Yet he could not shake from his brain and vision the warm recollection of those bronze slippers, that clinging gown, and all the feminine softness and pliancy of Dede in her pretty Berkeley rooms. Once again, on a rainy Sunday, he telephoned that he was coming. And, as has happened ever since man first looked upon woman and called her good, again he played the blind force of male compulsion against the woman's secret weakness to yield. Not that it was Daylight's way abjectly to beg and entreat. On the contrary, he was masterful in whatever he did, but he had a trick of whimsical wheedling that Dede found harder to resist than the pleas of a suppliant lover. It was not a happy scene in its outcome, for Dede, in the throes of her own desire, desperate with weakness and at the same time with her better judgment hating her weakness cried out:—

"You urge me to try a chance, to marry you now and trust to luck for it to come out right. And life is a gamble say. Very well, let us gamble. Take a coin and toss it in the air. If it comes heads, I'll marry you. If it doesn't, you are forever to leave me alone and never mention marriage again."

A fire of mingled love and the passion of gambling came into Daylight's eyes. Involuntarily his hand started for his pocket for the coin. Then it stopped, and the light in his eyes was troubled.

"Go on," she ordered sharply. "Don't delay, or I may change my mind, and you will lose the chance."

"Little woman." His similes were humorous, but there was no humor in their meaning. His thought was as solemn as his voice. "Little woman, I'd gamble all the way from Creation to the Day of Judgment; I'd gamble a golden harp against another man's halo; I'd toss for pennies on the front steps of the New Jerusalem or set up a faro layout just outside the Pearly Gates; but I'll be everlastingly damned if I'll gamble on love. Love's too big to me to take a chance on. Love's got to be a sure thing, and between you and me it is a sure thing. If the odds was a hundred to one on my winning this flip, just the same, nary a flip."

In the spring of the year the Great Panic came on. The first warning was when the banks began calling in their unprotected loans. Daylight promptly paid the first several of his personal notes that were presented; then he divined that these demands but indicated the way the wind was going to blow, and that one of those terrific financial storms he had heard about was soon to sweep over the United States. How terrific this particular storm was to be he did not anticipate. Nevertheless, he took every precaution in his power, and had no anxiety about his weathering it out.

Money grew tighter. Beginning with the crash of several of the greatest Eastern banking houses, the tightness spread, until every bank in the country was calling in its credits. Daylight was caught, and caught because of the fact that for the first time he had been playing the legitimate business game. In the old days, such a panic, with the accompanying extreme shrinkage of values, would have been a golden harvest time for him. As it was, he watched the gamblers, who had ridden the wave of prosperity and made preparation for the slump, getting out from under and safely scurrying to cover or proceeding to reap a double harvest. Nothing remained for him but to stand fast and hold up.

He saw the situation clearly. When the banks demanded that he pay his loans, he knew that the banks were in sore need of the money. But he was in sorer need. And he knew that the banks did not want his collateral which they held. It would do them no good. In such a tumbling of values was no time to sell. His collateral was good, all of it, eminently sound and worth while; yet it was worthless at such a moment, when the one unceasing cry was money, money, money. Finding him obdurate, the banks demanded more collateral, and as the money pinch tightened they asked for two and even three times as much as had been originally accepted. Sometimes Daylight yielded to these demands, but more often not, and always battling fiercely.

He fought as with clay behind a crumbling wall. All portions of the wall were menaced, and he went around constantly strengthening the weakest parts with clay. This clay was money, and was applied, a sop here and a sop there, as fast as it was needed, but only when it was directly needed. The strength of his position lay in the Yerba Buena Ferry Company, the Consolidated Street Railways, and the United Water Company. Though people were no longer buying residence lots and factory and business sites, they were compelled to ride on his cars and ferryboats and to consume his water. When all the financial world was clamoring for money and perishing through lack of it, the first of each month many thousands of dollars poured into his coffers from the water-rates, and each day ten thousand dollars, in dime and nickels, came in from his street railways and ferries.

Cash was what was wanted, and had he had the use of all this steady river of cash, all would have been well with him. As it was, he had to fight continually for a portion of it. Improvement work ceased, and only absolutely essential repairs were made. His fiercest fight was with the operating expenses, and this was a fight that never ended. There was never any let-up in his turning the thumb-screws of extended credit and economy. From the big wholesale suppliers down through the salary list to office stationery and postage stamps, he kept the thumb-screws turning. When his superintendents and heads of departments performed prodigies of cutting down, he patted them on the back and demanded more. When they threw down their hands in despair, he showed them how more could be accomplished.

"You are getting eight thousand dollars a year," he told Matthewson. "It's better pay than you ever got in your life before. Your fortune is in the same sack with mine. You've got to stand for some of the strain and risk. You've got personal credit in this town. Use it. Stand off butcher and baker and all the rest. Savvee? You're drawing down something like six hundred and sixty dollars a month. I want that cash. From now on, stand everybody off and draw down a hundred. I'll pay you interest on the rest till this blows over."

Two weeks later, with the pay-roll before them, it was:—

"Matthewson, who's this bookkeeper, Rogers? Your nephew? I thought so. He's pulling down eighty-five a month. After—this let him draw thirty-five. The forty can ride with me at interest."

"Impossible!" Matthewson cried. "He can't make ends meet on his salary as it is, and he has a wife and two kids—"

Daylight was upon him with a mighty oath.

"Can't! Impossible! What in hell do you think I'm running? A home for feeble-minded? Feeding and dressing and wiping the little noses of a lot of idiots that can't take care of themselves? Not on your life. I'm hustling, and now's the time that everybody that works for me has got to hustle. I want no fair-weather birds holding down my office chairs or anything else. This is nasty weather, damn nasty weather, and they've got to buck into it just like me. There are ten thousand men out of work in Oakland right now, and sixty thousand more in San Francisco. Your nephew, and everybody else on your pay-roll, can do as I say right now or quit. Savvee? If any of them get stuck, you go around yourself and guarantee their credit with the butchers and grocers. And you trim down that pay-roll accordingly. I've been carrying a few thousand folks that'll have to carry themselves for a while now, that's all."

"You say this filter's got to be replaced," he told his chief of the water-works. "We'll see about it. Let the people of Oakland drink mud for a change. It'll teach them to appreciate good water. Stop work at once. Get those men off the pay-roll. Cancel all orders for material. The contractors will sue? Let 'em sue and be damned. We'll be busted higher'n a kite or on easy street before they can get judgment."

And to Wilkinson:

"Take off that owl boat. Let the public roar and come home early to its wife. And there's that last car that connects with the 12:45 boat at Twenty-second and Hastings. Cut it out. I can't run it for two or three passengers. Let them take an earlier boat home or walk. This is no time for philanthropy. And you might as well take off a few more cars in the rush hours. Let the strap-hangers pay. It's the strap-hangers that'll keep us from going under."

And to another chief, who broke down under the excessive strain of retrenchment:—

"You say I can't do that and can't do this. I'll just show you a few of the latest patterns in the can-and-can't line. You'll be compelled to resign? All right, if you think so I never saw the man yet that I was hard up for. And when any man thinks I can't get along without him, I just show him the latest pattern in that line of goods and give him his walking-papers."

And so he fought and drove and bullied and even wheedled his way along. It was fight, fight, fight, and no let-up, from the first thing in the morning till nightfall. His private office saw throngs every day. All men came to see him, or were ordered to come. Now it was an optimistic opinion on the panic, a funny story, a serious business talk, or a straight take-it-or-leave-it blow from the shoulder. And there was nobody to relieve him. It was a case of drive, drive, drive, and he alone could do the driving. And this went on day after day, while the whole business world rocked around him and house after house crashed to the ground.

"It's all right, old man," he told Hegan every morning; and it was the same cheerful word that he passed out all day long, except at such times when he was in the thick of fighting to have his will with persons and things.

Eight o'clock saw him at his desk each morning. By ten o'clock, it was into the machine and away for a round of the banks. And usually in the machine with him was the ten thousand and more dollars that had been earned by his ferries and railways the day before. This was for the weakest spot in the financial dike. And with one bank president after another similar scenes were enacted. They were paralyzed with fear, and first of all he played his role of the big vital optimist. Times were improving.

Of course they were. The signs were already in the air. All that anybody had to do was to sit tight a little longer and hold on. That was all. Money was already more active in the East. Look at the trading on Wall Street of the last twenty-four hours.

That was the straw that showed the wind. Hadn't Ryan said so and so? and wasn't it reported that Morgan was preparing to do this and that?

As for himself, weren't the street-railway earnings increasing steadily? In spite of the panic, more and more people were coming to Oakland right along. Movements were already beginning in real estate. He was dickering even then to sell over a thousand of his suburban acres. Of course it was at a sacrifice, but it would ease the strain on all of them and bolster up the faint-hearted. That was the trouble—the faint-hearts. Had there been no faint-hearts there would have been no panic. There was that Eastern syndicate, negotiating with him now to take the majority of the stock in the Sierra and Salvador Power Company off his hands. That showed confidence that better times were at hand.

And if it was not cheery discourse, but prayer and entreaty or show down and fight on the part of the banks, Daylight had to counter in kind. If they could bully, he could bully. If the favor he asked were refused, it became the thing he demanded. And when it came down to raw and naked fighting, with the last veil of sentiment or illusion torn off, he could take their breaths away.

But he knew, also, how and when to give in. When he saw the wall shaking and crumbling irretrievably at a particular place, he patched it up with sops of cash from his three cash-earning companies. If the banks went, he went too. It was a case of their having to hold out. If they smashed and all the collateral they held of his was thrown on the chaotic market, it would be the end. And so it was, as the time passed, that on occasion his red motor-car carried, in addition to the daily cash, the most gilt-edged securities he possessed; namely, the Ferry Company, United Water and Consolidated Railways. But he did this reluctantly, fighting inch by inch.

As he told the president of the Merchants San Antonio who made the plea of carrying so many others:—

"They're small fry. Let them smash. I'm the king pin here. You've got more money to make out of me than them. Of course, you're carrying too much, and you've got to choose, that's all. It's root hog or die for you or them. I'm too strong to smash. You could only embarrass me and get yourself tangled up. Your way out is to let the small fry go, and I'll lend you a hand to do it."

And it was Daylight, also, in this time of financial anarchy, who sized up Simon Dolliver's affairs and lent the hand that sent that rival down in utter failure. The Golden Gate National was the keystone of Dolliver's strength, and to the president of that institution Daylight said:—

"Here I've been lending you a hand, and you now in the last ditch, with Dolliver riding on you and me all the time. It don't go. You hear me, it don't go. Dolliver couldn't cough up eleven dollars to save you. Let him get off and walk, and I'll tell you what I'll do. I'll give you the railway nickels for four days—that's forty thousand cash. And on the sixth of the month you can count on twenty thousand more from the Water Company." He shrugged his shoulders. "Take it or leave it. Them's my terms."

"It's dog eat dog, and I ain't overlooking any meat that's floating around," Daylight proclaimed that afternoon to Hegan; and Simon Dolliver went the way of the unfortunate in the Great Panic who were caught with plenty of paper and no money.

Daylight's shifts and devices were amazing. Nothing however large or small, passed his keen sight unobserved. The strain he was under was terrific. He no longer ate lunch. The days were too short, and his noon hours and his office were as crowded as at any other time. By the end of the day he was exhausted, and, as never before, he sought relief behind his wall of alcoholic inhibition. Straight to his hotel he was driven, and straight to his rooms he went, where immediately was mixed for him the first of a series of double Martinis. By dinner, his brain was well clouded and the panic forgotten. By bedtime, with the assistance of Scotch whiskey, he was full—not violently nor uproariously full, nor stupefied, but merely well under the influence of a pleasant and mild anesthetic.

Next morning he awoke with parched lips and mouth, and with sensations of heaviness in his head which quickly passed away. By eight o'clock he was at his desk, buckled down to the fight, by ten o'clock on his personal round of the banks, and after that, without a moment's cessation, till nightfall, he was handling the knotty tangles of industry, finance, and human nature that crowded upon him. And with nightfall it was back to the hotel, the double Martinis and the Scotch; and this was his program day after day until the days ran into weeks.

CHAPTER XXI

Though Daylight appeared among his fellows hearty voiced, inexhaustible, spilling over with energy and vitality, deep down he was a very weary man. And sometime under the liquor drug, snatches of wisdom came to him far more lucidity than in his sober moments, as, for instance, one night, when he sat on the edge of the bed with one shoe in his hand and meditated on Dede's aphorism to the effect that he could not sleep in more than one bed at a time. Still holding the shoe, he looked at the array of horsehair bridles on the walls. Then, carrying the shoe, he got up and solemnly counted them, journeying into the two adjoining rooms to complete the tale. Then he came back to the bed and gravely addressed his shoe:—

"The little woman's right. Only one bed at a time. One hundred and forty hair bridles, and nothing doing with ary one of them. One bridle at a time! I can't ride one horse at a time. Poor old Bob. I'd better be sending you out to pasture. Thirty million dollars, and a hundred million or nothing in sight, and what have I got to show for it? There's lots of things money can't buy. It can't buy the little woman. It can't buy capacity. What's the good of thirty millions when I ain't got room for more than a quart of cocktails a day? If I had a hundred-quart-cocktail thirst, it'd be different. But one quart—one measly little quart! Here I am, a thirty times over millionaire, slaving harder every day than any dozen men that work for me, and all I get is two meals that don't taste good, one bed, a quart of Martini, and a hundred and forty hair bridles to look at on the wall."

He stared around at the array disconsolately. "Mr. Shoe, I'm sizzled. Good night."

Far worse than the controlled, steady drinker is the solitary drinker, and it was this that Daylight was developing into. He rarely drank sociably any more, but in his own room, by himself. Returning weary from each day's unremitting effort, he drugged himself to sleep, knowing that on the morrow he would rise up with a dry and burning mouth and repeat the program.

But the country did not recover with its wonted elasticity. Money did not become freer, though the casual reader of Daylight's newspapers, as well as of all the other owned and subsidised newspapers in the country, could only have concluded that the money tightness was over and that the panic was past history. All public utterances were cheery and optimistic, but privately many of the utters were in desperate straits. The scenes enacted in the privacy of Daylight's office, and of the meetings of his boards of directors, would have given the lie to the editorials in his newspapers; as, for instance, when he addressed the big stockholders in the Sierra and Salvador Power Company, the United Water Company, and the several other stock companies:—

"You've got to dig. You've got a good thing, but you'll have to sacrifice in order to hold on. There ain't no use spouting hard times explanations. Don't I know the hard times is on? Ain't that what you're here for? As I said before, you've got to dig. I run the majority stock, and it's come to a case of assess. It's that or smash. If ever I start going you won't know what struck you, I'll smash that hard. The small fry can let go, but you big ones can't. This ship won't sink as long as you stay with her. But if you start to leave her, down you'll sure go before you can get to shore. This assessment has got to be met that's all."

The big wholesale supply houses, the caterers for his hotels, and all the crowd that incessantly demanded to be paid, had their hot half-hours with him. He summoned them to his office and displayed his latest patterns of can and can't and will and won't.

"By God, you've got to carry me!" he told them. "If you think this is a pleasant little game of parlor whist and that you can quit and go home whenever you want, you're plumb wrong. Look here, Watkins, you remarked five minutes ago that you wouldn't stand for it. Now let me tell you a few. You're going to stand for it and keep on standin's for it. You're going to continue supplying me and taking my paper until the pinch is over. How you're going to do it is your trouble, not mine. You remember what I did to Klinkner and the Altamont Trust Company? I know the inside of your business better than you do yourself, and if you try to drop me I'll smash you. Even if I'd be going to smash myself, I'd find a minute to turn on you and bring you down with me. It's sink or swim for all of us, and I reckon you'll find it to your interest to keep me on top the puddle."

Perhaps his bitterest fight was with the stockholders of the United Water Company, for it was practically the whole of the gross earnings of this company that he voted to lend to himself and used to bolster up his wide battle front. Yet he never pushed his arbitrary rule too far. Compelling sacrifice from the men whose fortunes were tied up with his, nevertheless when any one of them was driven to the wall and was in dire need, Daylight was there to help him back into the line. Only a strong man could have saved so complicated a situation in such time of stress, and Daylight was that man. He turned and twisted, schemed and devised, bludgeoned and bullied the weaker ones, kept the faint-hearted in the fight, and had no mercy on the deserter.

And in the end, when early summer was on, everything began to mend. Came a day when Daylight did the unprecedented. He left the office an hour earlier than usual, and for the reason that for the first time since the panic there was not an item of work waiting to be done. He dropped into Hegan's private office, before leaving, for a chat, and as he stood up to go, he said:—

"Hegan, we're all hunkadory. We're pulling out of the financial pawnshop in fine shape, and we'll get out without leaving one unredeemed pledge behind. The worst is over, and the end is in sight. Just a tight rein for a couple more weeks, just a bit of a pinch or a flurry or so now and then, and we can let go and spit on our hands."

For once he varied his program. Instead of going directly to his hotel, he started on a round of the bars and cafes, drinking a cocktail here and a cocktail there, and two or three when he encountered men he knew. It was after an hour or so of this that he dropped into the bar of the Parthenon for one last drink before going to dinner. By this time all his being was pleasantly warmed by the alcohol, and he was in the most genial and best of spirits. At the corner of the bar several young men were up to the old trick of resting their elbows and attempting to force each other's hands down. One broad-shouldered young giant never removed his elbow, but put down every hand that came against him. Daylight was interested.

"It's Slosson," the barkeeper told him, in answer to his query. "He's the heavy-hammer thrower at the U.C. Broke all records this year, and the world's record on top of it. He's a husky all right all right."

Daylight nodded and went over to him, placing his own arm in opposition.

"I'd like to go you a flutter, son, on that proposition," he said.

The young man laughed and locked hands with him; and to Daylight's astonishment it was his own hand that was forced down on the bar.

"Hold on," he muttered. "Just one more flutter. I reckon I wasn't just ready that time."

Again the hands locked. It happened quickly. The offensive attack of Daylight's muscles slipped instantly into defense, and, resisting vainly, his hand was forced over and down. Daylight was dazed. It had been no trick. The skill was equal, or, if anything, the superior skill had been his. Strength, sheer strength, had done it. He called for the drinks, and, still dazed and pondering, held up his own arm, and looked at it as at some new strange thing. He did not know this arm. It certainly was not the arm he had carried around with him all the years. The old arm? Why, it would have been play to turn down that young husky's. But this arm—he continued to look at it with such dubious perplexity as to bring a roar of laughter from the young men.

This laughter aroused him. He joined in it at first, and then his face slowly grew grave. He leaned toward the hammer-thrower.

"Son," he said, "let me whisper a secret. Get out of here and quit drinking before you begin."

The young fellow flushed angrily, but Daylight held steadily on.

"You listen to your dad, and let him say a few. I'm a young man myself, only I ain't. Let me tell you, several years ago for me to turn your hand down would have been like committing assault and battery on a kindergarten."

Slosson looked his incredulity, while the others grinned and clustered around Daylight encouragingly.

"Son, I ain't given to preaching. This is the first time I ever come to the penitent form, and you put me there yourself—hard. I've seen a few in my time, and I ain't fastidious so as you can notice it. But let me tell you right not that I'm worth the devil alone knows how many millions, and that I'd sure give it all, right here on the bar, to turn down your hand. Which means I'd give the whole shooting match just to be back where I was before I quit sleeping under the stars and come into the hen-coops of cities to drink cocktails and lift up my feet and ride. Son, that's that's the matter with me, and that's the way I feel about it. The game ain't worth the candle. You just take care of yourself, and roll my advice over once in a while. Good night."

He turned and lurched out of the place, the moral effect of his utterance largely spoiled by the fact that he was so patently full while he uttered it.

Still in a daze, Daylight made to his hotel, accomplished his dinner, and prepared for bed.

"The damned young whippersnapper!" he muttered. "Put my hand down easy as you please. My hand!"

He held up the offending member and regarded it with stupid wonder. The hand that had never been beaten! The hand that had made the Circle City giants wince! And a kid from college, with a laugh on his face, had put it down—twice! Dede was right. He was not the same man. The situation would bear more serious looking into than he had ever given it. But this was not the time. In the morning, after a good sleep, he would give it consideration.

CHAPTER XXII

Daylight awoke with the familiar parched mouth and lips and throat, took a long drink of water from the pitcher beside his bed, and gathered up the train of thought where he had left it the night before. He reviewed the easement of the financial strain. Things were mending at last. While the going was still rough, the greatest dangers were already past. As he had told Hegan, a tight rein and careful playing were all that was needed now. Flurries and dangers were bound to come, but not so grave as the ones they had already weathered. He had been hit hard, but he was coming through without broken bones, which was more than Simon Dolliver and many another could say. And not one of his business friends had been ruined. He had compelled them to stay in line to save himself, and they had been saved as well.

His mind moved on to the incident at the corner of the bar of the Parthenon, when the young athlete had turned his hand down. He was no longer stunned by the event, but he was shocked and grieved, as only a strong man can be, at this passing of his strength. And the issue was too clear for him to dodge, even with himself. He knew why his hand had gone down. Not because he was an old man. He was just in the first flush of his prime, and, by rights, it was the hand of the hammer-thrower which should have gone down. Daylight knew that he had taken liberties with himself. He had always looked upon this strength of his as permanent, and here, for years, it had been steadily oozing from him. As he had diagnosed it, he had come in from under the stars to roost in the coops of cities. He had almost forgotten how to walk. He had lifted up his feet and been ridden around in automobiles, cabs and carriages, and electric cars. He had not exercised, and he had dry-rotted his muscles with alcohol.

And was it worth it? What did all his money mean after all? Dede was right. It could buy him no more than one bed at a time, and at the same time it made him the abjectest of slaves. It tied him fast. He was tied by it right now. Even if he so desired, he could not lie abed this very day. His money called him. The office whistle would soon blow, and he must answer it. The early sunshine was streaming through his window—a fine day for a ride in the hills on Bob, with Dede beside him on her Mab. Yet all his millions could not buy him this one day. One of those flurries might come along, and he had to be on the spot to meet it. Thirty millions! And they were powerless to persuade Dede to ride on Mab—Mab, whom he had bought, and who was unused and growing fat on pasture. What were thirty millions when they could not buy a man a ride with the girl he loved? Thirty millions!—that made him come here and go there, that rode upon him like so many millstones, that destroyed him while they grew, that put their foot down and prevented him from winning this girl who worked for ninety dollars a month.

Which was better? he asked himself. All this was Dede's own thought. It was what she had meant when she prayed he would go broke. He held up his offending right arm. It wasn't the same old arm. Of course she could not love that arm and that body as she had loved the strong, clean arm and body of years before. He didn't like that arm and body himself. A young whippersnapper had been able to take liberties with it. It had gone back on him. He sat up suddenly. No, by God, he had gone back on it! He had gone back on himself. He had gone back on Dede. She was right, a thousand times right, and she had sense enough to know it, sense enough to refuse to marry a money slave with a whiskey-rotted carcass.

He got out of bed and looked at himself in the long mirror on the wardrobe door. He wasn't pretty. The old-time lean cheeks were gone. These were heavy, seeming to hang down by their own weight. He looked for the lines of cruelty Dede had spoken of, and he found them, and he found the harshness in the eyes as well, the eyes that were muddy now after all the cocktails of the night before, and of the months and years before. He looked at the clearly defined pouches that showed under his eyes, and they've shocked him. He rolled up the sleeve of his pajamas. No wonder the hammer-thrower had put his hand down. Those weren't muscles. A rising tide of fat had submerged them. He stripped off the pajama coat. Again he was shocked, this time but the bulk of his body. It wasn't pretty. The lean stomach had become a paunch. The ridged muscles of chest and shoulders and abdomen had broken down into rolls of flesh.

He sat down on the bed, and through his mind drifted pictures of his youthful excellence, of the hardships he had endured over other men, of the Indians and dogs he had run off their legs in the heart-breaking days and nights on the Alaskan trail, of the feats of strength that had made him king over a husky race of frontiersmen.

And this was age. Then there drifted across the field of vision of his mind's eye the old man he had encountered at Glen Ellen, corning up the hillside through the fires of sunset, white-headed and white-bearded, eighty-four, in his hand the pail of foaming milk and in his face all the warm glow and content of the passing summer day. That had been age. "Yes siree, eighty-four, and spryer than most," he could hear the old man say. "And I ain't loafed none. I walked across the Plains with an ox-team and fit Injuns in '51, and I was a family man then with seven youngsters."

Next he remembered the old woman of the chaparral, pressing grapes in her mountain clearing; and Ferguson, the little man who had scuttled into the road like a rabbit, the one-time managing editor of a great newspaper, who was content to live in the chaparral along with his spring of mountain water and his hand-reared and manicured fruit trees. Ferguson had solved a problem. A weakling and an alcoholic, he had run away from the doctors and the chicken-coop of a city, and soaked up health like a thirsty sponge. Well, Daylight pondered, if a sick man whom the doctors had given up could develop into a healthy farm laborer, what couldn't a merely stout man like himself do under similar circumstances? He caught a vision of his body with all its youthful excellence returned, and thought of Dede, and sat down suddenly on the bed, startled by the greatness of the idea that had come to him.

He did not sit long. His mind, working in its customary way, like a steel trap, canvassed the idea in all its bearings. It was big—bigger than anything he had faced before. And he faced it squarely, picked it up in his two hands and turned it over and around and looked at it. The simplicity of it delighted him. He chuckled over it, reached his decision, and began to dress. Midway in the dressing he stopped in order to use the telephone.

Dede was the first he called up.

"Don't come to the office this morning," he said. "I'm coming out to see you for a moment." He called up others. He ordered his motor-car. To Jones he gave instructions for the forwarding of Bob and Wolf to Glen Ellen. Hegan he surprised by asking him to look up the deed of the Glen Ellen ranch and make out a new one in Dede Mason's name. "Who?" Hegan demanded. "Dede Mason," Daylight replied imperturbably the 'phone must be indistinct this morning. "D-e-d-e M-a-s o-n. Got it?"

Half an hour later he was flying out to Berkeley. And for the first time the big red car halted directly before the house. Dede offered to receive him in the parlor, but he shook his head and nodded toward her rooms.

"In there," he said. "No other place would suit."

As the door closed, his arms went out and around her. Then he stood with his hands on her shoulders and looking down into her face.

"Dede, if I tell you, flat and straight, that I'm going up to live on that ranch at Glen Ellen, that I ain't taking a cent with me, that I'm going to scratch for every bite I eat, and that I ain't going to play ary a card at the business game again, will you come along with me?"

She gave a glad little cry, and he nestled her in closely. But the next moment she had thrust herself out from him to the old position at arm's length.

"I—I don't understand," she said breathlessly.

"And you ain't answered my proposition, though I guess no answer is necessary. We're just going to get married right away and start. I've sent Bob and Wolf along already. When will you be ready?"

Dede could not forbear to smile. "My, what a hurricane of a man it is. I'm quite blown away. And you haven't explained a word to me."

Daylight smiled responsively.

"Look here, Dede, this is what card-sharps call a show-down. No more philandering and frills and long-distance sparring between you and me. We're just going to talk straight out in meeting—the truth, the whole truth, and nothing but the truth. Now you answer some questions for me, and then I'll answer yours."

He paused. "Well, I've got only one question after all: Do you love me enough to marry me?"

"But—" she began.

"No buts," he broke in sharply. "This is a show-down. When I say marry, I mean what I told you at first, that we'd go up and live on the ranch. Do you love me enough for that?"

She looked at him for a moment, then her lids dropped, and all of her seemed to advertise consent.

"Come on, then, let's start." The muscles of his legs tensed involuntarily as if he were about to lead her to the door. "My auto's waiting outside. There's nothing to delay excepting getting on your hat."

He bent over her. "I reckon it's allowable," he said, as he kissed her.

It was a long embrace, and she was the first to speak.

"You haven't answered my questions. How is this possible? How can you leave your business? Has anything happened?"

"No, nothing's happened yet, but it's going to, blame quick. I've taken your preaching to heart, and I've come to the penitent form. You are my Lord God, and I'm sure going to serve you. The rest can go to thunder. You were sure right. I've been the slave to my money, and since I can't serve two masters I'm letting the money slide. I'd sooner have you than all the money in the world, that's all." Again he held her closely in his arms. "And I've sure got you, Dede. I've sure got you.

"And I want to tell you a few more. I've taken my last drink. You're marrying a whiskey-soak, but your husband won't be that. He's going to grow into another man so quick you won't know him. A couple of months from now, up there in Glen Ellen, you'll wake up some morning and find you've got a perfect stranger in the house with you, and you'll have to get introduced to him all over again. You'll say, 'I'm Mrs. Harnish, who are you?' And I'll say, 'I'm Elam Harnish's younger brother. I've just arrived from Alaska to attend the funeral.' 'What funeral?' you'll say. And I'll say, 'Why, the funeral of that good-for-nothing, gambling, whiskey-drinking Burning Daylight—the man that died of fatty degeneration of the heart from sitting in night and day at the business game 'Yes ma'am,' I'll say, 'he's sure a gone 'coon, but I've come to take his place and make you happy. And now, ma'am, if you'll allow me, I'll just meander down to the pasture and milk the cow while you're getting breakfast.'"

Again he caught her hand and made as if to start with her for the door. When she resisted, he bent and kissed her again and again.

"I'm sure hungry for you, little woman," he murmured "You make thirty millions look like thirty cents."

"Do sit down and be sensible," she urged, her cheeks flushed, the golden light in her eyes burning more golden than he had ever seen it before.

But Daylight was bent on having his way, and when he sat down it was with her beside him and his arm around her.

"'Yes, ma'am,' I'll say, 'Burning Daylight was a pretty good cuss, but it's better that he's gone. He quit rolling up in his rabbit-skins and sleeping in the snow, and went to living in a chicken-coop. He lifted up his legs and quit walking and working, and took to existing on Martini cocktails and Scotch whiskey. He thought he loved you, ma'am, and he did his best, but he loved his cocktails more, and he loved his money more, and himself more, and 'most everything else more than he did you.' And then I'll say, 'Ma'am, you just run your eyes over me and see how different I am. I ain't got a cocktail thirst, and all the money I got is a dollar and forty cents and I've got to buy a new ax, the last one being plumb wore out, and I can love you just about eleven times as much as your first husband did. You see, ma'am, he went all to fat. And there ain't ary ounce of fat on me.' And I'll roll up my sleeve and show you, and say, 'Mrs. Harnish, after having experience with being married to that old fat money-bags, do you-all mind marrying a slim young fellow like me?' And you'll just wipe a tear away for poor old Daylight, and kind of lean toward me with a willing expression in your eye, and then I'll blush maybe some, being a young fellow, and put my arm around you, like that, and then—why, then I'll up and marry my brother's widow, and go out and do the chores while she's cooking a bite to eat."

"But you haven't answered my questions," she reproached him, as she emerged, rosy and radiant, from the embrace that had accompanied the culmination of his narrative.

"Now just what do you want to know?" he asked.

"I want to know how all this is possible? How you are able to leave your business at a time like this? What you meant by saying that something was going to happen quickly? I—" She hesitated and blushed. "I answered your question, you know."

"Let's go and get married," he urged, all the whimsicality of his utterance duplicated in his eyes. "You know I've got to make way for that husky young brother of mine, and I ain't got long to live." She made an impatient moue, and he continued seriously.

"You see, it's like this, Dede. I've been working like forty horses ever since this blamed panic set in, and all the time some of those ideas you'd given me were getting ready to sprout.

Well, they sprouted this morning, that's all. I started to get up, expecting to go to the office as usual. But I didn't go to the office. All that sprouting took place there and then. The sun was shining in the window, and I knew it was a fine day in the hills. And I knew I wanted to ride in the hills with you just about thirty million times more than I wanted to go to the office. And I knew all the time it was impossible. And why? Because of the office. The office wouldn't let me. All my money reared right up on its hind legs and got in the way and wouldn't let me. It's a way that blamed money has of getting in the way. You know that yourself.

"And then I made up my mind that I was to the dividing of the ways. One way led to the office. The other way led to Berkeley. And I took the Berkeley road. I'm never going to set foot in the office again. That's all gone, finished, over and done with, and I'm letting it slide clean to smash and then some. My mind's set on this. You see, I've got religion, and it's sure the old-time religion; it's love and you, and it's older than the oldest religion in the world. It's IT, that's what it is—IT, with a capital I-T."

She looked at him with a sudden, startled expression.

"You mean—?" she began.

"I mean just that. I'm wiping the slate clean. I'm letting it all go to smash. When them thirty million dollars stood up to my face and said I couldn't go out with you in the hills to-day, I knew the time had come for me to put my foot down. And I'm putting it down. I've got you, and my strength to work for you, and that little ranch in Sonoma. That's all I want, and that's all I'm going to save out, along with Bob and Wolf, a suit case and a hundred and forty hair bridles. All the rest goes, and good riddance. It's that much junk."

But Dede was insistent.

"Then this—this tremendous loss is all unnecessary?" she asked.

"Just what I haven't been telling you. It IS necessary. If that money thinks it can stand up right to my face and say I can't go riding with you—"

"No, no; be serious," Dede broke in. "I don't mean that, and you know it. What I want to know is, from a standpoint of business, is this failure necessary?"

He shook his head.

"You bet it isn't necessary. That's the point of it. I'm not letting go of it because I'm licked to a standstill by the panic and have got to let go. I'm firing it out when I've licked the panic and am winning, hands down. That just shows how little I think of it. It's you that counts, little woman, and I make my play accordingly."

But she drew away from his sheltering arms.

"You are mad, Elam."

"Call me that again," he murmured ecstatically. "It's sure sweeter than the chink of millions."

All this she ignored.

"It's madness. You don't know what you are doing—"

"Oh, yes, I do," he assured her. "I'm winning the dearest wish of my heart. Why, your little finger is worth more—"

"Do be sensible for a moment."

"I was never more sensible in my lie. I know what I want, and I'm going to get it. I want you and the open air. I want to get my foot off the paving-stones and my ear away from the telephone. I want a little ranch-house in one of the prettiest bits of country God ever made, and

I want to do the chores around that ranch-house—milk cows, and chop wood, and curry horses, and plough the ground, and all the rest of it; and I want you there in the ranch-house with me. I'm plumb tired of everything else, and clean wore out. And I'm sure the luckiest man alive, for I've got what money can't buy. I've got you, and thirty millions couldn't buy you, nor three thousand millions, nor thirty cents—"

A knock at the door interrupted him, and he was left to stare delightedly at the Crouched Venus and on around the room at Dede's dainty possessions, while she answered the telephone.

"It is Mr. Hegan," she said, on returning. "He is holding the line. He says it is important."

Daylight shook his head and smiled.

"Please tell Mr. Hegan to hang up. I'm done with the office and I don't want to hear anything about anything."

A minute later she was back again.

"He refuses to hang up. He told me to tell you that Unwin is in the office now, waiting to see you, and Harrison, too. Mr. Hegan said that Grimshaw and Hodgkins are in trouble. That it looks as if they are going to break. And he said something about protection."

It was startling information. Both Unwin and Harrison represented big banking corporations, and Daylight knew that if the house of Grimshaw and Hodgkins went it would precipitate a number of failures and start a flurry of serious dimensions. But Daylight smiled, and shook his head, and mimicked the stereotyped office tone of voice as he said:—

"Miss Mason, you will kindly tell Mr. Hegan that there is nothing doing and to hang up."

"But you can't do this," she pleaded.

"Watch me," he grimly answered.

"Elam!"

"Say it again," he cried. "Say it again, and a dozen Grimshaws and Hodgkins can smash!"

He caught her by the hand and drew her to him.

"You let Hegan hang on to that line till he's tired. We can't be wasting a second on him on a day like this. He's only in love with books and things, but I've got a real live woman in my arms that's loving me all the time she's kicking over the traces."

CHAPTER XXIII

"But I know something of the fight you have been making," Dede contended. "If you stop now, all the work you have done, everything, will be destroyed. You have no right to do it. You can't do it."

Daylight was obdurate. He shook his head and smiled tantalizingly.

"Nothing will be destroyed, Dede, nothing. You don't understand this business game. It's done on paper. Don't you see? Where's the gold I dug out of Klondike? Why, it's in twenty-dollar gold pieces, in gold watches, in wedding rings. No matter what happens to me, the twenty-dollar pieces, the watches, and the wedding rings remain. Suppose I died right now. It wouldn't affect the gold one iota. It's sure the same with this present situation. All I stand for is paper. I've got the paper for thousands of acres of land. All right. Burn up the paper, and burn me along with it. The land remains, don't it? The rain falls on it, the seeds sprout in it, the trees grow out of it, the houses stand on it, the electric cars run over it. It's paper that business is run on. I lose my paper, or I lose my life, it's all the same; it won't alter one grain of sand in all that land, or twist one blade of grass around sideways.

"Nothing is going to be lost—not one pile out of the docks, not one railroad spike, not one ounce of steam out of the gauge of a ferry-boat. The cars will go on running, whether I hold the paper or somebody else holds it. The tide has set toward Oakland. People are beginning to pour in. We're selling building lots again. There is no stopping that tide. No matter what happens to me or the paper, them three hundred thousand folks are coming in the same. And there'll be cars to carry them around, and houses to hold them, and good water for them to drink and electricity to give them light, and all the rest."

By this time Hegan had arrived in an automobile. The honk of it came in through the open window, and they saw, it stop alongside the big red machine. In the car were Unwin and Harrison, while Jones sat with the chauffeur.

"I'll see Hegan," Daylight told Dede. "There's no need for the rest. They can wait in the machine."

"Is he drunk?" Hegan whispered to Dede at the door.

She shook her head and showed him in.

"Good morning, Larry," was Daylight's greeting. "Sit down and rest your feet. You sure seem to be in a flutter."

"I am," the little Irishman snapped back. "Grimshaw and Hodgkins are going to smash if something isn't done quick. Why didn't you come to the office? What are you going to do about it?"

"Nothing," Daylight drawled lazily. "Except let them smash, I guess—"

"But—"

"I've had no dealings with Grimshaw and Hodgkins. I don't owe them anything. Besides, I'm going to smash myself. Look here, Larry, you know me. You know when I make up my mind I mean it. Well, I've sure made up my mind. I'm tired of the whole game. I'm letting go of it as fast as I can, and a smash is the quickest way to let go."

Hegan stared at his chief, then passed his horror-stricken gaze on to Dede, who nodded in sympathy.

"So let her smash, Larry," Daylight went on. "All you've got to do is to protect yourself and all our friends. Now you listen to me while I tell you what to do. Everything is in good shape to do it. Nobody must get hurt. Everybody that stood by me must come through without damage. All the back wages and salaries must be paid pronto. All the money I've switched away from the water company, the street cars, and the ferries must be switched back. And you won't get hurt yourself none. Every company you got stock in will come through—"

"You are crazy, Daylight!" the little lawyer cried out. "This is all babbling lunacy. What is the matter with you? You haven't been eating a drug or something?"

"I sure have!" Daylight smiled reply. "And I'm now coughing it up. I'm sick of living in a city and playing business—I'm going off to the sunshine, and the country, and the green grass. And Dede, here, is going with me. So you've got the chance to be the first to congratulate me."

"Congratulate the—the devil!" Hegan spluttered. "I'm not going to stand for this sort of foolishness."

"Oh, yes, you are; because if you don't there'll be a bigger smash and some folks will most likely get hurt. You're worth a million or more yourself, now, and if you listen to me you come through with a whole skin. I want to get hurt, and get hurt to the limit. That's what I'm looking for, and there's no man or bunch of men can get between me and what I'm looking for. Savvee, Hegan? Savvee?"

"What have you done to him?" Hegan snarled at Dede.

"Hold on there, Larry." For the first time Daylight's voice was sharp, while all the old lines of cruelty in his face stood forth. "Miss Mason is going to be my wife, and while I don't mind your talking to her all you want, you've got to use a different tone of voice or you'll be heading for a hospital, which will sure be an unexpected sort of smash. And let me tell you one other thing. This-all is my doing. She says I'm crazy, too."

Hegan shook his head in speechless sadness and continued to stare.

"There'll be temporary receiverships, of course," Daylight advised; "but they won't bother none or last long. What you must do immediately is to save everybody—the men that have been letting their wages ride with me, all the creditors, and all the concerns that have stood by. There's the wad of land that New Jersey crowd has been dickering for. They'll take all of a couple of thousand acres and will close now if you give them half a chance. That Fairmount section is the cream of it, and they'll dig up as high as a thousand dollars an acre for a part of it. That'll help out some. That five-hundred acre tract beyond, you'll be lucky if they pay two hundred an acre."

Dede, who had been scarcely listening, seemed abruptly to make up her mind, and stepped forward where she confronted the two men. Her face was pale, but set with determination, so that Daylight, looking at it, was reminded of the day when she first rode Bob.

"Wait," she said. "I want to say something. Elam, if you do this insane thing, I won't marry you. I refuse to marry you."

Hegan, in spite of his misery, gave her a quick, grateful look.

"I'll take my chance on that," Daylight began.

"Wait!" she again interrupted. "And if you don't do this thing, I will marry you."

"Let me get this proposition clear." Daylight spoke with exasperating slowness and deliberation. "As I understand it, if I keep right on at the business game, you'll sure marry me? You'll marry me if I keep on working my head off and drinking Martinis?"

After each question he paused, while she nodded an affirmation.

"And you'll marry me right away?"

"Yes."

"To-day? Now?"

"Yes."

He pondered for a moment.

"No, little woman, I won't do it. It won't work, and you know it yourself. I want you—all of you; and to get it I'll have to give you all of myself, and there'll be darn little of myself left over to give if I stay with the business game. Why, Dede, with you on the ranch with me, I'm sure of you—and of myself. I'm sure of you, anyway. You can talk will or won't all you want, but you're sure going to marry me just the same. And now, Larry, you'd better be going. I'll be at the hotel in a little while, and since I'm not going a step into the office again, bring all papers to sign and the rest over to my rooms. And you can get me on the 'phone there any time. This smash is going through. Savvee? I'm quit and done."

He stood up as a sign for Hegan to go. The latter was plainly stunned. He also rose to his feet, but stood looking helplessly around.

"Sheer, downright, absolute insanity," he muttered.

Daylight put his hand on the other's shoulder.

"Buck up, Larry. You're always talking about the wonders of human nature, and here I am giving you another sample of it and you ain't appreciating it. I'm a bigger dreamer than you are, that's all, and I'm sure dreaming what's coming true. It's the biggest, best dream I ever had, and I'm going after it to get it—"

"By losing all you've got," Hegan exploded at him.

"Sure—by losing all I've got that I don't want. But I'm hanging on to them hundred and forty hair bridles just the same. Now you'd better hustle out to Unwin and Harrison and get on down town. I'll be at the hotel, and you can call me up any time."

He turned to Dede as soon as Hegan was gone, and took her by the hand.

"And now, little woman, you needn't come to the office any more. Consider yourself discharged. And remember I was your employer, so you've got to come to me for recommendation, and if you're not real good, I won't give you one. In the meantime, you just rest up and think about what things you want to pack, because we'll just about have to set up housekeeping on your stuff—leastways, the front part of the house."

"But, Elam, I won't, I won't! If you do this mad thing I never will marry you."

She attempted to take her hand away, but he closed on it with a protecting, fatherly clasp.

"Will you be straight and honest? All right, here goes. Which would you sooner have—me and the money, or me and the ranch?"

"But—" she began.

"No buts. Me and the money?"

She did not answer.

"Me and the ranch?"

Still she did not answer, and still he was undisturbed.

"You see, I know your answer, Dede, and there's nothing more to say. Here's where you and I quit and hit the high places for Sonoma. You make up your mind what you want to pack, and I'll have some men out here in a couple of days to do it for you. It will be about the last work anybody else ever does for us. You and I will do the unpacking and the arranging ourselves."

She made a last attempt.

"Elam, won't you be reasonable? There is time to reconsider. I can telephone down and catch Mr. Hegan as soon as he reaches the office—"

"Why, I'm the only reasonable man in the bunch right now," he rejoined. "Look at me—as calm as you please, and as happy as a king, while they're fluttering around like a lot of cranky hens whose heads are liable to be cut off."

"I'd cry, if I thought it would do any good," she threatened.

"In which case I reckon I'd have to hold you in my arms some more and sort of soothe you down," he threatened back. "And now I'm going to go. It's too bad you got rid of Mab. You could have sent her up to the ranch. But see you've got a mare to ride of some sort or other."

As he stood at the top of the steps, leaving, she said:—

"You needn't send those men. There will be no packing, because I am not going to marry you."

"I'm not a bit scared," he answered, and went down the steps.

CHAPTER XXIV

Three days later, Daylight rode to Berkeley in his red car. It was for the last time, for on the morrow the big machine passed into another's possession. It had been a strenuous three days, for his smash had been the biggest the panic had precipitated in California. The papers had been filled with it, and a great cry of indignation had gone up from the very men who later found that Daylight had fully protected their interests. It was these facts, coming slowly to light, that gave rise to the widely repeated charge that Daylight had gone insane. It was the unanimous conviction among business men that no sane man could possibly behave in such fashion. On the other hand, neither his prolonged steady drinking nor his affair with Dede became public, so the only conclusion attainable was that the wild financier from Alaska had gone lunatic. And Daylight had grinned and confirmed the suspicion by refusing to see the reporters.

He halted the automobile before Dede's door, and met her with his same rushing tactics, enclosing her in his arms before a word could be uttered. Not until afterward, when she had recovered herself from him and got him seated, did he begin to speak.

"I've done it," he announced. "You've seen the newspapers, of course. I'm plumb cleaned out, and I've just called around to find out what day you feel like starting for Glen Ellen. It'll have to be soon, for it's real expensive living in Oakland these days. My board at the hotel is only paid to the end of the week, and I can't afford to stay after that. And beginning with to-morrow I've got to use the street cars, and they sure eat up the nickels."

He paused, and waited, and looked at her. Indecision and trouble showed on her face. Then the smile he knew so well began to grow on her lips and in her eyes, until she threw back her head and laughed in the old forthright boyish way.

"When are those men coming to pack for me?" she asked.

And again she laughed and simulated a vain attempt to escape his bearlike arms.

"Dear Elam," she whispered; "dear Elam." And of herself, for the first time, she kissed him.

She ran her hand caressingly through his hair.

"Your eyes are all gold right now," he said. "I can look in them and tell just how much you love me."

"They have been all gold for you, Elam, for a long time. I think, on our little ranch, they will always be all gold."

"Your hair has gold in it, too, a sort of fiery gold." He turned her face suddenly and held it between his hands and looked long into her eyes. "And your eyes were full of gold only the other day, when you said you wouldn't marry me."

She nodded and laughed.

"You would have your will," she confessed. "But I couldn't be a party to such madness. All that money was yours, not mine. But I was loving you all the time, Elam, for the great big boy you are, breaking the thirty-million toy with which you had grown tired of playing. And when I said no, I knew all the time it was yes. And I am sure that my eyes were golden all the time. I had only one fear, and that was that you would fail to lose everything. Because, dear, I knew I should marry you anyway, and I did so want just you and the ranch and Bob and Wolf and those horse-hair bridles. Shall I tell you a secret? As soon as you left, I telephoned the man to whom I sold Mab."

She hid her face against his breast for an instant, and then looked at him again, gladly radiant.

"You see, Elam, in spite of what my lips said, my mind was made up then. I—I simply had to marry you. But I was praying you would succeed in losing everything. And so I tried to find what had become of Mab. But the man had sold her and did not know what had become of her. You see, I wanted to ride with you over the Glen Ellen hills, on Mab and you on Bob, just as I had ridden with you through the Piedmont hills."

The disclosure of Mab's whereabouts trembled on Daylight's lips, but he forbore.

"I'll promise you a mare that you'll like just as much as Mab," he said.

But Dede shook her head, and on that one point refused to be comforted.

"Now, I've got an idea," Daylight said, hastening to get the conversation on less perilous ground. "We're running away from cities, and you have no kith nor kin, so it don't seem exactly right that we should start off by getting married in a city. So here's the idea: I'll run up to the ranch and get things in shape around the house and give the caretaker his walking-papers. You follow me in a couple of days, coming on the morning train. I'll have the preacher fixed and waiting. And here's another idea. You bring your riding togs in a suit case. And as soon as the ceremony's over, you can go to the hotel and change. Then out you come, and you find me waiting with a couple of horses, and we'll ride over the landscape so as you can see the prettiest parts of the ranch the first thing. And she's sure pretty, that ranch. And now that it's settled, I'll be waiting for you at the morning train day after to-morrow."

Dede blushed as she spoke.

"You are such a hurricane."

"Well, ma'am," he drawled, "I sure hate to burn daylight. And you and I have burned a heap of daylight. We've been scandalously extravagant. We might have been married years ago."

Two days later, Daylight stood waiting outside the little Glen Ellen hotel. The ceremony was over, and he had left Dede to go inside and change into her riding-habit while he brought the horses. He held them now, Bob and Mab, and in the shadow of the watering-trough Wolf lay and looked on. Already two days of ardent California sun had touched with new fires the ancient bronze in Daylight's face. But warmer still was the glow that came into his cheeks and burned in his eyes as he saw Dede coming out the door, riding-whip in hand, clad in the familiar corduroy skirt and leggings of the old Piedmont days. There was warmth and glow in her own face as she answered his gaze and glanced on past him to the horses. Then she saw Mab. But her gaze leaped back to the man.

"Oh, Elam!" she breathed.

It was almost a prayer, but a prayer that included a thousand meanings Daylight strove to feign sheepishness, but his heart was singing too wild a song for mere playfulness. All things had been in the naming of his name—reproach, refined away by gratitude, and all compounded of joy and love.

She stepped forward and caressed the mare, and again turned and looked at the man, and breathed:—

"Oh, Elam!"

And all that was in her voice was in her eyes, and in them Daylight glimpsed a profundity deeper and wider than any speech or thought—the whole vast inarticulate mystery and wonder of sex and love.

Again he strove for playfulness of speech, but it was too great a moment for even love fractiousness to enter in. Neither spoke. She gathered the reins, and, bending, Daylight received her foot in his hand. She sprang, as he lifted and gained the saddle. The next moment he was mounted and beside her, and, with Wolf sliding along ahead in his typical wolf-trot, they went up the hill that led out of town—two lovers on two chestnut sorrel steeds, riding out and away to honeymoon through the warm summer day. Daylight felt himself drunken as with wine. He was at the topmost pinnacle of life. Higher than this no man could climb nor had ever climbed. It was his day of days, his love-time and his mating-time, and all crowned by this virginal possession of a mate who had said "Oh, Elam," as she had said it, and looked at him out of her soul as she had looked.

They cleared the crest of the hill, and he watched the joy mount in her face as she gazed on the sweet, fresh land. He pointed out the group of heavily wooded knolls across the rolling stretches of ripe grain.

"They're ours," he said. "And they're only a sample of the ranch. Wait till you see the big canon. There are 'coons down there, and back here on the Sonoma there are mink. And deer!—why, that mountain's sure thick with them, and I reckon we can scare up a mountain-lion if we want to real hard. And, say, there's a little meadow—well, I ain't going to tell you another word. You wait and see for yourself."

They turned in at the gate, where the road to the clay-pit crossed the fields, and both sniffed with delight as the warm aroma of the ripe hay rose in their nostrils. As on his first visit, the larks were uttering their rich notes and fluttering up before the horses until the woods and the flower-scattered glades were reached, when the larks gave way to blue jays and woodpeckers.

"We're on our land now," he said, as they left the hayfield behind. "It runs right across country over the roughest parts. Just you wait and see."

As on the first day, he turned aside from the clay-pit and worked through the woods to the left, passing the first spring and jumping the horses over the ruined remnants of the stake-and-rider fence. From here on, Dede was in an unending ecstasy. By the spring that gurgled among the redwoods grew another great wild lily, bearing on its slender stalk the prodigious outburst of white waxen bells. This time he did not dismount, but led the way to the deep canon where the stream had cut a passage among the knolls. He had been at work here, and a steep and slippery horse trail now crossed the creek, so they rode up beyond, through the somber redwood twilight, and, farther on, through a tangled wood of oak and madrono. They came to a small clearing of several acres, where the grain stood waist high.

"Ours," Daylight said.

She bent in her saddle, plucked a stalk of the ripe grain, and nibbled it between her teeth.

"Sweet mountain hay," she cried. "The kind Mab likes."

And throughout the ride she continued to utter cries and ejaculations of surprise and delight.

"And you never told me all this!" she reproached him, as they looked across the little clearing and over the descending slopes of woods to the great curving sweep of Sonoma Valley.

"Come," he said; and they turned and went back through the forest shade, crossed the stream and came to the lily by the spring.

Here, also, where the way led up the tangle of the steep hill, he had cut a rough horse trail. As they forced their way up the zigzags, they caught glimpses out and down through the sea of foliage. Yet always were their farthest glimpses stopped by the closing vistas of green, and, yet always, as they climbed, did the forest roof arch overhead, with only here and there rifts that permitted shattered shafts of sunlight to penetrate. And all about them were ferns, a score of varieties, from the tiny gold-backs and maidenhair to huge brakes six and eight feet tall.

Below them, as they mounted, they glimpsed great gnarled trunks and branches of ancient trees, and above them were similar great gnarled branches.

Dede stopped her horse and sighed with the beauty of it all.

"It is as if we are swimmers," she said, "rising out of a deep pool of green tranquillity. Up above is the sky and the sun, but this is a pool, and we are fathoms deep."

They started their horses, but a dog-tooth violet, shouldering amongst the maidenhair, caught her eye and made her rein in again.

They cleared the crest and emerged from the pool as if into another world, for now they were in the thicket of velvet-trunked young madronos and looking down the open, sun-washed hillside, across the nodding grasses, to the drifts of blue and white nemophilae that carpeted the tiny meadow on either side the tiny stream. Dede clapped her hands.

"It's sure prettier than office furniture," Daylight remarked.

"It sure is," she answered.

And Daylight, who knew his weakness in the use of the particular word sure, knew that she had repeated it deliberately and with love.

They crossed the stream and took the cattle track over the low rocky hill and through the scrub forest of manzanita, till they emerged on the next tiny valley with its meadow-bordered streamlet.

"If we don't run into some quail pretty soon, I'll be surprised some," Daylight said.

And as the words left his lips there was a wild series of explosive thrumming as the old quail arose from all about Wolf, while the young ones scuttled for safety and disappeared miraculously before the spectators' very eyes.

He showed her the hawk's nest he had found in the lightning-shattered top of the redwood, and she discovered a wood-rat's nest which he had not seen before. Next they took the old wood-road and came out on the dozen acres of clearing where the wine grapes grew in the wine-colored volcanic soil. Then they followed the cow-path through more woods and thickets and scattered glades, and dropped down the hillside to where the farm-house, poised on the lip of the big canon, came into view only when they were right upon it.

Dede stood on the wide porch that ran the length of the house while Daylight tied the horses. To Dede it was very quiet. It was the dry, warm, breathless calm of California midday. All the world seemed dozing. From somewhere pigeons were cooing lazily. With a deep sigh of satisfaction, Wolf, who had drunk his fill at all the streams along the way, dropped down in the cool shadow of the porch. She heard the footsteps of Daylight returning, and caught her breath with a quick intake. He took her hand in his, and, as he turned the door-knob, felt her hesitate. Then he put his arm around her; the door swung open, and together they passed in.

CHAPTER XXV

Many persons, themselves city-bred and city-reared, have fled to the soil and succeeded in winning great happiness. In such cases they have succeeded only by going through a process of savage disillusionment. But with Dede and Daylight it was different. They had both been born on the soil, and they knew its naked simplicities and rawer ways. They were like two persons, after far wandering, who had merely come home again. There was less of the unexpected in their dealings with nature, while theirs was all the delight of reminiscence. What might appear sordid and squalid to the fastidiously reared, was to them eminently wholesome and natural. The commerce of nature was to them no unknown and untried trade. They made fewer mistakes. They already knew, and it was a joy to remember what they had forgotten.

And another thing they learned was that it was easier for one who has gorged at the flesh-pots to content himself with the meagerness of a crust, than for one who has known only the crust.

Not that their life was meagre. It was that they found keener delights and deeper satisfactions in little things. Daylight, who had played the game in its biggest and most fantastic aspects, found that here, on the slopes of Sonoma Mountain, it was still the same old game. Man had still work to perform, forces to combat, obstacles to overcome. When he experimented in a small way at raising a few pigeons for market, he found no less zest in calculating in squabs than formerly when he had calculated in millions. Achievement was no less achievement, while the process of it seemed more rational and received the sanction of his reason.

The domestic cat that had gone wild and that preyed on his pigeons, he found, by the comparative standard, to be of no less paramount menace than a Charles Klinkner in the field of finance, trying to raid him for several millions. The hawks and weasels and 'coons were so many Dowsetts, Lettons, and Guggenhammers that struck at him secretly. The sea of wild vegetation that tossed its surf against the boundaries of all his clearings and that sometimes crept in and flooded in a single week was no mean enemy to contend with and subdue. His fat-soiled vegetable-garden in the nook of hills that failed of its best was a problem of engrossing importance, and when he had solved it by putting in drain-tile, the joy of the achievement was ever with him. He never worked in it and found the soil unpacked and tractable without experiencing the thrill of accomplishment.

There was the matter of the plumbing. He was enabled to purchase the materials through a lucky sale of a number of his hair bridles. The work he did himself, though more than once he was forced to call in Dede to hold tight with a pipe-wrench. And in the end, when the bath-tub and the stationary tubs were installed and in working order, he could scarcely tear himself away from the contemplation of what his hands had wrought. The first evening, missing him, Dede sought and found him, lamp in hand, staring with silent glee at the tubs. He rubbed his hand over their smooth wooden lips and laughed aloud, and was as shamefaced as any boy when she caught him thus secretly exulting in his own prowess.

It was this adventure in wood-working and plumbing that brought about the building of the little workshop, where he slowly gathered a collection of loved tools. And he, who in the old days, out of his millions, could purchase immediately whatever he might desire, learned the new joy of the possession that follows upon rigid economy and desire long delayed. He waited three months before daring the extravagance of a Yankee screw-driver, and his glee in the marvelous little mechanism was so keen that Dede conceived forthright a great idea. For six months she saved her egg-money, which was hers by right of allotment, and on his birthday presented him with a turning-lathe of wonderful simplicity and multifarious efficiencies. And their mutual delight in the tool, which was his, was only equalled by their delight in Mab's first foal, which was Dede's special private property.

It was not until the second summer that Daylight built the huge fireplace that outrivalled Ferguson's across the valley. For all these things took time, and Dede and Daylight were not in a hurry. Theirs was not the mistake of the average city-dweller who flees in ultra-modern innocence to the soil. They did not essay too much. Neither did they have a mortgage to clear, nor did they desire wealth. They wanted little in the way of food, and they had no rent to pay. So they planned unambiguously, reserving their lives for each other and for the compensations of country-dwelling from which the average country-dweller is barred. From Ferguson's example, too, they profited much. Here was a man who asked for but the plainest fare; who ministered to his own simple needs with his own hands; who worked out as a laborer only when he needed money to buy books and magazines; and who saw to it that the major portion of his waking time was for enjoyment. He loved to loaf long afternoons in the shade with his books or to be up with the dawn and away over the hills.

On occasion he accompanied Dede and Daylight on deer hunts through the wild canons and over the rugged steeps of Hood Mountain, though more often Dede and Daylight were out alone. This riding was one of their chief joys. Every wrinkle and crease in the hills they explored, and they came to know every secret spring and hidden dell in the whole surrounding wall of the valley. They learned all the trails and cow-paths; but nothing delighted them more than to essay the roughest and most impossible rides, where they were glad to crouch and crawl along the narrowest deer-runs, Bob and Mab struggling and forcing their way along behind. Back from their rides they brought the seeds and bulbs of wild flowers to plant in favoring nooks on the ranch. Along the foot trail which led down the side of the big canon to the intake of the water-pipe, they established their fernery. It was not a formal affair, and the ferns were left to themselves. Dede and Daylight merely introduced new ones from time to time, changing them from one wild habitat to another. It was the same with the wild lilac, which Daylight had sent to him from Mendocino County. It became part of the wildness of the ranch, and, after being helped for a season, was left to its own devices they used to gather the seeds of the California poppy and scatter them over their own acres, so that the orange-colored blossoms spangled the fields of mountain hay and prospered in flaming drifts in the fence corners and along the edges of the clearings.

Dede, who had a fondness for cattails, established a fringe of them along the meadow stream, where they were left to fight it out with the water-cress. And when the latter was threatened with extinction, Daylight developed one of the shaded springs into his water-cress garden and declared war upon any invading cattail. On her wedding day Dede had discovered a long dog-tooth violet by the zigzag trail above the redwood spring, and here she continued to plant more and more. The open hillside above the tiny meadow became a colony of Mariposa lilies. This was due mainly to her efforts, while Daylight, who rode with a short-handled ax on his saddle-bow, cleared the little manzanita wood on the rocky hill of all its dead and dying and overcrowded weaklings.

They did not labor at these tasks. Nor were they tasks. Merely in passing, they paused, from time to time, and lent a hand to nature. These flowers and shrubs grew of themselves, and their presence was no violation of the natural environment. The man and the woman made no effort to introduce a flower or shrub that did not of its own right belong. Nor did they protect them from their enemies. The horses and the colts and the cows and the calves ran at pasture among them or over them, and flower or shrub had to take its chance. But the beasts were not noticeably destructive, for they were few in number and the ranch was large.

On the other hand, Daylight could have taken in fully a dozen horses to pasture, which would have earned him a dollar and a half per head per month. But this he refused to do, because of the devastation such close pasturing would produce.

Ferguson came over to celebrate the housewarming that followed the achievement of the great stone fireplace. Daylight had ridden across the valley more than once to confer with him about the undertaking, and he was the only other present at the sacred function of lighting the first fire. By removing a partition, Daylight had thrown two rooms into one, and this was the big living-room where Dede's treasures were placed—her books, and paintings and photographs, her piano, the Crouched Venus, the chafing-dish and all its glittering accessories. Already, in addition to her own wild-animal skins, were those of deer and coyote and one mountain-lion which Daylight had killed. The tanning he had done himself, slowly and laboriously, in frontier fashion.

He handed the match to Dede, who struck it and lighted the fire. The crisp manzanita wood crackled as the flames leaped up and assailed the dry bark of the larger logs. Then she leaned in the shelter of her husband's arm, and the three stood and looked in breathless suspense. When Ferguson gave judgment, it was with beaming face and extended hand.

"She draws! By crickey, she draws!" he cried.

He shook Daylight's hand ecstatically, and Daylight shook his with equal fervor, and, bending, kissed Dede on the lips. They were as exultant over the success of their simple handiwork as any great captain at astonishing victory. In Ferguson's eyes was actually a suspicious moisture while the woman pressed even more closely against the man whose achievement it was. He caught her up suddenly in his arms and whirled her away to the piano, crying out: "Come on, Dede! The Gloria! The Gloria!"

And while the flames in the fireplace that worked, the triumphant strains of the Twelfth Mass rolled forth.

CHAPTER XXVI

Daylight had made no assertion of total abstinence though he had not taken a drink for months after the day he resolved to let his business go to smash. Soon he proved himself strong enough to dare to take a drink without taking a second. On the other hand, with his coming to live in the country, had passed all desire and need for drink. He felt no yearning for it, and even forgot that it existed. Yet he refused to be afraid of it, and in town, on occasion, when invited by the storekeeper, would reply: "All right, son. If my taking a drink will make you happy here goes. Whiskey for mine."

But such a drink began no desire for a second. It made no impression. He was too profoundly strong to be affected by a thimbleful. As he had prophesied to Dede, Burning Daylight, the city financier, had died a quick death on the ranch, and his younger brother, the Daylight from Alaska, had taken his place. The threatened inundation of fat had subsided, and all his old-time Indian leanness and of muscle had returned. So, likewise, did the old slight hollows in his cheeks come back. For him they indicated the pink of physical condition. He became the acknowledged strong man of Sonoma Valley, the heaviest lifter and hardest winded among a husky race of farmer folk. And once a year he celebrated his birthday in the old-fashioned frontier way, challenging all the valley to come up the hill to the ranch and be put on its back. And a fair portion of the valley responded, brought the women-folk and children along, and picnicked for the day.

At first, when in need of ready cash, he had followed Ferguson's example of working at day's labor; but he was not long in gravitating to a form of work that was more stimulating and more satisfying, and that allowed him even more time for Dede and the ranch and the perpetual riding through the hills. Having been challenged by the blacksmith, in a spirit of banter, to attempt the breaking of a certain incorrigible colt, he succeeded so signally as to earn quite a reputation as a horse-breaker. And soon he was able to earn whatever money he desired at this, to him, agreeable work.

A sugar king, whose breeding farm and training stables were at Caliente, three miles away, sent for him in time of need, and, before the year was out, offered him the management of the stables. But Daylight smiled and shook his head. Furthermore, he refused to undertake the breaking of as many animals as were offered. "I'm sure not going to die from overwork," he assured Dede; and he accepted such work only when he had to have money. Later, he fenced off a small run in the pasture, where, from time to time, he took in a limited number of incorrigibles.

"We've got the ranch and each other," he told his wife, "and I'd sooner ride with you to Hood Mountain any day than earn forty dollars. You can't buy sunsets, and loving wives, and cool spring water, and such folderols, with forty dollars; and forty million dollars can't buy back for me one day that I didn't ride with you to Hood Mountain."

His life was eminently wholesome and natural. Early to bed, he slept like an infant and was up with the dawn. Always with something to do, and with a thousand little things that enticed but did not clamor, he was himself never overdone. Nevertheless, there were times when both he and Dede were not above confessing tiredness at bedtime after seventy or eighty miles in the saddle.

Sometimes, when he had accumulated a little money, and when the season favored, they would mount their horses, with saddle-bags behind, and ride away over the wall of the valley and down into the other valleys. When night fell, they put up at the first convenient farm or village, and on the morrow they would ride on, without definite plan, merely continuing to ride on, day after day, until their money gave out and they were compelled to return. On such trips they would be gone anywhere from a week to ten days or two weeks, and once they managed a three weeks' trip.

They even planned ambitiously some day when they were disgracefully prosperous, to ride all the way up to Daylight's boyhood home in Eastern Oregon, stopping on the way at Dede's girlhood home in Siskiyou. And all the joys of anticipation were theirs a thousand times as they contemplated the detailed delights of this grand adventure.

One day, stopping to mail a letter at the Glen Ellen post office, they were hailed by the blacksmith.

"Say, Daylight," he said, "a young fellow named Slosson sends you his regards. He came through in an auto, on the way to Santa Rosa. He wanted to know if you didn't live hereabouts, but the crowd with him was in a hurry. So he sent you his regards and said to tell you he'd taken your advice and was still going on breaking his own record."

Daylight had long since told Dede of the incident.

"Slosson?" he meditated, "Slosson? That must be the hammer-thrower. He put my hand down twice, the young scamp." He turned suddenly to Dede. "Say, it's only twelve miles to Santa Rosa, and the horses are fresh."

She divined what was in his mind, of which his twinkling eyes and sheepish, boyish grin gave sufficient advertisement, and she smiled and nodded acquiescence.

"We'll cut across by Bennett Valley," he said. "It's nearer that way."

There was little difficulty, once in Santa Rosa, of finding Slosson. He and his party had registered at the Oberlin Hotel, and Daylight encountered the young hammer-thrower himself in the office.

"Look here, son," Daylight announced, as soon as he had introduced Dede, "I've come to go you another flutter at that hand game. Here's a likely place."

Slosson smiled and accepted. The two men faced each other, the elbows of their right arms on the counter, the hands clasped. Slosson's hand quickly forced backward and down.

"You're the first man that ever succeeded in doing it," he said. "Let's try it again."

"Sure," Daylight answered. "And don't forget, son, that you're the first man that put mine down. That's why I lit out after you to-day."

Again they clasped hands, and again Slosson's hand went down. He was a broad-shouldered, heavy-muscled young giant, at least half a head taller than Daylight, and he frankly expressed his chagrin and asked for a third trial. This time he steeled himself to the effort, and for a moment the issue was in doubt. With flushed face and set teeth he met the other's strength till his crackling muscles failed him. The air exploded sharply from his tensed lungs, as he relaxed in surrender, and the hand dropped limply down.

"You're too many for me," he confessed. "I only hope you'll keep out of the hammer-throwing game."

Daylight laughed and shook his head.

"We might compromise, and each stay in his own class. You stick to hammer-throwing, and I'll go on turning down hands."

But Slosson refused to accept defeat.

"Say," he called out, as Daylight and Dede, astride their horses, were preparing to depart. "Say—do you mind if I look you up next year? I'd like to tackle you again."

"Sure, son. You're welcome to a flutter any time. Though I give you fair warning that you'll have to go some. You'll have to train up, for I'm ploughing and chopping wood and breaking colts these days."

Now and again, on the way home, Dede could hear her big boy-husband chuckling gleefully. As they halted their horses on the top of the divide out of Bennett Valley, in order to watch the sunset, he ranged alongside and slipped his arm around her waist.

"Little woman," he said, "you're sure responsible for it all. And I leave it to you, if all the money in creation is worth as much as one arm like that when it's got a sweet little woman like this to go around."

For of all his delights in the new life, Dede was his greatest. As he explained to her more than once, he had been afraid of love all his life only in the end to come to find it the greatest thing in the world. Not alone were the two well mated, but in coming to live on the ranch they had selected the best soil in which their love would prosper. In spite of her books and music, there was in her a wholesome simplicity and love of the open and natural, while Daylight, in every fiber of him, was essentially an open-air man.

Of one thing in Dede, Daylight never got over marveling about, and that was her efficient hands—the hands that he had first seen taking down flying shorthand notes and ticking away at the typewriter; the hands that were firm to hold a magnificent brute like Bob, that wonderfully flashed over the keys of the piano, that were unhesitant in household tasks, and that were twin miracles to caress and to run rippling fingers through his hair. But Daylight was not unduly uxorious. He lived his man's life just as she lived her woman's life. There was proper division of labor in the work they individually performed. But the whole was entwined and woven into a fabric of mutual interest and consideration. He was as deeply interested in her cooking and her music as she was in his agricultural adventures in the vegetable garden. And he, who resolutely declined to die of overwork, saw to it that she should likewise escape so dire a risk.

In this connection, using his man's judgment and putting his man's foot down, he refused to allow her to be burdened with the entertaining of guests. For guests they had, especially in the warm, long summers, and usually they were her friends from the city, who were put to camp in tents which they cared for themselves, and where, like true campers, they had also to cook for themselves. Perhaps only in California, where everybody knows camp life, would such a program have been possible. But Daylight's steadfast contention was that his wife should not become cook, waitress, and chambermaid because she did not happen to possess a household of servants. On the other hand, chafing-dish suppers in the big living-room for their camping guests were a common happening, at which times Daylight allotted them their chores and saw that they were performed. For one who stopped only for the night it was different. Likewise it was different with her brother, back from Germany, and again able to sit a horse. On his vacations he became the third in the family, and to him was given the building of the fires, the sweeping, and the washing of the dishes.

Daylight devoted himself to the lightening of Dede's labors, and it was her brother who incited him to utilize the splendid water-power of the ranch that was running to waste. It required Daylight's breaking of extra horses to pay for the materials, and the brother devoted a three weeks' vacation to assisting, and together they installed a Pelting wheel. Besides sawing wood and turning his lathe and grindstone, Daylight connected the power with the churn; but his great triumph was when he put his arm around Dede's waist and led her out to inspect a washing-machine, run by the Pelton wheel, which really worked and really washed clothes.

Dede and Ferguson, between them, after a patient struggle, taught Daylight poetry, so that in the end he might have been often seen, sitting slack in the saddle and dropping down the mountain trails through the sun-flecked woods, chanting aloud Kipling's "Tomlinson," or, when sharpening his ax, singing into the whirling grindstone Henley's "Song of the Sword." Not that he ever became consummately literary in the way his two teachers were. Beyond "Fra Lippo Lippi" and "Caliban and Setebos," he found nothing in Browning, while George Meredith was ever his despair. It was of his own initiative, however, that he invested in a violin, and practised so assiduously that in time he and Dede beguiled many a happy hour playing together after night had fallen.

So all went well with this well-mated pair. Time never dragged. There were always new wonderful mornings and still cool twilights at the end of day; and ever a thousand interests claimed him, and his interests were shared by her. More thoroughly than he knew, had he come to a comprehension of the relativity of things. In this new game he played he found in little things all the intensities of gratification and desire that he had found in the frenzied big things when he was a power and rocked half a continent with the fury of the blows he struck. With head and hand, at risk of life and limb, to bit and break a wild colt and win it to the service of man, was to him no less great an achievement. And this new table on which he played the game was clean. Neither lying, nor cheating, nor hypocrisy was here. The other game had made for decay and death, while this new one made for clean strength and life. And so he was content, with Dede at his side, to watch the procession of the days and seasons from the farmhouse perched on the canon-lip; to ride through crisp frosty mornings or under burning summer suns; and to shelter in the big room where blazed the logs in the fireplace he had built, while outside the world shuddered and struggled in the storm-clasp of a southeaster.

Once only Dede asked him if he ever regretted, and his answer was to crush her in his arms and smother her lips with his. His answer, a minute later, took speech.

"Little woman, even if you did cost thirty millions, you are sure the cheapest necessity of life I ever indulged in." And then he added, "Yes, I do have one regret, and a monstrous big one, too. I'd sure like to have the winning of you all over again. I'd like to go sneaking around the Piedmont hills looking for you. I'd like to meander into those rooms of yours at Berkeley for the first time. And there's no use talking, I'm plumb soaking with regret that I can't put my arms around you again that time you leaned your head on my breast and cried in the wind and rain."

CHAPTER XXVII

But there came the day, one year, in early April, when Dede sat in an easy chair on the porch, sewing on certain small garments, while Daylight read aloud to her. It was in the afternoon, and a bright sun was shining down on a world of new green. Along the irrigation channels of the vegetable garden streams of water were flowing, and now and again Daylight broke off from his reading to run out and change the flow of water. Also, he was teasingly interested in the certain small garments on which Dede worked, while she was radiantly happy over them, though at times, when his tender fun was too insistent, she was rosily confused or affectionately resentful.

From where they sat they could look out over the world. Like the curve of a skirting blade, the Valley of the Moon stretched before them, dotted with farm-houses and varied by pasture-lands, hay-fields, and vineyards. Beyond rose the wall of the valley, every crease and wrinkle of which Dede and Daylight knew, and at one place, where the sun struck squarely, the white dump of the abandoned mine burned like a jewel. In the foreground, in the paddock by the barn, was Mab, full of pretty anxieties for the early spring foal that staggered about her on tottery legs. The air shimmered with heat, and altogether it was a lazy, basking day. Quail whistled to their young from the thicketed hillside behind the house. There was a gentle cooing of pigeons, and from the green depths of the big canon arose the sobbing wood note of a mourning dove. Once, there was a warning chorus from the foraging hens and a wild rush for cover, as a hawk, high in the blue, cast its drifting shadow along the ground.

It was this, perhaps, that aroused old hunting memories in Wolf. At any rate, Dede and Daylight became aware of excitement in the paddock, and saw harmlessly reenacted a grim old tragedy of the Younger World. Curiously eager, velvet-footed and silent as a ghost, sliding and gliding and crouching, the dog that was mere domesticated wolf stalked the enticing bit of young life that Mab had brought so recently into the world. And the mare, her own ancient instincts aroused and quivering, circled ever between the foal and this menace of the wild young days when all her ancestry had known fear of him and his hunting brethren. Once, she whirled and tried to kick him, but usually she strove to strike him with her fore-hoofs, or rushed upon him with open mouth and ears laid back in an effort to crunch his backbone between her teeth. And the wolf-dog, with ears flattened down and crouching, would slide silkily away, only to circle up to the foal from the other side and give cause to the mare for new alarm. Then Daylight, urged on by Dede's solicitude, uttered a low threatening cry; and Wolf, drooping and sagging in all the body of him in token of his instant return to man's allegiance, slunk off behind the barn.

It was a few minutes later that Daylight, breaking off from his reading to change the streams of irrigation, found that the water had ceased flowing. He shouldered a pick and shovel, took a hammer and a pipe-wrench from the tool-house, and returned to Dede on the porch.

"I reckon I'll have to go down and dig the pipe out," he told her. "It's that slide that's threatened all winter. I guess she's come down at last."

"Don't you read ahead, now," he warned, as he passed around the house and took the trail that led down the wall of the canon.

Halfway down the trail, he came upon the slide. It was a small affair, only a few tons of earth and crumbling rock; but, starting from fifty feet above, it had struck the water pipe with force sufficient to break it at a connection. Before proceeding to work, he glanced up the path of the slide, and he glanced with the eye of the earth-trained miner. And he saw what made his eyes startle and cease for the moment from questing farther.

"Hello," he communed aloud, "look who's here."

His glance moved on up the steep broken surface, and across it from side to side. Here and there, in places, small twisted manzanitas were rooted precariously, but in the main, save for weeds and grass, that portion of the canon was bare. There were signs of a surface that had shifted often as the rains poured a flow of rich eroded soil from above over the lip of the canon.

"A true fissure vein, or I never saw one," he proclaimed softly.

And as the old hunting instincts had aroused that day in the wolf-dog, so in him recrudesced all the old hot desire of gold-hunting. Dropping the hammer and pipe-wrench, but retaining pick and shovel, he climbed up the slide to where a vague line of outputting but mostly soil-covered rock could be seen. It was all but indiscernible, but his practised eye had sketched the hidden formation which it signified. Here and there, along this wall of the vein, he attacked the crumbling rock with the pick and shoveled the encumbering soil away. Several times he examined this rock. So soft was some of it that he could break it in his fingers. Shifting a dozen feet higher up, he again attacked with pick and shovel. And this time, when he rubbed the soil from a chunk of rock and looked, he straightened up suddenly, gasping with delight. And then, like a deer at a drinking pool in fear of its enemies, he flung a quick glance around to see if any eye were gazing upon him. He grinned at his own foolishness and returned to his examination of the chunk. A slant of sunlight fell on it, and it was all aglitter with tiny specks of unmistakable free gold.

"From the grass roots down," he muttered in an awestricken voice, as he swung his pick into the yielding surface.

He seemed to undergo a transformation. No quart of cocktails had ever put such a flame in his cheeks nor such a fire in his eyes. As he worked, he was caught up in the old passion that had ruled most of his life. A frenzy seized him that markedly increased from moment to moment. He worked like a madman, till he panted from his exertions and the sweat dripped from his face to the ground. He quested across the face of the slide to the opposite wall of the vein and back again. And, midway, he dug down through the red volcanic earth that had washed from the disintegrating hill above, until he uncovered quartz, rotten quartz, that broke and crumbled in his hands and showed to be alive with free gold.

Sometimes he started small slides of earth that covered up his work and compelled him to dig again. Once, he was swept fifty feet down the canon-side; but he floundered and scrambled up again without pausing for breath. He hit upon quartz that was so rotten that it was almost like clay, and here the gold was richer than ever. It was a veritable treasure chamber. For a hundred feet up and down he traced the walls of the vein. He even climbed over the canon-lip to look along the brow of the hill for signs of the outcrop. But that could wait, and he hurried back to his find.

He toiled on in the same mad haste, until exhaustion and an intolerable ache in his back compelled him to pause. He straightened up with even a richer piece of gold-laden quartz. Stooping, the sweat from his forehead had fallen to the ground. It now ran into his eyes, blinding him. He wiped it from him with the back of his hand and returned to a scrutiny of the gold.

It would run thirty thousand to the ton, fifty thousand, anything—he knew that. And as he gazed upon the yellow lure, and panted for air, and wiped the sweat away, his quick vision leaped and set to work. He saw the spur-track that must run up from the valley and across the upland pastures, and he ran the grades and built the bridge that would span the canon, until it was real before his eyes. Across the canon was the place for the mill, and there he erected it; and he erected, also, the endless chain of buckets, suspended from a cable and operated by gravity, that would carry the ore across the canon to the quartz-crusher. Likewise, the whole mine grew before him and beneath him-tunnels, shafts, and galleries, and hoisting plants. The blasts of the miners were in his ears, and from across the canon he could hear the roar of the stamps. The hand that held the lump of quartz was trembling, and there was a tired, nervous palpitation apparently in the pit of his stomach. It came to him abruptly that what he wanted was a drink—whiskey, cocktails, anything, a drink. And even then, with this new hot yearning for the alcohol upon him, he heard, faint and far, drifting down the green abyss of the canon, Dede's voice, crying:—

"Here, chick, chick, chick, chick, chick! Here, chick, chick, chick!"

He was astounded at the lapse of time. She had left her sewing on the porch and was feeding the chickens preparatory to getting supper. The afternoon was gone. He could not conceive that he had been away that long.

Again came the call: "Here, chick, chick, chick, chick, chick! Here, chick, chick, chick!"

It was the way she always called—first five, and then three. He had long since noticed it. And from these thoughts of her arose other thoughts that caused a great fear slowly to grow in his face. For it seemed to him that he had almost lost her. Not once had he thought of her in those frenzied hours, and for that much, at least, had she truly been lost to him.

He dropped the piece of quartz, slid down the slide, and started up the trail, running heavily. At the edge of the clearing he eased down and almost crept to a point of vantage whence he could peer out, himself unseen. She was feeding the chickens, tossing to them handfuls of grain and laughing at their antics.

The sight of her seemed to relieve the panic fear into which he had been flung, and he turned and ran back down the trail. Again he climbed the slide, but this time he climbed higher, carrying the pick and shovel with him. And again he toiled frenziedly, but this time with a different purpose. He worked artfully, loosing slide after slide of the red soil and sending it streaming down and covering up all he had uncovered, hiding from the light of day the treasure he had discovered. He even went into the woods and scooped armfuls of last year's fallen leaves which he scattered over the slide. But this he gave up as a vain task; and he sent more slides of soil down upon the scene of his labor, until no sign remained of the out-jutting walls of the vein.

Next he repaired the broken pipe, gathered his tools together, and started up the trail. He walked slowly, feeling a great weariness, as of a man who had passed through a frightful crisis.

He put the tools away, took a great drink of the water that again flowed through the pipes, and sat down on the bench by the open kitchen door. Dede was inside, preparing supper, and the sound of her footsteps gave him a vast content.

He breathed the balmy mountain air in great gulps, like a diver fresh-risen from the sea. And, as he drank in the air, he gazed with all his eyes at the clouds and sky and valley, as if he were drinking in that, too, along with the air.

Dede did not know he had come back, and at times he turned his head and stole glances in at her—at her efficient hands, at the bronze of her brown hair that smouldered with fire when she crossed the path of sunshine that streamed through the window, at the promise of her figure that shot through him a pang most strangely sweet and sweetly dear. He heard her approaching the door, and kept his head turned resolutely toward the valley. And next, he thrilled, as he had always thrilled, when he felt the caressing gentleness of her fingers through his hair.

"I didn't know you were back," she said. "Was it serious?"

"Pretty bad, that slide," he answered, still gazing away and thrilling to her touch. "More serious than I reckoned. But I've got the plan. Do you know what I'm going to do?—I'm going to plant eucalyptus all over it. They'll hold it. I'll plant them thick as grass, so that even a hungry rabbit can't squeeze between them; and when they get their roots agoing, nothing in creation will ever move that dirt again."

"Why, is it as bad as that?"

He shook his head.

"Nothing exciting. But I'd sure like to see any blamed old slide get the best of me, that's all. I'm going to seal that slide down so that it'll stay there for a million years. And when the last trump sounds, and Sonoma Mountain and all the other mountains pass into nothingness, that old slide will be still a-standing there, held up by the roots."

He passed his arm around her and pulled her down on his knees.

"Say, little woman, you sure miss a lot by living here on the ranch—music, and theatres, and such things. Don't you ever have a hankering to drop it all and go back?"

So great was his anxiety that he dared not look at her, and when she laughed and shook her head he was aware of a great relief. Also, he noted the undiminished youth that rang through that same old-time boyish laugh of hers.

"Say," he said, with sudden fierceness, "don't you go fooling around that slide until after I get the trees in and rooted. It's mighty dangerous, and I sure can't afford to lose you now."

He drew her lips to his and kissed her hungrily and passionately.

"What a lover!" she said; and pride in him and in her own womanhood was in her voice.

"Look at that, Dede." He removed one encircling arm and swept it in a wide gesture over the valley and the mountains beyond. "The Valley of the Moon—a good name, a good name. Do you know, when I look out over it all, and think of you and of all it means, it kind of makes me ache in the throat, and I have things in my heart I can't find the words to say, and I have a feeling that I can almost understand Browning and those other high-flying poet-fellows. Look at Hood Mountain there, just where the sun's striking. It was down in that crease that we found the spring."

"And that was the night you didn't milk the cows till ten o'clock," she laughed. "And if you keep me here much longer, supper won't be any earlier than it was that night."

Both arose from the bench, and Daylight caught up the milk-pail from the nail by the door. He paused a moment longer to look out over the valley.

"It's sure grand," he said.

"It's sure grand," she echoed, laughing joyously at him and with him and herself and all the world, as she passed in through the door.

And Daylight, like the old man he once had met, himself went down the hill through the fires of sunset with a milk pail on his arm.

CPSIA information can be obtained at www.ICGtesting.com
Printed in the USA
LVOW03s1744280914

406243LV00009B/180/P